Barbara Erskine is the author of *Lady of Hay*, which has sold well over a million copies worldwide, the best-selling *Kingdom of Shadows, Encounters* (short stories), and *Child of the Phoenix*, which was based on the story of one of her own ancestors. This was followed by *Midnight is a Lonely Place* and *House of Echoes* – which were shortlisted for the W H Smith Thumping Good Read awards of 1995 and 1997 respectively – plus her second volume of short stories, *Distant Voices*. Her most recent novel is *On the Edge of Darkness*. Barbara Erskine's novels have been translated into twenty-three languages.

Barbara Erskine has a degree in mediaeval Scottish history from Edinburgh University. She and her family divide their time between the Welsh borders and their ancient manor house near the unspoilt coast of North Essex.

BARBARA ERSKINE

MIDNIGHT IS A LONELY PLACE

HOUSE OF ECHOES

HarperCollins*Publishers*

This omnibus edition published in 2001 by
HarperCollins*Publishers*

HarperCollins*Publishers*
77-85 Fulham Palace Road,
Hammersmith, London W6 8JB

www.fireandwater.com

ISBN 0 00 764578 3

Printed and bound in Great Britain by
Mackays of Chatham plc, Chatham, Kent

MIDNIGHT
IS A
LONELY PLACE

FOR A.J.
WHO THOUGHT OF THE TITLE

'Where'er we tread 'tis haunted, holy ground.'

Byron

'C'était pendant l'horreur d'une profonde nuit . . .'

Racine

PROLOGUE

Her hair was the colour of newly frosted beech leaves;
glossy; rich; tumbling from its combs as he pulled her
against him, his lips seeking hers. His skin was tanned by
the sun and the wind, hers, naked against him, white as
the purest marble.

The heavy, twisted silver of the torc he wore about his
arm cut into her flesh. She did not notice. She noticed
nothing but the feel of his body on hers, the strength of
his muscular thighs, the power of his tongue as he thrust
it into her mouth as though he would devour her utterly.

'Claudia . . .'

He breathed her name as a caress, a plea, a cry of
anguish, and then at last a shout of triumph as he lay still,
shaking, in her arms.

She smiled. Gazing up at the sky through the canopy of
rustling oak leaves she was utterly content. The world had
contracted into the one small clearing in the deserted woodland. Child and husband were forgotten. For this man in
her arms, she was prepared to risk losing both; to risk
losing her home, her position, life itself.

He stirred, and, raising himself onto his elbows, he stared
down at her, his face strangely blank, his silvery eyes
unseeing.

'Claudia . . .' he whispered again. He rested his face
between her breasts. It was the little death; the death a
man sought; the death which followed coition. He smiled,
reaching his fist into her hair, holding her prisoner, tracing
the line of her cheek-bones, her eyelids, with his lips. What
would this woman's husband, a son of Rome, an officer

of the legion, say if he ever found out? What would he do if he learned his wife had a lover, and that the lover was a Druid Prince?

I

'I hate being famous!' Kate Kennedy confessed as she sat on the floor of her sister Anne's flat. They were sharing a takeaway with a large Burmese cat called Carl Gustav Jung.

When her biography of Jane Austen was published Kate had found herself a celebrity overnight. She was invited onto talk shows, she was interviewed by three national daily newspapers and two Sundays, she toured the libraries and bookshops of Britain and she met Jon Bevan, described by the *Guardian* as one of England's most brilliant young literary novelists and poets. The reason for all this interest? What the *Times Literary Supplement* called her 'sizzling exposé' of Jane's hidden sensuality; her repressed sexuality; the passion in those well-loved, measured paragraphs.

Three weeks after meeting Jon she moved into his Kensington flat and her life changed forever.

Her elder sister and former flatmate, Anne, had remained philosophical about being deserted. ('My dear, it was bound to happen to one of us sooner or later.') Herself a writer – a Jungian psychologist whose library, especially the Freudian bits, Kate had ransacked when writing *Jane* – she had watched with amusement as Kate coped with fame. And found it wanting.

'If you hate it so much, bow out. Become a recluse. Decline to appear, my dear. Cultivate a certain boorishness. And wear a veil.' Anne licked soy sauce off her fingers. 'Your sales would double overnight.'

'Cynic.' Kate smiled at her fondly. 'Jon says I'm mad. He loves it, of course.'

'I can see Jon giving up writing in the end to become a

media person,' Anne said thoughtfully. She wiped her hands on a paper napkin stamped with Chinese characters and, wrapping her arms around her legs, rested her chin thoughtfully on her knees. 'He's bad for you, you know, Kate. He's a psychic vampire.' She grinned. 'He's feeding off your creative energy.'

'Rubbish.'

'It's true. You've slipped into the role of housewife and ego masseuse without even realising it. You're besotted with him! It's months since you got back from Italy, but you haven't even started writing the new book yet.'

Startled by the vehemence of the statement Kate was astonished to find that she felt guilty. 'I'm still researching.'

'What? Love?' Anne smiled. 'And does Jon still think you're mad to write about Byron at all?'

Kate nodded fondly. 'Yes, he still thinks I'm mad. He thinks Byron is too well known. He thinks I should have plumped for someone obscure – and not so attractive,' she added as an afterthought. 'But I'm glad to say my editor doesn't agree with him. She can't wait for the book.' She shook her head wearily, giving Carl Gustav the last, carefully-saved prawn. She had been secretly pleased and not a little flattered to find that Jon was jealous.

'Is that why you chose Byron? Because he's attractive?' Anne probed further.

'That and because I love his poetry, I adore Italy and he's given me a chance to spend wonderful months travelling round Europe to all the places he lived.' Kate gathered up the empty cartons from their meal. 'And he was a genuinely fascinating man. Charismatic.' She was watching Carl Gustav who, having crunched his prawn with great delicacy, was now meticulously washing his face and paws. 'Actually, I am ready to start writing now. My notes are complete – at least for the first section.'

Anne shook her head. 'I suppose I can think of worse ways of earning a living!' She stood up and went to rummage in the fridge for a jar of coffee beans. 'Tell me, are you and Jon still happy?' she asked over her shoulder. 'Really happy.'

Kate nodded.

'Getting-married happy?'

'No.' Thoughtfully. Then, more adamantly, 'No, I don't think either of us are the marrying type. At least not at the moment.'

'But you can see yourself living with him for a long time.'

There was a moment's silence as Kate regarded her sister with preoccupied concentration. 'Why do you want to know?'

'I've been offered a job in Edinburgh. If I take it I'll have to give up the flat.'

'I see.' Kate was silent for a moment. So, it was burning bridges time. 'What about Carl Gustav?'

'Oh, he'll come with me. I've discussed it with him at great length.' Anne bent down and caressed the cat lovingly. He had always been more hers than Kate's. 'He's quite pro-Edinburgh, actually, aren't you, C.J.?'

'And he approves of the job?'

'It's a good one. At the University. A big step up that dreadful ladder we are all supposed to mount unceasingly.'

Kate turned away, astonished by the pang of misery that had swept through her at the thought of losing Anne. 'Have you told Mum and Dad about this?' she said after a minute.

Anne nodded. 'They approve and I can see them just as often from Edinburgh. It's not as though it's the end of the world, Kate. It's only four hundred miles.'

Kate smiled. 'Well, if C.J. approves, and Mum and Dad approve, it must be OK. Get rid of the flat with my blessing and I'll try and hang on to Jon for a bit!'

But she didn't.

It was sod's law, she supposed, that the day after Anne moved into her new flat in Royal Circus she and Jon had their first serious row. About money. Hers.

'How much are they going to pay you?' He stared at her in astonishment.

She pushed the letter over to him. He read it slowly. 'It's an American contract! You must have known about this for months.' He was hurt and accusing.

'I didn't want to tell you until it was definite. You know how long these things take –' She had saved the news as a surprise. She had thought he would be pleased.

'Christ! It's iniquitous!' Suddenly he was on his feet. 'I get paid a paltry few hundred dollars' advance for my last book of poetry and you –' he spluttered with indignation, – 'you, get that!' He threw the letter down.

She stared at him, shocked. 'Jon –'

'Well, Kate. Be realistic. You write bloody well, but it's hardly literature!'

'Whereas your books are?'

'I don't think anyone would dispute that.'

'No. I'm sure they wouldn't.' She took a deep breath.

'Oh, hey, come on.' Suddenly he realised how much he had hurt her. Silently he cursed his flash-point temper. He put his arm round her shoulders. 'Look, you know me. All mouth. I didn't mean it. You are bloody good. You do enough research! Take no notice. I was just miffed. No, let's face it, jealous.' He gave her a hug. 'I might even go so far as to swallow my pride and borrow some of that money off you.'

It was the first time she had heard even a hint of his financial problems.

He managed it by making her feel guilty. She saw that later. It was a subtle manipulation; a masterpiece of manoeuvring. She pushed the money at him; threw it at him; gave it to him and lent it to him, with every cheque tacitly apologising that she made money while he did not. When the end came she had less than a thousand left in the bank and no prospect, though he had promised faithfully to repay her, of any more until her next royalty cheque in the summer.

Even so, it was not the increasing pressure over money which came between them in the end. It was something sudden and quite unexpected.

It was a cold, miserable day in early December when Jon found her in the Manuscript Gallery of the British Museum standing looking down at the flat glass case where an open book stared up at her, Byron's crabbed, slanting hand, much crossed out, flowing across the page of the dedication to 'Don Juan'. The atmosphere of the gallery, the air conditioning, the strange false light with its muted hum were giving her a headache. She had been concentrating too long and the unexpected tap on her shoulder had given her such a fright she let out a small cry before she turned and saw who it was and remembered Jon had said he would meet her for a quick coffee.

The restaurant was, as usual, packed and as they sat down at a table near the wall she had no idea that this would lead to the outbreak of war. A couple of Japanese tourists, hung with cameras, inserted themselves, with bows and apologetic smiles, into the two spare chairs next to them. Coffee slopped into Jon's saucer. A tall man, his own legs had folded with difficulty beneath the table as he pushed himself into the corner opposite Kate. His tray balanced in one hand, a letter in the other, his long, lanky frame and floppy hair lent him an air of languid elegance, something to which one look at the keen darting of his eyes as he stared around the room immediately gave the lie.

Still thinking about Byron, she had not immediately sensed his excitement. 'You're coming with me, Kate!' He picked up the letter which he had put on the table between them and waved it at her. There was a gleam of triumph in his eyes.

'Coming with you? To the States?' Giving him her full

15

attention at last, Kate looked at him in surprise. 'I can't.'

The expression of baffled anger which for a moment showed in his face confirmed her sudden suspicion that he was not going to understand.

'Why?' He was hurt and astonished by her response. He had thought she would be as excited as he was. He scowled. Why was it that she never reacted the way he expected? 'This is the most important time of my life, Kate. My new novel being published in the States. A lecture tour. Publicity. Perhaps real money at last. Isn't that what you want for me?'

'You know it is.' Her tone lost its defensiveness. She regarded him fondly. 'I'm terribly pleased for you. It's wonderful. The trouble is I am writing a book too, if you remember. And I can't just swan off on a tour at the moment. My research is complete. My notes are ready. I am about to start writing. You know I can't go with you. It's out of the question.'

'For God's sake, Kate, you can start the book any time.' Jon flung the letter down. He had counted on her; he could not visualize himself without her. 'I'm not asking you to give it up. I'm not asking you for a vast amount of time. We would be in the States less than a couple of weeks.'

Kate glanced at the Japanese woman sitting opposite her. Her eyes tactfully lowered, the woman was unwrapping a vast multi-layered sandwich, from which tranches of ham and cheese and various highly-coloured salad leaves hung in festoons. The air filled suddenly with a mouthwatering aroma of cooked meats.

'You know as well as I do that a couple of weeks is a hell of a long time when you are writing,' she retorted crossly. Her headache had worsened, she felt tired and depressed and she could be as stubborn as he on occasions. 'Don't be an idiot, Jon. Anyway, you would get on much better without me.' Somehow he had managed to make her feel guilty.

'But I need you. Derek has got some terrific things lined up for me.' Jon stubbed at the letter with his forefinger. 'Telly in New York. And some wonderful parties. An interview with the *New York Magazine* and *Publishers Weekly*. You would meet everyone. He is expecting you to be there, Kate. We're an item on the literary circuit –'

A wave of impatience swept over her. 'I don't care if your publisher is expecting me, Jon. I don't care if the President of the United States is expecting me. You may be an item, but I am not. Nor am I a natty little accessory to complement your glittering image. If I tour New York it will be to publicize *Lord of Darkness*, not to be photographed smiling at your elbow. I'm sorry, but I'm going to stay here and work.'

Jon shook his head. His voice was suddenly bleak. 'You can't stay in the flat, Kate.'

'What do you mean? Of course I can.' Even then she took no notice of the warning bell clanging away at the back of her head.

He folded his arms, the familiar stubborn expression beginning to settle on his face softened by a hint of anxiety. 'Derek has asked me to lend the flat to Cyrus Grandini while I'm away.'

Kate was speechless for a moment. 'And who, may I ask, is Cyrus Grandini?' she spluttered at last.

'Oh, Kate.' He was impatient. 'The poet. For God's sake, you must have heard of him!'

'No. And I don't wish to share a flat with him.'

His reply was apologetic. 'There's no question of sharing the flat. I'm sorry, Kate, but I have agreed he can have it for two weeks.'

'But what about me? I thought it was my home too.' She fought to keep the sudden panic out of her voice.

'It is your home.' He sounded angry rather than reassuring. 'You know it is. Derek expected you to come to New York; so did I. I thought you would jump at the chance!'

'Well, I haven't.'

'Then you will have to find somewhere else to go for a couple of weeks. I'm sorry.'

So, that was it. She knew where she stood. A lodger. A lover. But not a partner.

She stood up, scraping her chair back on the floor with such vehemence that the Japanese man next to her nearly dropped his pastry. He too leaped to his feet, climbing from behind the table so that she could squeeze inelegantly past him. A wave of frustration and anger and unhappiness swept over her. 'If I go, I go for good,' she stated flatly as her neighbour subsided once more into his chair and reached rather desperately for his pastry.

'OK. If that's the way you want it.' He had turned away from her and sat, chin in hand, staring up at the horsemen from the Parthenon on the frieze on the wall above him, suddenly and shamefully near to tears. Correctly interpreting his rocklike stance the Japanese lady who had been preparing in her turn to rise and allow him to leave the table relaxed and took a large mouthful of sandwich.

It was after eleven when he returned to the flat that evening.

The front door led straight into the small sitting room where she was sitting reading, cosy in the warm light of the single table lamp. Outside she could hear the sleet hitting the window. The shoulders of Jon's heavy jacket glistened and sparkled with unmelted ice. 'Well, have you changed your mind?' he asked.

For a moment she was confused, still lost in the world of Lord Byron and his friends. Unwillingly she dragged herself back to the present. 'No. I haven't changed my mind.'

'It's not working, is it?' He stood in front of the electric fire and began slowly to unwind his long scarf.

'What isn't working?' She kept her eyes on the book

before her. Her stomach had clenched uncomfortably at his tone and the print blurred into an indistinguishable black haze.

'Us.'

She looked up at last. 'Because I won't go to the States with you?'

'That and other things. Kate, let's face it. You're too obsessed with your damn poet to have time for me. Look at you. Even now you can't take your eyes off some bloody text or other.' He swooped on her and grabbed it out of her hand. 'See!' He held it up triumphantly. '*Victorian Poets*!' He hurled it down onto a chair. 'He –' by implication Kate gathered that 'he' meant Byron, '– comes between us all the time. You have no time for us; for our relationship, Kate.'

'Jon –'

She was stung by the injustice of the remark but he swept on. 'No, hear me out. You're completely obsessive. You have no time for me at all.'

She leaped to her feet. It had taken her much of the afternoon to calm down after their exchange at the British Museum earlier. She had thought they could work things out amicably once he came home, once he had had time to think about the justice of everything she had said. 'You . . . you say that, when all you ever talk about is your own work. Your friends, your parties, your TV interviews! You admitted that you only wanted me to go with you to the States as an appendage! The Jon Bevan literary circus. The wonderful, clever, stunning novelist and poet Jon Bevan and his cute girlfriend who writes such glitzy biographies – though heaven forbid that they should be taken as seriously as Jon's *oeuvre*.' Her hands had begun to shake as she realised the implications of what she was saying. She was condemning their relationship unequivocally to death. There would be no going back on this, no making up, no withdrawing of hurled insults. 'You're right, Jon, this relationship is not going to work. It's over. Finished!' Pushing past him, she flung out of the room.

Their bedroom was very small. The double bed, pushed against the wall, left space for a desk – her desk. On it her laptop sat amongst piles of books and papers. Jon's desk was in the sitting room she had just left. Jon's sitting room. Jon's flat. She stared round in despair. Then she reached for her coat. Throwing it on, she turned and ran to the front door.

'Kate. Don't be childish. We can work this out.' Jon followed her. Suddenly he was terrified by what he had done. 'For Christ's sake, where are you going?'

'Out.' She was fumbling with the deadlock.

'You can't go out. It's nearly midnight and it's snowing.' His anger had gone. He saw himself suddenly as she must see him – selfish, arrogant, thoughtless, cruel. 'Kate, please –' He stretched out a hand towards her.

. She did not answer. Slamming the door behind her she had run down the steps and out into the street.

II

She missed him.

The flat was tidy, already empty though she was still there, and the days were ticking by. She had to find somewhere, somewhere she could afford, to live, to lick her wounded self esteem, to write.

She tried to justify what had happened; to explain it to herself. He was right. It had not been working. There had been too much conflict, too much competition between them. And all the sacrifices had been hers: her time, her concentration, her money and her commitment.

Well, now it was over. All her time, her concentration, her commitment could be focussed on one thing. One man. Byron. She stood, spreading honey on a slice of bread, watching the wholemeal crumbs disintegrate. Frowning, she tried to stick the crumbs back together. She couldn't stay in London, that was obvious. Her money – the money she had lent him – had been her sole source of income. She had spent a morning scouring her bank statement and building society book, calculator in hand, trying to see how far she could make the last few hundred pounds stretch. Thank God she had had the sense to stick some of it into a tax fund which, even for Jon, she had not touched. Without that she would be in trouble indeed. It was all her fault. She was a sucker, a classic, besotted mug. She had no one to blame but herself. And Jon. She had tried calling him names. It helped, but always she came back to the empty space in her life and the fact that she missed him.

But life had to go on, which was why, two days later, she found herself at Broadcasting House, where her old friend, Bill Norcross, ran one of the production departments.

'So, is what I hear on the grapevine true? You and Jon are a couple no more. The beautiful Kate Kennedy has turned at bay and bitten the hand that fed her.'

Bill leaned back in his chair and waved Kate into its twin, angled on the far side of his desk.

Swallowing a retort Kate sat down, aware of his eyes sliding automatically from the top of her black leather boots to the line of her hem. Secure in the knowledge that her thighs were thickly and unglamorously shrouded in black woollen tights she crossed her legs, deliberately provocative. 'He never fed me Bill. I paid my share,' she said calmly.

Bill grinned amiably. She was tall, like Jon, and with a similarity of build which had led many people to take them for brother and sister. Where on Jon the look was loose-limbed and laid back, on her it was elegant and graceful, an impression compounded by her long brown hair, tied loosely at the nape of her neck with a scarlet silk scarf, and by the slender fingers which at the moment dangled the pair of spectacles which she had put on to scrutinize Bill's face and then removed as though a ten second scan was enough for a lifetime.

'I need your help, Bill. I need somewhere to live for a bit.' She paused and gave him a slow, reluctant smile. 'I wondered if I could stay in your cottage.'

Bill frowned. 'My God! You must be desperate. Do you know where my cottage is?'

She laughed. 'It's up in North Essex, isn't it?'

'It's in the most beautiful corner of Essex, which is, to my mind, the most beautiful corner of England. But alas, at this time of year, it is also the most inaccessible and cold. I have only a minimum of so-called mod cons, the bedroom's full of rubble, the roof leaks and it's very damp and cold. You'd be miserable. Has Jon thrown you out?'

'In a manner of speaking.' She narrowed her lips. 'I thought we shared a flat, but apparently not.'

'So, you have split up?'

She nodded. 'The histrionics are over. We're both being frightfully civilised.' It hurt to talk about it.

She had known Bill for fifteen years, since they had been freshers together at university. He was one of her best friends, but she was not going to tell him about the money. What she had done with her savings to render her unable to pay a decent rent was none of his business. Besides, Jon had promised he would pay her back when he received his next advance. Or the next . . . Cheerful, generous, feckless, selfish bloody Jon! and she was the mug who fell for him!

Bill leaned back and folded his arms across his chest. A stout, balding man in his mid thirties, he had a humorous, likable face which to his chagrin, failed to convey anything other than a perpetual, cheerful bonhomie.

'Am I right in thinking Jon has relieved you of most of the dosh you made with *Jane*?'

She raised an eyebrow. 'Is that what he told you?'

'Not in so many words, no. I guessed. I've known you both a long while, after all, before you even met each other. Are you completely skint or can you afford some rent?'

'Some,' she said guardedly. 'But not London prices.'

'No. Near me. In Essex. Up at Redall Bay. My neighbours have a cottage they want to rent to someone for six months. It's a couple of miles from mine; a lot more civilized. Quiet.' He gave a sudden laugh. 'Quiet as the grave.'

'Would they rent it to me?'

'I'm sure they would. They were talking about it last time I was up there. They need the money. If I recommend you and if you can rustle up a cheque for three months' rent in advance I'm pretty certain I can fix it for you.' He leaned forward abruptly and pulled open a desk drawer. The sheaf of photos he threw onto the blotter in front of her were crumpled and much thumbed. 'It's bleak, Kate.

You'd better think hard about it. You would be terribly lonely.'

She picked them up with a glance at his face. 'I know it's bleak. I know the coast. I've been up there once or twice.'

The pictures featured a series of holiday scenes: people, boats, dogs, children, sand, shingle and always the sea – a grey-green, muddy sea. In one she saw a small cottage in the distance. 'Is that your place?'

He nodded. 'I don't go there much in the winter. I can't stand the cold and the desolation.'

'It looks lovely. But too crowded.' She glanced up at him mischievously. 'I want solitude. I am writing a book, don't forget.'

'What else?' With an expansive gesture of his arms Bill stood up. 'If I can find a tenant for Roger and Diana who can pay good solid money for the privilege of staying in that God-forsaken cottage of theirs freezing their balls off – saving your presence – I shall earn loads of Brownie points with them and they'll be in my debt forever. Give me a couple of days to phone them and send them your cheque and I can assure you that provided it doesn't bounce, they will welcome you with open arms.'

She stood up. 'Don't tell Jon where I'm going, Bill, assuming he's even remotely interested,' she said as she left. 'At least for now I want it to be a complete break. On my terms.'

'Bitch.' It was said with great affection.

'Well, why not. He's dropped me in it.' She was surprised at her own lack of anger.

'Silly sod.' Bill grinned amiably. 'I'll tell you what. I'll drive down with you at the weekend. It won't do any harm for my place to have a quick airing, then you can drop me at the station on Sunday night and I shall abandon you to the east wind and return here to my creature comforts.'

*　　*　　*

It did not take long to clear her stuff out of Jon's flat. There didn't seem to be much of it – apart from her books, of course.

They had discussed it all amicably in the end, just as she had determined that they should. They had been adult and businesslike and utterly calm in the division of their affairs – a divorce without the complications of a marriage – and with a cool kiss on her cheek Jon had departed for New York several days earlier than he had originally intended. He did not ask her where she was going; they had not mentioned the money.

A half-dozen boxes and suitcases packed into the back of her car, a carton of plants, carefully wrapped against the cold wind, and an armful of unwanted clothes. That was the sum total of her life in London which she ferried to the attic of Bill's house in Hampstead – all to be put in store except the plants which were to be pampered and coddled by him far from the East Anglian wind. That left her laptop and printer, her books, her boxes of filing cards and notes and a couple of suitcases packed with jeans and thick sweaters and rubber boots. It was not until she had piled them into her small Peugeot and gone for one last look around the flat that the small treacherous lump in her throat threatened to choke her. She swallowed it sternly. This was the beginning of the rest of her life. Slamming the front door behind her she pushed her keys through the letter box, hearing them thump onto the carpet the other side of the door with a dull finality which suited her mood exactly. She had not enquired how Cyrus Grandini would gain entry to the flat and Jon had not told her. Turning the collar of her jacket up around her ears she ran down the steps towards her car. She would pick Bill up at the Beeb on her way across London and then together they would head north-east.

III

The tide crept higher, drawn inescapably onward by the full moon lost behind ten thousand feet of towering cumulus. Softened by the sleet in the ice-cold wind the sand grew muddy and pliant beneath the questing fingers of water. The shingle bank was deserted, lonely in the darkness. As the water lapped the stones in silence, gently probing, a lump of sand broke away from the mound behind it and subsided into the blackness of the water. Behind it, a further fissure formed. Matted grass strained and tore, a network of fine roots pulling, clinging, interlocked. The grass hissed before the wind, grains of sand flicked into the air by a gust, veering round into the east. Now the wind and the tide were of one mind and, inexorably, the water crept forward.

The small pocket of clay, left on the floodplain of the River Storwell after the glaciers had melted, had two thousand years ago, been at the bottom of a freshwater marsh. Long ago drained, the marsh had gone and the rich pasture which replaced it had turned, over the centuries, to arable then to scrub and to woodland, and then, as the sea advanced inexorably on the eastern coasts of England, to shingle beach. Now, after nearly two millennia of change and of erosion the soil, sand and gravel which still separated the clay from the air and the light was only centimetres thick.

IV

Diana Lindsey's plump figure was swathed in a thick pair of trousers, an anorak and a vast lambswool shawl as she stood in the doorway of Redall Cottage watching her eldest son lighting the fire. She was a small fair-haired woman, pretty, with light green eyes and reddened, work-worn hands.

'Hurry up. Lunch will be ready soon, Greg. I've already wasted enough of this morning with all your fuss.' She cast a professional glance around the small living room. Watery sunlight poured through the window, illuminating the bright rag rugs on the floor and the small sofa and chair which had been pulled up around the fire. She was pleased with the room. They had only had twenty-four hours to tidy the place, to move Greg's belongings out of it and to replace them with a few pieces of respectable furniture: a table and two chairs for the kitchen; a small Victorian nursing chair for the bedroom where the double bed had been the only fixture; sheets, towels, a box of basic groceries – Bill's idea and well beyond the landlord's brief, but she had agreed with him that the place would be cold and lonely enough without finding there was no food or coffee in the cupboards and no shops for miles, and those there were, not open until Monday morning. The final touch had been to light the woodburner which was settling now to a steady roar, and fill a vase with winter jasmine for the kitchen table.

Greg latched the burner's doors and stood up. His burly presence filled the small room and he had to bend his head beneath the ceiling beams. 'Right. Satisfied now, Ma? Lady Muck will be comfortable as a bug in a turd here.'

'Don't be vulgar, Greg.' Her reproach was automatic. Bored. She went through into the kitchen and had a final look round there, too. The pots and pans and plates were almost unused – Greg had never bothered to cook anything except coffee as far as she could tell. The knives and forks and spoons she had brought over from the farmhouse. 'Right. Let's get back. Bill phoned to say they would probably be here by tea time. He wanted her to settle in before it got dark.'

'How wise.' Greg pulled open the front door. Behind them the flames in the woodburner dipped and flared and steadied behind the blackening glass of the doors. 'Shall I call Allie?'

Leaving his mother to head for the Land Rover parked at the end of the rutted track which led through the half mile or so of bleak woods separating the cottage from Redall Farmhouse, he turned and walked around the side of the cottage. The small, timber-framed building, painted a soft pink, nestled in a half-moon of trees. Behind it, short rabbit-cropped turf formed an informal lawn which straggled towards the sand and shingle spit separating the estuary of the River Storwell from the beach and the cold waves of the North Sea. It was a windy, exposed site, even today when the sun was shining fitfully from behind the broken cloud.

'Allie!' Greg cupped his hands around his mouth and bellowed for his sister. As his mother opened the door of the Land Rover and climbed in, he disappeared around to the far side of the cottage into the teeth of the wind.

Alison Lindsey, fifteen years old, her blonde hair tightly caught by a rubber band into a pony tail tucked into the neck of her yellow windcheater, was crouching in the lee of one of the shingle and sand dunes which stood between the cottage and the sea. She glanced up as her brother appeared and raised her hand, the wind whipping tendrils of hair into her eyes.

'What have you found?' He jumped down the small sandy cliff to stand beside her. Out of the wind it was suddenly very quiet, almost warm in the trapped sunlight.

'Look. The sea washed the sand away here. It must have happened at high tide.' She had been scrabbling at the sand; her fingers were caked with it. He could see where she had caught her nail. A small streak of blood mingled with the golden red grains stuck to her skin. She had dug away the side of the dune and pulled something free. 'See. It's some kind of pottery.'

He took it from her, curious. It was slipware, red, the glaze shiny with a raised pattern, hardly scratched by the sand.

'Pretty. It must be something someone chucked out of the cottage. Come on Allie. Ma's in a ferment. She wants to feed us all before she goes off to Ipswich or wherever it is she is going this afternoon, and I want to get out of here before Lady Muck turns up.'

Alison took the piece of pottery from her brother and wedged it into her anorak pocket. She glanced up at him. 'Why do you call her that? She's famous, you know. She's written a book.'

'Exactly.' He smiled grimly. 'And no doubt will feel herself superior in every way to us country bumpkins.' He gave a short laugh as he scrambled up the bank and turned to give his sister a hand, hauling her bodily out of the sandy hollow. 'Well, she'll soon find out that living in the country at this time of year is not the same as swanning out for the odd picnic in the summer. Then perhaps she'll go away.'

'And let you have the cottage back?' Alison surveyed him shrewdly, her green eyes serious.

'And let me have my cottage back.' He looked at her thoughtfully. 'Don't say anything to Ma, Allie, but I think between us you and I can find a way to chase Lady Muck away from Redall Cottage, don't you?' He smiled. 'Perhaps we can give the weather a helping hand. Scare her off somehow.'

'You bet.' She laughed. Then she frowned. 'But don't we need the money?'

'Money!' Greg snorted. 'Doesn't anyone think of anything else around here? For the love of Mike, there are other things in the world. We're not going to starve. Dad's pay-off and his pension are more than enough to last us for years. We can afford petrol and electricity and food. They can afford to buy booze. My dole money buys my paint and canvas. What does everyone want all this money for?'

Alison shrugged dutifully. She knew better than to argue with her elder brother. Besides he was probably right. She sternly pushed down a sneaking suspicion that his views were simplistic and wildly immature – he was, after all, twelve years older than she – and, pushing her wispy hair out of her eyes for the thousandth time as they reached the Land Rover, she pulled open the door and hauled herself into the front seat beside her mother.

In the farmhouse the third Lindsey offspring, Patrick, had been laying the table for lunch, walking silently around the kitchen in his socks as his father dozed in the cane chair before the Aga, two cats asleep in his lap. The silence of the room was broken only by the ticking of the grandfather clock in the corner and by the gentle bubbling from the heavy pan on the stove. The air was rich and heavy with the fragrance of the cooking chicken in its thick herb-flavoured gravy. Two years older than Alison, Patrick was the studious member of the family. Upstairs in his bedroom – the north-facing end room above the kitchen, according to Alison the best room in the house because of its size – computer, printer, calculating machines and hundreds of books vied with one another for space, overflowing from tables and chairs on to the floor and even from time to time out into the corridor outside his sister's room. At the moment Patrick was lost in thought, his mind still fully occupied with his school project. He noticed neither the noise of the engine as his brother drove up outside and parked the Land Rover around the side of the house, nor the speed with which Number Two cat, Marmalade Jones, jumped off his master's lap and onto the worktop where he proceeded to lick the pat of butter which Patrick had incautiously withdrawn from the fridge.

The opening door woke Roger, startled Patrick and gave the cat an unwonted and sudden attack of conscience.

'My goodness it's cold out there.' Diana went straight to the heavy iron pan simmering quietly on the Aga and peered inside it before she took off her coat.

'Bill rang.' Roger stretched and reached for the newspaper which had slid from his inert fingers as he slept. Indignant at the move, Number One cat, Serendipity Smith, slipped from his knees and diving through the open studwork which separated the kitchen from the living room, went to sit on the rug in front of the fire, staring enigmatically into the embers. 'They should be here by about three. Apparently she's an absolute cracker!' He grinned at his eldest son and gave a suggestive wink. 'You might try charming her, Greg, just this once. I can't believe as your mother's son you are completely devoid of the art.'

'Oh you.' Diana gave her husband a playful tap on the head.

Greg ignored them both. Sealed in an intense inner world of frustrated imagination he frequently missed his parents' affectionate banter. Walking through to the fire he stooped and threw on a log. 'Half the old dune behind the cottage has gone,' he called through to them. 'You know the one which shelters it from the north-easterlies. A few more tides like that one last week and we'll need to worry about the cottage being washed away.'

'Rubbish.' Diana, having hung up her coat was now tying a huge apron over her trousers. The apron sported a giant red London bus which appeared to be driving across the rotund acres of her stomach. She shook her head. 'No way. That cottage has been there hundreds of years.'

'And once upon a time it was miles from the sea, my darling.' Roger stood up. Painfully thin, his face was haggard with tiredness, a symptom of the illness which had forced him to take early retirement. 'Come on. Why don't I open a bottle of wine. That stew of yours smells so good I could eat it.' He smiled and his wife, on her way back to the Aga with her wooden spoon, paused to give him a quick hug.

'Show Dad the piece of china you found in the dune, Allie,' Greg called from the next room. His sister, still wearing her anorak, had seated herself at the table, her elbows planted amongst the knives and forks which Patrick had aligned with geometric neatness. She fished in her pocket and produced it.

Roger took it from her and turned it over with interest. 'Its unusual. Old I should say. Look at the colour of that glaze, Greg.' He held it out towards his eldest son. Reluctantly, Greg left the fire. Taking the fragment he turned it over in his hands. 'You could take it into the museum some time, kiddo,' he said to Alison. 'See what they say.'

'I might.' Alison stood up and they were all surprised to see her eyes alight with excitement. Her usual carefully-studied air of ennui had for a moment slipped. 'Do you know what I think? I think it's Roman. There's stuff just like it in the castle museum.'

'Oh, Allie love, it couldn't be. Not out here.' Diana had produced four glasses from the cupboard. She handed her husband the corkscrew. 'The Romans never came this far out of Colchester.'

'They did, actually. They've found a lot of Roman stuff at Kindling's farm,' Roger put in. He tore the foil from the top of the wine bottle. 'Do you remember? They found the remains of a villa there. Some rich Roman chap from Colchester retired here. They found an inscription.'

Alison nodded. 'Marcus Severus Secundus,' she said, intoning the words softly.

'That's right.' Roger nodded. 'There was an article about him in the local paper. And they found even older stuff too. Iron Age, I think it was, or Bronze Age or something. Are you still thinking of doing something archaeological for your project, Allie?' He smiled at his daughter.

'Might.' Her sudden burst of enthusiasm had apparently run its course. She sat down again and spread her elbows, scattering knives and forks. Patrick frowned, but he said nothing. He had learned a long time ago that a comment from him would produce a tirade of abuse from his sister which would upset everyone and end up with the whole meal being spoiled. It had happened before too often.

'I'm going to excavate the dune.' Alison's sudden announcement stopped Roger's hand in mid air as he poured the wine.

'That sounds a bit ambitious, old girl,' he said cautiously. 'There would be a lot of hard digging and you might not find anything.'

'I found something before.'

'In the same place?' Greg looked across at her, disbelieving. 'Why didn't you say?'

'None of your business.' Alison reached for a glass of wine which left Patrick without one.

'Hey, that's mine –'

'Pour yourself one.' When neither parent said anything she raised the glass defiantly to her lips and took a sip.

'What did you find, Allie?' Roger's voice took on the conciliatory tone he often used with his daughter – soft, persuasive, almost pleading.

'I'll show you.' She rose to her feet, and, her glass still in her hand, trailed towards the staircase which led from the living room behind the door in the corner by the inglenook.

'There's loads of books on archaeology in her room,' Patrick put in in an undertone when she was out of earshot.

'You haven't been in there again.' Diana was exasperated. 'You know she doesn't like it —'

'She nicked my Aran sweater. I needed it.' Patrick's mouth settled in a hard line, exactly like his sister's as Alison reappeared with a shoe box in her hand.

'Look. I found all these on the beach there, or in the cliff or in the saltings, and these two I dug up from the dune.' She tipped the contents of the box onto the table amongst the knives and forks. For once there was no comment about the shower of dirty sand which descended over the cutlery on Diana's scrubbed table top: several shards, a few pieces of carved bone and one or two unrecognisable fragments of twisted, corroded metal. 'I think it's a grave. A Roman grave,' she said solemnly.

There was a moment's silence.

Slowly Greg shook his head. 'No chance. If it's anything at all, it's one of those red hill things — to do with ancient salt workings. Not that that isn't extremely interesting,' he went on hastily after a glance at the rebellious set of his sister's face. 'Perhaps we should get someone over here who knows about these things.'

'No!' Alison rounded on him furiously. 'I don't want anyone knowing about it. No one at all. It's mine. My grave. I found it. You're not to tell anyone it's there, do you understand. Not anyone at all. I am going to dig there. Anything I find is mine. If you tell anyone it will ruin everything. Everything!'

Sweeping her treasures back into the box, she clamped the lid on it and flung out of the room.

'Let her be.' Diana turned comfortably to the stove.

'She'll grow bored with it when she realizes how much hard work is involved. And I'm sure there is nothing there. Nothing at all that would interest anyone sane, anyway.' She smiled tolerantly. 'Clear up that mess would you, Patrick darling and then let's eat, otherwise our guests will be here before we've finished.'

V

His nails had cut deep welts into the palms of his hand;
the veins stood out, corded, pulsating on his forehead and
neck, but his silence was the silence of a stalking cat. Not
a leaf crisped beneath his soft-soled sandals, not a twig
cracked. Soundlessly, he parted the leaves and peered into
the clearing. His wife's long tunic and cloak lay amongst
the bluebells, a splash of blue upon the blue. The man's
weapons, and his clothing, lay beside them. He could see
the sword unsheathed, the blade gleaming palely in the
leaf-dappled sunlight. He could hear her moans of pleasure,
see the reddened marks of her nails on his shoulders. She
had never writhed like that beneath him, never uttered a
sound, never raked his skin in her ecstasy. Beneath him
the woman he adored and worshipped would lie still; com-
pliant, dutiful, her eyes open, staring up at the ceiling, on
her lips the smallest hint of a sneer.

He swallowed his bile, schooling himself to silence,
watching, waiting for the climax of their passion. His sword
was at his waist, but he did not reach for it. Death at the
moment of fulfilment would send them to the gods together.
It would be too easy, too quick. Even as he watched them he
felt the last remnants of his love curdle and settle into thick
hatred. The punishment he would inflict upon his wife
would last for the rest of her days; for her lover he would
plan a death which would satisfy even his fury. But until the
right moment came, he would wait. He would welcome her
back to his hearth and to his bed with a smile. His hatred
would remain, like his anger, hidden.

*   *   *

Watery sunlight filled Roger's study, reflecting in from the bleak garden, throwing pale shifting lights across the low ceiling with its heavy oak beams. Greg flung himself down in his father's chair and stared round morosely. He would never be able to paint here. Somehow he had to get Lady Muck out of the cottage – his cottage – so he could go back. She must not be allowed to stay.

The small room was stacked with canvasses and sketch pads. His easel filled the space between the desk and the window; the table was laden with boxes of paints and pencils and the general debris he had fetched down from the cottage; a new smell of linseed oil and white spirit overlaid the room's natural aroma of old books, Diana's rich crumbling pot pourri and lavender furniture polish. Thoughtfully he stood up. He leafed through a stack of canvasses and lifted one onto the easel, then he sat down again, staring at it.

The portrait bothered him. It was one of a series he had done over the past two or three years. All of the same woman, they were sad, mysterious; evocations of mood rather than of feature; of beauty by implication rather than definition. This was the largest canvas – three feet by four – that he had tackled for a long time and it had given him the most trouble.

He sat gnawing at the knuckle of his left thumb for several minutes before he glanced round for brush and palette. It was the colours that were wrong. She was too hazy; too indistinct. Her colouring needed to be more definite, her vivacity more pronounced. He stood close to the canvas, leaning forward intently, and stabbed at it with the brush. He had made her too beautiful, the bitch, too seductive. He ought to paint her as she was – a whore; a traitor; a cat on heat.

His tongue protruding a little from the corner of his mouth, he worked furiously at the painting, blocking in the face, shading the planes of the cheeks, sketching lips and eyes, touching in the line of the hair, his anger growing with every brushstroke.

It was a long time before he threw down the brush, wiping his hands carelessly on the front of his old, ragged sweater. He stood back and stared at his handiwork through narrowed eyes, aware that as the sun moved lower in the sky, slanting first across the estuary and then across the bleak winter woods, the light was changing once again and with it her face. He glared down at the palette he had slid onto his father's desk, aware that the anger was leaving him as swiftly as it had come and wondering, not for the first time, where it came from.

VI

Turning the car off the road Kate found they were bumping along an unmade track through a wood. Before them the sky, laced with shredded, blowing cloud had that peculiar intensity of light which denotes the close proximity of the sea.

'I hope we don't have to go far down here,' she commented, slowing to walking pace as the small vehicle grounded for the second time on the deep ruts. Winding down the window she took a deep appreciative breath of the ice-cold air. It carried the sharp, resinous tang of pine and earth and rotting leaves.

'I'm afraid it gets worse.' Bill grimaced. 'And you'll have to leave your car at the farmhouse. Roger or Greg will run all your stuff up to the cottage in their Land Rover.'

The track forked. In front of them a rough wooden gibbet held two or three fire brooms – threadbare, broken. She brought the car to a standstill. 'Which way?'

'Right. My place is up there to the left – about half a mile. The farmhouse is down here.' He gestured through the windscreen and cautiously she let in the clutch once more. The track began to descend sharply. They bounced again into the ruts as the wood grew more dense. Pine was interspersed with old stumpy oaks, hazel breaks strung with ivy and dried traveller's joy and thickets of black impenetrable thorn.

The farmhouse itself stood at the edge of the woods, facing east across the saltings. Behind it a thin strip of field and orchard allowed the fitful sunshine to brighten the landscape before another wood separated the farmhouse gardens from the sea. There was no sign of any cottage.

She halted the car beside a black-boarded barn and sat for a moment staring out. The farmhouse was pink washed, a long, low building, covered in leafless creepers which in the summer were probably clematis and roses. Even in the depths of winter the place looked extraordinarily pretty.

'What a lovely setting.'

'Not too wild for you?' Bill glanced beyond the farmhouse to the mudflats. As far as the eye could see there was nothing but mud and water and grey-green stretches of salting. A stray low shaft of sunlight shone from behind them throwing a sunpath over the mud towards the water. The rich colour lasted a moment and then it had gone.

Bill opened the car door allowing biting, pure air into the warm fug. 'Come on. It will start getting dark soon. I think we should get you settled in.'

Kate surveyed her hosts as she shook hands with them. Roger and Diana Lindsey were both in their fifties, she guessed. Comfortable, quiet, welcoming. She found herself responding immediately to their warmth.

'I thought you would like some tea here before you go up to the cottage,' Diana said at once, ushering her towards the sofa. 'Make yourself comfy – move those cats – and then I'll give my son a call. He is going to take your stuff up there for you. It's a long walk carrying luggage.'

'And she's got a heap of it,' Bill put in. He was standing with his back to the fire, his palms held out behind him towards the smouldering logs. 'Computers and stuff.'

'Oh, my goodness.' Diana frowned. 'In which case you'll certainly need help.'

'Where is the cottage?' Kate, while enjoying the soporific comfort of the tea and the warmth of the fire, was eager to see it. Over the last couple of days her excitement, though partly dampened by the thought of how much she was missing Jon – a thought she had deliberately tried to erase – had been intense.

'It's about half a mile from here. Through the wood. You're right on the edge of the sea out there, my dear. I hope you've brought lots of warm clothes.' Solicitously Diana refilled Kate's cup, inserting herself between Kate and the staircase door where she had spotted a movement. The kids were spying. No doubt any moment now they would appear. She sighed. Kids indeed. She meant Alison and Greg. Patrick would no doubt be upstairs by now with his computers and would not reappear until called for supper. It was her elder son – a grown man, old enough to know better – and her daughter, who were, if she were any judge of character, going to cause trouble.

She glanced over her shoulder at Roger. 'Give Greg a call. I want him to help Miss Kennedy –'

'Kate, please.'

'Kate.' She flashed Kate a quick smile. 'He could start loading her stuff into the Land Rover.'

'I don't want to be a nuisance.'

'You won't be.' Was it Kate's imagination, or was there a certain grim determination in the way Diana said those words?

Greg, when called, turned out to be a man in his late twenties or early thirties, Kate guessed, which made him around her age or slightly younger. His handsome features were slightly blurred – too many beers and too little care of himself – and his thick pullover was smeared with oil paint. He shook hands with her amiably enough but she sensed a hint of reserve, even resentment in his manner. It was enough to make her question her first impression that here was a very attractive man.

'I'm sorry. It's a nuisance for you to have to drive me to the cottage,' she said. She met his eyes challengingly.

'But necessary if our tenant is to be safely installed,' he replied. His voice was deep; musical but cold.

Bill must have felt it too. She saw him frown as he levered himself to his feet from the low sofa. 'Come on, Greg. I'll give you a hand. Leave the others to finish their tea, eh?'

As the front door opened and the two men disappeared into the swiftly-falling dusk, a wisp of fragrant apple smoke blew back down the chimney.

'You can park your car in the barn, Kate,' Roger said comfortably. He leaned back in his chair, stretching his legs out towards the fire. 'It'll be out of the worst of the weather there. Pick it up whenever you want, and if you have any heavy groceries and things at any time give us a shout and we'll run them over for you. It's a damn nuisance the track is so bad. I keep meaning to ask our neighbour if he'll bring a digger or something up here and level it off a bit, but you know how it is. We've never got round to it.'

'I've come for the solitude.' Kate smiled at him. 'I really don't want to be rushing up and down. I'll lay in some stores at the nearest shop and then I'd like to cut myself off from the world for a bit.' The thought excited her. The great emptiness of the country after London, the sharp, clean air as she had climbed out of the car, had heightened her anticipation.

'You'll be doing that all right. Especially if the weather is bad,' Roger gave a snort which might have been a laugh. 'There is a telephone over there, however. You might find you're glad of it after a bit, but if you want peace you'd better keep the number quiet.' He looked up as the door opened.

'All loaded.' Bill grinned at them. 'I think what I'll do, if you don't mind, Kate, is begin to make my way back to my place. It's quite a walk from here. I'll leave you to Greg and I'll wander over tomorrow morning if that's all right. Then I can show you the way back on foot in daylight, and perhaps we can have a drink together before you drop me off in Colchester to catch the train for London.'

The Land Rover's headlights lit up the trees with an eerie green light as they lurched slowly away from the farmhouse into the darkness. Kate found herself sliding around on the slippery, hard seat and she grabbed frantically at the dash to give herself something to hold on to, with a worried thought for the computer stored somewhere in the back.

'Sorry. Am I going too fast?' Greg slowed slightly. He glanced at her. He had already taken note of her understated good looks. Her hair was mousy but long and thick, her bones good, her clothes expensive, but he got the feeling she wasn't much interested in them. The undeniable air of chic which clung to her was, he was fairly sure, achieved by accident rather than design and the thought annoyed him. It seemed unfair that she should have so much. 'I take it you're not the nervous type. I can't think of many women who would want to live out here completely alone in the middle of winter.'

Kate studied his profile in the glow of the dashboard lights. 'No. I'm not the nervous type,' she said. 'I enjoy my own company. And I've come here to work. I don't think I'll have time to feel lonely.'

'Good. And you're not afraid of ghosts, I hope.'

It had been Allie's idea, to attempt to scare her away with talk of ghosts. It was worth a try. At least until he thought of something better.

'Ghosts?'

'Only joking.' His eyes were fixed on the track ahead. 'This land belonged once to a Roman officer of the legion, Marcus Severus Secundus. There's a statue of him in Colchester Castle. A handsome bastard. I like to think he strolls around the garden sometimes, but I can't say I've ever seen him.' He grinned. Not too much too fast. The woman wasn't a fool. Or the nervous type, obviously. 'I'm sure he's harmless.' He narrowed his eyes, concentrating on the track.

Beside him Kate smiled. Her excitement if anything increased.

The cottage when it appeared at last seemed to her

delight to be a miniature version of the farmhouse. It had pink walls and creeper and was, she could see in the headlights as they pulled up facing it, a charmingly rambling small building with a peg-tiled roof and smoking chimney. Beyond it she could see the dull gleam of the sea between towering banks of shingle. Leaving the headlights on, Greg jumped down. He made no effort to help her, instead going straight round to the rear of the vehicle, leaving her to struggle with the unfamiliar door handle. When she at last managed to force the door open and jump down, he straightened, his hair streaming into his eyes in the wind. Before she realised what he was doing, he threw a bunch of keys at her. She missed and they fell at her feet in the dark.

'Butterfingers.' The mocking words reached her through the wind. 'Go and open the front door, I'll carry this stuff in for you and then I can get back.'

The door had swollen slightly with the damp and she found she had to push it hard to make it open. By the time she had done it Greg was standing impatiently behind her, his arms full of boxes. She scrabbled for a light switch and found it at last. The light revealed a small white-painted hall with a staircase immediately in front of her and three doors, two to the left and one to the right.

'On the right,' Greg directed. 'I'll dump all this for you and you can sort it out yourself.'

She opened the door. The living room, low-ceilinged and heavily beamed like its counterpart in the farmhouse, boasted a sofa and two easy chairs. In the deep fireplace a wood burning stove glowed quietly, warming the room. The other three walls each had a small-paned window, beyond which the black windy night was held at bay by the reflection of the lamp as she switched it on. She crossed and drew the curtains on each in turn. By the time she had finished Greg had brought in another pile of stuff.

44

'Well, that's it,' he said at last. He had made no attempt to tidy it or distribute things for her. All were lumped together in a heap in the middle of the rug. 'If you need anything you can tell us tomorrow.'

'I will. Thank you.' She gave him a smile.

He did not respond. With a curt goodnight he turned and ducked out of the front door, pulling it closed behind him. Resisting a childish urge to run to the window and watch him leave she saw the glow of the headlights brighten the curtains for a moment as they swept across them, then they disappeared. She was alone.

Walking out into the hall she pulled the door bolt across and then turned back. The sudden wave of loneliness in the total silence was only to be expected. She sighed, looking round. Somehow she had expected that Bill would be with her this first evening. Or that the new landlord would invite her over for supper.

It had all been such a rush up until now. The packing, the storing of her stuff, borrowing books from the London Library, arranging her new life, separating herself from Jon; she had had little time to think and she had welcomed her exhaustion each evening. It meant she did not dwell on things. Here there would be plenty of time to dwell unless she was very careful. She straightened her shoulders. There would also be plenty of time to work, but first she would explore her new domain.

The cottage was very small. Downstairs there was only the one living room with a small kitchen and even smaller bathroom next to it. Upstairs there were two bedrooms, almost identical in size. Only one had a bed. In that room someone had made an attempt at cosiness. There was a chest of drawers and a small Victorian chair upholstered in rubbed gold velvet, with a couple of soft cushions tossed onto it. There was a new rug on the sloping floor and a wardrobe, which touched the low beamed ceiling. Inside was a row of wire hangers. Kate went downstairs again.

Her initial excitement and sense of adventure was slipping away. The silence oppressed her. Taking a deep breath she went into the kitchen and reached for the kettle. While it boiled she lugged her two suitcases upstairs and left them. She would hang up the dresses and two skirts which she had brought with her later. All her other clothes – jeans, trousers, sweaters – she could stuff into the small chest of drawers tomorrow. She did not feel like unpacking this evening.

After sorting out some of her books and papers, stacking them all neatly on the table in the living room, and putting the food and the bottle of Scotch she had brought with her into the kitchen cupboards she felt too tired to do any more. She made herself some tea, selected a couple of tapes and sat down, exhausted, on the sofa near the fire, her feet curled up under her. Her hands cupped around the mug, she sat listening to the strains of Vaughan Williams on her cassette player, strangely aware of the giant heave and swell of the sea outside beyond the shingle bank, even though she could not hear it.

She should have felt pleased with herself. She was in the country at last. She was ready to begin work. She had the peace and quiet she desired – Greg's attitude had not left her in any doubt that her privacy would be respected – and yet there was a nagging sadness, a feeling of anticlimax which had not a little to do with Jon, curse him. Only three weeks before, she had been living with him, researching the book, settled, a Londoner at least for the foreseeable future, and now here she was in a small cottage on the wild north-eastern coast of Essex with strangers for neighbours, no money, no man, no fixed abode and only Lord Byron for company.

Glancing at the floor where her boxes of books lay in a pool of lamplight she stood up again restlessly. She went over and, groping for her glasses in the pocket of her jeans, she began wearily to tear the sticky tape from the top of one of them. She must stay positive. Forget Jon. Forget London. Forget everything except the book.

The door banging upstairs made her jump. She glanced up at the ceiling and she could feel her heart thumping suddenly somewhere in the back of her throat. For a moment she did nothing, then slowly she straightened.

There was no one in the house so it must have been the wind, but at the foot of the stairs she paused, looking up into the darkness, the thought of Greg's legionnaire suddenly in the forefront of her mind.

Taking a firm grip on herself she walked up onto the landing. Both doors stood open as she had left them. Switching on the light she peered into the bedroom where earlier she had put her cases side by side near the cupboard. She looked round the room, satisfied herself that nothing was amiss and turned off the light. She repeated the action across the landing, staring round the empty bedroom, her eyes gazing uncomfortably at the two windows which were curtainless. The glass reflected the cold light of the central naked bulb and she was very conscious once again of the blackness of the night outside.

Frowning, she went downstairs. There had been nothing that she could see to account for the noise. She peered into the bathroom and the kitchen and then turned back to the living room.

The room was distinctly chilly. Walking over to the woodburner she peered at it doubtfully and, seeing the reassuring glow from within had disappeared, she stooped and reached for the latch. The metal was hot. She swore under her breath and looked round for something to pad her hands. Finding nothing she tugged at her sleeve and, wrapping the wool of her jersey around her fingers, she jiggled the latch undone and swung the doors open. The stove contained nothing but a bed of embers.

She glanced round but she had already realised that her tour of the cottage had yielded no coal; no log basket. She had grown spoiled living in London; the subject of heating had never crossed her mind. Central heating arrived for her these days at the flick of a switch. The hot water and heating in this cottage, it dawned on her suddenly, probably all depended on this small stove. Why hadn't Greg mentioned it? Surely the first thing he should have told her was how to heat the place. She shook her head in irritation. The omission was probably deliberate. She would have had to be very dense not to have sensed his hostility and resentment. Teach the townie a lesson. Well, if the townie wasn't going to freeze to death she would have to find some fuel from somewhere. A swift search produced one box of matches in the kitchen drawer, – thank heaven for that. As a non smoker it had never crossed her mind to bring matches. But there were no fire lighters, and there was no torch. There was nothing for it. Cursing herself for her own stupidity she realised she was going to have to explore outside in the dark.

Firmly putting all thoughts of the unexplained noise out of her head, she pulled on her jacket and gloves and with some reluctance she walked into the hall, unbolted the front door and pulled it open, fastening the latch back as she peered out into the darkness.

The wind caught her hair and pulled it back from her face, searing her cheeks. It was fresh and sharp with the scent of the sea and the pine woods which crowded across the grass towards her. She stood still for a moment, very conscious that she was silhouetted in the doorway. Reminding herself that there was no one watching she stared out at the path of light which ran from her feet in a great splash along the track before it dissipated between the trees. On either side of it the darkness was intense. She could see nothing beyond the muddy track with its windblown grasses and tangle of dead weeds.

Reluctantly, she stepped away from the door and began to walk along the front of the cottage, one hand extended cautiously in front of her touching the rough plastered walls. As her eyes grew used to the dark she could see the stars appearing one by one above her, and patches of cloud, pale against the blackness, and she became aware slowly of the sea shushing gently against the shingle in the distance and the wind sighing in the trees. She was straining her eyes as she reached the corner and peered round. Half way along the wall there was a small lean-to shed which must surely be some kind of fuel store. Moving a little faster as her confidence increased, she felt her feet grow wet in the grass.

Her fingers encountered the boards of the lean-to at last – overlapping, rough, splintery through her gloves. She groped her way around it until she came to the open doorway where she stopped, hesitating. The entrance gaped before her, the darkness intensely black and impenetrable after the luminous dark of the night, but she could smell the logs. Thick, resinous and warm, the scent swam up to her. Stooping, she groped through the doorway. Her hands met nothing but space. She reached out further and suddenly her fingers closed around something ice cold. A handle. Whatever it was slipped from her grasp and fell to the ground with a clatter. She stooped and picked it up. A spade. It was a spade. Leaning it against the wall, she took a cautious step forward, bending lower, and found herself right inside the shed. There at last her groping fingers encountered the tiers of stacked logs, their ends sharp, angled, their sides rough and rounded. Cautiously she pulled at one. The whole pile stirred and she leaped back. 'From the top, you idiot.' She found she had actually spoken out loud and the sound of her voice was somehow comforting. Straightening a little, she raised her hands, groping for the top of the pile, and one by one she reached down four logs. That was all she could carry. Clutching them against her chest she stumbled out of the shed backwards and retraced her steps towards the corner of the wall. Once there the stream of cheerful light from the hall guided her back to the front door. She almost ran inside and throwing the logs down on the floor she turned and slammed the door shut, shooting the bolt home.

It was only as she looked down at the logs, covered in sawdust and cobwebs that she realised how frightened she had been. 'You idiot,' she said again. Shaking her head ruefully she began to pull off her anorak. What had she been afraid of? The silence? The wood? The dark?

She had been afraid of the dark as a child in her own little bedroom next to Anne's in their Herefordshire farmhouse. Night after night she would lie awake, not daring to move, hardly daring to breathe, her eyes darting here and there around the room, looking – looking for what? There was never anything there. Never anything frightening, just that awful, overwhelming loneliness, the fear that everyone else had left the house and abandoned her. Or died. Had her mother guessed in the end, or had she confessed? She couldn't remember now, but she did remember that her mother had given her a night light. It was a china owl, a white porcelain bird with great orange claws and huge enigmatic eyes. 'You'll scare the child to death with that thing,' her father, a country doctor with no time for cosseting his own family, had scoffed when her mother produced it from the attic, but Kate had loved it. When the small night-light candle was lit inside it the whole bird glowed with creamy whiteness and its eyes came alive. It was a kind bird; a wise bird; and it watched over her and kept her company and kept the spooks at bay. When she was older the owl had remained unlit, an ornament now, but her fear, tightly rationalized and controlled, had remained. Sometimes, even when she was a student at university, she had lain in her room in the hall of residence, the sheet pulled up to her chin, her fingers clutched in the pillow she was hugging to her chest as she stared at the dark square of the window. The fear had gone now. Only one hint of it remained. She always opened the curtains at night. With them closed the darkness gave her claustrophobia. Jon had laughed at her, but he had conceded the open curtain. He liked it open because he loved to see the dawn creeping across the London roofs as the first blackbirds began to whistle from the television aerials across the city.

Well, that Kate was grown up now, and on her own and not afraid. Pulling herself together, she gathered up the logs and, walking through into the sitting room, she stacked them neatly in the fireplace beside the stove. Opening it again she peered in. The embers were very low. She looked at the logs thoughtfully. If she put one of those in it would just smother the small remaining sparks and put the whole thing out. She had no fire lighters. What she needed was newspaper and some dry, small twigs to rebuild the fire. She stared round.

In the kitchen the vegetable rack in the corner was lined with newspaper. She grabbed it, showering a residue of mud from long-gone potatoes over the kitchen boards. There was enough to crumple into four good-sized wads. Stuffing them in around the log she lit it and, closing the doors, slid open the damper. The sudden bright blaze was enormously satisfying but she held her breath. Would the paper burn and then leave the log to go out?

She glanced over her shoulder at the room and shivered. It had lost its appeal somehow. Her lap top computer and printer lying on the table rebuked her; the boxes of filing cards, the notebooks, the cardboard boxes full of books. She glanced at her watch. It was eight o'clock. She was hungry, she was tired and she was cold. A boiled egg, a cup of cocoa and a hot bath, if the woodburner could be persuaded to work, and she would go to bed. Everything else could wait until morning. And daylight.

VII

It was bitterly cold and barely light. Well wrapped up in a Shetland sweater and thick jacket with two pairs of socks inside her boots and a pair of her younger brother's gloves, Alison Lindsey stood staring at the cottage from the shelter of the trees. It was in darkness. Downstairs the curtains were drawn, but upstairs both the front windows which looked down across the garden appeared to be uncurtained. She frowned, then plucking up her courage she sprinted across the grass. Heading straight for the log shed she ducked inside and groped around in the darkness. After a second she gave an exclamation of annoyance. Her tools had been moved. She kicked crossly at the firewood and leaped back with a mixture of fright and malicious satisfaction as one of the piles began to slip. Dodging the cascading logs she watched until they had stopped moving, waiting for the noise to die away. The dust settled, but there was no sound from the cottage. 'Lady Muck's asleep,' she whispered to herself and she gave a superior smile. She turned to the doorway again and then she saw her spade. It had been propped up in the corner.

Picking it up she peered out into the silent dawn. It was well before sunrise. The morning was damp and ice cold and there were still long dark shadows across the sea, stretching out into the black mist.

Running lightly she headed across the shingle and leaped down into the hollow on the seaward side of the dune. Her dune.

The tide in the night, she saw with satisfaction, had not been very high. The sea wrack on the shore, still wet with spume, was several feet short of her excavation and had come nowhere near the place where she was digging. Her tongue protruding slightly from between her teeth she set to, cutting the soft sand into sections and scooping it away from the side of the dune. From somewhere in the darkness along the shore she heard the scream of a gull.

Her hands were frozen after only a few moments in spite of the thick gloves and already her headache had come back. With an irritable sigh, she paused to rest, leaning on her spade as she blew on her wool-covered knuckles. The sand was crumbling where she had attacked it and as she watched, another section fell away by itself. With it it brought something large and curved and shiny. Throwing down the spade she bent over it and gently worked the object free of the sand. It was another section of pottery. Much larger this time. Large enough to hold the curve of the bowl or vase of which it had once formed a part. Through her gloves, as she dusted away the damp sand fragments, she could feel the engraved decoration. She stared at it for a long time, then carefully she put it to one side and attacked the sand with renewed vigour. Minutes later something else began to appear. It was thin and bent and a corroded green colour, like a rusty bit of old metal. Forgetting the pain in her temples she pulled at it in excitement. Thick as a man's thumb it was several inches long, with a rough knob at one end. Turning it over in her hands she stared at it for a long time, then, scrambling out of the hollow of her sheltered digging place she ran over the shingle towards the sea. The shingle was wet and smelled of salt and weed, the night's harvest of shells and dead crabs lying amongst the stones. Nearby she could see the gulls picking amongst them. Crouching down, her feet almost in the water, she swished the object back and forth in the edge of the tide and then she stared at it again. It was no cleaner. The greenness was a part of it. She took off her glove and ran a cautious finger over it, feeling a certain symmetrical roughness on the cold metal as though at some point in the distant past it had been carved, though now the incrustations of time and sea and sand had covered it forever.

Excited, she turned back towards the dune and stopped in her tracks. A freak gust of wind had risen. It had whipped the sand up and spun it into a vortex which danced for a moment across the beach and then dropped back to nothing. Behind her the first rim of the sun had appeared above the horizon. For a moment she hesitated, frowning. She was frightened, with the strange feeling that there was someone nearby, watching her. Shrugging, she huddled into her jacket, wedging her find into the pocket as she stared round. If there was someone there it would be a friend. Joe Farnborough from the farm, or Bill Norcross if he had decided to go for an early walk, or even Lady Muck herself or someone out walking their dog along the tide line.

Her spade was still lying where it had fallen in the sand and she took an uncertain step towards it. The skin was prickling on the back of her neck. It was a strange feeling, one she couldn't remember experiencing before, but instinctively she knew what it was. She was being watched! The words of a poem flitted suddenly through her head. Her mother had read it to her once when she was very small. The blood of the small, impressionable Alison had curdled as she listened wide-eyed, and the words had stuck. It was the only poem she had ever learned.

> When sunset lights are burning low,
> While tents are pitched and camp-fires glow,
> Steals o'er us, ere the stars appear,
> The furtive sense of Jungle Fear . . .

Primitive fear. Fear of danger which you cannot see.

She licked her lips nervously. 'Silly cow,' she said out

loud. It was herself she meant. 'Stupid nerd. Move. Now. What's the matter with you?'

The sun had risen further. A red stain began to spread into the sea and imperceptibly it grew lighter. She clenched her fists and took a step towards the spade. Her mouth had gone dry and she was shaking. With cold. Of course it was with cold. Gritting her teeth she jumped back into the hollow and grabbed the spade, holding it in front of her with two hands. The wind had begun to blow again and it lifted the skirt of her jacket, billowing it around her, whipping her hair into her eyes. The dust was spinning again, rising near her feet. She rubbed her eyes with the back of her wrist. The sand was lifting, condensing. Almost it was the shape of a human figure.

Slowly she backed away from the dune and, scrambling out of the hollow, she began to move towards the cottage. Seconds later she broke into a run. Hurtling across the lawn she dived down the side of the building, threw the spade into the shed and pelted down the track towards the trees.

In the dune the piece of red-glazed pottery lay forgotten, covered already by a new scattering of sand.

VIII

Kate lay for a moment disorientated, staring up at the heavily-beamed ceiling, wondering where she was. Her dream had been so vivid, so threatening. Huddling down into a tight ball under the bedclothes she tried to piece it together, to remember what had been so frightening, but already she was having difficulty recalling the details and at last with some relief she gave up the attempt and, sitting up, she gazed around the unfamiliar room. It was ice cold. A diffuse grey light like no light she had seen before filtered in from between the undrawn curtains. It was eerie; luminous. Dragging the quilt around her she climbed out of bed and going to the east-facing window, she peered out. The sea was slate black, shadowed with mist and above it a low sun hung like a dark crimson ball shedding no reflection and little light. It was a cold, unenticing scene without perspective. She shivered and turned back into the room. Gathering up her clothes she ran down the stairs on ice-cold feet and looked into the living room. There the curtains were still closed. After drawing them back she opened the doors of the woodburner and stared at it, depressed. The fire was out and the metal cold.

'Sod it!' She looked down at the single log. It was barely scorched from last night's paper blaze. To light it she would need firelighters, twigs, more paper . . .

Of course there would be no hot water either. Shivering, she abandoned the idea of washing and pulled on a pair of jeans. Thick socks and a heavy sweater and she was ready to forage once more in the log shed.

The outside world was bitterly cold. The garden – no

more than a piece of rough turf and a couple of small bare flower beds — appeared to surround the cottage in a small compact circle; beyond it in the cold early-morning light the grass grew wilder and more lumpy and matted before almost at once giving way to the dunes and shingle banks which backed the sea.

As she stepped out of the front door a movement at the side of the cottage caught her eye and she stopped, astonished to find that her heart was beating faster than normal again. The fear in her dream was still with her and the silence and emptiness of the woods unnerved her. Forcing herself to walk outside she peered around and realised, relieved, that what she had seen was a rabbit. Three rabbits. They all straightened for a moment as she appeared, their ears upright, their eyes bulging with terror and then they bounded back into the trees. She smiled, amused and not a little embarrassed by her own fear. She was going to have to take herself in hand.

In the doorway of the shed she stopped. The spade was lying across the threshold. Stooping she picked it up. There were clods of wet muddy sand attached to the shoulders of the blade. Someone had used that spade recently — certainly since she had come out to the shed last night. She surveyed the woods but as far as she could see they were silent and still. Even the rabbits had gone.

Shrugging her shoulders, she gathered up another armful of logs and, this time spotting the pile of neatly stacked kindling in the corner of the shed, filled her pockets with twigs and small slivers of wood to help light the fire.

Hot coffee and a blazing furnace in the woodburner did much to restore her optimism as did the discovery that there was an electric immersion heater in a cupboard in the bathroom as a backup to the more esoteric uncertainties of hot water from logs. She ate a bowl of cereal and then set about unpacking in earnest.

Several times as she glanced through the windows she

noticed that the day was clearing. The mist was thinning and the sun had gained a little in strength. By the time her bags and boxes were empty and she was storing them in the spare bedroom, the sea was a brilliant blue to match the sky.

Turning from the curtainless window her eye was caught by a stack of canvasses behind the door which she hadn't noticed earlier. They stood, face to the wall, in a patch of deep shadow. Curious, she turned one towards her. The painting was of the sea – a strangely surrealist, nightmare sea. With a grimace she pulled out another canvas. It repeated the theme as did the next and the next. Then came two more, scenes of the cottage itself, one in the autumn where a bland chocolate-box house was surrounded by a curtain of flame, the other a representation of the house as it would look beneath the nightmare sea. She stared at the latter for a long time and then with a shudder she stacked it back against the wall. They were all painted by the same hand, and a hand which commanded a great deal of talent and power, but she did not like them. They were cruel; twisted in their conception.

Closing the door with a shiver she ran down the stairs and back into the sun-filled living room where her books and papers were laid out on the table ready to start work. Putting the paintings firmly out of her mind she stood looking down at the table.

The book was there, in her head, ready to start and it was going to be even better than *Jane*. Kate smiled as she pulled her notepad towards her and switched on her word processor.

The knock on the front door two hours later took her by surprise. She had completely forgotten Bill.

'Hi!' He grinned at her as she led the way into the living room. 'How are you? Ready for lunch?'

She stared at him, miles away, reluctant to lose the mood, aching to go on writing.

Bill was watching her. 'Penny for them,' he said softly. 'You didn't hear a word I said, did you? I've boobed. I've intruded on the writer with her muse.'

'Oh, Bill, I'm sorry. Of course I heard you.' Kate dragged herself back to the present and gave herself a little shake. 'Blow the muse; she can go back in her box for a few hours. And yes, that's a super idea. I'd love lunch.'

The walk through the wood was thoroughly enjoyable and eagerly she looked around, noting the crisp air, the soft muddy track, the whispering fragrant pines, the winter-dead oak, and birch and hazel bright with young catkins, as she plodded beside him, her hands in her pockets, throwing off her preoccupation with the background of the poet's father, mad Jack Byron, in order to recount her adventures of the night before.

'That's typical of Greg, I'm afraid, not to tell you about the fire or leave you any logs,' Bill said, shaking his head. 'There's a petty streak to him. He's angry about having to give up the cottage for you.' He kicked out at a rotten branch which lay half across the track.

'I didn't realise he lived there.'

'Oh yes. Greg is a brilliant painter. He dropped out of university about six years ago, half way through getting a Fine Art degree, came home here and more or less squatted. That was before Roger had to give up work – I don't know if you realise, but he's got cancer.' He paused for a moment. 'Anyway, the Lindseys indulged Greg disgracefully, there is no other word for it, and I think Roger gave him some sort of allowance, but when he had to stop work himself there were a few heavy hints that Greg might get off his backside and get a job to help the family coffers. He was impervious to them all, I gather. He has lofty views on the sacredness of talent and the fact that the rest of the world owes him a living so he can indulge that talent. Poor Diana, I don't know how she's coped until now. The idea of renting the cottage did not go down well with old

Leonardo, as you can imagine. I gather he was dragged out kicking and screaming. So, don't take his animosity personally. But don't expect him to come calling with bunches of flowers either.'

Kate frowned. 'You might have told me all this before, Bill.'

'Why? Would you have changed your mind about coming?'

She shook her head. 'No, but it explains a lot.' She paused. 'I found some paintings in the bedroom. He must have forgotten them.'

'I doubt it. If he left them there, he left them there for a reason. Which means he wanted you to see them.' Bill glanced at her. 'His paintings are pretty grim, to my mind.'

She nodded. 'I didn't like them. There was one which showed the cottage under the sea. It was –' she hesitated, trying to find the right word '– morbid – threatening.'

'Take no notice. We'll ask Diana to take them away.'

'It seems wimpish to make a fuss.'

'Not at all. You're as much of an artist as he is, remember. A better one, because you are disciplined. And you are entitled to feel as sensitive and touchy as he is.' He grinned. 'Are you feeling sensitive and touchy?'

'Not in the least. Hungry covers it rather better.'

'Good. In that case, let's find your car and go eat.'

The farmhouse was empty. After a cursory glance through the windows to convince themselves that there really was no one at home they turned their attention to the barn. Kate's Peugeot was there, neatly parked next to an old Volvo estate.

'Diana's,' Bill said. 'They can't have gone far if they are all packed into that fiendish Land Rover, not if they value their teeth.'

By the time they had reached the end of the track and gained the metalled road, Kate was beginning to think he was right – and that perhaps when her next royalty cheque came she should sacrifice a few teeth in the interest of her car's springs and buy an ancient four-wheel drive of her own for the duration of her stay.

They ordered curry at The Black Swan, a delightful long, low, pink-painted pub a mile or two from the lane, and sat down pleasantly near to a huge inglenook fireplace with a gentle smouldering log which filled the room with the scent of spicy apple. Save for the smiling pink-cheeked girl behind the bar they were the only people there. 'So. Are you going to like it at Redall?' Bill sat down on the high-backed settle, and sticking his legs out towards the fire he gave a great sigh of contentment. He raised his pint glass and drank deeply and appreciatively.

Kate nodded. 'It's the perfect place to work.'

'The loneliness doesn't worry you?'

She shook her head. 'I must say it was a bit quiet last night. Just the sea. But I'll get used to it. It will be wonderful for writing.' Picking up her own glass – she had opted for a Scotch and water – she looked at Bill for a moment. In a thick brown cable-knit sweater and open-necked shirt he reminded her faintly of a rumpled sheepdog. 'Did you speak to Jon at all before he left, Bill?'

He glanced at her over the rim of his glass. 'Only once. He rang to ask me if I knew where you were going.'

'Did you tell him?' She looked away, not wanting him to see how much she wanted him to say yes.

'No.' There was a thoughtful pause as he sipped his lager. 'We had a few words on various themes related to male chauvinism – his – and misplaced chivalry – mine – and professional jealousy – all of us – and at that point I told him to bugger off to America and let you get on with your life. Did I do wrong?'

'No.' She didn't sound very certain.

She was thinking of their last meeting. Jon had been about to leave for the airport. The taxi was at the door, his cases stacked nearby and she, not wanting to say good-bye, not wanting to see him again before he went in case her resolution wavered, had arrived back at the flat thinking he had already gone. For a moment she had been tempted to turn and run – but he had seen her and they were after all both grownups. For a moment they had looked at each other, then she had smiled and reached up to kiss him on the cheek. 'Take care. Have a wonderful time. I hope it's all a great success.' For a moment she had thought he would turn away without a word. Then he had smiled at her awkwardly. 'You take care too, Kate, my love. Don't get too wrapped up in old George. And remember to look after yourself.' They were both hurting; miserable; stiff-necked. And that was it. Picking up his cases he had walked out to the cab and climbed in without a word or a backward glance. There was no way that she could know that there were tears in his eyes.

'I had an Irish grandmother, Kate,' Bill said after a moment's sympathetic silence. 'She was always full of useful aphorisms. One of her favourites was: "if it is meant to be it will be." I think it just about fits the case.'

Kate laughed. 'You're right. We need a break from each other at the moment.' She glanced up as a waitress appeared with their knives and forks, wrapped in sugar-pink napkins, a huge bowl of mango chutney and large pepper and salt cellars contrived to look like a pair of old boots. 'But if he phones again, perhaps you might tell him where I am this time.' She caught Bill's eye and they both smiled comfortably.

'Is there a woman in your life, Bill?' She hadn't meant it to come out quite so baldly as she sought for a change of subject, but he didn't seem put out.

'Only Aunty Beeb at the moment – the goddess I work for. There was one once, but she buggered off too.' He paused reflectively, taking another deep drink from his glass. 'You are not offering, I take it. Flattered and tempted though I would be by such a possibility, I think it would be bad for both of us.'

'I'm not offering. But I need a friend. Someone who will walk through the woods now and then and drag me to a pub for a curry.'

'Done. But not alas for a while after today. I've got a tight schedule until Christmas.'

She was astonished at how devastated she felt at his words. She had known he was going back to London and yet somehow she had counted on him being there again next weekend.

'Want another Scotch?' He had been watching her face closely and saw something of the loneliness which had shown in her eyes for a moment.

She nodded and held out her glass. 'Then we can drink to Lord Byron. By the time I see you again, he will be, with a lot of luck, several chapters long.'

After dropping Bill at Colchester station she took the opportunity to drive on into the town, curious about the place which would be her nearest large centre for the next few months. Pevsner, in the edition of the book she had briefly consulted in the London Library, had waxed lyrical about it, but nineteen-sixties red-brick shopping centres now seemed to vie with nineteen-eighties glass and concrete where much of what he had described must have been. Saddened, she turned her attention at last to the castle museum.

The huge squat building was shadowed already from the late afternoon sun as she made her way across the bridge and inside the great door to buy her ticket. The place was strangely empty. In the distance she could hear the disembodied, dramatic voice of a video loop — the sound effects and urgency of the narrative strangely out of place amongst the glass cases beneath the high-beamed roof of the castle. She walked slowly around the ground floor exhibits gazing at Bronze Age and Iron Age artefacts, gradually growing closer to the sound.

For several minutes she stood watching the video — which told of the Romans in Colchester — then turning away, she began slowly to climb the stairs. At the top were Roman exhibits, life-size models, colourful, larger than life panoramic pictures on the walls, and then another video enactment, this time of Boudicca's attack and the sack of the town.

Poor Boudicca. Kate wandered round slowly studying the exhibits, piecing together her life: the wife of Prasutagus; her children; the political background of first-century Britain; her husband's death; the rape of her daughters and her humiliation as she was flogged by a Roman — the final insult after years of unrest and dissatisfaction in a country under foreign occupation, which caused the revolt which had nearly ended the Roman occupation of Britain. What a story her life made. Suddenly Kate found herself watching the video with heightened excitement. What a biography it would make; what a book, when George Byron was finished . . . The burning of Colchester, the rampage of Boudicca's forces across Essex and Hertfordshire as they made their way towards London, and the final hours when she realised that all had failed and she took her own life. And Colchester was the centre of it all — a city where the flames had burned so hot that nearly two thousand years later a layer of blackened death was still clearly visible in the foundations of the town.

She watched the video through twice, alone in the darkened booth — seeing the huge sketched shapes of the warriors, hearing their shouts and screams, then she stood up and left, intensely aware suddenly of the vaults far beneath the castle which were all that remained apparently of the Temple of Claudius — the temple Boudicca had burned to the ground with most of the population of the town inside it.

She recognised this feeling: the tight, bone-tingling, breathless excitement as ideas jostled in her head, and under her breath she swore. She had had this feeling before, after she finished *Jane*; not until she had finished *Jane*. To get it now, while she was still at the beginning of *Lord of Darkness* meant she was going to suffer months if not years of suppressed, hidden frustration and worry in case someone else had the idea first; in case her publisher didn't like the idea; in case the idea took root in her sleep and developed and began to encroach on the work in progress.

Shaking her head in a small gesture of irritation she moved on past the exhibits. How could a woman – any woman – however hurt and humiliated, order the slaughter of other women, of children, of babies? What kind of person was she, this remote queen who offered human sacrifice to her gods before going to war?

She stopped abruptly. She was standing in front of a statue of a Roman citizen and her eye had been caught by the name. Frowning, she read the inscription: 'MARCUS SEVERUS SECUNDUS, one of the very few recorded survivors of the Boudiccan massacre. Instrumental in the rebuilding of Colchester after its sack in A.D. 60, he died full of years and honour and was buried next to his wife Augusta in the year A.D. 72. Their graves were excavated in 1986. See exhibit in case 14.'

So this was Redall's former owner. She stared hard at the stone face of Marcus with his patrician nose, slightly chipped, his warrior stance, the carefully sculpted folds of his toga and she wondered what kind of a man he had been. He had been one of those who had survived the massacre and returned to pick up the threads of his life. She felt another sudden frisson of excitement. Had he seen Boudicca? Could he have described the warrior queen of the Iceni with her flowing red hair and her massy torcs, her body armour and her war chariot?

She jumped suddenly as a disembodied voice, echoing

around the castle, announced that the museum would soon be closing and she gave Marcus a last regretful glance. But not too regretful. She had the feeling she would be coming back to see him again.

IX

The youngest son of the late King, he had stood head and shoulders above his brothers and he knew he had been the favourite. His love of learning, his memory, his wit had marked him out as a child for study and initiation. His priesthood gave him power. His royal blood marked him for destiny. That was why he had been given lands and authority, and why he was trusted as advisor at Camulodunum to the Roman settlers, even though his brothers led revolt in the west. He wore Roman clothes; he spoke their language; he assimilated their learning and their ways. And he had fallen in love with one of their women. But he hated them and he bided his time.

He frowned when he saw the detested overlords raising their temple in the heart of Camulodunum: a temple to Claudius; a temple to a man who had declared himself a god. But he kept his views silent. One day the time would come, one day the Romans would be expelled from the land of his ancestors. When that day came, he would kill Claudia's husband and he would take her back to his hall. But until then, ever the diplomat, he would smile.

His duties as druid were light. He was royal, rich, in love. The gods would understand. He would serve them in due time when the bluebells had faded and the blood ran more slowly in his veins.

The old priests disapproved. They frowned and shook their heads first at him, then at the signs from the gods; the gods who despised the Romans who would venerate a man and make him one of them.

He did not know that the gods, too, were growing angry.

It was almost dark as Kate drove down the track and into the barn and parked her car next to Diana's Volvo once more. The farmhouse, she had noticed at once and with a strange sense of loss, was in complete darkness. She had not realised until that moment how much she had been counting on being asked in to sit by their cosy fire and have a cup of tea before she set out on the walk through the wood to her cottage.

On the drive back she had found a farm shop open where she had managed to buy some bread and milk, crumbly local cheese and Essex honey and, to her great delight, some firelighters and matches.

Hefting her plastic carrier over her shoulder she was already on the track when she stopped. The torch was still in the car. Turning back she pulled open the barn door once more and, unlocking the Peugeot she rummaged in the glove compartment. The torch was there, and – experimentally she flashed it up into the high rafters – it worked. Comforted, she locked up again and set off at a determined pace into the woods.

The track ran straight for a few hundred yards and then curved eastwards, narrowing until there was only room for the rutted marks of the Land Rover's wheels. Her feet slipped and she found she needed the torch to see where to put them in the mud. The evening was very still. There was no wind and the trees were silent. In the distance she heard the warbling call of a curlew from the marshes. The sound echoed in the falling darkness and was answered by the shriek of an owl. She clutched her bag more tightly, her eyes riveted to the track.

May the gods of all eternity curse you, Marcus Severus Secundus, and bring your putrid body and your rotten soul to judgement for what you have done here this day . . .

The woods were still silent, the trees unmoving. The words, as clear and well enunciated as those of a BBC presenter, had been inside her own head. Kate stopped dead, a sheen of sweat on her skin, her heart hammering in her ears. She stared round, her eyes straining into the darkness between the tall tree trunks, very conscious of the smell of rotting wood and damp, dark earth which surrounded her.

Stupid. The darkness and the silence after the celluloid drama of the museum and the excitement of the new idea had set her imagination working overtime, that was all. She resumed walking, a little more quickly this time, her torch clutched so tightly in her hand that her fingers grew numb.

When the cottage at last came into view she was breathless. Fumbling in her pocket for her key she let herself in and turned on the light, then she put her shopping bag down on the kitchen table, ran upstairs and grabbed one of her empty boxes from the spare bedroom. Dragging it after her she went straight outside again and made for the log shed. Before she did anything else and before she lost her nerve completely she would stock up with firewood.

Flashing the torch beam around the small shed she piled logs into her box, and then a huge heap of kindling. The shed was very neat, the ranks of logs undisturbed beneath their net of spiders' webs save for a few that had fallen at the end of the pile, the spade still leaning where she had left it in the corner. With one last look round she turned off the torch and returned it to her pocket. She needed both hands for the box. Hefting it up with a groan she made her way out into the cold garden, conscious of the brooding woods so close to the front of the cottage. It was impossible to run with the box. As swiftly as she could she walked back indoors and then she dropped it on the hall floor. Turning she slammed the door shut and shot the bolt home.

Safe. She closed her eyes and laughed quietly to herself, embarrassed, alone as she was, by her own stupidity. Picking up the box again she hauled it into the living room and put it neatly by the stove. Then, drawing the curtains against the darkness she went back to the kitchen and put on the kettle. The phone rang as she was waiting for it to boil.

'Kate, my dear. Just checking to see that everything is all right.' It was Roger Lindsey. 'I'm afraid we've been out most of the day so I thought I would give you a quick call to make sure you have everything you need.'

'Thank you. I'm fine.' She took a deep breath, astonished at how pleased she was to hear the sound of his voice. 'I came by earlier to leave my car again so I saw you were out.'

'We were having lunch with some friends in Woodbridge. Nice people. They had read your book.'

'Nice people indeed.' She smiled wryly. 'Roger, tell me, how do I make this woodburner thing stay alight all night?'

She heard an exclamation of impatience. 'Didn't Greg show you? I'm sorry, my dear. Those things take a bit of getting used to, but once you've got the hang of it you can keep it going for months without it going out. Do you want me to come up and show you?'

She shouldn't drag him over when he was ill, when he had been out all day and must be tired, but suddenly the thought of a visitor was very tempting. 'Would it be an awful imposition? I've got a good whisky here.'

She heard him laugh. 'I'm on my way.'

It was scarcely fifteen minutes later that she saw the headlights of the Land Rover appear from the trees. Roger climbed out. 'Greg's away for a day or two. I'll give him a good bollocking when he gets back. He was supposed to show you how everything works.'

'He must have forgotten. I had so much stuff to bring in.' She closed the door behind him and led the way into the living room. She had put the whisky bottle on the table with two glasses. She poured, then she watched as he knelt before the stove and pulled the doors open. 'Start with a good blaze, like this,' he instructed. Magically a fire appeared beneath his thin hands. 'Then put on one or two of the logs. Like so.' He pushed two huge logs into the small cavity and miraculously they fitted. Then he closed the doors. 'Now, leave it for a while with the dampers open like this. Once the fire has caught properly – about two-thirds of the way down that glass, I should say – we close them tight. The secret is to get it burning slowly and steadily and then to cut off as much air as possible. You have to stack the logs in really tight last thing – that's an art you must practise I'm afraid, but you'll soon get the hang of it. It keeps this place really snug once it's working properly.'

He took the glass she offered him and sat down in one of the armchairs, gazing round the room. 'You've made it look very comfortable.'

The tall, thin man sprawling in the chair in his shabby cords and old tweed jacket was so reassuring and normal that Kate found the wave of nervous loneliness which had hit her earlier was receding fast. 'I gather your son used to live here. I'm sorry my coming here has upset him,' she said as she sat down opposite him.

'He's no business to be upset.' For a moment a shadow passed across Roger's face. 'He knows we need the money. Sorry if that sounds crude, but it's a fact of life. And it's nice for us to have a congenial neighbour.' He smiled comfortably. 'As you've gathered, it's fairly isolated up here. And to that end, Diana has instructed me to ask if you would like to come and have some supper with us on Wednesday. We quite understand if you'd rather not because you are working, but –'

'I should love to.' She replied so quickly she surprised even herself. 'I shall look forward to it immensely.'

'Good.' His smile was expansive, deepening the network of wrinkles around his eyes. 'You'll have the pleasure or otherwise of meeting our other two children, Allie and Patrick.' Draining his glass he stood up. 'If there's nothing else I suppose I'd better go home. Di will have supper ready soon.'

Stay, she wanted to say. Please, stay and talk to me. She liked his presence in the room. It was comforting. Solid. And safe. She said nothing. Smiling, she showed him to the door. 'I'll report back on my success or otherwise with the stove when I see you.'

'Do that.'

She watched as the Land Rover backed round and headed back up the track, the headlights bucking against the trees as it slid between the ruts. In a moment it was out of sight.

Closing the door and bolting it again she walked back into the living room. As though recognising the hand of a master the woodburner had settled down to produce a satisfyingly hot glow which was already warming the room. She looked round, pleased. Although Roger had gone something of the friendliness he had brought with him had remained; basking in it, she would make herself some supper, read a little, listen to some music, have a hot bath and go to bed early. Tomorrow she would spend the day with Lord Byron.

X

In the stillness of the night the tide lapped imperceptibly higher along the beach, round the headland and slowly, oh so slowly, into the backwaters of the estuary, licking at the mud, floating strands of trailing grasses and weeds, curling round the toes of sleeping geese and ducks. Rising.

In the dune the sand had dried. It was brittle, friable, ready to fall. Beneath it, only a centimetre down now, was the clay – clay which was plastic, impervious to air or water, and in the clay was the peat which held preserved the remains of four human bodies.

XI

She had been sitting at the word processor for two hours and she had not noticed that it was getting light. Now, arms and shoulders cramped and her head throbbing from her intense concentration, Kate sat back, took off her glasses and, dropping them beside her notes, stared out of the window. The mist had receded to leave a sunrise of breathtaking clarity. The narrow vee of sea visible between the shingle banks from her carefully positioned table glittered with blinding beauty. It was more than anyone could resist; besides, she needed a break. Donning jacket, scarf and boots she pulled open the front door and emerged into an ice-cold wind. Looking around she took a deep breath of pure delight. This was a place where Byron himself would have felt at home.

> Roll on, thou deep and dark blue Ocean – roll!
> Ten thousand fleets sweep over thee in vain . . .

The beach was still wet from the receding tide as she tramped northwards along it, murmuring the lines from 'Childe Harold', her head ducked against the sting of the wind and the glare, her cheeks tingling beneath the whipping strings of hair as they pulled free of her scarf. The words weren't quite right, of course. This wasn't an ocean and it was neither all that deep nor dark, but still the mood was right. It was exhilarating. She wanted to jump and run and dance, but the shingle and soft sand precluded all but the most undignified gallop. Stopping at last, exhausted, she turned and began to retrace her steps. With the wind and glare behind her she could slow down and appreciate the different colours and textures of the water: where the sand rose near the surface it was pale green, even yellow. Further out streaks of deep turquoise melded with grey and black and the intense sapphire blue of a child's painting of the sea. In the distance the shingle gave way to muddy sand and she could see dunlin and redshank at the water's edge. Save for them she appeared to be the only being alive in the world.

She came level with the cottage, appreciating from here how sheltered it was behind the shingle banks, only a narrow section of its face visible behind the waving grasses and heaps of sand. In front of her, beyond the dunes, the beach swept away around the corner. There a narrow inlet led into the shallow, muddy waters of Redall Bay with its network of small islands and tidal creeks.

By the last of the dunes she stopped. Part of it appeared to have fallen onto the sand, and in the hollow on its seaward side there were signs of recent digging. Curious, she walked towards it, her boots slipping in the deep soft mixture of stones and mud and sand. The top section, out of sight of the cottage, had had a neat transverse slice removed from it. About ten feet long and two feet deep the interlocking grasses had been sectioned away and below it the sand had been scooped loosely into piles. Jumping down into the hollow she stared at the exposed wall of the dune. The resulting scar in the sand looked too regular and neat to be the result of a child's game; and it had certainly not been caused by the tide, although further along the cut had been lengthened and randomly enlarged by a muddy landslip where tell-tale strands of weed and a scattering of whelk shells betrayed a recent high tide propelled by an easterly wind.

Intrigued, Kate ran her hand lightly over the sand face. Who had been digging here, and why? Was it something to do with sea defences? She turned and looked back at the beach. The receding tide looked gentle and benevolent now, but she was under no illusions about the force it could muster if wind and moon were right.

She was about to scramble out of the hollow to resume her walk when her eye was caught by something shiny sticking out of the sand. It looked like a piece of pottery. She picked it up and examined it, then, frowning, she looked at it more closely. It was thin, fine, red, decorated with a raised pattern and it looked very like the Samian ware she had seen in the museum only yesterday. But that was impossible. She turned and surveyed the sand face again. Was this some sort of abandoned excavation? She stared down at the piece of pottery in her hand almost guiltily. Perhaps she shouldn't have touched it. On the other hand it had been lying in the loose spoil, obviously overlooked. With another high tide it would have been buried and lost. Pulling her scarf off her hair she wrapped the piece carefully and put it reverently in her pocket, then she turned and examined the exposed sand again. It was in a very crumbly state. The lightest touch dislodged another shower of soil. A few feet to her left she spotted something dark protruding from it. Cautiously she touched it. Metal. Scraping at the sand with her fingers she tried to see what it was without disturbing it. The narrow twisted neck of metal stuck out at right angles from the sand. She must ask the Lindseys. They would know who had been excavating here, and why they had stopped. She eyed the piece of metal longingly. If she touched it and it was of archaeological interest then she might be destroying valuable evidence – on the other hand another tide might remove it even more irrevocably. As she was standing there, trying to make up her mind what to do, a small crack appeared of its own accord in the top of the dune. As she watched a lump of wet sand broke away and fell at her feet. A minute later another six-inch section fell, taking the metal object with it. She bent and picked it up. Twisted, corroded, the metal was heavy and cold in her hand. She could not begin to guess what metal it was. Not gold certainly. Bronze, perhaps, or even silver. She examined it in excitement and awe. In all probability she was the first person to touch it for over a thousand years – perhaps two, perhaps more. It was a torc.

MY LOVE

The voice in her head had spoken so loudly she thought it was real. Dropping the torc she put her hands to her ears, looking round.

There was no one there. An oystercatcher was plodding slowly along the tide line near her, dipping its beak into the sand.

She could feel her heart beginning to hammer in her ears again, as it had in the woods in the dark the night before. Taking a deep breath she bent and picked up the piece of twisted metal, then she scrambled out of the hollow. She stared round, her arm across her eyes to hold back her streaming hair, loose now she had removed the scarf. There was still no one in any direction as far as she could see. Besides the voice had been inside her own head.

Taking a deep breath she turned towards the cottage. Get a grip on yourself, Kennedy. You're imagining things, she told herself sternly. Too much fresh air, that's your trouble.

The panic had gone almost as soon as it had come. Out here in broad daylight, in the brilliant sunshine and the light, tossing wind with birds patrolling unconcerned along the tide line, her moment of terror seemed absurd. It was imagination, that was all. A visit to the museum, a new preoccupation with Boudicca and the events of nineteen hundred years ago, together with the isolated situation and already she was having hallucinations. Strong coffee would soon sort that out.

Slightly faster than she would normally have walked she retraced her steps towards the cottage. Only once did she look back. There in the dazzle off the sea a sand devil whirled in the hollow where she had been standing. She watched it for a moment. It looked almost like a figure. Then it disappeared.

Letting herself in out of the wind, she shook her hair back from her face and putting her finds down on the kitchen table she put the kettle on even before she removed her jacket and boots. While the kettle was boiling she went to the phone but there was no answer from the Lindseys.

Picking up her coffee and her two artifacts she carried them through into the living room and put them down on her work table. Automatically she turned on the word processor. Waiting for it to summon up her programme she picked up the torc and examined it again. It was large – large enough to go around the neck of a full grown man at a guess, and still heavy in spite of, or perhaps because of, its corrosion. She stared at it for a long time then carefully she placed it on the windowsill before sitting down before her keyboard.

When she next looked up it was nearly one o'clock.

This time Diana was in when she phoned. Her query about the digging on the beach was greeted by a moment of embarrassed silence. 'You were there this morning, you say?' she asked cautiously.

'I was walking on the beach.'

'Of course. I think the place you're talking about is where my daughter has been doing some digging. It's for an archaeological project at school. It's not a designated site of any kind.'

'I see.' Kate frowned. She could hear the defensiveness in the other woman's voice. 'It's just that there seemed to be signs of some kind of ancient usage –' Her eyes strayed towards the doorway into the hall. She couldn't see the windowsill where her finds were lying. 'I felt that probably someone qualified ought to take a look at it. It could be an important site.'

'I think you'll find Alison has that in hand. It's her project entirely, Kate.' Diana's voice took on an unaccustomed firmness. 'Please leave it to her.'

And keep your nose out! Kate muttered as she put down the phone. She wandered back into the sitting room and stood looking down at the metal torc. If Alison was going to inform the museum then that was fine. She would show them her two trophies at the same time. She picked up the piece of twisted metal and examined it once more. It was badly corroded and bent, but the basic design of intertwined strands of metal wire was clearly visible. She scratched at it cautiously with her fingernail. A pale gleam appeared. She hesitated, then she scratched at it again, this time harder. The faint scratch showed a distinctly silvery sparkle. It was silver. She was holding a silver torc.

I CURSE YOU, MARCUS SEVERUS, FOR WHAT YOU HAVE DONE HERE THIS DAY

The voice was so sudden and so loud she dropped the torc onto the table. Frantically she shook her head. The sound had been inside her ears; it came from her brain. From her head. From her soul. Frightened she stared round the room. Then taking a deep breath she picked up the twisted metal again. It was very cold beneath her fingers. As cold as it had been when she first picked it out of the wet sand.

'This is stupid.' She said the words out loud, and her own voice sounded light and insubstantial in the empty room. She carried the torc and the piece of pottery to the small table in the corner on which the lamp stood and pulling out the drawer she laid them both in it. Closing it firmly she turned the key.

Auditory hallucination is a condition engendered by various states of mind and various physical conditions. She had read about it in one of Anne's books. But which one of them, if any, applied to her? Picking up the bottle of Scotch she walked through into the kitchen and firmly closed the door behind her. The first thing she could do was restore her blood sugar levels to normal. Perhaps a cooked lunch would dispel whatever it was which was causing this to happen.

She was sitting at the small kitchen table, with a book propped up before her, eating baked beans on toast covered in melted cheese, when there was a loud knock at the front door. Pushing her plate away reluctantly she went to open it.

A girl stood on the doorstep, dressed in jeans and a bright blue anorak, her blonde pony-tailed hair blowing wildly in the wind.

'I've come to tell you to keep away from my dig.' The green eyes were furious, the face unsmiling. 'Mum says you've been poking around in the dune. Well don't. Just because you've rented this place it doesn't give you any right to go poking around in other people's affairs. Keep away from it.' The young face was pale and strained. Her headache had been worse this morning, too bad to go to school, too bad to get up until Diana had told her what was happening out at the dune.

'You must be Alison.' Kate raised an eyebrow but, firmly suppressing the angry response which was her automatic reaction to the girl's rudeness, she merely said, 'I'm sorry. I didn't mean to interfere in your excavation. Of course I won't go near it again if you'd rather I didn't.'

'Please don't.' Alison scowled.

'You've told the museum about your finds, I gather.'

'I'm going to soon.' The girl's chin was set determinedly. She was very like her elder brother, Kate decided suddenly. They were a good-looking family, but obviously not noted for their charm. 'I'm writing it up first and taking photos and things.'

'Good.' Kate smiled. 'That's exactly the right thing to do.' She took a step back, about to shut the door but Alison still stood there, hands in pockets, obviously wanting to say something else. 'Are you really a writer?' It came out at last.

'Yes,' Kate smiled. 'I am.'

'And you're writing about Byron, Dad said.'

'That's right.'

'So, why did you come here?'

'I wanted somewhere quiet so that I could concentrate on my work.'

'And you know about history and things.'

Kate nodded. 'A bit. I studied history at university.'

'So you know about the Romans.'

'A bit, as I said. I gather they came here.'

'And there were people here even before that.' Alison's brow wrinkled slightly. 'The Trinovantes lived in Essex before the Romans came. That's a Roman grave.' She nodded her head in the general direction of the beach.

'A grave?' Kate frowned. 'What makes you think that?'

Marcus. The thought had come unbidden and as swiftly it had gone. Marcus Severus's grave was found in somewhere called Stanway, which, she had seen on the diagrammatic map near his statue, was on the far side of Colchester, some twenty miles away.

'I just know.'

Kate looked at the girl, disquieted. 'Alison, when you've got some time, would you show me your dig? Show me properly. Explain what you've done – the digging looks very professional – and tell me what you've found.'

'You really want to know?'

'I do. Not to interfere. I'm interested.'

'OK. Do you want to come now?'

With a moment's regretful thought about her baked beans and her book Kate nodded. 'Hold on. I'll get my jacket and boots.'

The tide had receded a long way when they stood together side by side on the edge of the hollow looking at the excavated side of the dune. The wind was whipping the sand into little eddies which whispered amongst the thin dry grasses and the sun had gone, hidden behind huge threatening clouds. 'I found some bits of pottery – shards, they're called, and some metal objects,' Alison said slowly. 'They're at home. I'll show you when you come to supper if you like.'

'I would like.' Kate glanced at the girl. She did not seem to be showing any eagerness to jump down into the hollow. 'How did you know where to dig?'

'The sea started it. Half the dune collapsed. Then I began to find things.'

'What made you think it was a Roman grave?'

'That's where you find things. In graves. There was a villa on our neighbour's farm. It's under his field, very near us, and there was a Roman road to the village and another to the other side of Redall Bay.'

'Was there?' Kate was fascinated. 'Can we go down into the hollow? It'll be out of the wind and you can show me exactly how you've been sectioning the soil.'

Alison seemed reluctant, but after a moment she jumped down into the soft sand and approached the exposed face where she had been working. 'I've been very careful not to disturb anything. The trouble is the sand just falls away. You can't stop it. The wind and the sea erode this coast all the time. Even houses fall over the edge a bit further along from here, at Redall Point.' She raised her hand gently to the sand, and then drew back without touching it. 'I've left my tools in your log shed.'

'Oh, I wondered who the spade belonged to.' Kate pushed her hair out of her eyes and reaching into her pocket for her glasses squinted more closely at the surface of the dune in front of her. 'Look, do you see? Here, and here. There's a change in texture. The sand is more gluti-nous. It's stronger. I think there's an outcrop of clay and peat of some sort. You may have more luck excavating that. It won't crumble so easily.'

'No.' Alison took a step forward and examined the place Kate was pointing to. Then she shivered. Her headache had returned with a vengeance. 'It's too cold to work today. I think I'll go home now.' She turned away. As they scrambled out of the hollow into the full force of the wind again Kate saw the girl glance over her shoulder at the spot where they had been standing. There was an unhappy frown on her face as if she had seen something which puzzled her.

It was only after Kate had watched Alison disappear up the track through the woods and had let herself once more into the cottage that she realised that she had not said a word about her own finds. She walked back into the kitchen and looked with regret down at her plate. Then she scraped the congealed mess into the waste bin and put the kettle on. She had wasted enough time already today. Forget Alison Lindsey and her Roman grave. This afternoon she must go back to the world of the cold, bleak Aberdeen lodgings where the young George Gordon was learning the bible, and a lot more besides, at his nurse's knee.

Her eyes glued to the screen of her lap top Kate did not notice the room growing dark. Her fingers were cramped; her arms stiff and heavy and there was an cold spot somewhere between her shoulder blades which had begun to hurt quite badly. Taking off her glasses, she stretched her hands out in front of her and wriggled her fingers painfully. The fire had died again and the room was icy. Climbing stiffly to her feet she went through the now routine acts of lighting, filling and closing the stove and stood for a moment staring down at the blackened glass of the little doors. She had done it on automatic pilot, her thoughts still with Catherine Gordon and May Grey and their volatile confusing relationships with the boy in their charge, relationships which would leave him scarred for life.

Satisfied at some subconscious level that the fire would

now catch and warm her she went back to the table and, sitting down she began to read through the afternoon's work.

May the gods of all eternity curse you, Marcus Severus, and bring your putrid body and your rotten soul to judgement for what you have done here this day . . .

She stared at the words blankly. She did not remember writing them. She hadn't written them. They appeared in the text suddenly, arbitrarily, half way through a description of eighteenth-century Aberdeen.

Pushing her chair back she stood up abruptly, conscious that her hands were shaking. Turning away from the screen she went back to the stove. Opening the doors she knelt in front of it and held out her hands, trying to warm them. It's just a phrase that's been whirling round in my head. I must have read it somewhere and it's somehow lodged in my brain and I typed it out. Idiot. Idiot.

Her eyes went unwillingly to the table drawer. For several minutes she tried to resist the urge to go over to it, then, giving up, she rose and went to switch on the lamp.

Picking up the torc she took it back to the fire and, sitting down on the floor in front of the blaze she turned the piece of metal over and over in her hand. She was no expert, no archaeologist, but she knew enough to be fairly certain that this was a Celtic ornament; almost certainly silver and therefore once the property of a wealthy man; a man not a woman, judging by its weight and size. It was certainly not Roman, whatever Alison thought. So it did not belong to Marcus Severus. Had not belonged, she corrected herself at once. So, whose was it? What was it doing buried in the sand on the edge of Redall Bay? The British tribes who opposed Rome had been Celts. The Celtic world, which today is linked in the popular mind purely to Wales and Scotland and Ireland and Brittany, once covered the whole of Britain – the whole of Europe. East Anglia had been as Celtic as Gwynedd or Galloway. It had been the Saxon invasions that had overridden their traces in folk memory.

She sat back, leaning against the sofa, drawing her knees up, the metal in her hands. It was warm now. The places where she had rubbed and scratched it glinted faintly in the firelight. She closed her eyes. This part of the country – this part of Essex – had been as Alison said the land of the Trinovantes, the tribe who had joined Boudicca and the Iceni in their revolt against Rome. Disillusioned and cheated by their Roman overlords in Colchester, they had not hesitated in rising up against the foreign oppressor. Had this torc belonged to one of them? A highborn Celtic lord? A prince? Was that his burial mound out there on the beach, lashed by the winter sea?

And what had Marcus Severus Secundus to do with him?

The sound of hail rattling against the window made her look up. It had grown quite dark outside. The lamplight reflected in the glass and suddenly the room felt very cold. She glanced at the fire. With the doors open the stove had consumed the logs she had thrown on earlier. Only ash remained. Rising to her feet she put the torc back into its drawer, closed and locked it, then she went to the window and, shading her eyes against the reflection she looked out. The glass was cold against her forehead. Cold and hard. The evening was totally black. Against the rattle of the rain and the howl of the wind she thought she could hear the crash of waves on the beach. With a shudder she stepped back and drew the curtains across. Then for the third time that day she built up the fire.

She awoke in the early hours with a start. Her bedroom was very cold. The wind had risen and she could hear the sea clearly now. The waves crashing on the beach, the rush and rattle of shingle, and from the other side of the cottage – the western side – the thrash and creak of trees.

She peered across the room. She had left the landing light on – a relic of that old fear of the dark – and she could see the outline of the door, the comforting wedge shape of light. For a minute she lay there staring at it, then she reached for the bedside lamp. Propped against the pillows, huddled beneath the blankets with her book and her glasses, she felt warm and safe. She half relished the battering of the storm.

A stronger than usual gust of wind flung itself against the window and she heard the groan and rattle of the glass and suddenly she was aware of the smell of wet earth. Bitter sweet, cloying, pervasive, it filled the bedroom. It was the smell of gardens, of newly-dug flower beds, of ancient woodlands.

Groping for her dressing gown she reached for her slippers and padded across the room. Opening the door fully she peered out onto the landing. It was ice cold out there and unbelievably draughty. Frowning she went towards the stairs and looked down.

The front door stood wide open.

For a moment she stood transfixed. It was the wind. It must have been the wind, but the front door was on the sheltered side of the house. She ran down the stairs and threw the door shut. She had bolted it. Surely she had bolted it the night before? Sliding the bolt hard home she turned the key in the lock as well.

The kitchen and the living room doors stood open, the rooms beyond, dark. She glanced at them with sudden misgiving. Supposing it wasn't the wind that had thrown the door open? Supposing it was a burglar?

Come on, Kennedy. Who would burgle this place? She went to the kitchen door and switched on the light. The room was empty, just as she had left it a few hours earlier, her dishes stacked in the sink, the kettle still – she put her hand on the metal and saw it cloud fractionally beneath her palm – a little warm. Switching it on she turned and went back to the hall. Immediately the smell of earth grew stronger. She paused for a moment, sniffing. The front door

86

was shut and the smell should have lessened, but now it seemed to be coming from the living room.

It was as she put out her hand to the light switch that she realised that there was someone in the room. Her mouth went dry. She held her breath, listening, aware that the other person was doing the same thing, painfully conscious that she was standing silhouetted against the bright light of the hall.

It was a woman.

She wasn't sure how she knew; she could see no one, but suddenly her terror wasn't quite so sharp. 'Alison?' Her voice sounded ridiculously loud and shrill. 'Alison, is that you? What are you doing here?' She found the light switch, clicked it on and stared round, her heart hammering under her ribs. There was no one there. The windows were closed, the curtains drawn as she had left them the night before and the woodburner was glowing quietly in its hearth, nicely banked – this time it would last easily until morning. But if the fire was alight, and the glass behind the door of the stove glowing, why was the room so deadly cold and where was the strange smell coming from? Biting her lip, she stared round again, before going cautiously into the room and looking quickly behind the sofa, behind the chairs, in the corners, even behind the curtains. All was as it should be.

It was a last minute thought to check the drawer where she had put the torc.

The lamp was no longer central on the table. Had she pushed it to one side like that, so it overhung the edge? So that one small push would have sent it toppling to the ground? She put her hand to the handle of the drawer and then drew back. The knob was covered in earth. Wet, rain-soaked earth. Cautiously, with two fingers, she pulled open the drawer. The torc and the piece of pottery were still there. They did not appear to have been touched.

So it was Alison. She had suspected Kate's theft and

come back for her treasure. She probably had a key to the cottage. Hearing Kate moving about upstairs she had lost her nerve and run away. Shaking her head angrily, Kate wiped the handle of the drawer and pushed it closed. She gave one final look around the room and walked to the door.

She was about to switch off the light when she became aware of another scent in the room beyond the smell of the wet earth. It was rich, feminine, musky. The scent a sophisticated woman would wear. She gave a wry smile. Perhaps even rude, boisterous, teenage girls showed signs from time to time of one day growing up.

XII

The decision was made; the sacrifice would be at Beltane. So would the gods be placated at last; the choice of victim to be given to them; he who took the burned bread from the basket would be the one who would die the threefold death.

Nion laughed when he heard. He was young and strong and invincible. And he was in love. His body coursed with the red blood of passion. His skin took fire each time she touched him. His eyes hungered after her body even as she turned to leave him. It was known that one of the elderly druids would take the burnt morsel; one of the old men; one of the fathers, who was ready to go willingly to meet the gods.

The bedroom at the Hyatt Hotel in New York was stiflingly hot. Jon Bevan had woken suddenly, his body bathed in sweat. With a groan he brought his wrist up close to his face and scrutinised the luminous dial of his watch with eyes that felt as though they had been rubbed in hot sand. Four in the morning. Swinging his feet to the carpet he groped his way across the bedroom to the small bathroom and felt for the light switch. The bright white light was blinding. Groaning again he went in and ran the cold tap into the basin, plunging his hands in, sweeping the water over his face and shoulders. It wasn't cold. In fact it was tepid, but it was better than nothing.

What had woken him? He passed back into the bedroom and turned on the light beside the bed. The heavy double curtains were tightly closed. It was strange how he had got used to Kate's silly, paranoid need to have the bedroom curtains open at night; now he too felt claustrophobic with them shut. He lifted one corner and peered out but he knew there would be no stars there. His bedroom looked out onto a monstrous, cavernous well, surrounded by other windows, reaching up out of sight towards the heavens. Even when he had tried to crane his neck out while it was still daylight he had not been able to see the sky. He pulled up the window an inch or two. Cold air rushed into the room, and with it the smells and sounds of the city. The blast of a car horn, the distant wail of police sirens, a miasma of indistinguishable music, a shout from somewhere in the dark wall of windows in front of him, and carried on the cold air, rich and spicy and nauseating, the smell of a thousand kitchens cooking steaks and fries, burgers and beans and onions. At four in the morning, for God's sake! Pulling down the window he sat down on his bed with a groan. Last night's party at the Café des Artistes had gone on until ten. Then he and Derek had gone on to 44 where they had met up with some other writers. After that he could remember little. They had gone to Peace then on somewhere else he could no longer recall – drinking, talking philosophy which had become increasingly maudlin, composing lines of stupendous prose which they had scribbled on paper napkins and promptly lost and which by tomorrow would be forgotten, and best so. He gave a grimace, embarrassed even to remember it. And tomorrow there would be more of the same. A talk to a group of creative writing students, a signing session at Rizzoli's, lunch with ... who? He shrugged. Who cares. One of Derek's minions would turn up, usher him around, line him up, make sure his clothes were on straight and his hair brushed, present him on time – a minion who would be intense, humourless, dedicated to the art of not losing an exhausted author in New York.

With an exclamation of disgust Jon threw himself back

on the bed and crossed his arms behind his head. He would never sleep now. He groped for the TV remote and pressed it at random. Seconds later he switched it off again. He was not that desperate.

The trouble was, he was missing Kate. He was missing Kate most dreadfully, and the guilt he felt about the way he had treated her had not gone away. The thought made him furious with himself. He had been small-minded, jealous, insecure, unfair. He listed his faults mercilessly. Well, at least now he had a new American contract as good as under his belt and he could begin to pay her back some of the money he owed her. He glanced at his watch again, idly computing what the time was in England. Nine? Ten? Morning anyway. He pulled the phone towards him and began to dial Bill. Somehow he would persuade him to divulge her number. He had to speak to her. He was missing her too much.

XIII

The tide had turned but the wind still piled the sea in against the north-east-facing coasts of Britain. It filled Redall Bay, all but inundating the low-lying islands which were the abode of so many birds. It washed away a huge section of cliff, six metres long, further up the coast near Wrabness, bringing two oak trees which had been clinging desperately to the edge of what had once been a wood crashing to the sand. Rolling up the beach, it flooded into the hollow near the dune, worried at the soil and began to undermine the face of the excavation.

Two of the bodies lay on top of each other, the man face down, his face pressed into the seeping wetness of the clay, his head at an angle, bent against his shoulder. The garotte was embedded deep in the strange desiccated blackness which was all that remained of his skin. He was naked save for the strip of tanned tree bark tied about his arm. It was the bark of the ash; the tree which was his totem; the tree for which he had been named – Nion.

The woman lay across him, hunched, contorted by the agony in which she had died. The fabric of her clothing was strangely intact. In one or two places the colour was still visible, though darkened by the chemical processes of clay and salts and decomposition. And by the blood. Out of sight, beneath her as she lay across the other body was a sword. It was a short sword, but sharp, corroded now to razor-thin metal. One of her hands still clasped the hilt. The point was embedded between her ninth and tenth thoracic vertebrae.

XIV

Kate was stacking the dishes in the sink next morning when she happened to glance out of the window and saw Alison appear from the wood. The girl had a fluorescent green haversack over one shoulder and in her hand she carried a large red radio cassette player. Still exhausted and angry after her disturbed night Kate waited for her to approach the cottage, but Alison veered off the path and headed straight towards the shed.

Drying her hands Kate went outside. The storms of the night had passed and the day was bright and crisp with only the lightest wind blowing from the south.

'Good morning.' She stopped behind Alison as the girl groped inside the shed.

Alison jumped. She turned, her spade in her hand. 'Hi.' She did not look pleased to see her.

'I thought you might be going to drop in and say hello,' Kate said.

Alison shrugged. 'I thought I'd get on.'

'Fair enough. But first, haven't you got some explaining to do about last night?'

It had not been easy to sleep after the disturbances. Even with the front door locked and bolted and the lights on throughout the house Kate had only dropped off an hour or so before dawn and then her sleep had been restless and light.

'Last night?' Alison turned back to the shed and retrieved a trowel and a broom.

'It was you who came up to the cottage.'

'Me?' She had the girl's full attention at last. 'I didn't

93

come up last night. What on earth would I do that for?'

Kate frowned. The wide eyes looked genuinely puzzled.

'Someone came to the cottage last night. About three in the morning and let themselves in. They must have had a key.'

'Weird.' Alison shook her head. 'Did they steal anything?'

'No.'

'Why did you think it was me? I'm not a thief.'

'I know.' Kate tried to lighten the mood by laughing. The sound came out tightly; it betrayed her sudden misgivings. 'You would tell me, wouldn't you, because if it wasn't you, I need to know who it was.'

'Perhaps it was Greg. He's probably still got a key.'

'No, it was a woman. And she had earth on her hands. I thought perhaps you had been digging again.'

'At three in the morning?' Alison gave her a withering look. 'If it was a burglar you'd better tell the police or something. We've never had burglars here before.' The implication in her tone was that Kate had obviously brought the trouble with her. 'You'd better ring Dad.'

'Yes, perhaps I'd better.' Kate frowned. 'In fact I'll drop in and see him when I pick up the car. I need to go into Colchester this morning.'

She wasn't sure when she had decided she needed to go back to the museum. The idea had come so firmly, so ready-formed it was as though she had had it planned all along.

'He's not there now. They've gone to Ipswich for the day.'

'Oh.' Kate felt let down. Ever since she had woken up that morning she had kept a picture of the gentle, reassuring face of Roger Lindsey firmly before her. He would know what to do. 'Are you going to be all right here by yourself?' She turned to Alison who was juggling all her tools into her arms with her ghetto blaster.

'Of course. I always come up here by myself.' The voice was jaunty, firm. It belied the moment of uncertainty in Alison's eyes.

The museum was comparatively empty as Kate threaded her way through the Bronze Age and Iron Age exhibits towards the staircase. Over on her left she could hear the video playing to itself. Someone had pressed the button, activating the sequences and then they had left, leaving the sound to echo disembodied around the deserted gallery.

Marcus Severus Secundus stared blankly at the glass cases around him from dead stone eyes. His face was stereotyped – handsome, classic, the hair formally curled. Was there any likeness there, or had the statue been purchased off the sculptor's shelf by an admirer or a descendent – his son perhaps – to stand in memoriam near his tomb? She stood staring at him for a long time, trying to get behind those blank eyes. Then, gently, aware that she was breaking museum regulations, she raised her hand and ran her fingers across his face, touching the mutilated nose, tracing the line of his cheekbones, his jaw, his shoulder.

The glass case which contained the surviving contents of his grave was close by. She stood and stared down at it with a sense of shock. She had not expected to see bones.

'In an inhumation, rare at this period, excavated on site B4 at the third Stanway burial mound were found the remains of Marcus Severus Secundus and his wife Augusta Honorata. A survivor of the Boudiccan attack on Colchester in A.D. 60, Marcus Severus was a leader of the rebuilding of the town. In the grave were found symbols of his office, jewellery and small grave goods.'

Kate stared through the glass. The bones lay in heaps, displayed in a plaster replica of the grave. Neither skeleton was complete. Had they died together then, Marcus Severus and his wife? She squatted nearer the case to see better the jewellery which was displayed there. Two rings of gold, a necklace of turquoise and amber, two brooches, one silver, one enamelled and several hairpins. Those must have been hers. And his was the heavy signet ring, mounted beneath a magnifying glass through which she could see the engraving. It showed a rearing horse. And his also, presumably, was the large silver brooch with an intricate design and long embossed pin. Consulting the information cards at the far side of the display she read: 'Exhibit 4: A curvilinear brooch of native silver, Celtic. Probably dating from the first century B.C. An unusual find in a Roman grave.' So, what was Marcus Severus of the Roman Legion doing with a Celtic cloak brooch? Had he bought it? Or looted it? Or was he given it as a gift?

Leaving the museum at last she turned into the town centre. Having stocked up with fresh food, a couple of films for her camera, a large torch with two spare batteries and after treating herself to a glass of wine and a plateful of fettuccine and salad at a wine bar off the High Street she made her impulse buy – a bottle of silver polish. The weathered silver of the brooch in the glass case had given her the idea. That too must once have been a corroded unrecognisable lump of metal. It was probably wrong to clean the torc herself. She should leave it to the trained restorers at the museum, but if she were gentle, and very careful – she wanted to see if she could achieve that same soft radiance. The torc itself was locked in her car. She had not wanted to leave it in the cottage, giving Alison all day to look for it. Now suddenly she wanted to get back to it, to make sure it was safe.

A cold wintery sunshine flooded across the town as she retraced her steps to the car. To reach it she walked past the theatre and through the surviving arch of the Roman Balkerne Gate. There was a wonderful view of the Roman wall here, as she walked, laden with her parcels, across the footbridge over the scar which was one of the main dual carriageways into town, towards the multi-storey car park.

The drive down the track to Redall Farmhouse was alarmingly slippery. Twice the car slid out of control side-w·ys, where somehow it had clawed its way out this morn-in. Presumably other cars had made the track worse. She hoped that meant that the Lindseys had changed their minds and come home early, but there was no sign of them when she parked in the barn, transferred the torc from the locked glove compartment to her shoulder bag, unloaded all her shopping and finally changed her shoes for her heavy boots.

It took a long time to walk the half mile or so to the cottage through the mud. Several times she stopped to change arms, and rest with her heavy bags. In the slanting sunshine the wood looked beautiful. Without leaves, the trees were graceful, linear dancers in the wind and there were hidden flowers around her feet; dead nettle and winter heliotrope and speedwell with the occasional small clump of snowdrops tightly furled in bud. The scent of pine and wet vegetation and resin was sharp and exhilarating. It was, she realised suddenly, nothing like the earthy smell which had permeated her cottage the night before.

To her relief the front door was still locked. Letting herself in she dumped her purchases on the kitchen table and went on a careful tour of the place. Nothing had been touched. The hair she had, rather shamefacedly, stuck across the drawer was still there. No one had been in. The more she had thought about it during the day, the more certain she was that Alison had somehow been responsible for last night's intrusion. Who else could it have been? With a silent apology to her young neighbour in the dune for her suspicions that she would return, she transferred the torc back to its resting place. Only then, cheerful enough to whistle as she worked, did she unload her bags and put on the kettle.

XV

Alison had stood for a long time on the edge of her excavation surveying the damage the wind and tide had wrought on her carefully exposed soil face. The dune had almost broken up. Half the wall she had left the day before had fallen. It lay, a tumble of wet sand and soil in the bottom of the declivity, strewn with tangled seaweed and shells and the rotting half-eaten corpse of a large fish. At the sight of it she pulled a face. Stacking all her equipment on the edge of the hollow she jumped in. She lifted the dead fish out on a spade and hurled it back onto the beach with a shudder. Moments later a screaming gull was circling over it, its claws outstretched for a landing.

She turned back to the shambles before her and stared round. She had already spotted several more pieces of that strange red earthenware lying around in the loose soil and there were other things too. Small round things. Black. 'Coins!' Her shriek was echoed by the gull which danced into the air for a moment before returning to gorge itself on the cold white flesh of the fish.

There were thirteen that she could find. Wrapping them carefully in pieces of soft tissue which she had optimistically brought with her for just such a purpose she stowed them in the pocket of her haversack, then she turned back to the dig.

It was the silence she hated. A silence which seemed to block out the gentle constant noise of wind and waves. It was threatening. It entered her aching head like an entity, battering against her brain. She was pretty sure that it had given her the migraines which were the reason for her missing school, but this time she had thought of a way of defeating it; of keeping the headaches at bay. Half an hour later, to the deafening sounds of The Sex Pistols, she was intently sifting through the heaps of sand with her fork and trowel, systematically separating out anything of interest, when she paused, looking down at the patch of dark sand in front of her.

The dagger was half buried still, the hilt and transverse hand-guard badly corroded, but not so badly that it was not instantly recognisable. For a long moment Alison stared down at it without moving, then she dropped to her knees and reverently she began to scrape away the surrounding sand. The dagger was some fifteen inches long, the blade two inches wide at its broadest. She sat for a long time with it in her hands, staring at it, awed, as the voice of Johnny Rotten blasted across the beach, torn by the wind and dissipated across the water. When at last she stood up, she held her trophy awkwardly aloft and she reached for her haversack again.

The blast of ice cold wind took her completely by surprise. Whipping the haversack with its precious cargo out of her hands it flung it down the beach as, blinded by flying sand, she tried desperately to catch it. Her broom fell sideways in front of her and was blown away to end up wedged into the shingle at the end of the dune and her cassette player subsided slowly into the loose soil, where it continued to blast out its music into the roar of the wind before the heavy soil depressed the switches on the top and it fell silent.

The squall had gone almost as soon as it had come. Pushing her hair out of her eyes Alison scrambled out of the hollow and stared up the beach. She could see her haversack, lying in a dayglo heap amongst the tangled seaweed, fifty yards along the tide line. Running to it she caught it to her chest, panting. Then she turned.

Above the dune the sand was still spinning crazily in a

whirling spiral which extended about four feet into the air. For several seconds she watched as it spun out of the hollow and away from her down the beach towards the inlet into the bay. Then as swiftly as it had come, it disappeared.

She swallowed nervously. This place was getting to her badly. She forced herself to walk back and stared down at the spot where she had been working so peacefully only five minutes before. All her hard efforts had been undone. The sand was piled randomly once more, her broom and spade lying beneath it. Her trowel had gone. Her cassette player was half-buried and silent, her picnic – two chocolate bars and a can of Coke – had fallen into a pool of sea water.

'Shit!'

She jumped down into the hole. Salvaging her belongings she heaped them on the edge. Switching on the music again she was comforted to hear it blast forth apparently unharmed. The Cure did a great deal to restore her equilibrium. Tearing the wrapper, thankfully intact and seemingly undissolved, off a chocolate bar she began to eat it.

Two yards to her left, unnoticed and almost invisible in the clay from which it protruded, a human hand, clawed and shrivelled, began, in the cold damp air, the process of disintegration.

Behind her, a faint shadow hovered over her; when at last she looked up and saw it, it was the size and shape of a man.

XVI

Oh, she was beautiful, the mother of his son. He watched her as she lay, propped on her elbow on the far side of the low table picking idly at the figs heaped on the plate before her. Her hair was rich and thick, piled high on her head and held in heavy-plaited coils by four ivory pins. Her skin was creamy, soft; her breasts, heavy, luscious beneath the soft folds of her long tunic. He felt himself tense. They were breasts which had been touched by another man's hands; another man's lips. It was strange. The heat of his fury and bitter jealousy was contained utterly by the cloak of ice which had formed inside him. Contained and controlled but not extinguished.

If he had returned to Rome, to the house of his father, would things have been different? Had he been foolish to accept the gift of land in the first colonia in Claudius's province of Britain? Colonia Claudia Victricensis which had been Camulodunum. He chewed thoughtfully at a dried fig. The land had brought him wealth, respect, honour – the perfect conclusion to an exemplary military career. But his young wife had been dismayed. She had wanted to return to Rome. She and her sister hated Britain. One of the reasons she had wanted so much to go back had been a man. She thought he did not know, but that man had been the reason for Marcus accepting this distant posting in the first place. He smiled grimly.

It was only a few months ago that she had changed her mind about Britain, and at once he had begun to suspect.

Feeling his gaze upon her Claudia looked up at him. Her smile was empty. Cold. A sham. He returned it and he saw doubt in those lovely grey eyes. But only for a moment. She thought she was safe. She thought she was clever. Let her think it. He would bide his time. The moment had to be right. Only her lover would know the real reason for his death, for Marcus could not afford to allow the scandal which would erupt if it became public. Private grief and anger must be contained, must be subservient to the public good. Any flame which might ignite the fire of revolt must be extinguished quietly. There must be no explosion of hate between the native tribes and Rome.

But in private . . . He breathed deeply, holding his anger in with iron control. In private, in secret, there would be revenge.

And his wife's punishment, afterwards, would last a lifetime, and then through all eternity.

For a moment Kate had been tempted to make up a thermos of coffee and take it out to the dig to see how things were going but she changed her mind. She had had her morning off. This afternoon, or what was left of it, should be spent in serious work. Besides, Alison would, no doubt, not extend much welcome to any intruders in her private excavation. Perhaps later, Kate would stroll out to the beach for a little fresh air, but not now.

She had worked solidly for about half an hour when the telephone brought her back to the present. Taking off her glasses she went through to the kitchen to answer it.

'Kate. Hi.'

'Jon?' The lift of her spirits, the excitement at the sound of his voice after so long was a purely Pavlovian response she told herself sternly, a conditioning, from living with him and loving him. 'How did you get my number?'

'From Bill.' For a moment he sounded defensive, then meekly he said. 'I hope you don't mind.'

She smiled. 'No. I don't mind. Of course I don't mind. How is the tour going?'

'OK. Nearly over, thank Christ!' He sounded tired and depressed. 'How are you?'

'Fine. Getting a lot of work done.'

'Is the cottage nice?'

Was he asking out of politeness or did he really care? 'Yes, it is as a matter of fact. Very nice.'

'Bill says it's very isolated.'

'It is. It's a good place to work.' There was a lump in her throat. Suddenly she was missing him so badly it hurt.

'Good. The money I owe you will soon be on its way, Kate. I'm sorry it's been so long. Look, I fly to Boston tomorrow. Perhaps I'll try and ring you from there.' There was so much he wanted to say, so much he wanted to tell her, but he couldn't. For some reason he was tongue-tied. He loved her and he had blown it. 'Take care.'

That was all. He had hung up. She stared at the receiver in her hand, feeling suddenly very, very lonely.

She was too unsettled to go back to work. After only a few minutes' struggle with her conscience she stood up, threw down her specs and reached for her jacket.

The beach was deserted, side lit in the falling dusk by the last streaks of sunlight from a bruised sun, going down in a haze behind the estuary. Along the tide line the dunlin were busy, probing the sand with their bills. Far out to sea the mist was waiting, hovering on the horizon, for the dark. There was no sign of Alison.

Kate stood staring down into the excavation for a long time. The mess of tossed sand and mud, the tangled weed, the shells, all spelt out the intrusion of the sea into the girl's vision of a Roman grave. There was no sign now of her meticulous digging and brushing of the sand. The vertical lines caused by the cutting edge of her spade had been replaced by a horizontal stratum, the sand intermingled now by long pale streaks of clay and broader wedges of black, the remnants of the three-thousand-year-old peat bog which had covered the river valley here when the sea was still two miles away. Looking down at the mess Kate shivered. She could see the earthenware, lying abandoned in the trench. Alison had not thought that worth collecting for some reason; nor had she gathered up the piece of metal lying on a tussock of uprooted grasses.

Slipping and sliding Kate scrambled down into the trench herself and picked it up with a frown. It was a dagger.

She turned it over in her hands, looking thoughtfully at the pitted corroded blade. It was ice cold to the touch.

Marcus

It was a whisper in her ear. A sigh on the wind. It was her imagination. Behind her, above the wood, the stars were emerging as the sky grew dark.

Scrambling out of the hollow she turned and began to walk swiftly back towards the cottage, the dagger still held in her hand, point down towards the ground, as though it were still potentially sharp. Which it was.

Indoors she slammed the door against the swiftly coming darkness, locked and bolted it and put the dagger down on the kitchen table, then she reached for the phone.

There was no answer from Redall Farmhouse.

She let it ring for several minutes, then at last she put the receiver down. If Alison wasn't at the farmhouse, where was she? Thoughtfully she walked into the living room and switched on the table lamp. She had begun to draw the curtains when she glanced at the stove. She couldn't believe it! It was out. And there were no logs in the box.

'Damn!' She stared down at it in dismay. She didn't want to go out, even to the log shed. She did not want to open the front door again. Suddenly she was shivering and to her astonishment she found she was near to tears.

Idiot. Idiot woman. Missing Jon. Frightened of your own shadow! Come on Kennedy where's your guts? What would sister Anne think of you if she could see you now? Firmly she put her jacket back on.

In the early dusk she could just see the nearest trees, their trunks glistening from the damp as she turned resolutely towards the shed, the empty box in her arms.

Alison's tools lay in the doorway higgledy piggledy as though she had thrown them down in a great hurry. Kate groped in her pocket for her new torch and shone the beam into the darkness of the shed. It caught the trowel lying on the ground, just inside the door. She bit her lip. What had made the girl leave so suddenly that she had left possibly her best find yet lying in the grave, and the tools of her trade, at first so neatly put away, thrown haphazardly down?

Better not to think about that. She had probably grown bored on her own. With a half-smile Kate remembered the ghetto blaster. Swiftly she tidied up the tools, then she loaded the box with logs and kindling. Now that it was heavy she could not spare a hand for the torch. Reluctantly she switched it off and pushed it into her pocket. After the bright torchlight the garden seemed very dark, but after all, she could see quite clearly by the light streaming out of the kitchen window.

And the headlights.

She paused, easing the box higher into her arms, watching them coming down the track, jerking up and down as the Land Rover slithered through the woods across the clear grass area and jerked to a stop outside the front door. Invisible in the darkness Kate waited as the door opened and the driver climbed out. He went to the cottage door and pushed it open.

'Hello?'

To her disappointment the voice was a deep baritone. Not Roger. Greg.

'Hello.' Kate had the satisfaction of seeing him jump violently as she came silently round the corner of the cottage, the box in her arms. 'Good evening.'

'Christ, you frightened me!' He looked at her for a

moment, then long-ingrained chivalry, drummed into him by his father over the years, prevailed over intentional boorishness as he saw the weight of her load. 'Here. Let me take that.'

She handed over the box gratefully and preceded him into the cottage. 'I've been in Colchester. The fire's out, I'm afraid.' She pushed the front door closed, making sure the latch had engaged, then she went through into the kitchen and drew the curtains, cutting off the cascade of light which shone out onto the grass. The garden sank into darkness.

'I've come up to find Alison. Is she here?'

Kate swung round and stared at him. 'You mean she's still not at home? I've been to see if she was digging out there, but there's no sign of her.'

They stared at one another, the hostility which crackled between them suddenly muted. Greg lowered the box to the ground. 'Are you sure?'

'Of course I'm sure.'

Behind Kate the phone rang from the kitchen. She turned to answer it. Greg followed.

It was Roger. 'Tell Greg she's with a friend. Silly child didn't think to leave a note. Apparently she went up through the woods to the Farnboroughs'. She's spending the night with them.'

'I knew she would be OK.' Greg shook his head in exasperation when she told him. Then he leaned across to the counter and picked up the box of matches lying there. 'Do you want me to light the fire for you while I'm here?' His voice was curt, almost as if he were offering against his will.

'Would you.' She did not allow herself to sound too grateful. 'The lighters are over there. I'll get us a whisky.'

'All done.' Greg came back moments later. 'Good lord, what's that?' He had spotted the dagger lying on the table near the coffee pot. Curiously he picked it up and examined it. 'Where did you find this?'

'In Alison's excavation.'

He frowned. 'I thought she asked you not to touch anything there.'

'She did, and I had no intention of doing so. This was lying on the ground at the edge as though she'd dropped it. Another tide and it would have been lost.' She poured the two drinks and pushed one towards him. 'I told you, I went out to see if she was still there. There's a terrible mess at the excavation.'

He raised his glass and sipped the whisky, still holding the dagger. 'I thought she was doing it carefully.'

'She was. She showed it to me only yesterday. It must have been that storm last night. It's full of seaweed, and half the side has fallen in. I expect that's how that came to light.' She nodded in the direction of the dagger.

Putting down his glass he examined it more closely.

'Is it Roman do you think?' He glanced up.

Kate missed the sudden amusement in his eyes. She shrugged. 'I don't know. I don't think so. I think it might be earlier but I'm not an archaeologist. I do think she ought to get some experts here. She could be doing irreparable damage, poking around the way she is.' She still had not mentioned the torc.

'The way you describe it the sea will do a lot worse than anything she could do. At least she's saving a few things this way.' Greg put the dagger down. 'You'd better bring it when you come to dinner tomorrow.'

'I shall.' She met his eye. For a minute they studied one another, measuring each other up.

'So. How are you liking Redall Cottage?' he said at last.

'Very much. But I'm sorry you had to leave so I could come.'

'You mean you'd like me to move back in with you?' He raised an eyebrow suggestively.

'No.' She did not flinch. 'I'm paying for my privacy.'

'And I'm interrupting it.' He put down his glass.

'Not for another thirty minutes. I allow myself the occasional break. Have another?' Picking up the bottle she gestured towards the glass. He intrigued her. Handsome, boorish, presumably talented, he was something of an enigma.

'Why not? I can hardly get done for drunk driving in that thing. No one would notice the difference.'

As Kate led the way through into the sitting room he followed her. She poured his whisky then she glanced at him. 'Someone broke in here last night.'

'Broke in?' His expression was bland; politely interested. If he was surprised he didn't show it.

'They seemed to be looking for something.'

'Have you told the police?'

She shook her head. 'Whoever it was had a key.' She sat down, cradling her glass on her knee.

'Oh, I see. You think it was me.'

'No. It was a woman.'

That did surprise him. 'You saw her?'

She shrugged. 'Not quite. But I know it was a woman, and I smelt her perfume. I thought at first it was Alison messing about, but now I'm not so sure. Perhaps it was a friend of hers.' She paused. 'Or of yours.'

He did not rise to the remark. 'Is anything missing?'

'No. At least, nothing of mine.' She took a sip from her glass, not looking at him. 'Did you mean to leave those pictures upstairs?' she asked after a moment. She sat staring at the woodburner. The fire inside roared like a wild beast.

Greg raised his foot and kicked the damper across. 'I did. There's no more space in the farmhouse. Why, don't you like them?' He threw himself down into the chair opposite her. There was a challenge in his eyes.

'Not much.'

'Too strong for you, eh?' He looked puzzled suddenly. 'Did you mean to imply that one of them is missing?'

'No, they were all there, I think. And yes, I suppose so,' she conceded. 'They are disturbing.'

'They depict the soul of this place. The cottage. The bay. The land. The sea. The sea will drown all this one day, you know.'

'So I gather.' She refused to be rattled by the dramatic declamation. 'And sooner rather than later if that digging is anything to go by.'

He frowned. 'It's strange. None of us knew that was there. Allie found it a while back – the signs of the dune having been dug by men and not just being natural – then only a few weeks ago a great section split off like a ripe rotten fruit and it started spewing out all these bits and pieces.' His voice was quiet, but his choice of words was deliberate. He had not taken his eyes off her face. 'It exudes evil, this place. It's in my paintings. I'm amazed Allie can't feel it. But she's an astoundingly insensitive kid. Perhaps it's because she anaesthetizes herself all the time with that noisy crap she calls music.'

Kate smiled. 'I saw the scarlet machine this morning.'

He was right. She had felt it. The evil. She gave an involuntary shudder and was furious to see that he had noticed. He smiled. Pointedly he put down his glass and, standing up, he went to the stove. Opening the doors he loaded in another log. 'Do you want me to get in touch with the police about your visitor?'

She shook her head. 'Nothing was taken. I'm sure it was a schoolgirl prank. I'll bolt the door in future.'

'And you're not worried about staying here alone?' He raised an eyebrow. 'Perhaps it wasn't a burglar at all. Perhaps the woman you saw was a ghost. I told you this place was haunted. Haunted and evil. The locals won't come near it.'

Was that it, then? Was this all a ploy to frighten her

away? She laughed. 'Being a writer of history I'm happy to live with ghosts.'

'I trust you're not tempting providence with that remark,' he said. Throwing himself down in his chair again he crossed his leg, left ankle on right knee and sighed. 'I used to find it very oppressive here after a while. My paintings would change. They would grow more and more angry. Whilst I am by nature quite a sunny chap.'

She was watching him closely.

'At the farmhouse I paint differently. With more superficiality,' he went on thoughtfully. 'If I ever paint a masterpiece it will be in this cottage.' For a brief moment it was as though he was talking to himself. He had forgotten she was there; forgotten he was trying to scare her. Remembering her again he glanced at her. 'Art, it seems, must wait for commerce.'

Straight from the hip. She took it without flinching. 'Don't you sell your paintings then?'

'No.'

The reply, loaded with scorn, was succeeded by a long silence. She did not pursue the subject. Studying his face as he stared morosely into the flames she was conscious suddenly of the lines of weariness around his eyes and the realisation that Greg Lindsey was a very unhappy man. The moment of insight struck her dumb. The silence dragged out uncomfortably as she, too, stared into the flickering fire.

The crash from upstairs brought them both to their feet. 'Shit! What was that?' Greg put down his glass.

She swallowed. She had heard a crash like that before and her investigation had found nothing. 'The wind must have blown the door shut,' she said at last. 'I'd better look.' She did not move. The room seemed suddenly warm and safe. She did not want to climb the stairs.

The noise seemed to have shaken him out of his introspection. He looked at her, noting her white face and anxious eyes and was astonished at his own reaction. He should have been pleased that she was scared but his studied hostility wavered and for a brief second he felt a wave of protectiveness sweep over him. 'I'll check.'

Taking the stairs two at a time he went first into the spare room. The room was empty save for her cases and boxes, and his own pictures, standing where he had left them behind the door. He noted briefly that they still faced the wall, then he ducked out of the room and switched on the light in the main bedroom. After the stark business-like aura of the living room downstairs with its computer and books, the bedroom – his bedroom – shocked him by its unaccustomed femininity. He glanced round. Nothing was out of place. Both doors had been open. Nothing appeared to have fallen – he checked the painting on the wall. One of his, it was uncharacteristically pretty, depicting the bluebells in Redall Wood. He scowled at it. His mother must have brought it over, for it used to hang in the spare room at the farmhouse. Having ascertained that there was no reason for the bang that he could see, his gaze travelled more slowly around the bedroom for the second time, noting her towelling bathrobe, thrown across the bed, her slippers near it, both a bright flame which would suit her rather mousy colouring. He found himself picturing her in the robe for a moment. On the chest of drawers lay a heap of silver bangles – she had been wearing them the day she arrived, he remembered – and next to them a glass filled with winter flowers she must have gathered in the wood. The naturalist in him noted periwinkle, small velvety-red dead nettles and a sprig of daphne she must have found in what was once the cottage garden. Continuing his quick perusal, he studied the small collection of cosmetics. On neither occasion that he had met her so far had she been wearing any makeup at all, but obviously when the occasion demanded she was happy to gild the lily. He turned to the low windowsill where she had put several paperbacks – poetry and social history, he saw. No reader of fiction, this author.

'Have you found anything?'

Her voice behind him in the doorway made him jump guiltily.

'Nothing. Both doors were open. Nothing seems to have fallen over. The windows are closed.'

'Could it have been outside?'

'The chimney, you mean?' He smiled. 'I think we would have noticed if it had fallen through the roof.'

'What was it then?' Her voice betrayed her irritation. From the landing she had seen him studying her things. His interest made her feel vulnerable and angry.

'Perhaps it was the ghost of Marcus. I've often heard things here.' When she did not rise to the remark, he headed back towards the stairs, glancing at his watch. 'Look, Kate, I should be going back. There's nothing here. Nothing to worry about. I'll take a look at the roof as I leave, and get a few more logs in for you. It was probably out in the trees – a branch coming off or something. Acoustics are often unaccountable.' He descended the stairs ahead of her. 'If you're worried, give us a ring and Dad or I will come back and check things for you.'

'There won't be any need. I shall be all right.'

Marcus

She shivered at the name which had floated unbidden into her head, watching as Greg pushed his feet into his boots and reached for his jacket. Half of her wanted him to go. He had been perfectly polite, but she could sense his dislike. The other half was afraid. She did not relish the idea of being alone.

Which was crazy. She had rented the cottage for six months and she wasn't planning to have any lodgers. She had to get used to being alone, and get used to whatever funny noises the countryside had to throw at her. As if to test her resolution the sharp scream of a vixen rang out as he opened the front door. He turned and studied her face. 'You know what that is, I suppose.'

The bastard! He expected her to be frightened. 'I know,' she said. She managed a smile. 'I've lived most of my life in the country, Greg. Because I have, or had,' she corrected herself as she remembered yet again the full implications concomitant with moving out of Jon's flat, 'a London address, it does not make me a townie.'

She thought he had the grace to look slightly shamefaced as, with a bow and a mock touch to his forelock, he headed for the Land Rover. She did not hear his parting comment as he hauled himself behind the wheel: 'And fuck you too, Lady Muck!'

It was only after she had watched the tail lights disappear into the trees that she realised he had neither given the roof a glance as he left, nor fetched her in the promised extra logs.

'Bastard.' She said it out loud this time. She glanced at the log box. There were still a few there but not enough, after the blaze he had initiated, for the night. She would have to go out again into the dark.

The torch was sitting where she had left it on the counter in the kitchen. Next to the dagger. She looked at her jacket hanging on the back of the door and she reached a decision. When the fire died she would have a bath – heated by electricity – and she would go to bed. Nothing and no one was going to get her out of the front door again until it was daylight.

With an immense feeling of relief she shot the bolt on the door and walked back into the living room. She made sure the damper was closed – make the wretched thing last as long as possible – put on an Elgar tape – the Enigma Variations – loud – and then she poured herself another whisky.

* * *

113

She had worked for another couple of hours on the book, and was printing up a rough copy for herself when she remembered the silver polish she had stashed away in the cupboard under the sink. Switching off the computer with a sigh of relief she stacked the pages neatly away and went to the drawer. The torc looked greenish-black as she lifted it out and examined it again in the bright kitchen light. Shaking the bottle of polish she smeared some of the mixture cautiously onto the metal and began to rub it gently with the corner of a duster. Ten minutes later she gave up. Her more and more energetic rubbing had had no effect whatsoever. Disappointed, she laid duster and metal on the counter when the phone rang.

'Hi, Kate.' Jon's voice was so strong it sounded as though he was in the next room. 'I'm in Boston. How is Lord George?'

'Going well.' She found she was smiling. 'What about your tour?'

'OK. A bit tiring. Nearly over now, thank God. I'm taking five at the hotel. English tea and muffins before I get ready to go out this evening. What are you up to?'

'I'm cleaning an ancient British torc with modern British silver polish and its having no effect whatsoever.' Leaning against the counter, the phone comfortably tucked against her ear she turned and surveyed her handiwork.

'Sounds fun.' The response from across the Atlantic was muted. 'May I ask where you got an ancient British torc?'

'It was lying on the beach.'

'I see.' She could tell he didn't believe her. 'There isn't an ancient Briton wearing it, I suppose?'

'Not at the moment, no.' She smiled to herself again. 'You'd love it, here, Jon.' It was a tentative feeler; a peace offering.

'The parties are good, are they?' The irony in his tone reminded her that they were no longer supposed to be friends. Or lovers.

So, why had he rung her again?

She knew better than to ask.

'There's no one to party with, here. Just the birds and I believe there are seals round in the bay.'

'And the occasional ancient Brit.'

'You got it.' She mimicked what she hoped was an American insouciance. 'Actually the ghost is Roman.'

There was a moment's silence.

'You sounded almost serious,' Jon said cautiously.

'Did I?' She reminded herself how quick he was to pick up nuances; his sensitivity was one of the things she loved – had loved, she corrected herself sharply – about him. It made his actions over the last few weeks harder to bear.

She laughed lightly. 'How silly. Only joking.'

'I see.' He was still thoughtful. 'You are all right?'

'Yes. Fine.'

'OK. Well, enjoy yourself kiddo. I'll give you a ring in a day or two.'

For the second time he had not given her time to say goodbye. The line had gone dead and she was left staring at the receiver once again. Replacing it slowly she went thoughtfully back to the table and picked up her duster.

The blast of cold air behind her, smelling heavily of wet earth, took her completely by surprise. She whirled round. The front door must have blown open in spite of her care in locking and bolting it. She peered out into the hall. The door was as she had left it. The hall was dark and deserted.

Come on, Kennedy. Either a window has come open or the wind has blown back down the chimney. She found she was whispering to herself as she looked into the warm, dimly-lit living room. There was still a faint glow coming from the stove, though the log box was empty. The room was cooling, but the scent of earth was not coming from there. It was coming from upstairs.

Her bedroom window must be open. She frowned. She had opened it earlier to stare out at the sea, watching the mist drifting in across the still, grey water as night came in from the east. Obviously she had not latched it properly. Her hand on the stair rail, she began to climb.

Both doors at the top were open. Both rooms were in darkness. Reaching the top she clicked on the light. The window in her bedroom was shut as she had known in her heart it would be, and the curtains were tightly drawn across. She sniffed. There must be a patch of damp in the house which the rain had activated somehow. Ducking out of the room she peered into the other across the landing. The smell was stronger there and the air was cold. Bitterly cold. The room had a north-facing window, she reminded herself as she went to examine it. It was closed and judging by the cobwebs welded over the catch, had not been opened for a long time.

Slowly she surveyed the walls, looking for the telltale signs of discoloration on the wallpaper. Tiny lemon yellow flowers on brown green stems romped across the uneven walls and between the oak beams without a sign of damp.

Switching off the lights she walked downstairs again, sniffing. The smell was still strong. A sweet, cold smell like a newly-turned flower bed after rain. With a shrug she walked back into the living room and turning over the tape, threw herself down in the armchair nearest the fire.

When she awoke 'In the South' had finished, the fire was out and the room was ice cold. Her head ached and for a moment she was too stiff to move. Forcing herself to her feet she groaned and reached for the switch on the table lamp. Turning it off she made her way to the door. A warm bed and a heap of soft pillows to cuddle into, that was what she wanted. In the doorway she turned and surveyed the room before flicking off the light switch on the wall and plunging the room into darkness. It was as she made her way into the bathroom and reached for her toothbrush that she realised she had not had any supper. Two whiskies was not exactly a nutritious way to end the evening. Perhaps that accounted for her splitting headache. She frowned. She was beginning to drink too much. She contemplated getting herself something to eat and realised that she wasn't hungry. She also realised that she had not switched on the immersion heater so there was not enough hot water for a bath. With a sigh she bent over the basin and splashed some tepid water into her face. All she wanted was sleep. Food and bath could wait until morning. That was one of the joys of living on your own, she recognised suddenly. You could please yourself. Cook or not cook. Wash or not wash. Sleep when you wanted. And just at this moment that was all she wanted.

It was as she put her foot on the bottom step of the staircase that she saw the movement upstairs. She froze, 'Is there anyone there?' Her voice sounded thin and frightened in the silence.

There was no answer.

'Who is it?' She called again. Her desire for sleep had vanished.

She was answered by the rattle of rain on the windows as a squall of wind hurtled in from the sea.

'Christ, I'm seeing things now,' she muttered to herself. Tired eyes. Too much computer, that was the problem. It was the logical explanation but it still took an enormous effort of willpower to force her up the stairs, throwing on all the lights when she reached the top. The place was empty, the windows closed against the storm. She sniffed hard. The scent of wet earth seemed to have disappeared, though when she pushed back the curtains and stared out at the blackness she could see the rain coursing down the panes of glass.

Undressing as fast as she could she slipped between the sheets, leaving the light on the landing switched on against the dark. She lay, wide awake, clutching one of her pillows to her chest, her eyes straining out through the door to the small expanse of wall – painted a dark Suffolk pink and bisected by one pale oak beam – which she could see from the bed. And she listened to the rain.

XVII

'Are you awake, Sue?' Alison stared through the darkness of her friend's bedroom towards the bed by the far wall.

'Yes.'

They had been whispering and giggling for the last two hours. Twice Sue Farnborough's mother, Cissy, had come in and shushed them wearily and told them to go to sleep; now she had gone to bed herself and the house was in darkness. For the last twenty minutes or so the silences between the two girls had been growing longer and longer.

'Do you think I should tell them at home?'

'About what happened at the grave?'

'Of course, about what happened at the grave.'

'No. They'll interfere. Parents always do. Are you going to go back?'

Alison hesitated for only a second. 'Of course I'm going to go back. I'm going to finish the excavation.'

'By yourself?'

'You could come with me.' Alison sounded almost eager.

'No way. That's not my scene.' Sue was adamant.

'Oh, come on. You'd enjoy it. It's fun.'

'It doesn't sound fun to me.' Sue grinned maliciously in the darkness. 'You were so scared you nearly wet yourself. You told me as much.'

'I didn't.'

'You did. And why else did you come here? Running all the way through the woods instead of staying at home and waiting for your mum to get back from Colchester. You were really chicken.'

'I wasn't.'

'You were. Are you going to school tomorrow?'

'No. I'm still not feeling well.'

'You're skiving off, you mean. Well, I'm going, so shut up, Allie. I want to get some sleep.' Sue reached in the darkness for the headphones of her Walkman and switched on the little machine beneath her pillow. The blast of Sisters of Mercy at full volume in her ears seemed an unlikely lullaby but within minutes she was asleep.

Across the room Alison lay awake, staring towards the curtained windows, listening to the rain. Beneath the borrowed duvet she had begun to shiver again.

XVIII

There was a scattering of wet, sandy earth on the kitchen table. Kate stared at it. The torc lay where she had left it, next to the duster and the jar of silver polish. She touched the soil with her finger. It was wet and cold. She sniffed. The smell was there but very faint now – the smell of a newly-turned garden.

Or a newly dug grave.

She shook her head. She had not slept well. The room had been cold and the noise of the wind and rain lashing the windows had woken her several times from her uneasy, dream-laden sleep. Her head was so heavy she could not even think straight as she walked over to the sink, filled the kettle and switched it on. Perhaps after a cup of coffee she would find an explanation for the mess on the table. There had to be a reason. Earth does not just materialise on a kitchen table. It must have fallen from the beamed ceiling, perhaps released by creeping damp and rain, or it had been swept in on a freak gust of wind under the front door or down the chimney.

She spooned Nescafé into a mug and poured in the water, watching the swirl of brown granules clinging to the blue pottery dissolving as she stirred. It scalded her tongue when she drank but the caffeine shot into her system with gratifying speed. Putting down the mug she picked up the torc and stared at it closely. There was no sign of the effort she had made to clean it. Even the scratches she had made with her nail had disappeared. The metal was as greenish-black and corroded as ever. Wrapping it carefully in the duster she carried it upstairs and through into the spare room. Only one of her suitcases boasted a key. Locking the torc inside it, she pushed it into the corner and, closing the door behind her, she made her way downstairs again. She put the polish away and going to the sink rinsed out a J cloth under the hot tap. It took only a few minutes to wipe up the earth, rinse the cloth again and put it away before she dragged out her boots and jacket and throwing open the front door went outside with her log box. It was a bright sunny morning. High, white, wisped clouds raced across a vivid blue sky from the west and behind the cottage the sea glittered blindingly.

The rain had blown into the shed and many of the logs were soaked. Rummaging in the back she found a few that were dry and carried them indoors. Three times she made the trip back and forth, until there was a satisfactory pile beside the stove. Then she brought in kindling and a final armful of logs to put in the stove itself. Satisfied that she had enough fuel for twenty-four hours at least she stared down at the stove. There was no point in lighting it now. There was one more thing she had to do before she settled down to work for the day. It had been gnawing at the back of her mind since she had cleared up the soil in the kitchen.

Locking the front door behind her she wedged the key into the pocket of her jacket, and pulling on her gloves she headed across the short grass at the back of the cottage towards the beach. A flock of tern rose and wheeled as she appeared on the shingle banks and ran slipping and sliding towards the sand. The beach was wet still from the tide and trailed with weed. A line of shells, white and pink and glabrous in the bright sunlight, marked the line of the high tide. The air was so cold it made her eyes water as she turned right and followed the line of dunes towards Alison's excavation.

For a long time she stood on the edge staring down into the declivity. Another huge chunk of the dune had broken away and she could now see clearly the different strata in the bright sand. There were pale lines of clay, different shades of sand and gravel and now, clearly visible, a thick black crumbling layer of peat.

There was a strange dryness in her mouth as she half jumped, half slid into the hollow. A spray of bladderwrack lay draped across the bottom of the trench and, half-buried in the sand, something bright red caught her attention as she peered nearer. Frowning, she kicked at the sand fall. Alison's ghetto blaster lay there beneath a pile of seaweed. Stooping she pulled it free. The 'on' button was still depressed. Alison had been back this morning early and had gone again. Putting the machine on the edge of the hollow she stared round. What could have happened to make her abandon her precious cassette player? There was no sign of the girl's tools, but perhaps they were buried in the latest sand fall. She stepped closer to the face and cautiously she drew off her glove. The peat was soft, layered, compressed. It smelt, when she withdrew her fingers, of wet garden soil. She swallowed hard. 'Alison?' Her shout was whipped up by the wind and carried only a few yards before it was dissipated and dissolved. 'Alison?' She shouted louder. Scrambling up to the edge of the hollow she put her hand to her eyes against the glare and stared round. The beach was empty.

She turned round. There could be no question of the girl being there, under the sand, but for a moment her imagination was playing the wildest of tricks. She could see where it was soft and loose, where it had fallen, and where, in the bottom of the hollow, a long mound lay compressed beneath the clay. A mound that had the shape of a human grave.

She stared at it. Alison would not have come back in the dark. She was safe at her friend's house when Diana had rung last night. Whoever – whatever, she corrected herself swiftly – lay down there, it was not a twentieth-century

123

fifteen-year-old schoolgirl. Kate stepped towards the mound cautiously. It was her imagination again working overtime. From a different angle the mound was just a part of the sand, shadowed by the low sunlight. She could see the worm casts on it now, and the sprinkling of loose peat which had fallen from the sand cliff.

'What are you doing here?' Alison's voice, harsh and angry, broke into her thoughts so sharply she jumped.

'Oh thank God!' The words were out of her mouth before she could stop them. 'I thought perhaps you had had an accident —'

'You thought I was buried in there?' The note of disdain quivered a little at the end. Alison stepped white-faced from behind the edge of the dune. There were dark circles under her eyes.

Kate smiled. 'Only for a second. It was when I saw your radio.'

Alison's gaze switched to the cassette player. She did not move towards it. 'I forgot it,' she said after a moment.

'So I see. I'm afraid it was buried in the sand. I think the tide probably got it.'

'Why did you come here?' Alison's voice was markedly less aggressive as she stood looking down at Kate. She still had made no move to jump down into the hole, or to pick up her radio.

'There was something I wanted to check.' Kate scrambled up beside her. 'The different lines of strata being exposed. Do you see? The sand fall last night is revealing the line of a peat bog which is probably thousands of years old.'

Alison's eyes strayed to the dark streaks in the sand for a moment. Still she had not moved. 'Did you see anything moving?' she asked. 'When you came. Was there anything — anyone here?'

Kate looked at her sharply. 'What sort of thing?'

Alison shrugged massively. 'I don't know. Yesterday,

when I was here. There was something.' She looked away evasively. 'I don't suppose it was anything. Maybe a bird-watcher or a naturalist or something . . .' Her voice trailed away.

'But you didn't see them clearly,' Kate prompted.

'No.'

'Did you smell anything strange? Wet earth.'

Alison stared at her. 'The whole place was wet.'

'True.' Kate smiled.

For a moment they both looked down at the excavation in silence. Then, 'Are you going to do some more work on it today?' Kate asked at last.

Alison shrugged. 'Might. But I've got work to do to catch up for school.' She was shifting restlessly from foot to foot. She had not wanted to come today but something had made her do it. She could not stop herself.

'That's tough. I wondered why you weren't at school,' Kate said. 'Have you been ill?'

Alison nodded, but offered no further explanation. Kate did not pursue it. 'I think it's going to rain. Better to leave any digging for another day.' For some reason she would feel much better if Alison were not here alone on the beach. The thought of the child digging away in isolation in this lonely grave appalled her. And it was a grave. Alison was right.

'You said you were going to take some photos. Would you like me to do it for you later, when the sun is right?' she asked at last.

Alison peered at her through wildly blowing wisps of hair. 'Would you?'

'Of course. I should think by about midday the light would be better. I'll come out then. I'll bring the film with me this evening and whoever goes into town next could get it developed.'

'Great.'

Was it her imagination again or was there a marked

lessening of enthusiasm? 'Allie, did something frighten you yesterday?' Kate asked gently.

'No, of course not!' The flash of red in Alison's cheeks and the defiant glare belied her words.

'I just wondered.'

'Why, does it scare you?' Pitying. Disdainful.

'It does a bit. Yes.'

'Why?' Again the aggressive, derisive note. But beneath it, Kate sensed there was a plea. And she knew suddenly that she must not reinforce the girl's fears. She shrugged. 'I don't know. Perhaps it was, as your brother said, that I've grown used to living in a town. One forgets the country noises. And I've never stayed so close to the sea before.'

To her relief Alison's face cleared. 'You'll get used to it,' she replied. For the first time she smiled. 'Will you really take the photos for me?'

'Of course I will. No problem.' Kate hesitated. 'Do you want to come back to the cottage for some coffee before you go home?'

Alison's nod and the speed with which she gathered up her ruined ghetto blaster and turned away from her excavation spoke volumes. Following her, Kate turned and glanced over her shoulder only once towards the dig. A cloud of gulls hovered over the place where she and Alison had been standing. Then with a wild screaming and shrieking, they wheeled as one and flew straight out towards the sea.

'Why did you lock it? We never bother.'

Out of sight of the dunes Alison was once more her supercilious self.

'Habit, I suppose,' Kate replied easily. 'After all, someone did break in.' She pushed open the door. 'Black or white?' She walked ahead into the kitchen.

'White please.' Alison had not followed her, nor had she given any acknowledgment of Kate's comment. She had walked through into the living room. 'You've let the wood-burner go out,' she called.

Kate closed her eyes for a moment and took a deep breath. 'I know, but it's laid all ready to light. Do you want to do it for me?'

She reached for the coffee jar and stopped. There was a trail of black peaty soil on the worktop.

'Oh Christ.' She didn't realise she had spoken out loud.

'What is it?' Alison appeared behind her in the doorway.

Kate took a deep breath. 'Nothing. I spilt something, that's all.'

'Where are the matches?' Alison bent and rummaged in the cupboard under the sink. She had taken off her jacket and brushed back her hair with her fingers.

'There, on the dresser.' Kate was still staring at the trail of wet earth amongst the mugs. 'Allie, don't bother to light it now, OK? When we've had our coffee, I'll walk back with you. I need to drive into Colchester this morning.' Again the thought had come unprompted. Perhaps this time it was because suddenly she didn't want to be alone in the house.

'What about the photos? You promised.'

Damn the photos!

'That's OK, I'll do them later, don't worry. In fact the later I leave it, the better the light will be. We'll get more definition. I'll still have the film for you by this evening.'

She lifted two mugs out of the earth and rinsed them under the tap before reaching for the coffee jar.

'What's all this mess on the side here?'' Alison had seen it. Staring down at it critically she ran a finger through it, leaving a clean trail on the varnished wood of the work-top.

Kate shook her head. 'I'm not sure. It must have come in when I brought the logs in earlier.'

The answer seemed to satisfy Alison. Turning away she returned to the living room.

'Do you like using a computer?' Her voice came through the door as Kate waited for the kettle to boil.

'Yes, quite. It makes correlating notes and chronologies and things much simpler.' Kate carried the mugs of coffee through. Alison was standing at her table looking down at her books and notes.

'My brother Patrick is a computer wizard,' the girl said. 'Most of the time, he's a nerd, but he is tops on computers.'

'Will he be there tonight?'

'Yeah.'

'And will Greg?'

Alison shrugged. 'No one ever knows what Greg is going to do.'

'I see,' Kate said dryly. 'Well, I'm looking forward to coming to dinner with your parents. They seem so nice.'

'They are, I suppose.' Alison finished her coffee and put the mug down. 'I'm going. Do you want to come with me?'

The challenge in her eyes was hostile again and suddenly Kate was tired of the child. 'I'll be ready in about half an hour,' she said. 'If you want to wait for me, that'll be nice, if not, I'll follow you over later.'

For a moment Alison hesitated, obviously reluctant to walk back alone, then with an exaggerated sigh she flung herself down in one of the chairs. 'OK. I'll wait.'

'Thanks.' Kate smiled. She gathered up the mugs and left the girl sitting there.

The door to the spare room was open and the boxes and cases in there had been strewn all over the floor. Kate stared at the scene for a moment in dismay, then she turned and called down the stairs. 'Alison, did you do this?'

'What?' The girl's voice was puzzled.

'Do all this? For God's sake!' Her case, the case with the torc was still locked, she could see that from the doorway.

Alison ran up behind her and looked round. 'What a mess.'

'All these boxes and things. I left them tidy.'

'Oh.' Alison avoided her eye. 'Well, it wasn't me. How could it have been? I haven't been upstairs at all.'

Kate found her heart was hammering rather too loudly in her chest. There had to be an explanation. This child or her brother must have done it. Perhaps while she was on the beach Greg or the unknown computer wizard had sneaked in and messed up the place. Turning, she flung open her bedroom door. Nothing in there appeared to have been touched. Everything was as she had left it.

Seeing her white face Alison frowned. She too suspected that it must have been Greg. Last time she had seen him, he had still been planning to try to scare Kate out of the cottage. He was keen on her idea of making Kate think it was haunted. Could he have done all this? Had he already taken things this far? Staring round she felt herself shiver. If it was him, then it was working. She narrowed her eyes for a moment. Was it Greg down on the beach as well? Was he behind what had happened yesterday?

Suddenly she was furious. She turned and running down the stairs she opened the front door. 'Come on. I need to get home,' she called. 'There's nothing wrong. Let's go.'

If it was Greg she would get even, if it was the last thing she ever did. The bastard! The unmitigated, double dealing, swindling bastard! He had really scared her. And he owed her a new radio cassette player.

129

XIX

'You shouldn't have come.' Nion took her hands. 'You take too many risks. What if you were seen?'

She broke free and ran a few steps in front of him to the edge of the water, skipping like a child. 'Who is there to see? He's out all day. The slaves are too busy to care. The child and his nurse think I am visiting my sister.' She pirouetted, laughing. 'I've never been so happy. I can't believe this is happening. Me, a staid Roman matron, and you –' she stood in front of him, staring into his face and rested her hands for a moment on the folds of his cloak, '– you, a prince of the Trinovantes.'

Nion laughed, throwing back his head, his strong teeth white in his tanned face, the laugh lines at eyes and mouth carving deep into the square features.

Around them the dunes stretched for miles; sand, spun and blown by the wind into hollows and ridges, the shingle thick and clean as the tide drew back. Nearby, her mule waited patiently beside the horse, which stood between the shafts of his chariot, grazing listlessly on the salt sand flowers and grasses. They were alone. Quite alone. He caught her against him, burying his face in her hair.

'I want you to come away with me. One of my brothers is in the west. We could go to him there. Your husband would never find you.'

She tensed, raising her face slowly to his and he read the conflicting emotions in her eyes. Desire. Hope. Excitement. All three blazed in their sea-grey depths, but there was doubt there too. Doubt and fear. 'I can't leave the boy.'

'Then we'll take him with us.'

'No.' She shook her head sadly. 'No. He would never allow his son to go. Me —' she hesitated. 'I don't know if he would come after me, but he would search the whole earth for his son.' Her eyes brimmed with tears. 'And I could not ask you to leave this — your home.' His land, his woods, his pastures, his fields, his water, the salt pans which made him rich, all worked by the men of his people.

She shivered as she looked up again and raised her lips towards his. His gods were powerful, cruel, demanding. Sometimes she wondered if they had given their blessing to their servant's union with a daughter of Rome, or if they were jealous, biding their time, waiting to punish her for her presumption.

Behind them the sun glittered on the sea, turning it the colour of jade. As his hands moved down to release her girdle she forgot her fear; she forgot everything, drowning in the pleasure of his touch.

'We'll have to give you a season ticket at this rate!' The man in the ticket office at the museum greeted Kate with a cheery smile.

She smiled back. 'I think you might. Or a job!' She was still wondering why she was here. Was it the thought of the next book, bubbling uncontrollably in her subconscious, or was it just the fascination of that strange, half-excavated pit on the beach beside her cottage? She refused to admit that she felt a slight reluctance to stay in the cottage alone. She could not allow that. But perhaps it was a little of all three. She was feeling guilty. She shouldn't be here. She should be working with George Byron and his irritating, hysterical mother.

Retracing her steps upstairs she went to stand once more in front of the statue of Marcus Severus, gazing into his face as if somewhere there in the cold, dead eyes she would find the answer to her riddle. For he had something to do with that grave on the shore, she was sure of it. Marcus

Severus Secundus and Augusta, his wife. Thoughtfully, she turned to the display case where his bones lay exposed to view. There was no answer there. Nothing but the gentle hum of the lights and in the distance, the muffled and unreal shouts and screams of the video replay of Boudicca's massacre.

As she parked the car in the barn later she glanced at Redall Farmhouse with a certain amount of longing. They were there this time; she could see smoke coming from the chimney and there were lights on in the kitchen. They were expecting her to supper; supposing she knocked and went in now? Perhaps she could help prepare it, or sit out of the way by the fire sipping tea or better still whisky, until the appropriate time. But she couldn't, of course she couldn't. She glanced at her watch. It was barely three o'clock. She had another five hours to wait before she could knock on their door.

Shouldering her bag she turned up the track into the woods. The early sunshine had gone. The sky was growing increasingly wintry and as the wind rose a quick light shower of sleet raced through the trees. She shivered. At least the fire was ready to light at home.

Home. She hadn't thought of the cottage as home before, but for now that's what it was. She could draw the curtains against the coming darkness, have tea and a hot bath and do a couple of hours' work before setting out on the walk back through the dark.

Opening the door she dumped her bag on the floor and glanced round, unconsciously bracing herself against signs that anyone had been inside. There were none. The cottage was as she had left it. The kitchen was spotless, the doors and windows closed and the air smelt faintly of burned apple wood. Relieved, she unpacked her shopping and went to light the woodburner, then slowly she went upstairs.

Pulling open her cupboard she looked through the

clothes she had brought with her. Since she had arrived in north Essex she had worn trousers and thick sweaters, but she wanted to change into something a little more formal tonight. More formal, but still practical, bearing in mind that she had a long walk through the muddy woods. She pulled out a woollen skirt and a full-sleeved blouse and threw them on the bed.

It was then that she remembered her promise to Alison to photograph the grave. She glanced at the window. It would soon be getting dark and the sky was already heavy with cloud. Perhaps she could leave it until tomorrow. But she wanted to keep her promise. She needed to win the girl's trust, for the sake of what was left of the site. She hesitated for a moment longer, then reluctantly she went to find her camera. She loaded a new roll of film and with a wistful glance at the fire she grabbed her anorak and set out into the cold.

The beach was very bleak. Turning up her collar, she put her head down into the wind and walked as swiftly as she could back towards Alison's dig, firmly resisting the urge to glance over her shoulder at the coming darkness. The wind had blown the sand into soft ridges, rounding the sharp corners, drying the surface of the soil so the different strata were harder to see. Squinting against her hair which whipped free of its clip into her eyes she raised the camera and peered through the viewfinder. She doubted if anything would come out even with the flash, but at least she would have tried. She took the entire roll, shooting the dig from every angle, and trying, rather vainly, to get a few close-ups of the sand face itself. She did not see the dark, withered stumps which had been a man's fingers; nor the black protrusion which was his femur, broken and splintered and already crumbling back into the sand.

Safely back inside the cottage she locked the door with a sigh of relief and, taking the film out of the camera, put it into its plastic case and tucked it into her shoulder bag.

She was damp and thoroughly chilled. Slotting a tape of Vaughan Williams' Fifth Symphony into her cassette player and turning it up loudly, she climbed the stairs and went back into her bedroom, pulling off her scarf and shaking out her wet hair as she began slowly to undress. Putting on her dressing gown she paused, listening, as the music downstairs grew quiet. She could hear a strange buzzing from the spare room. She frowned. For a moment she hesitated, biting her lip. What was it about this damn house which made her so jumpy? It was a fly, that was all, awoken by the morning sunshine. Taking a deep breath she flung open the door and switched on the light. The room was deserted. A quick glance showed that her cases and boxes were undisturbed; Greg's pictures stood where she had left them, face to the wall behind the door, and she was right, a couple of bluebottles were crawling across the window. As the light flicked on they buzzed angrily against the glass. Shaking her head she backed out and closed the door. Tomorrow she would deal with them.

The bathroom was very cold. With a shiver she pulled the cord to switch on the wall heater and, putting the plug in the bath, she turned on the hot tap. As the windows steamed over she closed the curtains then she tipped some foaming bath oil into the steaming jet of water and stood back, twisting her hair into a knot on the top of her head as she watched the bath fill with fragrant froth. Lying back in the warmth was ecstasy. With a groan of pleasure she submerged all but her head and closed her eyes.

She hadn't noticed the bluebottle in the corner of the window frame. As the light and warmth woke it up it crawled from beneath the curtain and buzzed angrily towards the strip light over the basin. She opened her eyes and watched it, irritated. The discordant buzzing spoiled her mood. After dashing itself several times against the mirror it took off and made a low swift circuit of the bathroom. Involuntarily she ducked as it swooped over her head. 'Damn and blast!' She flicked foam at it. She would not let it spoil her bath.

As the water began to cool she turned on the hot tap hopefully, knowing before she did it that the tank would not yet have heated up again. As she expected it was cold. Heaving herself to her feet she stepped out onto the bath mat and wrapped a towel around herself. Wiping the steam from the mirror she peered at her face. Out of the corner of her eye she could see the bluebottle on the frame of the mirror. She flipped at it with her hand and it took off, swooping up to the light. It was then the phone rang. Wrapped in the towel she picked it up in the kitchen.

'Kate, I was worried. Are you OK?'

'Jon?' Her heart leaped as she sat down, shivering. 'God, I wish you were here.'

'I thought so. Something is wrong isn't it? I could hear it in your voice yesterday.'

She could have bitten out her tongue. Why had she said it? It was over between them. Anyway, what was the use of worrying him when he was so far away? 'Nothing is wrong,' she said hastily. 'I just meant you'd like it here. The big skies, the sea, the silence. They would appeal to you.'

'Perhaps I'll come and see you when I get back.' There was an echo on the line this time – a pause between each sentence; it made them both sound awkward and they didn't talk for long. After she put the phone down she sat looking at it thoughtfully for several seconds. If it was all over between them, why did he keep ringing?

At a quarter to eight she switched off her computer and the desk lamp and standing up, she stretched. As she worked she had been conscious of the wind rising outside the cottage. It rattled the windows and from time to time she heard the spatter of rain against the glass.

Carefully she built up the fire and shut the doors as tightly as she could, closing the dampers right down so the stove would be snug and still alight when she came home later, then reluctantly she began to pull on her jacket and boots. With one glance behind her into the living room where she had left the single lamp on the side table burning to welcome her home, she stepped out into the night and pulling the front door shut behind her, she turned the key in the lock. For the last hour, she realised, she had been hoping that the phone would ring and Roger would suggest he came to fetch her. It would only take him ten minutes in the Land Rover. She sighed. Clutching her torch firmly she switched it on and directed the beam up the muddy track into the trees.

It took her half an hour to walk the half mile through the wood. The track was muddy and slippery and the wind had scattered the springy resinous branches of the pine trees on the ground, making the path treacherous in the unsteady torchlight. Several times she stopped and glanced around, shining the torch into the trees. The narrow beam showed only wet, black trunks, deep shadows and a tangle of matted undergrowth.

Diana opened the door with an exclamation of surprise. 'Kate, my dear, you haven't walked! Greg said he was going over to pick you up half an hour ago.'

Greg, she thought. I might have guessed. She smiled, realising suddenly that her face was so cold it was hard to make her muscles work. 'I wish I'd known, I would have waited for him,' she said. She followed Diana inside, shed her wet outer garments and found herself ushered towards the dreamed of inglenook. Within minutes she had been settled into the warmest corner of the sofa with a whisky in her hand and a cat on her knee.

The room smelled gloriously of burning apple logs, and cooking; she sniffed in anticipation; garlic, oregano, tomatoes – something Italian then. Lying back with her head against the cushions she smiled at Roger who had seated himself opposite her. 'This is heaven. It's not worth cooking for myself. I've been living on baked beans and tinned soup for the last few days.'

'So, how is your book going?' Roger smiled. At the Aga Diana had lifted the lid off a pan and was stirring gently.

Kate took a sip of her whisky, feeling the warmth flowing through her veins. 'Quite well. From the work point of view coming here was a good move. It's given me the time to concentrate.'

'Not much else to do over there, eh?' Roger smiled. He cocked an eye at the door as it opened and Greg appeared. 'I thought you were supposed to be fetching our guest,' he said sharply.

Greg grimaced. 'I'm sorry. I didn't realise the time. I was on my way out now to get you.'

Kate eyed him cryptically. She did not believe it. He had meant to leave it so late that she had to walk. She said nothing, however. She did not want to spoil the mood of the evening. 'Don't worry,' she said easily. 'No harm done. I enjoyed the walk.'

'Well, you can be sure he will drive you back after supper,' Roger put in quietly, and hearing the note of steel in his voice Kate realised that Greg's father was as aware as she was that his omission was deliberate. She relaxed back in the cushions further with a sigh of pleasure, her hand gently stroking Serendipity Smith into a state of ecstasy, surprised to acknowledge how relieved she felt that she would not have to face the cold wet trees alone again that night.

It was when Alison and Patrick appeared that Greg, who had been morosely drinking beer in the corner chair, looked up. 'Did you remember to bring the dagger you found in Alison's dig?' he asked. Though his voice was quiet there was a hostile edge to it that Kate picked up immediately.

She frowned. 'I did indeed.' Carefully, so as not to disturb the cat, she leaned down to the soft leather shoulder bag which lay at her feet and rummaged inside it. The iron dagger was wrapped in a piece of newspaper. Lifting it out she held it up to Alison. 'I found it lying on the sand,' she said. 'I only moved it because the tide was coming in. It would have been lost.'

For a moment Alison hesitated. She took the newspaper packet with obvious reluctance. 'Thanks.' She put it down without opening it. 'I had put it in my haversack. It must have fallen out.'

Kate raised an eyebrow. 'Aren't you going to look at it?'

'Later.'

'What's wrong, Allie? Lost interest already?' Greg's challenge brought a flush of angry pink to Alison's face.

'Of course not.'

'You weren't there today.'

'I was.' The retort was flashed at him furiously. 'That just shows all you know. *She* saw me. Didn't you?'

'I did,' Kate acknowledged.

'So, what do you think of Allie's dig?' Roger interposed quietly, long used to stepping into the quarrels of his children.

'Remarkable.' Kate sat forward. 'I hope Alison is going to get some experts up here soon. The tide is taking away the sand very fast. If she's not careful the whole thing will have disappeared before it's properly recorded.'

'Did you remember to photograph it?' Alison's question stemmed not so much from interest, Kate sensed, as the desire to catch her out. It was with some satisfaction that she nodded. She reached again into her bag and produced the roll of film.

'I'm afraid the light wasn't as good as I'd hoped. It may not have come out, but it's better than nothing.'

Alison took the film and threw it down on the table near her. 'Thanks,' she said again.

'It was very good of you to take them for her,' Roger put in. He had been watching his daughter with a frown.

'Alison, have you told anyone yet about your finds? Kate is right. Someone expert on these matters needs to come and see it soon.'

'She'll do it when she's ready,' Diana put in from the kitchen. 'Don't pester the child. Give her a chance to write up her project on her own first, if that's what she wants.'

Kate turned in her seat, resting her arm along the back of the sofa so she could see Diana who was grating parmesan at the kitchen table. 'It really is getting quite urgent,' she said almost apologetically. 'A few more high tides and the tumulus will have gone.'

'So that's what it is. A tumulus,' Greg put in. 'It seems to me we have our own expert here on the premises.'

'I'm not an expert,' Kate turned back, conscious that the cat on her knee was becoming increasingly irritated by her apparent inability to sit still. 'Far from it. But I do think it could be important.'

MARCUS!

The voice seemed to echo round the room.

Digging its claws into her knee the cat leaped off her lap and streaked out of sight up the stairs.

The others looked at it in astonishment.

'Sorry. I hope he didn't scratch you,' Roger said with a puzzled smile. 'I can't think why he did that. He seemed to like you.'

'It's probably the smell of mum's cooking,' Patrick put in his first comment of the evening.

Had none of them heard it then, apart from the cat? The pain of the voice which seemed to ring round the room had rung so loudly in her ears. The anguish. The fear.

Completely disorientated, Kate realised that Greg was watching her closely. 'Perhaps you don't really like cats,' he put in softly. 'They often go and sit on people who don't like them out of sheer perversity.'

'Of course I like them,' she snapped. Her hands were

clenched tightly around her empty glass. Noticing, Roger levered himself to his feet. 'Here, let me get you another one, Kate. Forget the moggy. He's a damn nuisance.' His voice was soothing. 'So, tell me, how do you like Redall Cottage?'

'Did you see the ghost again last night?'

Greg's question floated into the conversation before she had time to answer Roger's.

'What ghost?' Diana asked. 'There's no ghost there, Kate. Take no notice of my son. He's trying to wind you up.'

'Would I?' Greg smiled. 'Of course there's a ghost there. Kate and I were discussing the unpleasant atmosphere at the cottage when I was up there last night. Weren't we? And she told me she'd seen it.' He appealed to her to substantiate his claim. 'We both believe it has something to do with that grave on the beach.'

Alison had gone white. 'Shut up, Greg.'

Her brother looked at her. As their eyes met, he raised an eyebrow very slightly. Guiltily Alison looked away. He had explained it all to her an hour ago, when she had challenged him on the subject, how he was going to drive Lady Muck out of the cottage; how she was already nervous of being on her own out there; how it would take only one or two small things – noises perhaps, or strange happenings in the cottage – to send her screaming into the night. But he hadn't mentioned the grave.

Kate was watching Greg closely. He was a handsome man, with, at first glance anyway, an honest face and guileless eyes. She had noticed how he could hold her gaze with his own, steadily, the humour and challenge trembling just behind the mask. But it was a mask. He was playing with her.

'If it is a ghost it is a nice one.' She smiled at him. 'And it wore a beautiful scent.'

Alison bit her lip. 'Stop joking about it. It's silly.' Her

voice had risen in something like panic. 'When's supper going to be ready? I'm starving.'

From the far end of the room where she was laying the kitchen table Diana looked up and smiled. She had been listening to the exchange and had half guessed what Greg was up to. 'It's ready now. Come and finish this for me, Allie. Then we can eat. Greg, come and pour the wine. And Roger and Patrick, sit where you are till I call you. I know you both. The moment you think I'm about to announce the meal you will disappear on some urgent errand and I shan't see you for hours.' She turned to drain the pasta.

The room was busy, bustling, warm. Kate took another sip of her whisky. She was beginning to feel lightheaded. Had none of them heard it? Or had the voice, somehow, come from Greg?

Suddenly she realised that he was standing in front of her. He put out his hand for her glass. 'Come. Let me take you in to dinner,' he said, extending his arm.

She scrambled to her feet. 'Thank you.' He was about her height, broadly built and solid; she could smell his aftershave. With a sudden feeling of shock she realised he was really a very attractive man. Strangely conscious of the firm touch of his hand beneath her elbow she let him escort her to the table, where she found herself seated between him and his father.

'If there are ghosts, then there are two of them.' Kate was enjoying herself. 'And they are Roman,' she added as Diana laid a dish of paté on the table in front of her. 'One would be your Marcus Severus Secundus, and the other, the one I think I saw, might have been — perhaps — his wife, Augusta.'

Roger laughed. He dug his knife into the butter and carved himself off an unfashionably large corner. 'Good lord! How on earth have you come to that conclusion?'

Kate turned to Greg. 'You said Marcus haunted Redall

Cottage,' she said. 'I went to the museum and saw the exhibits about him and his wife. That is how I know her name.'

Greg grinned. He reached for the butter himself. 'I think there must have been a beautiful villa here in their day. It's strange. You make him sound almost approachable. I can't say I've ever been on first name terms with him. I don't think he was at all a pleasant character.'

'Why do you say that?' Kate hadn't taken her eyes off Greg's face, trying to read his expression.

'Greg.' Diana reproved her son from the end of the table.

'I'm sorry, Ma, but I think Kate should be warned. She is, in a way, Marcus's guest, after all. And if he and his wife have introduced themselves, it would seem that they are going to seek a closer acquaintance with her.'

There was a moment's silence.

'The dagger belonged to him,' Alison put in softly. 'He used it to kill people.'

Kate glanced at her, in spite of herself giving a little shiver of apprehension. Alison was staring down at her plate. Her headache had come back.

'I'm glad to be rid of it then, ' Kate said. She forced herself to sound cheerful. 'It will be safer here out of his reach with you looking after it. I was talking to a friend in the States on the phone this evening and telling him about it,' she went on, determined to show that she was in no way upset by the sudden atmosphere in the room. 'They don't have Roman ghosts in America. He was quite jealous.' Were they in it together, Greg and Alison? Were they all having a good laugh at her expense? 'In what way is he unpleasant?' she pressed Greg. She watched him closely. If he told her at least she would know what to expect.

He shrugged. 'They say that on certain nights, when the tide is high and the moon is full, you can hear the screams of his victims –'

'Greg, that is enough!' his father put in abruptly. 'You are frightening your sister.'

'Rubbish. Allie's as tough as old boots. It would take more than that to frighten her,' Greg retorted. He turned to Kate. 'And I'm sure our lady historian is not frightened by ghosts. They are, after all, her stock in trade. She should be very pleased to be able to rent a couple so reasonably.'

So there you had it. The barb which had betrayed him. Kate smiled. Suddenly she felt more cheerful. She could handle Greg Lindsey. Taking another mouthful of Diana's delectable home made paté she turned back to him. 'Why should they haunt the grave on the beach? They weren't buried there, and I'm fairly certain that it's not a Roman burial.'

'How do you know it's a burial at all?' Patrick put in another of his rare remarks. 'Allie hasn't found a body has she?'

'No, I haven't!' Again the panic. Unexplained. Sudden. Overwhelming. Alison clenched her fists against the sudden pounding behind her eyes.

'And she probably won't. The sand dissolves bodies,' Kate put in. She hadn't looked at Alison. 'Like at Sutton Hoo. Although that is a Saxon burial and therefore probably much later, it must be the same principle. The salts in the sand dissolve everything except the shadow. And archaeologists can only find that if the site has been undisturbed.' She caught sight of Alison's strained look and hastened to add: 'The trouble with Redall beach is that now it is right on the edge of the sea. The tide and the wind have already damaged the site beyond any hope of finding that kind of evidence.'

The peat. The peat strata in the dune. The words floated into her mind as she stared down at the paté on her plate. The peat was newly exposed, only the edge was crumbling, smelling of sweet garden earth . . .

She dropped her fork. The others were looking at her.

'I'm sorry.' She smiled, scrabbling for it. 'It's all this talk of ghosts. I think you are at last making me nervous.'

'And that is unforgivable,' Diana put in firmly. 'I'll have no more of this nonsense. I have known that cottage for most of my life. It is not haunted. It has never been haunted and we will not discuss it any more.'

Kate stole a glance at Greg. He had meekly turned his attention to his plate.

At the end of the meal as the others made their way back to the fire Diana put a hand on Kate's arm. 'Stay and help me make the coffee. I haven't had the chance to talk to you properly yet.' She smiled as she lifted the kettle from the hob and carried it to the sink. Neither woman spoke as the water ran into the kettle, then with a glance over her shoulder Diana beckoned Kate nearer to the stove. There was a hiss of steam as she put the dripping kettle onto the hot plate. 'I think you have gathered that Greg is trying to scare you away from Redall Cottage,' she said quietly. 'I am so sorry he has decided to be childish like this. He can't forgive me for making him move out. It's got nothing to do with you. It is me he is angry with.'

Kate turned to the table and began to stack the plates. She glanced at the far end of the room where Roger was choosing a CD from the pile on the stereo. Greg was bending over the fire, coaxing some fresh logs into a blaze.

'I had guessed that was what was going on,' she said after a moment. 'He and Alison are both in it, I think. Don't worry, I can handle it.'

'You're sure?' Diana frowned. 'It seems so feeble to say I can't do anything about it, but whatever I say to them, they will go on if they think it's working.' She banged two of her dishes together crossly and carried them over to the sink. 'I hate to think of you out there on your own. It's so far from anywhere.'

'You don't think they would harm me?' Kate looked at her in astonishment.

'No. No. Of course I don't think that. Neither of them would hurt a fly. But they might think it amusing to frighten you.' She shook her head. 'Oh, my dear, I am so sorry. I feel dreadful about this. Greg is not an easy person . . .' Her voice trailed away helplessly.

Kate felt a surge of anger. Impulsively she put her hand on Diana's arm. 'Please, don't upset yourself. I told you, I can cope.' She grinned. 'It was real ghosts I wasn't sure about. I can deal with imposters. I expect I can play them at their own game.' Diana looked at her gratefully and Kate smiled again. 'Just so long as I know it's them. And just so long as I know you and Roger are there – a touch of sanity at the end of the phone.'

'You can be sure of that.'

'Then there's no problem.' She picked up the coffee jug and carrying it to the sink ran some hot water into it to warm it. Greg and his father were sitting down now, one of either side of the inglenook. The two younger Lindseys had vanished. Quietly, the sound of music floated through the long, low-ceilinged room.

It was nearly midnight when reluctantly Kate climbed to her feet and announced that she ought to go home. Roger had been asleep in his chair for the last twenty minutes and Diana, for all her animated conversation, looked exhausted.

Greg stood up immediately. 'I'll drive you back. You don't want to walk up through those woods on your own at this time of night.' He grinned.

Kate glanced at Diana and she smiled. The implication was clear. More ghosts. 'Thanks. I wouldn't say no to a lift. It's surprising how long that path can be when you're tired.'

The sky had cleared. It blazed with stars and there was a fine layer of frost on the windscreen. Greg opened the door for her then he fumbled about under the driver's seat for a scraper. 'It won't take a moment. Did you leave the stove banked up?'

She smiled. 'I think I'm getting the hang of that beast at last. It's voracious in its appetite for attention, isn't it?'

'It is indeed.' A small circle cleared in the frost – apparently all he required to see the narrow track – he climbed in beside her and slammed the door. The engine started reluctantly, revving deafeningly in the silent darkness. Shoving the gearstick forward Greg turned the vehicle around and headed for the trees. A sheen of frost lay on the damp ground and the spinning wheels shattered crazy patterns into the thin veneer of ice on the puddles between the ruts.

Kate hung on grimly as the Land Rover slithered around.

'The friend you mentioned in the States,' Greg said suddenly, out of the silence. 'Your boyfriend?'

'He was.'

'What happened?' He hauled at the gear lever as the tyres spun.

'People grow apart.'

'But you keep in touch.'

She looked sideways at the handsome profile, trying to interpret the cryptic tone and she felt a small shiver of excitement. 'Yes,' she said firmly. 'We keep in touch.'

To her surprise he did not speak again until they arrived. Jumping down from the high seat she leaned in to thank him, but he was already climbing out.

'You'd better let me check everything is all right,' he said. 'The least I can do.'

'There's no need. I'm sure the ghosts have gone.' She smiled at him, but she gave him her key. Buoyed up with the knowledge that Diana and Roger were on her side she was curious to know what he would do next.

The lamp in the living room was still alight as they went in, and so, to Kate's relief, was the woodburner. Greg glanced at it almost approvingly and she saw him take note of the huge pile of logs next to it. If he was amused by her foresight he gave no sign. 'It all looks OK to me. Do you want me to check upstairs?'

'No need. Thanks, but I'll be fine. I'm not afraid.' She hadn't taken off her coat, waiting pointedly by the door. He gave a final glance around. 'OK then. I'll see you around.'

'Thanks for bringing me home. And thank your parents again for me, for a lovely evening. I really enjoyed it.'

'Good.' For a moment he paused, looking at her. It was there again, the humour, just behind the sober, almost stern exterior and for a moment she thought he was going to stoop and kiss her cheek as his father had done. If he was, he changed his mind. He gave a curt half-bow – the Englishman's salute – and turned away.

For a moment she stood watching as he climbed back into his vehicle and, flooding the darkness again with the arcing headlights, turned it and headed back into the trees. Closing the door she gave a sigh of relief. The cottage was warm and safe. The fire was lit, the water hot – she had left the immersion heater on to be sure – the door was locked, and she had allies. Marcus was a trick. A figment of someone else's imagination.

XX

Switching out the lamp she turned towards the kitchen. A cloud of angry flies rose and buzzed around the light, hitting the ceiling, banging against the walls as she stared at them in disgust. Where were they coming from? She glanced round. She had left no food out, nothing to tempt them. Besides, it was winter. She walked over to the dresser, and then she stopped. A trail of wet peat lay over the pale wood surface. There was more on the floor in front of the cupboards and more again in the sink. She stared down into the stainless steel bowl and felt her stomach lurch as she saw maggots in the filth that lay there. The room, she realised suddenly, was once again full of that sweet, intense odour of rich earth. A smell which she had not noticed at all as she opened the door.

She clenched her fists. Greg. This was something to do with Greg. Somehow he had arranged all this while she was out. One of his friends must have come to the cottage, using his key, while they knew she was safely at the farmhouse and had had all the time in the world to prepare a little surprise for her.

Furious, she turned both taps on full, watching the black soil and maggots swirl away down the drain. Then she set about clearing up the rest of the mess. About the flies she could do nothing. Several energetic minutes with a rolled up newspaper only bagged a couple. Tomorrow she would buy a spray.

Turning off the light at last and closing the door firmly behind her she paused at the foot of the stairs, looking up. Her mouth had suddenly gone dry. What had they done up there? Cross and very tired she walked firmly up, and turning on the light in her bedroom she stood in the doorway and stared round, holding her breath. As far as she could see there was nothing wrong. With a sigh of relief she went in and going to the bed she pulled back the lace cover. The sheets were undisturbed. Relieved that they had not succumbed to a childish urge to defile her bed in some way she looked round carefully, searching for any signs of intruders, but there were none. The room was as she had left it. The only smell in there was from the sweet-scented stems of daphne in the glass on the table by the window. Walking over to the window she drew back the curtain, and opening it she leaned out. The night was clear as crystal. The starlight was so bright she could see every detail of the garden and the hedge and across the dunes towards the sea which lay luminous and still, the movement of the waves on the beach dulled into a slow, heavy, rhythmic beat like the steady breath of a sleeping animal. She stood for a long time, her elbows on the ice-cold sill, then at last, shivering, she closed the window and turned back towards the bed.

The creak of the door on the landing made her jump out of her skin. She spun to face it, her heart thundering beneath her ribs. There was someone there; someone hiding in the spare room. Taking a deep breath she glanced round for some kind of a weapon to defend herself with. There was nothing that she could see save a wire coat hanger lying on the chair. Picking it up she held it out in front of her as, white knuckled, she tiptoed to the door. She had not quite shut it and it was easy to creep into position behind it and from there peer round onto the dark landing. She frowned. In the narrow stream of light which fell from her bedroom across the rush mat and up onto the wall on the far side, she could see the door of the other room was still open. The room beyond it lay in darkness. For a moment she was tempted to slam her own door closed and jump into her bed, putting her head under the pillow and praying that whoever it was would go away. But that was impossible.

'Greg?' Her voice came out as a squeak. She cleared her throat and tried again. 'Greg? Come on. I know there's someone there.' Flinging her own door back against the wall she walked openly onto the landing and pushed open the door opposite. 'For God's sake, stop messing about. It's one o'clock in the morning. Come on. The joke's over!' She flicked on the light and peered round. For a moment she was too horrified by what she saw to react.

Her boxes and cases had been strewn all over the place; Greg's pictures had been thrown over, the stretchers broken, the canvas slashed and all round the room was a dusting of black earth. The smell of it was overpowering, sweet, rich, cloying. Clutching the door, leaning against it for support she found she had begun to shake; her knees were on the point of giving way. She could feel the bile rising in her throat. Whoever had done this, whoever had been there had wrecked everything in the room. Her eyes strayed to her locked suitcase. It had been torn apart at the hinges. The duster in which the torc had been wrapped was shredded and the pieces lay scattered across the floor. As far as she could see the torc itself had gone.

'Oh God!' Her lips were dry, her palms wet.

Turning, she peered down into the darkness of the stairwell.

'Where the hell are you?' she screamed. She ran down the stairs and flung on the lights in the hall. 'Where are you?' The front door was still locked and bolted as she had left it – the key lying in the dish on the hall table. She ran into the living room. It, too was as she had left it, the windows closed. The kitchen was deserted too, save for a cloud of bluebottles which rose as she turned on the light and homed in at once in their endless circling of the ceiling.

She picked up the phone. It rang for a long time before Diana answered, her voice muzzy with sleep.

'Diana, I'm sorry to ring so late.' Kate was unaware of how her voice shook. 'Can I speak to Greg? You warned me. You warned me and I thought I could cope but this is too much. He's got to come and clear all this up now!'

'Kate, what's happened?' Diana, sitting up in bed at the farmhouse reached for the bedside light. Beside her Roger groaned and opened his eyes.

'The place has been smashed up. My cases – his pictures – his own pictures – have been shredded!' Kate swallowed hard, trying to make herself breathe more slowly; trying to regain a little calm. 'Please, just tell him to get here!' She slammed down the phone and turned to survey the kitchen. At first she had thought it was all right – clean – but now she could see that she had missed a patch of earth on the dresser behind a pile of oddments – a kitchen timer, a couple of books, a pen. She stared. A maggot was wriggling across a shopping receipt she had tossed down when she came back from Colchester, its white gelatinous body dotted with grains of fibrous peat. For a moment she thought she was going to vomit where she stood. She closed her eyes and took a deep breath, feeling the chill of sweat on her face. Slowly she backed away from the dresser. Slamming the door on the kitchen she went to open the stove. She stood over it, holding out her hands, waiting for the sound of the Land Rover. It was a full twenty minutes before she heard the engine and saw the reflection of the headlights through the curtains.

Her legs were so weak she could hardly reach the front door. Fumbling she inserted the key and pulled back the bolts to let Diana and Roger and Greg into the hall.

'What's happened?' Diana put her arm round her. 'Oh, my dear, what's happened?'

'Ask him.' Kate nodded at Greg, ashamed to find she was near to tears.

'I don't know what the hell you think I've done,' Greg retorted sharply. He walked into the living room and peered round. 'What has happened?'

'Upstairs.' Kate pulled herself together with difficulty. 'The spare room.'

She and Diana remained in the hall while Greg ran up the stairs two at a time followed more slowly by his father. For a moment there was silence, then they both heard Greg's string of expletives.

'Would he really do that?' Kate asked. 'Destroy his own paintings?'

Diana looked at her with a frown. Releasing Kate she climbed up after the men.

Greg was standing in the middle of the room, one of his canvasses in his hand.

He spun round as Diana came in closely followed by Kate. 'Who did this?' His lips were white.

'I thought you would be able to tell me that,' Kate retorted. 'It was your plan, wasn't it? To scare me witless so that I would leave and you could come back here.'

'Do you think I'd destroy my own paintings?' He shouted. 'Do you think I would do this? Christ Almighty! This was one of my best pieces.'

It was the picture of the cottage under the sea.

'Why did you leave it here then?' Kate flashed at him. 'If it was so precious, why not take it with you?'

'Because – because it belonged here.' He glared at her. 'Because I had meant to have it framed to hang here.' He looked down at the torn, bent remnant in his hands.

'Obviously your bully boys got their orders wrong.'

'What the hell do you mean?' he shouted. 'Where have you got this idea from? Ma, I suppose?'

'You can't deny you meant to scare Kate away,' Roger put in. 'I could not believe anything so childish of you when your mother said she thought that was what you were up to. But she was right. I saw it tonight at dinner.'

He leaned against the wall, his hand going surreptitiously to his chest beneath his jacket. His face was grey with exhaustion.

Greg stroked the painting in his hand with a gentle forefinger. 'I don't deny Allie and I were going to have a bit of fun, talking about ghosts and that. It was going to be worth it.' He flashed a grimly defiant look at Kate. 'But this – No.'

'Then who did it?' Kate whispered.

They looked at each other.

'Vandals?' Diana took a few steps forward, and stooping, picked up a small sketch which had been torn free of a book which had rested with the paintings against the wall. She looked down at it sadly.

'Vandals would not have contented themselves with one room, surely,' Kate said. 'And nothing has been stolen as far as I can see.' She stopped. The torc. The torc had gone. Unless it was lying with the rest of the rubbish buried somewhere in the debris.

Roger was watching her face. 'Is something missing?' he asked.

'Maybe. Something I found on the beach. I had locked it in that suitcase.'

'Something from the dig?' Greg turned on her accusingly.

She shrugged. 'I was going to take it to the museum. I was pretty sure Alison wasn't going to bother and that site is too important for a child to be playing about destroying what is left of it. I'm sorry, but I really felt that. It was a torc. It was important.'

She walked into the room and picking up the suitcase tossed it aside, pushing at the drift of papers underneath with her foot. A clot of peaty soil fell off the case at her feet. Something was wriggling about in it. She stared at it for a moment then she turned away.

'Oh God!' Diana covered her eyes in disgust.

'I think we'd better call the police.' Roger sighed. 'If

Greg had nothing to do with this, and I don't believe in a million years he did, then obviously it is a matter for them.'

'But no one broke in,' Kate said quietly. 'The door was locked. The windows were all closed.'

'They were. I checked downstairs.' Greg threw his damaged painting into the corner with some force. 'What a pity you didn't let me check upstairs too. I might have saved you some of the shock. I'll ring the police, Dad.' Forcing his way past them he disappeared.

Diana reached for Kate's hand. 'You must come back and stay with us, my dear. You can't possibly stay here alone after this.'

Kate didn't argue. Following the others down the narrow staircase she ducked into the kitchen long enough to retrieve four tumblers and the bottle of whisky then she followed them into the living room, where Greg, having rung the police, was stoking up the fire. 'They'll be here as soon as possible,' he said. He straightened and faced Kate. 'I owe you an apology. Dad was right. It was unspeakably childish of me to try and frighten you away, but I swear to you, I had nothing to do with this.' His shoulders slumped slightly as he accepted a glass of whisky from her. She had added no water to any of them. 'I may have been offhand about my paintings up there, but some of those were very special. To me, at any rate. I would not have damaged them.'

She gave him a watery grin. 'I believe you.'

'Kate dear.' Roger sat down in the armchair near the fire. 'I think perhaps you should check all your belongings. Make sure nothing else is missing.' He glanced across at the table where her laptop computer and the printer sat amongst a litter of books. 'Though I can't believe anyone would have broken in and missed that. That of all things they would have taken, surely.'

Kate nodded. 'Thank God they didn't. But you're right. I'll check. I had some silver bangles and rings in the bedroom. I didn't notice if they were still there.' She moved towards the door, then she hesitated. Upstairs was suddenly somewhere hostile.

Without saying anything Greg followed her. 'I'll go first,' he said.

Nothing in her bedroom had been touched. There was no sign that anyone had been there at all. They searched carefully, then ventured once more into the spare room. 'I was going to look for the torc,' Greg said. 'But perhaps we'd better not touch anything else. They will probably want to fingerprint everything in here.'

She stared round. The bluebottles were still here as well, their angry buzz vibrating in the silence as they divebombed the single light bulb in the centre of the ceiling. She shook her head. 'I don't understand. I just don't understand,' she said.

He shrugged. 'Who can tell why people do things. There are so many reasons. I think this person was angry. For some reason he was angry.'

'He was searching for something he couldn't find perhaps.'

'But what. Money?'

'If it was money he would have looked in the bedroom. Under the chair seats. Up the chimney.' She gave a weak smile. 'I remember when my sister's flat was burgled. That was what they did. No. It was something in here, he wanted. Something specific.'

'The torc?'

'But how would he have known it was here. I was the only person who knew about it.'

They looked at each other.

Marcus

The word had not been spoken out loud, but it was there, hanging in the air between them. Kate shook her head. Marcus as a personality was an invention; an invention she and Greg and Alison had thought up between them in a strange spontaneous way; the creation of a fertile mind, hers, fed by the promptings of two devious ones, theirs.

'So, who else knew about it?' Greg prompted softly. 'You thought of someone, just then.'

'Only Marcus,' she said.

XXI

The police spent a long time searching the spare room at the cottage and it was after four before the tired men climbed into their vehicle and drove along the bumpy track back to Redall Farmhouse followed by the Lindseys' Land Rover. Kate stood for a moment watching the taillights of the police vehicle as it disappeared away into the woods, then she followed the others back inside. Her head was spinning and she was exhausted. She had grown to love Redall Cottage, she realised, in the short time she had been there, in spite of her occasional nervousness, and suddenly what confidence she had in the place had been smashed. It was as if a new friend had turned round and kicked her in the teeth.

Diana had paused to wait for her in the entrance hall. 'You can sleep in Greg's room, Kate. He's gone straight upstairs to make up the bed for you.'

'But what about him?' Kate followed her into the warm familiar room. The fire had died to ash but it was still cosy, still redolent with coffee and wine and the faintest suspicion of oregano and garlic from their supper so many hours before.

'He will be perfectly all right,' Roger put in sternly. 'He has appropriated my study through there as his studio.' He indicated a room off the entrance hall which she had not so far seen. 'He can camp in there. You look completely exhausted, my dear. I suggest you go straight upstairs and sleep. We'll talk in the morning.'

In spite of her tiredness Kate found herself staring around Greg's bedroom as she sat wearily down on the bed, but if she was looking for some clue to his personality amongst his belongings she was disappointed. The room had obviously been – and still looked like – the spare room of the house. The furnishings, though comfortable and charming, had that strange air of not belonging to anyone in particular which spare rooms acquire. The style was too feminine to be Greg's; too masculine to be a woman's room. She looked down at his things on the table by the window. In front of the small, square Edwardian dressing mirror lay a scattering of belongings. Besides the obvious brush and a comb there were cufflinks – so, he dressed up formally when he wanted to – somehow she couldn't quite picture it. There was a paintbrush, seemingly unused, several pencils of differing hardness, a pile of small change, a crumpled train ticket issued at Liverpool Street, a chain of paper clips, some Polo mints in a scruffy remnant of silver paper and an exquisite enamelled snuff box. She picked the latter up and stared at it for a moment, enchanted, then she continued her weary scrutiny of the room. The walls were covered with a pretty flowered wallpaper and criss-crossed with beams, the ceiling was low, the furniture mainly Victorian. It was small and comfortable and safe.

It took her only two minutes to undress, donning the cotton nightshirt she had stuffed into her shoulder bag with her toothbrush, and slide gratefully into the bed.

Pulling the duvet up over her head Kate closed her eyes. Minutes later she opened them again. She was too tired, too stressed, her brain too active to sleep. Hugging the pillow she lay looking towards the window at the blackness of the sky and the tears began to run down her cheeks. Outside, across the grass, the mud gleamed in the starlight as slowly the tide crawled in across the saltings.

It was daylight when she fell at last into a fitful doze and well after eleven before she awoke, rocketed out of her uneasy dream by the sound of loud pop music from the room next door. Sitting up slowly she swung her feet to the floor, rubbing her face wearily in her hands. From downstairs, as Johnny Rotten paused momentarily to draw breath, she could hear the sound of a vacuum cleaner.

Ten minutes later, her face washed in cold water, her hair brushed and fully dressed in her skirt and blouse of the night before, she ran downstairs. The sitting room half of the large living area was deserted — even the cats were missing. Peering through the oak studs which divided the room she saw that Roger sat alone at the kitchen table. He was reading *The Times*. The sound of the vacuum had shifted to the furthest recesses of the house as he looked up and saw her. He smiled. 'Coffee is on. Come and have a cup. You look as though you could do with one.'

'Thank you.' She sat down opposite him. She wondered for a minute how he had managed to get hold of a newspaper so early — surely they weren't delivered out here — then she remembered the time. It was already nearly midday. Time and plenty for any of her hosts to have gone out, half way round the county and returned if they had wanted to.

He pushed a cup towards her before folding his paper and setting it neatly beside his plate and leaning forward on his elbows. 'I had a long talk with the police this morning on the phone. After due reflection overnight they seem to think as you did that Greg probably did it himself, or at least that he was responsible. There was absolutely no sign of a break-in and he is the only person besides Di and myself, and you of course, to have a key to the cottage.'

Kate stared at him. 'But surely, he wouldn't destroy his own pictures.'

Roger sighed. 'It's difficult to tell sometimes what is going on in my son's mind, Kate. I often think he hates his talent.' He poured some more coffee into his own cup. 'My dear —' he paused, searching for the right words. 'I would of course understand if you decided that you wanted to leave, and I would be more than happy to return your rent.

All of it. I am extremely embarrassed by everything that has occurred. But if you still want to stay —' He hesitated. 'If you still want to stay at the cottage I shall get someone over there today to change the locks, and I will see to it myself that no one has a key but you for the rest of your tenancy. I can't apologise enough for all the distress this must have caused you.' He smiled. He looked exhausted. His face, beneath dry, paper-thin skin was drained of colour.

Impulsively Kate reached over and put her hand over his. In the daylight her fear had evaporated. 'I think I would like to stay. It's so lovely here and my book is going so well.' She glanced at the window, framed in blue gingham curtains. 'Of course, it's easy to say that now, with the sun shining outside and the house busy with people.' She looked down into the depths of her coffee. 'I'm not sure how I will feel in the dark, on my own.' She shrugged apologetically.

'Give it a try.' He turned his hand over to take hers for a moment. 'You can change your mind any time. And if you're nervous, you know we can be there very quickly. One of us will always come if you call, I promise.' He stood up. 'Greg is out. Come and look at his pictures.'

She followed him towards the study and paused in the doorway looking round as Roger made his way towards his chair behind the desk and threw himself down in it. 'He has talent,' he said tiredly. 'It does not excuse him, but maybe it helps us to understand him a little.'

Kate walked slowly round the room. She had already formed a view of Greg's talent from the paintings at the cottage, but this selection reinforced it tenfold. He was very good indeed. 'Who is this woman?' Curious, she held out a small portrait. It was one of several of the same subject.

Roger shrugged. 'I don't recognise her. They are all recent, though.'

Kate stared down at her. The woman had large, oval, grey eyes, too large for her face – they were the same in each painting – and looped chestnut hair. In every case she was dressed in blue, but there was no detail of what she was wearing, just a blur, a hint of shoulders, arms, no more. She shivered and put the painting down. 'He's good.'

Roger nodded. He gave a small conspiratorial smile. 'Don't tell him I showed you. Come on. We'll start on the potatoes and after lunch we'll take you back to the cottage.'

She couldn't help a feeling of slight trepidation as she let herself into the cottage later, but the presence of both Roger and Diana at her heels reassured her, as did the arrival twenty minutes later of the locksmith. While he fixed the door, the others worked upstairs with her, tidying the spare room and cleaning it.

Roger checked the two windows. 'Do you want him to fit window locks while he's here?' he asked doubtfully examining the window frame. There was no sign of a forced entry anywhere in the house.

Kate shrugged. 'It seems a bit like overkill –'

'Perhaps they could be screwed down. It would be less expensive,' Diana interrupted. 'I think we should take every precaution. And there should be a larger bolt on the front door as well as a dead lock.'

It was nearly dark by the time they had all gone. Kate looked round. Strangely she was relieved to see them go. Comforted that the house was now defended like Fort Knox and reassured that her strange experiences were in some way due to Greg she had found herself longing for them to leave; after twenty-four hours without writing she was suffering from withdrawal symptoms.

Taking a cup of coffee to her desk she sat down and pulled the pile of typescript towards her. Pen in hand she began to read.

Outside, the winter day had sunk into a cold sullen night. Once or twice she looked up towards the windows, listening. She had decided against having them screwed shut in the end. It seemed so sad to have to lose the reassuring noise of the sea and the fresh air.

At this moment however there was no sound from outside at all. No wind, no sea. A total silence enveloped the cottage, broken only by the quiet hum of her computer and the pattering of the keys beneath her fingers. The shrill ring of the phone from the kitchen made her jump violently.

It was Jon. His voice was light and sociable again, casual, as though he had no real reason to make a transatlantic call to her at all. 'How are you?'

'So, so,' she replied. She sat down on the high stool. 'Actually, not so good. I've had a burglary.'

'You're not serious. Oh my God, Kate, are you OK?' The real concern in his voice made her wish for the second time that she hadn't told him her news.

'Yes, I'm fine. They didn't take anything except –' she paused, ' – do you remember last time you phoned I was cleaning a torc?'

'Belonging to an ancient Brit?' Superficially light-hearted though the words were, she could still hear the worry in his voice.

'They took that. And they smashed up some paintings.'

'Kate, you can't stay there –'

'No. No. I'm fine. I have the phone, and they've changed all the locks. I am bolted and barred like someone in Holloway, except that I am the only one with a key. It was probably local kids who thought the cottage was empty. I don't suppose they will be back.'

'Have the police been? Are you sure you're all right? Oh God, Kate, I wish I were closer.' The warmth of his voice filled the kitchen. 'Take care, my darling, won't you.'

She hung up thoughtfully. My darling, he had called her. My darling. He still loved her.

She was aware suddenly that the wind was getting up

outside. She could hear the soft moaning of the tree branches from the wood, but it didn't matter. Suddenly nothing mattered any more. Feeling unaccountably happy, snug, knowing there was a good supply of firewood in her box, and with a brand new lock and a bolt top and bottom on the front door, she smiled. The sound made her feel all the more secure and cosy.

She went back to her book. It was hard to concentrate; her mind kept wandering back to Jon, but eventually the narrative captured her again and she was drawn back to the childhood of her poet. Catherine Gordon was something of an enigma in her relationship with her son, her love as twisted and deformed as the poor club foot of her child. Kate leaned back in her chair, chewing the end of her ballpoint. A squall of wind hit the cottage. She felt the walls shudder and heard the sudden crack of rain against the window as she sat forward, her hands on the keys and began writing again. A minute later she stared at the screen in horror.

May the gods of all eternity curse you, Marcus Severus, and bring your putrid body and your rotten soul to judgement for what you have done here this day . . .

Christ! she whispered. *Oh Christ!*

Another squall hit the windows and she flinched as though the wind and rain had hit her. Quickly, as though afraid it would burn her, she switched off the computer and pushed back her chair. Her hands were shaking.

I didn't write that.

But she had, like some robotic amanuensis, taking down dictation. She stared round the room. It was very still. The squall had retreated as fast as it had come and the night outside was silent once again. All she could hear was the pumping of her pulse in her ears. She grabbed her cassette player and inserting a cassette with trembling hands, she switched it on. The sound of Sibelius filled the room as taking a deep breath, she moved over to the stove and bending down, opened the doors to stare at the warm glow of the smouldering logs.

'I am tired, that's all,' she whispered to herself. 'It's been a long day. I need sleep. A lot of sleep.' She poured herself a small whisky with a hand that was still far from steady. Sipping it slowly she stood for several minutes in front of the stove.

Only very gradually did she become aware that there was someone standing behind her. Her knuckles white on the glass, the hairs on the back of her neck prickling with fear she held her breath, not daring to move. 'Alison?' Her voice was hoarse with tension. It was a woman. She was certain it was a woman. 'Alison, is that you?' Slowly she turned round.

The room was empty. She stared at the closed door. It had warped slightly over the years and already she had learned the sound of its squeak as it opened or shut. It was distinctive; loud. And she had not heard it.

'Come on, Kennedy. Pull yourself together.' She took a gulp of the whisky, feeling the heat of it burning her throat and creeping through her veins. It gave her the courage to walk over to the door and pull it open. Outside, the hall was deserted. The front door was still barred and bolted as she had known it must be. There was no one there. Resolutely, her glass still in her hand she climbed the stairs and flicking on the lights she peered into her bedroom. It was empty. The room was tidy. For a moment she hesitated in front of the spare room, then taking a deep breath, she flung the door open and switched on the light. The room was as they had left it earlier. Tidy, neat, almost empty, her cases stacked against the wall. The remnants of Greg's paintings were gone – retrieved to the makeshift studio in his father's study. Both windows were shut. The blue-bottles had disappeared. Of the torc there was still no sign.

With a sigh of relief she went heavily back downstairs and into the living room.

Oh God, it was there again! The smell of earth and with it that sweet, indefinable scent. Shaking her head wearily she went over to the stove, piled in as many logs as she could and slammed the doors shut.

'Go to hell, Marcus, wherever you are, and leave me in peace!' she said out loud.

She turned round to switch off the desk lamp and let out a scream, knocking her empty glass to the ground.

A woman was standing in the corner of the room.

In the fraction of a second that she was there Kate saw her auburn hair, her stained, torn, long blue gown, and she knew that somehow, somewhere, she had seen this person before. And then she was gone, leaving only the scent of earth and with it the cloying, flowery perfume.

A taste of acid in her mouth, Kate backed towards the door. She reached it and backed into the hall, her eyes on the spot where the woman had stood. She didn't believe in ghosts. No one sane believed in ghosts. Only to joke with the Lindseys. It was her imagination; she was too conscious of the black stormy night outside the windows and it had created this vision inside her head. That was it. Who was it who had said we are all mad at night? Was it Mark Twain? She shook her head. Whoever it was was right.

Or it might be the whisky. Perhaps she had been drinking too much. And the rest of the bottle was in the living room where – it – had been standing. Too bad. She could do without it. She took the stairs two at a time and running into her bedroom she slammed the door. She was still shaking, but not so much she couldn't drag the Victorian chair, heavy for all its neat smallness, across the room and wedge it under the handle. Why, oh why hadn't she insisted on having a bolt fitted to her bedroom door as well while the locksmith was about it this afternoon?

It was only as she pulled off her clothes and dived into bed, pulling the covers up over her head, that she remembered that ghosts can walk through walls.

XXII

In his bedroom Patrick frowned. The mathematical formula he had been working on wasn't going to come out. Somehow he had to try it another way. He paused for a minute, staring into space. He could hear the music from Allie's bedroom blaring down the passage. Even with two doors closed in between it was deafening. He sighed. Yelling would do no good. If anything it would make her turn it up louder. He frowned for a minute pondering on how she had persuaded Greg to fork out for a new radio cassette. Their father had said that the insurance would probably pay in the end, but why had Greg put his hand in his pocket so fast? He puzzled over it for a few minutes more but already his mind was going back to the figures on his screen.

Around him his books, their spines all neatly aligned, were gleaming, friendly companions in the semi-darkness. The only light in his room came from the anglepoise lamp on his desk and from the screen of the computer.

He thumped the enter key a couple of times and tried again, conscious suddenly of the sound of the sea in the distance and the whine of the east wind and the patter of rain on the window.

Before him the screen shivered. He frowned and rubbed his eyes. A letter had dropped from the top of the screen to the bottom. Then another, then another.

'Oh, no! Oh fucking hell!' He stared at it in disbelief. 'Not a virus! Not a fucking virus!'

Holding his breath he tapped at the keys frantically, trying to save what he had been doing, but already the screen was blank and the cursor was moving purposefully up to the top left hand side once more. Slowly a message appeared.

May the gods of all eternity curse you, Marcus Severus Secundus and bring your putrid body and your rotten soul to judgement for what you have done here this day . . .

Patrick stared, clutching at the wooden arms of his chair. For a moment he sat without moving, reading the message through and through again, then he stood up with such violence that his chair fell onto the floor behind him.

'Allie! Allie! I'm going to wring your bloody neck!' He hurled himself at the door. 'What have you done to my computer, you stupid, silly cow?'

He pounded the six short strides down the passage and threw open her bedroom door.

After the comparative darkness of his room, hers was a shock. At least six light bulbs blazed in there – two spotlights, a ceiling light and three desk lamps, sitting at strategic angles on the floor. No wonder she had migraines!

His sister was lying on her bed, still fully dressed, a dazed look on her face as she listened to her Sisters of Mercy tape for the thousandth time.

Patrick flung himself on the machine and pulled out the cable. 'You cow! Do you realise what you've done? You've only fucked up my project, that's what!'

'What?' She stared at him blankly. The sudden silence after the blare of music was strangely shocking.

'The message on my computer. Very funny! Very droll! Let's all have a good giggle!' He was almost spitting with fury.

'What message?' She lay back again and put her arm across her eyes. 'I haven't touched your silly computer.'

'Then who has?'

'I don't know and I don't care. Get out of my room.'

'Allie.' His voice was suddenly very quiet. 'I am warning you.'

'I told you, I don't know anything about it,' she repeated. 'Get out.'

He leaned forward and seized her arm. 'Come with me.'

'No!'

'Come with me!' He dragged her off the bed.

'Paddy! You're hurting me!' she wailed as she followed him unwillingly down the passage and into the womblike darkness of his room.

'There. Explain that!' He flung his arm out in the direction of the screen.

She leaned closer and peered at it.

'It looks like maths,' she said. 'I haven't a clue what it is.'

'Maths?' He pushed her aside. The screen was neatly ordered, the formula complete. Nothing flickered. He stared at it in disbelief. 'But it all fell off. There was a message – a curse –'

'Bullshit!' she said rudely. 'Can I go now?'

He didn't hear her. He was running his finger over the screen. 'I saw it. A message. A curse –'

But Allie had gone, slamming the door behind her.

XXIII

'I hope it doesn't snow too hard. I'd hate for you to miss your last talk,' Sam Wannaburger, Jon's American editor, said apologetically as he hefted up the heavy case. 'I'm just so glad you agreed to come out and see us.' He had collected Jon from his hotel in a pickup the size of a pantechnicon and driven him in the general direction of south-west. They had stopped at last at a white-painted clapboard house set back from the main street in a small town somewhere in deepest Massachusetts. The floodlights had been switched on, illuminating the graceful lines of the house and its surrounding fir trees, making it look ethereal, floating in a sea of whiteness – for here the grass and the sidewalks were already covered in two or three inches of soft white fluffy snow. 'Anyway, it's too late to worry about it now. We'll have good booze, good talk, good food. It won't matter how hard it snows! And if we can't get back to the big city in the pickup we'll leave it to AmTrak to get us there!' Sam clapped Jon on the back and pushed him none too gently up the path towards the front door.

It was a wonderful house. Huge, converted, so Sam told him proudly, from an early-nineteenth-century carriage house. The fireplace alone was about twelve feet across, the logs burning in it cut to scale; the huge, soft sofas and chairs around it built obviously for seven-foot Americans. The house smelled of hothouse flowers and – Jon hid a smile as he raised his head and sniffed surreptitiously like a pointer – could that really be apple pie?

Sam's wife was thin to the point of emaciation, and so

elegant she looked as though she would break if she moved too fast. Her hand in Jon's was dry and twiglike, her life force, he thought vaguely as he smiled into her bright birdlike eyes, hovering barely above zero. She was one of those Americans who filled him with sadness – dieted, corseted, facelifted and encased in slub silk which must have cost old Sam a few thousand bucks, and looking so uncomfortable that he hurt for her. It was so incredibly sad that, for all her efforts – perhaps because of them – she looked years older than dear old rumpled, slobby Sam with his beer belly and his balding scalp and his huge irrepressible grin. I wonder, he thought idly as he saw her stand on tiptoe and present her rouged cheek to her husband for kissing – a kiss which left a good two inches of cold air between them – if she ever kicks off her shoes and has a good giggle. The thought reminded him of Kate and he frowned. Worried about the burglary he had tried to ring her three times from Boston after his last quick call and on none of them had she picked up the phone. Automatically he glanced at his watch and did the calculation. Six p.m. in Boston meant it was eleven or so in the evening at home. He glanced at Sam. 'Could I try and call Kate one last time. It's eleven over there. I'm sure she'll be at home by now.'

'Sure.' Sam beamed. 'Let me show you your room. You've your own phone in there.' He lifted Jon's case and led the way up a broad flight of open stairs which swung gracefully from the main living room up to a corridor as wide as a six-lane motorway. Jon's bedroom was not as large as he had feared but it was luxurious beyond his wildest dreams – bed, chairs, drapes, carpet, toning, matching, blending greens, until he had the feeling he was walking in a woodland womb. He smiled to himself at the metaphor. Ludicrous. Overblown. Outrageous. Like the room. Like his host. And wonderfully welcoming. He sat on the bed as Sam left him and pulled the phone towards him.

Twenty minutes later, showered and dressed in a clean shirt and a cashmere sweater Kate had given him for his birthday last year, Jon ran downstairs and accepted a large whisky mac from his host. His call had been a dead loss. After a great deal of hassle and toing and froing between the ladies of AT&T and the British exchange, they had established that the phone at Redall Cottage had gone suddenly and totally dead.

XXIV

The priests had walked in solemn procession to the sacred place in the circle of trees on the ridge above the marsh. Nion was not senior among them – he was young – but his royal blood gave him a certain precedence as they made their way, robed and solemn, to their appointed places in the circle.

Nion glanced round. The faces of his teachers, his friends, his colleagues, were taut, their thoughts turned inwards, their bodies bathed and dedicated to their purpose. He grimaced, trying to turn his own mind to prayer and meditation. The choosing of the sacrifice was a ceremony he had taken part in only once before. On that occasion the sacred bread had been baked on the flame and broken as laid down by tradition centuries old. The scorched piece, the piece which belonged to the gods, had been chosen by an old druid of four score summers or more – a man dedicated and ready for whatever the gods decreed. But even he, when he drew out the burned portion and knew that he was to die, had betrayed for a brief moment a flash of terror, before he had bowed his head in acceptance.

The ceremony was strictly ordained. The man was honoured by his colleagues, crowned with gold. In the hours that remained he would bid farewell to his family, order his affairs and at the last divest himself of all his raiment, bathe in waters sanctified with herbs and spices, then, drinking the sacred, drugged wine of death he would kneel willingly for the sacrifice: the garotte if his death was dedicated to the gods of the earth, the rope if to the gods of the sky, and the third death, the death by water if to the gods of the rivers and seas.

Now Nion watched, his head covered, as were those of the others, as the bakestone was blessed and heated. His mouth was dry with apprehension, even though the choice was preordained. He stole a glance at the oldest druid there, a man as frail as a windblown reed, his bald pate beneath the linen veil wrinkled as an old, dead leaf. Almost certainly he would be chosen, the bread passed in such a way that his would be the burned piece. How did he feel, knowing that by the next dawn he would be dead?

Nion closed his eyes and tried to concentrate on prayer, but at noon he was to meet Claudia. His body, strong, vigorous, lusty, quivered at the thought. Sternly he reprimanded himself, and brought his thoughts back to the scene before him.

The bread was cooking now, the fragrance sharp on the morning air. His nostrils picked up the acrid smell of scorching and he swallowed nervously, his eyes going once more automatically to the old man who had blanched to an unhealthy shade of buttermilk.

He watched, arms folded beneath his cloak, as the bread was allowed to cool and broken into small pieces — twenty-one, seven times three — one for each of them, and put into the basket. Slowly it was carried round the circle. Slowly. Slowly. One by one the hands went in. The choice was made. The hands came out. One by one the faces relaxed into relief and the portion was eaten. The old one's turn came. He put in his hand, shaking visibly, and withdrew it. Nion saw him turn the fragment over and over in disbelief. Then his face relaxed into a toothless smile. So, the gods had rejected an old, frail man. In the face of the threat from Rome such a sacrifice was not enough.

Nion's stomach knotted sharply in fear. He noticed suddenly that several men were watching him surreptitiously from beneath their headdresses.

The woven bowl was coming closer. His hands were sweating. Only five more portions remained. Then it was before him, held in the hands of the archdruid who had baked the bread and taken the first piece himself. For a moment Nion hesitated. He raised his eyes to the other man's face and read his fate even before he had put his hand in the basket.

The bread fragment he took was crumbling, still warm from the bakestone, and it was burned black.

The tide was high at six in the morning and the wind was from the north-east, crossing the Urals, dripping ice across the continents, whipping the sea into angry peaks of foam.

Tossing in her bed, Alison was dreaming uneasily. All around her the cold wet earth was pressing down, clogging her nostrils, crumbling into her eyes, filling her ears so she could no longer hear, weighing her into the damp sedge. Hiding her. Hiding the truth. The truth which must be told. With a cry of panic she sat up, untangling herself from the duvet. She stared round the room. It was pitch dark and she could hear the rain pouring down in the garden outside. When it grew light there would be a puddle on the windowsill.

Still dazed by her dream, she stood up and reached for her clothes. There was something she had to do; something urgent. The pounding behind her eyes was insistent, like the beat of the tide upon the shore, driving her, pushing her against her will. Opening the door she stood for a moment on the landing, listening. The house was silent. Her parents slept at the far end in a bedroom which looked out across the woods. Next to her, Greg and beyond him, Patrick, always slept like the dead until they were awakened. She shivered violently. Today was a day for awakening the dead.

Scarcely knowing what she was doing she hauled on her waterproof jacket and forcing her feet into her boots she opened the door and peered out into the icy morning. The wind was roaring in from the north-east full in her face as she pulled the door shut with difficulty behind her and set off in the darkness towards the track through the woods. All she knew was that she had to get to the grave; she had to get there before the tide washed it away.

She had to save it.

XXV

Kate had slept in the end, too exhausted to do anything else, but she too had awoken at six to the sound of rain against the windows. It was steady rain this time, hard and unrelenting and behind the sound of it she could hear the wind.

She didn't want to get up. There was something frightening downstairs, something which when daylight came she would have to confront, but until then she was going to stay where she was, safely tucked up in her bed with the lights on. Wearily she reached for her book and lay back huddled against the pillows.

When she dragged herself out of bed an hour later and pulled back the curtains all she could see was blackness, alleviated only by the streaks of rain sliding down the glass. But she couldn't go back to bed. She was too conscious of the silence outside her door.

Pulling on a pair of jeans and a thick sweater she went out onto the landing and peered down. All seemed as usual down there. She stood for several seconds, then taking a deep breath she ran down and flung open the living room door. The room was empty. The woodburner still glowed quietly. All was as it should be. Lights burned in every room – God knows what her electricity bill would be when she left – but all was quiet. There were no strange smells, no figures lurking in the shadows.

Her face doused in cold water and a mug of strong coffee at her elbow she poured some muesli into a bowl and reached into the fridge for some milk. She was a first class prize idiot with a powerful five-star imagination – how else could she be a successful writer – and a bad dose of nervous collywobbles. All she needed was food, coffee – both being attended to – and then a bracing walk in the rain to clear her head. Then in the cold light of day, probably with more coffee, she would switch on the computer again and get back to young George and his mother.

The knock on the front door took her completely by surprise. Greg stood outside, his collar pulled up around his ears, rain pouring off his Barbour jacket. His hands were firmly pushed into his pockets.

'You see. No key. I had to knock,' he said grimly. The wind snatched the words from his lips and whirled them away with the rain. 'May I come in, or am I too dangerous to allow over the threshold?'

'Of course you can come in!' Kate stood back to let him pass and then forced the door closed behind him. 'Why the sarcasm?'

'The sarcasm, as you call it, was perhaps engendered by two hours of questioning by the police last night who seem under the impression that you still think I robbed the cottage.' He pulled off his jacket and hanging it on the knob at the bottom of the banisters, shook himself like a dog. 'I just thought I would come and thank you in person for your vote of confidence and, incidentally, collect one or two of my things which I would rather not leave here any longer.'

Kate could feel her antagonism rising to match his. 'I assure you, I didn't tell the police it was you. If they thought so they must have got the idea somewhere else,' she said furiously. 'And I must say, I wonder if they aren't right. It seems the sort of half-baked stupid thing you would do to try and get me out. That was the idea, I take it? To get me out.'

'It would be wonderful to get you out.' He folded his arms. 'As it happens, I think the wind and the weather will do it for me. Now, if you don't mind, I should like to collect my property and then I shall leave you to your triumph behind your locked doors.'

'What property exactly have you left behind?' They were facing each other in the hall like a couple of cats squaring up for a fight. 'It seems to me you cleared everything out on Wednesday night.'

'The torn paintings, yes. There are two more here. On the walls.' He strode past her into the living room. There in the corner, hanging near the window, was a small portrait sketch of a woman. Kate had hardly noticed it. He took it down and laid it on the table. 'There is another upstairs. If you will permit me.' Still unsmiling, he turned away and ran up the stairs two at a time.

Kate shrugged. How petty could you get! In spite of herself she walked across to the picture and looked down at it. It was the woman whose portrait she had seen over and over again in the study at Redall Farmhouse, but in this version her figure was full length, her garment clearly drawn.

He had come back into the room again in time to hear her gasp. 'What is it?'

She looked up at him, her face white. 'You've seen her. You've see her here.' She was accusing, taut with shock.

'Who?' In his hand he held the small picture of the blue-bells which had been hanging in her bedroom. She glanced at it regretfully. It was so unlike his usual style. She had really rather liked that one.

'The woman in the picture. I saw her. Last night.'

He frowned. 'You can't have. I made her up. She came out of my head. She's a pastiche of styles – something I was doing for fun. A doodle.' A doodle of a face which had come without his bidding and which had tormented him.

'A doodle of so much importance that you can't leave her here with me.' Kate spoke so softly he had to strain to hear.

179

'That's right,' he said. His voice was aggressive. 'What do you mean you saw her last night? You had a visitor, did you? Are you sure she wasn't a burglar or a vandal?'

'She was a ghost.'

She said it so flatly that he wasn't sure he had heard her correctly. For a moment he stared at her. He was the one who was supposed to be doing the frightening; the one who had decided to use ghosts to scare her away, and yet, with that one small sentence she had sent a shiver down his spine, a shiver which had raised the hairs on the back of his neck.

A moment later he shook his head. She was trying to play him at his own game. Fine, if that was the way she wanted it. 'Where did you see her?'

'There. Almost where you are standing. Your sketch is monochrome, but her dress was blue, like the other pictures you've done of her, the ribbons and combs in her hair were black.'

Greg had to fight very hard the urge to move to another part of the room. 'Supposing I admit that I have seen her.' In his dreams; in his head; even in his heart. 'Doesn't it frighten you, sharing the house with a ghost?'

For a moment she paused, as if she were considering. She looked him in the eye. 'I suppose, if I'm honest it does, yes.'

'But you're going to stay, just to spite me.'

'If you don't mind my saying so, you have a very inflated idea of the importance you hold for me,' she said seriously. 'I'm staying because I came here to write a book; because this is my home for the next few months and because –' she hadn't meant to add this, but it came out anyway ' – I have nowhere else to go. I can't afford London rents at the moment.' None of his business why.

'So, you're staying.'

'So, I'm staying.' She glanced at the painting under his

arm. 'I'm sorry you're taking that. I liked it.' The remark was a concession.

He did not rise to it. It was a trifle, a pretty sketch of which he was not proud. 'I am sure you can buy yourself a print if you need bluebells on your walls.'

She narrowed her eyes. 'I don't think I'll bother,' she said dryly. 'Now, if there is nothing else, I would like to get back to work and I expect you have to report to a police station somewhere.' She smiled sweetly and was rewarded with a scowl.

'No, I am sorry to disappoint you but they did not arrest me. Nor any of my friends.'

'I'm sure it is only a matter of time.' She stepped past him and went towards the front door.

The wind had changed slightly and as she opened the door, rain swept into the hall, icy, harsh, cruel. She stood back and he walked out without a backward glance. By the time he had climbed up into the Land Rover she had closed the door and walked back into the kitchen.

She was thoughtful. Every shred of intuition told her that he was not lying; that the break-in had had nothing to do with him. But the picture? What did the picture of the woman mean?

She waited until he was safely out of sight before donning her weatherproof jacket and her scarf. Her enthusiasm had gone but she was determined to go out anyway, to clear her head, to get rid of the terrible throbbing behind her temples and, dragging her mind back to the book, to straighten out her thoughts about the next chapter. Somehow she had to rid herself of the images of the last few days. The cottage had ceased to be an impersonal place to work and think. It had become tied up with personalities: with Greg and Alison; with Roger and Diana – and, God help her, with Marcus and the lady in a blue gown.

The grass clung wetly to her legs above her boots, soaking her trousers. Then she was on the short turf and then the sand. The tide was on the ebb, but the angry white-topped waves still lashed the beach, sucking at the stranded weed, filling the air with the sharp, cold smell of far-off ice.

Turning her back doggedly on the dig Kate walked into the wind, her hands pushed firmly to the bottom of her pockets. The cold was so fierce it stung her face, it hurt to breathe. She clamped her lips tight across her teeth and, head down, walked firmly forward, scarcely aware of the beauty of the sea beyond the beach where the air was crystalline, the colour of mother-of-pearl, and the heaving mass of water had the solid shine of polished pewter. Somewhere nearby a gull screamed. She looked up and saw it weaving and circling effortlessly on the wind, part of the fearsome force of it.

> There is a pleasure in the pathless woods
> There is a rapture on the lonely shore,
> There is a society, where none intrudes,
> By the deep sea and music in its roar . . .

It was elemental; wonderful. As always, Byron had the words to convey the power of the scene; if only she in her turn could bring his images into her book . . .

The sand whirled around her feet in eddies, loosened by the sleet. Ahead she could see the body of another gull, one which had lost the battle with the elements, lying wet and bedraggled on a patch of wet shingle. A tangle of weed lay near it, and it was not until she was close, staring down sadly as she compared it with the beautiful wild beauty of its colleague above her head that she saw the cruel pull of nylon fishing line around its legs. Overwhelmed by anger at the thoughtless, careless arrogance of man she stooped to touch the mottled grey brown feathers. It wasn't even an adult bird. This must have been its first winter, its first joyous tussle with the elements. The bird's body was cold and hard, the feathers clamped scalelike against its body. Shivering, she straightened and walked on.

She did not walk for very long. The opaque mist on the horizon was drawing closer; the wind strengthening. She could see a faint shadowing across the waves which was a shower of hail sweeping down the coast and towards Redall Bay. Turning, she walked briskly back, more comfortable now that the wind was behind her.

She had not intended to walk as far as the grave, but somehow she could not resist it. One glance, to see if it were still there. Each tide now was a threat. Each storm, each wind.

Her shoes sliding on the side of the dune she was nearly there when the first shower of hail hit her. Sharp, biting, the ice cut her hands and face, tearing at her scarf as she scrambled the last few feet and stood looking down into the hollow below the exposed face of the dune to find that she was not the first person there. Alison was kneeling on the sand, her hands ungloved, hanging at her sides, her eyes fixed on the exposed face of the working. One glance at the trail of wet weed and shells showed Kate that the early morning tide had come nowhere near the edge of the excavation this time. It was still safe.

She hesitated, unsure whether to creep away, not wanting to intrude and risk a mouthful of abuse. The girl was unmoving. Kate frowned. She took a step closer. There was no sign of any spades or trowels, no ghetto blaster, no tools of any kind. Still Alison had not moved. Her hair whipped wildly around her head; her jacket flapped, unzipped, around her body.

'Alison?' she called, uneasily. She paused, waiting for the girl to turn and swear at her for intruding upon her private thoughts, but Alison didn't stir.

'Alison!' she called again, more sharply this time, and she began sliding down the side of the hollow. 'Alison? Are you all right?'

Alison gave no sign that she had heard. She was staring at the sand and peat face of the dune.

'Alison?' Her voice rising in alarm Kate put her arm around the girl's shoulders. 'Alison, can you hear me?' She shook her gently. The girl's body was rigid and cold beneath the flapping parka, clad, beneath it, in only a tee shirt and thin sweater. 'Alison, what's the matter?'

Behind them another shower of hail swept in from the sea. The hailstones rattled against the wiry grass, shushing into the sand, battering their faces. To Kate's horror she saw that Alison neither blinked nor moved as the hail hurled itself against her face and slid down her cheeks. 'Oh God!' She glanced round wildly, half hoping that there would be someone else around, someone who could help, but knowing already that there was no one on the beach at all. 'Alison, you must listen to me!' She grabbed the girl's hand which was ice-cold and began to chafe it vigorously. 'Alison, you've got to stand up. Come on. You can't stay here. You'll catch pneumonia. Come on. Stand up.'

Alison gave no sign of hearing her. She stayed totally rigid except for the hand which Kate was tugging which was limp and cold as death.

Kate stared round, her hair tangling across her eyes, her own face ice-cold with sleet. In only a few moments the sea had changed from pewter to the colour of black ink; opaque, thick, sinister in its uneasy movement. Far out there was no distinction now between sky and water. All were black and threatening.

'Alison, come on. The weather is getting worse.'

Dropping the girl's hand Kate moved in front of her. Alison's face was frozen into immobility, the eyes staring straight ahead, not reacting when Kate brought her hand sharply towards them. 'Right.' Kate spoke with some force. 'I'm sorry to have to do this.' She pulled back her hand and gave Alison a sharp slap. The girl did not react. She did not even blink. Behind them another curtain of hail raced across the sea, embedding itself in the sand, turning the beach a glittering white.

Kate stared at her in despair, then dragging off her own jacket, she pulled it roughly around Alison's shoulders. Without the padded, fleece-lined protection, the cold enveloped her like a curtain, wrapping itself around her, embedding itself in her lungs, clawing at her bones, but she ignored it. She pulled Alison's arm around her neck and heaved at her, trying vainly to raise her off her knees. 'Stand up, blast you. Stand up,' she cried through gritted teeth. 'You've got to move, Alison, or you're going to die of cold.' She struggled desperately against the dead weight of the girl. Alison was barely two inches shorter than she was, and although not plump she was solidly built. Nothing Kate could do seemed to shift her from her knees.

'Please.' Stopping her futile effort Kate stood back, wiping the streaming sleet from her face, feeling the ice soaking through her own sweater. 'Please, Allie, you must try. Stand up. I'll help you. Then we'll go to the cottage. It's warm there. Warm and safe.' In spite of herself she glanced at the streaming sand around them. Just at this moment she was not prepared to think what could have sent Alison into this state. She did not dare.

Taking a deep breath she pulled the girl's arm around her shoulder once more, and putting her own around Alison's waist, she heaved at her, rocking her sideways slightly to try and gain some momentum. As though sensing the movement for the first time, Alison stirred. 'That's it. Help me. Try and stand up.' Kate was elated. Taking another deep breath she renewed her efforts with the last of her strength and this time Alison tried feebly to scramble up. 'Good. And another step. Good girl.' Kate pushed her frantically, terrified she would fall again as, unsteadily, Alison rose to her feet, leaning heavily against her. 'Good, that's it. Now, we've got to get you out of here. One step at a time. Steady. That's it.' Sweat was pouring off her face in spite of the icy downpour as, somehow, Kate half guided half pushed Alison up the bank and onto the beach. Still the girl's eyes hadn't moved; still she did not appear to register anything going on around her, but she was stumbling forward, guided by Kate's desperate tight grip around her waist, hanging from Kate's shoulders like a giant rag doll.

Twice they had to stop while Kate fought to regain her breath but slowly they drew nearer to the cottage. Somehow Kate managed to prop the girl up against the wall as she groped for her new, shiny keys then at last the door was open and they were inside out of the hail. Slamming the door closed with her foot, Kate half carried, half dragged Alison into the living room and unceremoniously tipped her onto the sofa. Gasping as she tried to regain her own breath she ran upstairs to her bedroom and dragged a blanket off her bed. Gathering up her dressing gown on her way out of the room she ran downstairs again. Alison lay where she had left her, half on the sofa, her legs still trailing across the floor.

'Right, let's get you out of those wet clothes.' Awkwardly Kate bundled the girl back against the cushions and began to pull off the soaking sweater and tee shirt. Then the slip of cotton which was her bra. Somehow she forced the cold unbending limbs into her towelling dressing gown, trying to rub some warmth into the wet slippery skin which reminded her horribly of the feathers of the dead gull. She pulled off the girl's boots and then her jeans and socks, and somehow lifting her legs onto the sofa, tucked her up in the blanket, making a cocoon out of which the girl's head, with its straggly wet hair, poked like the head of a startled doll.

'Phone.' Aware that her own teeth were chattering Kate turned towards the kitchen. Shaking, she waited for the number to connect her to Redall Farmhouse. It was only as she tried for the second time that she realised that there was no dialling tone. The line was not dead – she could hear it alive, hissing slightly, resonating as though there were someone the other end. But the number made no impression on the echoing silence. 'Oh, no. Please.' It was a sob of desperation. She took a deep breath and punched nine nine nine. The line remained silent, expectant, as though someone the other end were listening as desperately as she was. 'Hello?' She shook the receiver. 'Hello, can you hear me? Is someone there?' But no one answered. A fresh wave of ice hit the kitchen window. Slowly she hung up. She had never felt more alone.

She went back to the living room and stood looking down at Alison. The girl's face was unchanged, her muscles somehow frozen in the same look of astonished terror. She was not blinking. Her pupils did not appear to be reacting to the dim light of the sitting room. They were still pinpoint small, staring. Reaching into the blankets Kate felt her hand. Was it marginally warmer? She thought so. What was one supposed to do with cases of hypothermia? No alcohol. Wasn't that what they said? Hot water bottles. She had no hot water bottle and she was pretty sure that she would have seen one if there was one in the house. Somehow she did not think it was something that Greg, or even his parents would consider a necessity. So, what else could she use? A hot brick. Wasn't that what people used in the old days? A hot brick wrapped in flannel. She gave a grim smile. There was neither brick nor flannel in the cottage that she had seen. Then she remembered the stones outside, edging what had once been the drive. Large smooth stones, pebble shaped, perhaps off the beach. One of those would do, surely, wrapped in a towel. She turned and ran back to the front door. Pulling it open she stared out at the storm. The clear morning had turned into a vicious darkness lashed by squalls of hail and sleet which tore at her clothes, reminding her that she, too, was chilled to the marrow and wet through. She dived out and heaved at one of the stones. About ten inches long and shaped like a pillow, for a moment she thought it was stuck fast. Then it came up out of the icy ground with a small sucking noise and she carried it back inside, staggering under its surprising weight. She laid it gently on top of the wood-burner, and opening the doors, stacked in some more logs. 'Not long, now,' she said over her shoulder. 'I'm getting something to warm your feet. Would you like a hot drink?' She glanced round at the girl. 'You're safe now, Allie. Come on. Try and wake up.' Sitting down on the edge of the sofa she put her hand on Alison's shoulder. The girl flinched. The movement was so sudden and so violent that Kate jumped. She frowned. 'You're safe, Allie,' she repeated gently. 'There's nothing to be afraid of.' She found herself looking towards the window. Outside, beyond the streaming sleet as it slid down the glass, she could see nothing. What had happened out there in the dune? She wished fervently that Greg was still around. Or that he would remember something and come hurtling back in his Land Rover. Perhaps she should try the phone again.

As she stood up Alison grabbed her wrist. Kate gave a little cry of fright. The girl was staring at her now, her eyes suddenly fully focussed in her white face. 'Don't leave me.' Her voice was hoarse, barely audible.

Kate breathed a sigh of relief. 'You're all right. You're safe.'

'No.' Alison shook her head. The movement seemed to hurt her and she flopped back, her eyes closed for a second. Kate frowned. She was relieved that the awful horrified stare had gone, but the monosyllabic answer had chilled her. 'Why are you not safe?' she asked softly. 'What happened? Do you want to tell me?'

For a moment she thought Alison had not heard her but slowly the girl's eyes opened. 'They're free,' she whispered. Her fingers clutched with surprising strength at Kate's hand. They were still ice-cold. 'I've released them.' Her words were slurred, as though she were slightly drunk. 'They've been waiting. Claudia. Claudia wants her revenge.'

'Claudia?' Kate stared down at the white, pinched face, puzzled. 'Who is Claudia?'

Alison smiled shakily, but her voice when it came out was surprisingly strong. 'Claudia is a whore; a traitor. She's an animal. She deserved to die.'

Kate stared at her in horror. 'Alison, do you know where you are?'

The green eyes opened. They roamed the room unsteadily then they focussed on Kate. For a moment the girl said nothing, then abruptly she burst into tears.

'Oh, Allie, love, don't. I told you, you're safe.' Kate was astonished at the strength of the wave of compassion which swept through her. Leaning forward she put her arms around Alison and held her close. The girl seemed as frail as a bird suddenly, every bone sticking out beneath the warmth of the dressing gown, her body still radiating a terrible chill. 'Listen, let me go upstairs to fetch a towel. I've heated a stone up for you. I can put it near your feet to warm you up once I've wrapped it.' Glancing at the stove Kate began to rise.

'No!' Alison clutched at her again. 'Don't leave me.'

Kate subsided onto the sofa beside her again. 'There is nothing here to frighten you, Alison,' she repeated gently. 'You're safe.'

As though to emphasise her words an extra loud gust of wind shook the cottage. A puff of smoke blew out of the open stove into the room, bringing with it the pungent aroma of burning oak and apple. Kate glanced at the window, wondering for a moment if it would hold against the force of the storm. Something moving on the sill caught her eye. Water. There was water on the sill. The window was leaking. She moved slightly, without letting go of Alison's hand and craned sideways to see better. Sure enough, a puddle had formed on the wood. She stared. Floating in the puddle were bits of leaf and soil and there, wriggling around the edge were several maggots.

For a moment she thought she was going to be sick.

'What is it? What's happened?' Her voice rising shrilly in panic Alison clutched at her harder. 'What have you seen?'

'Nothing. Nothing at all.' Wincing at the pain of the girl's clawed fingers Kate tried to free herself. 'Some rain leaking in, that's all. It's hardly surprising, the wind's so strong.' Somehow she forced herself to sound calm. 'Listen, I must go and get something to mop it up. I'll stick a towel on the sill. There must be a leak in the window frame. Then why don't I make us a hot drink. I'm sure you'd like something, wouldn't you?' How she kept her voice steady, she didn't know. Firmly she tried to unfasten Alison's fingers. She was like a child, clutching desperately at her mother's skirt. The moment Kate managed to dislodge one hand the other grabbed at her again. 'Allie, there's nothing to be frightened of,' she repeated.

Allie nodded frantically. 'There is. There is, don't you understand? Claudia is free. Claudia and . . .' she hesitated, frowning, her head suddenly cocked to one side as though trying to hear something from far off, in another room. 'Claudia and . . . and . . . Claudia and . . .' Her voice was fading. A look of puzzlement appeared on her face. 'What was I saying?'

'Nothing, Allie. Nothing at all.' Kate forced her voice to a calmness she did not feel. The child was hallucinating. Was that a symptom of hypothermia? She did not know. The vagueness, the fear, were they all part of it? Oh God, they needed a doctor. 'Allie, I want to go and ring your mother. You'll be quite safe here. I'll only be in the kitchen. Look, if I leave both doors open you'll be able to see me all the time –'

'No!' Alison's voice slid up into a scream. The sound made Kate's skin crawl.

Alison was fighting with the blankets. 'I'll come with you. I don't like it here. That window. She is going to come through that window.' She flung out her arm. Kate looked where she was pointing. There was more earth in the puddle now. Earth and peat and — she could feel the bile rising in her throat as she saw a movement at the edge of her vision.

Suddenly her mind was made up. 'OK. Let's go into the kitchen. Come on. I'll help you. We'll make a hot drink and I'll try and phone.'

Please let it work. Please God, let the phone work.

Her arm around Alison, she helped the girl shuffle through to the kitchen and sat her, still cocooned in the blanket, on a stool.

Quietly, she closed the door and turned the key, then, her hand shaking with fear, she picked up the phone.

The line was still dead.

XXVI

Defiantly leaving his car in a parking space reserved for the disabled right next to the castle gates Greg strode towards the entrance. He glanced at the sky. Snow and sleet showers, they had forecast, turning to unseasonably heavy snow later. That probably meant sleet out at Redall Bay, but you never knew. Sometimes it settled. Whatever happened it would be worse in Colchester. It always seemed to snow heavily there.

It was a long time since he had been in the museum. He stared round, confused. The huge hall with its peripheral exhibits had vanished. Instead it was sectioned, partitioned, intimate, the lighting low and seductive and from some distant corner he could hear the tinny insistent blare of videoed commentary. He frowned. Why couldn't the buggers leave things alone? He could have found his way to Marcus blindfold before. Now, God knows where he was.

He was upstairs, near yet more video crap. With an impatient glare at the booth from which sounds of massacre were emerging, Greg stood in front of the statue and stared long and hard at its face. Then he, as Kate had done, moved to the exhibit and looked down at the man's skeleton. She had been right. It was not Marcus himself who was buried at Redall. So who was it? His eyes strayed to the other remains. Smaller, though not significantly so; Marcus's wife had strong, well-formed bones. His art school study of the skeletal form had been fairly rudimentary, but it was thorough enough for him to give an educated guess that she had been young when she died. How, he wondered. Illness? Injury? Childbirth? He glanced at the inscription. There was no clue there, no notes beyond the bare minimum. He stared down at what was left of Marcus's skull. Was his story written there, in the imprint of his bones? His loves, his hates, his triumphs, his disasters? He brought up his hands and rested them against the cold glass of the display case. 'Come on, you bastard, cough.' He hadn't realised he had spoken out loud until he saw a woman near him turn and stare. She caught his eye and hurriedly turned away. He grinned absentmindedly but already his attention was back on Marcus. Rich, successful Marcus who had made good after the Boudiccan defeat; who had returned to Colchester and to Redall and bought land, probably when prices were rock bottom, like today – he grimaced – was that how it had been? Or had he just helped himself to some property he fancied and marched in? Had Redall's former owner died in the rebellion, leaving his lands wasted and deserted, or did he sell at a profit? He leaned closer to the glass, resting his forehead against it and closed his eyes.

HATE
ANGER
FEAR
FURY

The emotions sweeping through him obliterated every other thought in his head. They swirled round him, shimmering with colour: Red! Black! A vicious violent orange! He was spitting, shouting, tearing at the air, aware in some distant part of himself that there was foam at the corners of his mouth, hearing howls of anguish in his ears and realising they were his own.

Then, as suddenly as they had come, the noise and the colour and the pain were gone and he was conscious of a sudden total silence around him.

Christ, had that been him? Had he really screamed out loud, or had it all been inside his head? The tape in the booth had reached its end and was silent for a few minutes before it marshalled itself for yet another enactment of the conversation between two Romans as the hordes closed in. The hall echoed with silence and cold.

The quick, anxious tap of heels on the floor did not intrude on his shock and terror until he felt a timid hand on his arm. 'Are you all right? Would you like me to fetch someone?' The woman who had been watching him was staring anxiously into his face. 'I saw you staggering about. I thought perhaps –' She faltered as he stared at her, blankly. 'I don't know, but I wondered if you were epileptic or something . . . ?' Her anxiety petered out and she blushed crimson. 'I'm so sorry.'

He gazed at her vaguely. 'I'm all right. Thanks. It must be the heat in here.' He stared round, confused. The hall was cold. Very, very cold.

Slowly she was backing away. She would hurry as soon as she was out of sight and run downstairs and perhaps send up one of the attendants. Well, when they came, whoever they were, they would find that he wasn't pissed. In fact he had never been more sober.

He reached out a hand towards the glass case and then withdrew it quickly as though it had stung him. Whatever had attacked him, overwhelming him with its vile emotions, had come from behind that glass.

XXVII

There was no escort, no guard to watch over him. They trusted him absolutely. The gods had spoken; there was no question but that he would obey. Last minute private farewells were common; what more natural than that a man should say goodbye to the world.

'NO!'

Her scream of agony echoed across the dunes and marshes, the sound rising and falling across the land and the sea until it was lost in the clouds beyond the horizon.

'Claudia – my love –'

'No! I won't let them! What kind of barbaric gods do you worship that they can do this? You can't go back to them. You can't! You can't . . .' She burst into tears.

'Claudia. I have to. The gods have chosen me.' His voice was firm, his strength surprising, even to himself.

'I hate your gods!'

'You mustn't. You must honour them as I do. And obey. To be chosen for the Great Sacrifice is the highest honour possible.'

'Honour! I thought your people sacrificed their prisoners! Their slaves! What kind of honour is it to die like them?' The tears were running down her face, streaking the saffron eyeshadow she had so cheerfully applied before she left home.

'The greatest. The gods have demanded the blood of a prince.' He spoke calmly, his need to reassure her in some strange way giving him courage. 'Maybe we offended them, my dearest, with our love,' he said gently, touching her face with the tip of his finger as though trying to memorize

the position of her nose, her mouth, her eyes for all eternity.
'Perhaps it is best like this. Your gods too, I hope, will be appeased and honoured by my death.'

'No.' She shook her head blindly. 'No. I worship For-tuna. She does not demand the death of her followers. She wants them to live, and be happy. No, I won't let you die. If you die I want to die too.'

'No!' He took her shoulders and shook her gently. 'Claudia, you must live. For your son's sake. You can't leave him. And for my sake. To carry my memory in your heart. You must be strong. You are a daughter of Rome, remember?' It was something she took such pride in, her noble breeding. As he hoped, the words reached her.

She straightened her shoulders a little and raised her head, though tears still streamed down her face. 'You're not afraid?'

'Of course I'm not afraid.' He smiled sternly. 'I am a prince and I am a priest. Why should I be afraid to meet my gods?' He reached up to the heavy silver brooch which fastened his cloak. 'I want you to have this. Wear it for me and don't grieve too much.'

She took it with a shaking hand and pressed it to her lips. 'When . . . when will it happen?'

'At dawn. As the sun shows over the eastern edge of the world.'

'Where – ?' It was barely a whisper.

'At the sacred marsh.' He smiled sadly. 'On the land that belonged to my fathers and my fathers' fathers. In the place where the gods congregate and this world and the next run side by side.' He took a deep breath. 'You must go now.'

'Not yet.' Her voice slid up in agony.

'Please, Claudia Honorata. I wish to bid you farewell without tears. I want you to be as full of honour and courage and pride as you would have been had you been my wife.' His voice was stern.

She closed her eyes for a moment and took a deep breath. 'If that is your wish, husband of my heart.' She forced a tight, meaningless smile and, raising her face, she kissed him on the cheek. He took her hands and pressed them to his lips, then, unable to trust himself further he turned away and ran towards his chariot.

The phone was still not working. Three times she dialled, her hand sweating, slipping on the receiver, and three times she was greeted with the strange echoing silence, the conviction that at the other end someone was listening to her heavy breathing.

'What's wrong?' Alison was shaking visibly.

'The phone doesn't seem to be working.'

'You mean we're cut off?' The girl's voice slid into a squeak.

'It's all right, Allie. It doesn't matter. You're safe here. Safe and warm.' Kate forced herself to smile reassuringly. 'I'll make that hot drink now. What would you like?' She glanced at Alison, who shrugged.

Picking up the kettle Kate walked across to the sink to fill it, staring out of the window as she did so. The trees in the wood, only just visible through the streaming sleet, were bent double before the force of the wind. There was a strange darkness in the sky which was heavy with brownish cloud. Snow. It was snow cloud.

She turned on the tap. There was sand in the sink. Sand and peat and — with a shudder she snatched the kettle away, letting the stream of water swish round the sink to wash the maggots and soil away. She glanced at Allie, hoping she had noticed nothing. The girl's eyes were closed and she was swaying slightly on her stool.

With a grimace Kate filled the kettle and went to plug it in. 'Do you want to go back by the fire next door?' she asked gently. 'You can lie on the sofa and have a snooze.'

'No.' Allie shook her head. 'I want to stay with you.'

'OK.' Kate reached down two mugs. Her hand hovered over the coffee jar then moved on to an unopened tin of drinking chocolate. Diana must have put it there when she stocked up the cottage with groceries. Chocolate was rich, soothing, comforting. It would do them both good. She levered off the lid with a spoon and tore back the paper seal. The tin was full of earth. A fat white maggot wriggled indignantly at the sudden light. With a scream Kate hurled the tin across the room and it hit the wall with a crash.

Alison jerked upright. 'What is it?' She stared at the red tin which had rolled into the corner leaving a trail of powdered chocolate across the floor.

Kate rubbed her eyes. She was shaking like a leaf. 'I'm sorry. It slipped out of my hand. How silly . . .'

Somehow she forced herself to pick it up. She sniffed the remaining contents cautiously. It smelt good; rich, sweet and clean. 'Luckily there's enough left to make us a drink.' She was imagining things. Stupid. She had to be calm and strong for Alison's sake. She took a deep breath. 'Allie, who is Claudia?'

'Claudia?' Alison turned towards her. The colour had returned to the girl's face a little now and she seemed more alert but there was a strange blankness somewhere behind her eyes which made Kate uneasy. 'I don't know anyone called Claudia. Why?'

'I thought you said –' She stopped with a sigh. 'No. Perhaps I heard you wrong. It doesn't matter. Look, the drink is ready. Let's both go next door and sit by the stove.'

The sleet was lashing the panes and she could see the puddle on the sill was larger now. It had begun to drip onto the floor. Putting down the chocolate she went back into the kitchen for a cloth. Alison was still perched on her stool. 'Come on. I'll put some more logs on. Do you want me to help you?'

Alison shook her head. 'Is it . . . is it all right in there?'

'Of course it's all right. The window is leaking a bit that's all.' She reached for the cloth. 'I'll mop it up and then I'll stoke up the stove.'

She approached the window cautiously, peering at the sill. There were still flecks of soil floating in the water, but the maggots had disappeared. With a sigh of relief she mopped up the water and wedged a clean drying-up cloth into the angle between the sill and the window frame to catch the melted sleet as it seeped through, then she turned to the stove. There were only three logs left in the box. She opened the door and wedged one of them into the stove, and opening the dampers roared it up a little, then she plumped up the cushions on the sofa. Behind her Alison had shuffled as far as the doorway. She was peering into the room.

'Has she gone?' she said.

'Who?' Kate swung round.

'—' Alison's deep breath was cut off short and her shoulders slumped. 'I don't know. There was someone here . . . or was she on the beach . . . ?'

Kate walked over to her and put her arm round her shoulders. 'There's no one here, Allie,' she said softly. 'And there's nothing to be afraid of. You got very cold on the beach and I think you've had a touch of hypothermia. That sometimes makes people imagine things. Come and sit down and put your feet up then have a drink. You'll feel better soon, I promise.' She would not look at the corner where she had seen the figure of the woman. That, too, was imagination. 'I'll tell you what, why don't we have some music.' She went to her pile of cassettes and shuffled through them with a small half-smile at the thought of what Alison was going to think of Vaughan Williams or Sibelius or Bach when her tastes were so demonstrably different. Her hand hovered over the tapes. Fauré's Requiem. How had that got there? It was Jon's. She stared at it for a moment, then she opened its box and took it out. Was it some atavistic need for prayer that made her choose it? Whatever it was it would do no harm. As she slotted it into the cassette player her eye was caught by the pile of typescript on her desk. She shrugged. Now was not the time to worry about work. Perhaps if Alison fell asleep she would be able to do some writing. It was obvious at the moment that the girl could not walk anywhere, so there was nothing she could do but keep her warm and wait. But later, when Alison was better, should they try and walk back to the farmhouse, or should they wait for Roger and Diana to miss the girl and come looking for her? She felt so alone without a telephone; so thrown back on her own resources.

As the ethereal strains of the *Introit* and *Kyrie* filled the room Alison sank back without protest and closed her eyes. Kate watched her surreptitiously from the chair opposite. The log was burning well. Soon she would have to put on another. Then there would be only one left. Her gaze turned to the window sill. The tea towel was still dry and there was no sign of any movement there.

The tentative knock on the front door was almost lost in the strains of music but at the sound of it a shot of adrenalin propelled Kate out of her chair in a panic, every nerve stretched. She looked at Alison, but the girl didn't seem to have heard it.

Patrick stood on the doorstep, a yellow cycling mac over his thick jacket, his hair plastered to his head, his cheeks pink with the effort of bicycling down the wet muddy track.

'Hi. Mum wondered if Allie was here. Your phone's out of order, did you know?'

'Yes, I did and yes, she is.' Kate pulled him into the hall and closed the door. 'Thank God you've come!' She glanced over her shoulder into the living room. Alison still appeared to have heard nothing. Her eyes were closed and her face had relaxed into sleep. 'Come into the kitchen where we can talk.' Kate led the way and closed the door silently behind them. To her shame she found that her hands were still shaking. 'Listen, something very odd has been happening. I found Alison out in the dunes, kneeling in the excavation in some sort of trance. You've got to fetch your parents and the Land Rover to take her home. She's OK, more or less, but she's not well enough to walk. I think she ought to see a doctor.'

'Oh hell.' Patrick's thin face was a picture of worry. 'The reason I came on the bike was because Greg's taken the Land Rover. No one knows where he's gone. The Volvo won't make it through the woods. It's a quagmire. And there's been a severe weather warning on the radio. It's going to snow hard.'

'Damn!' Kate gnawed at her thumbnail.

'What's wrong with Allie? What was she doing out at the dig in this weather?' Patrick asked thoughtfully.

'I don't know. She had no spades with her or anything. She seemed to be in a state of shock.' Kate eyed him. She had barely spoken to this intense young man before, but what she had seen she liked. He appeared to be steadier and calmer than either his brother or his sister – far more like his father in fact. 'Something happened to her out there, Patrick. I don't know what it was, but it scared the hell out of her. She's still frightened. And so am I.' She hadn't meant to add that last bit.

Patrick was eyeing her warily. 'She started something when she messed about with that grave, didn't she?' he said. His voice was pleasant, light, calm. 'She's stirred something up.'

Kate swallowed. 'I suppose it's possible,' she said cautiously.

'Do you think it's Marcus's grave?'

Kate shook her head. 'I don't see how it can be. They found his grave near Colchester somewhere.' She hesitated. 'I think it's a woman's grave.'

'I see.' He frowned. He seemed unsurprised. He didn't ask her how she knew. He was more concerned with turning over this new set of possibilities in his mind. 'You mean the ghost is not a joke. A woman really does haunt this cottage. Do you think Allie saw her?'

Kate nodded. 'Her name is Claudia.'

Patrick's eyebrows shot up. 'How do you know that?'

'Allie was muttering about her. She doesn't remember now, but she said the name several times.'

'Wow.' Patrick looked awestruck. 'Oh, Jeez. I wish Mum and Dad were here.' He glanced up and swatted exasperatedly in the air as a bluebottle divebombed the light near him. Kate stared at it. Something cold had lodged in the pit of her stomach. Where were they coming from, the bluebottles – and the maggots?

As if reading her thoughts Patrick grinned. 'You often get them in old houses in the winter,' he said comfortably. 'They hibernate or something. There are probably dead mice under the floorboards. You've heated the place up a lot so they've woken up.'

He was right of course. Kate shuddered. Had she really begun to wonder, deep down in the innermost part of herself, if the maggots and the soil and the flies had somehow come out of the grave? She gave a feeble grin. 'I was beginning to think the worst.'

'Have you really seen her? Claudia?' Patrick's eyes were like his brother's. They were deep grey-green, all-seeing, but unlike Greg's they were sleepy, gentle. Misleading. She could feel them boring into her soul.

'Yes, I've seen her.'

Once again he seemed to accept her answer without surprise. There was no mockery or disbelief in his voice when he asked his next question:

'Do you think she smashed up the house?' He held her gaze.

She shrugged. 'I've never really thought about the idea

of whether or not I believe in ghosts, before. They seemed a nice idea — at a safe distance.'

'Scientifically, the idea is untenable, of course.'

She smiled. 'Is it? I wonder.'

'Psychokinetic energy is something that is measurable, I believe, and has been shown to be capable of hurling things about a bit. That is what poltergeists are. They are often connected with the presence of a teenager. All our frustrated angst.' He smiled and Kate found herself thinking with a certain wry amusement how very much more mature this intense boy was than his elder brother.

'Allie is a bit of a prat,' he went on, 'but she's a nice kid. There's nothing malicious about her. She wouldn't do this on purpose.' He was speaking from the safe platform of two years' superiority. He glanced up as an unusually strong gust of wind hurled a shower of hail against the window and he shuddered. 'Can I see the room where it happened before I go?'

'Help yourself. On the left at the top of the stairs.' She stayed in the kitchen as he ran up, listening to the sound of his feet overhead. A couple of minutes later he came down again. 'It's all tidy.'

'She got what she wanted.'

'Allie?'

'No. Not Allie.'

His eyes widened. 'I didn't realise that something was missing? I thought Mum said they hadn't taken anything.'

'They — she — took the silver torc which I found in the grave.'

'Wow.' There was a pause as he thought this over. Then, 'It can't have been a ghost. It must have been a real thief after all.' He sounded disappointed. 'Ghosts can't steal things.'

'They can.' Unnoticed by either of them Alison had appeared in the doorway. She was clutching the blanket around her shoulders like a cloak. Her face was transparent in its whiteness. She walked uncertainly to the stool and dragged herself up onto it. 'She wanted the torc because it was his.'

'Whose?' Patrick stared at his sister.

'—'

Again she had begun to speak and stopped without uttering a word as though the word – the name – had been snatched from her lips. 'I don't know. But she loved him.'

Patrick shot a quick look at Kate. It seemed to be a plea for understanding. 'Listen, Allie. I'm going to go home and get Mum and Dad. You ought to be in bed or something.'

'I'm OK.' Belying her words, Allie's body gave an involuntary shudder.

'Will you bring them back as soon as you can?' Kate asked quietly as she went with Patrick to the door. 'Please. I don't think we – she – should be here alone.'

She watched as he pulled on his bright yellow cycling mac. She didn't want him to go. She wanted to catch at his sleeve and shout at him to stay. She wanted him to barricade himself inside with them. Stupid. What was there to be afraid of?

'She needs a doctor, Patrick. She's OK I think, as long as she keeps warm, but I don't know about these things. I'd feel much happier if someone took a look at her.'

He nodded. 'Don't worry. Mum used to be a nurse. She'll know what to do. I'll be home in ten minutes. If Greg's not back with the Land Rover we can ring Bob Farnborough up on the main road. He's got a four-wheel drive which will do.' He turned away into the sleet then he stopped. 'It will be OK. Don't worry. Just keep the door locked.'

She stared at him. As their eyes met she realised he was scared too and that he was as aware as she was that doors would not keep Claudia, if it was Claudia, out.

XXVIII

At the bottom of the hollow the sand was stained by the peat as it leached out of the exposed face of the dune and dispersed in the icy puddles. The rain and hail washed at the leathery skin, keeping it moist, preserving it momentarily from the air, rendering it supple again. Strands of hair, long, coppery, still silken after more than nineteen hundred years washed across the blind face which stared up at the darkness. Her arm, lying across his chest was twisted, broken, the fingers outstretched. As the cold air touched them they drooped and grew supple again, caressing his shoulder, skin melting into skin, lips into lips, dry brittle bone crumbling to become one with the sand.

A squall from the sea, hitting the dune face, brought down more sand. The soft, wet mixture of peat and soil swirled in the icy water and slowly the silver torc which lay in the loose grip of Nion's fleshless fingers sank out of sight once more.

XXIX

Standing at the window looking down into the street Bill sighed. He hated London in the rain and this cold, blustery hail was the worst kind of rain. It was too wet to turn to snow and settle, too cold to bear against the face, suitable only for turning the muck and leaves and litter which blew in the gutters into a disgusting soup. He could hear the rainwater gurgling down the gutter near the window. It sounded like a bath emptying and was extremely depressing. He was trying to make up his mind about going to the cottage. He had been looking forward to a break all week. After careful manipulation of his diary he had managed to clear all Monday and half of Tuesday so it could be a long weekend. The best kind. But now the weather looked as though it was doing its best to screw the whole plan. He walked back to his desk and picked up the glass of wine from his blotter – a remnant of yesterday's party, the bottle retrieved from a fridge on the next floor. It was up to him. He had only himself to please. Did he really want to go flogging up the A12, taking a risk on whether this cold wet rain would turn to snow when he left the outskirts of London? Of course that in itself was tempting. He could think of worse places to be marooned than Redall Farm Cottage in the run up to Christmas, and if he took enough food and booze he could disappear there for several days happily. He walked back to the window, battling with his conscience. He had a tight schedule in the second half of next week. Christmas was getting close and he couldn't really take the risk of missing any time in the office. He watched two London buses inch past beneath his window, their domed scarlet roofs slick with sleet which for a fraction of a second remained unmelted then turned to water before his eyes and ran in streams down the windows.

Behind him the phone rang. He paused to drain his glass before going to the desk and lifting the receiver.

'Bill, it's Jon Bevan.'

Bill eased himself into his chair with a raised eyebrow. 'Hi. When did you get back?'

'I'm not back. I fly home tomorrow. Bill, I'm a bit worried. I can't raise Kate. Her phone is out of order. Do you have the number for the people at the farmhouse?'

'Sure.' Bill reached for a bulging, shabby filofax, something he was comfortable with only now that they were truly out of fashion. 'How is it going out there?'

'Not bad. I wanted to check if I would be welcome at Redall.'

'Can't help you there. I haven't spoken to anyone there this week.'

'So, you don't know about the burglary?'

'Burglary!' Bill frowned, shocked. 'At the farmhouse?'

'No, at Kate's cottage. She sounded edgy when I last spoke to her. Almost frightened. It's been worrying me.'

'Frightened?' Bill stared at the agitated, circular doodle he had been sketching on the pad in front of him. He added a couple of swirls, and then an eye. 'I should think so, if she was burgled. Did they take much?'

'I don't think so. Something she dug up in the sand, that's all. I'm sure she's all right. I'm sure there's nothing to worry about.'

Bill laughed. 'I'm sure there isn't but I'll give the Lindseys a ring and check. I was wondering whether I should drive up this evening, funnily enough. I'm not sure though. The weather is pretty bad over here.'

'It's bad here too.' In Massachusetts Jon glanced out of his bedroom window at the thick, white snow which whirled across the garden blotting out the view of the maples on the far side of the lawn. 'I think you should go, Bill. Look, if you do, will you ring me when you've seen her? Or get her to ring me from somewhere. Hang on. Let me give you the number here.'

Bill copied it down. 'I'll get back to you as soon as I've spoken to Diana, OK? Don't worry, old son, I'm sure Kate is all right.'

He tried her number first. It was, as Jon had said, dead. Then he rang the farmhouse. It was some time before someone picked up the phone.

'Greg?' Bill had been about to hang up. 'It's Bill Norcross. Can I speak to Diana?'

'Sorry. They all appear to be out.' Greg's voice was distant. 'What can I do for you?'

'I just wanted to check what the weather was like your end. I was planning on coming down today.'

'It's windy and hailing and the forecast is lousy. I should stay tucked up by your fire in London if I were you.'

'Have you seen Kate at all?'

'I have indeed.' Greg's voice became even colder.

'Is she all right? Her phone is out of order.'

'She seemed admirably well when last I saw her. Fighting fit, you might say. Did you report it?'

'I'm about to.'

'Good. Well, as soon as it is mended you can ring her and ask her for a weather forecast on the hour, can't you?'

Bill frowned. 'I'll do that. Thanks, Greg.' He hung up. The pencil with which he had been doodling snapped in two. He stared down at it in surprise. 'Bastard,' he murmured to himself. 'Bastard.'

It was nearly two hours after Patrick had left Kate and Alison on their own that Kate, glancing out of the front window saw an ancient vehicle slither to a stop outside. It was driven by a stranger but she saw Diana and Roger climbing out, closely followed by Patrick.

'Thank God,' she murmured. Alison was lying, wrapped in blankets once more, on the sofa. The girl appeared to be asleep.

Running to the door Kate pulled it open.

'Where is she?' Diana's face was white with strain. She pushed past Kate and went into the living room.

'Hi, Mum.' Alison opened her eyes.

'What happened exactly? Roger paused in the hall and caught Kate's arm. 'Sorry, let me introduce you. This is Joe Farnborough. He kindly drove us up here.'

Kate glanced at the tall, white-haired man who was staring down at her with undisguised curiosity. Catching her eye he grinned, his eyes silver in a tanned weather-beaten face. 'Young Allie got herself in a spot of bother, has she?' he asked.

She shrugged. 'I think she'll be fine. But she ought to be at home.' They followed Diana and Roger in to the living room and found them bending over Alison. Diana was holding her hand. 'I'm OK, Mum. Honestly.' The girl looked white and strained but her voice had regained some of its strength and with it its peevishness. 'Don't fuss. Just take me home.'

'But what happened, Allie?' Roger sat down, pushing the blankets aside. 'Come on, you must tell us.'

Alison shook her head. 'I'm not sure. I went out to the grave. I wanted to see it. It was early. It was still dark.'

'You went out when it was still dark!' Diana repeated, shocked.

Alison nodded. 'I don't know why. It was just something I had to do. I took a torch. The woods were wet and cold and it was very dark and I was scared.' Her voice trembled. 'When I got to the cottage I saw that all the lights were on. That made me feel better. I thought I would knock and ask Kate to come with me. But I couldn't.' She burst into tears. 'I wanted to, and I couldn't.'

Kate stared at her, appalled. 'Allie, why not? I would have gone with you.'

'I don't mean I couldn't because I didn't want to. I wanted to, but she wouldn't let me.'

There was a moment's silence. Kate met Roger's gaze. It was thoughtful; she guessed that Patrick had already told them about Claudia.

'Who wouldn't let you, Kate?' Diana asked gently.

'Someone. Her. I don't know. He wants to stop me, but she wants to tell me something. They're fighting in my head.' She put the heels of her hands to her temples, still crying. 'She wants me to know.'

'She wants you to stop digging up her grave?' Patrick put in from the doorway. 'That's it, isn't it?'

'No.' Allie sat up. 'No, that's the point. She wants me to. She wants me there. She wants me to find . . . something.' She lay back again.

'Well, whatever it was that happened, I suggest we get you back home, young lady,' put in Joe Farnborough from the doorway. 'I don't want to hurry you folks, but I must get into town and collect some stuff before this weather gets any worse.'

'Of course, Joe. I'm sorry. It was so good of you to come like this,' Diana started to bustle. 'Roger, can you carry her?'

'No need, Mum. I can walk.' Sniffing miserably, Alison swung her legs over the side of the sofa and stood up.

Kate watched as she was ushered out of the door and into the back of the Land Rover – a model even more ancient and muddy than the Lindseys' own. It was Patrick who turned and looked at her. 'Dad. Can Kate come with us? I don't think she ought to stay here alone.'

Roger swung back towards her. 'Of course. That goes without saying. You must come with us, Kate, my dear. We have got to discuss all this very seriously. And if nothing else, we've got to report your phone out of order and get it fixed before you can stay here alone.' He unhooked her jacket from behind the door and held it out to her.

Kate closed her eyes in relief. For a moment she had thought they were going off without her and she had known she would not have the strength of will to call after them. The urge to stay in the cottage was as strong as the urge to leave it. Turning back into the room she began to switch off the lights. She closed the doors on the stove and glanced round. The water had begun to seep back across the windowsill under the cloth. At the edge of it she could see a few dark specks of soil and there, in the shadows, something small and white wriggled purposefully towards the edge of the sill. She turned away sharply and grabbed her shoulder bag. As an afterthought she picked up the pile of typescript that sat on her desk, and with it the diskette from her computer. Then she followed Roger outside and banged the front door closed behind her.

XXX

Diana had gone downstairs. Alison slid down in her bed. Beside her, out of sight under the duvet was an old, well-worn teddy bear with one ear. All the lights in the room were on.

A couple of minutes later Greg appeared in the doorway. 'Are you awake, Allie?'

She pushed the teddy bear even further down the bed. 'What?'

'Look. We ought to talk.' He came in properly and shut the door. Sitting down on the edge of her bed he folded his arms. 'I know I said we ought to scare her off. Kate, I mean. I know I said a lot of things about her being in the way. And I meant it. She's a pain.' He lapsed into silence for a minute, staring thoughtfully down at his feet.

'She was nice to me,' Alison put in at last. There was none of the usual stridency in her voice.

'What really happened, Allie?' He looked at her again. 'Out there. You weren't just trying to scare her, were you.'

'No.' Her voice was very small.

'So. What happened?'

'Nothing.'

'It can't have been nothing.' He put his hand for a moment on the hump of her shoulder beneath the duvet. 'Come on. You can tell me.'

'It's the truth. Nothing happened. I didn't see anything. It was just feelings.' Her mouth began to tremble. She sat up and defiantly retrieved the teddy, hugging it tightly against her chest. In her dayglo green nightshirt, with her hair all over her face, she looked about six.

Greg was astonished by the wave of affection which swept over him. 'What sort of feelings?' he asked gently.

She frowned. 'Fear. Anger. Hate. They all sort of hit me, all jumbled up inside my head in a sort of red whirl. It hurt.' Her eyes flooded with tears.

He stared at her but he wasn't seeing her. He was seeing a short, grey-haired woman in a pale blue puffa jacket which went ill with her high heels. 'I saw you staggering about . . . I wondered if you were epileptic or something . . .' the voice echoed in his head.

Under the thick layers of Viyella shirt, lambswool sweater and ancient tweed jacket he could feel the tiptoe of goose flesh up his arms. His mouth had gone dry.

'What is it?' Her eyes were huge and round, the pupils dilated. 'What's wrong?'

'Nothing. Nothing's wrong, sweetheart.' He never called her that. The endearment frightened her even more than the strange preoccupation on his face had done.

He stood up. 'Listen, Allie. You must get some sleep. OK? Lie down again and I'll tuck you in.' He leaned over as she slid down on the pillows, pulling the duvet up to her chin and patting it with awkward, unaccustomed tenderness. 'Shall I turn out the lights?'

'No!'

He glanced at her sharply. The muffled word, filtered through the threadbare fur of the teddy bear, held a note of real terror.

'OK. No sweat.' He tried to smile. 'Sleep well, prat.' That was more like it. More normal. Sort of.

Downstairs the others were sitting around the fire with mugs of steaming tea. Greg took up position with his back to the inglenook – a speaker addressing a meeting. 'We have to fill in that excavation. Alison must not go up there again, and I think, personally, that Kate ought to move out of the cottage.'

'So that you can move back in.' Kate's words were mild

enough, but he saw a hardness in her face which spoke a great deal about her determination to stay, and did he but know it, of her increasing unease in his company.

He sighed. 'No. As a matter of fact I have no desire to move back in at the moment. But do you really want to stay there? After everything that has happened? I can't believe you are getting much work done if you keep being interrupted.'

'As a matter of fact, I am working very well at the moment, thank you,' Kate retorted. 'And it would be very small-minded of me to resent the time I've spent with Alison. She's a nice, intelligent girl. I'm getting fond of her. I don't know why she stayed out at the dig like that – I'm sure she will explain when she feels better – but it has not put me off staying at Redall Cottage in any way. Those locks you have put on for me make me feel as though I were living in Fort Knox.'

'I agree about filling in the excavation,' Roger put in. He leaned back on the sofa comfortably. 'There has been nothing but trouble since Allie found that place. I suggest we get Joe up there with a bulldozer to flatten it.'

'No!'

Kate hadn't realised the word came from her own mouth until she saw everyone staring at her. 'No,' she repeated more softly. 'I don't think we should do that. It's an important site. Much better we get in touch with the local archaeological society or the museum or someone quickly and get them out here to see what is really there.'

'I don't think we want to know what is really there,' Greg said abruptly. 'Don't you agree, Dad? Allie is upset enough as it is.'

'She's not upset at the idea of it being a grave,' Kate retorted.

'Excuse me, but I think she is. She may be a brash, tiresome kid on the outside, and she certainly has loads of guts, but inside she is hurting. This whole thing is upsetting her a lot. You've seen yourself how it's stimulated her imagination. It's bad for her. Ma,' he appealed to his mother, 'you must back me up.'

Diana frowned. She had been listening to the whole exchange in silence. 'You're both right in a way. She is obsessed by that place and I don't think that is good for her, but I don't think the right answer is to try and bury it. It would still be there and she would know it.'

Kate nodded. 'Better to get it excavated properly – a rescue dig can be arranged very quickly, you know. Then we'll all know the truth.'

'The truth about what?' Greg's voice was very quiet. 'What is it that's so important we know? I don't think there is anything there that we need to know about. Nothing at all.'

XXXI

The light was strangely cold. In the cool dawn before the sunrise the marsh was laved with a pale veiling of mist which lapped across the grasses and reeds in a silent, muffling shroud.

Nion stood at the edge of the pool. Bathed, dressed in his finest array, he was ready. Behind him the two priests stood, the tools of their trade openly displayed before them on a wooden altar – a rope, a knife. They waited now, in prayer, respectfully watching his preparations. When the moment came he would tell them.

He frowned. Why only two priests? He had expected them all, a circle of attendants, not this quiet, almost shabby affair unwitnessed and unsung. Slowly he began the business of preparation. Around his neck he wore two torcs. The great twisted golden torc, the symbol of his royal blood and priesthood, and below it one of carved silver which Claudia herself had given him. He took off the first, pulling the heavy gold over his warm skin, feeling the constriction, swallowing, closing his mind to what was to come. He took the torc in his hands, gently running his fingers across the intricate design on the metal, admiring it for the last time. It was truly a worthy gift to the gods. He held it up above his head, half expecting an early stray beam from the still-hidden sun to catch the gleaming metal. None came. He murmured the words of offering and then hurled it with all his might into the mist-covered water. It was gone before him to the world beyond. Next came the silver. Pulling it from his neck he touched it to his lips, then he hurled it after the first. He turned and gathered up *his weapons. Sword, spear, dagger. One by one he raised them in offering, balanced across his palms, and threw them. Beneath the curling white of the mist they sank into the cold brown water and began to settle inexorably into the mud.*

His clothes next. He unfastened his cloak, folding it carefully into as small a bundle as possible, doing it slowly, meticulously, perhaps stretching out the last few moments before the rim of the sun showed above the sea. Pinning the bundle with his cloak pin he hurled it after his weapons. Next came the bag of coins, his leather belt, his armlets, his tunic. Finally he was naked, save for the strip of woven ash bark around his arm, his birthright and his name sign. The cold air played across his skin. He frowned. He would not want the priests to think that his shiver was one of fear. Imperceptibly he straightened his shoulders, his eyes, like theirs, upon the eastern horizon which with every second grew brighter. Behind him he was conscious suddenly that one of the priests had reached to the altar and taken up the garotte. He was winding it onto his hands.

Nion clenched his fists. The sun had still not appeared but out there, beyond the cold waters, hidden by the mists, the gods were waiting.

The phone at Redall Cottage was working again by late afternoon. Roger drove Kate back there in the Land Rover through the heavy sleet and slush and toured the cottage with her room by room. 'It all looks all right,' he said at last. He had insisted on lighting the stove and carrying in a new supply of logs. 'Are you really quite sure you feel happy about staying here?' On the kitchen table stood a cardboard box full of tins of food, a jar of coffee, a bottle of Scotch, some matches and several other things that Diana had extricated from her own larder. 'Just in case you get trapped by this awful weather they're forecasting,' she had said to Kate. Taking her aside she too had asked her yet again if she wanted to stay with them, but Kate was adamant. 'I must work. Really.'

Roger looked round, seemingly reluctant to leave. 'Are you sure you're happy about this?' he asked again.

'Perfectly happy.' She grinned at him. 'Really. I want to get back to work.'

'Good.' He gave a gentle smile. 'Well, you know where we are if you want anything.'

She stood at the door to watch him drive away into the woods, then she turned back to the house. Nothing had been decided about the excavation. Greg had wanted it buried deep beneath the sand; Roger and she had wanted to call the Colchester archaeological people and Alison, when at last she had woken up had become totally hysterical at the thought of anyone touching it at all. In deference to her tears Diana had vetoed any action at least for a day or two and reluctantly, Kate had had to acquiesce. It was after all their land; their dune.

She glanced at her watch. It was nearly four. She put on the kettle and then hauling herself onto the stool, she reached for the phone. Anne was in.

'Hi, stranger. I was wondering how you'd been getting on.' Her sister's voice was cheerful.

'I'm fine. How's Edinburgh?'

'Wonderful. Better than I had hoped even. The job is quite fascinating and I love the city and C.J. loves the flat. It's huge compared with our old one, and there's a walled garden at the back. He's in seventh heaven. At least he was until the snow started.' She laughed. 'So tell me about the wilder shores of East Anglia.'

'A bit strange, actually.' Kate paused, watching the steam begin to rise from the kettle spout. 'Anne. Are there such things as poltergeists?'

There was a moment's silence the other end of the line. 'Now there's a fascinating question. Why do you ask?'

'Various reasons.' Kate smiled wryly. There would be

no turning back now until Anne had wormed the last tiny detail out of her. She took a deep breath. 'Let me tell you the story then you give me your opinion . . .'

It took a surprisingly long time to tell. Anne listened in silence, clicking her fingers once at Carl Gustav as he flexed his claws provocatively against the back of an armchair. He beamed at her and leapt onto her lap, cuddling down for a long stay.

'From what you say and your initial question you suspect the activity is centred around Alison, am I right?' she said at last.

'That's how it works, doesn't it? Teenage angst and all that. Frustrated energy.'

'That's how it works. ' Kate could hear the smile in Anne's voice. 'If it works. The bangs you have described sound to me as though they could just be wood splitting. You've probably heated up the cottage more than anyone in ages and it's falling apart. Had you thought of that? I suppose it could be explosions of psychic energy if one believes in such things. I've certainly read about them. But the rest. The soil. The maggots. Ugh. That doesn't sound like poltergeist activity either, to be honest. More like a horror novel.'

Kate pursed her lips. 'Anne, this is not a novel! Come on. I want your help.'

'Well, then, perhaps the sudden heat has woken them up. Wasn't that what someone suggested to you? That sounds more realistic. But even more likely it sounds to me like some kind of practical joke, Katie, love, and if the brother – Greg, did you say his name was? – is anything like as angry as you say, I should look no further than him. He sounds a very unhappy and frustrated man.'

'You don't think any of this could be supernatural then?'

'I think it's unlikely. Even the ghost you think you saw. You were tired; you could have imagined it. The smells are easily explained. They hang around for months, even years in houses sometimes. And maggots for God's sake! What are you supposed to think? That they are coming from a two-thousand-year-old grave? How long do you think the flesh lasts on bones? How long do you think any organic matter survives at all? Besides, how would they have got into your cottage?' Anne fondled Carl Gustav's ears. Kate could hear his purr down the telephone. It made her feel suddenly terribly lonely.

'How do I handle it, big sister? I don't want to leave this cottage. It's wonderful. I love it and I'm working well.'

'Has anything happened since you had the locks changed?'

'Yes.'

'And you don't believe the maggots are breeding on something terribly dead beneath the floorboards?'

'No.' Kate looked down at her feet. The cottage floors, she had established, were uncompromisingly concrete.

'And you don't think Alison could have slipped a matchboxful onto the windowsill while you were out of the room?'

'No. I don't.'

'I think I'm going to need notice of this one. It's tricky.' Anne laughed out loud. 'Intriguing but tricky. You're not scared?'

'I don't think so.'

'You don't sound very certain.'

'Well, would you? In the middle of nowhere? It's beginning to get dark. There's a bluebottle in here now.' It hadn't been there a few minutes ago, she was sure, and yet there it was, circling the light.

'Well, take comfort that there is nothing supernatural about bluebottles. You may not find out where they are coming from, but as sure as eggs is eggs, they are coming from the maggots who in turn are coming from some source of putrid flesh –'

'What did you say?' Kate interrupted her, her voice tight with fear.

'I said putrid flesh.'

'"Your putrid body and your rotten soul,"' Kate quoted slowly. 'Those are the words which keep going round and round in my head.' She was suddenly very scared.

'It's a coincidence. Have you never heard of synchronicity?' Hearing the fear in her sister's voice, Anne was immediately reassuring. 'Besides, it's hardly a coincidence when one is talking of maggots. Listen, love, I have got someone coming to supper. I really ought to get on or they will be having sardines on toast. Can we talk again tomorrow? I'll look up something about poltergeists and teenage werewolves to give you some ammunition to throw at young Alison, but if I were you I should have a stiff drink, bolt every door, check for matchboxes of maggots under the sideboard and lose yourself in the book. And if you're really, really scared I want you to ring me at once. Any time. Understand? Must go.'

She had hung up before Kate had a chance to say goodbye.

'Anne. Anne?' She shook the receiver. Anne had gone but the line still sounded as though it were open. She listened for a moment longer. 'Oh no. Not again.' She felt a moment of quite irrational panic as she jiggled the phone, hung up and lifted the receiver again. The line had not disconnected. It was live. There was no dialling tone. She put it down again and lifted it a second time. The same thing happened.

In Edinburgh Anne stared at the phone on the table in front of her and bit her lip. It was unlike Kate to be afraid of anything; very unlike her. To hell with the guests. Kate was more important than a perfect soufflé. She reached for the receiver again and dialled Kate's number.

The line was dead.

*   *   *

Bleakly Kate stared round the kitchen. Damn and blast it. It didn't matter, of course. Tomorrow she would walk up through the woods to the farmhouse and report the phone once again. There was no reason she should want to phone anyone again tonight. As Anne had said she should have a drink, check for maggots, and then go back to work.

It was a quarter to midnight when at last she turned off her computer, stretched and stood up. Her eyes were weary and her brain felt scrambled. She stared down at the pile of printed pages on the desk then she picked up her glasses and put them on again, reading through the last section one more time. It was good. It was exciting, alive, tremendous. Exhilarated, she stood up and wandered through to the kitchen and reached for the new bottle of whisky. The Lindseys, it appeared, drank Johnnie Walker. She poured herself half an inch and went back into the living room. Damn it, with the phone cut off no one could ring her either and she had, she realised suddenly, been hoping for another call from Jon. She sighed. She missed him so much.

The sharp bang above her head hardly made her jump at all. She stared up at the ceiling again and slowly she leaned forward to the table and reached for the bottle. 'Sod off, Marcus,' she murmured. 'You're either psychic energy or you're a splitting beam. Either way you are not my problem.'

XXXII

Greg found Allie in the kitchen next morning. She was sitting at the table, still wearing her dressing gown. Her face was pale and strained. He sat down opposite her and reached for the coffee pot. 'How are you feeling, prat?' he asked.

She glared at him. 'Awful.'

'Did Ma say you ought to see the doctor?'

'No. She thinks I'm all right. Just tired.'

'Didn't you sleep?'

'What do you think.' She put her arms on the table and rested her head on them.

'We are going to ring Joe today and ask him to bring a tractor up to flatten the dune,' he said gently. 'Dad agrees that that would be best. It's only a matter of days anyway before the sea takes the whole lot away.'

'You can't.' She stared up at him aghast, her fair hair flopping across her eyes. 'You can't do that. It's an archaeological site. You won't be allowed to.'

'No one is going to know. I'm sorry, Allie, but my mind is made up. There are things there which are best left untouched. If you think about it you'll agree.'

'No!' She jumped up, scraping the chair legs across the stone slabs. 'No. I won't let you! You can't. You mustn't!'

'Allie –'

'No.' Her voice had risen to a shriek. 'Don't you see. People have got to know. They must know the truth!'

'The truth about what?' He frowned.

'The truth about –' She shrugged, subsiding once more. 'The truth about what is in the grave. The truth about what happened there. The truth about –' She stopped dead. It was as though the name on her lips had been snatched from her. 'The truth about whose grave it is,' she improvised. 'You must not touch it. No way. If you even think about ringing Joe I shall phone the museum and tell them. They will put a preservation order or something on it.'

'What on earth do you know about preservation orders?' Greg asked. He could feel his anger rising. He had been a fool to tell her. He should have rung Joe and they could have gone ahead with it without telling her. After the event it would be too late to stop it.

'I don't know anything about them, but I know you can get them. You can get them to stop farmers ploughing up their fields when there are special things on them.'

'Well, there is nothing special about this. A few old bits of pottery and stuff in a dune on the edge of the sea. Big deal. It's better forgotten.'

'No.' Her eyes narrowed. She looked like Serendipity when he had a mouse or a bird and he thought someone was going to try to take it from him. 'No. You are not to touch it. The truth has to come out.'

Greg stood up, picked up his cup of coffee and found the cup was rattling on its saucer. 'Please yourself.' He wandered through towards the sofa and sat down next to the cats who were ensconced firmly in a manner which denoted profound rejection of an outside world where the sleet slanted out of a slate sky and the wind knifed round corners and through unresisting flesh. He felt extraordinarily upset. Adrenalin flooded through his body; he felt a dry sickness in his throat. His hands, clenched around the cup were shaking slightly and he was angrier than he had ever been. He took a deep breath trying to steady his breathing. What on earth was the matter with him? He didn't care one way or the other about the damn grave and being tactically defeated by Alison was no big deal. She did it all the time and mostly he tolerated it. He took a swig of the coffee and leaned back, closing his eyes.

Behind him she was still sitting at the table. She sniffed, surreptitiously wiping the back of her hand across her eyes. Her head was throbbing and her face felt puffy from lack of sleep. There was still something she had to do but she could not remember what it was. She stared at the window wearily as a gust of wind threw more hail at the glass. The kitchen was cold. She glanced at the Aga. It was lit. The kettle on the hot plate was steaming gently, so why was it she could not stop shivering? Standing up shakily she went to where her brother was sitting and perched on the arm of the sofa. 'I'm going to ring the archaeological people.'

He glanced up at her. 'You're a fool. They won't want to know. Anyway, what the hell could they do in this weather?' As if to reinforce his remark another gust of wind shook the house. The fire flared up. Several sparks shot out onto the hearthrug. Automatically Alison got up and stood on them one by one. 'They will want to know.'

'They will not want to know. Anyway, by the time they get here there will be nothing to see. I expect the sea will have done all the excavating for you.' He drained his cup, watching as she tramped methodically over the carpet to make sure she had extinguished the last spark. She turned towards the door.

'Where are you going?'

'To phone.'

'Now?' He sat up.

'Yes, now.'

'Allie, you mustn't.'

'Why not?' She swung round to face him, her hair hanging in curtains across her face. 'Just why are you so against it?'

'Because I think it will only cause more trouble.'

'What kind of trouble?' She raised her chin slightly in the defiance which was more natural to her than this haggard exhaustion.

He stood up. 'Leave it alone, Allie. Please. Look let's wait at least until Monday. With the weather like this they won't be able to get here anyway. Even better, leave it until the spring. Then they can come and see if it's still here.'

'That's the whole point.' She stamped her foot. 'Don't you see? They must get to it before it is washed away. They have to find out who is buried there, and why.'

'No.' His face had closed, his voice was harsh. 'No. No one must ever find out.'

'Why on earth not?' She stared at him in astonishment and was frightened to see the implacable rage in her brother's face. 'Greg, what is it? I don't understand.' His eyes were hard, the pupils contracted to tiny pinpoints although the light in the room was low. Behind him the two cats leaped from the sofa of one accord and vanished behind the Aga.

'Greg?' Her voice was pleading. 'What is it? You're frightening me.'

For a moment he went on staring at her, as though his hatred of her were too great to contain, then visibly he seemed to shake himself free of whatever strange emotion had gripped him. 'I'm sorry. I don't know what's wrong. I don't give a screw what you do about your stupid grave, Allie. Do what you like.'

He was shaken. It had happened again, the strange feeling that there was some kind of alien being inside his head, battering at his skull – an alien with terrible, raging emotions. Leaning back against the cushion with a groan he put his hand over his eyes.

With a nervous glance at him Alison escaped thankfully into her father's study. The telephone books were piled on the floor by his desk. She pulled up the swivelling chair and sat down, reaching for the local directory. All round her her brother's paintings were stacked against the walls, and on the easel. The room smelt strange, its own comfortable familiar smell eclipsed by oil and turpentine and wonderful arcane scents of varnish and paint and linseed. She flipped open the book and began to look for the number under Archaeology. There was nothing there. She tried again under Colchester. It was several moments before she found it. Holding her finger under the number she reached for the phone, aware that Greg had come into the room and was standing in the doorway watching her.

Her fingers tightened on the receiver. Ignoring him she began to dial. She listened for several minutes, frowning, then she jiggled the rest and dialled again.

'What is it. Is something wrong?' Greg's voice from the doorway was almost mocking.

'I can't get a dialling noise.' She shook the receiver and tried again. 'It sounds as if there is a crossed line. As if someone is listening on the other end.'

He smiled. 'Perhaps they are,' he said quietly.

XXXIII

Bill leaned forward and stared through the windscreen. He was bitterly regretting having set out for the cottage. Just as he was leaving the office the afternoon before, someone had come in and talked to him for hours. By the time they had gone it was getting dark and he had decided to postpone his decision until the morning.

A desultory sun was shining when he woke up at nine. He stared thoughtfully out of the window at the distant view of Hampstead Heath and then back at his bedroom which was untidy and smelled frowsty. He glared at the socks he had taken off the night before and thrown into the corner. Perhaps a weekend in the clean, bracing East-Anglian air would do him good.

The sun had disappeared almost as soon as he had joined the A1. By the time he was on the M25 the sky was overcast, deep, brown-bellied clouds massing overhead. When he got to Chelmsford it began to snow. Wet, sleety snow which swished beneath the tyres and clogged the windscreen wipers. The traffic was slow – not because there was a lot of it; unusually for a Saturday morning it was light, but because the visibility was appalling. Silently Bill cursed himself for his stupidity in setting out at all. He leaned forward and pressed a cassette into the deck, not taking his eye off the sleety road. He would drive as far as Colchester, park the car, give himself a drink and a meal at The George and then make the decision whether to go on or go back.

XXXIV

Kate dreamt again that night. In the midnight shadows on the beach something threatening stalked the darkness. She ran, glancing behind her over her shoulder, aware that the threat was growing closer and closer all the time. She could hear herself sobbing out loud as she tried to draw breath, pushing herself with the last of her strength as she felt the sand slip and lurch beneath her shoes. She was going to make it. She stretched out her hand, hearing the footsteps pounding ever closer behind her on the sand. She was home.

She reached out to the door and became aware suddenly that someone was standing in the doorway, holding out his hand to her. It was Jon. She saw his smile, saw his hand, felt the brush of his fingertips and then she stumbled. Her hand grasped at the thin air and the door began to close, with her still outside in the darkness, alone . . .

Kate awoke with a groan, her face wet with tears. Her head was hammering like a water pipe and her mouth was dry. She tried to sit up, groaned again and lay back on the pillow wishing she were dead. She lay still for several minutes then she realised she was going to have to get up to go and have a pee. Staggering a little, she managed to grope her way downstairs. The chill in the cottage told her at once that she had forgotten to stoke up the woodburner. Her face washed, her teeth brushed, and her hair combed, she felt only marginally better. She put the kettle on and then went through into the living room. Drawing back the curtains she found it was daylight outside – but only just.

The sleet which sheeted down out of the east was back-dropped by clouds the colour of pewter; she could feel the beat and push of the wind against the cold windowpane. She glanced down at the sill. The surface was quite dry. There was no sign of anything untoward lurking there.

Back in the kitchen she made herself a cup of black coffee. As she sipped it she lifted the phone and listened. Still no dialling tone. Still nothing but the strange interplanetary echo. Slamming it down, she winced slightly as the crash reverberated up her arm and through her skull.

She forced herself to get dressed, donning a shirt and thick sweater over trousers and two pairs of socks. Then she dragged on her jacket, scarf and gloves. Her boots were by the front door. Before she left she relit the stove and left it burning nicely in the hope of having a warm cottage to come back to. With a bit of luck someone would give her a lift back from the farmhouse.

Patrick opened the door to her. 'Hi.' He smiled, his face lighting up at the sight of her. 'Come in.'

The thought that he was pleased to see her warmed her. 'How's Allie?' She followed him into the hall and pulled off her boots.

'She's all right. A bit weird, but she'll live.'

For a moment she wondered whether to ask him to expand on this rather cryptic reply but she thought better of it. 'Patrick, could I possibly use your phone? Mine has gone on the blink again.'

'Sure. There's one in the study.' He indicated the door on his right. 'Phone away then come into the kitchen. The others are there. I'll tell them to pour you a coffee.'

With a grateful smile at him she opened the door into Roger's study. The phone was on the desk. Shaking her head free of her woollen scarf she made for it.

'Can I help you?' The quiet voice nearly scared her out of her wits. She swung round. 'Greg! I'm sorry. I didn't realise that there was anyone here.'

'So I gather.' He was sitting on the arm of a comfortable, shabby old armchair near the window, a sketchpad in one hand, a pencil in the other, the pale paper illuminated by one of the shaded wall lights. She couldn't see his face in the shadow.

'I wanted to borrow the phone.'

'So. You don't trust us, eh? Going to ring the museum yourself, were you?' His voice was harshly sarcastic.

'No, I wasn't.' Indignantly she glared at him. 'I said I would do nothing until we had discussed it further, and I meant it. Besides, if I was going to phone someone about the grave I would hardly walk all the way over here through this foul weather in order to do so. I have in fact come to report my phone out of order again.'

'I see.' He gave her an amicable grin. 'Well, I'm afraid you are out of luck. This one is kaput also.'

She was astonished at the sudden wave of fear which swept through her. For a moment she thought her legs were going to give way. She leaned on the desk. 'Are you sure?'

'See for yourself.' He half turned away from her, going back to his drawing.

She picked up the receiver and listened. The sound was the same. That strange echoing silence which seemed to connect to distant spheres. Putting it down she found the palm of her hand was slick with icy sweat. 'Have you reported it?'

'I believe Dad is driving up to the village later. He will no doubt do so then.' He glanced up. Her face, which had been pink and shiny from the wind and rain had gone white. 'Are you all right?'

'Yes, of course.'

'It worries you that much? Not having a phone?'

'Yes.' She forced herself to smile.

'You're scared, out there on your own, aren't you?' His voice was very soft.

'No. Not scared.' She took a deep breath. 'But I am inconvenienced. I need the phone for my work. I need to speak to my editor; and I need it for research.'

'Busy lady.' He put down the sketchpad and stood up slowly. 'And of course you want to phone the man in America. Well, I'm sure it will be mended soon. The wiring is old. They are always having trouble with phones round here. Next year, I gather, our exchange will be updated to the space age. Heaven knows what will happen then. If they keep the same old telegraph posts and fraying wires it will still go off if it rains.' He paused, eyeing her thoughtfully. 'So, how is your book progressing?'

'Do you really want to know?'

'I would not waste time asking unless I wanted to know.' He shaded in part of his drawing, the strokes of his pencil sure and firm.

'Then thank you. The book is going well.'

'Good.' He glanced up. 'Kate. You saw Allie, yesterday. You know the state she was in. Please use your influence to dissuade her from going on with this archaeological plan of hers. It's upsetting her too much. She's having nightmares – all kinds of horrors. She's imagining god-knows-what monsters climbing out of the grave. You must see how bad it is for her. It's like some awful horror movie.'

Thoughtfully Kate moved round the desk and took Roger's chair. She leaned forward, her chin on her elbows. 'It's not knowing what's there that is worrying her, Greg. If you cover it up and bulldoze it all into the sea the effect will be the same. It, whatever "it" is, will still be there because it's inside her head. It would be much better to get some professionals in to look at it. They may say "Look this is all nonsense. This is no more than a spoil pit. There was no grave here," or they may say, "Yes, this was a grave, an Iron Age cremation perhaps. Look. It's all gone. There's nothing left except a few shards and some metalwork". Her worst fears would be laid to rest. And I am sure they would enlist her help. Help her with her project. Encourage her. Talk about it. That's the best course of action, I really do believe it. The worst thing you could do is pretend that there is nothing there.'

'Quite the psychologist, aren't we.'

She refused to let herself be roused by his deliberately mocking tone. 'No. I think it's common sense.' She stood up. 'Patrick said there would be some coffee in the kitchen. Are you coming through to get some?'

He shook his head, not raising his eyes from his sketchpad.

'Then, if you'll excuse me, I think I will. It was a long walk through the woods and I'm very chilled –'

'Kate.' He had put down his pad. 'Tell me something. Do you think it's all her imagination?'

She held his gaze for a full half-minute. 'Not completely. No.'

'That's a little ambiguous, if I may say so. Do I gather you still suspect me?'

'There is a particularly irritating phrase which is in this case I think suitable. If the cap fits.'

'Obviously you think it does.'

Walking towards the door she shrugged. 'I find it hard to make up my mind, Greg. Put it this way. If it isn't you, then I think that maybe we should all be worrying with Allie.'

'Let me show you something before you go and get your coffee. ' Greg stood up. He went across to the desk and rummaged in the bottom drawer under a pile of notebooks of his father's. Bringing out a photograph wallet he laid it on the desk. 'I had your pictures developed at Boots.'

She glanced up at his face then she felt in the pocket of her jeans for her spectacles. Reaching for the wallet she flipped it open and pulled the photos out. The room was silent as she studied them. When she looked up at him again her face was even whiter than before. 'You could have faked these.'

'Oh come on. I would hardly bother to go that far.'

'Have you shown them to Allie?'

'Obviously not.'

She looked down at them again. They had come out well in spite of the strange light. Every grain of sand was visible, every line of strata, every trail of weed and every shell. In three of them there was, clearly visible, something else, something which she had not seen when she took the pictures.

'What do you think it is?'

Greg was leaning over the desk beside her. He pointed to one of the pictures. 'It looks like something spinning: a dust devil; a whirlwind perhaps. What did it look like when you took the pictures?'

She shook her head mutely. 'I didn't see it. I didn't see anything odd at all.' She gave an involuntary shiver. 'The light wasn't very good. To be honest I didn't think they would come out.' His head was very near hers as they leaned towards the desk. She was surprised to feel a strange tingle of something like excitement as his shoulder brushed hers. Cross with herself, she moved away sharply. Taking one of the photos she carried it to the lamp where he had been sitting. The entire periphery of the photo was clear and fully in focus but about one third of the way down, slightly to the left of centre was a strange, swirling, bright mass. 'Do you think my camera was letting in the light somehow?' she said slowly. She held the photo closer to the lamp.

'I don't think so. The whole picture would have been spoiled. If you look at the edges of that thing you can see everything completely clearly. Here. Try this.' He picked up a magnifying glass which had been lying on the desk. 'You see, the thing, whatever it is, is clearly superimposed on the background. It was in front of it, blocking it off.'

Taking the glass from him she squinted through it. 'What is your theory?'

'I think it's an energy field.'

'And where do you think the energy is coming from?' Her question was guarded.

'The way I see it, there are only three possibilities. The first is a human source. You.' He glanced up at her. 'Could you have been projecting some kind of force field? Repressed anger, perhaps? Indignation? Frustration?' He grinned. 'I should imagine you've been feeling all three since you arrived at the cottage.'

'Very probably,' she retorted tartly. 'But not in sufficient quantities, I think, to create a whirlwind.' He was standing very close to her again, staring down at the picture in her hand. This time she did not move away. 'What are your other two suggestions?' she asked.

'That it was just that, a whirlwind, and somehow you missed seeing it. Or the energy came from the earth.'

'The former is out of the question.' She hoped he hadn't noticed the sudden tremor in her voice.

'And the latter?'

'Earth energy? Like ley lines, you mean?'

'That or perhaps from some external source in the ground.'

There was a long silence as she digested his words. 'Greg. What are you trying to say?' When she looked up at him his face was very close to hers. He was, she noticed for the first time, unshaven. The shadow of beard was a rich golden colour, far brighter than his hair.

He shrugged. 'I'm just wondering whether perhaps it could come from something that is buried there.'

'Something or someone?'

'It is someone, I'm afraid.'

'But we can't be sure. And surely it is the best reason to try and find out.' Again the slight tingle of excitement as his hand brushed her shoulder.

He reached for the photo. 'I think we can be sure, Kate. Look at this other one. See what you think.' He turned to the desk and shuffled through the prints. 'Here. Look at that corner. On the sand face.' His forefinger was smudged with a grainy smear of cobalt blue. Taking the print her hand accidentally touched his. He did not move away.

She stared through the magnifying glass, angry to find her hand was shaking suddenly. 'What am I supposed to be looking at? There's no sand devil on this one.'

'There. Wait, let me point with a pencil. Look.' The fine point also trembled slightly, she noticed. She screwed up her eyes, staring at the fine definition of the photo. The sand, the lines of peat, the shells, all were startlingly clear, and there, at the edge of the photo was something protruding from the sand face.

'Dear God!' she whispered.

'It's part of a hand, isn't it,' Greg said softly.

She looked him straight in the eye. 'Did you put it there?' Their faces were only eighteen inches apart.

'No.'

This time she believed him. Suddenly there wasn't a shadow of doubt in her mind. She could feel the fine hairs on the back of her wrist standing on end as it held the photo. 'We have to go out there and see.'

'Yes.'

'What did you tell Allie about the photos?'

'That I put them in too late for the one-hour service so they would be a couple of days. She seemed quite relieved.'

'She's terrified of the place. She wants nothing to do with it anymore,' she said thoughtfully. 'And yet she still wants it excavated. That's strange. Dangerous.'

He nodded. 'So, we are on the same side.'

'Is it a question of sides?' She shook her head thoughtfully. 'No, Greg. The grave must be investigated, surely you can see that. If there is a body on the beach, a coroner has to be informed for a start, however old it is. Probably the police too, for all I know.'

'It's hardly a murder enquiry!'

He had said the words laughingly. Throwing back his head he took the print from her, all the anger gone, his thoughts a delicious mixture of clandestine intrigue with a bulldozer, coffee in the kitchen and the woman standing so near to him. She was, he realised suddenly, really very beautiful when she wasn't being so stroppy.

The sudden drop in temperature took them both by surprise. It was as though someone had opened a freezer door nearby. For a second the atmosphere in the room was electric.

'*Marcus.*'

The whisper came from Kate's mouth. Without realising it she had clutched at his arm. 'Oh, sweet Jesus, Greg, what is it?'

He shook his head. 'God knows. Come on. Obviously we've touched a chord somewhere. Let's get out of here. And not a word to the others. Not yet. Not until I've had a chance to think.' Dropping her arm, he opened the door and ushered her through it into the hall.

She followed him, glancing back over her shoulder as she did so. The room looked perfectly normal. There was nothing there to frighten them; nothing out of the usual at all. The temperature, she realised as she closed the door behind her, was as warm as it had been before. Only one thing was different. The smell of paint and varnish and linseed oil had been eclipsed totally by an all-pervading smell of wet, cold earth.

XXXV

Her eyes were blinded by tears as she parted the clump of elder with a shaking hand and peered through. She could see him standing only a few yards from her, naked now, his arms raised in salute towards the eastern sky, his fists clenched against the crimson clouds. Behind him the priests were waiting. She saw the golden knife, the ligature, the bowl which contained the sacred mead. As she watched, he turned. For a moment she saw his face. His expression was closed, cold, impassive, as though his spirit had already fled.

The priest stepped forward with the bowl. With a bow he handed it to Nion. The young man turned back towards the east. He raised the bowl towards the red clouds. On the distant horizon, two miles away, where sea met sky, crimson colour bled upwards from below the rim of the earth. Behind him the priest raised his knife. They all waited, motion suspended, their eyes on the distance where the sun would appear.

Claudia bit back her tears. She clenched her fists. He would not see her, or hear her pain. Her eyes, too, went to the horizon. As she watched, the smallest segment of scarlet appeared out of the crimson mist.

Nion tensed. His knuckles whitened on the rim of the bowl. For a fraction of a second he seemed to thrust it further towards the sun, then he threw back his head and began to drink. She saw the movement of his throat; she saw the golden liquid spill over the side of the bowl, onto his chin, run down his arms and splash onto his chest. He drained the bowl to the dregs and flung it into the *marsh, then he crossed his arms on his breast and knelt.*

Behind him the two priests stepped forward. She saw the red reflection of the sun glinting on the knife blade as it was raised. And she saw the garotte as it was slipped swiftly and dextrously about his throat.

The meal had been excellent. Bill sat for a long time over his coffee. At his side *The Times* lay beside his cup, neatly folded to expose the crossword. In the last hour he had managed only two clues and he was feeling discouraged. He glanced up at the window. Outside the sleet appeared to have stopped. A slash of palest stone-washed denim blue had appeared between the clouds. Staring up at it he felt a sudden uplift of his spirits. Damn it, it was only twenty miles or so further.

Slotting a couple of carriers full of Marks and Spencer food into the boot of his car he tucked four bottles of wine in beside them and slid into the driver's seat.

He had no problems until he reached the track down through the Redall woods where the slush and rain had turned it into a quagmire. Parking on the side of the road he climbed out. Behind him a tractor was lumbering along the road. It drew to a halt behind his car. Bill walked up to it. 'Hello, Joe. Do you think I'd be mad to take the car down to the cottage?'

Joe laughed. He scratched his head. 'I reckon you were mad to come at all,' he shouted over the clatter of the engine. 'I tell you what. You come and leave your car up at the farm and I'll run you down to yours. Best that way.'

Bill gave up the effort of competing with the huge engine. With a grin he gave a thumbs up sign and turned back to his car. At least this way he wouldn't get trapped by the weather.

It was an hour later that Joe delivered him to his door. Waving his good Samaritan off he inserted his key in the door and pushed it open with his shoulder. The smell of cold and damp assailed him at once and he grimaced. 'Bloody fool.' He meant himself.

The front door led straight into the living room. The furnishings were shabby and not very pretty – good enough for weekends, but not so good they would get nicked. It always depressed him a little when he arrived, but he knew from long experience that once he had put a match to the fire – a resolution he had never once broken was to leave it laid ready when he left for London at the end of each trip – and turned on the lights and the radio the little house would spring to life. He found he was humming as he walked through into the kitchen – basic with an old, deep sink, a barely functional electric cooker and a pine table and chairs which were probably by now worth a fortune as antiques. Once he was settled he would dig out his wellies and stride out through the mud to visit Kate.

It had never crossed his mind that she wouldn't be at home. He peered through the windows of her cottage. The woodburner was alight. He could see the glow of the fire through the closed doors. He shaded his eyes as he leaned closer. Her desk was untidy, as though she had got up and left it in the middle of some work. And the lamp on the table in the corner was switched on. He glanced over his shoulder towards the beach. Perhaps she had gone for a walk.

His wellingtons sliding wetly on the sand and shingle, he made his way down towards the sea, standing on the foreshore at last, shading his eyes as he stared up and down the beach. The rain and sleet had drifted inland. Overhead the cloud was still thick, but it was higher now, and there was still the odd patch of blue. His hands wedged firmly into his pockets he threw his shoulders back and inhaled deeply. It was a rash move and led to a spasm of coughing, but at least he was getting the desired fresh air. He chuckled to himself, and turning north up the beach began to walk briskly over the sand. The sea was sullen, heaving menacingly on the horizon, a shifting solid mass of seemingly waveless water. The tide was midway up, he guessed, creeping nearer half-heartedly, dribbling each progression of weed and shells onto the beach before sliding back into the black depths to gather itself for another inroad onto the sand.

He didn't walk far. The wind in his face was not strong but it was bitingly cold. Turning, he glanced back the way he had come. There was no sign anywhere of Kate. No footprints on the sand to show where she had passed. Disappointed, he retraced his steps. Blow fresh air. You could get too much of that. He walked down the beach as far as the end of the dunes and climbed up to get a view across the estuary. It was alive with geese. Bustling with activity. He could hear them now, gossiping, squabbling, murmuring to each other as they spread out across the still water onto the low-lying islands and the saltings. He grinned to himself. He liked the geese. They were jolly chaps, and with them there it wasn't possible to feel lonely. He couldn't understand why people had to shoot them. But then some people would kill anything that moved, given half a chance. Shrugging himself deeper into his thick quilted jacket he turned away and pulled up short. There was a woman standing in the distance on one of the other dunes. His heart leapt. 'Kate!' he shouted. 'Over here.' He waved.

She had her back to him. He could see she was huddled into some long garment. Her hair was tearing free of its fastenings.

'Kate!' He put his hands to his mouth and bellowed. The trouble was the wind was blowing from her to him, carrying his voice away. Behind him some of the geese looked up from their grazing and he heard a volley of anxious alarm notes. He leaped off the dune and ran back through the deep, soft sand towards her, feeling the sweat break out on his body beneath the heavy jacket. Puffing, convinced he was about to have a heart attack, he scrambled up the dune where she had been standing. She was nowhere to be seen. He stared down. Half the dune had fallen away onto the beach. He could see where the tide had washed the sand into mounds of weed-covered spoil. A dead crab lay on its back amongst the debris. He wrinkled his nose. Slithering and jumping he made his way back onto the beach, staring round. Where the hell had she gone? Out at sea the evening was beginning to draw in. He could see the mist which preceded the coming darkness hovering on the horizon.

Crossly, he made his way back towards her cottage. Obviously she hadn't seen him. Well, he couldn't blame her for going in. It was becoming much colder. He could feel the icy chill on his body as his sweat dried. Suddenly he felt very alone.

The cottage was still deserted, the front door locked. He stared at it in disbelief. Perhaps it wasn't Kate he had seen after all? It must have been someone else. But who else would be out there on the beach in this weather at this time of day? It had certainly been neither Alison nor Diana. One was too short, the other too well-built. Although the figure he had seen had been too far away to recognise he had been able to see that she was tall and willowy, her figure emphasised by the way she had pulled her coat tightly around her.

Disappointed, he turned away from the door. He might as well walk up to Redall Farmhouse and see if he could cadge a cup of tea there. Maybe that was where she was anyway. Pulling his collar up more tightly around his ears, Bill set off towards the trees.

XXXVI

'Where is Allie?' Diana looked around the kitchen as though it was only the first time she had noticed her daughter's absence. It was two hours since they had finished lunch – a meal to which Kate had been invited without hesitation and one which she had accepted with equal alacrity. Alison had appeared for the first course but she had barely touched it and, making her excuses, had retired upstairs to sleep. 'Run and see how she is, Patrick, will you, dear?' She and Kate had finished the dishes together and a new kettle of water was brewing on the Aga. 'She ought to eat something.'

Patrick vanished upstairs. Diana smiled. 'I know I'm being silly to worry, but I can't help it. She's not right yet.'

'Do you think you ought to take her to the doctor?' Kate lined up six mugs on the table.

Diana's reply was interrupted by Patrick's shout. 'Ma! She's not up here.'

Diana stared across the room towards the staircase. 'What do you mean she's not up there? Of course she is.'

'She's not. And she's not in the loo. I've looked everywhere.' Patrick reappeared.

Roger had been dozing by the fire. Pushing a heap of cats off his lap he stood up. 'She must be somewhere. This is not a very big house. You had better find her.' He could not keep the anxiety out of his voice.

'She's gone.' Diana threw down the oven glove she had donned to pick up the kettle. 'She's gone back to that bloody grave.'

'No.' Kate's whisper was lost as Roger threw his news-paper down.

'She can't have. She wouldn't be so stupid. God! It will be dark in another hour.' He strode to the door.

'Look for her jacket, darling.' Diana was standing in the middle of the floor, frozen with fear.

'It's gone.' He was rummaging through the stack of coats and waterproofs on the pegs inside the front door. 'So have her boots.'

Greg had disappeared into the study with his cup of coffee after they had finished the meal. At the sound of Roger's raised voice he opened the door and peered out. 'What's up?'

'It's your sister. She seems to have gone out.'

Greg's eyes sought Kate's. His face was suddenly very grim.

'Kate and I will go and look for her,' he said. 'We'll take the Land Rover. Don't worry, Ma. She'll be all right. She's not a fool. If she's taken her coat and boots she'll be warm enough and it shows she is being sensible.'

'I'll go with you.' His father was reaching for his own coat but Greg put his hand on his arm. 'No, Dad, no need. Honestly. Kate and I will find her. You stay here with Ma. You never know. She may just have gone for a walk in the garden. We may be panicking for nothing.' He smiled into the silence. None of them believed that; they all knew where she had gone.

The Land Rover was cold. Hauling herself into the pas-senger seat Kate dug her hands deep into her pockets, wait-ing in the silent vehicle as Greg walked round to the driver's side and pulled open the door. He climbed in and reached for the ignition key, glancing at her. 'How long do you reckon she's been gone?'

'It could have been hours. Would we have noticed if she'd gone out while we were still eating?'

He shrugged. 'She had to come through the living room

to reach the front door. The trouble was we were talking so hard I don't suppose we would have noticed her even if she had jumped up and shouted at us.' He rammed in the gear and eased the car away from the side of the house. 'Did you throw in the blankets?'

Kate nodded. Her stomach was cold and shivery. Her mouth had gone dry. 'Something out there is calling her.'

'Well, they can call away. She is not going.' Greg swung the Land Rover onto the track, feeling the tyres slipping sideways as they tried to grip the mud.

Under the trees they were suddenly aware of how soon it would be dusk. The shadows beneath the pine and larch were softly black; in the distance the wood was dark. The headlights cut a swathe through the undergrowth, lighting up patches of yellow where willow whips were already showing signs of spring to come in spite of the cold.

'Do you think we should check for footprints, to make sure she did come this way?' Kate asked tentatively. She grabbed at the door to try and stop herself sliding off the seat.

'We know she came this way,' Greg shot her a quick look. 'Fasten your seat belt, then you won't get thrown off if we tip over. This track will be impassable if we get any more rough weather.' He whirled the wheel round as the vehicle skidded sideways into a pothole.

'Perhaps if you went a bit slower.'

'We've got to get there before she does. Hell's teeth!' He hauled at a gear lever, forcing them back onto the track. A spatter of raindrops hit the windscreen as they brushed some trailing ivies and clematis, the bare, woody branches of traveller's joy already showing tiny new buds. Ahead, on the track something moved. He slowed the Land Rover and they both peered through the streaked windscreen. 'What was it? Is it Allie?' Kate leaned forward eagerly.

He shook his head grimly. 'Deer.' He pulled the wheel round. 'Christ, how far has she got?'

'Is there another way? Could she have taken a short cut?'

'I don't think so. This is the short cut. Everyone always goes the quickest way.'

Kate looked across at him. The worry was clearly etched into his face, the lines between nose and mouth drawn tight and deep, the frown lines between his eyes accentuated in the near-darkness. For all his constant bickering with his sister he obviously loved her deeply. She felt a wave of something like affection for him. Curbing her instinct to touch his shoulder in an attempt to give him some sort of comfort she stared ahead through the windscreen once more. 'She'll be all right. We'll find her.'

'Indeed we will.' His voice was grim.

They drove on for several minutes in silence, then Kate let out a cry. 'There she is! Look. Over there.'

Greg swung the Land Rover off the track towards the figure sheltering beneath a tree. They had drawn up beside it and Greg was already opening his door before they realised at the same moment that it was not Allie. The figure which staggered towards them was that of a man. Suddenly Kate recognised him.

'Bill!' She leaped out of her seat and ran round the vehicle, slipping in the mud. 'Bill, what are you doing here?'

'Watch out. He's hurt.' Greg caught her arm, stopping her in her tracks. In the light of the headlamps they could both see the stream of blood running down his face.

'Bill?' Her stomach turning over with fright, Kate put her hand on Bill's arm. 'Bill, are you all right? It's Kate.' The look he turned on her was completely blank.

'I'll get one of those blankets.' Greg turned and sped back to the car. Returning, he pulled the warm rug round Bill's shoulders. 'Can you walk, old chap? Come on. Only a few steps. Kate, open the back door. Help me boost him in. Christ, what's happened to him?'

Her mouth dry with fear, Kate helped Greg push Bill up

onto a back seat. He was a big man and his limbs did not appear to be co-ordinating properly. She could feel him shivering under the thick blanket. She climbed in beside him, fumbling for his hand. When she found it she chafed it gently, appalled at the chill of his skin. 'I think we should get him to hospital, Greg,' she murmured.

Greg nodded. 'As soon as we've found Allie. Has he had a fall? Hold on. I'll get the other torch and the first aid box.' Rummaging in the box at her feet he glanced into the darkening woods. Kate was staring at Bill's face. That look of blank terror; the fixed, pinpoint pupils, the chilled skin. It was the same as Alison. Identical. She glanced at Greg who had slipped onto the narrow seat opposite them. 'This is how Allie looked when I found her.' She felt Bill give a small shudder.

'Christ!' Greg bit his lips. 'Look, can you cope in the back? We've got to go on and find her.'

'We'll be OK. He's not quite as cold as she was.' Even so, she could hear his teeth chattering. She bent to open the first aid box. It was difficult rummaging in it in the unsteady light but she managed to find antiseptic and some dressings. As gently as she could she swabbed the blood off his forehead, wincing at the bruises on his hairline. He sat unmoving, seemingly oblivious to what she was doing, though he flinched once or twice as the swab did its work. Taping a dressing across his forehead, she was carefully mopping some of the blood that had dripped down his cheek when he gripped her wrist with sudden, ferocious strength. 'Alison!' he gasped.

'Have you seen her?' There was a strange cold sickness building in Kate's stomach. She left her hand in his. His fingers were very strong but they were still very cold.

Bill shook his head, bewildered. He put his hand to his temple and drew it away, looking at his fingers as though he expected to see blood. He did not seem to realise there was a dressing there. 'She hit me.'

Greg had climbed into the driving seat. He turned, his elbow over the back. 'Alison hit you!'

'I tried to stop her. She was with someone. The woman I saw on the beach.' To her horror Kate saw Bill's eyes fill with tears. 'I wanted her to come with me,' he went on. He was mumbling slightly. 'I tried to stop her. I took her arm and it was then she turned on me. Her face was −' he shook his head back and forth several times '− it was ferocious. She grabbed a fallen branch. It was a big one. Out there. Pine or fir or something. She lifted it up and crashed it down on my head. I must have lost consciousness. I don't remember anything else until you came.'

'You're imagining it! Allie couldn't, wouldn't do such a thing!' Greg said, horrified.

Kate glanced up at him.

'What woman did you see with her, Bill?' she asked.

He shrugged. 'I saw her in the distance on the beach. She was tall. Thin. I thought it was you. She was wrapped up tightly against the wind. Her hair was long, falling down, all sort of dishevelled. She was angry. I could feel her anger.'

Greg's eyes flicked from Bill's face to Kate's. He wondered briefly if he looked as frightened and shocked as she did.

She met his eye. 'You'd better drive on, Greg,' she said. Her voice had gone husky.

He hesitated for a moment. Then he nodded. Turning round he reached for the ignition.

Kate put her arm round Bill's shoulders as the Land Rover lurched forward again and she felt him slump against her, shivering. As calmly as she could she edged another blanket out of the pile Greg had thrown on the floor in front of her and tucked it round him. Then she groped for his hand again and held it tightly.

It took them another ten minutes to reach the cottage. Greg swung the Land Rover to a standstill on the grass, directing the headlights past the building, down towards the beach. Kate leaned forward, staring ahead across the back of the seat. 'I can't see her.'

Greg reached for the torch and swung his door open. 'You stay here. I'll go down to the grave.'

'I should come with you.'

'You can't.' His voice was curt. Then he relented. Coming round to the back he swung the rear door open for her. For a moment he looked into Kate's eyes. He held out his hand to help her out, and she felt him squeeze her fingers. 'You've got to stay with Bill. Take him into the cottage. Get the kettle on or something. I won't be long. We know where she'll be.'

'Be careful, Greg.'

'I will.' For a moment he stood gazing at her then he leaned forward and gave her a swift kiss on the lips.

She watched the torchlight receding into the distance. After a few moments it disappeared. The Land Rover was silent save for the ticking of the engine as it cooled. Kate swallowed. For a moment she didn't move. Bill didn't stir. Taking a deep breath she groped in the pocket of her jacket for the keys. She could see a pale glow of light from the window to the right of the front door where she had left the lamp switched on.

'Where are you going?' Bill jerked awake as she turned away.

'To open the cottage. You'll be more comfortable there. It's warm. Do you think you can walk?'

'Where's Greg?' He seemed aware for the first time that Greg had gone.

'He's looking for Allie –'

'On his own?' The fear in the man's voice made her skin crawl.

'He'll be all right. Greg's a big chap. And he knows he has to be careful because you've warned us.' She was astonished at how reassuring her own words sounded.

'Shall I go and open the door first? Then I'll come back for you.'

'No.' Bill's fingers clamped around her wrist. 'I'm coming with you.'

To her relief the house was still warm. Propping Bill against the wall, she switched on all the downstairs lights and drew the curtains. Then she looked at him properly for the first time. His face was a mass of purple bruises. There were lacerations in his scalp she had not seen in the dim torchlight. His sweater and anorak were torn and soaked with dried blood. She schooled her face carefully into a reassuring smile, hoping he had not seen her horror as she saw the extent of his injuries. 'Bill you must lie down.'

'No. No, I want to stand for a minute.' He pushed himself away from the wall. 'Can we have something hot to drink? I'm so cold.'

'Of course. She took his arm and ensconced him on the stool in the kitchen while she reached for the kettle. All the time her ears were straining for sounds outside the house. She had locked the front door and drawn the bolt.

'I ought to try and clean up those cuts for you a bit better,' she said as she reached down a couple of mugs.

'Don't bother. I'll be all right.' Beneath the bruises his complexion was returning to a more normal shade. His hands though, when he reached for the coffee, were still shaking visibly.

'Can you tell me any more about it, Bill?' she asked quietly as she sat opposite him. 'About the woman. Did she say anything?'

He shook his head. 'Not a word. She just sort of hovered in the background.'

'Hovered?'

'Well, watched. You know. Her face was impassive. Uninvolved. She didn't seem to care what Allie was doing.' His voice trembled again.

'Bill.' Kate leaned forward and touched his hand reassuringly. 'Allie is not herself. She had an accident of some sort on the beach.' She hesitated. 'I don't think she knew what she was doing. As for this woman.' She bit her lip. 'God knows who she is. Bill?' She realised suddenly that his attention had been distracted. He was staring at the curtained window, his head slightly to one side.

'Did you hear that?' he said.

'What?' She held her breath, listening.

'I thought I heard something – a shout – I don't know.' He put his head in his hands.

'Shall I go and look?' There was nothing she wanted to do less than open the front door but Greg was out there, alone.

He shook his head mutely. 'You can't help him,' he said after a minute. 'No one can.'

'What do you mean?' She stared at him, whitefaced.

He shrugged. Suddenly he laughed but she saw a tear slide down his cheek. 'I came over to ask you to supper. I bought some wine and there's an M&S gourmet meal waiting back at my place.'

She leaned forward and reached for his mug to refill it. 'That's a lovely thought. I shall look forward to it.'

'But not now. Now everything is changed.'

He was like a child talking. Working it out, plaintive that his plans had been spoiled. She looked at him, frightened. Bill was strong, reliable, always there to lean on. This shaking, shocked man was not the Bill she knew.

'We'll do it tomorrow,' she said, keeping her voice bright. 'Perhaps for lunch. I'd like that.'

'Yes. For lunch.' His voice was dull. He pressed his hand to his head again. 'I feel sleepy, Kate.'

'Why don't you lie on the sofa? I'll stay with you and keep you company.' She rose and took his hand.

He followed her through into the living room and lay down obediently, his long legs hanging over the arm. She pulled a rug over him, and arranged a cushion gently under his head. He looked very uncomfortable on the small piece of furniture, but he curled up on his side and closed his eyes without a word. She sat down opposite him, watching him uneasily. Almost certainly he had concussion; perhaps a cracked skull. And there was nothing she could do to help until they managed to get him to a hospital.

She leaned back in the chair, gazing into the fire. The house was silent. She strained her ears, trying to hear through the walls, listening for sounds from outside. There was nothing save a gentle scraping of the rose tree at the window which faced the sea. Where was Greg? Why was he taking so long?

XXXVII

Standing on the shingle bank Greg shone the torch ahead
of him into the sleet. All he could see were silver needles
slanting across the dark; beyond, he could hear the sea
above the howl of the wind. The whole world seemed
insubstantial, moving. Sand. Shingle. Water. Grasses. All
swayed and shifted, formless in the torchlight.

'Allie!' Greg yelled. His voice was puny against the
roar of the elements. 'Allie. Where are you?' Why hadn't
they questioned her more? Why hadn't they tried to
find out why she had run out into the cold at dawn to
come here by herself? Why hadn't they asked her more
about what happened? He shuddered violently. What
had made her attack Bill, a man she had met dozens
of times? Was it that she hadn't recognised him, or had
the attack come from someone else; the woman with
her. And who was the woman? Oh Christ, let her be
all right!

He moved forward, his boots slipping on the wet stones,
and swept his torch around again. Nothing. There was
nothing.

Shivering, he forced his way into the teeth of the wind,
emerging between the dunes onto the beach and turning
towards the grave. In the roaring darkness he could see the
flash of breakers and hear the suck of the water as they
pulled back against the wind. Beneath his feet the ground
seemed to be shaking.

'Allie!' His fear, under control in front of Kate, was
rising by the second. Fear for Allie and fear for himself.
He had walked on this beach a thousand times in every

weather, at midnight and in the day but never before had he found it so ball-breakingly terrifying.

His steps slowed as he approached the grave. He could feel his heart thundering beneath his ribs and he felt cold and sick. The torch was slippery in his hands as he thrust it ahead of him, seeing the beam slide waveringly towards the edge of the excavated hollow.

'Allie?' His voice was growing hoarse. 'Allie? Prat! Where are you?'

It was dark in the hollow below the beam. The rushing hail and wind seemed to speed across it, leaving the gaping blackness very still.

Sliding in the wet sand he climbed to the edge and looked down, directing the beam swiftly up and down the digging. For a moment his heart stood still. A black cavern seemed to open up beneath his feet, leading down and down forever. The torch hovered for a long moment over it, then he forced it to move on and saw that it was just a trick of the light, a lie perpetrated by the shadows. There was nothing there but a slightly higher ridge in the sand, which had cast that deep impenetrable shadow. Beside it lay the usual scattering of shells and weed. The grave site was empty. He felt a rush of relief and at the same time a sharp pang of disappointment. He had half expected – hoped – to find her kneeling there, just as Kate had found her. He leaped down into the hole. The torchlight showed up every bump and indentation in the sand, but he could see no footprints, just the pitting of the rain.

Crouching down out of the wind he directed the torch at the sandface, running the beam of light along the strata. It was smooth now, wet, compacted. There was no sign that he could see of any remains. No bones. No hand reaching out from the sand, the broken fingers beckoning in supplication. He felt his body shaken by another uncontrollable shudder. Standing up he swung the torch round. Where was she? Where in the name of Christ was she?

This damn grave. If she hadn't found it all would have been well. He aimed a vicious kick at the sand and with a sharp sense of pleasure saw a large section of the sandface break away and fall. He kicked again. It would only take a few minutes. The sand was so soft. They would think it was the sea. Behind him the tide was hurling itself ever closer across the beach. Gritting his teeth, he drew his foot back for another kick at the base of the sand cliff when he heard a sound behind him. He swung round, holding his torch out before him, like a weapon.

'Allie!' His voice came out as a croak. 'Allie?' He tried again. 'Where are you?'

The destruction of the dune forgotten, he scrambled, slipping and stumbling back into the wind. The torch beam was growing less sharp. He shook it angrily and slapped it against his palm. His hands were ice cold and wet, his fingers growing numb.

The darkness was empty. She could be anywhere. In the woods; on the beach; in the marsh. Anywhere. Helplessly he turned slowly round, staring into the tearing darkness, feeling the ice-cold fingers of sleet sliding down inside his collar, fighting the battering of the wind, hearing the throb of it in his ears.

She could be back at the cottage by now. His hand tightened on the torch. Supposing she had gone there? Supposing she was hiding in the woodshed or amongst the trees, waiting for Kate to come back? She liked Kate. She seemed to trust her. Surely that is what she would have done. Turning, he began to retrace his footsteps, his back to the sea.

It was then he thought he saw a figure at the very edge of his torch beam.

It was a man.

As the figure moved sharply backwards Greg's feeble torchlight caught the glint of what looked like a knife blade before he vanished into the darkness.

XXXVIII

'Bill?' Kate's whisper sounded strangely loud in the silence of the room. 'Bill, are you asleep?' He was lying on his side, huddled beneath the blanket she had tucked around him, his head on the pillow she had brought down from her bed. One of the cuts had reopened on his temple and she could see a slow trickle of black blood soaking through the dressing onto the flowered pillowcase, adding to the entwined cornflowers and poppies an obscene decoration which shone slick and oily in the light of the lamp. 'Bill?' She knelt down next to him. His sleep frightened her. It was too deep, too sudden and she didn't know what to do.

She squinted at her wristwatch. It was seven o'clock. Two hours since they had left Redall Farmhouse, perhaps an hour and a half since they had reached the cottage. So where was Greg? She stared up at the curtained window, straining her ears. The whole cottage was full of the sound of the wind and the sea. The walls seemed to vibrate beneath their combined assault. Trickles of draught played across the floor, shifting the curtains uneasily, flaring the flames in the stove, teasing the fringe on one of the cushions on the chair.

Taking Bill's hand in hers, she stroked it gently, appalled by the heavy coldness. Slipping her fingers around his wrist she felt for the pulse. She thought there was something there, but it was terribly faint, barely a fluttering beneath her chilled fingers. Too frightened to touch him any more she tucked his hand under the blanket and stood up. The stone still lay on the hearth where she had put it after bringing it in earlier for Alison. Humping it up onto the top of the stove she opened the doors and pushed on another log. Then she turned to her cassette player. The Requiem was still there. As the music filled the room she glanced back at Bill.

It was a long time since she had prayed. Not since she was a small child and had knelt beside her bed, her hands folded neatly and fervently beneath her chin, and prayed for a pony. It had never materialised and her faith which for a short time had blazed inside her, had shrivelled with disappointment and died. She wasn't sure she knew how to pray now. Our Father, which art in Heaven. Save Bill. Please, save him and keep us safe. Deliver us from evil. For thine is the kingdom. She kept her eyes open, scanning the room, trying to allow the music to soothe and comfort her. Behind her on the windowsill the puddle of water inside the frame had broadened. A drip fell from the ledge onto the floor. Then another.

The 'Pie Jesu' finished. The room fell into silence which was broken only by the sharp click as the player switched itself off. Even the wind seemed momentarily to have died away. For a while Kate sat without moving, then she stood up. She picked up the towel she had fetched from the bathroom and wrapped it round the hot stone.

'Bill?' she whispered. 'Bill? Are you asleep?' The heavy warm bundle clutched in her arms, she stood looking down at him. His face was remote, white, utterly composed. The wound on his temple had stopped bleeding now. She could see where the blood had clotted into a dried crust on his skin. 'Bill, I'll put this by your feet. It will help keep you warm.' But she couldn't. His feet were hanging over the edge of the sofa. She lifted the blanket and eased the towel-wrapped stone in near his knees. His trousers were damp. Perhaps she should try and take them off. Then, wrinkling her nose, she realised what had happened. He had peed all over himself as he lay there on the sofa. Closing her eyes she tucked the blanket back over him.

She had never tried to find the pulse in anyone's neck before, but she didn't really expect to find it. The total emptiness in the room told her that he was dead. Turning away she sat on the floor in front of the fire and wrapped her arms around her knees, as the tears poured down her cheeks.

XXXIX

He had been hiding in the reeds, lying on his stomach where he had a good view of the proceedings, close enough to see the rivulet of drugged mead running down the man's chin, dropping into the hollow of his collar bone and on down his chest. As the garotte tightened, he stood up, slowly, in full view, his hands on his hips. He saw Nion's eyes open; he saw the realisation dawn, saw the man's hands flail towards his throat as he tried to tear away the ligature and he began to laugh. 'It was not the gods who ordered your death, Nion, prince of the Trinovantes!' he shouted into the sunrise. 'I arranged it all, I and the priests I bribed. You die to avenge my honour at the expense of your own.' He could see the flesh bulging on either side of the knotted cord around the young man's throat. He could see the trickle of blood as his struggles grew more frantic. 'No man lies with my wife and lives. Not prince, not druid, not Briton, not Roman! And no god will greet you and lead you across the Styx. You die dishonoured.'

'Marcus!'

The scream from the far side of the sacrificial site sounded like that of a wild bird. He swung round, numb with shock, as behind him the priest plunged the knife into Nion's back. For a second his wife's beauty stunned him, illumined as she was by the rose gold rays of the rising sun, then the hatred congealed again in his breast and he stared at her with cold loathing as she gazed wildly past him, towards Nion.

For a moment the young man straightened, his dying gaze fixed on the sun. His hands dropped away from the garotte around his throat. As the light died from his eyes his knees buckled and he fell forward into the waiting mud.

She was standing knee deep in the rushes, her blue gown wet, clinging to her body, her hair unbraided, loose on her shoulders, her face crazed as she ran towards him, her arms upraised, her nails clawed like those of an animal.

'May the gods of all eternity curse you, Marcus Severus, and bring your putrid body and your rotten soul to judgement for what you have done here this day!'

As her cry echoed across the marshes a flight of duck rose from the reeds, soaring above their heads and setting off towards the rising sun, a vee of glittering green and gold as they rose into the fresh light of the new morning.

Greg was running. His breath was catching in his chest, rasping in his throat as he propelled his feet forward through the soft sand, the weakening torchbeam moving wildly back and forth in front of his pounding feet.

'Allie!' His cries were almost inaudible. His throat was dry and there was no breath left for shouting. 'Allie, for the love of Christ, where are you?'

The sea was coming closer. His feet were wet. There was a trail of seaweed clinging to his shoe. He splashed on, feeling the icy water immerse him to the knees, then draw back, leaving the cold against his flesh under the wet cloth like a burn. 'Allie!' He veered away from the sea, feeling his feet on firmer sand now, pounding up the beach. 'Allie!'

The man had gone again. Twice he had glimpsed him, a shadow in the greater darkness, and each time the torch had picked out the blade of the knife.

Stumbling to a standstill he stared round, his chest heaving, feeling the ice in the hail rasp against the delicate linings of his nostrils. His face felt raw, as though it had been flayed of several layers of skin. He bent forward, switching off the torch for a moment as he rested his forearms against his thighs, his whole body heaving with the effort of drawing in those painful, shuddering breaths. Beside him another wave toppled onto the beach, racing towards him, stopping just short of his feet, showering him with spray. He straightened, his ribs a straight-jacket of pain, and stared round. Without the narrowing, confining point of light from the torch, the horizon had suddenly enlarged. The darkness was no longer so absolute. He could see the tangled luminous lace of the white water on the heaving darkness of the sea; he could see the glint of the wet sand, the heavy umber of the clouds bellying over the water. His head throbbed and spun and he staggered as his eyes focussed in horror on the man who had appeared again only a few feet from him now. He could see him clearly. The strong, patrician face, the hair plastered to his forehead by the rain, the heavy, sodden garment clinging to his body, the forearm naked beneath a swathe of darker material with the raised dagger clutched in his fist.

ANGER
HATE

Probing, thrusting, expanding, rage whirled within the confines of Greg's brain. The torch fell from his fingers as he raised his hands to his head and tore at his flesh, trying to free himself from the pain. He stepped backwards. His foot, tangled in a lump of gelatinous weed, slid and turned over. The sudden shaft of agony in his ankle forced him down abruptly onto one knee and he felt his arms flail sideways.

The figure was suddenly closer. It was smiling and the deep-set cavernous eye sockets, which for a fraction of a second had seemed empty, blazed with light.

Greg felt all the air wrenched out of him. He could feel the suspension of his lungs — rigid, straining to take in another breath which would not come. His head was whirling. His eyes were growing dim. The white had gone from the sea. All he could feel was the cold. A strange, all-encompassing cold which came from deep inside him and was working its way, layer by layer through his body towards the surface. When it reached his brain he would die. He knew it clearly. And, just as clearly, he knew that this was what had happened to Alison and to Bill. He would die here on the beach of hypothermia and no one would ever find him because the tide was coming in. He raised his eyes to the face of the man who stood over him but the figure had gone. The night was empty. High above the bulbous obscenity of cloud a waxing moon sucked at the sea and spewed the tide ever higher across the land.

XL

With shaky determination Kate reached for her scarf and wound it around her head. She grabbed her thick jacket and her gloves, and with a last desolate look at Bill, she picked up her torch and opened the front door. She had to find Greg.

She stopped for a moment at the corner of the cottage, gathering her strength, then, not giving herself any more time to think, she launched herself down the track towards the dunes into the teeth of the gale.

The excavation was deserted. She stood at the edge of it staring down, her eyes narrowed against the cold, her back to the wind, feeling the damp seeping through the shoulders of her jacket. The wall of sand opposite her had fallen away at one point, and in the torchlight she could see huge patches of discoloration in the exposed strata. She stared at it blankly. The outline of the body was quite clear in the torchlight. It was crouching in the foetal position, exposed in the sand and peat where the wall of the excavation had fallen. She stared at it. For a moment she was too shocked to react. The torch in her hand was wet between her gloved fingers. She steadied it desperately. Had Alison seen this? Was this what had tipped her over the edge into a madness that had driven her to attack and kill a man? She swung the beam round frantically, turning into the wind again, searching for Greg, but she could see nothing in the streaming darkness. Beneath her feet the ground shuddered as the waves crashed onto the beach. The tide was high, within yards of where she stood. She could feel the spray soaking her back as each new wave thundered up the sand and shingle. She had never felt so alone.

'Greg!'

Her tears were scalding her icy cheeks; she dashed them out of her eyes with the back of her arm. Where was he? She didn't have the first idea where to look. The dunes and beach and marshes stretched for miles in both directions. Had he walked along the sea's edge looking for Allie, or had he turned back inland towards the cottage, or even back into the woods?

She swung the beam back towards the dune face. It was still there, the body, crouched in silhouette in the wet peat. Beneath it the first trickles of frothy water, thick with weed were seeping into the hollow. Unless the tide turned now the dune would be lost. She turned away. She didn't care. It would be a good thing if it were never seen again as far as she was concerned. Defiantly she began to walk along the edge of the tide, turning northwards, keeping an unsteady parallel course to the sea. If she walked north for fifteen minutes, then inland a hundred yards or so and back, still parallel to the sea, she wouldn't get lost. That would be better than wandering aimlessly amongst the dunes. Shutting off her torch, she rammed it into her pocket. The sea had a strangely luminous quality about it and she found she could see quite easily as she walked. Better to save the torch until she needed it. She did not specify to herself what such a need might be.

There was a movement in the darkness ahead of her. She stopped, squinting into the wind. Alison? It wasn't Greg, of that she was sure. She could feel her breath quickening in her throat. Alison was still out here in the dark. Alison, who had killed a man. Her hand closed over the body of the torch, but she didn't switch it on. Slowly she moved closer to the spot where she had caught a glimpse of movement.

The figure had moved. She was slightly to Kate's left

now, almost behind her. And she was beckoning. Beckoning back towards the grave. It wasn't Allie. This woman was taller, slimmer and she was wearing some sort of blowing, willowy garment – a skirt in spite of the weather, and it looked like a long skirt. Kate's mouth had gone dry. She found her breath was coming in small, tight gasps. Was this the woman Bill had seen with Allie – the woman who had watched the girl attack him and not lifted a finger to help?

'Claudia?'

It was a whisper. Please God, don't let this be happening. Don't let her be real. Kate took a few steps backwards. The woman seemed to follow her. Adjusting her fingers carefully along the body of the torch until her thumb found the switch, Kate drew it out of her pocket. Sliding the switch across she lifted the torch in one quick movement and shone it straight into the woman's face. She did not react. The beam went straight through her. Kate could see the streaming grasses and the blowing sand behind her as if her figure was made of glass.

'Help!' The voice was distant, almost obliterated by the wind. 'Help me, someone! Kate!'

Keeping her eye on the woman, Kate backed away. The woman seemed to follow her. Her face was clearly visible. It was a youngish face, pale in the torchlight, the cheekbones high, the hair unravelled, whipping around it. She could see the colours clearly for all their transparency. The bright blue of the gown with the stains upon the front, the redness of her hair, the strange golden eyeshadow on the deepset eyes.

'What is it? What do you want?' Kate's voice was shaking. She was vividly conscious of the cry from behind her but she did not dare to turn her back on the figure. It didn't seem to threaten her in any way but her own terror was so great she was incapable of doing anything other than backing slowly away from it. Slowly, the figure was holding out its hands, but at the same time it was fading. The background behind it was growing stronger. It was her torchbeam, she realised suddenly. It was weakening. 'Oh no. Please don't run out.' She switched off the beam and switched it on again, keeping it directed desperately at the figure. But the woman had gone. She directed the beam up and down, seeing it waver as her hands shook. There was nothing there. Nothing but the violence of the night. She swung round and began to run towards the place from where the voice had seemed to come, the torchbeam swinging violently up and down as she moved and then she saw him. Greg. He was sitting on the edge of the sand, almost in the water.

'Greg. Oh Greg, thank God!' She flung herself down beside him, almost knocking him backwards on the sand, tears streaming down her face. 'Greg. Greg.' She couldn't do anything but repeat his name over and over again as she clutched at his jacket.

His arm went round her and he pulled her against him. 'It's OK, Kate. It's OK. Calm down.'

'I saw her. I saw the ghost. Claudia. She was standing by the grave. And there's a body there, Greg. A body.' Sobbing, she pushed her face against his sleeve. His jacket was wet and cold, and she could feel him shivering through it. 'Greg. Bill's dead.' The words were muffled through the green waxed material, but he heard them clearly enough.

'Oh sweet Christ.' He hugged her closer against him. 'Listen, Kate. You have to help me. Strange though it may seem I'm not sitting here with my feet in the sea for fun. Something has happened to my ankle. I've got it caught in something. Have a look, there's a love. Each time I try and lean forward to free myself I go all peculiar.'

He had lain there watching the tide rising higher and higher, swimming in and out of consciousness. He was not catatonic like Alison, nor dazed like Bill, but he knew, as he lay back, resigned to the cold that was creeping through him, that he was well on his way to unconsciousness. Then he had seen the crazily flashing light of Kate's torch for a second in the dunes behind him. The sight had given him the shot of hope which had sent the adrenalin coursing through his veins again.

Kate crouched forward. She held the torch close to his ankle. 'It's fishing line. All wound round your foot. The hook has gone through your shoe.'

She felt her stomach clench at the sight of the blood soaking into the sand around his foot. The line had tangled around a whole pile of jetsam weed which had snagged against something which stuck out of the sand. She tugged at it, careful not to touch his foot, but it was immovable, tethering him there in the path of the tide.

Greg eased himself forward on his elbow. 'Can you free it? I've got a knife somewhere in one of my pockets. Inside, here.' He tried to drag the zip down from his chin but his hands were cold and slippery and he could feel another wave of nausea and dizziness building.

'I'll look for it.' She left his foot and came close to him again. The knotted ends of her scarf were fluttering wildly in the wind. He could feel them drumming against his cheek as she knelt beside him, her eyes narrowed. 'Wait, I'll have to get my gloves off.' She gave him the torch and he saw her pulling at the fingers of her glove with her teeth. He switched off the torch. He could see how weak the battery was, and he ducked suddenly as a stronger than usual wave hurtled up the beach and crashed almost over them, covering them both in icy spray. The glove was off and she had the heavy zip in her hand now, coaxing it down. He could feel the cut of the wind as it slid inside and froze his skin. Her hand followed and he felt her fingers rummaging against the jacket lining. Easing his position slightly, he lifted himself onto his other elbow and put his free arm around her shoulders, trying to borrow some of her warmth. But her jacket was slick and cold with rain. She glanced up at him, her face only inches from his and he saw her smile grimly in the darkness. 'Hang on in there. I'll find it. You've got more pockets than the Artful Dodger.'

'Keep searching. I wish I were feeling better. I'd take the chance to make a massive pass at you!' He gave a wan grin.

'In this cold I might just reciprocate.' Her hands were methodically searching each of the deep pockets on the inside of his jacket. Another wave broke across them and she heard herself gasp at the cold.

His arm tightened around her. 'It's getting closer.'

'It must be nearly high tide. It was in over the edge of the grave.'

'There's an easterly wind. It's pushing it higher than usual.' He glanced up at the sky over her head. 'Thank God the moon, wherever it is, isn't quite full. We're not into springs or I would have been a goner by now.'

The pain from his foot was hitting him in pulses, travelling up his leg and receding but always constant from his ankle down. He did not dare to try and waggle his foot. The pain when he had done that had caused him to faint. When he had woken up it was because a wave had broken across his face; he had come to, choking. He did not dare to contemplate what the pain would be like when Kate freed him. If she could free him. Perhaps he would pass out again – God's own anaesthetic. He tried to concentrate on her hand roaming the pockets of his jacket. He was not so far gone that the old system had not reacted a little to the questing hands of a beautiful woman. Her hair smelt of woodsmoke and ash from the woodburner, and her body, pressed close to his, had the slightly musty smell of wet wool, but under it all he could smell the faintest traces of whatever scent she had put on that morning – whenever that was, and her own indefinable smell, the smell that registered subconsciously and made you like or hate, love or loathe, or remain purely indifferent to every human being you met. In her case, in spite of the aggravation she had caused him, he found it extremely attractive. He lay back a little, trying to ease the weight on his elbows, jumping as the movement jarred his leg.

'Sorry. Did I hurt you?' She had noticed.

'Not you. The hook.'

'Found it.' At last her fingers had closed over the knife. She pulled it out of his pocket and sat back. Catching hold of his zip she dragged it up. 'Can't let you freeze to death.' She shook her head as another deluge of cold spray poured over them. Officially, the tide had turned half an hour before, but nobody seemed to have told the sea. She glanced at his face. 'I'll try not to hurt you.'

He forced a grin. 'Listen, if I keel over, just go on and do it. Cut the line, and get the hook out while you can and stop the bleeding.' He paused to catch his breath as another spasm of pain took him. 'Don't try and move me though. I'm heavy.' Another wan grin. 'When I come to, I'll be able to wriggle away from the sea. Then you can go and get help.'

'OK, boss.' She put her hand on his for a second and squeezed it. Then she picked up the torch.

Whatever happened she mustn't drop the knife. She tried to pull open the blade with cold, wet fingers but they slipped off uselessly. Swearing, she tried again, hands shaking. Behind her Greg had lain back on the sand. His eyes were closed. His face in the torchlight was almost transparent. She breathed on her fingers for a moment to warm them and then, half unzipping her jacket, pushed her hand under the opposite arm to dry her fingers on the wool of her sweater and bring some feeling back. The next time she tried to prise open the blade the knife opened easily. With a sigh of relief she edged down his body until she was opposite his feet. His free leg was hunched up beneath

him where he had tried to drag himself away from the
approaching water, his other leg stretched out, the foot
twisted, the patch of blood beneath it washed away now by
the tide. Holding the torch close to the foot, Kate studied it.
Her hands were shaking and she felt suddenly very sick.
The first job clearly was to cut away the tangled fishing
line where it was wrapped around the ankle. She inserted
the knife blade flat against his sock and pulled tentatively
against the nylon line. Nothing happened. She pulled
harder. Greg groaned. Kate bit her lip. 'I'll cut away this
bit from the rest. That way I won't hurt you so much.' She
felt around beneath his foot amongst the weed. Another
wave swamped her hands and she clutched desperately at
the knife, waiting for the water to draw back again. How
had he got it tangled so tightly? It was as if someone had
tied the line around and around the foot, tethering him to
something buried in the beach. She scrabbled with her
hands in the sand. There were shells and an old dead crab
tangled amongst the weeds, then the ice-cold, wet sand,
then her fingers encountered something hard. A balk of
timber completely buried. The line seemed to come from
under it. She pushed the knife blade against the timber and
gave a ferocious jerk. The line parted. Cautiously, she felt
for the next bit. That was easier. It came away at once as
did the next. But the final strands, wound round his foot
seemed to be pulled tight. Of course, he had done that
himself, struggling to free his foot. Shaking the water out
of her eyes she worked steadily, strand by strand until at
last the final piece fell away. He groaned again. She ignored
it. Gently she felt around his shoe. The fish hook in his
foot was the largest of several that had been knotted into
the line. Curved and barbed they lay glittering in the torchlight, all except the one which disappeared into the side of
his trainer. She studied it for a moment, biting her lip.
Then she turned, shining the torch for a moment onto
Greg's face. 'Shall we try and drag you back away from

the sea before I do anything else? I've cut the line that's holding you.'

Lifting himself on his elbows he nodded. 'I'll be too heavy for you, Kate. Just help me while I edge back.' He crooked his good leg up, wedging his heel into the wet shingle and sand and pushed. Sweat broke out on his forehead. Grimly clenching his teeth he did it again, painfully inching his body back away from the sea's edge. The drag on his bad foot was agony. He could see Kate bend over him. He knew she had gone behind him and he felt her hands under his shoulders. One more good pull and he would be out of reach of the waves, where the line of wet debris showed the tide had at last begun to pull back. The pull was agonising. He bit back a cry, then everything went black.

'Greg! Greg? are you all right?' Kate laid him gently down. 'Greg?'

His eyes were closed. She stared round in the darkness, feeling suddenly terribly alone. But she knew what she must do: get the hook out, now, while he was unconscious. Biting her lip in concentration, she wedged the torch so the beam shone on his foot and groped in her pocket for the knife. The trainer laces were easy after the fishing line; and the fabric of the shoe itself was not much tougher. Cutting carefully round the hook she managed to remove the shoe and straighten the twisted foot which was blackening and swollen. She wondered if it was broken. Swallowing the wave of nausea which threatened to overwhelm her, she gently lifted the remaining flap of the shoe and stared down at the hook. It had gone completely through his foot. There was no question of trying to pull it out the way it had gone in. The cruel barb on the end of the hook was half out of the top of his foot, wedged between two tendons. 'Dear God.' For a moment she wondered what to do. There was no choice. Taking as much care as she could not to jolt his foot further, she sliced the remaining length of line where it was knotted around the hook and began to ease the hook into the cold white flesh, pushing it right through his foot.

What kind of bastards left this stuff lying around on the beach to ensnare anyone or anything who walked there after them? She thought of the gull, drowned and cold, its feet laced together with nylon mesh. And this – a line of hooks abandoned by someone who had no doubt decided to go off to the chip shop somewhere down the coast and couldn't be bothered to take his line with him. The heat of anger which washed through her as she worked took her mind off the task she was performing. She wanted to push her hair out of her eyes – long strands of it had pulled free of her scarf – but she ignored them grimly. She had to do this and somehow bandage his foot before he came round, and before, she glanced at the torch, the battery failed. The hook slipped free surprisingly easily. Behind it the wound began to ooze with fresh, dark blood. She tore off her scarf then she fumbled in her pockets, searching for the small pack of tissues she had wedged there days earlier. They were still there. She tore several out of the cellophane and folded them carefully into two pads, one for the entry wound and one for the exit, then she bound them in place with the scarf. She wound the ends round and round his ankle, trying to tie it tightly, then she knotted it again and again. As she wrenched the last knot tight the torchbeam gave up and went out. She flopped back on the beach, wrapping her arms around her legs, her head on her knees, and sat quite still for a moment. She was shaking so much she could not move but Greg's groan brought her to her feet. She crouched next to him and reached for his hand. 'All over. The hook's out and I've straightened your foot.'

'Feels like hell.' He tried to sit up and failed. Closing his eyes he concentrated hard on staying conscious. 'What do we do now?'

Kate shook her head wearily. 'I suppose I ought to try

and go for help. We can't move you.' She glanced up without enthusiasm at the stormy blackness of the shore behind them.

His hand tightened on hers. 'I don't like the idea of you wandering around out there on your own. Listen, let me get my strength back a bit, then maybe I can walk.'

Kate smiled wistfully. 'No chance. You've damaged your foot horrendously.'

Greg was silent for a moment. 'If you could find me something to lean on. Some driftwood perhaps. There's masses of stuff chucked up on the beach. If we take it slowly, I'll manage to get back to the cottage.'

The word cottage triggered something in both their minds. Kate collapsed on her knees on the sand beside him and suddenly her eyes were filled with tears again. 'Bill's at the cottage.'

'I know.' He reached over and touched her face. 'But so is the Land Rover.' Somehow he kept his voice firm. 'You have to drive us back to the farm.' He did not mention Alison. 'Have you ever driven a four wheel drive?'

She shook her head wordlessly.

'Well, that doesn't matter. It's easy enough. I was just wondering how far you could get it on the sand.' He thought silently for a moment, then he gave a deep sigh. 'No. It's not worth trying. There's so much mud and soft stuff around. If you got bogged down, that would be our last chance gone. Our only hope is walking sticks.' Somehow he forced a bracing note into his words.

'I'll go and look along the tideline.' Kate wiped her nose on her sleeve – just like a small child, he thought affectionately – and she climbed wearily to her feet. 'I'm not going far. I'm not going out of sight.' She was reassuring herself as much as him.

'There's no need. It's surprisingly easy to see when one's got one's night vision. I can see lots of junk down there now.' He reached out and touched her hand. 'Only for

God's sake be careful where you walk, Kate. I don't want you treading on some more of those bloody hooks.'

He watched as she made her way cautiously back down to the tideline. What had happened was a blur; a nightmare which was coming back to him in sudden flashes. He could remember putting his foot down on something slippery; he could remember it sliding away from under him and he could remember going down on one knee in the icy water. That much was clear. He had been running away from something. Or someone. He frowned, cudgelling his memory.

Kate was walking slowly away from him, bending low, groping in the mess of tidewrack. She found an old tree branch and lifted it triumphantly, but it snapped as soon as she put any weight on it and she hurled it away.

She was right at the edge of his vision now. Greg frowned, sitting up straighter, trying to keep her in sight. She was a darker patch in the darkness. Every now and then as she straightened and looked around he could see her face, a pale blur beneath the flying hair. He lost her. Then he saw her again, several yards from where she had been. She was standing upright now, staring out to sea. It was strange. She seemed taller now. Taller and broader, and something had happened to her hair. He glanced back at where he had seen her before and his heart stopped still. She was still there. She had been squatting at the tide's edge, and now she jumped back as a wave hurled itself up the beach. He could see something in her left hand. He glanced back. The other figure was there. Near her. Watching her. The man with the knife.

Christ Almighty!

'Kate! Look out!' Greg's voice bellowed out into the wind. 'Kate, for God's sake look out. Behind you.' She couldn't hear him. Her back was turned and the roar of the wind and water would have deadened all but a foghorn at that distance. 'Oh Christ!' Desperately, Greg leaned forward, trying to drag himself onto his knees. 'Kate!' The bastard was nearer her now. He was moving effortlessly towards her. In a minute he would be right behind her.

'Kate!' His voice had risen to a scream. 'Kate, for God's sake, run!'

He half rose to his feet, lurching forward, and had put his weight on his injured foot before he realised what he had done. With a cry of despair he pitched forward onto his face. He was unconscious before he hit the ground.

XLI

Diana was stirring a pot of stew listlessly over the hotplate of the Aga. Made from leftovers from lunch to which she had added fried onions and dried herbs from the jars on the dresser, potatoes and mushrooms and carrots, it smelt delicious. The two cats were sitting side by side behind her, respectfully watching her every move, their admiration of her cooking technique obvious in every alert glance.

Patrick was sitting at the table behind her. His fingers drummed on the table top rhythmically and slowly, a drum roll for the march to the scaffold.

'Stop that, Paddy!' Diana's voice was sharp.

He stared at her and then looked down at his hand as though he did not know he owned it. 'Sorry.'

'They should have been back by now.' She clattered her pans together. 'They should have found her.'

'It's pretty stormy out there, Ma. They might have got the Land Rover stuck. Or they might have decided to stay at the cottage.'

'Or they might not have found her.' Diana turned to face her husband as he walked through towards the kitchen. 'Is the phone working?'

He shook his head. His face was lined with weariness and, as she watched, she saw his hand go surreptitiously to his chest under the flap of his jacket.

'Roger, darling. Go and sit down.' The displacement activity at the Aga forgotten she flew to him and threw her arms around him. 'Come on. Rest. You're wearing yourself out.'

'I should be out there with them, looking.' He shook his

head crossly, but he allowed her to steer him towards the fire.

'I'll go.' Patrick followed them. 'I'll take the bike and see where they are.'

'No.' Diana shook her head forbiddingly. 'No, Paddy. You stay here with us.'

'Let him go, Di.' Roger threw himself down in a chair and leaned back, his eyes closed. 'He can get to the cottage and check if they're there.'

'No.' It was a wail of misery. 'No. I want him to stay here. I don't want all my children lost.' Diana sat down abruptly, blinking hard, the strain only just contained.

'I won't get lost, Ma. I know the track like the back of my hand.' Patrick put his hand on her shoulder.

Her fingers sought his and tightened over them. 'But the storm . . .'

'If something has happened – I mean if the Land Rover has broken down, or the track is blocked or something, they have no way of telling us with the phones down. If I go, I can be back in half an hour and I can put your mind at rest.'

'He's right, Di.' Roger didn't open his eyes. 'Let him go.'

Her hand slid helplessly from her son's. He gave her shoulder a squeeze and stepped towards the door.

'Take no risks, Paddy.' Roger opened his eyes. 'No risks at all. If you see anything you can't cope with, come back at once, do you hear?'

'Sure, Dad.'

'No heroics.'

Patrick grinned. 'I'm not the superman type, Dad. Besides, what am I going to find? Mud. Trees. Snow. Cheer up. I won't be long.' He dived out into the hall and came back, dragging on his oilskin jacket. 'Have we got a decent torch?'

'I'll get it.' Diana went back into the kitchen. She

rummaged in a drawer. Patrick followed her. 'Don't let Dad go out,' he whispered. 'He's looking awfully pale.'

'I won't.' Finding the torch she switched it on, testing the beam. 'At least it's got batteries. Paddy, I know it's silly, but there have been some strange things going on at that cottage. You will be careful, darling, won't you?'

Patrick nodded. 'Promise.' He kissed her on the cheek and rammed the torch down into his pocket. Minutes later he had let himself out into the sleet.

The cold took his breath away. The ice on the wind felt as though it were cutting his face as he pulled on his gloves and went over to the barn, dragging back the heavy door to find his bike.

The narrow beam of his headlight lit up first the trees arching across the track as the bike slid and bucked over the potholes, then the slushy track itself where the latest set of tyre marks were clearly visible, not yet obliterated by the wet. Patrick concentrated hard on riding the machine without getting thrown off into the undergrowth, his eyes narrowed against the weather, searching out the least hazardous route, peering into the distance for a glimpse of the Land Rover. He was not feeling nearly as brave now he was out here alone. His thoughts kept jumping back to Alison, with her crazy eyes, to Kate's cottage – he thought of it as Kate's cottage, not Greg's – and the mess someone had made there. Was there someone out here in the woods? A maniac on the loose? Or was there really someone or something out there at the grave?

After a particularly bad skid in the thick mud he stopped, trying to catch his breath, bracing his foot against a tree root, aware that all his muscles were trembling with effort and shock. He stared round. The woods seemed awfully dark. The wind was howling between the trees, the sound sometimes rising to a banshee wail, sometimes falling to a moan. Leaning forward, he gripped the handlebars tightly and taking a deep breath, pushed off once more, forcing the pedals round with every ounce of strength he possessed. He would not think about the darkness where the light beam did not reach.

It was with enormous relief that he saw at last the squat outline of the Land Rover parked outside the cottage, silhouetted against the rectangle of a lighted window. Leaning the bike against the wall he hammered on the door. He waited, rubbing the back of his wrist against his nose, pushing his wet hair out of his eyes, then he knocked again. He frowned. Splashing his way through the puddles, he made his way to the front window, but it was curtained and he could see nothing. He turned back to the door and knocked again, hammering this time with his fist. 'Kate! Greg! Hey, let me in!'

At last he heard a sound. Somewhere inside a door banged.

'Kate! Greg! Come on. It's bloody freezing out here!' He paused, sniffing, to listen again. The silence inside the cottage was absolute, in contrast to the roar and scream of the elements outside.

Suddenly he was frightened. 'Kate! Greg! Why don't you open the door?' he shouted once more. He began pounding on it again with both fists. 'Come on. Please.' His voice cracked and slid up into the alto range, something which normally would have embarrassed him terribly. As it was he didn't even notice. He could feel tears pricking at the back of his eyes. He ran back to the window and knocked, pressing his face against the glass, but the flowery curtains with their pale sun-stained linings obscured any view of the inside of the room. He turned back and ran past the door, making this time for the windows at the side of the cottage. The bathroom window was slightly open. He inserted his arm and jiggled the arm of the latch free, letting the window swing outwards a little. The wind caught it and slammed it back against the wall, but it didn't matter.

The gap was large enough for him to climb in. He tried to get his knee up onto the narrow sill but his oilskin caught. Swearing to himself he unzipped it and tore it off, feeling the rain and wind blast against his body as he bundled the unwieldy garment up and tossed it in in front of him. Then he levered himself up onto the windowsill, and, holding his breath, squeezed himself in, dropping awkwardly onto the floor. The bathroom was dark. He scrabbled around the wall until he found the door and beside it the pull cord for the light. Tugging at it, he switched it on and stared round. The bath had a scattering of dark wet earth in the bottom. The tap was dripping slightly and he could see the trail scoured by the water in the soil. He frowned. Kate struck him as the sort of person who would meticulously wash out a bath after her, but perhaps like Greg she was also the type to get easily distracted when she was being creative; he forgot to change his clothes and wash and even eat when he was painting.

Tiptoeing across the floor again he opened the door a crack and peered out into the hall. It was dark out there, but he could see a thin line of light showing from the living room. Opening the door further he peered up the stairs. Everything there was dark and silent.

Suddenly he was shy of having broken in. It seemed a terrible intrusion to be in someone's house without their knowledge. He cleared his throat loudly, then realising how frightening that might be if Kate were on her own in there, he called out nervously. 'Kate, are you there?' He knocked on the door and jumped himself at the loudness of the hollow sound he made. 'Kate, it's Patrick.'

He crept across the hall and pushed the living room door open. The room was empty save for a figure lying on the sofa, covered by a rug. He felt a rush of relief. She was asleep. That explained it. He had crept right into the room before he realised that the feet and legs hanging over the arm of the sofa were those of a man.

'Greg?' He moved closer. The air in the room was stale and faintly unpleasant. It was very hot in there. Glancing at the stove he registered that it was glowing with heat. 'Greg?' He pulled the corner of the blanket away from the man's face and gave a small cry of horror. The flesh of Bill's face was discoloured and puffy; his eyes, half open beneath flaccid lids, were glassy and dim. A small stream of saliva had run from the corner of his mouth onto the pillow where it had dried in a sticky trail amidst the black crusts of blood. He was very obviously dead. Patrick reared back, repelled, swung away from the body and vomited onto the floor. 'Oh God! Oh God – oh God – oh God!' He leaned over and vomited again. Groping in the pocket of his jeans for something to wipe his mouth on, his fingers encountered the oily rag which he had used earlier to wipe the dipstick on the Volvo as he checked the engine for his father. He brought it to his face, mopping his mouth and his brow and his eyes, leaving a smear of dark oil across his cheeks. His eyes on the body he backed away from it towards the door. Where was Kate? He reached the hall and slammed the door shut, leaning against it. He felt desperately cold and shivery despite the heat in the house, and his legs were shaking violently. For a moment he thought they were going to collapse under him. He sat down on the bottom step of the stairs and took a deep breath, followed by another. Then he half turned, screwing his neck round so he could gaze up into the darkness of the upper landing. 'Kate?' His voice was husky, barely a whisper. 'Kate, are you up there?'

Somehow he hauled himself to his feet and he began to climb. Above him a door slammed again. 'Kate?' His voice wavered unsteadily. 'Kate, it's Patrick.' He could hear the wind more clearly up here. It was howling around the windows and behind it, a deep, subliminal beat, was the roar and crash of the sea. He reached the landing, straining his eyes into the darkness as he scrabbled along the wall for a light switch. He found it and flipped it on. Both bedroom doors were wide open. The air up here was ice cold in contrast to the fug downstairs. He frowned. In some recess of his mind he was registering that heat rises. It should be hotter up here, unless a window was open somewhere.

'Kate?' He tiptoed towards her bedroom door. Then he stopped. As the shock of what he had seen downstairs wore off a little his brain had begun to function again and the significance of what he had seen dawned on him. No fall could have caused the injuries he had seen on Bill's head and face. The man had been beaten to death. Bill had been murdered and the murderer was wandering round in the dark, perhaps up here now. He thought about the sound of the slamming door. Both doors on the landing were open. He swallowed, tasting once more the sharp, bitter flood of bile in the back of his throat. Kate. What had happened to Kate?

Taking a deep breath he flung wide the door to her bedroom and stared in. The light was on. The room was empty. He looked round, his hand clutching the door handle so tightly that his finger joints cracked. Apart from the bed which had been stripped of its blankets, the room seemed undisturbed. Peaceful. It was full of the scent of some unidentifiable perfume – not Kate's. He sniffed, puzzled. It was pleasant. Nice even, but it disturbed him. He could feel the hairs on the back of his neck stirring, like the hackles of a dog. He didn't like it. He turned away from the door and went across the landing to the other room. The light showed it to be empty with only a few stacked suitcases and cardboard boxes piled near the window on the far side of the floor. There was no sign of Kate. The windows in both rooms, he noticed suddenly, were tightly shut. So which door had he heard banging, and why the cold? He shuddered.

The kitchen. He hadn't checked the kitchen. 'Kate!'

Suddenly he found his voice again. 'Kate, where are you?' Taking the short flight of stairs two at a time he threw himself at the kitchen door. The room was empty. He stared round frantically. She had to be here. Please God, let her be here somewhere.

But there was nowhere for her to hide, nowhere else she could be. On the table in the middle of the room he noticed suddenly the bottle of Scotch they had given her. It lay on its side, empty. The lid, he found after a moment's hunting, was on the floor in the middle of another patch of damp wet earth; a cautious sniff told him the damp was whisky.

'Oh God! Kate! Greg!' He glanced round wildly, then turning on his heel, he ran to the front door and tore it open. All he could think about was getting home as fast as possible. Dad would know what to do. Dad would somehow make it all right.

Outside, the darkness was opaque, wet, like the bottom of the sea. He could see nothing, hear nothing but the wind. He was searching frantically for his bicycle when he heard the door bang behind him. Terrified he looked round. The bicycle wasn't there. He couldn't find it. It was gone.

For a moment in blind panic he thought of taking the Land Rover. He had driven it before, on the track. He ran towards it, scrabbling at the door handle and, dragging it open, looked inside. There were no keys in the ignition. With a sob of frustration he slammed the door and looked round again.

Where was his bike? It must be here. Desperately he ran a few steps up the track and suddenly he saw it, right in front of him. He couldn't stop in time and he had fallen over it before he knew what was happening. It bruised his shins, and he felt the warm trickle of blood down his leg, but he ignored it, dragging the machine upright, fumbling numbly for the pedal. It was only when he was once more on the track through the trees, his face streaming with rain and tears that he realised he had left his oilskin where it had fallen on the bathroom floor in the cottage.

XLII

Halfway back along the track the back tyre of Patrick's bicycle punctured. The machine ploughed deep into the mud and stopped. Panting, Patrick tried desperately to force it on, then, giving up, he dismounted and let out a string of expletives. It was impossible to ride with a flat tyre when the track was in this state. He was nearly in tears. Around him the woods seemed to be closing in. He grabbed the front lamp and slid it off its bracket, directing it around him in a long sweep. The trees hung over him, Arthur Rackham fingers clawed, ready to snatch at his flesh, their trunks twisted into leering faces, sleet dripping from their boughs like acid, trying to eat away his face.

With a sob he hurled the bicycle away from him and began to run, his boots slipping and sliding, his body pouring with sweat, the cycle lamp, clutched in his hand, illuminating the puddles, throwing blinding reflections from the black, treacly mud, sparkling from the sleet crystals which had caught in the undergrowth. After a hundred yards or so he had to stop, doubled up with an agonising stitch in his side. He put his hand to his hip, gasping. It was then he saw a figure in the shadows.

He froze, the stitch vanishing as though by magic. Slowly he straightened. He fought the urge to switch off the torch. Whoever it was would have seen where he was by now anyway. Slowly he swept the light around in an arc, playing it on the slick black of the branches, seeing the shadows shrink back and regroup just beyond the reach of the beam. He was holding his breath. If it was Kate or Greg they would have come forward at once when they saw him. The picture of Bill's battered, dead face swam up before his eyes and he thought for a moment he was going to black out. He took several steps backwards, feeling twigs and thorns tearing at his jersey, but he felt safer with the narrow trunk of a spruce at his back, solid between his shoulderblades. At least no one could get him from behind. Under the tree the smell of resin was clean and sharp and strong. It cleared his head a little. Once again he swept the torch round. There was no one there. No one in sight. He crouched lower trying to steady his breathing which sounded deafening in his ears.

He wasn't sure how long he stayed there. Perhaps five minutes, perhaps much longer, but suddenly he realised that he was shivering violently. The sleet was soaking into his thick sweater and he was ice cold. There was no sign of any movement in the trees. Whoever it was had long gone. Cautiously, he forced his cramped legs to move, crawling out of his hiding place and straightening up. He swept the rapidly-dimming lamp round once more. Nothing. He looked left and right up the track, seeing it disappear into the distance and he felt a sudden moment of total terror. Which way was home? In his panic he had lost his bearings completely. He closed his eyes. Idiot. Nerd. Keep calm. He knew this track like the palm of his own hand. Look for a landmark; he had always prided himself that he could recognise any tree in the wood.

He swept the lamp around again, concentrating this time on the vegetation. But it all looked so different in the dark; so sinister. For a moment he was afraid he was going to cry. His eyes were stinging suspiciously; he had never felt so desolate or so lost in his whole life, but as he cast one last desperate glance around, he spotted the lone pine. It was a tree they all knew well – a tree which rose head and shoulders above the others in the wood, an ancient Scots pine whose distinctive shape had been out of range of his torch as he flashed it around. With a sheepish grin of relief he headed towards it, realising that he was barely ten minutes from the farmhouse.

As he rounded the barn he caught sight of someone crouched in the lee of the wall and he stopped abruptly. Whoever it was was not moving. He glanced at the house, reassured by the comforting sight of light pouring from the downstairs windows, then he looked again at the figure. His cycle lamp had barely enough strength to light the path at his feet, but he shone it warily in the direction of the barn wall.

'Allie?' His voice was hoarse. 'Allie, is that you?' He took a few steps closer. 'Allie?' He ran towards her. 'Allie, what is it? What are you doing out here? What's wrong?' Catching his sister by the arm he swung her to her feet.

She stared at him. Her eyes were hard and blank. There was a deep scratch down one side of her face from her temple to her jaw and her hands, he saw as he pulled her towards him, were raw and bleeding.

'Come in, Allie.' His voice was urgent. 'Come in. Quickly.' He glanced over his shoulder. There was a murderer out there in the woods and by the look of things he had already attacked his sister.

Pushing open the front door he half carried, half dragged Alison in. 'Ma!' He propelled her into the living room. 'Ma!'

Diana flew towards them. 'Dear God! Alison! What happened to her?'

Patrick bit his lip. He shook his head, for a moment unable to speak, watching as Diana guided Alison towards the chair next to the fire and knelt beside her, chafing her hands.

Behind him his father had risen from the kitchen table where he had been staring blankly at *The Times* crossword for the last forty minutes. After a first horrified glance at his daughter, Roger turned to his son. He was appalled at the expression on Patrick's face. Putting his arm round the boy's shoulders he guided him back to the kitchen and sat him down at the end of the table. Without a word he reached into the cupboard and produced a bottle of brandy. Pouring a quarter of an inch into a tumbler from the draining board he pressed the glass into his son's hand. 'Drink first. Then tell me,' he instructed.

Patrick took a sip from the glass. His eyes started to stream. 'It's the brandy. Making my eyes water,' he whispered. 'It's the brandy.'

His father's hand was on his shoulder. 'It's OK old chap. It's OK. Take your time.' Roger glanced over Patrick's head towards his wife. She was tucking a blanket around Alison's knees. The girl had not spoken or moved since she had sat down.

'Give her some brandy, Di,' Roger called. He pushed the bottle across the table.

Diana looked at him. Her face was white as she left Alison's side. She stood for a moment staring down at Patrick. 'What's happened to them, Roger? What in God's name has happened to them?'

Patrick took another gulp from his glass. He was clutching it so tightly his knuckles shone white through his chapped skin. Taking a deep shuddering breath he looked up at his father. 'Bill Norcross is dead. He's at the cottage. He's been murdered.' His eyes flooded with tears again and this time he made no effort to hide them. 'His head is all bashed about, and his face . . .' He drank again, the glass trembling so much in his hands his parents could hear it banging against his teeth. 'I couldn't find Kate or Greg. I called and called. The cottage was empty so I came back, then I got a puncture and I saw someone skulking in the woods . . .'

Roger sat down abruptly. His face was grey. He closed his eyes as a wave of pain shook his body. 'Try the phone again, Di. Perhaps by now they've reconnected it.'

For a moment she didn't move, then she turned and ran towards the study.

Alison watched her with blank eyes. 'The truth has to be told,' she said slowly. She pushed the blanket away and staggered to her feet.

Her mother stopped abruptly in the doorway. 'Allie? What do you mean. Did you see what happened?'

Alison smiled. 'It was Marcus. She's told me everything. It was Marcus. He killed them all.' Stooping, she picked up Serendipity who was curled up on the sofa, and cuddled him in her arms.

'Killed them all?' Diana whispered. Her mouth fell open in horror. 'Killed who?'

Alison smiled again. She kissed the top of the cat's head. 'All of them. All in the same grave.'

'Who?' Roger was suddenly there behind them. He grabbed his daughter's arm and swung her to face him. The cat gave a yowl and fought free of her grip, leaving a long scratch along her arm but she didn't appear to notice. 'Alison! Answer me. Who has been murdered? Where is your brother?' Diana's gasp of horror was lost in his next shout. 'Alison! Can you hear me? Who has been murdered?'

'All of them.' She smiled vaguely. 'Did you expect him to let them live?'

Roger swung round to face his son. 'What does she mean? Did you see the Land Rover? Did Greg get to the cottage?'

Patrick nodded. 'It was parked outside.'

'So he must have seen the –' he paused. 'He must have seen Bill there.'

'I suppose so.' Patrick took a deep breath. 'Someone had put plasters on his face. He was tucked up on the sofa. Someone had tried to look after him.'

'Greg and Kate perhaps.' Diana clutched at the thought. 'They must have found him. Tried to help him.'

'We need the police.' Roger frowned. 'Did you try the phone?'

Diana shook her head. She was staring at her daughter who had not moved. Alison was standing before the fire, her arms hanging loose in front of her. From the scratch on her left forearm the blood dripped slowly and steadily onto the carpet.

Roger strode past her towards his study. In thirty seconds he was back. 'It's still dead.' His face was grim. 'I'll have to take the car and try and get help from Joe's.'

He glanced at Patrick who was still sitting at the kitchen table, staring deep into his empty tumbler.

'Paddy!' His voice was sharp as he used the baby name for his son which Patrick hated so much.

Patrick jumped. He looked up at his father. There was bewilderment in his eyes.

'Patrick, your mother must stay here and look after Alison. I'm going to leave you here to take care of them both. I want you to lock the door behind me, and bolt it. You are not to let anyone in. Anyone at all, do you hear?'

'Dad, you can't go.' Patrick rubbed his sleeve across his face. He was shivering again in the soaking wet clothes. 'Let me take the Volvo. I know how to drive it.'

'He's right, Roger. You can't go.' Diana looked from Alison to her husband and back in an agony of indecision. 'It should be me.'

'No. Alison needs you.' Roger shook his head.

'I can do it, Dad,' Patrick said quietly.

The fact that Roger hesitated even for a second showed more clearly than any words just how weak and ill he was feeling, but he shook his head slowly. 'Not in this weather. It's too dangerous. And it's not as though I have to do anything but sit there and let the car do the work. I'll drive it up to the road and along to Joe's. Joe will do the rest and bring me back.' He hesitated, seeing the strange mixture of emotions cross his son's face and reading them all. Relief that he did not have to go out again; worry about his father; indignation and mortification that he was not considered old enough to cope.

Roger sighed. 'Get the car out of the barn for me, there's a good chap.' He smiled. 'I'll get my coat.' He took Patrick's arm and drew him to one side. 'You'd be more use here, old chap. If anything happens.' He glanced at his son's face and knew that the sop he had just thrown to the boy's pride was in fact the truth. 'You're stronger than me. You can protect them better. I want you to load the shotgun and keep it in here near you.'

Patrick stared. Then he nodded. 'I'll get the car.'

Unhooking the keys from the small rack behind the door he pulled it open and peered out. He didn't want to go out again. Outside was hostile and frightening. It had lost all the safety and charm he had known all his life – the secret wonder of the black sky sewn with stars, the rushing clouds, even the rain and snow. He had loved them all for that special clean fresh smell that comes at night, that quietness which enfolds the countryside and wipes out for a few hours all the brash horror of the twentieth century.

Shutting the door behind him Patrick sprinted across to the barn. Pulling open the heavy double doors he groped for the light pull and dragged it on, flooding the huge, shadowy building with a harsh blue light from the double strip of lights which hung, crazily crooked, from their chains and electric cables twenty feet above the ground. There was an uneasy rustle from above him in the rafters and he heard a querulous piping cry. Some bird, roosting there out of the wind, was bitterly resenting his intrusion.

He opened the door of the car and slid behind the steering wheel, slamming the door behind him and ramming down the locks. It was bitterly cold in there. His breath fogged the windscreen. Glancing through it with a frown he pulled out the choke and turned the key. The faithful old car started first go and he sat there for a few minutes, teasing the accelerator with his toe, feeling the cold engine warm slowly into life. Frowning with concentration he engaged reverse gear, and craning over his shoulder, he backed the car out through the impenetrable trails of its own exhaust and swung it backwards towards the house, parking it neatly outside the front door. Mission accomplished.

Climbing out he hesitated for a moment then he reached in and turned off the engine. Locking the door, he let himself back into the house. No point in leaving the car there, engine running.

He watched his father wrap himself in coat and muffler and turned away, pretending not to see Roger slipping a bottle of pills into his pocket. He didn't need reminding that his father was in terrible pain. The strain of his face and the pallor of his skin told it all.

'Here.' Roger handed him a key. 'The gun cupboard. I'm serious, Paddy. Load it and keep it near you. And check every door and window is locked and bolted after I've gone. I'll be back as soon as I can.'

'Be careful, Roger.' Diana ran to him and threw her arms around his neck. 'I shouldn't be letting you go like this. Oh, darling, be careful.'

He smiled grimly. 'I will. Don't worry.' He turned to the door and pulled it open. In the few short minutes since Patrick had come in the sleet had turned to snow. It whirled down out of the sky and already it was settling in the sheltered corners of the garden. He frowned as he peered through it then he turned. 'Where did you leave the car?'

'Right there. Outside.' Patrick gestured past him. He frowned and took a step past his father.

The car had gone.

Patrick's mouth fell open. He stared round helplessly. 'But I left it here. Here.' He stood where he had parked it. In the light spilling out from the front door the faint rectangular outline in the snow where the car had been parked was clearly visible. He looked up at his father, distraught.

'You didn't put the brake on,' Roger said slowly. He was frowning. The patch of gravel where the car had been was totally level.

'I did.' Patrick contradicted hotly. 'Of course I bloody did! And I locked it. It's been taken. He must have been watching me all the time.' He could feel the hair standing up on the back of his neck. 'He must have broken in and hot wired it.'

'It only took me three minutes to come out after you parked it, Patrick,' his father said slowly. 'No one could break into a car that fast. Not without taking a sledge hammer to the window and we'd have heard that. The brakes can't have been on.' He was staring down at the ground.

In the thin covering of snow there was no sign of any car tracks.

XLIII

Marcus stared at the woman who was his wife and his eyes were hard. She had never looked so beautiful. Her hair was wild, loose in the wind, her eyes fiery as she ran towards him. He gave a cold smile, his arms folded across his chest, aware of the priests drawing away from them, aware of the body sinking slowly, face down, in the soft mud of the marsh. The blood red of the sunrise spilt across the reeds, reflecting in the still waters around them. She was running towards him, but it seemed to take forever for her to reach him, to lift her hand, her nails clawed, towards his face, to duck beneath his raised arm and snatch the sword snugly sheathed at his belt. He stepped back to protect himself and she laughed. The sound made his blood curdle. She raised the sword. 'Curse you, Marcus. Curse you. Curse you. You will not keep me from him.'

The sword seemed to catch for a moment against the flimsy stuff of her gown. Then it was free, sliding into her belly like a knife through cheese. She stood for a moment, upright, strong, proud, her fists still clenched around the hilt as she pulled it towards her, not acknowledging the pain, a daughter of Rome, then slowly her knees began to sag as the blood splashed out over her skirt.

Kate swung round, her eyes straining in the darkness. She had the feeling someone was standing behind her. 'Greg?' She glanced round wildly, but she couldn't see him; she had walked farther than she thought. The beach was deserted. There was no sign of him sitting on the sand. Her heart began to pound unsteadily as if she had been running and she felt her mouth go dry. She clutched the piece of drift-wood she had picked up from the tide edge, feeling it cold and wet and solid against her fingers and slowly she began to retrace her steps, straining her eyes into the darkness. Dear God, where was he? She could feel little trickles of panic running up her back. He couldn't have gone. He wouldn't have gone. He had to be there somewhere. She dashed the sleet out of her eyes, realising as she did so that it was more like snow now, light and feathery, caressing her skin where before it had been hard and sharp.

There it was again. The strange conviction that there was someone near her. Someone beside her, close beside her, so close she could feel the heat of his body, sense his bulk. 'Idiot!' In her fear she spoke out loud. She veered towards the sea trying to free herself of the feeling and felt a wave breaking over her boots, showering her with spray. She jumped back out of reach of the next and felt it again – the absolute conviction that there was a man standing beside her. She stopped walking and stood quite still staring round. There was no one there. It was some trick of the wind and the weather. Gritting her teeth she turned her back on the sea and began to walk up the beach. 'Greg!' Tucking the piece of wood beneath her arm she cupped her hands around her mouth. 'Greg! Where are you?' Trudging wearily on she scanned the darkness again. She frowned. She had suddenly realised that she was heading back towards the sea. Somehow in the dark she had turned completely round and, without noticing it, she had strayed back below the high water mark in a lull between waves. The roar of the sea and the wind had disorientated her and now she could see a wave racing towards her. She froze. It towered up above the rest like a tidal wave. Tsunami. The word flashed into her mind unsought. Desperately she turned to run but she couldn't. She seemed to be rooted to the spot. It was as if someone were holding her, forcing her forward towards the onrushing water. She could almost feel the grip on her arms, propelling her onwards.

'Greg!' She heard her voice rising into a scream as the towering water seemed to lift above her head. 'Greg!'

As the water crashed forward over her, knocking her backwards onto the shingle the last thing she heard before the roaring filled her ears was a man's laugh.

She awoke to find Greg bending over her. 'Thank God you're all right. Oh Christ, Kate, I don't know what's going on.' He was lying beside her, she realised, his body shielding hers, one arm across her almost as though they had been making love. He must have dragged himself towards her over the wet shingle, his poor useless foot agony as he moved. 'I saw the wave. I saw him push you. I thought you were dead.' He clutched at her hand, holding it against his chest.

Desperately she tried to clear her head so she could think. 'Who pushed me?'

'Marcus. It was Marcus, Kate. I saw his toga, his cloak, I saw his sword. He was beside you, then he pushed you towards the sea and I saw that great bloody wave rising up . . .' He leaned forward and laid his head on her chest. It was a strangely comforting feeling – completely unsexual. She reached up and stroked his hair.

'Marcus doesn't exist, Greg. He's not real. He's a statue. A joke. An imaginary ghost.'

'There was nothing imaginary about him.' He was mumbling into her jacket. 'He was real. I saw him push you. I saw you shoot forward towards that wave. He was real, he tried to take over my mind. He's done it before, and each time I've pushed him away. I didn't realise what was happening; I didn't understand. But now, for some reason he wants us both dead.'

She lay back for a moment, staring up at the sky, her eyes narrowed against the softly drifting snow. It was falling harder now, settling higher up the beach out of reach of the water, clogging the dunes, drifting before the wind. 'Why? Why does he want us dead?'

He shook his head. 'I don't know. It's something to do with that bloody grave. We've disturbed him.'

'It's not his grave. He's buried in Colchester.' She rolled towards him, dislodging his head so that he was lying face down next to her. Gently she put her hand on his back. 'Can you turn over? Let me help you to sit up. We've got to try and find some shelter.' Where was her carefully garnered piece of wood? She glanced round but there was no sign of it in the darkness. The sea must have snatched it from her before it tossed her back on the beach. She dragged herself up to her knees, groaning. Her whole body seemed to be one big bruise. She was soaked to the skin and already she could feel herself growing seriously cold. If they were not careful they were both going to die of hypothermia.

Greg, with a small sigh had lain back on the sand and closed his eyes. For a moment she felt total panic. He was dead. He had just died, next to her, between one moment and the next, like Bill. 'Greg!' Her voice rose to a scream.

He opened his eyes and smiled. 'You have a plan?'

Her relief was so overwhelming she nearly kissed him. 'We have to keep moving. However much it hurts you. It's the only way to stay alive. Sod Marcus. If he comes near us again we'll pray or something. Doesn't that chase off ghosts? We'll make the sign of the cross. The sign against the evil eye. They are always doing that in historical novels and it always works.'

Greg's smile deepened. 'Do you know what the sign against the evil eye is?' He seemed to be content to lie there. Like her, a moment before, he could feel the soft engulfing peace of the snow closing over him.

'I'm sure I can work it out. Come on, Greg. Move. You've got to move. Try and roll over. If you crawl, you can keep your weight off the foot. Come on. You mustn't give in.'

With a groan he obeyed her, swinging himself over until he was lying with his face pressed into the cold, wet sand. A shaft of pain shot through him and he felt the heat of his own sweat like a mantle flowing over his cold body. With a grunt he dug his elbows into the sand and dragged himself forward a couple of feet. Falling flat again he groaned out loud. 'It's going to take me a while, like this.'

'It may take all night, but we're going to do it.' She was grim. 'If you can't do it that way you'll have to stand up and lean on me.'

'It's tempting, but I think if I try and stand I'll pass out again.' He clenched his fists and with a superhuman effort dragged himself forward again. Then he collapsed. 'It's no use. I can't do it. You've got to go for the Land Rover. It can't be far to the cottage.' He raised his head with an effort and squinted into the whirling snow, willing it into view.

'I can't leave you, Greg.' She was kneeling in front of him.

'You must or we'll both die. I'll be OK. I'll keep moving forward, like this, parallel with the sea. Don't attempt to drive down onto the soft sand. Keep to the firmer stuff away from the dunes. Just get as near as you can. Realistically, we'll only survive if we get into the Land Rover. I've had it and you're soaked through. Even if it does get bogged down we'll have a chance in there and they'll find us more easily.' He dragged himself up onto his elbows. 'Do it, Kate. Here, take the keys. They're in my pocket.' He groped painfully inside his Barbour and withdrew them with numb fingers. Dropping them into her palm he forced himself to smile.

Her hand closed over them. She looked at him in despair. He was right. He couldn't get back on his own.

She climbed to her feet and began to drag off her jacket.

'No, don't be a fool.' He shook his head angrily. 'You need it as much as I do. The slightest move leaves me pouring with sweat. I'll be all right. You keep it on and get back as fast as you can.'

She nodded grimly. For a moment longer she hesitated, then she turned and began to run unsteadily back down the beach, the wind behind her now, which made it easier, without the snow and sleet in her eyes.

Her exhaustion seemed to have reached a plateau where pain and chill had withdrawn behind some automatic programmed response. On and on she went, sometimes slowing to a walk, sometimes jogging, faintly aware that part of her was listening over her shoulder for the sound of pursuit. But pursuit by whom? Marcus?

Snatching great lungfuls of air, she pounded on, driven by her fear. She had to get back to the cottage. She had to find the Land Rover. There was no question of getting lost with the sea constantly at her left hand, crashing on the shore, drawing infinitesimally back, worrying the sand like an animal reluctant to abandon its prey, yet glancing up the beach again she found she was beginning to panic. Where was the cottage? Surely she should be able to see the lights from the windows by now. She had left them on. She remembered distinctly. She had left them on because she could not bear to leave poor Bill in the dark. Tears flooded her eyes and she brushed at them with the wet, icy sleeve of her jacket and stopped.

Bending double she drew in great rasping gulps of air, not daring to look behind her, keeping her eyes strained into the darkness. Then, suddenly she saw it. The rising silhouette of the dunes against the white of the distant trees, and the angular black shape which was a roof. There was no sign of any light from the upstairs windows.

She swallowed, willing her heartbeat to slow down as she turned her back on the sea and looked for the track between the dunes. The cottage garden was white with snow; beneath the wall it had drifted in the wind and was heaped into shallow piles already several inches thick. Not giving herself time to think she followed the wall towards the front and peered round it. The Land Rover stood where they had left it. She closed her eyes and sank against the wall, weak with relief. It was only at that moment that she realised that she had half expected it to have gone. Leaving the shelter of the wall she walked towards it, then she stopped abruptly. The front door of the cottage was wide open.

'Bill.' Her lips framed the words silently. Her stomach was churning suddenly and her legs seemed incapable of co-ordinated movement, but somehow she forced herself to walk towards the door. Light poured out of the hall, showing the snow white and clean. There were no signs of any footprints.

She crept to the door and peered in. The sitting room door was open and she could see the curtains blowing against the window. The cottage stank of vomit. 'Allie?' Her voice came out as a croak. 'Allie?' she tried again. 'Are you there?'

The effort of will required to force herself to walk forward and peer into the room was enormous, but somehow she managed it. It was as she had left it. Bill still lay on the sofa; nothing had been touched. Cautiously she stepped inside. The woodburner had cooled down. There was no welcoming glow from it now. The room was distinctly chilly. She took another step forward, pressing her forearm against her mouth and nose in an attempt to filter out the evil smell in the room and stopped, overwhelmed with horror and disgust. The blanket which she had drawn over Bill's face had been pulled back. His face, blue and puffy was turned towards her, his eyes half open, staring blindly straight at her. In front of him on the floor was a pool of vomit.

Turning she ran back towards the front door, trying

desperately to control her own retching. She tore out of the house and running to the Land Rover, slumped over the bonnet, her head cradled in her arms, her stomach feeling as though it were somersaulting against the back of her throat. For several seconds she stood still, fighting her nausea, her legs trembling, then at last she managed to grope in her pocket for the keys. She found them and staggered to the driver's door, trying desperately to insert one in the lock. It was several seconds before she realised that the door was not locked. Dragging it open she pulled herself onto the seat and slammed it shut. Then she burst into tears.

Her glasses. She had lost her glasses. Sniffing frantically she groped in her jacket with shaking hands until at last she found them, pushed into an inner pocket. Rubbing her eyes with her wet sleeve, she put them on and leaning forward she inserted the key into the ignition. Fumbling with the unfamiliar gears, she slammed the gearstick back and forth until she managed to find first and at last she pulled the heavy vehicle round to face the sea and jerkily she began to drive towards the dunes.

'Come on. Come on. Please don't get stuck, you bastard, please don't get stuck,' she begged, her voice husky as she peered forward desperately through the streaked windscreen.

The Land Rover lurched across the grass and down onto the sand, its tyres slipping and sliding but somehow keeping a grip on the shifting, wet surface of the beach as she threaded her way at a snail's pace between the dunes, the headlights catching a whirling wall of sand and snow and sleet. When at last she saw the sea, it was a barrier of angry white rising in front of her, hurling itself at the land. Biting her lip she tore the wheel round, heading north now, keeping the vehicle moving at a steady walking pace, every muscle tense as she willed the wheels to keep their traction. Where was he? Oh please God, let her find him. She had never felt so lonely in her life, with her eyes straining frantically ahead, scanning the beach and the dunes to her left as she looked for Greg's hunched figure on the sand. She hadn't been too long, surely? She cursed the time she had wasted weeping like some useless, spineless feeble fool, and desperately she pulled the vehicle further away from the sea as it lurched into a weed-strewn rutted pool and ground to a halt. 'Oh, no!' She juggled the clutch and accelerator desperately, trying hard not to drive in deeper. 'Please. Please, come on.' She wrenched the gear levers back and forth frantically as the car rocked forwards and lurched to a standstill again, the wheels spinning. 'Damn you!' She hit the steering wheel in fury. 'Come on. Come on!' In the cold remorseless beam of the headlights the beach was unrelentingly empty of life. Sleet whirled in the double light beams, the sand gleamed coldly and beyond it, even above the sound of the engine, she could hear the angry roar of the sea. Biting her lips in concentration she tried a new combination of gears and suddenly, wonderfully, the old vehicle lurched into life and dragged itself out of the hollow, shaking itself free like some great hippopotamus which had been wallowing in the mud. 'Be careful.' Kate was talking to herself openly now. 'Be careful you silly cow. Look where you're going. Next time you won't get out.' Her hands gripping the wheel so tightly her knuckles cracked, she leaned forward again, peering into the shadows at the edge of the headlight beams.

Midnight: the witching hour, in this empty, godforsaken, lonely place.

Where in the name of God was he?

XLIV

'Allie?' Diana leaned over her daughter's bed. 'Allie, can you hear me, darling?' The child was cold again, her skin clammy, but she wasn't shivering. After her first outburst she had said nothing at all as her mother led her upstairs, ran a hot bath and helped her undress. Normally Allie would have protested wildly at the thought of Diana even coming into the bathroom while she bathed but now she stood meekly while Diana undressed her, lifting her arms obediently like a small child as her mother pulled off her sweater and tee shirt, and stepping quietly into the bath. Sitting down she drew up her knees and hugged them, resting her chin on them, eyes closed, as Diana sponged her back with warm water. 'Do you want to lie back for a bit to thaw out?' The child was so thin. How had she not noticed that she was losing so much weight? Diana went on sponging, watching, horrified, as the scented water trickled down Allie's staring ribs and around the prominent knobs of her backbone. 'Allie, did you hear me? Do you want to lie down and have a bit of a soak?'

The shake of the head was barely visible.

'Come out then. Let's get you into bed,' Diana spoke briskly. 'Then I want you to tell me what happened. Did you see Greg and Kate?'

Alison stood woodenly whilst her mother towelled her dry and moved her limbs with the same automaton jerkiness as before as her nightshirt was pulled over her head. Obediently she allowed Diana to lead her to her bedroom and there she climbed into bed. It was only as Diana put the teddy into her arms that she showed any emotion at all. Clutching the toy against her chest she turned on her side, pulling her knees up below her chin until she was curled in the foetal position, and she began to cry.

'Allie, sweetheart.' Sitting on the bed beside her, Diana put her hand on the girl's shoulder. She felt helpless and afraid. 'Sweetheart, please. Don't cry. You're safe now.'

But Alison went on crying, sobbing into the teddy bear's fur until at last she fell asleep.

Diana sat there for a long time, her hand on her daughter's thin shoulder then at last she stood up. Turning off the main light she left the small bedside lamp burning and, leaving the door ajar, she tiptoed out of the room.

The living room was empty. 'Roger? Paddy?' She went quickly to the study. That too was empty. 'Roger?' Her voice rose in panic. 'Patrick? Where are you?' She retraced her steps to the front door and pulled it open. The front garden and the grass which led down to the saltings were a uniform white beneath the whirling darkness. There was no sign of her husband or her son. Closing the door again she bolted it and walked slowly back to the fire. They must have both decided to go up to the main road after all. She stared round the room. The two cats were sitting together on the sofa, a pair of recumbent lions, shoulder to shoulder, staring into the embers of the fire. The sight of them reassured her, but for the first time for years she found herself wishing they had a dog. If there was someone out there in the woods a dog would at least alert them. Her gaze went thoughtfully to the shotgun which Roger had left propped in the corner, a box of cartridges on the chair beside it.

Unable to sit down and relax she walked through into the kitchen and began to tidy it. She was on automatic pilot. Her entire concentration was fixed outside the house, listening.

* * *

'We should have brought the gun, Dad.' Patrick was scared. He kept as close as he could to his father as they walked up the track. At their feet the torch beam was searching the ruts for any sign of footprints or tyre marks.

'It's not thick snow. It's hardly settled here, under the trees. If he'd come this way we would have spotted something by now.' Roger was indignant rather than scared.

He did not believe that there was a murderer skulking in the woods. Whoever had attacked Bill would be long gone by now. He stopped, glaring down at the pale circle of torchlight as it rested on a patch of muddy pine needles gleaming with watery sludge. It made no sense, all the same, to take unnecessary risks. The car had not come this way. Of that he was convinced. And they had left Diana alone in the farmhouse. Better to go home and search again outside the door where the car had been standing. A stranger might after all, have driven off across the garden. No, he halted that train of thought. There had been no trail of destruction through the bare flowerbeds. The other possibility was that he had driven across the lawn and down onto the marsh. The garden was more exposed on that side of the house. Perhaps the snow had indeed hidden the tracks or they had missed them in their initial panic at finding the car gone.

He led the way back, swinging the torchlight left and right this time, scanning the darkness between the trees, conscious that Patrick was so close beside him that he could feel the boy's shoulder brushing his own. He found himself wishing suddenly for both their sakes that Patrick was small enough to be held by the hand.

Outside the front door they stopped. Roger drew a deep sigh of relief. The pain was coming back. He could walk no further. He followed Patrick to the door and waited, leaning against the wall while Patrick banged on it, thankful that the darkness hid his face.

The door opened within seconds and Diana fell on them

both. Hugging them to her she dragged them to the fire. 'Thank God! Did you get through? Is the doctor coming? And the police?'

She looked from one to the other and her face fell. 'You didn't get there, did you?' she said in a small voice. She sat down abruptly.

Roger sank down beside her and took her hand. He shook his head. 'The car's gone, Di. It's been stolen.' He leaned back and closed his eyes.

'So he was here. Right here outside this house.' Her eyes went to the curtained window near her. She closed them weakly, slumping against Roger's shoulder. 'What are we going to do?'

'Nothing. Not tonight.' Roger was suddenly so tired he could hardly speak. 'We'll just have to pray that Greg and Kate are together and safe. Greg will look after her . . .'

His voice trailed away as he thought suddenly about Bill. Bill was a man; a big man and he had not been safe.

'It will help no one if we go searching for them in the dark. Far better to keep ourselves safe here until daylight. We'll check again that all the windows and doors are locked and wait it out. There is nothing else we can do.'

'I'll check, Dad.' Patrick had been standing looking down at his parents. He fought off the wave of fear which had been building inside him as he realised suddenly and completely that they were as helpless and afraid as he was; that for the first time that he could remember they were not going to be able to bail him or themselves out of the situation.

His father looked up at him and their eyes met. 'It'll be OK.' Roger gave a wan smile. 'We'll sort it all out in daylight.'

'Sure, Dad.' Patrick turned towards the stairs. Then he stopped. 'Greg's going to be all right, isn't he?'

'A great big chap like Greg? Of course he is.'

'But he wasn't in the cottage.'

'I expect they were looking for Allie.'

'And he doesn't know she's safe.' Patrick's voice rose unsteadily. 'They'll go on looking, Dad. Greg won't give up.'

'They'll be all right, Paddy.' Diana forced herself to stand up. 'Greg is not a fool. He'll realise there is nothing he can do in this weather. He and Kate will go back to the cottage or they'll come here. Now you go upstairs and check everything's all right, while I put the kettle on. Don't wake Allie, but double check her window too.'

She watched her younger son nod and turn away. Then she glanced down at her husband. His face was grey, his eyes shut. Miserably she pulled the rug from the back of the chair where she had folded it that morning – yesterday morning, she corrected herself as she glanced at her watch – and she tucked it round him, then she went to the Aga and slid the kettle onto the hotplate.

XLV

Kate stopped the Land Rover and closed her eyes. There
was no sign of him. She had driven up and down the beach
three times slowly, edging the vehicle closer and closer to
the water's edge, taking it as far to the north as she dared,
far beyond the area where they had walked. He must have
wandered up into the dunes where, she knew, she did not
dare to try and drive. All she could do was go back slowly,
further from the tideline this time, hoping he had seen her
lights and was even now trying to drag himself towards
them.

Cautiously she let in the clutch, turning this time towards
the sea for one last sweep of the boiling waves with the
headlights. It was then she saw him. He was kneeling at
the water's edge, waving at her.

'Greg!' Incautiously she accelerated towards him and for
an awful moment she felt the wheels lose their grip and
spin, then she was near him. Drawing to a halt she leapt
out. 'I couldn't find you.' Shaking her hair back out of her
eyes she ran to throw her arms around him.

For a moment he didn't move then she felt him return
the hug, his mouth against her hair. 'Kate. Oh, Kate,' he
murmured. For several seconds they clung together, then
gently she freed herself.

'Come on. Try and stand. We'll put you in the back so
you can rest your leg along the seat.' He was desperately
cold. She could feel the chill from his body through his wet
clothes. 'Come on, Greg. You've got to stand up. I can't
lift you.'

He was staring at the vehicle. 'But I saw you. I saw you

out there.' He gestured behind him, towards the sea. 'I heard you call me. I was crawling towards you, then this wave came and drenched me again.'

She glanced up. 'You've lost your bearings and come right back down the beach. Come on. Stand on your good leg. I daren't bring the car any closer to the edge. You'll have to hop.'

'I can't.' He subsided onto the wet sand again with a groan. 'I've had it. I can't move.'

'You can. You've got to. ' She gritted her teeth. 'Come on. You can't give up now.' She hauled at his arm. 'I'll find something for you to lean on. You've got to try, Greg.' She was growing frantic.

'OK, OK.' He tried to shake his head. Spray and sleet were cold on his face; tears and sweat, hot. The salt mixture ran into his eyes, blinding him. He could see someone standing behind her. Why didn't she help? It was a woman. Not Allie. Not Ma. 'Give me a hand. Please.' His words were slurring. He felt Kate's arm strong under his; then her shoulder as he hauled himself up. The other woman was helping, no, she was gone. Where was she? He felt his knees buckle. He could not put his left foot on the sand. The rush of the waves filled his head; dimly he could see the outline of the Land Rover. The back door was open. Inside it was safety, warmth, rest. With a superhuman effort he launched himself towards it with three massive hops on his good leg, throwing himself half in through the door. Then he lost consciousness again.

'Greg! Greg!' Kate bent over him. 'Come on, one more effort.' The car was a haven. She wanted them both inside and the doors locked. Behind them the beach was hostile, threatening.

She glanced over her shoulder and saw the shadow; the woman hovering near them. Her skin crawled. The blue dress was still stained; it did not blow in the wind; the sleet did not seem to wet the woman's hair, but she was watching them and Kate could smell her scent. Over the wind and the sleet and the salt smell of sea and sand and weed she could still smell that flowery perfume. She felt sick. Her terror was so great she could not move for a moment. Only a groan from Greg jerked her back from her terrified fascination. She turned. 'Get in, Greg. Get in quickly,' she said urgently. 'Just crawl. Quickly.'

Something of the panic in her voice reached him through the black haze. His hands scrabbled at the seat in front of him; somehow he dragged himself along it and lay, panting, clawing at it to give himself purchase. Behind him Kate caught him round the hips and shoved at him with all her might. Without regard to his injured foot she caught his knees and folded them in behind him and slammed the door on him.

Spinning round she stared out into the night as a new flurry of snow whirled in across the beach. Where was she? She could see nothing now. Desperately she turned and fled round the car, grappling with the driver's door handle, dragging it open and flinging herself into the seat before slamming the door behind her and banging down the lock. With a cry of relief she slumped back to try and get her breath.

The white shape which hurtled onto the bonnet was so close in front of her she let out a scream. She saw a huge, bloodshot eye. Something crashed down on the windscreen and she saw a splintering crack shiver down the glass. 'No!' she flattened herself against the back of the seat, bringing up her arm instinctively to protect her face. 'No! Please! *Greg!*'

Greg stirred. He found himself lying face down on the rough rug spread on the back seat. He clutched at it convulsively and felt an agonising pain shoot up his left leg which appeared to have been folded in half beside him on the floor. 'Kate?' His voice was indistinct, muffled in the rug. 'Kate, where are you?'

'Here!' Her whisper barely reached him. 'Greg. Help! Look!' The fear in her voice reached him through the swimming veil of pain. With an enormous effort he raised his head. Somehow he managed to move sideways, dragging himself up into a sitting position. His teeth were chattering and his body was seized by a wave of violent rigors as he tried to focus on Kate. 'I'm here. I'm here.' He clutched at the back of the seat.

Her eyes still fixed on the windscreen she did not turn round. 'Look.'

It was still there — a huge, flapping white object. Again she saw the eye, yellow, threatening, and then a vicious curved beak. Kate flinched, raising her arm to protect herself, closing her eyes in terror as with a resounding clang a sharp blow descended on the already shivered windscreen.

'Kate — ?' Greg's voice was blurred and indistinct.

'It's a gull!' She was sobbing with fear and relief. 'It's a huge gull.' For a moment the whirl of flapping wings and the cruel eyes and vicious beak resolved themselves into a clear outline, the webbed feet scrabbling for a foothold on the bonnet, and then it had gone, launching itself off into the wind and out of sight.

Kate reached for the ignition. Her hands were shaking so much she could hardly start the engine. Frantically she grabbed at the gear lever and shoved it forward. The Land Rover jerked and stalled.

'Well done.' It was almost a chuckle from the back. Kate started the engine again. Forcing herself to be calm she engaged reverse gear and let in the clutch with more care. The Land Rover backed away from the sea, the headlights sweeping the beach. 'I can't see it. There's no sign.'

'I don't think we'll send out a search party. Let's get out of here. Can you see all right? See if you can get back to the track.' Greg gritted his teeth as a new wave of pain hit him. Ignoring it he pulled at the rug on the seat and dragged it around his shoulders. The dim interior of the Land Rover was beginning to swim around him once more.

'I think we're on our way.' Kate glanced back at the sea. Was the tide retreating at last? It seemed to be farther away, certainly, and the force of the wind seemed less. Cautiously she turned the vehicle south, keeping parallel to the waves, and began to drive back towards the cottage. Straining forward to see through the slivered glass, she watched the beach; it was impossible to see where the sand was firm. All she could do was pray as at last she swung the wheel and headed up towards the dunes. It all looked so different in the headlights; the snow and the spinning sand eddies shifted and disguised the landmarks. Nothing was where it should be. She felt the Land Rover lurch sideways suddenly and she clutched at the wheel. For a moment she thought they were going to stop, then the wheels regained their grip and they were on their way again. Moments later she saw the lights of the cottage in the distance behind the dunes and muttering a short prayer of thanks, she headed doggedly towards them, threading her way round the dunes, following the path she had taken so often on foot, until at last she felt the vehicle drag itself onto the snow-covered grass.

The front door was still open but she ignored it. She had no wish to go in there again, with poor Bill still lying on the sofa. Instead she headed up the track towards Redall Farmhouse, driving more quickly now as they lurched uncomfortably over the ruts and skidded in the ice-fringed puddles, once or twice crashing over fallen branches as she drove on with gritted teeth. The petrol indicator, she had just noticed, was bouncing around the empty level. She could not believe it. They could not run out of petrol now. Not here. 'Hang on, you bastard. Just hang on.' She chewed on her lip furiously, ducking automatically as they brushed beneath the low overhanging branches of a stand of larch and slithered back onto the main track.

Through the cracked and murky windscreen she didn't see the shadow which appeared right in front of them on the track until it was barely feet from her front bumper. She slammed on the brakes, fighting to control the sliding vehicle, spun the wheel and heard with a cry of misery the resounding crack as they crashed into a tree. She was wearing no seat belt and the jolt sent her flying forward against the windscreen.

It was several seconds before she sat up, feeling herself cautiously. There was a bump the size of an egg on her forehead and she felt as though she had been kicked in the ribs by a horse but she was alive.

The headlights were directed at an angle up in the air. They had landed against a tree, with the back wheels in some sort of ditch. Even from here she knew there would be no way of getting the car out. 'Damn.' She struck the steering wheel with the flat of her hand. 'Damn, damn, damn! Greg? Are you all right?' She dragged her aching body round to look at him. He had been thrown to the floor by the impact and lay there huddled below the seat not moving. 'Oh God!' Stiffly she groped for the door handle and tried to push it open. It appeared to be jammed. She peered out again. What was it she had seen in front of her like that? She shivered. Whatever it was had gone – a figment of her overwrought imagination probably – and now the woods were empty as before.

'Greg. Greg? Are you all right?' She wrestled with the handle. 'Greg. Can you hear me?'

It was no good. She couldn't open it. She glanced across at the other door. It looked as though it might be easier to open. Climbing across into the passenger seat she pulled at the handle. After a moment it swung free and she managed to climb out. One glance past the headlights showed the front wing was buckled, the radiator had gone and the front tyre was flat. 'Damn!' She kicked the tyre as hard as she could, then she turned and dragged at the rear door.

It was locked. Shaking with panic she crawled back in the front, knelt on the seat and reached down towards him. In the darkness she couldn't see his face. 'Greg? Greg, can you hear me?'

Her small torch was still there, in her pocket. Switching it on she directed it down. He was lying face down on the floor, his body hunched, his arms trapped beneath him as though he had made no effort to save himself at all when he was flung forward. Somehow she managed to scramble over the seat and putting her arms around him, she propped him up on the floor between the seats. He groaned but he did not open his eyes. For a moment she sat still, gazing out at the harsh beam of the headlights which lit up the woods. Soon the battery would fade and they would go out. She glanced at her watch wearily. It was after two. There was nothing for it. She was going to have to leave him and go for help on foot.

Gritting her teeth she wedged the torch into her pocket, tucked the rug more closely round Greg, lowered her window half an inch for air and climbed out into the cold. 'I'll be back as soon as I can. Hang on,' she whispered. She glanced up and down the track, shining the puny, swiftly-fading beam into the trees. The only sound was the drip of melting snow and the occasional rattle of leaves.

It couldn't be more than a quarter of a mile — ten minutes' walk at most. She set off up the path, keeping to the middle of the tyre ruts, feeling her boots slip repeatedly in the icy puddles and frozen mud. Her shoulders were crawling with terror. Tensely she hunched them, sure that any moment she would feel a hand reach out and touch her, turning round repeatedly as she walked, to look into the dark. There was no one there. The silence grew deeper as the sleet slackened and the dripping of the leaves began to diminish, but always with her was the sound of her own laboured breathing and the steady flap and squeak of her rubber boots.

The sight of a light in the distance was so sudden, so wonderful, she stopped and rubbed her eyes. It was a square light, pale blue, a light shining through an upstairs window at Redall Farmhouse. With a sob she began to run, squelching through the slush, brushing the wiry branches of larch and spruce out of her way as they tangled and whipped across in front of her.

She was gasping as she ran across the snow-covered grass and flung herself towards the door, reaching frantically for the bell.

For several seconds there was no response to her frenzied ringing, then she heard footsteps on the other side. 'Who is it?' Patrick's voice was muffled.

'It's me, Kate. For God's sake let me in.'

She listened to the sound of locks being turned and the two bolts being drawn, then at last the door was open and she fell into the hall.

'Kate, thank God you're all right. But where's Greg?' Diana, still dressed, her face drawn with exhaustion, clutched at her arm.

'He's in the Land Rover. I skidded into a tree. He's hurt his foot, and I think he may have knocked his head. It's only a few hundred yards up the track. You've got to help me bring him home.'

'Dear God!' Diana looked helplessly at her younger son. There was only Patrick left to help. Roger had gone to bed at last with two of his painkillers and when she had glanced into their bedroom an hour ago he had been fast asleep, his face still white and drawn as he lay clutching the pillow in the light of the shaded bedside lamp. Allie too was asleep, breathing harshly, her mouth a little open, her expression strangely hard, although her colour had returned to normal. Quietly shutting the door on her, Diana had walked downstairs thoughtfully. The sight of her daughter had filled her with unease.

Patrick had been asleep in the chair by the fire. She had

pulled a rug over him and left him there, near the comforting embers. She had been sitting at the kitchen table drinking her third cup of coffee when Kate's frenzied knocking and ringing had startled her to her feet, awakened Patrick and sent them both into the hall to stand behind the bolted front door.

'Sit down, child and get your breath back,' Diana commanded as Kate staggered into the living room. She was soaked and muddy and her hair hung in tangled rats' tails around a face that was transparent with exhaustion.

'I think he's safe for now. I locked the doors and he's got a rug, but after Bill –' Suddenly she was crying. 'You don't know about Bill –'

'We know, Kate.' Diana put her arm round Kate's shoulders. 'Paddy went over to the cottage before the snow got so bad. Paddy, fetch the brandy, quickly,' she commanded. 'Don't try and talk, Kate, till you've got your breath back. Then we'll work out how to fetch Greg.' Her eyes went to the window. He was alone out there. Alone and injured.

'Alison –' Kate said suddenly. She tried to sit up but Diana pushed her back against the cushions. 'Don't worry about Alison, my dear. She's safe. She came home by herself. She's upstairs in bed now. All we've got to do is fetch Greg, then we can all rest.'

There was a moment's silence. They were all thinking about Bill. Poor, kind Bill. Kate wished he wasn't alone at the cottage. But there was nothing they could do for him, whilst Greg needed help urgently.

'Did Alison tell you what happened?' She opened her eyes and studied Diana's face. Exhaustion and worry were etched on the other woman's features.

'Not really. She was too cold and tired. Time enough to question her in the morning.' Diana was silent for a moment as Patrick reappeared with a tray. On it were three glasses and a bottle of cognac. He poured them each a liberal dose and handed one to Kate, then another to his mother. The fact that she said nothing when he took the third himself filled him with misgiving. He sipped it cautiously and felt his eyes stream as fire spread down his throat. 'How can we fetch Greg? Could we somehow use your car, Kate?'

Kate shook her head. 'The track is almost impassable. That's why I skidded.'

'Is there any way he could walk? You said it was only a few hundred yards.'

'He's hurt and he's got no strength left. We've got to carry him, somehow.'

'Carry him?' For a moment Greg's mother was stunned. She looked at Patrick and then at the exhausted young woman sitting on the sofa. There were three of them. Could they do it? Greg was a tall, sturdily-built man. He weighed at least fourteen stone. But if the alternative was to leave him out there all night . . .

'We'll carry him,' she said firmly. 'It's not far. Between the three of us, we'll manage. Once Kate has got her breath back and downed that brandy. I'll get my boots and gloves.'

'Aren't you going to tell Dad?' Patrick asked. He was biting his lip with anxiety.

'Your father is asleep. We'll be back before he even knows we've gone,' Diana said firmly. 'There's no need to disturb him. We can lock the house. Allie is asleep too. They'll be quite safe.'

Kate took a sip of brandy and closed her eyes. She could feel warmth flooding back through her veins, but with it came a wave of total exhaustion. She did not think she could even stand again, never mind help carry Greg back to the farmhouse. She was willing energy back into her body as she took another sip. When she opened her eyes Patrick was watching her. 'You OK?' he asked quietly. 'Ma's gone off to get her scarf and things.'

'I'll manage.' Kate grimaced. 'Paddy, could I borrow some warm socks? I've had half the North Sea in my boots and my feet are so cold they don't even recognise me any more.'

'Sure.' He grinned, thankful to be asked for something so easy to achieve. 'I'll get them.'

As soon as he was gone she leaned back against the cushions and closed her eyes again, feeling the room spin and tilt suddenly. She opened them hurriedly as Patrick came back with a pair of thick woolly football socks and a towel. 'These warm enough?'

She nodded, suddenly realising that she was sitting there in their living room with her muddy, wet boots stuck out in front of her on the rug. Patrick followed her gaze. 'Don't worry. Ma didn't.' He grinned again. 'Shall I pull them off for you?'

'Would you? I don't think I have the strength.'

She lay back as he bestrode her legs with his back to her and professionally drew off first one boot then the other. A shower of muddy wet sand fell on the rug. Kneeling down he peeled off her socks. Her feet were white and wrinkled and ice-cold.

'Poor feet.' He smiled. Reaching for the towel he rubbed them vigorously until she snatched them away in agony, then he pulled on the socks. 'I'll see if I can find some new boots. What size?'

'Five and a half. Six.' She sat forward on the edge of the sofa. 'I think I'll wash my face. That will wake me up a bit.'

'OK. I'm sure I can find something that'll fit you. At least they'll be dry.'

In the bathroom Kate leaned over the basin towards the mirror and stared at her face. She was drawn, grey, her eyes hollow and haunted. Pushing her hair back with both hands she splashed cold water over her face for several seconds then she reached for a towel. She would make it.

Whatever it was out there would not attack three of them. She would see to it that Patrick took his gun – she had not missed the fact that he had it in his hand as they opened the door to her earlier – and they would bring Greg back. The whole exercise would be over in less than an hour and then they would all be safe.

It took two. He was conscious when they finally reached the Land Rover and he was able to greet his mother with something like good humour, forgetting the terror he had felt when he came to, to find himself alone. A combination of the fireman's lift, a sling seat made out of the rug and frequent rests, brought them back to Redall Farmhouse shortly after four in the morning.

Diana unlocked the door and walked in first, glancing round nervously as Greg stood on one foot in the doorway, clutching at the door frame. 'Everything looks all right. They must still be asleep.' She put her shoulder under Greg's arm. 'Come on, big son. Come and sit down. Let's look at you and see the damage.'

Behind them Patrick quietly rebolted and locked the front door and leaned the gun in the corner. He had seen the way Kate kept looking over her shoulder, and the relief on her face as they reached the farmhouse again. And he had felt it too, the atmosphere out in the woods; the certainty that they were being followed.

A large purple bruise had developed on Greg's forehead where he had hit it on the back of Kate's seat when the car skidded, but apart from that and his exhaustion and chill he seemed remarkably unscathed. Only his foot was badly damaged. He had been tucked up on the camp bed in Roger's study, heavily dosed with aspirin against the pain, when Patrick spoke quietly to Kate at last. His mother had gone upstairs to check on Alison.

'You'd better tell me what happened.'

'I have told you.' Kate frowned at him. Her face was white and drawn. She picked up the mug of hot chocolate

Diana had made her and sipped it, blowing the steam gently.

'No you haven't. Not what happened before. Where did you find Bill?'

Kate took another sip of the chocolate, feeling the sharp sweetness flood around her mouth, comforting her with its memories of childhood.

'He was near the track, on his way here. He'd been to the cottage to find me and when he found it empty he thought he'd try Redall Farmhouse.'

'Did he . . .' Patrick hesitated, overwhelmed suddenly by the image of the dead man lying on the sofa in the cottage, 'Did he manage to tell you what happened?'

Kate hesitated. 'He was very confused. Almost unconscious.' She took a deep breath as though to speak then paused again. How could she tell Patrick that Bill had accused Alison of attacking him? 'He seemed to think it was two women,' she said at last guardedly.

'Women?' Patrick repeated, shocked.

Kate nodded. 'He was in an awful state, Patrick. I don't think he could remember much. We put him in the Land Rover and took him back to the cottage, then Greg went off on his own to try and find Allie. As you can imagine we were very worried.' She paused again. Her hands had started shaking quite badly. Clutching the mug of chocolate against her chest she gave Patrick a shaky smile. 'I didn't know what to do for Bill. I kept him warm and still and tried to stop the bleeding, but he lapsed into unconsciousness.' Suddenly she was fighting her tears. 'I didn't know what to do. If I'd known something about first aid . . .' She put down the mug, mopping at the tears which were streaming down her face. Patrick stood up and quietly fetched a box of Kleenex from the kitchen. He put it beside her on the arm of the chair. 'I saw him, you know,' he said softly. 'I don't think first aid would have helped. I should think he had a fractured skull. You musn't blame yourself.'

Kneeling in front of the fire he reached for the poker and prodded the logs. 'Allie said it was Marcus who killed Bill,' he said after a minute. He was staring into the smoky embers. 'She said he had killed some other people as well.' His voice was flat and tired, beyond expression.

'Marcus?' Kate replied automatically. She did not sound convinced.

'Someone must have done it.' Patrick's face crumpled suddenly. He screwed up his eyes furiously, fighting his own tears, keeping his back to her as he stabbed at the logs.

'There's nothing we can do until daylight anyway.' Levering herself to her feet, Kate came and knelt beside him. She put her arm around his shoulders, feeling the boy's trembling body go rigid beneath her touch. 'We ought to try and get a couple of hours' sleep,' she said after a pause. 'We're all safe here. Whatever — whoever it is — can't get in; the doors are locked and you've got a gun. Why don't you go to bed?'

He shook his head wordlessly.

'Lie on the sofa then. With the gun beside you.'

'What about you?' He still had not looked at her. She could see the wet trail of tears on his cheek.

'If you're down here, can I borrow your bed?' Her fatigue was so great, she realised suddenly, that it was doubtful if she could make it up the stairs.

'Of course.' He looked at her at last and gave a watery grin. 'Sorry. I'm being pathetic.'

'No you're not. You're being very brave.' She dragged herself to her feet. 'Try and get some sleep. We'll need to have our wits about us in the morning.'

Somehow she pulled herself up the stairs. Every bone and muscle in her body was aching; her head throbbed and her feet hurt as she dragged herself up the final steep steps and made her way towards Patrick's room. At Alison's doorway she paused and peered in. A dull light was spilling out across the landing from the bedside lamp. Diana was sitting on the girl's bed, looking down at her sleeping form. She glanced up and put her finger to her lips. Then she stood up and tiptoed to the door.

'Patrick said I could use his bed for an hour or two,' Kate whispered.

Diana nodded. She took Kate's arm and ushered her down the passage and into Patrick's room. Switching on the light she stared round at the mess of books and papers and for once without comment shook her head before swooping on the bed and dragging a pile of books and tapes into a heap on the floor. 'I'll get you some sheets,' she offered wearily.

'No. Please. Don't bother.' To forestall her Kate threw herself down on top of the duvet, still fully dressed. She was too tired to think, to move, to stand another second. She shut her eyes. Immediately her head began to spin unpleasantly, as though she had had too much to drink. She forced them open with a groan as Diana pulled a cover over her.

Diana looked down at her for a moment, then she turned away and switched off the light. 'Rest, Kate. We'll talk in the morning,' she whispered, and she tiptoed out and pulled the door shut behind her. Somewhere outside a pheasant shrieked its alarm call into the pre-dawn darkness and fell silent again.

XLVI

The heavy ornate brooch was solid silver. A crude native design, but it had been his; the Briton's. He had known it all along. Bending over her he tore it from her gown and pinned it onto his own cloak with a sneer of triumph. Stupid bitch. Had she thought to frighten him with her curses? Did she really think she could pursue him into eternity?

He stood looking down at her for a moment, wondering how he could have loved her so much, making no attempt to draw the sword out of her body, anger and hatred boiling in his veins like vitriol, then he stooped and picking her up under the arms he dragged her towards the edge of the marsh. One thing he could do for her, sweet wife of his, companion of his bed, mate of his loins, mother of his son – send her to Hades with her seducer. With a massive heave he lifted her from the ground and hurled her a few feet into the marsh, watching with satisfaction as her body fell almost over the spot where her lover had disappeared. She lay there for a while, her blue gown spread across the mud, the sword still protruding from her body, her hair a splash of auburn in the light of the rising sun, then slowly, almost imperceptibly, she began to sink.

Hands on hips he watched, a sneer curling his lip. Vengeance; sweet, healing vengeance. And no one would ever know. Slowly the clouds were drawing back; the sky was turning blue. It was going to be a beautiful day. He put his hand to his belt and felt for the dagger he wore there, opposite the empty sheath which had held his sword. Taking the hilt between his fingers he stroked it for a moment, then he drew it out, feeling the weight and balance of a well-loved, trusted weapon.

Then he turned towards the priests.

'Are you and Alison going to work on your projects together today, Sue?' Cissy Farnborough looked at the top of her daughter's head, which was all she could see as the girl sat at the table, her face buried in a fat paperback.

Don't read at table. She wanted to say it, but how could she with Joe sitting there on the far side of the cornflakes packet, as deeply buried in the *Sunday Telegraph*? She sighed. 'Sue!' she tried again, louder this time, more irritated. 'Did you hear what I said?'

Sue looked up. Her unbrushed hair stood out round her head like a disorganised halo; her nightshirt, adorned with a particularly ugly picture of some hirsute pop star's face in close up, was crumpled and distinctly grubby. 'I don't know what she's doing. She missed school last week. I'll ring her later,' she said ungraciously.

'Please do. I should like to know if there is someone extra for lunch.'

'You always make too much anyway,' Sue commented tartly. She buried herself back in her book. Cissy pursed her lips. She turned to the kettle and switching it on, reached for the jar of coffee. Her husband and her daughter had tea at breakfast, and as usual Joe had insisted on a full, cooked, death-by-cholesterol blow out. She shuddered as she glanced at the greasy frying pan. He wouldn't even let her grill his bacon. 'I work for my living, woman,' he had growled when she suggested a slight moderation to his diet. 'These namby pamby doctors don't know anything about life on the land. They're writing for city folk; desk pilots. Men who never shift their backsides off their chairs from one end of the month to the other. They should try and do some real work. See what that does for them!' She had given up. It was a well-worn theme. A combination of rural arrogance and resentment against her father, who had been an accountant in London before he retired. Spooning the coffee into her cup she stirred it thoughtfully, rehearsing her own dissatisfaction silently as she turned to look out of the window. She had married beneath her; both her parents had thought so. And unfortunately they had made no secret of their opinion. She had defended Joe, stuck up for him, passionately supported him, slept with him and finally married him, and of course they had been right. He had gone to a minor public school in Suffolk but he was not what she would call educated; he was not interested in anything but the farm; he never read anything except the Sunday newspapers and he despised education in others – especially his wife. Susie was different. Nothing was too good for her, but even there he never supported Cissy when she tried to make the child do her homework. 'Leave the girl alone,' he would say impatiently every time Cissy tried to get Sue to switch off her Walkman or the television and concentrate on work. 'She's pretty. She'll find herself a man soon enough. She doesn't need all this crap!'

'There's no marmalade, Ciss!' Joe emerged from the paper looking wounded, the lid of the jar in his hand.

'Blast!' Cissy mouthed the word silently. Why, why, why did he always manage to find fault. Why was there always something she had forgotten?

'Don't call me Ciss,' she snapped back. Cecilia Louise. That was what her parents had christened her. But Joe had never called her Cecilia in his life. At first she had thought it funny to be called Cissy, but the joke had soon palled. Now it just added to the weight of resentment.

'Go and ring Alison now.' She turned on Sue as always, her anger and helplessness directed against her daughter instead of its true target. 'And get dressed. You look like a slut.'

To her surprise Sue got up at once, and she saw Joe

glance at her surreptitiously from behind the paper. Perhaps she had spoken more forcefully than she had realised.

'I will put marmalade on the list,' she said calmly. 'You will have to wait until I go to the shops again. There's plenty of jam in the pantry.' She smiled at her husband. 'Or Marmite.' She saw him shudder visibly, but to her surprise he said nothing. Meekly he larded his toast with butter and ate it plain. Well, if that was supposed to make her feel guilty it was not going to work. What were another few ounces of butter going to matter after the load of fat he had ladled into his body over the years?

She turned and looked out of the kitchen window. It was vile outside. The sky was almost dark even though it was after nine. The wind from the east was flattening the trees in the orchard beyond the kitchen garden, and there were thin, melting drifts of snow over the grass. She shivered. It was still sleeting. On the bird table outside the window a flock of small birds fought over the bowl of melted fat and seed she had put out for them. The only thing about Joe's diet which did please her was the amount of fat which dripped from his food and which she could make into bird pudding. She half smiled as she watched two robins squabbling with some sparrows. On the snowy grass beneath the bird table about fifty small birds foraged about for the seed she had scattered there.

'Mum! Their phone's out of order.' A querulous wail came from Sue as she slammed down the receiver. 'Hell and shit and fuck!'

Joe looked up. 'Go to your room, Susan,' he bellowed.

'But Dad. Allie's got my notes. I've got to speak to her.'

'I don't care what she's got.' Something had at last pierced his lethargy. 'No child of mine uses language like that in my house.'

Cissy sipped her coffee, for once uninvolved. Let them work it out. Sue's friendship with Alison was one she cultivated assiduously. The Lindseys were a pleasant family.

Well spoken; well educated. Their lack of money was not their fault – poor Roger was so ill – but still Diana managed to run that house with a grace and style which Cissy envied.

She turned away from the window and surveyed the thunderous scene at the table. 'I'll drive you down to Redall Farmhouse when I've put the lunch on,' she said peaceably. 'Then you can collect your notes and Allie can come back with us if she wants. In fact, they all can. I've got a huge joint this week. As you say, there will be plenty for every-one and it would be nice to have them over. In weather like this it's not as though anyone can be doing anything outside.' She smiled at her husband and her daughter, sud-denly cheerful. Her depression had lifted as swiftly as it had fallen. The Lindseys would cheer them all up.

XLVII

Kate awoke suddenly with a start and lay staring up at the ceiling wondering where she was. Her head was spinning. Nothing about the room was familiar; she could not place it at all. A dull light was filtering through the closed orange curtains. She stared round at the overflowing shelves, the untidy desk with its computer, the posters on every inch of available wall space and then she closed her eyes again, defeated. She hadn't the energy to sit up, but she knew she must. She lifted her wrist towards her face and squinted at her watch. A quarter past nine. She realised suddenly that under the duvet she was fully dressed. Cautiously she moved on the bed, easing herself nearer the edge, with a view to swinging her legs over the side, but every part of her body ached and for a moment she lay still, trying instead to force her brain into gear. What had happened last night? Why couldn't she remember?

She turned her face towards the door as a faint knock sounded. It was Patrick. He grinned. 'Sorry it's such a mess in here. I've brought you some tea.'

Of course. Suddenly it was all flooding back. The horror and the fear; the cold and exhaustion. She levered herself up onto her elbow, and pushing the hair out of her eyes reached for the cup. 'You're a saint. I didn't realise how thirsty I was. How is everybody?'

'Alive, I guess.' Patrick pulled the chair out from his desk and swivelling it round sat astride it, facing her. 'What's happening to us? What are we going to do?'

She sipped at the scalding tea and thought for a moment. 'We're going to have to get up to the main road. We need help. A doctor; the police.' She paused, frowning. 'How is Greg?'

'His foot is all inflamed. Mum says he ought to be in hospital.'

The wave of anguish which swept over her surprised her. Greg was the only strong one amongst them; the only one who could protect them if ... If what? If they were attacked?

Almost as though he had read her thoughts Patrick shook his head. 'Whoever murdered Bill must be long gone by now. In our car. It was stolen yesterday. I'm going up to the Farnboroughs' on foot. It won't take me more than an hour.'

She drank some more tea, feeling it flowing through her veins like some kind of elixir of life. 'You can't go on your own. I'll go with you. A quick wash and something to eat –' she was surprised suddenly to realise just how hungry she was, '– and I'll be ready for anything. What's the weather like?'

Patrick stood up. He leaned across his desk and pulled back the curtains, letting in a dim brownish light. 'Not very nice. It's still windy and there's been quite a bit of snow. They are forecasting blizzards –' He broke off suddenly.

'What is it?' The lurch of panic in Kate's stomach told her she was not nearly as calm as she had thought. All her fear was still there, under the surface, waiting to flood back through her.

'The car!' Patrick's voice was strangled. Putting down the cup Kate lurched out of bed and went to stand beside him. 'Where? Damn it, my specs are in my jacket.' She screwed up her eyes as she looked out across the snow-covered grass towards the edge of the saltings.

'Out there, on the marsh.' Patrick's voice was awed.

The Volvo was standing some hundred yards from the grass and sand at the edge of the salting, balanced on high sections of grass-topped mud. Beneath its wheels, the tide was rippling merrily out of the creek leaving a curtain of weed draped on the car's bumper.

'Is there anyone in it?' Kate could only make out the outline from this distance.

'I don't think so.' Patrick sounded distracted. 'How could it have got there? No one could have driven it.'

'Not even at low tide?'

'Kate, look at the height of the ground it's standing on! Those are like little islands. At high tide those grass patches are above sea level. They must be four feet off the ground. There is no way that car could have got there, no way.'

'The tide must have carried it. There was a terrific wind last night –'

'Blowing this way. Off the sea. That's a car, Kate. A bloody great Volvo. It's not a Dinky toy. If it got in the sea it would sink.'

'Yes. Of course.' She pushed her hands deep into her pockets, aware that she was shivering. 'Can we walk out there? When the tide's gone out a bit?'

He nodded absently. 'I'll have to tell Dad.'

'I'll come downstairs.'

She stood back and watched as he headed for the door. He was in a daze. She glanced back at the window. The car was still there, the windscreen glittering in a stray, watery ray of sunshine.

On her way downstairs she glanced into Alison's room through the open door. The girl lay unmoving, her hair spread across the pillow. The teddy lay on the floor, a hot water bottle near it. Kate stood for a moment watching her. She had a feeling Alison was not asleep.

'Allie?' she whispered. 'Allie are you awake?'

There was no reply.

Roger was sitting at the kitchen table, a cup of coffee in front of him, which judging by the skin on the top was cold and unappetising. Diana was standing near him watching the toaster.

'Did you manage to sleep?' She smiled at Kate and indicated the coffee pot on the hob.

Kate made for it gratefully. 'A bit.'

'Pour Greg one too, will you Kate, and take it through to him. I think he'd be glad to see you,' Roger said. He mustered a valiant smile. 'Then you and I and Paddy will grab a bit of breakfast. By then the tide will be low enough to make our way out to the family barouche. Those bastards. I can't think how the hell they got it there, but it won't be worth a tinker's ha'penny after the tide has been in it.'

'The insurance will pay, Dad.' Patrick had emerged from the study.

'Let's hope so.' Roger's face was grim as he watched Kate make her way across the room with the two mugs of coffee.

Greg was propped up against a pile of pillows and cushions on the camp bed in the study. Someone had made a makeshift cage across his foot to keep the weight of the bed-clothes off it, and though Kate could see the pain in his face as he grinned at her, he looked immeasurably better than he had the night before.

'How are you?' She knelt to hand him the coffee, and then sat down on the floor beside him. 'I hear the foot is not too good.'

'I'll live.' He reached out a hand to her. 'And that fact I owe to you. It hasn't escaped me that you saved my life about five times last night. That's some debt I owe you.'

'Don't be silly.' Embarrassed she looked down into her coffee. It was thick and black and rich.

'I know. Anyone would have done it.' He was laughing.

'Probably. Yes.'

'Well, thanks anyway. If I had been you I would

331

probably have left me there to rot and thought it served me right after the way I've buggered you about.'

She smiled. 'Poetically put.'

There was a moment's silence. Then Greg reached out to her again. 'Kate, I had the most peculiar dream while I was asleep. I think we are all still in terrible danger. I've told Paddy and now I'm telling you. You'll think I'm hallucinating; you probably think I was hallucinating last night –'

'If you were, then we both were,' she put in softly. 'We both saw that figure.'

'Was it because we were expecting to?' He shook his head and, releasing her hand, reached for his coffee cup again. 'When you came here I decided to scare you away. You know that. The joke, if it was a joke, got rapidly out of hand. We all began to imagine things . . .' He paused, his attention riveted to the depths of his cup. 'In that state, maybe, what I saw was dictated by my own mind . . .' He paused again. 'Thomas De Quincey puts it rather neatly, if I remember it right. "If a man who only talks about oxen becomes an opium eater, then he will dream about oxen" – is that right?' He cast her a quick glance under his eyelashes, and did not miss the look of astonishment in her face. '"And if a man who is a philosopher has an opium dream then it will be . . . *humani nihil* –"'

'"*Humani nihil a se alienum putat.*"' Kate finished for him. 'Well, well, I would never have suspected that you had read *The Confessions*.'

He smiled, the look of mischief cutting across the greyness of pain. 'Well, I used to be quite literate, you know. I even know what it means. "He believes nothing human strange" – yes?' He waited for her comment. When she said nothing he went on, 'I even read up my Byron when I heard what Lady Muck was up to in my cottage.'

'Lady Muck?' She was even more astonished.

'If you'd known I called you that you would have left me to the sharks.'

'Indeed I would.' Thoughtfully she took a sip of coffee. 'You haven't told me yet what you dreamed of. What phantasmagoria haunted you?'

'Marcus.'

She bit her lip. 'Who else?'

'He tried to get me, you know, on the beach. He tried to take me over. I fought him . . .' He paused. 'In my dream he was trying to get inside my head again.' He shifted his weight uncomfortably in the bed. 'It was the most awful dream I have ever had in my life, and yet I can't remember more than a few bits.'

'You were awoken perhaps by a stranger from Porlock.' Kate smiled at him, trying to tease him out of his bleak mood.

'All right, all right. Believe it or not, I know that one too. All I remember is that he was trying to get inside my head, and that if I had let him he would have got into this house. And that was what he wanted. To get to us. Because we know his secret.'

She was watching him. 'And what is his secret?'

He glanced at her looking for signs of disbelief or scorn. 'That he killed Claudia. But there's more to it than that. Much more. Otherwise why would he be so angry? And so desperate?'

The silence in the room grew uncomfortable. There had been no humour in his eyes; no relieving lightness. What she had seen there, behind the narrowed grey-green irises, was fear. She swallowed, plaiting her fingers together nervously.

'Who do you think killed Bill?' she asked at last. Her voice was husky.

Greg heaved a sigh. 'I don't know what to think. Has Allie said anything, do you know?'

'Patrick told me she said it was Marcus.'

'Did you tell them what Bill said?'

'No.'

Greg eased himself higher against the pillows. His foot was throbbing painfully, stabs of hot pain shooting up as far as his knee. He had not needed to see the inflamed, discoloured flesh to know it was infected. 'Has she woken up?'

'I don't think so. She was fast asleep when I came down. Greg, I think the important thing is to get a doctor here for you – and for her. Patrick and I are going to walk up to the main road.' She glanced at the window. 'It doesn't seem quite so frightening in daylight.'

He reached out and touched her hand again. 'I'm so sorry this has all happened, Kate. Poor old Byron.'

She gave a rueful smile. 'He'll wait.'

'You know,' he hesitated. 'I think I'm quite glad you came after all.' Leaning towards her he kissed her forehead gently. He ran a finger down the line of her cheek. 'You've got good bones. When all this is over I'll paint your portrait.'

She smiled, surprised at the shiver of excitement which had whispered across her flesh in spite of her exhaustion. 'Am I supposed to take that as a compliment?'

'Oh, yes. People who know me well would kill for such a compliment.' The humour in his eyes was hidden very deep – a mere quirk of the eye muscle.

She studied his face for a moment, then half reluctantly she stood up. 'We know where the car is.'

'Oh?'

She laughed. A tight little laugh which hovered for a moment on the edge of hysteria. 'It's out on the saltings; in the middle of the water. No one could have driven it there.'

He said nothing, his gaze holding hers, then he too gave an uncomfortable laugh. 'Well, well. Perhaps he was only used to driving chariots; a Volvo must be a bit different.'

334

'You don't seriously think —'

'I don't know what I think.' His patience snapped. 'For Christ's sake, what can I do from here? Just be careful. Make Paddy take the gun and watch every step of the way. We don't know what we're dealing with. There is someone out there who is out to kill. It seems to me it doesn't matter much if he's a real flesh-and-blood homicidal maniac or a ghostly one, the effect seems to be the same.'

'So you don't think it was Alison.' She had turned towards the door.

'Of course it wasn't Alison. She wouldn't have the strength even if she wanted to kill someone. And she had nothing to do with the car.' He slumped back, over-whelmed by helplessness and frustration and pain. She looked down at him, hesitating for a moment longer, then silently she opened the door and slipped away.

Roger pushed a fresh cup of coffee at her across the table as she walked back into the kitchen. 'Allie is awake. Diana and Paddy are with her.' He gestured her towards a chair. He looked only slightly more rested than the night before; there was still an alarmingly blue tinge about his lips as Kate sat down opposite him.

'How is she?'

He shook his head. 'I thought I'd wait till they came down. She doesn't want us all up there crowding into her room.' Besides, I can't face climbing the stairs again, not yet. The thought, though unspoken, showed clearly in his eyes.

Kate looked away, painfully aware how sick he was. 'As soon as Paddy comes down I think we should go for a doctor.'

'And the police have to be informed.' He looked down into his coffee mug, stirring thoughtfully, watching the movement of the liquid, with its miniaturized reflection of the overhead lamp. 'I know you all have some crazy idea that there is a ghost out there, Kate. Get real, as Allie

335

would say. Ghosts do not beat large, strong men to death.'
He looked up at her at last. 'Be careful. Please be careful —'
He broke off, and she saw his face light with a smile which
hovered around his mouth for a few seconds and then
died. Following his gaze, she swivelled round on her chair.
Alison was standing by the staircase door. Wearing her
nightshirt, her hair tumbled on her shoulders, she was
staring round the room as though she had never seen it
before.

'Allie?' Roger stood up, pushing his chair back over the
floor tiles with a scraping sound which tore at the nerves.
'Are you all right, sweetheart?'

She moved her head slightly, as though she were having
difficulty focussing, and looked towards them vaguely, her
body swaying from side to side. Behind her, Patrick
appeared in the doorway. His face was white. 'Allie?' He
dodged round her. 'Allie, sit down. Sit down and I'll get
you something nice to drink.' He gestured at Roger and
Kate frantically behind his back.

They glanced at each other. The atmosphere in the room
was suddenly electric. Alison took another step forward,
placing one foot in front of the other with enormous care
as though the floor were swaying like the deck of a ship.
As she moved towards them the two cats, who had been
asleep near the fire, leaped off the chair where they had
been entwined and streaked across the floor. Within
seconds they had both disappeared through the cat flap.
Kate stared after them, puzzled. Their eyes had been wild;
their hackles and tails fluffed up in terror. Frowning, she
glanced back at Alison who had stopped again and it struck
her suddenly that the girl looked as though she was drunk.

Roger had the same thought. 'Alison? His voice was
sharp. 'What is the matter?'

'She attacked Mum,' Patrick murmured, his voice husky.
He reached the table and slid behind it, putting it between
him and his sister. 'She's gone mad. Oh, Dad, what's

336

happening?' His face was white and strained. He looked frightened.

Roger flicked a glance at him and then looked back at his daughter. Her face was completely blank. She took another step forward, her hands out in front of her as though she were groping in the darkness.

'Alison!' Roger's voice rang out loudly. 'Answer me! What's wrong?' He shot a look at his son. 'Where is Di? Is she hurt?'

Patrick shook his head. 'Shocked. She's coming –'

He was interrupted by a sudden, slow laugh. The sound, he realised with a sudden shiver, came from Alison, but it was not her voice. Kate felt the hairs on the back of her neck stir as she stared at the girl.

'No one,' Alison spoke slowly, her voice husky. 'No one is going to leave this house. No one is ever going to find out what happened.' Behind her Diana appeared in the doorway. Kate heard Roger's sharp intake of breath as he glanced at his wife. Her face was discoloured with a massive purple bruise. She slid into the room, and stayed where she was, her back to the wall, her hurt and bewilderment and fear obvious in every angle of her body.

Roger swallowed. 'Allie, darling. I think we should have a talk. Why don't you sit down. We'll all have a hot drink –'

She did not appear to have heard him. Slowly and painfully she took another step. Kate was watching her eyes. They were blank; totally blank.

'Roger.' She stepped closer to him, her voice barely a whisper. 'I think she's asleep.'

Roger glanced at her sharply then he looked back at his daughter, narrowing his eyes. 'Dear God, I think you're right! What do we do?'

'Isn't it supposed to be dangerous to wake them?' Kate threw a pleading look towards Diana.

It was Patrick who acted. 'If she's asleep she can't see

337

us,' he said quietly. He took a cautious step towards his sister, and then, as she failed to react he took another. Slipping round behind her, he put his hands lightly on her shoulders. 'Come on, Allie, back to bed.' She ignored him. 'Allie. Come on. You must lie down –' He increased the pressure slightly, trying to turn her round. She tensed, then suddenly she swung round out of his grip, letting fly with a massive punch which grazed Patrick's shoulder as he leaped out of the way.

'All right, Alison, that is enough.' Roger moved with surprising speed. He caught her wrists, and pulled her towards a chair. 'Awake or asleep you are not behaving like that in this house.' Taken by surprise she took two steps with him then she stopped and shook him off. He reeled back. Though weak with illness he was a tall man, and still fairly heavy and his daughter had flicked him away as though he were half her size. Her face was still blank; all expression completely wiped from her features.

'She's like a robot,' Patrick whispered. He slipped across to his father's side. 'Are you OK, Dad? She hasn't hurt you?'

Roger shook his head. They all had their eyes fixed on Alison's face which remained impassive. Kate frowned. Was she asleep? Or was it something else? The girl stood immobile for several minutes; no one moved or spoke, then out of the corner of her eye Kate saw Diana slip from the room. Moments later she reappeared, a canvas belt in her hand. As they watched she tiptoed up behind Alison and gently she began to slide the belt around her, over her arms, obviously intending to pinion them at her sides. Alison did not react. Gently, Diana pulled the belt tighter, just above the girl's elbows. 'Fetch a blanket, Roger. Wrap her up tightly,' she commanded. 'Quickly. Before she wakes up.'

Alison stepped forward at the sound of her voice as if becoming aware of the restriction for the first time. She tried to move her arms and a look of frightened puzzlement flashed across her face to be followed immediately by a roar of rage. She turned round, lashing out with her hands and almost without effort, snapped the belt. The expression on her face was one of pure anger. She turned towards the table and reached out. Too late Kate saw the bread knife lying beside the loaf; she jumped to move it but Alison was there first and her hand was on the knife handle before Kate's. Kate grabbed her wrist, and for a moment their eyes met across the table. Kate felt a shaft of terror stab through her; the eyes which bore into hers were not Alison's; they were no longer expressionless; no longer asleep; they were cold, calculating and very angry.

'Allie —' she gasped. 'Please.'

Alison laughed. A deep throaty laugh. Twisting her arm effortlessly beneath Kate's grasping fingers she snatched the knife up and turning, lunged at her mother. She missed and for a moment she was off balance. Seizing his chance Patrick threw himself at her and they fell to the floor, wrestling.

'Paddy —' Diana's scream rang across the room as the blade caught his forearm and a splash of blood flew across the rush matting, but he did not let go. They fought on furiously, Patrick kicking and struggling as Alison began surely and steadily to overpower him. 'Roger, do something!' Forgetting her husband's weakness Diana screamed again but it was Kate who snatched up the folded table-cloth from the dresser and flung it over Alison's head. At the same moment Patrick wriggled free of his sister's arm lock and put his foot on her wrist, pinning it to the floor while he snatched the knife from her. It was only then that they realised that Greg was in the room, hobbling on a walking stick, his face white with pain.

'Here.' He handed something to his mother. 'Quickly. It's Dad's sedative.' Her hands shaking visibly, Diana opened the box he had given her and took out a syringe. She glanced at Roger, then filling it she approached her writhing daughter and, pulling the nightshirt up, planted the needle in the girl's buttock. Alison let out a scream of rage, only half muffled by the tablecloth Kate was holding round her head. It was followed by a stream of abuse which only very slowly subsided into silence. It was several minutes before her clenched fists relaxed and she slumped to the floor. Cautiously Kate removed the tablecloth and looked down. Alison's face, flushed from the struggle was relaxed at last; she was breathing quickly and lightly, her hair spread across the floor. Slowly Patrick stooped and pulled his sister's nightshirt down to cover her bottom, then he turned and picking up a drying up cloth from the draining board he staunched the blood flowing from his arm.

'Don't, Patrick. That's germy,' Diana's comment was automatic; her eyes had not left Alison's face.

'Did you hear what she was screaming?' Greg lowered himself into a chair, his head swimming from the effort of dragging himself from the study.

'It was some foreign language,' Roger said after a moment's hesitation.

'Not just any foreign language.' Greg looked at Kate. 'Go on. Tell them. What was it?'

Kate shook her head. 'I'm not sure —'

'Of course you're sure. You heard what she said. It was some sort of Latin. Go on admit it. You heard her.' He stared round at them all. 'You all heard her. It was Latin!'

Patrick bent down to pick up the knife. He stared at it for a moment as though he couldn't believe he held it in his hands. 'Allie would never have done that; she couldn't have done that. No girl could be that strong.'

Diana picked up the broken belt. It had snapped in two places. They all stared at it. 'How long will that injection last?' Roger asked softly. He glanced up at his wife. The sedative had been left by the doctor for him.

'Not long. I didn't expect it to work so quickly. She was

looking down at Alison's slumped body. 'I only used a tiny dose. Oh, Roger, what are we going to do with her?' Her voice shook with tears.

Roger moved to put his arm around her shoulders. 'I don't know.' His whole body was slumped with defeat.

'There is something you should know.' Greg looked from one to the other and then at Kate. His face was full of compassion. 'Before he died Bill told us that it was Alison who had attacked him.'

'No!' Diana's protest was half a scream, half a moan.

'I'm afraid that is what he said,' Kate added. 'But it wasn't Alison, was it? We all know that. Those eyes weren't Alison's.'

'What are you saying?' Diana rounded on her.

'You know what she's saying,' Greg said. He stared down at his sister's recumbent form. 'She's possessed.'

'No.'

'What do you call it then?' He reached across towards her but she drew back. He shrugged. 'That was not Alison speaking; they are not Alison's actions. Kate's right. They are not even her eyes.'

Diana burst into tears. 'What are we going to do?'

Greg looked at Kate and then at his father, who had sunk into the chair at the head of the table, his face grey with fatigue. 'We have to find a doctor.'

'No!' Diana turned on him. 'We are not getting a doctor, or the police. I am not having Allie taken away from here –'

'What about my foot?' Greg's voice was mild. 'And Dad. I think the doc should look at him.' He paused. 'Allie needs help. Badly. You know she does.'

'No.' Diana shook her head. Tears were pouring down her cheeks. 'No, we'll sort this all out ourselves. It will be all right. Allie will be fine when she's had a sleep. Your foot will be all right, Greg. It's better already, you said so yourself and your father only needs to rest –'

341

'Di.' Roger looked up. He rubbed his hands wearily across his cheeks and they all heard the rasping sound of his palms on the twenty-four-hour beard. 'We can't handle this ourselves. You know that better than I do. There is a dead man out there in the cottage. A dead man, Di. He's not imaginary. He's not going to sort himself out.'

'Allie didn't move the car, Ma,' Patrick put in suddenly. 'There must be someone else out there.'

'Patrick and I will go and phone from the Farnboroughs'.' Kate stood up. 'I think we should go now.'

'Take the gun, Paddy.' Roger nodded. 'Greg and I can take care of things here.'

Patrick looked from one parent's face to the other, uncertainly, then he turned to Kate. 'OK?' he whispered.

XLVIII

The kitchen was spotless, the joint in the oven, the potatoes roasting slowly beneath it. Cissy looked round with a pleased smile. Even Joe's Sunday papers had been marshalled into a more-or-less tidy heap at the far end of the kitchen table. There would be nothing now to jog her conscience if she and Sue drove down to Redall Farmhouse and had a cup of Diana's wonderful specially ground coffee from the shop in Ipswich, by her untidy, ash-spattered inglenook.

She often wondered why she liked Diana's house so much; the living room at Redall was just that – a room for living, always knee-deep in newspapers and sewing and cats, with Greg's paints and Patrick's books lying around in heaps. The untidy and often dusty surfaces were always filled with fresh flowers, though; even in the depths of winter Diana managed to find something in the woods and the house always smelled of coffee and home-baked bread and drying herbs, and even if there was the occasional whiff of cat, it was all wonderful.

She sighed, looking round her own kitchen. However hard she tried she could not be comfortable with Diana's mess. Not in her own house. She had tried to dry flowers, but they dropped shrivelled little petals all over the floor; she tried to bake bread, but the sight of the cloth-draped pans of dough rising on the side irritated her; and the results, though smelling good, were as heavy as lead.

'Sue!' She stood at the foot of the stairs and called up. 'Do you want to come down to Redall?'

'Coming.' For once Sue was in contact, the Walkman

343

for some reason (no batteries, her mother concluded) abandoned on her bedside table. Available for human communication, Sue appeared. 'Great. Are they coming back for lunch?'

'I hope so. Get your gloves darling.' Cissy looked critically at her daughter's attire – black leggings, black tee shirt, black jumper which came to her knees in front and only just covered her bottom behind, black scarf knotted around her head and black eye liner – and she sighed. When she had got up that morning the child had looked like a pretty teenager. Now she looked like a zombie from the swamp.

With an exasperated sigh Cissy collected the keys of the Range Rover from the hall table and led the way outside. It was a cold, damp morning, the sky heavily overcast; any moment the snow would start again. They climbed into the Range Rover and Cissy started the engine, letting it run for a few moments as she switched on the windscreen wipers to clear the screen, and rubbed at the condensation with a duster.

'I hate this weather.' Sue leaned forward to turn on the radio, flicking through the stations.

Her mother winced as Radio One blasted into the quiet cold. 'Must you?'

'Oh come on, Mum. You'll be telling me you want to hear the birds next.'

'Why not?' Cissy shrugged, unequal to the argument. With a sigh she released the handbrake and swung the heavy vehicle out of the yard and onto the road. The sanders had been down in the night and the two-lane road was slushy with yellow mud; there were no other cars in sight as she drove cautiously the couple of miles to the turning which marked Redall Lane. 'I hope their track is not too bad,' she murmured as she turned in. 'I can't think why Roger doesn't get it tarmacked. Anyone would think they wanted to get cut off from the world, down here.'

'They haven't got enough money for things like that,' Sue put in. She crossed her ankle across her knee, leaning against the door, trying to be casual and comfortable as the car lurched over the potholes. 'If Dad was any kind of a neighbour he would do it for them. It wouldn't cost him anything – he's always doing the farm roads and it would make no end of difference to the Lindseys.'

Cissy caught her breath, about to retort that things didn't work like that – Joe would never do it, and Roger would never accept anyway – when she thought better of it. The young sometimes saw with shining clarity what needed to be done, and often they did it. It was adults who loused things up with their dithering and self-imposed rules. She bit her lip at the choice of words which had spilt into her mind. A fuck up. It described so much of her life; and Joe's. A fuck up from beginning to end. Well, why shouldn't they help someone else for a change? Joe could easily say he had over-ordered gravel or tarmac or whatever they used to make roads; a white lie to save Roger's pride.

'What are you smiling at?' Sue was staring at her, defying her to tell her to sit in a ladylike fashion. Sue smiled even more broadly. Well, fuck that too. The child could sit how she liked. It was her life.

The Range Rover slithered round the first of the steep corners without mishap and moved steadily towards the next. Daringly, Cissy accelerated a little, longing to be there. Overhead the trees arched beneath a fine mist of snow, their leaves crumpled and stripped to skeletons by the frost. The wet ruts gleamed darkly, reflecting no light from the sky. She flicked on the headlights with an irritated exclamation. The next moment she let out a scream as the arcing flash of the lights illuminated a figure in front of them on the track. Jamming on the brakes she wrestled frantically with the wheel as the heavy Range Rover began to slide.

'Oh God!'

Desperately she fought for control, conscious of Sue being flung sideways against the window with a resounding crack.

'Oh God!' Her voice rose to a scream again as the figure seemed to fill her vision, his hands raised, then the car swung sideways over the edge of the track and spun into the ditch, slamming Cissie's head against the steering column as the engine stalled.

In the silence that followed the voice of Bruce Springsteen floated suddenly from the radio over the sound of the ticking engine and the hiss of steam from the shattered radiator.

XLIX

Patrick was clutching the gun under his arm. He was breaking all the rules; it was loaded and it was unbroken, but Kate had not commented on the fact as she followed him out of the door and they heard Diana bolt it behind them.

'Shall we go and look at the car?' Patrick turned to her questioningly. His face was pinched and white and she was astonished to feel a wave of something which she suspected was quite maternal. For all his attempts at being grown up he was still a little boy in some ways and he was looking to her to be the adult. Great. She wanted someone's hand to hold too.

She stopped and listened. The air was raw and cold; it smelt of damp pine trees and mud, catching in her throat, clammy against her face.

'We might as well,' she said slowly. 'It will only take a few minutes.' She was not anxious to set off up the dark track any more than he was.

They made their way across the rough grass to the sandy strip of ground which bordered their garden and the marsh and stood for a moment looking out across the mudflats. 'The tide is out far enough. I'll go and look.' Patrick handed her the gun. 'Will you wait here?'

She nodded. The gun was surprisingly heavy; she doubted if she could raise it to her shoulder and hold it steady even if she had to, but it felt reassuring in her gloved hands. Watching steadily, she narrowed her eyes against the wind as Patrick, protected by long boots, leaped from tussock to tussock, making his way out onto the mud, splashing every now and then through narrowing streams

347

of water, scrambling up sandy, muddy dunes which rose out of the sea like little islands. He reached the car and she saw him peer in through the windows, circling it cautiously. He groped in his pocket and, producing the key, he unlocked the passenger door, easing himself inside. She held her breath, watching. Behind her the garden was totally silent. She imagined Diana and Greg watching from the kitchen window and the thought comforted her.

Only seconds later Patrick was climbing out of the car again. Carefully he relocked the door – something which struck her incongruously as being immensely funny, and began to make his way back towards her. He was muddy and out of breath when at last he stood beside her again.

'It was locked. There was no sign of anyone forcing the door and pulling at the wires under the dashboard. Everything was as it should be. No mud; no water; no scratches. In perfect nick.'

'Should we be pleased?' Kate asked wryly.

Patrick bit his lip. 'How did it get there, Kate?'

She shrugged. 'Better not to ask at the moment. Let's concentrate on getting up to the road.' Pushing the gun at him she turned away from the sea.

He nodded. 'There's a short cut. Let's take that. I'll show you.' He led the way back across the grass.

In the house Greg turned away from the window. Behind him, his father had thrown himself down on the sofa. Within seconds he had fallen asleep. With a compassionate glance at Roger's exhausted face, Greg hobbled back to the kitchen. 'They've gone. Listen, Ma, what are we going to do about Allie? She is not going to sleep for very long.'

He gave her a careful look under his eyelashes, knowing what he would do – lock her up somewhere safe – and knowing that his mother would not hear of it. 'We have to accept that she might be dangerous. I know it's not her fault; it's not her, for Christ's sake, but we have to be careful.'

'What are you suggesting?' Diana's voice was hoarse with fatigue.

'Is there a key in her bedroom door?'

'You know there is. She's always locking herself in.'

'Then it won't be any hardship for her if we take her up and lock the door when she's safely tucked up in bed. For our own peace of mind.'

To his surprise she merely shrugged. 'All right.'

He glanced at his father and then back at her. 'You and I are going to have to do it, Ma.'

She nodded. For a moment she sat still, visibly wilting, then as he watched she straightened her shoulders and looked up. She gave a brave attempt at a smile. 'Sorry, Greg. I'm being no help. You're right, of course.' She stood up. 'I'll get her upstairs.'

'You can't do it on your own.'

'Of course I can –' Diana stopped short. For a moment neither of them had been looking at Alison but now, as they spoke, they realised that the girl had opened her eyes.

'Allie?' It was Greg who spoke first. 'Are you all right?'

Her eyes were wide, frightened, bewildered. Her own. He glanced at his mother and saw that she had seen too. She went towards the girl and kneeling put her arms round her. 'Allie, darling. You gave us such a fright.'

'Did I fall over?' Alison struggled to sit up, leaning against her mother.

'You had a dizzy spell, old thing,' Greg replied. He grinned at her reassuringly. 'Better now?'

'I . . . I think so.'

'Bed, sweetheart.' Diana's voice was firm. 'Then I'll bring you up something to eat.'

Alison climbed unsteadily to her feet and stood for a moment, rocking slightly, looking around her in a daze. 'He's gone, hasn't he.' she said at last.

'Yes, he's gone.' Greg shook his head sternly at Diana

as she opened her mouth to speak. 'Nothing to worry about any more little sister.'

Alison smiled. 'Nothing to worry about,' she repeated obediently. She still looked dazed.

Diana took her arm. 'Come on, darling. Upstairs. You'll catch cold down here.'

Greg watched as they crossed the room, then he sat down, aware again suddenly how badly his foot was throbbing.

It was several minutes before Diana reappeared. 'She lay down at once and she seems to have gone to sleep again.'

'Did you lock the door?'

She nodded. 'Oh, Greg, I hate to do it.'

'It's not going to hurt her. And better that than a repeat of – whatever happened before.'

She nodded. Pulling herself together she moved purposefully towards him. 'Right. Let's look at that foot.'

'Shouldn't we wait for the doctor?'

'So he can amputate? Come on. Put your leg up on the chair.' They both knew she had to keep herself busy somehow.

Gently she pulled away the bandages. They studied the swollen foot. 'I'm going to have to drain that.' She glanced up at him.

He managed to muster a smile. 'Can you face it?'

'Of course. I'll get the first aid box.'

It was in the study. Switching on the light, she peered round looking for the box she had left on the desk. It did not seem to be there. With an exclamation of annoyance she began to search the room then suddenly she stopped. It was cold in there – extraordinarily cold – and she could smell earth; damp earth. She frowned, fighting a sudden urge to run out of the room. 'Greg? What did I do with the first aid?' Her voice was unnaturally loud as she called over her shoulder. The door behind her was closed. Surely she hadn't closed it? She almost ran towards it, grabbing at the handle. It wouldn't open. 'Greg!' Her voice rose to a scream. 'Greg!' There was someone behind her. Someone very close to her. She could smell a strange perfume; sweet, cloying, and the cold was even more intense now, cutting into her fingers as she wrestled with the door latch. 'Greg!' Her voice broke into a sob. Whirling round she raised her arms in front of her face to ward off whoever was there.

The room was empty. She stared round, stunned. She had been so certain; she had heard her, felt her, smelt her; a woman. She knew it had been a woman. Sobbing with fear she turned back to wrestle with the latch. The door swung open with ease.

'Ma? Are you all right?' She could hear Greg's voice calling her; not worried, not afraid, just curious. Hadn't he heard her screams then? Swallowing hard in an attempt to steady herself, she looked back into the room. The first aid box was on the shelf by the door where she would have seen it straight away if she had looked. Grabbing it she slammed the door behind her and went back into the living room.

'Couldn't find it for a minute.' She gave Greg a bright unnatural smile. 'Right. What I need is some boiling water and the TCP and I'm ready for you.' She hunted out a towel from the drawer while the kettle boiled, putting it gently under Greg's foot, fussing about laying out her equipment on the table.

He put a hand on her arm. 'Are you OK?'

She nodded. 'I'm fine.'

'It's going to be all right.' He gave her a reassuring smile. 'There's an explanation for all this; nothing can bring Bill back, but I know it had nothing to do with Allie. Once the police get here they'll sort it all out, you'll see.'

She nodded again, concentrating on sorting out her dressings and bandages.

She boiled the razor blade for several minutes, then,

washing her hands first with soap and water, then in the TCP she waited for it to cool before picking it up. 'Don't look.'

He grinned. 'If I don't look I might find you've chopped my foot off.' He gritted his teeth as she laid the blade against the stretched swollen skin. She hardly seemed to apply any pressure at all but suddenly the wound was erupting in a froth of yellow-green pus. He swallowed hard, averting his eyes in spite of himself, wincing as he felt the pressure of her fingers pressing out the last of the poison. She swabbed the wound again and again, holding the cotton wool with a pair of tweezers, then at last it was over. He felt the cool, clean dressing on the fiery skin, and then the bandage.

'Thanks.' He spoke through gritted teeth, amazed to find he felt dizzy with pain.

She had noticed. 'Rest a minute and I'll make us both a cup of tea.' She was gathering the swabs and throwing them into the bin, clearing up the mess, wiping down the table. Collecting the kettle, she was half way to the sink when the lights went out.

'Shit!' Greg stared round. 'It must be a fuse.'

'Don't you move.' Diana put a hand on his shoulder as he started to get up. 'Wait there and I'll go and look in the cupboard.'

The room was dim without the lights; the windows allowed a grey, dismal daylight to filter in from the garden where, they realised suddenly, it had started snowing again – soft white flakes this time, drifting down out of the heavy sky.

The loud crash upstairs made them look at each other in alarm.

'Allie!' Greg said. 'She's woken up.' He glanced at his father. Roger had not stirred, his head cushioned on his arm.

'I'll go.' Diana put down the kettle, horrified and

ashamed to find that she was afraid – afraid of going to her own daughter.

'Be careful. Remember she's not herself,' Greg said softly.

She glared at him. 'Who are you suggesting she is?'

'I don't know. No one. I'm just saying, take care. She's been through a lot and she's had awful nightmares and I don't think she knows what she's doing half the time at the moment.'

Another crash followed the first and they both looked up. 'That came from Patrick's room,' Diana whispered.

'Take the rolling pin,' Greg murmured as she moved towards the upright studs which divided the living room from the kitchen. 'Just in case.'

'To hit my own daughter?' She stopped.

'If necessary, yes. For both your sakes.' He levered himself to his feet. 'Damn and blast this foot. I'm coming with you.'

'No, Greg –'

'Yes. Give me a walking stick from the hall. I'll be fine as long as I don't put too much weight on it.' He was staring up at the ceiling.

She brought it without further argument and then led the way to the staircase, pulling open the door which hid the dark stairwell. Looking up she listened, aware that Greg was right behind her, breathing painfully as he tried to balance with the stick.

Holding her breath she began to climb the stairs. At the top she peered cautiously down the passage. It was empty. Alison's bedroom door was closed as she had left it. The key was in the pocket of her trousers. She closed her hand around it and with a glance over her shoulder towards Greg, she moved stealthily towards the door and listened. At the far end of the passage the door to Patrick's room stood slightly ajar.

Biting her lip as she tried to move soundlessly, Diana led

the way down the passage towards it. Behind her Greg felt the sweat break out on his forehead as he forced himself to walk softly after her. Without lights the upper hall was almost dark; the black beams threw wedges of shadow across the soft pink of the ceiling. The curtains, though open, blocked whatever light filtered in from the heavy sky. The garden was totally silent. Even the sound of the wind had died. Diana tightened her grip on the rolling pin, slowing as she approached the door, reluctant to go in.

Behind her Greg frowned. He could feel the skin on the back of his neck crawling. He put his hand out and gripped his mother's arm. 'Let me,' he whispered.

She did not argue. Flattening herself against the wall, she let him pass and watched as very slowly he pushed open Patrick's door with the end of the stick. Peering over his shoulder she could not at first see anything, then slowly her eyes began to make out the dark interior of the room. 'Hell, look at his books.' Greg spoke out loud. He pushed the door back against the wall and took a step inside. The contents of every bookshelf had been tipped into the centre of the floor. There was no one there.

'Allie did this? Why? How did she get out?' Diana spoke in a whisper. The room smelled faintly of lavender.

Greg shrugged. He ran his stick under the bed, grunting with pain as his foot caught his weight, then he pulled open the cupboard door. There was nowhere in the room for anyone to hide. Pushing past him Diana pulled back the curtains, letting in a little more light. It revealed nothing but the shambles of books in the middle of the carpet. 'Some of them are torn,' she said sadly as she stood surveying the mess. 'He'll be so upset.'

'Where is she?' Greg turned and hopped back onto the landing. One by one he threw open the other doors – his own room, his parents', the bathroom. All were empty. It left only Alison's. 'She must be back in there.' He glanced at his mother. 'Shall I look?'

She nodded bleakly. He put his hand on the door knob and turned it. Nothing happened. 'It's locked,' he said in a whisper. 'Is there a bolt on the inside?'

She shook her head. 'I've got the key.' She put it into his hand. He frowned. With only a slight hesitation he inserted it into the lock and turned it as quietly as he could.

Alison's room too was dark, the curtains closed, the light which had been on beside her bed now off like the others. Greg stood in the doorway peering into the darkness, trying to see. If only they still had a torch that worked. His ears, straining in the silence adjusted to the sound of breathing. It was slow and steady and came from the bed. He groped in his pocket suddenly as he remembered his matches. Pushing his stick at his mother, who was immediately behind him, he struck one and held it high. The light was small and barely touched the room, but it was enough to see the hunched form of his sister in the bed. Wincing with pain he took a shuffled step forward and held it near her face. For a brief second, before it went out, he saw her closed eyes, the dark lashes on her cheek, her fist, clutching the blanket below her chin. Holding his breath he waited, half expecting her to leap from the bed with a scream, but nothing happened. The silence extended and filled the room again. All he could hear was her slow, heavy breathing, and behind him his mother's, quicker, lighter, exuding fear. Carefully he withdrew another match. The rasping sound as he struck it seemed to echo deafeningly as it flared and steadied, but Alison's lids did not flicker. He watched her for several seconds before raising the match high and glancing round the rest of the room. As far as he could see it was as it should be: her clothes lay in heaps on the floor, tapes and books in confusion on the chairs and table, but nothing seemed out of the ordinary. Nothing but the smell. As the frail light went out again he sniffed. The room was full of the heavy, spicy odour he had smelt before in the study. His mouth dry he began to back out. Diana moved with him. Without a sound he pulled the door closed and relocked it, then, taking his mother's hand, he led her towards the staircase.

Safely downstairs he subsided into one of the deep armchairs beside his sleeping father. He realised suddenly that he was shaking again. A sheen of sweat iced his skin as the pain, which had seemed dulled upstairs, swept up his leg and took hold of him again. He lay back and closed his eyes, fighting to remain conscious.

'I'll check the fuses.' Diana's voice reached him through the roar in his ears. She groped in his pocket for the matchbox, paused for a moment to rest a gentle hand on Roger's head, then she had gone.

Greg had allowed himself to slide away into the spinning kaleidoscope of pain, settling deeper into something approaching sleep when he felt a glass being pushed into his hand. 'Brandy.' The voice was crisp and commanding. 'Come on, Greg. I'm sorry, but I need you awake.'

He opened his lips obediently and felt the fire on his tongue. For one more minute he resisted, then, choking, he felt himself propelled into full consciousness.

'There are no trips out and I've tried all the fuses. Nothing works.'

Opening his eyes he realised the room was full of candlelight. He was still disorientated. 'Did you smell the perfume?'

'What perfume?' She sounded irritated. 'Did you hear me, Greg? The electricity is off. All of it. And I can't find out what's wrong.' Her voice rose slightly and he realised that it was fear that he could hear. Desperately he took a grip on himself and swigged another mouthful of the brandy. Fire shot through his veins this time, and he felt his head clearing rapidly. 'It's the wind and the snow,' he said as steadily as he could. 'You know we are always being cut off when the weather's bad. We've got the fire, and the Aga and candles. There's nothing to worry about.'

'No.' She didn't sound convinced. 'What happened upstairs, Greg, it wasn't Allie, was it.' She sat down on the arm of the chair beside him. He could feel her trembling as she leaned against his shoulder. He reached for her hand and pressed it gently. 'No. It wasn't Allie.'

'Then who – ?'

He shook his head. 'The wind? An earth tremor? Perhaps the shelves were under too much stress. Perhaps it was the cats. Where are they? Those two are quite capable of knocking a million books when they play scatty cats round the house.'

'When they were young, perhaps.' She sniffed. 'Not now. Not for ages. Normally they are here, by the fire.' Suddenly her eyes filled with tears. 'I haven't seen them since Allie came back.'

Greg frowned. Now that he noticed, their absence was a tangible thing. He took it for granted that one or the other or both would always be there, in the chair where he was sitting now, or on the sofa with his father, or on the rocking chair beside the Aga. The room without them was unfurnished; empty. Threatening. 'I expect they've gone out before the weather worsens,' he said, trying to comfort. 'They won't have gone far, not when it's like this. They're soft little buggers, for all they like to think they're so tough.'

'Oh Greg!' A sob escaped her in spite of all her efforts to sound calm. 'What's happening? The car; the cats; Allie; Bill – I can't bear it.'

He put his arm around her. 'Just a sequence of strange coincidences,' he said as firmly as he could. 'And some bastard out there who will be behind bars before much longer if Paddy and Kate have anything to do with it.'

'They will get through?' It was a plea.

'Of course they will get through.' He wished he felt as positive as he sounded.

L

Sleet hit the side of the dune, lodging in the crevices of sand, standing a moment, half snow, half ice, then melting into the cracks and crannies. A further lump of sand fell away, and behind it the black peat, spongy, sweet, no longer encased in its jacket of airtight clay and meeting daylight for the first time in nearly two thousand years, began to wash in a black streak down the face of the excavation.

Deep down the great golden torc, symbol of Nion's royal blood, settled further into the subsoil. Torn from its silver companion by its weight and accepted by whichever gods there were in that black underworld, it would never again see the light of the sun.

Far above, the sea was meek, restless, the waves brown from the sandbanks which the storm had chewed over and rearranged in the night. Overhead a skein of geese, flying low and fast, sent their ringing bugle cries out into the wind where they were lost.

Another high tide, another storm and the dune would be gone, the peat and the clay mingling in the churning depths of the North Sea, its secret hidden forever. Another slice of soft black soil peeled off and slid away and the air, corroding, acid, insidious, touched the arm which lay there cushioned on what had once been a raft of flowering rushes. Around the humerus, loose where once it had clung tightly, lay the twisted semi-circle of a priestly arm-ring.

* * *

'Come on, through here.' Patrick turned and gave Kate his hand. They were both panting now, exhausted from the scramble through the tangled, wet undergrowth.

'You are sure you know where this short cut goes?' Kate climbed after him, hearing her jacket rip once again on a trailing bramble as she levered herself up the slippery bank to stand beside him in a clearing.

'Of course. Greg and I used to come this way all the time. It doesn't go anywhere near the lane; it cuts off the whole corner and comes out just below the Farnboroughs' place.' Patrick looked round. It was quite dark in the clearing; the trees, glistening with sleet, hung low above their heads and they could hear the hiss of rain on the leaves of a holm oak. The air smelled of wet earth and beech mast and rotting leaves.

Kate shivered. She glanced at Patrick again. He had slung the gun across his back; in his hand was a stout staff which he had pulled from a thicket as they dived into the woods. Both gave her comfort. She glanced behind her again. Not for the first time she had the feeling that they were being watched. Her fist tightened on her own stick. Not as long as Paddy's, but just as sturdy, she held it in front of her as she looked from side to side into the shadows.

Patrick saw her glance. 'There's no one around.' He did not sound very confident. 'If there were we'd hear the birds go up. Pheasants. Pigeon. They make a hell of a din if they are disturbed – you heard when we set them off. And there are magpies down here. They would all let us know if there was anyone around – or anything.'

She nodded. 'I wish we had a dog with us all the same.'

Patrick nodded. He grinned. 'A detachment of paras wouldn't go amiss either. Come on. It can't be much further. Once we're on the road we'll feel better.'

So, he was feeling it too. Kate looked behind her again. There was no sign of the way they had come. The tangle of brambles and dead brown grasses and nettles had closed without leaving any sign of where they had forced their way through. She felt a moment of panic. 'Which way?'

'Upwards. The road is quite a lot higher than Redall. It's uphill all the way, I'm afraid. We're bound to hit the road somewhere between Welsly Cross and the Farnboroughs'. We can't get lost.'

'No?' she grinned wanly. 'I hope those aren't famous last words.'

He was about to set off again when he stopped. He gave her a long look, his thin face drooping with exhaustion. 'You look absolutely whacked.'

She smiled. 'So do you.'

'It will all be over soon, won't it?'

'Of course it will.' Trying to reassure him did nothing for her own confidence. She glanced up at the sky. Where she could see it, between the interlaced branches of the thicket, it was growing increasingly black. 'We ought to get on.'

'I know. It was an excuse to get my breath back.' He hitched the gun higher onto his shoulder then he turned and led the way with more bravado than confidence up the high slippery bank which led out of the thicket and, he hoped, towards the north.

Ten minutes later he stopped. 'There ought to be some kind of path. But I suppose it could be overgrown.' He sounded doubtful.

'Have you got a compass?' It was the sort of thing all boys in the country festooned themselves with as far as she could remember.

He shook his head. 'I know this path like the back of my hand.'

She refrained from comment.

He bit his lip. 'It's getting so dark.'

'I know. There's more snow on the way. You can smell it.'

He smiled. 'And to think Greg thought you were Lady

Muck from the town. You know more about the country than he does in many ways.'

'I can believe it —' She broke off as she saw a movement out of the corner of her eye. She spun round, staring into the shadows of the trees. 'What was that?' she whispered.

'Where?' He swung the gun off his shoulder.

'I thought I saw something move.'

They stared in silence for a moment, side by side.

'Probably a rabbit or a deer,' Patrick said softly.

He slipped the safety catch off the gun with a barely perceptible click.

She strained her eyes into the distance, trying to penetrate the murky depths of the scrub. There it was again, a shadow against the shadows, upright. Human. 'There.' Her whisper was scarcely audible. Inside her warm jacket she could feel her skin growing cold. 'There is someone there.'

'What shall we do?' Patrick's voice rose in panic and she was reminded suddenly that he was only a schoolboy and that he was probably far more scared than she was. If that were possible.

'I don't know. He must have seen us.'

'Do you think he's got a gun?'

She shook her head. 'I doubt it. We'd know by now.'

'Shall I shoot at him; try and scare him off?'

'I don't know.' She had started to shake again. 'Supposing it makes him angry?'

'If it does and he comes at us, at least we'll see who he is. And I can shoot him for real.' She saw Patrick's finger curling round the trigger.

She had only taken her eyes off the shadow for a second. Now as she looked back it had moved closer. It was tall; dark. To her horror she saw that it was moving quite swiftly, seeming to have no problem with the rough, tangled undergrowth. 'Yes. Go on, shoot.' She could hear her voice shaking with fear.

The report from the gun was colossal. It reverberated

through the woods, echoing from the trees, temporarily deafening her. A pheasant rose shrieking into the sky, followed by a pair of pigeons, their wings smacking loudly. Patrick lowered the gun cautiously, feeling in his pocket for his cartridges. 'Where is he now? Did I hit him?' To his chagrin he didn't know whether or not he had aimed at the shadowy figure. He had been too frightened to think.

'I can't see.' She stared into the trees, forcing her eyes to focus into the darkest corners. There was nothing there.

With shaking hands Patrick reloaded the gun. 'If I've killed someone I'll go to prison.'

'Not if he murdered Bill, you won't.' She touched his shoulder reassuringly. 'I don't know if it was anyone. It could have been a shadow.'

'Should we check?'

She hesitated then she shook her head. 'Let's get onto the road and fetch the police. They can look.'

Slowly, more nervously now, they began to make their way forward again. Minutes later Paddy stopped so suddenly Kate cannoned into him. 'Look.' He pointed ahead.

She followed his finger and caught her breath. He was there again. On the rabbit track in front of them. Beside her Patrick raised his gun. She saw the barrel wavering as he felt for the safety catch and slid it back.

She stared at it. It was no more than a shadow; she could see no features – no face at all, just a silhouette. But it was a man.

He had disappeared before Patrick could move his finger to the trigger. 'Where is he?' He was frozen, the gun to his shoulder.

'Gone.' Kate could feel herself trembling. 'He vanished as I was watching. Paddy, keep the gun at the ready. Let's walk on slowly.'

She stepped forward, so close to Patrick he could feel her jacket brushing against his arm.

'One shouldn't walk with a loaded gun,' he whispered.

'This is an emergency. Just don't trip up.' They were there already; where it had been standing. She looked down. There were no footprints in the mud.

'Marcus?' She breathed the name out loud.

Patrick lowered the gun. 'I don't like this, Kate. And we should have been at the road by now.' He glanced over his shoulder. 'We're lost.'

'How big are these woods?' She was still scouring the ground for signs of footprints. She could see rabbit here and there, where it was soft, and the deep, sharply-cut slots of a deer, but none that had been made by a man.

'Hundreds of acres. The other side they're conifer plantations. They go for miles.' He shivered visibly.

'Can you find your way back to Redall?' She glanced at him. The boy was near to tears.

He shook his head. 'I don't know where we are.'

'Right.' It sounded confident. 'Let's think. Your original plan of following the rising ground sounds a sensible one. We can't stay out here all day; we've got to keep moving. Let's do that. Let's move only upwards, then, if as you say, we cross the road we'll be fine.' She was trying to picture the map in her head. The sea would be to the east; the estuary to the south. That left only two directions: north where the road ran east-west towards the coast, or due west where presumably the woods spread out until they reached the bleak, agricultural prairie lands east of Colchester and south of the soft wooded folds of the Stour valley.

'Come on. We can't get lost, Paddy. Not here. This is hardly uncharted country. We're just getting tired and cold.'

'And frightened,' he put in. She wished he hadn't.

'All right, and frightened.'

'You think it's Marcus, don't you.'

She shook her head. 'I don't know. I don't know what

to think. I don't want to think any more. Let's save our strength for walking.'

He hesitated, about to say something, then he changed his mind. Breaking the gun he lowered it to his side. 'OK. Lay on Macduff. Which way would you say is up?'

She glanced round. 'Straight on up this rabbit track. Shall I go first?' It was only wide enough for them to go in single file. She saw him hesitate, and knew he was longing to say yes, but chivalry or male pride, or the possession of the gun or a bit of all three won and he shook his head. 'I'll go. You can protect my rear.' The giggle he gave was a little hysterical.

Two minutes later he stopped with a gasp of terror. The shadow on the track was barely ten feet in front of them. A swirl of icy wind swept round it, whipping leaves and soil off the ground, howling up through the branches of the trees, gaining in strength until it rose to a scream as the hatred and anger hit them like a tangible force. Kate heard Patrick cry out and she saw him reel to one side, the gun flying into the air. For a moment she couldn't breathe. She could feel a constriction round her throat. Her feet refused to move. She wanted to run, to run faster than she had ever run in her life before but she couldn't take even the first step. There was an enormous bang somewhere inside her head and suddenly everything went black.

LI

Fat, confident, unsuspecting, the priests died like sheep, their throats cut like butter, their indignant, protesting whimpers still on their lips as they fell. So much for the power of their gods! He wiped his knife on a fold of his cloak and sheathed it with a triumphant smile. That was the end of the matter. The Britons, the whore, all dead, all gone to Hades and perdition. No one would know. The land would not tell. The men of the Trinovantes, who would give an arm each for a reason to fall on Rome, would never find reason for rebellion from him. This small drama would die as it had flourished on the edge of the mud. If men had disappeared, it would be assumed that the gods had called for more than one sacrifice; they were greedy these British gods; they lapped blood like dogs in the arena.

He folded his arms and stared out across the marsh, towards the eastern sky. It was clear now of cloud. The sun shone cold and hazy, clean like the blade of his knife, the light incising the wind. The heaviness of salt was in the air, overshadowing the flat, sallow smell of mud, cleansing it, purifying it with the incense of the northern seas. His eyes flicked down at the rushes which grew at the marsh's edge; they were green, the ends tipped with spiky, iridescent flowers. Nothing disturbed them. There was no sign that anyone had passed that way at all. He flexed the muscles of his fingers slowly, staring down at his hand. Four lives, snuffed out like flames, as though they had never been. And no one would ever know.

* * *

It was the sound of a shot which awoke her. Loud, close, exploding in her brain. Then silence. A long long silence where she floundered painfully in nothingness. A shot. It couldn't have been a shot. Who would be shooting? The sound must have been in her head. A part of the nightmare. A part of the pain. Giving up the struggle to make sense of nonsense Cissy slept again.

'*Mummy!*'

A cry this time, floating into her head like a dream. 'Mummy, I'm hurting. Help me.'

The sound spun round and round, and finally lodged in some part of her brain which was capable of a reaction. Cissy forced her eyes open with a groan. 'Susie?' She tried to move. There was a tight band around her ribs, preventing her from breathing properly. 'Susie?'

'*Mummy.*' The word was followed by a sob.

The sound cut through the last of Cissy's confusion. Christ! She'd crashed the car. She lifted her head with difficulty and stared round, trying to make sense of a world upside down. No, not upside down. On its side. The car was on its side and she was hanging from her seat belt. She looked down. Red. Blood. An awful lot of blood. Dear God, had Sue been wearing a seat belt at all? The child was below her, huddled in the well in front of the passenger seat.

'Are you all right?' Somehow she managed to make her voice work calmly in spite of the pain in her ribs which was, she realised, excruciating.

'We've crashed!' The reply was couched in the tone of a complaint.

'I can see that, darling.' Cissy bit her lip, trying to keep herself under control. 'Darling, I don't see how I can move. Are you hurt? Try and move each one of your arms and legs in turn. See if they're all right.' Her eyes were heavy. She wanted to close them, to slide away from the pain.

'They're OK.'

'And your head. Does that hurt?'

Sue moved it from side to side experimentally and her eyes filled with tears. 'Yes.'

'And your neck?'

'Yes.'

'But not so badly you can't move.'

'No.'

'Is there any way you can climb out?' The windscreen had gone, she realised hazily. That was why it was so cold. She was shaking now, her whole body shuddering in tight, agonised spasms. 'If I undo my seat belt I'm going to fall on top of you.'

'Is the car going to explode?' Sue was crying so hard she had not heard anything.

'No, darling, of course it's not going to explode. Range Rovers can't explode.' If they could, presumably it would have done so by now. 'Please, Susie, I want you to try and be brave. We have to get ourselves out of here. See if you can wriggle out of the windscreen. Then see if you can stand up.' She was finding it hard to breathe now. 'This is an awfully big adventure.' Who had said that? Peter Pan, was it? But he was talking about death. 'Please, darling. You must get out. If you can't help me, you have to go down to Redall and get help. If I . . .' she swallowed and choked, '. . . if I pass out, you musn't be frightened. I think I've broken some ribs. It's not serious —' please God '— but it's very painful. I think we've got to cut the strap.' Everything was spinning round her. She frowned, trying to focus. She couldn't see Susie at all now. Or hear. Why couldn't she hear? She tried to lift her head and look round, but her eyes were blurred with tears. Hands. Where were her hands? Why couldn't she use her hands?

'I'm out, Mummy.' Susie's voice was further away, but it seemed to be stronger. 'I think I'm all right.' Suddenly her face was there, close to Cissy's. 'Can you climb out?'

Cissy tried to think. Climb out. It seemed like a good

idea, but how? She seemed to be suspended by her pain, swimming in space.

'I . . .' She tried again. 'I'm all right. My ribs. I think my ribs are hurt.'

'It's the seat belt. You're hanging in the seat belt.' Susie's voice was extraordinarily strong. 'I'll see if I can cut it with something.'

'No.' Shaking her head hurt. Perhaps her neck was broken too. Her thoughts were scattered, like a flock of pigeons after a bird scarer has gone off. Regroup them. Bring them in. Make sense. 'Can't cut it. You've got to undo it.'

'Mum, I can't. Look, you're pushing down on the slot.' Susie's hair was sweeping her face. 'We've got to lift you up somehow. Can you pull yourself this way?'

The girl's hands were cool, competent. She would make a good nurse. Cissy pondered her hands for a few seconds. 'Mummy!' The voice was cross now; impatient. 'Concentrate. You can't hang there. We've got to get you out. Put your hand up here. Where mine is. That's it. Now hold on. There. Tightly.'

She'd make a good commander too; firm. Positive. Calm. Lost in her endless pop music, it was easy to forget what the child was like as a person. She had become a shadow, walking round the house jerking to an unheard rhythm –

'Mummy!'

Silly girl. Giving orders. Silly orders.

'Mummy! Put your hand here.'

Impatient too. Stroppy little cow her father called her. Joe. Joe! Where was Joe?

She must have called out loud. Susie's face was there, in front of her again. Concerned, swimming in brightness. 'Dad will come soon, but we have to get you out.'

Susie had seen the slight dribble of blood at the corner of her mother's mouth. It terrified her. It should be Cissy comforting her, not the other way round. She glanced yet again over her shoulder into the dark trees. There had been no sign of him, the kook who had stood in the middle of the track in front of them and caused her mother to skid, but he must still be out there. He must have seen them crash.

Marcus

The name floated into her mind. Allie's Marcus. The dead Roman from the grave on the beach.

'Mummy!' Her terror gave her strength and she turned back to the smashed windscreen, leaning against the bonnet, trying to get a purchase on her mother's shoulder. 'When I say, try and take as much of your weight as you can here, on the doorframe. I'll see if I can free your belt.' She took a deep breath and reached into the car through the shattered glass. There was blood on the seat belt; the catch was slippery, hard to press, the belt strained beneath her mother's weight. She curled her fingers round the release and braced herself. 'Now. Now, go on, lift yourself as much as you can. NOW!' Frantically she pressed, wrenching the catch. Nothing happened. 'Don't let go. Pull up harder!' It must open. It must.

Pull. Cissy closed her fingers around the windowframe where Susie had positioned them. Pull. Good idea. Take her weight. Take the strain off her ribs. She pulled again and the pressure had gone.

'Done it!' The shriek in her ear was ecstatic. Then she was falling. Frantically she clung on again. Susie's arm around her took her full weight and she felt the girl stagger; the arm closed around her and the pain was renewed in force but somehow she was half out of the windscreen. Flailing with her hands she felt grass and brambles; her weight was sliding her out of the car across the bonnet to the ground and suddenly she was lying on the mud, huddled, hips high, hugging her pain.

'Well done!' Susie was triumphant. 'Now sit up comfortably. Lean against the bank here.'

The girl glanced up into the trees again. There was something there. It moved slightly in the darkness of the shadows. She stood up, letting her mother slump back to the ground, her eyes straining to see what it was.

'Who's there?' Her voice was shaking. 'Greg? Paddy?' Please let it be one of them. They must be near the farmhouse. She glanced round, confused. How far had they come before they crashed? She couldn't remember.

It was there again. The movement in the trees. She could feel her mouth, dry as sandpaper; she couldn't breathe properly. Her knees were beginning to shake. 'Mummy.' It was a reflex action, this desperate whisper for help. She knew her mother couldn't hear her. 'Mummy, can you see him?'

The figure was tall; the face, dark, aquiline, cruel. Strange, she had always thought ghosts would be transparent, insubstantial, traversable should they cross one's path. Without fully realising she had done it, she sank to the ground beside her mother and reached for Cissy's hand. 'Mummy. Help me. He's coming.'

Cissy heard her. She tried to move her fingers but they didn't seem to work; her words of reassurance were lost as blood seeped into her throat.

LII

Joe frowned and glanced once again at his wristwatch. Strange that they weren't back.

He could smell the beef. The whole house was full of appetising scents which made his juices flow. Perhaps she didn't realise the time; she always got carried away, did Cissy, when she went down to Redall; something about that house that made one forget the time – he had felt it too. But if she was bringing them back, surely they should be here by now? He glanced at his watch once again; it was after three. The meat would be ruined. He glanced at the oven and shook his head. Tempted though he was to start without them perhaps he'd better get down there and see what was wrong. Grabbing an oven cloth off the rail he pulled open the door and pulled out the meat pan. The meat was dry, shrunk on the bone, the potatoes almost black. He shook his head sadly and pushed the trays of food onto the counter. Spoiled anyway.

Outside he glanced up at the sky. The light was nearly gone already, the cloud black and threatening, the wind – he sniffed knowledgeably – coming a degree or so round to the north. That would bring real snow; the kind they hadn't seen for four years on this coast. Thoughtfully he hauled himself up into the old Land Rover which stood by the barn and leaned forward to turn the key.

At first he didn't recognise what he saw; his eyes refused to make sense of the axles, the wheels, the exhaust which were all he could see of his Range Rover, on its side in the ditch. In the headlights, through the driving sleet, all he could see was a pattern of shiny mud and steel. Then he realised and his stomach turned over. He skidded to a halt, and leaving the headlights trained on the wreck, he levered himself out of the driving seat and jumped down into the slush. 'Cissy?' Dear sweet lord, where were they? 'Susie my love?' He jumped into the ditch and clambered round to the far side of the vehicle, his boots sliding and squelching, catching in the brambles.

The black silhouette of the wreck cut out the powerful beam of his headlights and it was a moment before his eyes adjusted enough to the dim light to see Cissy, sitting, leaning against the bonnet, her eyes closed. Susie was curled up close to her, her arms wrapped around her knees, rocking slowly from side to side.

'Susie?' Joe called.

The girl tightened her grip on her knees. 'She's dead.' She did not look up. 'She's dead.' Tears were streaming down her face.

Joe scrambled closer and knelt down beside her, his craggy face white. He could hardly see for tears himself. 'No. No, baby, no.' Tearing off his gloves, he reached past her and gently he took Cissy's wrist in his own. It was cold. 'Ciss? Ciss, my love? Come on.' His fingers were rough and split, no good for this sort of thing. Persistently he felt all over her wrist, pressing the soft cold skin until suddenly he felt a faint flutter.

'She's not dead, Sue.' He was trembling as much as his daughter. 'Nearly, but not quite. Help me lift her. We'll get her into the back of the Land Rover.'

He scooped her up into his arms as though she were no weight at all, and slipping and sliding, carried her back to the track. The open back was full of old tools and sacks and bits of twine. 'Hop in, Susie. Take your Mum's head in your lap. Keep her comfy.' His calmness now that there was something to do was infectious. Susie obeyed him, sitting on the floor, pulling sacks over her mother's inert body.

Joe walked back to the driving seat and pulled himself into it. One look at the steep, icy track down which he had slithered only minutes before told him they were unlikely to make it back that way. 'I reckon we'll take her down to Redall. Diana will know what to do to keep her comfy. She used to be a nurse. Then if their phone is still not working I'll get back on the back lane to phone for an ambulance. Hold her now, Susie my love. You'd almost got there, you know. We're only a few hundred yards from Redall.'

He refused to consider the possibility that she might be dead. He had felt a pulse. He was sure of it. Letting in the clutch with infinite care he dragged the Land Rover back onto the track and headed on down towards the farmhouse.

Diana had seen them coming, but not until Joe emerged from behind the wheel did she open the front door. 'Joe? Thank God! Where are the police? Are they coming?'

'The police?' Joe shook his head, preoccupied with his own sorrow. 'I haven't called them yet, nor the ambulance. I reckoned I'd leave her here with you and try and get back up through a side track. It's all too slippery up there even for this old girl.' He slapped the vehicle with a gnarled hand as he walked round the back and tenderly lifted Cissy out.

'Cissy!' Diana cried. 'What's wrong with her?' Behind her Roger rose wearily to his feet. He peered over her shoulder.

'We crashed the Range Rover.' Susie scrambled out after her mother. 'She's dead. I know she's dead!' She burst into tears again.

'Bring her in. Quickly.' Diana glanced out into the darkness of the woods. Dusk was coming early. The snow was feathering down out of a bruised, blackened sky. The woods were silent.

'Put her down on the sofa.' She stared down at Cissy's white face, and then, as Joe had done, reached for her wrist. 'Where are Paddy and Kate? Didn't you see them?'

More practised than Joe, she found a pulse almost at once. It was faint but steady.

Behind them Greg emerged from the study. Quietly he shut the front door and bolted it. The candles in the living room flickered.

Standing around the sofa Greg, Roger, Susie and Joe stared down at the still figure lying there. Diana sat beside her, cautiously running her hands over her still form, refraining from any comment about the way Joe had man-handled his wife out of the Land Rover. If her neck or back were injured it was too late to say anything now. There were bruises on her face, a cut on her lip – please God that was where the blood was coming from – livid bruises on Cissy's shoulders and ribs as Diana opened her blouse.

'Joe, I think you should go back and phone for an ambulance now,' Greg said as he watched his mother's hands. 'And we need the police. Somebody has beaten Bill Norcross to death.'

The action of Joe's jaw lifted his scalp until his whole face seemed to slip back in surprise, but still he did not take his eyes off his wife. 'You reckon they attacked Cissy?' He looked at Greg at last, a deep flush spreading up from his neck across his face.

'No, Dad. We skidded. There was a man –' Susie stopped short.

'A man?' Greg turned to scrutinize her face.

'What man, Susie?' Joe grabbed her and turned her to face him. 'You didn't say anything about a man.'

'He . . . he appeared in front of us.' Susie started crying

374

again. 'Mummy jammed on the brakes and we began to spin round. I banged my head on the window.'

'What did he look like, Susie?' Greg kept his voice gentle.

'He was dressed in a long cloak thing. He had a sword . . .'

'A sword!' As Greg and Diana looked at each other Joe's words were an incredulous echo.

'And you saw no sign of Kate or Patrick?' Diana was feeling down each of Cissy's legs. Nothing broken there at least.

'No.' Susie shook her head violently.

'They had a gun,' Greg put in.

'I think I heard a gun going off,' Susie broke free of her father's hands and went to kneel beside her mother. 'Just after the crash. There was a big bang.'

Diana closed her eyes briefly. Somehow she managed to keep her hands steady as she took the rug which Greg handed her and pulled it up over Cissy's inert form. Standing up she turned to Joe. 'You must go and get help, Joe. We'll look after her as best we can but she needs a doctor. I think she's only bruised, but she might be concussed. She must have an X-ray.'

'But she'll be all right?' Joe looked down at her miserably. He felt lost and abandoned.

'I hope so.' Diana smiled at him; she rested a hand on his arm. 'Susie can stay here; I'll take care of them both, Joe, I promise.'

He nodded. For a moment he hesitated self-consciously, wanting to stoop and kiss his wife, then awkwardly he turned away.

Greg hopped after him. In the hallway he spoke in low, urgent tones. 'Joe, there's a maniac out there. Be careful for God's sake. Paddy and Kate set out hours ago to ring from your place. Keep your eyes open for them, and tell the police what's happened.'

Joe nodded curtly. He reached out to open the door. 'You take care of them all here.'

'I will, don't worry.' The grimness of Greg's tone was reassuring.

Joe paused on the doorstep. The world was totally silent, wrapped in whirling snow. For a moment he hesitated, unwilling to cross the few yards of white ground to his Land Rover, then shaking his head, he strode forward, hearing Greg bolt the door behind him.

Walking round to the back he reached in over the tail gate for his gun, wedged into clips which had been screwed onto the vehicle's frame. Wrenching it free he pushed back the lid on the box which sat beneath the side seat. His cartridges were there; left after the last shoot. He could lose his licence for carelessness like that, but who was to know. Almost kissing them he stuffed them into the baggy pocket of his jacket and climbed behind the wheel. Laying the gun on the seat next to him he reached for the key which he had left in the ignition, his eyes on the windscreen which was blanked out with snow.

The key clicked uselessly.

He turned it again and again without success. Behind him the door of the house opened again. Greg had obviously been watching from the study window. 'What's wrong?' His voice was muffled by the snow.

'Darned battery's flat. Hold on, I'll try the starting handle.' He climbed out, glad that someone else was there. The silence of the woods was becoming oppressive.

The metal was cold through his gloves as he inserted it and swung it round. The engine remained dead. 'Damned bloody thing!' He tried again, feeling the sweat start on his forehead.

Behind him Greg was watching the trees. He could feel his skin prickling with fear. Someone – or something – was watching them. He was sure of it. 'Joe,' he called quietly. 'Joe, bring the gun and get in here.'

'I'll just give it one more try.'

'No, Joe. Don't bother. Grab your gun and come in.'

There was something in the urgency of Greg's tone which stopped Joe in his tracks. He straightened. He could feel it too now, a building panic crawling across him. Leaving the handle where it was he reached in and grabbed the shotgun, then turning, he sprinted the few yards back to the farmhouse. Greg slammed the door behind him and threw the bolts across. Both men stood for a moment in the small hallway and listened. There was no sound from outside. 'You reckon he's out there?' Joe whispered.

Greg nodded.

'You've seen him?'

'Kate and I saw him down on the shore.'

'And Norcross is dead?' It seemed only just to have sunk in. 'Are you sure?'

'Quite sure.' Greg's tone left no room for doubt. 'What the hell do we do now, Joe? We have to have help.'

'I could take your car. I reckon that old Volvo would have a good chance of getting up the back lane.'

Greg shook his head. 'Our old Volvo is out on the marsh, Joe. Don't ask how it got there, and our Land Rover is smashed up; it hit a tree.'

Joe stared. 'You mean there are no cars working? None at all?'

'And no phones.'

The two men stared at one another. 'You reckon he did it. He caused Cissy's crash.'

'And Kate's. He tried to kill me on the beach.' Greg paused. 'Wait, Joe. I've just remembered. Kate's little car. The Peugeot. It's in the barn. I don't know if it would make it up the lane, but it might be worth a try.'

'Right.' Joe dug down into his pocket and came up with two cartridges. 'I'll put a couple of these up the spout, then we'll have a go. Is the barn unlocked?'

Greg shrugged. He rummaged in the drawer of the table.

Two small padlock keys on a large ring appeared and he pressed them into Joe's hand. 'I'll come with you. Hold on while I get my boots.'

'No.' Joe shook his head. 'I reckon I'll be quicker on my own. You look after your dad and the women.'

'I don't know if she left a key in it.'

'If she didn't I reckon I'll smash the window and hotwire it. I'm sure she'll forgive me in an emergency. My Cissy needs a doctor. No car door is going to come between me and that.'

Once more Greg unbarred the door and pulled it open. It was beginning to grow dark. The shadowed woods were in stark contrast to the brilliant whiteness of the lawn. Somewhere in the distance a pheasant let out its manic alarm cry. Joe tightened his grip on the gun. He gave a quick thumbs up sign to Greg then he turned and ran towards the black barn.

The padlock hung open from the hasp. Joe stared at it. His hackles were stirring again, like the back of a frightened dog. Cautiously he put his hand to the door and pulled it open a fraction. There was a strange smell in the barn. He sniffed. It smelt hot, petrol, with something else – like cordite. And smoke. There was smoke. He had time only to step back half a pace before a fireball of yellow and gold heat erupted out of Kate's car and blew him backwards into the garden.

'Christ Almighty!' Greg had not had time to close the door when he saw the man's figure fly backwards away from the barn doors. Fire and smoke were already erupting from the barn roof, sparks jumping into the air to be lost in the snow.

'Greg? What is it? What's happened?' Diana ran to join him followed by Susie. Behind them Roger closed his eyes. For a moment he stood without moving, then slowly he dragged himself after them to the door.

'Daddy!' Susie's hysterical cry was followed by a wild

sob as she saw the figure on the grass begin crawling towards them. 'I'll go.' Diana pushed past Greg. In seconds she was kneeling beside him.

'I'm all right. I'm all right. Just shaken.' Joe was coughing violently, his eyes streaming. 'Find the gun. Quickly. Find the bloody gun. And be careful, it's loaded.' He staggered to his feet and began to move towards the house.

Greg watched in an agony of frustration, seeing his mother running towards the blazing building. 'Get me my stick,' he yelled at Susie. 'Quickly. Get me my stick!'

Grabbing it from her he had begun to hobble towards Diana when he saw her duck into the smoke and reappear a moment later, the shotgun under her arm.

Pushing past his son, Roger ran out into the snow. 'Di –'

'Get in, Joe.' Greg thrust the man behind him and ran after his father, his eyes on the barn. Smoke was pouring through the roof; a series of small explosions were rocking the building. Diana reached them, gasping. For a moment they all stood staring at the fire then Greg took his mother's arm and pulled her away. 'Get back inside quickly.'

'Oh Greg.' Her eyes filled with tears. Miserably, she went to Roger, who put his arm around her and guided her back towards the house.

In his impatience Greg had put his foot down for a couple of steps. The pain sliced through him like a knife and he swore viciously. 'Just thank God the wind is blowing away from the house; the snow will damp down any sparks. But we've lost the barn, Dad. Nothing can save it.'

They stood in the doorway for a moment watching in despair as the first flames licked out through the black boarding. Diana's eyes filled with tears. 'I loved that barn. It was lovely. And my roses! My poor roses. They'll be burned.'

'I expect their roots will be all right.' Roger tried to

sound reassuring. Gently he pulled her in and closed the door. 'Go and sit down with Joe. Greg, can you manage to get us all a brandy?'

'Are you hurt, Joe?' Trying to forget the pain of her precious plants, and the small birds who always roosted in the barn at dusk Diana turned towards him, scrutinising the black smudges across his face.

He shook his head. 'Just bloody shocked.' He sounded angry more than anything else. 'What bastard would do a thing like that? That place must have been booby trapped!' He threw himself down on a chair. 'I reckon I could do with that brandy, thanks Greg.' He looked at Cissy. 'How is she?'

'Much the same.' Diana sat down beside her and put her hand on Cissy's forehead. Aware that her own heart was thundering in her ears with the shock of what had happened she slipped her fingers down to take the pulse beneath Cissy's ear. It was stronger now and steadier.

She looked up to find Greg standing behind her with a glass.

She reached up for it. 'So. What happens now?'

'I'll go on foot. That's what happens now.' Joe swallowed his brandy in one gulp and held out the glass for a refill. 'I'm not letting any murdering bastard do that to me and get away with it.'

'You can't go in the dark, Joe.' Greg glanced at the windows. 'It would be madness. Kate and Paddy will have reached your place by now. If they can't get in, I'm sure they will hitch up to the Headleys' or Heath Farm. They will get help far more quickly than you can.'

'And if they haven't made it?' Joe's question was brutally direct. 'What if he got them?'

'He hasn't got them, Joe.' Greg looked at his mother. 'Paddy had a gun. He wouldn't be afraid to use it.'

His eyes strayed thoughtfully to Sue. She said she had heard a shot. But you can't shoot ghosts. The thought kept straying back into his mind. A gun would have no effect on Marcus. No effect at all.

As if she had read his mind, Diana glanced at him. 'A ghost couldn't set fire to the barn, Greg. Or move the Volvo. That must have been a real man.'

'A ghost?' Joe stared at her. 'What does a bloody ghost have to do with all this? Are you telling me a bloody ghost ran my wife off the road?'

'I don't know what we're telling you, Joe. I just don't know.' Greg was white with frustration. He threw himself down on the chair again. 'Oh, Christ, I wish I could walk! Where are Kate and Paddy?'

LIII

Kate was lying on her face, her head cushioned on her arms, aware slowly that a small trickle of blood somewhere in the hair above her left temple had dried into a crust. How long she had been lying there she wasn't sure, but in the interval she had grown very cold. Cautiously she raised her head, expecting to feel at any second an icy hand on her back, but there was nothing, just the long, lingering catch of the bramble which had scratched her head as she fell. Her hand closed in the mud, crisp now with incipient ice, and she realised she was shaking.

'Paddy?'

There had been no sound since the gun went off. Her terror had led to paralysis of will. She could not move or speak. Some atavistic instinct told her that shamming death was her only protection. How long that state had lasted she didn't know. She moved her hand slightly, trying to bring her wrist, with the narrow, gold watch, within sight without raising her head more than a few inches.

'Paddy?' She tried again, louder this time.

'Here.' His voice was muffled, but not too far away.

'Are you all right?'

'I think so. I've lost the gun. I fell.' She could hear tears in his voice. 'Has he gone?'

'I don't know.' She raised her head higher, trying to see. 'I think so.'

'Where are you?'

'Here.' She rose cautiously to her knees, wishing she could stop herself shaking. She could actually hear her teeth chattering. 'I'm here. Keep talking and I'll see if I can find you.' The light had nearly gone.

There was a rustling somewhere to her left. She swung round. 'Is that you?'

'Yes. I'm OK. Here.' He clung to her for several seconds and she could feel the chill of his body against her own. 'He's gone,' she whispered. 'I can't feel him around any more.'

'Which way do we go?' He pulled away from her and she could feel him grasping at his dignity almost as though it were armour, and shrugging it on again.

'We should have brought a compass.' She tried to make the remark light. 'We can still follow the contour of the land, though. Keep going up.'

'That doesn't seem to work.'

'Paddy, what else can we do? We can't stay here all night.' She had only just realised that it was snowing again; proper snow this time, light and feathery and relentless; a pale glimmer at her feet showed where it was settling.

'Do you know any prayers?'

The question caught her by surprise. 'Well, the Lord's Prayer, of course, everyone knows that.'

'That's what one says to ward off evil, isn't it? To keep him away.'

Kate reached out and took his hand. 'We could say it together if it helps. You're right. It's supposed to keep evil spirits away. I'm not much of an authority on prayer.'

'Or evil spirits, I expect.' He forced a small laugh. 'Do you know it in Latin? *Pater Noster*. All that. He must speak Latin if he's a Roman. We don't do Latin at my school.' Again the strained little laugh. 'It never crossed my mind that I might need it.'

May the gods of all eternity curse you, Marcus Severus, and bring your putrid body and your rotten soul to judgement for what you have done here this day.

Kate rubbed her face with her hands. The words were

383

trapped in her brain. They were not external. If they had been Paddy would have heard them too. And the words were in English.

'I think he understands our language,' she said carefully. They had both accepted, she noticed, that it was Marcus they had seen, not some flesh and blood intruder in the woods. 'I think if we are communicating with him or with anyone else it is in our heads.'

'But you could tell him to sod off in Latin?' He said it so hopefully she heard herself laugh out loud.

'I did the kind of Latin one learns in the hope that it will facilitate one's grasp of literature,' she said apologetically. 'I don't think I ever learned to say sod off.' She paused. 'I do know the *Pater Noster* though.'

'Say it.'

'*Pater Noster, qui es in caelis, sanctificetur nomen tuum. Adveniat regnum tuum. Fiat voluntas tua, sicut in caelo, et in terra. Panem nostrum quotidianum da nobis hodie. Et dimitte nobis debita nostra, sicut et nos dimittimus debitoribus nostris. Et ne nos inducas in tentationem: sed libera nos a malo . . .*' She stopped.

There was a moment's silence. 'Go on,' he whispered.

'That's it. Or at least, that's all I can remember. But that's the important bit. *Libera nos a malo.* Deliver us from evil.' It didn't matter. There was no one out there listening now. She was sure of it. He had gone. 'Paddy, let's try and find the gun. It can't have gone far.' It was almost dark. The light was failing fast.

'I think it fell over there. Don't tell Dad it went off. He'll never let me use it again.'

'It probably saved our lives,' she retorted tersely. 'I can see it. There. In those nettles.'

The snow was thicker now, drifting down, here a pale drifting cloud, there driven by the wind into a stinging curtain.

Patrick retrieved the gun cautiously, and broke it under

his arm. He looked round. 'There's no sign of a path. I can't even see which way we came.'

'This way.' Kate didn't hesitate. She pushed through some brambles and began to climb a small incline, her borrowed boots slipping in the snow.

'Wait.' Patrick was staring round. 'Look. Through the trees.'

'Where?'

'There. I can see a light.'

'Thank God!' It was a heartfelt prayer. Side by side they scrambled towards it, sliding and slipping downwards now, out of the eye of the wind into the shelter of the woods again.

'It's gone. I can't see it.'

'There. There it is.' Patrick stopped. 'It's Redall. Oh, Kate, we've come round in a circle. We're back where we started. He's not going to let us escape.' The disappointment and fear in his voice were palpable.

She bit her lip, angry with herself as much for the stupidity as for the overwhelming rush of relief which had swept over her. 'Can't be helped. We'll go back in and see if we can find a compass.'

'Right. ' He nodded firmly.

'Then we'll have to try again. And this time we'll stay on the main track.'

'Agreed.' He gave her a broad grin. 'A hot drink first, though. Yes?'

'Yes.' She put her arm around his shoulder.

LIV

Jon opened the door of his flat and peered in. It smelt stale; unlived in. Cyrus, he had heard only yesterday before he flew out of Kennedy, had stayed there just two days before having a massive fight with the sponsors of his London visit, and flying back to the States.

Dropping his bag on the floor, Jon pushed the front door closed behind him with his foot and stooped to pick up his mail. Wearily he walked across to the table and threw it down. On the windowsill a vase of dead flowers stood in a circle of sticky yellow pollen. He went to pick it up and carried it through to the kitchen, wrinkling his nose at the stench from the stale water. On the worktop was a set of keys. Turning on the tap so it ran into the vase, flushing away the slimy green deposits which clung to the rough porcelain he picked up the keys and looked at the tag. A small black cat. Kate's keys. He smacked them down on the counter. Two days! Two lousy days Cyrus had stayed and he had as good as thrown her out for that! Well, he had paid back the first half of her money now, at least.

Going back to the living room, he flung himself down on the sofa and reached onto the table beside him to punch the answer machine. The calls went on and on. He listened wearily, his eyes closed. The procession of voices through the cold half light of the afternoon was like a review of his life. 'Hi Jon. Call me when you get back' . . . 'Jon, if you're there around the 18th we're having a get together . . .' 'Jon, don't forget, twelve thirty on the 23rd at the Groucho . . .' 'Jon . . .' 'Jon . . .' 'Jon . . .'

He stood up and went to pour himself a Scotch. The bottle – all the bottles on the tray, he noticed wryly – were empty.

'Shit!'

'Jon. This is Bill. Just to let you know all the phones down at Redall seem to be out of commission. I'm going down this morning – it's about ten on Saturday morning now – to see what's going on.'

Jon switched off the machine. Reaching for the phone he dialled Bill's number. It rang on in the silence. He re-dialled – Bill's cottage this time. 'Come on, answer.' Jon drummed his fingers on his knee. Abruptly he cut the connection. He tried the Redall Cottage number. The line was still dead. Swearing under his breath, he dialled the Lindseys'. That, too was silent. He slammed down the receiver and stood up. What the hell was going on up there?

Turning to his bags, he found the bottle of duty free Talisker he had picked up at the airport. Uncapping it he poured himself a slug.

Why the hell did he care so much anyway? Kate was part of history. They had not got on. The affair was over. Finished. Kaput. There was nothing left to rekindle. She wasn't interested in him any more, however friendly she had been on the phone. That was just politeness; typical Kate, not wanting to hurt anyone's feelings. He would probably never see her again.

He drained his glass and poured some more. Outside the window with its veil of sooty net the London street grew dark. A steady wet sleet had begun to fall. Setting down his glass Jon went to switch on the tall, chrome lamp in the corner. Then he reached for the road map.

LV

HATE
ANGER
FURY

raging inside her head. There were no words, no form; a maelstrom of whirling pain.

'*Mummy!*'

The cry was muffled, agonised. It fell into the black silence of the room, unheard.

'*Mummy, help me!*'

They were inside her head, locked in battle. He, Marcus, always the stronger, tearing at the core of her brain, wanting her, using her, needing her voice, her arms, her strength.

And she. Claudia. She would not give in. The truth must be told. Nion. Betrayed. Insult to the gods. *Nion. Nion. Love of my life, partner of my soul.*

Tear them out. Be rid of them. Be free of them. Nails. Rip them out with her nails. Tear her head open.

'*MUMMY. HELP ME!*'

'*Let the truth be told. I will have the truth told.*' The scream is louder now. Claudia is gaining in strength. '*The grave is open. The secret is out. The people of Britain shall avenge our death. The fall of the Empire will not be revenge enough. May the gods of all eternity curse you, Marcus Severus Secundus, for what you have done . . .*'

'No, no, *NO!*'

Alison sat up violently, her hands to her temples. Her nails were red with her own blood. She stared round the room. The lights were no longer on, but she could see quite clearly. The woman was standing by the window, her blue gown moving gently as though the wind were blowing from behind her, her feet in the soft dune sand, her hair tangled in its combs. She seemed to see right through the wall, through the house, through the darkness and the snow.

Alison cowered against the wall. Blood. There was blood everywhere; down the front of the woman's dress; on the floor on her own sheets and – she looked down suddenly, seeing without trouble in the darkness, all over her own hands.

Her own scream blocked out the sound of voices. She screamed on and on, out of control, out of her head now, watching herself from the doorway, watching the group of people downstairs rise from the kitchen table, pick up their candles and head towards the stairs. Diana was there first, the flame of her candle shivering and trailing smoke.

'Alison. Alison, darling! Oh Christ, what's wrong with her?'

She could see her mother's arm around her, see her mouth moving, but she felt nothing. He was there now, inside her head again. Laughing. Why was he laughing? Laughing at the blood and the pain. Laughing at her: the woman by the curtains. She was indistinct now, a shadow from a distant past. Nothing more. Disappearing. Vanquished. Crumbling back into the sand. Part of the forgotten time . . .

'*Pater noster* . . .' It was Patrick's voice, trembling, in the shadows. '*Libera nos a malo. Ave Maria. Libera nos a malo.*' The words slid into a sob of pain.

'Her face. Christ, Di, look at her face.' Breathless, Roger had joined the group on the landing, peering over his wife's shoulder. 'Shut up, Paddy!' He turned on his son. 'I won't have that sentimental crap uttered in this house!'

'Go away, all of you.' Diana tightened her grip on

Alison's shoulders. 'Go away. I'll see to her.' She glanced up, scarcely able to see through her tears. 'Kate, will you stay. The rest of you go downstairs.'

For a moment Roger opened his mouth, about to speak, then he changed his mind. He handed Kate his candle and turned away. He was shaking visibly as he ushered the others down.

Obediently Kate went to the bathroom for a facecloth and, wringing it out brought it back to the bedroom. Diana wiped the blood from Alison's hands, then gently she guided her back to bed. 'You're safe now, sweetheart. Quite safe.'

'What about her face?' Kate was holding the candle steady.

'I'll leave it for now. They're only superficial scratches.' Diana glanced at her wearily. 'I'm not letting you and Paddy or Joe leave this house again tonight.'

'Someone must get help, Diana.'

'Time enough in daylight. Everything must wait until then.'

'But what about Greg? What about Cissy?' Kate had been appalled at the sight of Cissy Farnborough lying, barely conscious, on the sofa by the fire.

'She'll be all right. I can take care of her. There is someone trying to kill us all out there, Kate!' Diana pulled the sheet up around Alison's chin and tucked it in. 'I am not letting anyone else set foot outside this house.'

Kate looked down at Alison. The girl was quiet now, lying very still on her blood-stained pillow, breathing long, even breaths as though she were asleep again. 'What do you think happened?' she asked in a whisper.

'She had a nightmare.' There was a desperate set to Diana's chin.

'I think it was more than that.' Kate walked further into the room. The small intimate space, lit by the two candles was icy cold. On the floor in front of the curtains lay a scattering of sand. Kate stared down at it for a moment, frowning, then she turned away. 'Why did your husband swear at Paddy for praying?'

'He doesn't believe in God. He stopped believing the day he discovered he had cancer.'

'And does he believe in evil? In possession? In ghosts?'

It was Diana's turn to shiver. 'He's a reductionist and a fatalist. He believes in nothing that cannot be scientifically proven.'

'How strange.' Kate's eyes were fixed on Alison's face. To her, Roger had come across as a man with poetry in his soul. And he was a man who still, in extremis, cried out the name of Christ even though it meant nothing to him.

'Do you pray?' Diana sat down on the edge of the bed and laid a gentle hand on her daughter's forehead. It was very cold.

'Not very often. But it was me who taught Paddy the words to say. Outside in the dark it seemed the right thing to do. He thought Marcus would understand the Latin.'

'And did he?' The note of irony Diana was aiming at somehow failed to materialize; the question came out straight.

'I don't know. But the words made me feel better. A shield. A talisman against evil.'

'He's got us trapped here, hasn't he?' Diana looked at her suddenly and for a moment she could no longer hide her panic. 'Every one of the cars is damaged; the phone won't work; no one knows what's happened. Bill and Cissy tried to help us and look what happened to them.' A tear slid down her face. 'And Allie. What's happened to Allie?'

Kate knelt beside her and took her hand. 'I think we should take Allie downstairs. I think we should all stay together.'

'She's right.' Greg's voice from the landing made them both jump. He hobbled in and stood looking down at his sister. 'I'll ask Joe to come and carry her down then I think you should make a huge cauldron of soup for us all.' He was looking at his mother. He glanced at Kate who was still kneeling on the floor. 'Everything will seem a bit less fraught in the morning, then we can send for reinforcements.'

Kate gave him a watery smile. 'You make it sound easy.' The flickering candlelight, made her face look ethereal. She had, he noticed not for the first time, a frail, pre-Raphaelite beauty, emphasised by her disordered, tangled hair and helped, he supposed wryly, by the submissive posture, on her knees at his feet.

'It will be easy. Everything is always better in daylight.'

'Don't tempt providence!' As if realising that her position put her at a disadvantage, she scrambled to her feet. Standing, she was as tall as he. 'Greg.' She put her hand on his arm, her voice barely a whisper. 'Look, by the window. On the floor.'

He raised an eyebrow, then picking up the candle, he limped across and surveyed the carpet.

'Sand. It could have come from Allie's shoes.'

'But it didn't. I was up here earlier and it wasn't here.'

'How can you be sure?'

'I just am.' She shrugged. 'I notice things like that. After the cottage.'

'What are you saying?' Diana turned to look at the carpet.

'She's saying that some sand has blown in the window and that it would be better if we all went downstairs and sat round the fire,' Greg said firmly.

'Don't patronise me!' Diana snapped. She stood up. 'What does the sand mean?' She looked at Kate.

'All right, I'll tell you,' Greg said slowly. 'It means that I don't think we are dealing with a human killer. I don't think there is anyone out there in the woods or on the beach. I think our enemy is a man who has been dead for

392

nearly two thousand years; a man who is very, very angry because we have disturbed a grave in the sand. And I think we are all in terrible danger.'

LVI

'I must have been mad to come, quite mad!'

Anne Kennedy walked along the line of small cars, the keys in her hand as she peered through the driving snow to try and find the vehicle she had been allocated. In her other hand were the handles of a large canvas holdall, a road map bought from the car hire desk in the airport terminal, the strap of her shoulder bag, and there were three books balanced in the crook of her elbow.

It had not been snowing in Edinburgh. This was ridiculous. Sisterly love had overstepped the bounds. There it was. Number 87. A small, neat, bright red Ford Fiesta. With relief she slotted the key into the lock and pulled the door open. The car smelled of plastic and air freshener. It was blessedly spotless. Tossing her bag and her books onto the back seat she climbed in and closed the door then she fumbled for the light switch. She had to find out how to get from Stansted out to the east coast before the snow piled too thick in the country lanes.

Her last conversation with Kate had worried her a great deal, as had the fact that Kate's phone was still out of order. It had been with enormous relief that she had found two visiting lecturers to look after her flat and wait upon C.J.'s every whim, so that she could head south for a three-day break to reassure herself that all was well. Now she was not so sure that she had done the sensible thing. England, with its usual paranoia about any weather pattern one or two points either side of the norm showed every sign of closing down completely. The forecast was becoming increasingly hysterical and to make matters worse, Kate was not even expecting her, thanks to the incompetence of the telephone engineers who swore each time she rang them that the line had been checked and was working perfectly.

She took one last look at the road map, memorised the formula – A120 east towards Colchester, A12 north towards Ipswich and then A120 again – switched on the engine and turned out the light. It would take, she reckoned, about an hour, perhaps an hour and a half at most. She glanced down at the dashboard clock. It was nearly nine already.

The roads were unpleasant but by no means impassable as she drove east, the windscreen wipers carving arcs in sleet which turned white and sparkling in the reflected headlights of oncoming cars. The road was more or less straight and she made far better time than she expected, bypassing Dunmow and Braintree and turning north at last on the main dual carriageway which cut through the flatlands of East Anglia towards Suffolk. The radio played quietly in the background with once a break for the weather forecast – dire: overnight snow would thicken with easterly gales tomorrow causing drifting, and piling high tides onto the beach with the full moon – and a news update, then it lapsed once more into Brahms and Schumann.

It was ten past ten when she pulled into a layby in front of a multi-armed signpost and, flicking on the light, consulted her road map again. It showed Redall as a small dot on the shore. Leading to it was a broken line which denoted a track of some sort. To reach the track she had to negotiate about four miles of intricate lanes. She scowled. The snow was harder now and though the little car had bowled gamely through the worst it could throw at her so far, there were signs of it drifting now she was on a deserted road. There were no car tracks visible; and at the foot of hedges a deceptively soft bank was building up on both sides of the road.

'Oh, well, plough on.' She muttered to herself. She had already pinpointed a pub on the mainish road which looked as though it was only half a mile or so from Redall. Perhaps she should make for that first.

The tyres slithered uncomfortably as she engaged first gear and pulled out into the middle of the carriageway, but once she got going the car held the road. Left. Left. Right. She repeated the turnings to herself out loud as she negotiated each increasingly narrow lane with more and more care. She should be nearly there now. There should be a pub on the next bend.

There wasn't. She drove on. The turning she knew should appear within a couple of hundred yards did not materialise. The lane turned inland again and wound infuriatingly back on its tracks, climbing up and down steep hills which had no right to be there at all. She must have missed a turning somewhere. 'Damnation!' She pulled up and consulted the map again. It looked so straightforward on paper. Left, left, right. A straight bit, a bend, the pub and then a few more bends until the top of the track. She wound down the window and stared out. The wind was ice cold, clean, cutting. Ice crystals seared her skin. All she could hear was silence and then, almost subliminally, in her bones, the distant moan of the wind. Hastily she wound her window up again. She preferred the steamy, incestuous fug of the little car with its canned music – Schumann had now given way to a Beethoven Sonata.

She had begun to ponder the possibility of having to spend the night in the car – not a pleasant prospect without rugs or thermos – when she saw the lights of a house loom out of the snow ahead. It was no pub, but at least the occupants might be presumed to know where they were.

They did, and it was a good five miles from Redall. 'You turned the wrong way back there, my dear.' The elderly man who opened the door in his dressing gown had invited her into his hallway to consult her map with her. 'What you had better do is go on down here,' he stabbed at it with a nicotine-stained finger, 'and then turn back along the estuary road.'

'Are you on your own?' A pale wispy woman in a worn eau-de-Nil bathrobe, her straggly hair in rollers, appeared at the top of the stairs. 'You shouldn't drive around on your own on a night like this.'

'I know.' Anne managed a bright smile. 'I didn't realise the weather was going to be so bad.'

'Would you like a cup of tea before you go on?' The woman was descending the stairs now, one step at a time, painfully.

Anne was sorely tempted but she shook her head. 'It's kind of you, but I think I had better go on. It's settling quite deep and I don't want to get stuck.'

'Well, you go carefully,' the old lady nodded. 'And you watch out for the Black Dog on the marsh.' She chuckled as she watched Anne pull up her collar and run out to the car.

'Black Dog!' Anne muttered to herself as she restarted the engine. She had heard of the phantom Black Dog of East Anglia; she gave a wry grin. She had not expected to run into the supernatural quite so soon.

As the car slithered down the lane and turned at last onto a slightly broader road which showed signs of having been recently sanded, the snow lessened and a patch of clear sky revealed a high, cold moon, only a fraction off the full, sailing amongst a trail of huge, bulbous clouds. Cautiously Anne accelerated a little, following the winding road with care. The woman had described this as the estuary road, and suddenly Anne saw why. A steep incline, where the car tyres spun wildly for a moment gave way to a flat straight stretch and she found she was looking down on a broad river estuary, glinting like silver in the moonlight. She brought the car to a standstill and stared. It was breathtaking. A landscape of white and silver and polished steel. And completely deserted. She had not, she realised, seen another car for over half an hour now. Turning her back with regret on the view, she set off again, more slowly this time, determined not to miss the turnings which would take her across the arm of land which led behind Redall Bay.

The track was in the right place. There was no doubt she had reached it at last, but it was obvious that that was as far as the little car was going. The wind had piled the snow across the turning in heaps four feet deep. She climbed out and looked round in despair. The moonlight was so bright now that the road was clearly visible in both directions for several hundred yards. She had passed a farmhouse some half a mile back. Perhaps she should drive back there and ask their advice? She glanced at her watch. It was after eleven. Not too late, surely, to knock on the door.

But the farmhouse, when she reached it, was in darkness and her repeated knocking brought no answer.

She shivered. The moon was half veiled now and the clouds were building once more. In another few minutes it would have gone. Climbing back into the car, glad of its lingering warmth, she sat back for a moment and thought. There were only two alternatives. Either she could drive on to the next village and beg a room at the pub or she could leave the car on the road and walk down the track to Redall.

Pulling back onto the road she drove slowly back to the top of the track and stopped. It was clearly visible, in spite of the snowdrifts, winding into the trees. She put on the light again and stared down at her map. The track could not be more than half a mile long, less probably. She measured it with her thumbnail. It was crazy to go away now she had got here. She glanced up at the sky again, peering through the windscreen. The moon was clearly visible now, lighting the whole place like day. The banks of snow cloud she had seen over the estuary did not seem to have advanced at all. It would be easy to see her way down the track.

She made up her mind. Climbing out of the car she pulled her bag out with her. There was a bottle of Laphroaig in there, produce of Scotland. She had not forgotten her sister's fondness for malt whisky and if she fell in a snowdrift, to hell with all the received wisdom about cold and alcohol, she would drink it herself. Turning off the lights she locked the car and, shouldering the bag, with a rueful glance down at her far-from-waterproof Princes Street boots, she turned towards the trees.

For the first twenty-five yards the moonlight lit the path with brilliant clarity and it was easy to put the thought of Kate's poltergeist out of her mind. The snow was soft but not very thick and she found the going easy, though it was strange how quickly her bag grew heavy. Then abruptly the track turned at right angles into a densely growing copse and the moonlight, deflected by the trees, shone elsewhere. The path at her feet was black. In spite of herself she glanced over her shoulder into the deeper shadows. It was very quiet. The wind had died and she could hear nothing but the steady crunch of the snow beneath her boots.

She stopped to swing her holdall onto the opposite shoulder. Without the steady sound of her own footsteps the night was eerily quiet. No wind; no patter of leaves; then, in the distance she heard the manic tu-wit, tu-wit of an owl, followed by a long wavering hoot. It was a primitive sound which brought a shiver to the back of her neck. She walked on, unaware how tightly her knuckles were knotted into the straps of the bag on her shoulder.

Her eyes were used to the darkness now and she could make out more detail. The gnarled oaks, their solid profiles clearly recognisable, the tangled mass of less easily identifiable copse which crowded to the edge of the track, the dense curtain of some creeper or other — traveller's joy, perhaps — which hung in clusters over the path. The track turned again and she found the snow at her feet bathed in moonlight once more. With a sigh of relief she quickened her pace, slithering out of control as the track steepened, staggering to keep her feet.

It was then she saw the upturned car. Cautiously she approached it, her heart thumping uneasily, pushing her way through the broken branches. The skid marks were still visible beneath the snow, and the dark stains which in daylight would probably be blood. Her mouth had gone dry as she peered round the upturned bonnet. There was no one there. Relieved, she touched the cold metal and saw the drift of snow which had settled on the inside console. The crash must have happened a while ago and whoever had been in the car had gone.

The loud crack of a breaking twig stopped her in her tracks. She looked round. She could hear her heart thundering in her ears. She glanced up at the sky. The moon was almost gone. In another few seconds it would be swallowed by the thick, snow-heavy band of cloud which was drifting steadily in from the sea. It was nearly midnight and she had never felt so lonely in her life.

The skin on the nape of her neck began to prickle as she walked on. She tried to view the feeling objectively. It was a primitive reaction to fear of the unseen; or was she sensing something out there in the dark? Something watching her. Swallowing hard, she made herself go on. Surely it could not be far now to the farmhouse? A flicker in the strength of the moonlight made her glance up again. Only a few seconds more and the moon would be gone. She held on to her bag more tightly, refusing to quicken her pace. A fear of the dark was an irrational primitive throwback; this was the twentieth century. There were no wild beasts out there, queuing up to eat her, no enemy tribes, no evil spirits, no ghosts. She was a rational, liberated modern woman; a scientist.

But in at least one of the books in her bag there was a very convincing argument that ghosts and spirits were real entities.

The darkness when it came was total. Her step faltered – a logical reaction to sudden blindness which would pass as soon as her night sight came back. She knew the path was clear; she had been able to see twenty feet in front of her a moment before, so why had she stopped? Why was she convinced that there was someone standing there on the path immediately in front of her? Why did she have this terrible urge to turn and run back the way she had come?

'Come on, Anne!' Like her sister she was prone to addressing herself out loud. 'Get a move on. Your feet are getting cold!' The sound of her voice seemed shocking in the silence; an intrusion. 'You'll be singing "Onward Christian Soldiers" in a minute,' she went on conversationally. 'Go on, you bastard.' She was no longer addressing herself. 'If you're out there, show yourself, whoever you are.'

This was ludicrous. There was no one there. No one at all. She gritted her teeth and walked on, concentrating grimly on the wild beauty of the night. She could understand Kate's enchantment with this place. The silence, the clean pure air which came, she supposed, straight from the arctic ice, the occasional glimpses before the moon had gone, of glittering, still water through the trees. She pictured the cottage where Kate was by now probably tucked up cosily in bed. A warm stove, oak beams, pretty, chintzy curtains, an old bed with a soft feather mattress and an old-fashioned patchwork quilt. When she arrived there would be coffee and food and whisky of course, and a long night of gossip with their toes tucked up near the fire –

She snapped suddenly out of her reverie. In the distance

she could hear the sound of galloping hooves. It was coming closer. The creak of leather, the hiss of breath through a horse's nostrils. She flung herself back off the path, feeling the ground shake beneath the rider as he hurtled up the track and then he was gone. Shocked, she stared back the way she had come. She had seen nothing. How could anyone ride at that speed in the dark? And why? What was so important?

With a heavy sense of foreboding she slithered back onto the track, renewing her grip on her bag, aware suddenly of a new smell in the fresh coldness of the air. A foul, acrid smell. The smell of burning.

She stood for a moment looking at the still smouldering barn, feeling the heat striking out from the black stinking ashes, then she walked slowly towards the farmhouse and banged on the door.

For a long time nothing happened. No lights came on. There was no sound. She was beginning to panic that there was no one there when at last she heard the sound of a door opening somewhere inside.

'Who is it?' A man's voice sounded strangely hollow from behind the door.

'Hi. I'm sorry to arrive so late. My car couldn't make it down the track. I'm Anne Kennedy. Kate's sister.' It felt faintly ridiculous, speaking to a bolted door. She wished they would hurry up and open it. There was something not right out here, something frightening in the air. 'Please. May I come in?' She tried to keep the panic out of her voice.

'Wait.' The voice was curt. Almost rude.

Anne stared at the door in disbelief. It had not crossed her mind that they might not let her in. She glanced behind her at the dull white sheen which was a snow-covered lawn.

'Anne? Is that you?' Suddenly Kate's voice came from behind the door. The flap of the letter box rose and a torch shone out into the darkness. 'Crouch down, so I can see your face.'

'For God's sake, Kate. Of course it's me. I sincerely wish it wasn't!' The last of her stamina was going. Anne bent over and stared into the letter box. 'What is the matter with you all?'

'It's her. Let her in.' She heard the muffled words as the letterbox sprang shut followed at once by the sound of bolts being drawn back.

'Quickly. Come in.' Kate pulled her over the threshold into a darkened hall. Anne was dimly aware of a guttering candle on a saucer as someone closed the door behind her and shot the bolts across once more, then she was ushered into a candlelit living room. It was warm, and smelled of wonderful cooking and it was full of people.

She stared round, doing a double take. 'It's like the hospital at Scutari,' she blurted out. 'Kate, love, what's been happening?'

A woman, wearing a sling and with a black eye lay on the sofa; a girl, wrapped in rugs was lying on pillows in the corner; a man, his bandaged foot propped up on a stool sat beside the fire. Behind her the two men – one man and a boy, she corrected herself as she glanced at them – who had opened the door with Kate were standing staring at her as if she had just appeared from Mars. Two other people and a girl stood nearby, all looking at her. 'What is happening here? What's wrong?'

'Oh, Anne!' Kate threw herself into her arms. 'I've never been so pleased to see anyone in my life!'

'The *dea ex machina*, come to rescue us, I presume.' The words came from the man with the injured foot.

Anne stared at him blankly then she turned to Kate. 'You'd better explain,' she said.

LVII

He rode fast, leaning forward on his horse's neck, the brooch, the native brooch which had pinned her gown, holding his own cloak now against the wind. The prince of the Trinovantes had paid the price and gone to his gods and the hell-cat woman with him, with her curses and her hate. Well, let her curse. Who would ever know what had happened here today? There were no witnesses, no survivors. Her sister, simple docile girl that she was, would believe him when he told her Claudia had fled with her lover to his brothers in the west. She would be shocked, but she would believe him. And she would understand the need for divorce. He smiled as he rode, and raised his hand to flog his horse on faster as it scaled the rise in the track, its hooves throwing up clouds of dust. He had already decided that he would remarry. Her sister was much like her to look at, much younger and more biddable by far. She could take over his household and raise his son; provide him with more sons if she did her duty well. And he would see to it that the prince's tribe came no more to Colonia Claudia Victricensis. They incubated sedition and plotted with the Iceni against Rome. A burning straw would ignite the mood against their overlords, but it would not be his straw; no uprising would be of his instigation. Nor hers. Claudia. The woman he had treated as a goddess. No one would ever know what had occurred here today. She would never tell; she had taken her betrayal and her fury with her to her muddy, inglorious death.

*   *   *

'There are ten people in this house.' Roger stood with his back to the fire, looking down at the others as they sat round him. Allie still had not spoken. She was asleep on a pile of cushions and pillows in the corner and no one suggested waking her. Sue was sitting beside her, holding her hand, her eyes closing as she nodded sleepily in the warmth of the room. 'I cannot believe that we can't vanquish whatever is threatening us here tonight. Anne. You are, I gather, the expert,' he bowed in her direction. 'And we seem to be agreed that our enemy is not human. Can I ask you to take the floor and tell us what the hell to do!' He moved to his chair and sank into it with a groan.

Anne felt a thousand times better than she had walking on her own through the woods, but now that the full horror of the situation had been explained to her even a bowl of hot soup had not managed to dispel the chill which had settled in her stomach. She shook her head. 'I'm a psychologist, not a psychic. I know very little about ghosts. As far as I know I've never seen one.' Then what or who was the mysterious horseman who had thundered past her on the track? No one in the house knew anything about him.

'You must help Allie, Anne,' Kate put in from her seat on the floor. She was leaning against the side of Greg's chair, gazing into the embers. His hand was resting lightly on her shoulder.

'I think she's possessed,' Greg said quietly. 'Her strength, her voice, her actions. None of them belong to Alison.'

'Greg. Don't!' Diana's voice was anguished. She glanced across at the two girls. Sue's head had fallen forward; her grip on Alison's hand had loosened and her fingers were slack. She was dozing. Alison moved her head restlessly from side to side and then lay still again. Her eyes were not properly closed. Beneath the half-open lids the whites showed as pale slits.

Anne bit her lip. They were all looking at her and she

didn't know what the hell to say. 'Has she been seen by a doctor recently?' she asked at last. 'There are quite a few conditions which could fit some of what has happened to her. For instance, has she had a head injury in the last few months? Even quite a mild knock could do it.' She looked from Diana to Roger and back. Diana shook her head. 'And there has been no organic damage at any time as far as you know? Cysts, lesions, tumours, anything like that? Has she complained of headaches?'

'Yes, she has.' Patrick and Greg spoke simultaneously.

'But you're on the wrong track there,' Greg went on. 'Quite wrong.'

'Not necessarily.' Anne looked at him seriously. 'There could be a medical reason for her suffering these strange blackouts and we need to rule them out if we can.' Again she looked at Diana. 'Is there any family history of schizophrenia or genetic disorders as far as you know?'

Diana shook her head.

'And there is no possibility that she is taking drugs?'

'None at all.' Diana pressed her hands to her cheeks. 'I was a nurse, Anne. Do you think I haven't thought of these things? Besides, Allie is not the only one to have had strange experiences.'

Anne paused. She bit her lip. She had felt on reasonably safe ground talking in medical terms. 'OK,' she went on carefully. 'Let's explore some other possibilities and find out exactly what we are talking about. I take it that nothing has happened actually inside this house.' Her eyes rested speculatively for a moment on Greg's hand on Kate's shoulder.

'Except for Allie going peculiar; but that probably happened, as Kate said, on the beach.'

'And my books on the floor,' Paddy put in.

'And I smelt her perfume. It was in your study, Roger.' Kate hugged her knees more tightly.

Roger raised an eyebrow. 'What does she use? Chanel?'

'Something with flowers – jasmine and musk and amber. And with it there is always the smell of wet earth.'

Anne looked at her carefully. 'How often have you smelt this?'

'Often. In the cottage too.'

'And it always precedes some kind of phenomenon?'

Kate shrugged. 'Not always. Sometimes that is all there is.'

'And him. Marcus. Does he have a smell too?'

Kate looked up at Greg. He shook his head. 'I can't say I've noticed. When he's around one is too shit-scared to notice anything.'

'Is it mass hysteria?' Diana said slowly. 'Are we all infecting each other?' She was shivering in spite of the heat of the fire.

Anne shrugged. 'It's possible. How many of you have actually seen something?' She looked at Roger, who shook his head almost regretfully. 'Diana?'

'No. It's all hearsay – except for what happened to Allie, of course.'

'Kate and I have seen both Marcus and Claudia,' Greg said slowly. He caressed Kate's neck gently. 'Cissy and Sue saw him clearly. Allie obviously has seen them both. Paddy – ?'

'I felt him,' Patrick said slowly. 'And we saw him out there. I shot at him. And he wrote a message on my computer.'

'He wrote it, or you wrote it without knowing you'd done it?' Anne asked.

'I don't know. I don't remember doing it. But how would a Roman know how to use a computer?'

Anne smiled. 'He wouldn't.'

'I wrote something strange on my computer too,' Kate added. 'A curse. "May the gods of all eternity curse you Marcus Severus Secundus for what you have done here this day . . ."'

407

She spoke the words quietly, but they hung in the room for what seemed an uncomfortably long time. Kate sat still, her eyes on the fire. 'I wonder what he did to her.'

'It must have been something pretty awful,' Greg said softly.

'Murder. I think he murdered her. Her dress is covered with blood.'

'And it's her grave Alison has uncovered in the dunes.'

Anne shivered. Pulling one of the cushions from the end of the sofa she threw it down in front of the fire and sat down on it, hugging her knees just as her sister was doing. 'Just supposing you are right,' she said thoughtfully. 'What are we assuming here? That Alison's excavation has uncovered a long-dead crime? That a murdered woman is still crying out for vengeance after two thousand or so years and that for some reason she and the man who murdered her are attacking everyone in sight. That they are capable of clubbing a man to death, burning down a barn, throwing a car into the sea, cutting off the phone, manifesting soil and maggots and perfumes and physically threatening anyone foolish enough to go outside?'

'It sounds a pretty grim scenario, put like that,' Roger commented wryly. 'But for want of a better theory, and because it is more or less midnight, which is traditionally the witching hour, and because whatever has happened has scared the daylights out of a fairly large, responsible group of people, most of whom are otherwise sane adults, I would say it sounds fairly convincing for now.'

'Perhaps Kate is right and we should pray,' his wife put in tentatively. 'I appreciate your intellectual opposition to prayer, darling, but it would seem to be the only option left, and traditionally, to use your word, it is the only sensible response.'

'It's the only possible response,' Patrick muttered.

'Rubbish,' Roger retorted. 'The sensible response is for

us all to get some sleep. In the morning we will have some breakfast and some of us will walk up the track with Joe and call the police. There has, after all, been a murder committed. If there is anyone out there, and I doubt if by now he is still there, my judgement is that he is human. Some kind of maniac on the loose from somewhere. Poor Bill happened to be in the wrong place at the wrong time. The police will get him. But for the rest of us to end up basket cases because of what has happened is insane in itself. I am sure we will find a concrete explanation. You do what you like. I am going to bed.' He stood up.

No one else moved. 'There aren't enough beds for everyone, Roger,' Diana put in absent-mindedly.

'Then whoever wants to can stay down here by the fire. There are lots of rugs. No one need be too uncomfortable.' Roger stooped and threw a couple of logs onto the fire. It roared up the chimney in a shower of sparks. 'Joe. I suggest you take my son's bed as he shouldn't climb the stairs. Kate, you and Anne —'

'We'll stay down here, Roger, thank you. I'm very comfortable by the fire.' Kate smiled at him.

'Me too.' Patrick put in.

Kate glanced up at Greg. 'You go and lie down in the study, Greg. Rest your foot. We'll keep watch. If anything happens we can call you.'

He reached down and put his hand on her shoulder again. The touch was only light, a brush, no more. 'Thanks, but I think I'll stay here. I'm too comfortable to move.'

When the elder members of the group had gone upstairs, Anne seated herself on the chair Roger had vacated. 'Have any of you heard the weather forecast?' she said quietly. 'It's unbelievably bad. I don't know whether being near the sea makes it better, but they are predicting blizzards for tomorrow. It's not going to be easy to go for help.'

'You think we should try now, before it gets too bad?' Greg leaned forward.

She shrugged. 'I don't know what to think. I just wanted to warn you.'

'I don't think we should go out again,' Kate put in. 'We've been lucky so far.' Her eyes strayed down to Greg's foot. 'But I don't think we should risk anything else.'

'I think we should open a bottle of wine.' Greg levered himself to his feet. 'If we're going to stay awake we may as well enjoy ourselves, and if it helps us sleep that would be no bad thing.'

He hobbled across to the kitchen. Then he stopped suddenly. 'Where are the cats?'

Paddy shrugged. 'I haven't seen them.'

Greg frowned. 'Are they upstairs?'

'If they're like C.J. they will be in the middle of the best bed,' Anne commented. 'No cat is going to be anywhere else in this kind of weather.'

'They don't usually go upstairs.' Greg bent down and hauled a bottle out of the wine rack in the corner. 'It's too cold most of the time. The cosy places are all in here round the fire or the Aga.' He took the corkscrew out of the drawer and tearing the foil seal off the bottle, he began to wind into the cork. 'We're all used to fifteen blankets and duvets each and night storage heaters and things but that is hardly up to feline standards. Here, Paddy, carry this for me, there's a good chap, and we need some glasses.' He hopped back to the fire and sat down again with a groan. He put his hand on Kate's shoulder again, more firmly this time, and he let it rest there. 'Cheer up, we're all safe now.'

She shook her head. 'I keep thinking of poor Bill in the cottage, all alone.'

She accepted a glass from Paddy and took a sip. 'I can't believe any of this has happened. It's ridiculous. It's not possible. Things like this don't happen to people in real life.' Greg's hand was still on her shoulder. Without thinking, she reached up and grasped his fingers. They were warm and reassuringly strong as they returned her grip.

'I'm afraid they do happen to ordinary people,' Anne put in. She smiled at Patrick as he gave her a glass. 'But I'm glad to say there is usually a mundane explanation for even the strangest phenomenon. I'm inclined to think that most of your weird goings on here have been a combination of ordinary things. Cars skid in bad weather; they crash on steep icy lanes. People imagine they see things when the weather is bad. Oh, yes, they do, Kate. And people infect one another with something like hysteria very easily when they're scared and you've had something real to be scared about. A man has been murdered.'

'But before he was murdered. When I phoned you. All the things we discussed.' Kate shifted slightly to lean against Greg's good knee.

'Poltergeists.' Anne nodded. 'Centred on Alison. I think that is very possible. She seems to be emotionally very disturbed at the moment.' She glanced at the two girls who appeared to be sleeping soundly on their makeshift bed in the corner.

'So you consider poltergeists to be real?' Greg asked.

'Yes. I do, in that they are an outward manifestation of inward conflict; the energy created by the brain is quite astounding, you know.'

'Astounding enough to throw a large car out into the saltings? Astounding enough to set fire to a barn?'

'The latter could easily have been a prowler, Greg.' Kate had accepted the loss of her car with astonishing calm; after everything else that had happened it seemed almost unimportant on the scale of things.

Paddy was half way through his own glass of wine when he looked up suddenly. 'The cats couldn't have been in the barn, could they?'

'Of course not. They never went there except bird-nesting in the summer. They can't get in when the door's locked anyway.'

'Of course they can. There are – or were – loads of holes they could get in through.'

'They won't have been there, Paddy, don't worry,' Anne put in, hearing the panic so near the surface in Patrick's voice. The boy was very near the end of his strength. 'The first hint of trouble and they would have been away. Cats are psychic about these things.'

There was a moment's silence then Greg let out a short bark of laughter. 'Not entirely a happy choice of words under the circumstances.'

She grimaced as she hauled herself to her feet. 'Sorry. Listen, is there a loo downstairs? I don't want to disturb anyone who's asleep.'

'Just across the passage, behind the study.' Kate gestured towards the door. 'Here, take this candle.'

The passage was very cold after the heat near the fire. Sheltering the flame with her hand, Anne pushed past the coats and boots, past the closed study door. She could feel the draught from the front door on her neck. They should have a curtain for it. The passage was cluttered with things: carefully she held the candle up, trying not to trip over baskets and shoes, walking sticks, a box of cat food, an old electric fire – heating this house was obviously a problem – a box of what looked like stones, some rolls of Christmas paper and a box of decorations, obviously ready to go up, and – she stopped. Something had moved ahead of her, just out of candle range. It must be one of the cats. She raised her hand a little trying to throw the dim circle of light a little further from her. There it was again. Something in the shadows. But not on the floor; this was full height. Human height. 'Who's there?' To her disgust her voice was shaking.

There was no reply. No sound save the slight moan of the wind under the front door. She could no longer hear the voices from the living room.

'Who is it?' she repeated, louder this time. She was

rooted to the spot. Without going closer the weak candle-light would not reach the door; without light she was too afraid to take even one step closer. 'Oh, shit, come on. Don't mess about. Who is it?'

She could smell it now. The perfume. Rich, exotic, crude, with a strong overlay of wet earth. She swallowed, conscious that her hands were shaking; the candlelight had begun to tremble.

'OK, Lady Claudia. Let's see you.'

Somehow she forced herself to take a small step forward. Her stomach was churning, her knees wobbly. The candle-light licked across the doorway, showing another row of hooks, another huddle of raincoats and jackets. Nothing more. No ghost. No Roman lady. She took a deep breath, feeling her hands ice cold and clammy as she reached for the doorhandle and pulled it open. The small cloakroom was neat, with pale green curtains, a thick rag rug, a green towel, and soap. She wedged the candle onto the high windowsill and turning, began to unzip her trousers. It was then she looked down into the small handbasin. There was a scattering of black soil in the bottom and amongst it, throwing fat, unwieldy shadows in the candlelight, wriggled several maggots.

LVIII

Snow had settled in the dunes. The streaming moonlight cast long, colourless shadows over the sand. As the clouds drifted inexorably in from the north-east, the sky, backlit to opal and then to dull pewter, lowered closer to the land. No night birds called; only the wind in the trees behind the cottage disturbed the silence of the grave as it lay now lapped in its mantle of snow.

The young man looking down at it cast no shadow; he left no footprints. Like the woman he loved he sought revenge. No kind god had received his soul as sacrifice, for with his dying breath he had vowed to return and that vow had kept him from his love. There was no need to comb the furthest galaxies; Marcus Severus Secundus was anchored to this spot by blood. The blood of his victims. His hate had kept them apart through the centuries. The young man smiled. They had all three been released by the meddling of the girl and through her this secret charnel house would be made known to the world and his vengeance would be made sweet.

In front of him the moon was shrouded suddenly in a cloak of cloud. The darkness had returned to the land and with it came the snow. Thick, white, whirling, dissolving the shadow which was all that remained of the druid, Nion, save his need for revenge and his love.

There was a hair in her mouth. She pawed at it, screwing up her face, and opened her eyes to find a head next to hers on the pillow. Frowning, she stared at it. Sue. It was Sue, her tangled hair strewn across the pillow, fast asleep, cuddled up beside her on the floor. Alison moved her head slightly. A violent pain slammed away behind her temples, but she could see dimly in the candlelight. Candlelight? Had they been to a party? A disco somewhere? Why was she on the floor? 'Sue!' She shoved at the girl next to her with her elbow. 'Sue!' The whisper was louder this time. Somehow she managed to sit up, her head spinning. She could just see Sue's mother asleep on the sofa. Why? Why were they all asleep by the fire in her own house? There was no one else there. The fire was burning merrily – she could feel its warmth. 'Sue!' Not a whisper this time, but a peremptory call.

Sue opened her eyes. 'What?'

'How long have you been here?'

'I don't know. Hours. Are you all right?' Sue sat up and looked at her hard.

'Of course I'm all right. Why?'

'They said you'd gone funny.'

'What do you mean, funny?'

'I don't know. All kinds of funny things are happening. Mum crashed the Range Rover, look at my bruises! And we saw your ghost. The Roman. He was horrible.'

'You saw him?' Alison's eyes rounded. She sat up and hugged her knees with a shiver. 'Is that why you're here?'

'I think so. Dad found us. He wasn't even angry. I think he's scared.'

There was a moment's silence as they considered this. Sue bit her lip. 'Mum's asleep.'

They both looked at the sofa.

'Where's everyone else?'

'I don't know.' There was a rising note of hysteria in Sue's voice.

'They can't have gone.'

'Of course they can't have gone.' Sue did not sound too sure. 'Shall I look?'

'No! Don't leave me!'

Hugging one another, the two girls stared round, frightened, as on the sofa Cissy muttered in her sleep. Inside the room the silence was overwhelming. Even the fire seemed quiet, the sweet smoky smell of burning apple logs slowly giving way to the overpowering aroma of wet earth.

LIX

Greg and Patrick were peering down into the washbasin in disgust. Behind them in the dark corridor, Kate stood clutching Anne's hand. 'You saw her, didn't you, Claudia.'

Anne shrugged. 'I didn't exactly see her . . .'

'But you smelt her scent. You sensed her. You saw the earth, the maggots that drop off her everywhere she goes!'

Anne swallowed hard. 'Let's go back to the fire. Surely you've seen enough.' The candlelight was flickering crazily on the ceiling of the small cloakroom as the two heads bent over the washbasin.

'Yuk!' Patrick's one word said it all.

Greg turned with a grimace of pain, balancing on his stick. 'You're right. Let's go back.'

They made their way into the candlelit living room to find Alison and Sue sitting upright in their rugs. Both girls looked dishevelled and scared.

'Greg? What is it? What's happening?' Alison's voice had taken on a strangely high timbre.

He gave her a long searching look, then he lowered himself back into his chair, wincing as he lifted his foot onto its cushion with a grimace of pain. 'We seem to be orphans of the storm!' he replied. Somehow he managed to keep his voice cheerful. 'So, how are you both feeling?'

'Lousy. I've got a really grotty head.' Susie's face was whiter than her companion's.

'And you, Allie?'

Alison shrugged. 'I feel a bit spaced out. Tired. Who's that?' She had noticed Anne.

'Sorry. I forgot you hadn't been introduced,' Kate put

417

in quickly. 'This is my sister, Anne. She picked a really vile weekend to come and stay with me.' She walked over to the two girls and knelt beside them. 'Do you want anything to eat? Diana made some soup. It's on the stove.'

Alison shook her head vehemently. 'I couldn't eat anything. I feel sick.'

'So do I.' Sue's whiteness had by now progressed to a shade of green. 'In fact, can we go and sleep in your room, Allie?'

'No!' Patrick's shout startled them all.

'Why not?' Alison stuck out her chin.

'Well . . .' Patrick floundered with a desperate look towards Kate. 'Won't you be warmer down here, near the fire?'

'I don't think they'll come to any harm upstairs, Paddy,' Greg put in quietly. 'Not if they're together. Why don't you go up, girls. It's a good idea. Take those rugs with you to keep you warm. Sue's had a nasty shock with the car crash, and Allie's probably still suffering from exposure. A warm bed is the best place for both of you.'

The others watched in silence as the two girls climbed to their feet, and collecting armfuls of rugs and cushions, made their way to the door. Their unaccustomed silence was unnerving as they disappeared upstairs.

'You shouldn't have let them do that, Greg,' Paddy said as soon as the staircase door shut behind them. 'You know it's not safe.'

'What's not safe?' Cissy's voice from the sofa was weak but perfectly lucid.

Greg grimaced at his brother. 'Paddy was thinking about the noise those two make when they get together. It is the middle of the night.'

Cissy lay for a moment staring at the ceiling. 'I was on my way to ask you to lunch,' she said suddenly. 'Someone jumped out in front of the Range Rover. I remember trying to miss him, and skidding . . .' She looked up at Kate who sat down on the edge of the sofa beside her. 'Did I hit him?'

Kate smiled reassuringly. 'No. No one was hurt except poor old you.'

'Joe . . . ?'

'Joe is upstairs asleep. Where you should be.'

'Have I broken my ribs?'

'Diana thought they were only badly bruised. You need to rest. I'm afraid we couldn't get hold of a doctor – the phones are still not working – and it's started to snow so hard Joe thought it better to stay here till morning.' It sounded convincing and it was, after all, the truth.

'The joint,' Cissy cried suddenly, distracted. 'My lovely joint will be burnt. What a shame.' She put her hand to her head suddenly. 'Oh, God, I'm so tired –'

'You could sleep in Paddy's room, Mrs Farnborough,' Greg said. 'If you feel you can manage the stairs.'

She did. With Kate and Anne to help, Cissy washed her face, painfully removed her torn, bloody blouse, wrapped herself in Diana's bathrobe and subsided into Paddy's bed. In spite of her pain she was asleep almost as soon as her head touched the pillow. On the landing outside, Kate and Anne looked at each other, their faces shadowed by the candle in Kate's hand, then Kate opened the door of Alison's bedroom and peered in. The two girls were huddled in the narrow bed, their heads very close on the pillow. Both were fast asleep. 'They seem all right,' Kate said softly as she closed the door on them.

Patrick had thrown on a couple more logs and the fire had sprung back into life. Kneeling before it, the poker in his hand, he was prodding it viciously as the two women returned to the room.

'Everything all right up there?' Greg asked.

Kate nodded. 'Everyone seems to be asleep.'

'No strange smells or earth where there shouldn't be any?'

She shook her head.

'Thank God. Perhaps we can settle down for some sleep too.'

'I think we need to talk.' Anne said thoughtfully. 'And besides, I don't think we should all sleep. The unconscious mind is very vulnerable when it is asleep. We need to stay on our guard.'

'So you admit all this is supernatural.' Greg watched her through narrow eyes as she settled on a cushion near the fire.

She shrugged. 'I was trying to keep an open mind, but I certainly saw something out there . . .' She paused. 'I think you were right, this is some kind of phenomenon which is centred on Alison. I read some books about ghosts and poltergeists after I spoke to you, Kate. Your story intrigued me. There seem to be two theories: one, that all the strange events occurring are somehow centred on or created by the unconscious mind of, in this case, a teenage girl. That doesn't make them less real, but they are subjective rather than objective phenomena. The second theory is that real spirits or ghosts – however you define them – are involved. In other words, external forces.' She hesitated. 'There are respected authorities who believe that poltergeists are actually disembodied spirits who feed off the emotional energy of people. Pubescent and teenage kids often have a lot of that to spare. If one believes one of those theories, one must also believe that the forces at work are powerful – powerful enough to light fires, move heavy objects and manifest physical symptoms like the soil and maggots which keep turning up here.' She glanced from one to the other. 'Poltergeists don't usually hurt people. They are mindless and mischievous rather than malicious, perhaps taking their character from the person upon whom they are centred.' Again she looked round. The others were watching her in silence. 'Spirits, ghosts, whatever you call them can be a different matter. But even there, in the books

I was reading anyway, where deaths have occurred, it is usually through a heart attack or a fall as someone ran away or reacted in terror – something indirect. Nowhere did I read of an actual physical attack, where someone was beaten to death.'

'Unless the spirit had possessed a human and was using his or her strength to do it,' Greg said slowly.

'If we are assuming Marcus possessed Alison,' Kate interposed, 'But surely it's the other way round. He was feeding her with his own strength. That is the point. She could never have done what she did on her own.'

'Does it matter how she did it?' Patrick put in suddenly. 'What matters is how to stop it happening again, and to make Marcus go away.'

'You're right, Paddy.' Anne drew up her knees and wrapped her arms around them, gazing into the fire.

There was a long silence.

'So?' Greg said at last. 'How do we do it?'

Anne shrugged. 'I wish I knew. If we had a priest we could try bell, book and candle. Holy water. That kind of thing.'

'We haven't got a priest.' There was irritation in Greg's voice. 'Even if we believed in all that mumbo jumbo. We have got a psychologist – someone who understands the human mind. So, why don't we assume that Alison is behind all this – that somehow she has attracted this ghost – and approach the problem through her.'

Kate glanced at her sister, and then at him. 'He had a go at you, Greg, didn't he? You said you felt him trying to take you over.'

Anne shot him a quick look. 'Why didn't you say before?'

'Because I'm still not sure it wasn't my imagination, that's why.'

'Tell me how it felt.'

Greg frowned. 'It felt like someone going ten rounds

with boxing gloves on inside my head. It felt unspeakably frightening. I was overwhelmed with rage and hatred which weren't mine.' He stared thoughtfully at the burning logs. 'The first time it happened someone came up to me and he left; the second time I fought him off. I wondered if I was going out of my mind.'

'And Allie couldn't fight him. She didn't know how to start,' Kate put in quietly.

'He used her until he had drained her energy,' Greg went on thoughtfully. 'So, how do we fight him?' He looked at Anne.

Anne closed her eyes. 'The trouble is I'm not a clinical psychologist. I'm not a psychotherapist. I'm particularly not a parapsychologist. I'm not sure that I know where to start.'

'Start by talking to Allie.'

She shook her head. 'That's easy to say, but heavy-footed probing can be terribly dangerous.'

Paddy got up. He wandered restlessly over into the kitchen and picking up the kettle, he carried it across to the sink and began to fill it. 'You said we shouldn't go to sleep. You think Marcus might possess one of us?' He was trying not to let his fear creep into his voice.

'I think it unlikely, but I think we should be on our guard.'

'What about the others upstairs? They are all totally unprotected.'

Kate bit her lip. 'Shouldn't we go and wake them?'

Anne shrugged. 'Your father and mother didn't seem worried about the risk. Nor Joe. They are older, of course. Maybe they don't have any energy to spare. Susie and Cissy —' She frowned. 'It may be that their experiences have already depleted their energies so much that they would be no use to him anyway.'

'I'll go and look at them all again.' Kate climbed to her feet.

The staircase was cold and dark as she stood looking up, the candle in her hand. She shaded the flame as it flickered and put her foot on the bottom step. Behind her, through the open door, she could see Paddy filling the teapot. By the fire, Anne and Greg stared morosely into the flames.

She took another step and then another, staring up ahead of her. The landing smelt as it usually did, clean and slightly mothbally – from the linen cupboard she guessed. She stood, waiting for the candlelight to steady, watching the shadows running along the pink walls. From behind the closed door to Greg's room, she could hear a steady, throaty snore. Joe. Taking a deep breath, she put her hand on the latch and gently pushed the door open a fraction. The room was pitch dark, but the sound of the snore, suddenly loud in her ears, was reassuringly steady. She pulled the door closed and turned to the end of the passage. The master bedroom. All was silent. She hesitated. It seemed a terrible intrusion to look into Diana and Roger's room, but she knew she must. None of them could rest until they were sure all was well. Steadying her shaking hands as best she could, she pulled down the latch and pushed the door open. A small nightlight burned on the bedside table. By the light of its flame she was just able to see the two heads on the pillow. All seemed quiet. That left Alison and Susie. For the second time in an hour she opened their door and looked in, walking right into the room and holding her candle near the bed to see the two sleeping faces. Both were peaceful, their cheeks slightly flushed, their faces poignantly young and vulnerable as they slept. Tiptoeing out of the room, she glanced behind her at the dark square which was Patrick's door. Cissy.

The room was still a mess. Paddy had taken one look at his tumbled books and had turned and walked out of the room. He had not, as far as she knew, been back. She could see the hunched form of the woman in his bed.

She was moving restlessly, and as Kate watched, she began to murmur. Kate froze. Her hand was shaking violently as she held the candle and she saw the shadows leap and dance across the walls. The temperature had dropped several degrees.

Who are you?

The words hovered on her lips, but she said nothing out loud. Secretly glad no one could see her, she made the sign of the cross over Cissy's head and closed her eyes for a moment in prayer. When she opened them again the room seemed to be warmer. Backing out, she closed the door silently and left Cissy to it.

Putting the tray of mugs down on the hearth in front of the fire, Paddy threw himself down in a chair. His face was grey with fatigue as he glanced at his brother. 'It's going to be all right, isn't it, Greg?' His voice wavered for a moment.

Greg studied the boy and his expression softened. ''Course it is.'

'Try and get some sleep, Paddy.' Kate slipped into the room, closing the staircase door behind her. Reaching for one of the mugs, she cradled it against her chest, hoping they would not notice her shaking hands.

The boy nodded. Leaning back in his chair he closed his eyes.

Silence fell over the room. Greg too could feel his lids drooping. He glanced from Anne to Kate and back. There was a strong family resemblance between them. Their colouring and build were similar as was, at this moment, their look of total exhaustion. He sighed. Sleep. That was what they all needed. Sleep and tomorrow to awake and to find it had all been a ghastly nightmare.

LX

Jon woke with a start. He stared round, trying to locate the sound that had startled him; the phone, the quick, imperious tone of an English telephone, so different from the depressing monotone of the American. With a groan he dragged himself to his feet and pulled on his robe. Christ, what time was it? He stumbled across the bedroom and reached for the light switch as he made his way into the living room.

'Jon? My dear, I'm so sorry to wake you at this hour.'

So it really was the middle of the night. For a moment he couldn't place the voice, then it dawned. Kate's mother. 'Hello Anthea. How are you?' He tried to keep the weariness and jet lag out of his voice.

'I'm well, dear. Forgive me for ringing you so early but I'm so worried.'

'About Kate?' Hadn't she told her parents that they had split up?

'About both of them. Anne was supposed to be flying down to stay with Kate in this cottage she's rented. I can't get in touch with either of them and apparently the weather is appalling over there on the east coast.'

Jon leaned across and lifted the curtain with a cautious finger. The street light outside showed thick snow drifting down; it was settling. He frowned. If it was as bad as that in London, what on earth would it be like in deep country? 'I'm sorry, Anthea. I only got back from the States yesterday. I haven't been able to contact them either. The phone down there is out of order.' He tucked the receiver under his ear and reaching out for the whisky bottle unscrewed it deftly. 'I'm sure they're all right.'

'You really think so?' There was a slight quiver in the woman's voice. 'I've had this bad feeling. I can't explain it, but I'm sure something's wrong.'

He poured a double into the unwashed glass left on the tray from the night before. Then he put it down untouched. 'Anthea. Did Kate say anything to you about what's been happening out there? Anything to worry you particularly?' Would she have mentioned the burglary? Knowing Kate, probably not, if it would worry her mother, but then he hadn't spoken to her for several days. Supposing something else had happened?

'She rang me a couple of times. She said she was very happy, but I could tell she was keeping something back.'

Jon smiled grimly. So much for hiding things from one's parents. He could still remember the unerring way his mother unearthed his misdeeds when he was a boy, homing in on them like a bloodhound.

'Jon, dear. I know you and Kate weren't getting on very well. She told me she was probably not going to move back to your flat. Is that still true?'

'I don't know, Anthea.' He raised the glass to his lips at last. 'I was hoping I could talk her into changing her mind.'

'You know there's a man down there.'

'A man?' The tone of her voice had implied volumes. He found his body was reverberating suddenly with shock.

'An artist. Anne thinks she's fallen for him. Jon, I spoke to Anne yesterday before she flew south. She was very worried about Kate. She said all kinds of awful things had been happening. She said Kate sounded upset and frightened. She said someone had broken into her cottage and smashed it up. Apparently she was talking about ghosts and evil spirits and things —'

'Hey, slow down.' Jon frowned. Anne obviously did not share her sister's compunction about frightening her

426

mother. 'I'm sure she was exaggerating. Kate told me about the break-in. It wasn't that bad. Kids, the police thought.'

'Evil spirits. Anne said evil spirits. Jon, please. You have to go there and see everything's all right. Please.'

Jon glanced at the window. 'The weather is appalling, Anthea. I doubt if I'd make it. They were telling people to stay off the roads –'

'Please, Jon. I know you're worried too.'

He thought for a moment. 'As you said, Kate and I aren't together any more.'

'I see.' Her voice was very small. Disheartened. 'So you don't care –'

'Oh, come on, Anthea. Of course I care.' It was true. He finally acknowledged the truth of the statement. He did care, very much indeed. 'Look, I'll tell you what. I'll ring the station and see if the trains are still getting through. If they are, I'll see how near I can get, and see if I can find someone locally who can get me out there. But I can't promise.'

'Snow doesn't last very long at this time of year, Jon. It's too early. The ground isn't cold enough. It'll all be gone by tomorrow.'

Jon gave a wry smile. 'Not quite tomorrow, Anthea. Look, I will do my best.'

The trains were running. Just. But it was afternoon before he eventually reached Colchester and there the train stopped, disgorging dozens of disgruntled passengers into the snow. By the time Jon reached the front of the queue there were no taxis to be seen. He shivered, humping his canvas carryall higher onto his shoulder, and looked round. If he found a taxi at all he was going to need one with the courage of a madman to take him out to the coast. He glanced at the payphone. Should he ring Anthea and tell her he had got this far? One look at the queue of disconsolate people waiting for the phone made his mind up. He would call her tomorrow.

The taxi driver who eventually picked him up was more help than he had dared hope. After studying Jon's map with him, he looked up and smiled. 'They've got the main roads cleared, mate. I can get you pretty close.' He glanced down over the back of the seat at Jon's shoes. 'Do you want to stop off and get some rubber boots before we start?'

Jon grinned. 'Sounds like good advice.'

He bought boots, a torch, a half-bottle of whisky and a long woollen scarf whilst his driver waited unrepentantly on the yellow lines ("Can't see 'em, mate, with all this snow."), then he climbed in beside him, loaded with shopping bags.

'Scott of the Antarctic.' The man grinned again.

Jon laughed. 'I just got back from the States. It was pretty bad there too.'

'But they can manage, right?' The driver pulled away from the kerb. 'Here the whole bloomin' country grinds to a halt after an hour's snow. And me. I reckon I'll pack it in after I get you there.'

'If you get me there.'

'I'll get you as far as The Black Swan on the main road. It's as good a place as any to give up if you're going to. You might hitch a lift with a farmer. Their tractors can get through anything.'

It was a comforting thought as the car slithered its way east, the windscreen wipers pushing laboriously at the wedges of caked snow which clogged the glass. Jon shivered. He was tempted to broach his whisky, but it seemed unfair to drink alone and he wasn't about to offer it to his driver, not while he was still driving at any rate.

Every now and then a pair of headlights, dim against the white-out ahead, approached them, passed and disappeared into the murk. The driver was sitting forward, leaning over his wheel, staring ahead.

'It's getting bad, isn't it?' Jon voiced his worry at last.

'You're not wrong.' The taxi did a little shimmy sideways and the driver spun the wheel. 'Stupid thing is, we're nearly there. Can't be much further.'

'Do you think we should stop?'

'Not here. No. Pete Cutler doesn't give up if there's a decent pub within sniffing distance!' The broad shoulders quivered as he chuckled. 'We'd freeze to death if we stopped here, mate. I reckon it's about another two miles. Yes!' He let out a whoop of triumph suddenly as some landmark loomed in the distance and vanished. 'Hang on. We'll make it.'

From the way Pete locked the taxi and followed him inside the long, low, pink-washed pub, Jon had the feeling his driver was not about to turn round and drive back to Colchester. He was right. 'I'll ring them back at base and tell them I'm camping down here at the old Sooty Swan for the night. Mine's a pint of strong.' He winked and disappeared into the passage beyond the saloon bar. Jon pushed open the door. A fire was burning brightly in the huge hearth, but the room was empty. It was several minutes before a figure appeared behind the bar. 'Didn't think I'd see anyone in tonight,' the landlord greeted him cheerfully. 'How did you get here? Hitched a ride with Father Christmas, did you?'

Jon smiled. 'Something like that. A whisky for me, please, landlord, and a pint of strong for my mad driver and something for yourself.' He hitched himself up onto a bar stool. 'I don't suppose there is any way I can finish my journey from here, is there? I'm trying to get to Redall Bay.'

The landlord was concentrating on drawing the pint. He frowned and sucked in a lungful of air through the gap in his teeth. 'Tricky one, that. You'd need a four-wheel drive, I reckon. You going to see the Lindseys, are you? Or are you a friend of Bill Norcross? I saw he was down this weekend.'

'I'm a friend of Bill's, yes. And of Kate Kennedy. I don't know if you've met her? She's staying at the cottage.'

'Writer lady?' He set the glass on the counter and began to draw a second pint, presumably for himself. 'He did bring her in here, yes. A week or so back.'

'They've been cut off without phones for a couple of days, so I couldn't ring.'

'Unaccountable things, phones.' The landlord put the second glass on the counter. 'Always ring when you don't want them, and won't when you do. Do you want something to eat, sir, while I have a think about what you can do?' He selected another glass and held it up to the row of optics.

'I'd love something.' Jon was cheering up by the second. He turned as the door opened. 'Your drink, Pete.' He took a moment to survey his companion who until now had been no more than a pair of broad shoulders and a round, red face, with a huge, lopsided grin. Pete was a large man altogether – not the ideal shape, Jon thought idly, for a life cramped behind the wheel of a cab. His brilliant blue eyes, surrounded by the gold wire rims of his spectacles, were topped by thick sandy eyebrows and he was wearing two clashing bright red sweaters beneath his anorak.

The two men moved to the fire and sat down. 'Food.' Jon handed him the menu. 'The least I can do is buy you a meal after you got me this far.'

'That's uncommon nice of you.' Pete grinned. 'Any luck with a tractor?'

'The landlord is thinking.'

'Straining himself, is he?' Pete leaned back on the settle with a hefty sigh. 'I've known Ron Brown here for six years. He's a good bloke. He'll fix you up. You know, I reckon I'm starting to enjoy this.'

A chicken pie with baked potatoes, several drinks and much mutual backslapping later, Pete had wheedled Ron into lending them his old Land Rover. 'I'm a professional driver, mate!' he said, not for the first time. 'You know it'll be safe with me.'

'In this weather and with you pissed as a newt? I'd lose my licence letting you have it.'

'Then what say we borrow it without telling you.' Pete heaved a contented sigh and patted his stomach. 'I've had a nice time here. And I've heard a good story. I reckon I would like to go and do a spot of ghost hunting to round the evening off. In fact, why don't you close up and come too? You're not getting any more customers tonight.'

Both men had listened avidly to Jon's story about Kate's ghost, a story he had shamelessly embellished in the interests of camaraderie.

'No fear, I'll head for my bed, thanks.' Ron shook his head. 'I don't fancy going anywhere in this and you wouldn't either if you had any sense at all.' He stooped and groped under the counter, standing upright again to toss a bunch of keys to Pete. 'Just get it back to me in one piece tomorrow, boys, OK?'

Jon stood up. 'Thanks. We will.'

On the doorstep they nearly changed their minds. The wind had risen and the snow was driving straight at them; there was a sting in it which cut into Jon's face.

He hesitated. They could always wait until morning, when the sanders had been through, and go then. He glanced at Pete who was obviously thinking the same thing. Their eyes met.

'A bit of an adventure?' Pete said with a grin.

Jon nodded with a sudden surge of high sprits. He was right. This was an adventure.

They found the old Land Rover (the registration made it more than twenty years old, Jon calculated) in a lean to garage round the back of the pub. Facing away from the wind, it was surprisingly sheltered round there, and little snow had driven in under the roof. The two men climbed in and Pete, who had patted the bonnet as though greeting an old friend, inserted the key into the ignition.

'Are you sure you're OK to drive?' Jon looked at him dubiously. He wasn't worried about there being any other cars on the road, but he was imagining what it would be like if they skidded into a ditch.

'Right as rain.' Pete started the engine first go. 'Don't worry. I blotted up that beer with chicken pie and coffee. I'm all right. Not that any one will be driving their best tonight. You just keep your eyes skinned for this track down to the bay.'

The Land Rover backed out easily, its huge tyres holding their own in the slippery yard and gripping the road easily. They backed out past Pete's taxi – now covered in snow – and turned onto the road again. The pub behind them, with its thatched roof and string of coloured lights looked reassuringly cosy as it faded abruptly behind them and disappeared.

'A mile, he said.' Jon leaned across to peer at the milometer. He snorted. 'I wonder how many times this baby has been wound back.'

'Probably only once. I reckon Ron has had her most of her life.' Pete was leaning forward again, a frown between his bushy eyebrows. He did indeed seem remarkably sober suddenly.

'A mile will be a guess, I suppose,' Jon went on thoughtfully. 'People are notoriously bad at judging distances.'

'No, I think he's right. Look.' Pete slowed the Land Rover down in the middle of the road and stopped. They peered out into the darkness. A track led down steeply into the trees on their right, the features of the route flattened and hidden by the snow. Nearby was a notice, the message obliterated. They could see a car, almost hidden under the snow, parked close in beneath the trees.

'Private road to Redall Bay?' Pete glanced at Jon. 'Want to take a shufty?'

Jon let himself out onto the slippery tarmac with its coating of impacted ice and snow and slid across to the notice. Brushing off the snow with his sleeve he peered at it. 'Private R—d to Red—-ay.' The words, blistered and worn were just visible. He walked over to the other car. Pushing the snow from the windscreen he peered in. 'Europ-car.' He could just read the sticker on the windscreen.

'That's it.' He climbed back in. 'And that must be Anne's car. She must have hired it at the airport. She got this far safely, anyway. What are we going to do? Try and drive?'

Pete screwed up his face. 'Ron said it was a bastard of a track even when the weather's all right. I can't think why folks put themselves through such sweat. Why not get someone to come in and flatten it for them and tip a load of tar? It wouldn't cost the earth and they'd save a few axles.' He pulled the Land Rover into the side of the road. 'I vote we walk.'

'All right by me.'

Jon grinned at him. His relief when Pete had enthusiastically volunteered to join in the expedition had been so overwhelming it had surprised him. He had not realised how much he had been dreading the thought of braving a long walk from the pub through the darkness alone. He did not believe in Kate's story about a ghost for one minute, but the incredible loneliness of the night, the snow, the silence, the wind, were all a bit unnerving.

Tucking the Land Rover in under the fir trees next to the red Fiesta, they reached into the back for the canvas holdall – Jon's – and a plastic carrier containing four cans of lager, donated by Ron as a farewell gesture. They locked up and stood looking down the path.

'Ready?' Pete grinned at his companion.

'Ready.'

Jon forced himself to smile back, but suddenly he had begun to shiver.

LXI

They were there again. Nightmare voices. Hatred and anger, forcing her from her bed, until she stood, listening, in the centre of the room. Listening to something far away. The sea. The sea was the danger now. She could hear the roar of the waves, see the walls of spume crashing across the dunes.

Tell them. Tell them my story.

Claudia was the stronger now. Her voice rising above his in the howl of the wind.

Tell them. Tell them. Let the people judge.

Then he was there. Marcus. His voice the louder. Hatred. Anger.

'*No!*'

Spinning round slowly, Alison raised her hands to her head and clutched at her hair. They were fighting; fighting inside her; fighting for the last of her strength.

The grave. She must go to the grave.

She must save it from the water.

She must die.

Die with the bitch whore in the clay.

Live.

Die.

The door opened quietly and she walked out onto the landing, her bare feet warm on the thin carpet. Turning towards the stairs, she began to walk down, seeing nothing but the vision in her head. In the dark at the bottom of the stairs her fingers went unerringly to the latch on the inside of the door, though it was pitch dark there, without lights. The door opened and she stepped into the living room. Silently she moved between the sleeping figures towards the hall.

By the fire Paddy stirred uncomfortably in his chair, but, worn out, he did not open his eyes, even when the cold draught from the open front door stirred the logs into flame in the hearth.

Still barefoot she stood on the doorstep staring sightlessly out into the snow. Something made her pause – in her sleep some inner guardian directed her to step into boots and jacket – then she was gone, closing the door softly behind her.

In the living room the others slept on.

LXII

Their boots sliding in the snow, Jon and Pete tramped slowly down the track. Pete's cheerful patter had finally died away and apart from the occasional heartfelt curse as he slipped in the hardening ruts, he had fallen silent. Jon stopped every now and then to stare gloomily ahead. The snow had lessened now, and he could see clearly all round them. The moon, high above the clouds cast a flat, white radiance across the woods. He was sure they were lost.

The track they had been following seemed suddenly to have petered out and they had been forced for the past twenty minutes or so to follow what could have been a rabbit path through the undergrowth. Whatever it was it was narrow and full of brambles, and the thick snow had on several occasions piled in over the top of his boots.

Behind him Pete cursed again. Jon grinned. Stopping, he turned. 'Can't be far now.'

'No? I reckon this place of yours is like some kind of Brigadoon. It only appears every hundred years or so.'

'Please God, you're wrong.' Jon's reply was heartfelt. He shuddered as a gust of wind tore at his clothes.

A hundred yards further on the woods began to change. The thick oak and hawthorn copse became more sparse. The air grew if anything colder and, turning a bend in the track Jon and Pete found themselves at the edge of the dunes.

Narrowing his eyes against the wind, Jon stared round. 'Now where?'

'I can hear the sea.' Pete cupped his hand around his ear. 'Just over that sand. Bloody hell, it's close.'

They scrambled up to the top of the dune and found themselves overlooking the beach. Huge lines of angry breakers creamed up the shore, crashing onto the sand, and over the water they could see racing towards them the brown, bellying clouds which carried the snow.

'Another five minutes and we'll have a white-out.' Jon turned to Pete, worried. 'Which way do you think?'

'Left.' Pete spoke unhesitatingly. 'You said the farmhouse looked over the estuary. We've come too far to the east. We've got to the sea for real here.' Turning he began to tramp along in the lee of the dune. 'Come on. We'll get some shelter down here. God help us when that lot hits land.'

It seemed like hours before they saw the cottage looming before them in the darkness. Eyes screwed up against the snow Pete grabbed at Jon's arm and pointed. 'Found the bugger!'

Jon grinned with relief. At last. Thank God. Kate.

Hurrying now with new energy the two men fought their way up the dunes and across the snow-covered garden, ever aware of the crash of mighty waters behind them. The tide, as the forecast had warned, was going to rise and rise.

Ducking round towards the front door they found themselves sheltered at last from the wind. 'I hope to God she's there.' Jon didn't like the look of the dark windows. The cottage felt empty. Even from here he was pretty sure that they would find no fire; no one at home. And who could blame her? If he was living here, within spitting distance of the North Sea and he had heard a forecast like the one they were broadcasting today he would have packed and moved out on the spot.

The snow in front of the front door was smooth and clean. No sign of footprints. Raising his hand to the knocker, Jon surreptitiously crossed his frozen fingers.

The door swung open. His heart sank. 'I suppose this is

the right place?' There should have been locks and bolts. There were locks and bolts. His hand located them on the inside of the door as cautiously, he pushed it open. 'Hello!' He called. 'Kate?'

Silence.

He took a step in. 'Kate, are you there?' His searching fingers found a light switch and he clicked it up and down several times. 'No light.'

Pete had followed him into the hall out of the wind. 'Bit ripe in here, mate.' Pete sniffed hard. 'Somebody's puked.' He reached into his pocket for the torch and shone it around the hall. 'There's obviously no one here. I reckon your girlfriend moved out – for the night at least.' Stepping forward, he pushed open a door and shone the light inside. 'Kitchen. Bloody electric cooker. No electrics.' He was trying that light switch as well. He turned and made for the door on the opposite side of the hall. 'Living room. With a wood stove. We could light that at least. Oh my God!' The roving beam of light was directed at the sofa.

'What is it?' Jon pushed through the door behind him and peered over his shoulder. 'Oh Christ!' Both men stood where they were for a moment, their eyes fixed on the shape beneath the blanket on the sofa. It was Jon who stepped reluctantly forward. Behind him Pete shone the torch onto the battered face.

Jon closed his eyes. For a moment he thought he was going to throw up, but somehow he controlled himself as he turned and staggered out of the room. There was no need to check if the man was dead.

Pete followed him. 'Know who he is?'

Jon nodded. 'Bill Norcross. The friend I was telling you about.'

'Shit.'

'As you say.' They moved back into the kitchen and Jon sat down at the counter, his gloved hands to his face. 'What the hell happened in there?'

'I'd say he'd been beaten. Bloody hell, Jon, mate. Where's your girl? Where's her sister?'

Jon shook his head. Suddenly he was shaking like a leaf.

Pete reached onto the dresser. The fading torch beam had revealed a whisky bottle lying in a mess of earth. It turned out to be empty. 'You sit here, mate. I'll take a look round the rest of the place.'

Jon shook his head. 'I'll come with you.'

'There's no need.' Both men were thinking the same thing. Were Kate and Anne up there somewhere?'

'No. But I'll come all the same.'

They took the stairs two at a time. It was Pete who pushed open first one door then the other. Both rooms were empty. They stood in Kate's bedroom and stared round. Sand and earth had drifted across the floor. The bed was unmade – blankets piled in a heap in the middle of it – and there was earth there as well. The room was full of the sweet, damp smell of it. And something else. Scent. The overpowering stench of it had completely blocked out the unpleasant smell that was seeping up the stairs from below.

'No one here.' Pete stated the obvious. 'I reckon they got out all right.'

Jon sat down on the bed. His fingers trailed across the disarrayed sheets and he found Kate's nightshirt, tangled amongst the pillows, beneath which presumably she had folded it at some point. He recognised it. It was blue with cheerful scarlet stripes. Smart. Almost masculine. He remembered the way her long, slim legs emerged from the indecently high hemline. Oh, God, Kate. Where was she? 'What do we do?' Holding the nightshirt against his chest, he found he was suddenly feeling very weak.

'Go and look for this farmhouse. It shouldn't be too far away. That's where they'll be.' Pete's voice was strong. Confident. Not for the first time, Jon thanked whichever fate had dictated that this particular Colchester taxi driver should be with him tonight.

Closing the front door behind them again, they stood outside the cottage and stared round. There was no clue to which direction to go. Any path there might have been had long since been covered by the snow. Pete shone the torch around once and was about to switch it off when he saw the tracks. A set of footprints. Recent footprints which had passed close to the door and went on across the snow back towards the sea.

'Someone's been past here within the last ten minutes or so, while we were inside,' he commented.

Kate? Anne?

The two men bent their heads towards the wind and set off the way they had come, heading back towards the snow covered dunes.

LXIII

'Where is she?' Roger burst into the room and stared round at the sleepy figures sprawled around the fireplace. 'Where in God's name is she?'

'Who, Dad?' Greg stretched with a groan. They had all fallen asleep in the end, Anne and Kate and Paddy too. In the hearth the fire had died to cold embers. He shivered violently.

'Alison. Where is Alison?'

'She's not upstairs?' Greg asked the obvious.

It was Paddy who stood up first, stretching. 'I'll go and look.'

He disappeared through the door into the hall. Roger threw himself down in Paddy's vacated chair and bent forward, rubbing his face wearily in his hands. He seemed to have aged ten years in the last few hours.

Kate stared at the greyness of his skin, the transparency of his face and she bit her lip. 'Shall I make us all some tea?' she said, standing up. 'And let's get the fire going.' She walked across to the window and pulled back the curtain. It was still dark. Thick snow had fallen and judging by the sky, there was more to come. She could hear the wind buffeting against the glass. In the distance the trees were thrashing their branches, and she watched as a cascade of dislodged snow fell to the ground.

She was filling the kettle when Paddy came back into the room. 'She's nowhere through there. Her boots and jacket have gone. I can't believe she came past us in the night, but she must have, while we were all asleep. Sorry, Dad.' He slumped on the sofa, crestfallen.

'Sorry!' Roger roared. 'Sorry! Is that all you can say?' Behind him Susie had appeared in the doorway. Her hair was tangled and her face was still crumpled with sleep. The large bruise on her forehead from the car crash had turned a deep blue.

'Sorry! You know where she's gone, don't you! God only knows how long she's been out there. Go outside, Paddy. See if you can see footprints.'

'Outside?' Patrick looked at him doubtfully. He nodded. Dragging himself to his feet again he disappeared and moments later they all felt the rush of cold air as he pulled open the front door.

'There's no sign.' He called from the hall. 'No tracks at all. Just birds and rabbits and a fox.'

They heard the door slam.

'Not that it matters. We all know where she's gone.' Roger's face was livid suddenly, the dry skin flushed with colour. 'To that damn beach. I'm going to have that dune bulldozed. I'll have it destroyed utterly!'

Was it Kate's imagination or was there a sudden frisson in the air, a charge of fear – and triumph. With a shiver, she hunted for the tea caddy. 'That's what he wants,' she said over her shoulder. 'That's what Marcus wants.'

'And once he's got what he wants, perhaps he'll leave us alone!' Roger rocked back in the chair, and threw his head back, closing his eyes.

'He might, but Claudia won't.' Paddy came and sat down next to his father. 'The only way to put an end to this, Dad, is to get the dune excavated properly. Then we'll know the truth.'

'And you think that will put a stop to all this horror?' Diana had appeared in the staircase doorway. She was still wearing her crumpled smock; there were smears of blood on it, but whose, Kate could not remember. She turned to the kettle which was steaming gently, willing it to boil. 'I can't believe you are all sitting there, doing nothing, when

Alison is outside in all this snow. For pity's sake is no one going to do anything? I'm going to find her!'

'No, Ma.' Paddy staggered to his feet again. The boy was white with exhaustion himself. 'You've got to stay to look after the others. I'll go.' He looked mutely at Kate.

'I'll come too.' She found she had spoken automatically. 'Of course I will.' She glanced regretfully at the kettle.

'No, Kate. Drink something first.' Roger's voice was suddenly very weak. 'Both of you. And have something to eat. For all we know she has been out there for hours. Five minutes isn't going to make any difference.'

'I'll go with you, too.' Anne stepped forward. 'Safety in numbers, and all that.' She gave a weak grin.

It was nearly ten minutes later by the time they had all drunk mugs of steaming tea, eaten a wedge of bread and marmalade each and dragged on boots and coats and scarves. As they headed for the door, Paddy glanced at the gun.

'Take it.' Greg had hopped after them. His foot was stiff and throbbed agonizingly this morning. 'We'll be all right here.'

Paddy looked at his brother. Greg gave a watery grin, then he punched him gently on the shoulder. 'Take care of yourself, Paddy; and take care of the girls.' He turned to Kate and touched her hand. She smiled at him, but it was a thin, tired smile. She had no strength left for more. The air was bitingly cold. She wondered how she would summon the strength to go even ten feet, never mind the best part of a mile.

Greg watched them go. All three were exhausted, he knew that. His brother could hardly lift the heavy gun he had so bravely hefted onto his shoulder. He glanced beyond them towards the woods. Was there anyone there, watching them, or were they as deserted as they seemed? He shuddered. The wind was increasing, coming from behind the house, tearing in across the marsh from the sea.

He watched until they were out of sight, then turning, he closed the door. Shooting the bolts across seemed a terrible act of treachery with them outside, but there was nothing for it. He hobbled back into the living room and stared at his father, shocked. Roger was lying back against the cushions, struggling to catch his breath. His face was blue and he was sweating profusely. Diana was bending over him.

'Ma –'

'It's all right, Greg.' Her face was as white as a sheet. 'Your father has had a bit of a turn, but he's OK now.' She stroked his face gently. 'Rest, love. She'll be all right. They'll find her.'

'They will, Dad.' Greg knelt by his father's knees. The syringe, empty now of painkiller, was lying on the arm of the chair. 'They'll all be fine. It's broad daylight now, and the weather is a bit better.' It was a lie but he doubted if his father would know it.

Roger managed a slight grin. He patted Diana's arm as she pulled a rug over him. 'Better now, love,' she whispered. She kissed the top of his head. He had relaxed visibly, lying back against the cushions and his colour was better. Taking Greg's arm she pulled him towards the kitchen end of the room.

'I'm fairly sure he's had a slight heart attack,' she whispered.

Greg started back towards his father but she caught his sleeve. 'No. I'm sure he knows, but don't say anything. Can you go upstairs and wake Joe? He's got to try and go for a doctor.'

Greg nodded. With a glance at his father's white face he dragged himself across to the door and pulled it open. The staircase was dark. Putting his hand on the rail he set his teeth grimly and somehow he hauled himself to the top, sweat pouring off his face as he dragged his injured foot up, step by step, after him. Joe was snoring loudly when

Greg limped into the darkened bedroom and shook him awake but it took him only a few minutes to shake off the deep sleep and climb to his feet. 'Right. Don't worry. I'll get there.'

He too was fortified with a marmalade sandwich and a mug of scalding tea before letting himself out into the cold.

'I hate to see you going out on your own, Joe,' Greg murmured as he stood with him on the doorstep. He was leaning heavily on his stick.

Joe smiled grimly. 'Don't you worry about me.' He carried his gun, broken, beneath his left arm. 'You take care of the others. Your Dad and Cissy and Sue. I don't like leaving you on your own here –'

'We're safe here, Joe.' Greg did his best to sound confident. 'Don't worry about us. Just get us some help for Dad.'

Joe nodded. Pulling the collar of his coat up around his ears he stepped out into the dark.

LXIV

The footprints were filling up as they watched, disappearing beneath a new layer of snow. Pete was slightly ahead, walking fast, his head down against the wind. Around them the landscape was uniformly white: shore, sea, sky, a formless, cold frame without definition.

'She went this way,' Pete had slowed almost to a standstill. He was casting around him, like a dog searching for a new scent. 'Then the footsteps seem to stop.' They stared around desperately, both men doubled over, studying the snow. 'I can't see . . .'

'Here.' Jon had walked closer to the sea and suddenly he spotted the tracks again. Lighter this time, and scuffed, as though she had been running.

Kate.

He shaded his eyes against the imagined glare and stared past the dunes towards the sea. The beach stretched in both directions, the shape of the dunes flattened by the snow, and in the cold emptiness nothing moved.

'Kate!' His shout was swallowed by the wind, muffled by the snow. It had no resonance, as though he had shouted through several layers of cotton wool. The sound would not have carried more than a few yards. 'Kate!'

Pete made no comment. He had moved on, head down against the wind, his face immobile now with cold, trying to see new footprints through the whirling snow.

'She was heading towards the sea,' Jon shouted at him at last. 'Why?'

'Lost her sense of direction? Panic?' Pete had stopped, his hands rammed down inside his pockets. 'Poor woman must be in terror of her life.' He shook his head. 'Shall we go on?'

'Of course we go on.' Jon was shaking. 'We go on until we find her.'

He plunged on, across the snow, sinking now and then through the white blanket into softer sand. 'Kate!' His voice rose and dissipated into nothing, whirled to shreds on the wind. 'Kate!'

The voices were still warring inside her head. Standing staring down into the snow-filled grave, Alison saw nothing of the snow, nor of the two figures floundering against the wind.

'Kate!'

The word whirled past her and was lost. It meant nothing.

Whore

Murderer

They were inside her head, both of them, sucking her energy. Soon she would be drained and they would go.

'It's not Kate!'

She did not hear the words; did not see the two men who stood now, one each side of her.

'Who then?'

Jon shrugged. 'I don't know.' Tentatively he reached over to touch her arm. 'Are you all right?'

Alison ignored him. She did not see or hear him. Her gaze never left the drifting snow at her feet.

'Hey, kid, are you OK?' Pete's touch was stronger. He took her by the shoulders and shook her gently.

Alison did not react. Claudia's face was white against the snow, her gown, still stained with blood, as blue as the sky. She could feel the woman's need, the longing, the fear and hate: *May the gods of all eternity curse you, Marcus Severus Secundus, for what you have done here today.*

She was winning now: Claudia.

'What's wrong with her?' Pete glanced at his companion.

'God knows, but the kid's freezing.' Jon wriggled out of his jacket and wrapped it around Alison's shoulders. 'Let's get her back to that cottage.'

'I don't know that that's such a good idea.'

'Maybe not, but where else can we take her?'

The two men looked at one another for a moment across Alison's bowed head.

She could not hear them. He was there now, his fury blistering inside her skull. *The grave. Destroy the grave!*

With a sob she wrenched herself free of Jon's arm. Staggering a few steps from him, she aimed a kick at the snow-covered sand. 'Destroy it!' The voice which came from her lips was guttural; low pitched. A man's voice, for all the words were clearly English.

Jon stepped back in surprise. Then, regathering his wits, he moved forward again to pick up the jacket which had slipped from her shoulders and wrap it once more around her. 'Come on. You must keep warm.' His own voice was shaking with cold.

'No!' She shook him off with ease. 'Keep away from me.' She threw the jacket down on the snow and leaped down into the shallow hollow below the dune with a sudden, last surge of energy. 'The sea will take it soon.' She threw back her head and laughed. 'The sea will take it at last! Two thousand years it has taken for the tide to come and tonight it will wipe the slate clean!' She stood staring at the sea, her hair streaming back from her forehead, her eyes fixed on the horizon. Jon and Pete, surprised into silence, stared with her. The wind was strengthening from the east, whipping the snow in across the water, building the waves, pushing the sea higher and higher up the beach.

'Alison!'

The cry barely reached them. For a moment none of them reacted, then Jon turned. Three figures were hurrying towards them, heads down into the wind, almost lost in the white whirl of snowflakes.

'Kate?' As he recognised her Jon felt his heart leap inside his chest. Relief, joy, worry – all three seemed to swirl around his head as he stepped towards her. She was accompanied by a young man – a boy he saw as he looked closer – and Anne.

'Jon?' Her astonishment stopped her in her tracks.

'Hi.' He found he was smiling. He shrugged. 'It's a long story.'

She stared at him for a moment, overwhelmed with relief, wanting to throw herself into his arms, then her glance moved on past him, resting briefly on Pete before she turned to Alison.

'Allie? Allie, are you all right?' Her questions to Jon could come later. The fact that he was there, on the beach in the snow, spoke volumes. She slid down the side of the dune after Patrick who had thrown his arms around his sister.

Alison shrugged him off viciously, and he staggered back, bewildered. 'She's gone, Kate.' There were tears running down his face. 'She's gone. She's not here. It's not her.'

'Allie!' Kate took Alison's hand and chafed it in her own. 'Allie, come on. Fight it. Please. You have to fight it. Come back to us!'

'What's wrong with her?' Pete slid down beside them.

'She's ill. She doesn't know what she's doing.' Pushing her hair out of her eyes, Kate began to button the jacket across Alison's chest. 'We have to get her back out of the wind. She's no strength left.'

'She seemed to have plenty of strength to me, love.' Pete grimaced. 'She nearly pushed me across the beach.'

'But don't you see, that's not her!' Kate cried. 'That's not her strength. He's possessing her. He's draining her. We have to get her away from here.'

'I'll take her.' Jon did not waste time asking her what she was talking about. He lifted Alison off her feet and turning, began to tramp inland, with his back to the wind.

He knew the exact moment when the strength went out of her. He could feel it draining away as he walked. Physically, she seemed lighter suddenly – a bag of bones in his arms where moments before he had held a rigid, angry body. He clutched her more closely, glancing down at her face as he cradled her against his chest. Her eyes were closed, her face white, a child's face, when a moment before it had seemed to belong to someone else entirely. He shuddered and suddenly there was a hand on his arm. He glanced sideways and met Kate's eyes. She smiled as she stumbled along at his side. 'Thank God you're here.' Did he hear the words against the wind or did he imagine them? He wanted to reach out and touch her, but all he could do was smile and stagger on, feeling the weight of the girl dragging at his arms. Suddenly, her head lolled back and her eyes rolled open. He stopped, horrified, staring down at her face. She was limp now, cold inside the roughly-buttoned jacket.

'Jon, what is it?' Kate was beside him, looking down at Alison's face.

He met her eyes. 'We've got to get her inside quickly, Kate.'

Wordlessly she nodded. Tucking the jacket more closely around Alison's inert body, she followed as Jon walked on across the snow through the dunes, his shoulders hunched against the wind.

In the cottage he carried her straight upstairs and laid her gently on Kate's bed, then he stood back as Kate pulled the blankets over the girl and chafed her hands.

Pete appeared in the doorway behind them. He had pulled the front door closed, and then, firmly, shut the door to the living room before climbing the stairs.

'What happened to Bill?' Jon asked softly. His eyes were fixed on Alison's face.

Kate did not look up. 'He was attacked. In the woods near here.'

'Attacked?'

She went on rubbing Alison's hand. 'He said it was a woman. Two women. We brought him here. But the phones were out. We couldn't get help.' Her voice was shaking; he saw a tear fall onto the blanket. Stepping forward he put his hand on her shoulder and gave it a gentle squeeze. 'Judging by the bruises on his face no one could have helped, Kate. I should think his skull was fractured in a dozen places.'

'He said Allie did it.' The words were out before she could stop them. She heard both men gasp and at last she looked up. 'She couldn't have done, could she? She couldn't . . . He was a big man. She's only a child . . .'

The room was very silent. The girl on the bed, her face white, her hair strewn damply across the pillow, did not move. Her hand in Kate's was limp and cold. Kate leaned back against Jon, her eyes closed. She was suddenly so weary she couldn't move. Alison's hand dropped from her fingers. For a moment it lay on the blanket where it had fallen, then suddenly it convulsed into a fist. The girl's eyes flew open. Her voice when she spoke was strong and triumphant.

'Listen,' she said. 'Listen. The tide is rising at last.'

LXV

When Boudicca swept across the country and burned the city she still called Camulodunum, he was one of the few who managed to escape. Taking his new wife and his child, he rode out of the town in good time and waited in safety as the smoke of rebellion rolled across the country. A spark had ignited the revolt as he had known it would. But it had not been his doing. Claudia's curse had not touched him. The sacrifice of an unknown, unsung prince to the gods of a British bog had sunk unnoticed into the mists of time. He was triumphant. Later, when the revolt was quelled and Nion's tribe had gone, lost in the slaughter of a proud and rebellious people, he would obtain the land.

He asked for the marsh where the whore he had called his wife had died, as a reward for his services to Rome and it was given to him with much more. He grew rich and fat; he bought more land; he owned two villas. He watched his son grow; the boy who had rich auburn hair and eyes of glass grey like his mother, and once a year he rode east, to the edge of the land and he stood looking down into the marsh, staring at the irises and bog cotton which blew in the knife-blade wind. Others, unseen strangers, still offered sacrifices to the gods of the marsh — pots of coins, small pieces of jewellery, even weapons. He offered nothing. He did not throw down a rose to commemorate the love which had gone; he did not hurl a dagger to the gods of hate. He merely stood and stared at the shifting, watery scene glittering in the sunlight, and, before he turned to go, he spat upon her curse.

*   *   *

'The storm is getting worse.' Diana turned from the study window, letting the curtain fall. She looked down at the bed where her husband lay. His face was grey with pain. His hands were clawing restlessly at the blanket she had pulled over him.

'Don't worry. Joe will make it.' His voice was growing noticeably weaker. 'He's a stubborn old bugger. I can't see him letting a mere blizzard get the better of him. And the kids will be all right.'

Diana forced herself to smile. 'I know.' She turned back to the window so that he couldn't see her face. Drawing back the curtain a little she peered once again into the whirling snow. He was out there somewhere. Marcus. She could feel him. Evil. Waiting. Waiting for what? To use them? To draw on their energy? And no door could keep him out. She turned back to Roger. His eyes were closed and she watched him for a moment. The energy was draining out of him almost visibly. Their evil visitor would find no food in him. She shuddered. He was dying. She could not pretend to herself any longer. He was dying before her eyes. She wanted to throw herself at him and hold him, to will her own strength into him, but she couldn't. She could do nothing but wait and watch. Shaking her head miserably she tiptoed towards the door and let herself out of the study into the cold hall. She could feel the draught blowing under the front door. It was icy; a drift of snow had somehow slipped under the draught-proofing and lay in a white veil across the stone tiles. Closing the door behind her silently she went through into the sitting room.

Cissy and Sue were seated on the sofa near the fire, side by side. Automatically her eyes went to the chair nearest the inglenook where normally in weather like this the two cats would be lying, in a heap of black and white fur. There was no sign of them. Greg was standing in the kitchen, leaning on the back of one of the bent oak chairs. He seemed to be gazing into space, 'How is he?' he asked as she wandered listlessly over to him.

She shrugged. 'Not good.'

He looked at her hard. 'Joe will get through, Ma.'

She tried to smile. 'I'm sure he will. But I don't think it will be in time for your father, Greg. We have to prepare ourselves.'

He put his arm round her, pulling her close against him. 'It was bound to happen one day. We knew he hadn't got long,' he said gently.

She nodded dumbly.

'He always said he wanted to go here and not in hospital.'

'I know.' It was a whisper.

'Shall I go and sit with him for a bit?' He dropped a kiss onto the top of her head. 'You get some sleep; you look completely flaked out. I'll call you if he needs you.'

She nodded. With a glance at the two dozing on the sofa, she went to the door at the foot of the staircase 'The moment he needs me, Greg,' she repeated softly.

'I promise.'

The staircase was cold and the upper floor of the house dark as she climbed wearily up to the bedroom she had shared with Roger for so many years. For a moment she stood in the doorway looking round, vividly aware in some inner part of herself that he would never walk through this door again. On the floor, in the corner, a pathetic reminder that Christmas was barely two weeks away, a pile of presents lay, partially hidden by a rug.

She walked across to the low window and stared out. It was growing light, but the snow was thick now, whirling through the air, blotting out the horizon. In this east-facing bedroom you could usually see across the dunes towards the sea, but today she was conscious of nothing but grey and white – a moving, whirling mass of nothing. Disorientated, she turned – and stopped short.

The woman by the bed was so clear she could see every detail of her clothes, her hair, her skin, her eyes. For a moment they stood there, their eyes locked together and for the first time Diana knew that Claudia could see her as clearly as she could see Claudia.

'Sweet Blessed Jesus!' The words were out of her mouth before she knew she had spoken. 'What do you want?'

For a fraction of a moment longer they stared at each other, then Claudia was gone.

'Ma.' Greg's voice from the foot of the stairs was urgent. 'Ma, come quickly.'

Diana whirled back to the door conscious with some part of her brain that the room smelled of a sweet, sickly perfume. 'What is it? What's wrong?'

'He wants you.' Greg hobbled ahead of her towards the study. Roger was lying propped up against the pillows and cushions. He was breathing with difficulty and his cheeks, which for so long had been colourless, had a livid, painful colour to them.

'He's here, Di,' he said slowly. 'That bastard is here, in this room. He's real.'

Diana glanced at Greg.

'Marcus,' Greg mouthed. 'He's seen Marcus.'

Diana knelt at the side of the makeshift bed and took Roger's hand. 'He can't hurt you, love.'

'Too damn right. I've nothing for him. It's the kids he wants. He wants their energy. But he's not going to get it.' He gripped Diana's hand so hard she winced. 'I'm going to fight him on his own ground.' The breath was rasping in his throat.

'Roger –'

'He didn't bargain for that, did he. I'm going after him. To hell, if necessary. ' He looked from his wife to his son and back. 'Don't worry. I'm sane. Dying, but sane. I've never believed. Not in heaven or hell or God or Satan until now. But this bastard has made me realise there is somewhere out there. If his soul can survive there, black as it is, then so can mine!' He laughed weakly and Diana buried her head in the blanket near him, trying to smother her sobs. 'I'm going to find out what it's all about. And if he can come back then so can I. I shall return to tell you.'

'Dad –' Greg tried to interrupt, but Roger talked on, his words slurring together now as the drugs took a stronger hold on his pain.

'No, my mind is made up. I am going to find out why she cursed him. She's here, you know, in the house now. She was his first wife. She's come to help me. She wants me to find him. I shall get him. I shall win –'

'Dad!' Greg knelt down stiffly on the other side of the bed, wincing as his foot dragged on the ground. 'Dad, don't talk like this.'

'Why?' Roger turned and looked at him. His eyes, though unnaturally bright, were perfectly lucid. 'After what that bastard has done to my daughter, you think I am going to let him get away with it?'

'No, of course not, but –'

'But nothing. My mind is made up. I am going after him. A quest. A glorious quest through the realms of the after-life. How do you like that idea?' He sounded delirious as he laughed again, clutching at Diana's hand. Then he began to cough.

'Roger –' Desperately she tried to soothe him. 'Get some water, Greg, quickly. Roger, darling, please, calm yourself. You're going to be all right.'

'Balls!' The word was gasped through another spasm of coughing. 'Do me the kindness of treating me like an adult, Di. I know. You know. Greg knows.' He paused, breathless, and sipped gratefully as Greg held a glass of water to his lips. 'Thanks son. Look. Better this way than lingering for months in some goddam awful hospice. I love Redall. All of it. I was born here. My father was born here. Not many families can say that nowadays. I'd like to think that you or Paddy will make your home here too. This place is in our bones,' he smiled grimly. 'Who knows, perhaps we are descended from Marcus himself. I'm bound hand and foot to this place – its history is in my blood.' He looked at Diana. 'What I'm trying to say, love, and making a frightful hash of it, is that I'm happy to die here. And I'm not going anywhere. I'll still love you, whatever happens. And I'll stick around. Not to frighten you. Just to watch over you and keep Marcus in line.' He closed his eyes, exhausted.

Diana looked up at Greg. Her eyes were blinded by tears. 'Greg –' She mouthed his name but no sound came.

Greg was biting his lip. Neither of them said a word as, holding a hand each, they watched Roger's face lose the colour which had animated it, as he dozed again. Around them the room seemed to grow darker in the candlelight.

'A quest,' Greg said at last, trying to keep his voice steady. 'I like that idea.' He frowned. If it were possible – to travel through time and space – to treat death as a mere doorway – that would only be comforting if one expected to find angels on the other side.

But Marcus was a demon.

LXVI

The waves threw off the snow, thundering up the beach in clouds of spray. The sea had reached the soft sand now, the sand which was never covered by the tide, sucking greedily at the ground and spitting out the residue with each successive incursion. Peat and soil swirled and dissolved; sand turned to brown liquid, dispersed and vanished, to be deposited again on a distant shore. In the dune the grave welcomed the first deep wave which seeped into its heart, whisking away a trowel and a brush, tearing at the remaining bones, grinding them, stirring them, flushing out every trace of what had been. Another followed and then another and then the sea overwhelmed, passing onwards towards the calm, ice-bound estuary where, long before, the geese had gone, flying inland away from the storm.

Joe stood panting at the top of the track and wiped his forehead with his sleeve. He could barely see now for the weight of snow on his eyelashes; his face was frozen stiff and his tears seemed to turn to ice as the wind whipped them from his eyes. He looked round, exhausted. Two cars were parked at the edge of the road. Drawn up under the trees. Anne's he supposed; but whose was the other? He walked over to it, and swept the snow off the snow-covered bonnet. Ron's Land Rover from the pub. He frowned and glanced back the way he had come. Whatever Ron had come for, he had left no trace. His tracks had long ago been covered over.

Wearily he turned up the road and began to trudge

towards home. Twice he stopped and looked behind him. A dozen times in the wood he had had the feeling that he was being followed. Each time he had stopped and raised the gun, sweeping it menacingly around at the undergrowth. But there had been no one there. No one at all. Only the silence and the wind and the occasional crash of snow falling from the trees.

It took him another hour to trudge the few hundred yards home, grope in his pocket with deadened hands for the key to the back door, and let himself into the blessed warmth and stillness. The house was very quiet. Stamping the snow off his boots he shrugged himself out of his coat, leaving it where it fell on the kitchen floor and he went over to the wall telephone. Picking it up, he listened. The familiar dialling tone rang out almost deafeningly in his ear.

Nine nine nine.

He had never dialled it before. Shaking his head wearily, he waited for a moment before asking for police and ambulance. The woman on the other end of the line was dubious. 'They'll be with you as soon as possible Mr Farnborough, but the weather is so bad! They're still forecasting hurricane force winds and blizzard conditions. The helicopter can't take off. It will be down to the police to try and get through with a medical team.'

'Do your best, love.' Joe found he had sunk down onto the wooden chair left neatly against the wall. Near him Cissy's apron hung on the back of the door. He shook his head. 'Things are bad down there. Very bad. There's a man murdered. Another man dying. Please. Help us.'

He sat still for a long time after he had hung up. There was nothing more that he could do. He could not go back. He had agreed to wait so he could guide the police vehicle down to the farmhouse. Leaning his head against the wall he closed his eyes wearily.

In two minutes he was fast asleep.

LXVII

Kate glanced up at Jon as they stood side by side looking out of the bedroom window of the cottage. She still wasn't entirely sure how or why he had appeared – explanations would come later – but she was comforted and happy that he was there. Behind them Alison was sleeping deeply. Downstairs in the kitchen Pete and Patrick were rummaging in the drawers of the dresser for candles and matches.

Patrick didn't like being down here. He was acutely conscious at every moment of the dead man lying on the sofa in the next room. Bill who in life had been a genial, popular visitor at Redall Farmhouse was in death a terrifying threat.

They were half-way up the stairs when Alison screamed.

'Shit, what was that?' Pete was close behind Patrick who stopped dead, his face white. 'That was Allie.'

'OK, son, I'll go. You wait here.' Pete pushed past him, taking the rest of the stairs two at a time.

In the bedroom Jon and Kate were standing over the bed. Kate had clutched at Jon's arm – her fingers were white as they sank into his sleeve. Alison was lying on the bed thrashing back and forth as though in pain, her hands clasped to her head. 'Mummy!' she screamed again. 'Mummy, help me!'

Anne sat down on the bed. She caught Alison's wrists, trying to pull them away from the girl's face. 'Allie. Allie, please, listen to me. You're dreaming. Don't be afraid. Wake up. Allie, wake up.' Alison was raking at her temples with her nails. A streak of blood appeared across her forehead, then another. 'Allie, don't, you're hurting yourself. Please.'

Alison did not hear her. They were there again, inside her head. Only this time he was laughing. *Gone! Gone under the sea at last! Now you're forgotten. Forgotten forever, you and your priest lover!*

Claudia's screams inside her head were so loud she thought her brain would burst; pain and anguish swirled about her; a tide of blood washed back and forth behind her eyes, and now, suddenly, there was another voice — a man's voice — the voice of Claudia's lover. At last he had come. He was there with them. And he was strong; stronger than Marcus, his fury uncontrollable.

With a groan Alison pulled at her hair, sitting up, rocking back and forth with such violence that Anne slipped off the bed to the floor. 'Alison!' She scrambled to her feet. 'Can you hear me? Listen!' She grabbed at the girl's hands again. 'You must be strong. Come back to us, Allie. Open your eyes and come back. Whatever it is you're fighting, you must be strong.' She gasped as Alison tore her wrists free and went back to attacking her own face with her nails. 'Alison, please!' She looked wildly at Jon. 'We've got to tie her hands. She's going to scratch herself to pieces. Please, help me, quickly.'

Jon looked round wildly. It was Kate who pulled the belt from her bathrobe which still hung on the back of the door. It took three of them to hold her still, but somehow they managed it, tying her wrists together and tucking her firmly down with the sheets. When they had finished both Anne and Kate had been badly scratched themselves. 'She's as strong as three men!' Anne stared down at the girl who was still throwing herself back and forth beneath the sheets. She rested a hand on Alison's damp forehead.

Alison did not feel it; she did not know what was happening to her. There was no room for thought inside her head now. No room for her at all. She had ceased to fight them. They had her strength. That was all they wanted.

Jon was shivering. The temperature in the room, he

461

realised suddenly, had dropped violently. Surreptitiously he retrieved his jacket which had fallen to the floor when they put Alison into the bed. 'What is it? What has happened to her?'

Kate looked at Patrick who had slid into the room behind Pete. 'Marcus has got her.' She gave a nervous laugh. 'My Roman. Remember? He killed Claudia, who we think must have been his wife, and now he's haunting us.' She looked down at the bed. 'He's possessed her, Jon.'

'No!' Anne shouted. 'No! He can't have her. Fight, Allie, fight!' She put her lips close to Alison's face. 'Concentrate, Alison. Think! Think about anything. Use your brain. Fight.' She took Alison by the shoulders and shook her gently. 'Don't give in. Don't let him win. Oh God!' She threw her hair back off her face with a furious jerk of her head, clenching her fists in her frustration. 'I don't know what to do. I don't know how to help her! Alison. Listen to me. Fight!'

Pete, like the others, was staring at Anne. His gaze left her face at last and slid down to Alison's restless form. His mouth had gone dry. He probably looked as bad as the others. They were all white-faced, cold. He cleared his throat. 'This kid should be in hospital, Anne,' he said at last. 'Where will we find the nearest phone?'

Kate shook her head. 'The phones aren't working.' Was it her imagination or was Alison calmer now? She stared down, terrified, at the girl's tortured face.

Shadows.

Whirling shadows filled with hate.

Inside her head Allie stared into the darkness helplessly and saw the three prowling, amorphous figures. She could feel someone's hands ice cold on hers, hear a voice shouting her name, but she could not react. They were like lions circling their prey: the woman, the two men, hungry in their hatred for living energy to sustain them.

Why me?

Did she cry out loud? She didn't know, but as her mind rebelled the figures drew back.

FIGHT

A voice reached her out of the stormy roar of hatred, a woman's voice. *FIGHT, ALISON, USE YOUR BRAIN.*

Too tired. She was too tired to fight. She was empty. They had sucked her dry.

In the dark the shadowy figures had begun to fade. Their concentration had left her. They were turning elsewhere; questing, hungry. Others must be found, and soon, to feed their lust for hate.

'We'll need to get back to the car.' Jon went back to the window. Anything to get away even for a moment from the torment of the girl on the bed. He took a deep breath and stared out. He found he was shaking. 'The snow is settling very thickly.' He glanced back at Pete. 'Take a look. Do you reckon the roads will still be passable?'

Pete joined him, staring down into the murky light. After a moment he rubbed his eyes. 'Tell me my eyes are going, mate,' he muttered under his breath. 'But is that the sea down there?'

In a low-lying corner of the garden, below the dunes, a line of dark water had appeared. As Jon watched it broadened slightly, strewn with ripples, lapping at the snowy grass. He craned his neck sideways, narrowing his eyes as a fresh flurry of snow hit the window. Beyond the belt of trees he could see the broad, icy spread of the estuary, the mud and dunes smothered in a uniform blanket of snow. The water was lapping higher, free of the ice, creeping round the back of the cottage as the wind drove the sea inland.

He turned to the bed. 'Patrick. Come and look at this.'

The boy came. He stared out into the garden. 'Oh shit!'

'Are we going to be cut off?'

Patrick nodded. 'Once it's here there's nothing to stop

463

it. It must have gone over the sea wall at Redall Point.'

'Right.' Pete looked at Jon. 'That settles it. We all have to leave. Fast. We'll make a stretcher to carry the kid.'

'What about Bill?' Kate looked from Jon to Pete and back.

'We'll have to leave him, Kate.' Jon put his arms around her and held her close. 'He won't know, love. Or if he does, he'll understand. We can't take him with us.' He lowered his voice. 'Our lives are in danger. That water is coming in very fast. We have to get Alison away.'

They built a stretcher using a rake and a broom handle from the log shed, winding sheets around them to make a hammock and padding it with blankets. Pete carried Alison down the stairs and laid her down on it outside the front door. They wrapped two more blankets around her, then Jon and Pete picked her up. 'It works,' Jon grinned at Kate.

She was about to close the door when a thought struck her. She hesitated for a moment outside the door of the living room. Bill was there. But so were her notes for the book. She couldn't leave them to the floods. Bill would understand. Screwing up her courage she pushed open the door and peered round it. Nothing had changed in the room. The smell of vomit was all-pervasive. As quickly as she could, she ran to the desk. Picking up her notebook, backup disks and her volume of poetry she rammed them into the inner pockets of her waterproof. One last look round and she turned back towards the door. By the sofa she stopped. ''Bye Bill. God bless.' Her voice sounded strange in the silent room.

Whirling round she ran out, closing the door behind her. Slamming the front door she ran after the others who were already disappearing into the wood. Inside the cottage the silence was suddenly intense.

Slowly the scent of jasmine drifted down the stairs and through the empty rooms.

LXVIII

'Ma, go and take a break. I'll sit with him.' Greg put his hand on his mother's shoulder. Roger was asleep, his breath coming in harsh rasping gasps.

Diana shook her head. 'I'll stay, Greg.' She looked up at him through her tears. 'It could happen at any time now.'

Greg bit his lip. Silently he knelt beside her, ignoring the pain which shot from his foot through every nerve in his body. 'It's what he wanted. To be at home,' he repeated softly.

'I know.' She laid her head for a moment on her husband's chest.

Roger opened his eyes. 'Not gone yet,' he whispered. 'I'm trying to think –' he paused, barely able to speak. 'Famous last words –'

'How about Sod you, Marcus, I'm coming to get you,' Greg said bitterly.

'Greg!' Diana was horrified.

'No. He's right,' Roger whispered. 'It gives me – a goal.' His eyes closed and for several seconds he struggled for breath.

'Hush now, love.' Diana put her hand on his forehead. 'Save your strength.'

'What for?' The grim humour kept on coming. 'I won't need strength – where I'm going.' He managed a faint smile.

'That's right. Sock it to him, Dad.' Greg had a tight hold of his father's hand.

Around them the room was growing colder. Diana

shivered. The candle burning low on the table beside the bed flickered violently.

'Greg.' Roger opened his eyes again. 'Get the archaeological boys in. Get them to turn over that grave. Every inch. Find out what it is that bastard is trying to hide and tell the world.'

Another gust of wind seemed to blow through the room. The candle flared again and then went out, trailing smoke.

Diana let out a small cry of distress.

'He doesn't like it!' Roger gave a croaky laugh. 'He wants to keep that grave a secret. It's up to you, Greg. Everything is up to you now –' His voice trailed away. In the faint light flickering through the window the room was all shadows.

For a moment the silence was so profound Greg stared round, afraid. It was as though he were seeing the room through a sheet of glass. Uncomprehending, he kept on clutching his father's hand, then suddenly he realised where the silence came from. Roger's harsh breathing had stopped. Blinking back his tears he bent and kissed the cold hand in his. 'Ma –'

'I know.' She was sobbing quietly. 'He's gone. Oh, Greg –'

Neither moved for a long time, then slowly and painfully, Greg climbed to his feet. He put his arm round Diana's shoulders. 'Come through to the warm. I'll make you some tea.'

She shook her head. 'I don't want to leave him –'

'He'll be all right. You must come. It's so cold in here –'

Somehow he managed to help her up. For a moment they both stood looking down at his father's face, relaxed now, looking younger and happier than it had for a long time, then suddenly Diana tore herself away from Greg's arm.

'All right, you bastard!' She screamed into the room. 'Are you satisfied now? You've killed another man. But

466

he's better than you. A good man, and he'll hunt you down. He'll follow you to hell and back if he has to!' She burst into tears again. 'Now get out of my house! Get out and don't come near any of us again!'

'Ma.' Greg caught her hand. 'Ma, come away. This isn't doing any good.'

'Isn't it?' Through her tears she turned on him like a spitting cat. 'Well it's doing me some good! I want that bastard Roman out of here for ever. He's not taking my house. He's not taking my children! We'll tell the world about him. We'll tell the world he's a murderer and a liar and a cheat. He killed that poor woman. He killed Bill. And now he's killed my Roger –' She broke down in sobs.

Somehow Greg managed to pull her away. In the sitting room Cissy had managed to get to her feet, her face white. 'Diana –?'

'Dad's dead.' Greg steered his mother towards the sofa and pushed her down. 'Please, Cissy, put on the kettle. She needs some tea. And some brandy.'

'Oh, my dear, I'm so sorry.' Cissy touched Diana on the shoulder, then she limped across the room to the Aga. She was shaking violently. Her arm, roughly bandaged and in a sling, hurt like hell, but she ignored it as she manoeuvred the kettle onto the hotplate. As she did so, there was a deafening bang from upstairs. She spun round. 'What was that?'

Greg was standing over his mother. At the sound he had turned. In two painful strides he was at the door.

Behind him Susie curled up on her chair and buried her face in a cushion. Cissy ran to her and put a protective arm around her.

Diana's face was white, her eyes glassy. 'It's begun,' she whispered.

'What has?' Greg opened the door and peered up the stairs.

'Your father and Marcus.'

Greg swung round. 'You don't believe that –'

'Your father is trying to protect us.'

Greg stared at her for a moment. Then he turned, and hauling himself with difficulty up the banisters, he disappeared upstairs. There was a long silence. Three pairs of eyes were fixed on the door. Then they heard him coming back. He appeared and closed the door behind him. He was shaking with the effort of negotiating the stairs on his injured foot. 'Nothing,' he said. The words were no sooner out of his mouth when there was another bang, louder than the first.

Diana let out a sob. 'Roger. Be careful.'

'Ma –' Greg went and sat down beside her. Putting his arm around her he pulled her against him tightly. 'It's probably the house timbers expanding or contracting in the cold. It's not Dad –' He glanced at Cissy. 'The brandy.'

Cissy, her face white, nodded. She collected bottle and glasses from the dresser and brought them back to the fire. Her hand shook so much as she poured it that the liquid spilled on the hearth. She handed Diana half a tumblerful. Not noticing, Diana took a sip. She coughed violently and handed the glass to Greg who drank in turn. They were all waiting, ears straining for another bang.

The silence lengthened. It was several minutes before they realised that the familiar smell of woodsmoke and polish in the room had been replaced by the scent of jasmine.

LXIX

*He saw her often in his dreams, the wife who had betrayed
him. He saw her laughing. He saw her in her lover's arms.
He saw her again and again in her blue gown, the splash
of scarlet dripping down her skirts, her eyes open in wild
agony and hate. And again and again he heard her curse
him. A woman's curse. A dying curse, made before the
gods themselves. He would awaken shivering, sweat sheen-
ing his body and if Augusta woke, he would claim it was
a touch of the marsh fever. He was scared of dying. While
he was alive she could not touch him, but in death they
would be equals. And the priest. Her lover. What of him?
Was he there too, waiting? Waiting to avenge the greatest
betrayal of all, a false message from the gods. He stared
into the darkness and he was afraid.*

The second time they stopped to rest Kate felt for Alison's
pulse. The girl was getting weaker all the time, her life
force draining visibly as they watched. She glanced at Anne.
'What can we do?'

Anne shrugged miserably. She felt helpless. All her knowledge of the human mind had deserted her. She had no
basis to work from. This was not covered by any category
she had read about. This was no chemical imbalance of
the brain; it was not multiple personality disorder; it was
not schizophrenia; it was not any kind of manic state.
Marcus was an external force, a parasite implanted inside
the girl's head and she had no parameters within which to
work. 'I wish I was religious. I feel a priest would be more
help than anything else,' she said slowly. 'Or a medium of

some sort as a go-between. Our culture doesn't give us weapons to fight this any more. I don't know what to do.' She looked at Jon and then at Pete, kneeling in the snow. The sleet, driving into their faces had turned without their realising it to rain. The wind, stronger than ever, had a warmer feel now. Behind them, like an ever-present enemy, the water lapped higher, flowing in amongst the trees, stealing imperceptibly through the undergrowth.

'Is he still there?' Kate murmured to her sister. 'Is he still inside her?'

Anne shrugged. 'I don't think so. She's calm; her strength has gone.'

'Then where is he?' Kate looked up into Jon's eyes as he bent over her to look at Alison.

Jon gave a wan smile. 'I don't know,' he said.

Anne stood up, stiffly. The woods were very silent; the trees seemed to be listening, shrugging off the hissing rain and wind.

'Perhaps with the grave flooded, he's left completely.' Patrick stood up too. Jon and Pete bent to pick up the stretcher and slowly the small procession began to move on. Kate paused a moment, staring back the way they had come. He wasn't here now. The woods were empty. But that didn't mean he had gone for good. Something deep inside her told her that he was still around, somewhere. Waiting.

LXX

'Dear God, what's happening!' Diana shrank against Greg. The room had grown dark. The rush and roar of the wind filled the chimneys, scattering ash into the room.

'Susie!' Cissy shouted suddenly, her voice shrill with panic. The girl had fallen from the chair. She was struggling on the ground, her hands to her throat as if she were trying to prise fingers loose from her neck – fingers they could not see. The candle which had stood on the table beside the sofa flared suddenly and went out. An acrid trail of smoke drifted across the room.

'Susie!' Diana flung herself towards them. 'Oh God, it's happening again.'

Susie was thrashing backwards and forwards on the rug, beating her heels on the ground, fighting for breath.

Mine

I have her

Mine

HATRED

ANGER

She could see nothing, feel nothing but the pain inside her head as three formless shapes tried, parasitic, greedy, to fasten their empty, gaping souls to hers.

'*Mummy* – !' Her shriek of pain and fear died in her throat as she writhed once more in a spasm of agony.

'Susie!' Cissy was on her knees, pulling at the girl's wrists, trying to drag her hands away from her face.

'It's what happened to Allie.' Greg knelt down beside

them. He looked at the girl for a moment then he stared round the room. 'He's here. He's here, in the room with us.' He turned back to his mother.

'Stop her hurting herself, Cissy,' Diana commanded, her voice surprisingly strong. 'You bastard, Marcus!' She turned and shouted at the ceiling. 'Can't you see, there's no point. It's over. We know. We know what you did –'

'That is the point,' Greg put in quietly. He was holding Susie's small hands in his own. 'We don't know what he did. We think we do. We think he murdered Claudia and now his conscience is making him pay the ultimate price, but we don't know.'

'*No! No! NO –!*'

Susie screamed so loudly that both Greg and Cissy shrank back, releasing her hands, staring down at her in fear and horror as she sat up, her body rigid, clawing at her eyes.

Greg recovered first, pulling her hands away from her face. 'He's using her in some way. The only way we can stop it is to find out what it is he is trying to say. And the evidence must be in that grave. We have to go and see as soon as the weather has improved enough to have a go ourselves. Never mind the archaeologists. This is between us and Marcus and Claudia. We need to know the truth. For all our sakes.'

'He'll try and stop you,' Diana put in softly. 'He wants whatever is in that grave to stay hidden.'

'Tough. It's not going to. Besides, he's tried to stop me before and he failed,' he grinned bitterly. 'I defeated him, remember? And I mean to get at the truth.' He climbed awkwardly to his feet, swearing softly as a shaft of pain shot up his leg from his throbbing foot. 'Do you hear that, Marcus Severus Secundus?' Like his mother, he was shouting at the ceiling. 'I'm not afraid of you, and I mean to have the truth!'

In answer the wind screamed ever more loudly down the chimney, scattering sparks.

'Where are you, Roger? Oh, please help us!' Suddenly Diana was crying. 'Fight him for us. Make him go away.'

'Ma –' Greg put his arms round her.

'No. He promised. He's there. I'm sure he's there. Help us Roger. Please.' She was trembling violently.

There was a long silence. Greg bit his lip. Wherever his father had gone, he had not lingered here. The silence thickened around them. He could feel the skin on the nape of his neck prickling.

There was a presence in the room. But it was not his father. It was a female presence. Greg shivered, staring round. Claudia. He could sense her near him, the woman in blue, the woman whose image he had so often conjured up with pencil and brush. 'Claudia's here. Speak to her.' He seized his mother's arm. 'Go on. Tell her we mean to find the truth. Tell her we will avenge her.'

'Greg –'

'Go on!' He turned round slowly himself, as if expecting to see the woman somewhere concealed in a corner. 'Do you hear me, Lady Claudia? We are going to learn the truth about your death. That's what you want, isn't it? That's what this is all about.' He paused, panting, half expecting to hear a voice answering his, but the only response came from the wind. 'Claudia!' He shouted the name again.

Surely he could smell it: the jasmine scent she wore.

And something else.

Tobacco.

He bit his lip with a glance at his mother. Had she smelt it too? It was two years since his father had given up smoking – the day his cancer had been diagnosed – but suddenly he could smell his tobacco in the room. Was he here, after all, fighting for them as he had promised or was it wishful thinking, this strange blend of scents? Ashamed at the sudden tears in his eyes he moved a few paces towards the window and looked out, trying to control his emotions.

In the space of an hour the scene out there had changed. The snow had turned to rain. The garden, so recently locked in a brittle, short-lived frame of ice had become a living, dripping sea of water. From trees and bushes the soft snow slid in lumps or melted as he watched, desperately trying to swallow his tears. The rain, sliding down the window was carrying the premature winter away with it as swiftly as it had come. The flowers of winter jasmine had freed themselves from a frosting of ice and drooped, yellow and orange from slender green stems.

Somehow he managed to get a grip on himself.

He was turning back towards Diana when out of the corner of his eye he saw a movement in the trees. He stiffened, a shot of adrenalin flooding through his stomach. Marcus? Claudia? His father? He waited, holding his breath.

His relief when he saw the small group of figures emerge from the trees, carrying between them what looked like a stretcher, was enormous. 'It's Kate and Paddy,' he called, trying to keep his voice steady. He limped to the door and, fighting the bolts, he pulled it open. The blast of cold air carried the sweet, clean smell of melt water before it, as the soaked, exhausted figures staggered across the lawn. He did not question who the two unknown men were as they trooped in; enough that they were all safe.

He stared down at his sister's face and he grew cold, his relief stillborn.

'What happened, Kate?' He looked up and met her eyes.

'We found her at the grave again,' she said wearily. 'Marcus had her.' She flung herself down on the sofa beside Anne who had collapsed there as soon as she walked in. It was only then that she saw Susie lying in front of the fire. 'Oh no?' Her plea turned to a sob.

'They'll be all right.' Diana was cradling Alison's head against her breast, kneeling beside the stretcher where Pete and Jon had lowered it to the floor. Behind them Paddy bolted the front door again and then subsided where he was onto the mat, sliding down to sit with his back against the wall, staring into space. He had reached the limits of his endurance.

Blowing on his freezing fingers Jon went quietly over to stand behind Kate and put his hands on her shoulders. It was a reassuring gesture and she leaned back, grateful for his strength. Raising her eyes wearily she found Greg staring at her. His white face was stiff with shock.

'This is Jon Bevan, Greg,' she said slowly, beginning to grapple with the zip on her wet jacket. 'He and Pete came to look for us. They went straight to the cottage. They found Allie.'

'Jon Bevan?' Claudia, Marcus, even his father were forgotten as Greg, oblivious suddenly of everyone else in the room, focussed his attention on Jon's face. 'The poet?'

'That's right.' Jon stepped round the sofa and held out his hand.

Greg stared at it. He did not make any attempt to take it. 'So, you've come to play ghostbusters with us, have you?' he said coldly. 'And what are your qualifications for sending Marcus Severus Secundus back to the hell he surely came from?'

Jon lowered his hand. Slowly he began to peel off his sodden jacket. 'Perhaps a poet can communicate with the dead; I'm sure he can do it at least as well as a painter,' he replied stiffly. 'We are supposed to speak a universal language which transcends the ages.'

'I thought you and Kate were finished,' Greg pressed. He was shaken by the sudden arrival of this man whom he had thought long gone from Kate's life.

'Greg!' His mother interrupted, her voice sharp with anxiety. 'Help me with Allie! Quickly!' Alison's head had fallen back on Diana's arm and her eyes had rolled open.

Unnoticed by any of them the smell of tobacco in the room strengthened.

'Christ!' Greg helped his mother lower her to the floor. Bending low he put his ear to her mouth. 'She's still breathing.' He swivelled to face Jon, his face growing hard again. 'Well? What do we do, poet?'

Jon ignored him. He like the others, was staring down at the two girls lying near one another on the floor. Only the occasional terrified sob from Cissy punctuated the silence of the room. Diana's eyes had filled with tears. She was drained, too tired even to speak. With Alison's hand in hers she sat helplessly on the floor gazing at her daughter's face.

There was a long silence. Kate looked at Jon. She had not noticed the hostility between the two men, nor the electric atmosphere as the tension between them flared, but she could feel the cold in the room which was suddenly palpable. It was swirling clammily round them. He was there. He hadn't gone. She could feel the strength of the alien mind reaching out, the tendrils of anger and hatred threading through the air, feeding on the energy of hate.

'NO!'

She didn't realise she had cried out loud until she saw the others staring at her, their faces full of fear. 'He's looking for someone else –'

'Fight him. Don't let your mind go empty. Fight him hard. Recite something. Concentrate.' Anne caught her arm. 'Fight him. He's drained those two like ... batteries ...' She spluttered with anger. 'And he needs energy from somewhere else. Fight him.' She looked round. 'Where's Paddy?' Her voice sharpened with fear.

'Oh God! Don't let him have gone into the study! Don't let him have found his father –' There had been no chance to tell them Roger was dead, no way of breaking the news gently. Diana scrambled to her feet and pushing past Pete, she ran to the door. She stopped abruptly. Patrick was slumped against the wall in the passage outside.

'Paddy! Her voice rose to a shriek. The boy opened his eyes. 'Paddy. Are you all right?' Flinging herself down beside him she hugged him tightly.

He nodded vaguely. 'Tired.' He could barely speak.

'Tired and very brave.' Jon had followed her out. He extended a hand to the boy. 'He's OK.' You could tell from the eyes. Alison's blank stare did not compare with this blurred, sleepy moment of disorientation. 'Come on, old chap. Stand up and come to the fire.' He smiled at Diana. 'He's OK. I'm sure he's OK. Just exhausted.'

Diana nodded. Behind the door in the study Roger lay, cold, on the camp bed. She had to tell Patrick that his father had died. She had to tell the others. Tears filled her eyes but she said nothing as Jon helped Paddy through to the fire and lowered him into a chair. Now was not the moment. She couldn't face even talking about it. Not yet.

They all stood huddled together, looking round. A spatter of rain hit the window. From the icicle above the porch a steady chain of drips began to fall onto the step. Inside, the temperature was still dropping. They stared at one another.

Anne frowned. 'He's still here. Looking for energy,' she whispered. 'I can feel him.' She shuddered. 'My God, I've never felt anything like this before.' She stared round at the frightened faces. 'Concentrate. Fill your minds with something. Think hard. Recite poetry. Anything. Don't let him in. Recite! All of you together. Now. Something you all know. Quickly.'

For a moment the room was totally silent. Then Diana, her daughter's hand clutched in her own, began slowly to intone the words of a nursery rhyme. 'The owl and the pussy cat went to sea, in a beautiful pea green boat . . .'

With a shaky smile Cissy joined her and after a minute

Pete joined in. 'They took some honey and plenty of money wrapped up in a five pound note . . .'

Was it their imagination or was the room growing less cold?

'Go on. It's working,' Anne whispered.

'Again. Again. Another.' Diana had screwed up her eyes as if she were praying. 'Humpty Dumpty sat on the wall, Humpty Dumpty had a great fall. All the king's horses and —'

They all felt the sudden easing of tension in the room.

'He's gone.' Greg's whisper cut them short.

There was a moment's silence.

As swiftly as it had come the cold prowling menace had left, and with it the strange, sudden, enigmatic smell of Roger's tobacco.

For the time being the encircling shadows were empty.

LXXI

The police Land Rover slid and bucked down the track with Joe in the front between the two uniformed constables. Behind them Doctor Jamieson clung on for grim death to the back of the seats as they skidded through the increasingly wet slush. 'Not far now.' Joe peered through the windscreen. 'Down through those trees and we're there.'

A gust of wind rocked the car sideways and the driver swore as he fought to keep it on the track. In front of them the radio crackled and spat with interference. The younger constable, Bob Garth, grinned at him, his face grey with fatigue. He had already been on duty for forty-eight hours. 'You reckon your ghost will be waiting for us then, do you?'

Joe had told them the whole story as far as he knew it. It was greeted with solemn interest by the two policemen. The doctor, an old friend of the Farnboroughs', was more forthcoming. 'If I didn't know you better, Joe, I'd tell them to breathalyse you. I've never heard such a load of bollocks. You've all been letting the solitude get to you.'

'I've heard stories about Redall Bay before,' Bob Garth put in. 'A lot of the locals reckon it's haunted. If not by the Black Dog then by a whole range of sinister things. You won't catch them going down on the marsh or the beach in the dark. When I was up here the other night I reckoned it felt strange. There was something very funny about all that business at the cottage.'

'The ghosts the locals are afraid of were invented by the smugglers to keep the revenue men away,' the man at the wheel put in. Mat Larkin had lived nearby all his life. 'You don't want to believe a word you hear about them.'

'I suppose not.' Joe did not sound too sure. He too was local born and bred.

'Nearly there now.' Mat swung the Land Rover expertly round a slippery bend. The wheels skidded in the wet slush, throwing muddy white spray across the bushes.

'Looks peaceful enough now.' All four men peered through the windscreen at the farmhouse as they drew up outside. Climbing out, both Joe and the doctor instinctively hung back allowing the two policemen to go first. A face at the window showed them that they had been seen. Seconds later the front door opened.

'Come in. Quickly. For God's sake, look! He's tried to take Susie too!' Cissy, near hysteria, grabbed the doctor's arm.

Joe stood looking down, paralysed with fear as Hal Jamieson knelt and felt the girl's pulse. He pulled up her eyelid and peered at her eye and then laid his hand on her forehead. 'She's asleep,' he commented tersely. 'Heavily asleep.' He turned to Alison and frowned. His examination this time took longer. He glanced at Diana. 'Her temperature is low and her pulse is weak. She's suffering from exhaustion. They should both be in hospital – Good God! What was that?'

The crash upstairs was louder than any before. They all looked at each other. Greg gestured towards the staircase. 'Up there,' he said weakly.

Glancing nervously at one another the policemen disappeared and the others heard their footsteps pounding up the stairs and along the landing.

A few minutes later they returned. 'Nothing.' Bob Garth sat down at the kitchen table and felt in his pocket for his notebook. The sooner they had taken statements the sooner they could be on their way. He glanced up with a shiver. There was something nasty here. He could feel it.

Kate talked to him first. As calmly as she could, she related everything that had happened since she had arrived at the cottage, watching as she did so, the doctor examine Greg's foot, rebandage it and nod to himself in apparent satisfaction. He moved on to Cissy.

'And you actually saw this figure?' Bob turned the page on his notebook. His mouth had gone dry. 'You are a writer, Miss Kennedy. Are you sure you haven't imagined some of this?'

'No, she bloody hasn't!' Greg had been listening. 'You heard that bang yourself! Did you imagine that?'

'I think,' Hal Jamieson put in, 'that all this is academic at the moment.' He straightened with an exhausted sigh. 'What we need to do is to get these people out of here to hospital. Cissy needs an X-ray, Alison should have a CAT scan, in my opinion as soon as possible, and both girls need a complete checkup before I'll be happy with them.'

'We can't take everyone, sir,' Mat Larkin put in.

There was a moment's silence. Kate felt her heart sink. For a moment she had thought it was all over; that they were safe.

'I don't suppose we could get your old banger going, Joe?' Bob Garth put in. 'Supposing we give it a jump start?'

Joe nodded. 'It's worth a try.' He felt in his pocket for the keys.

Kate gnawed at her fingernail as they waited, looking from one tense face to the other as, through the closed door, they heard the sound of Joe gunning the dead engine. Nothing happened. Again he tried. Again nothing, then they heard the sound of the two bonnets slamming shut. 'No go, I'm afraid. The old girl seems to have had it,' Joe said grimly when they were back inside. 'I'm sorry.'

'OK. You take the injured to hospital, Mat,' Bob Garth said firmly, overcoming his own reluctance. 'I'll stay here to check on the cottage and see about poor Mr Norcross.'

'Yes. You must get us out of here!' Cissy clutched at

Larkin's sleeve. 'You've got to get us out of here. He's after my daughter –' Her voice slid up the scale hysterically. 'You've got to save us!'

'It's all right, Cissy. We said we'll take you,' Jamieson put in comfortably. 'And Diana and the girls. And Greg. That foot is not all that good.'

'And Joe,' Cissy put in, sobbing wildly. Her voice rose dangerously again. 'You have to take Joe –'

'I'm not going,' Greg interrupted her. 'You said my foot was OK, Hal. It can wait. I'm not leaving Redall. But take Joe. That's fine by me.'

'I'm afraid that's all we can manage,' Mat put in, worried. 'The doctor has to come back with us. He's needed elsewhere, and that makes eight of us already –'

'Don't worry.' Kate caught Anne's eye and saw her sister grimace. 'We'll be all right. I think it is the two girls who are most at risk. We'll hold him off.'

There was an uncomfortable silence then Bob Garth grinned. 'I'll look after you all, Miss Kennedy, don't fret.' He would not allow himself to feel afraid.

They watched as the large police vehicle turned and churned its way up the path into the trees. 'You must have been sorry there wasn't room for you.' Greg looked curiously at Pete who had watched them from the window.

Pete shook his head. 'I reckon I'll hang around until this is all over. If you and the constable are going out to the cottage I think it would be a good thing if someone stayed here to keep an eye on the boy and the ladies.'

Greg gave a half-hearted humourless laugh. 'I think they would consider that remark patronising at the least and sexist more than likely.' He led the way back into the farm house.

'I doubt it, sir.' Bob Garth put in. 'Don't forget. We have a murderer on the loose somewhere –'

'Haven't you taken anything in!' Greg swung round on him. 'We are not looking for a man –'

'Greg.' Kate put her hand on his arm.

He shook it off angrily. 'No! We are not looking for some escaped lunatic or a robber or a psychopath. We are trying to stop a man who died nearly two thousand years ago —'

'Quite, sir.' Bob managed to keep his face impassive. 'But whoever we are looking for, dead or alive, he is still a real threat. I think this gentleman is right. Someone should remain here.'

'Well, I'm going with you.' Kate stepped forward. 'I was a close friend of Bill's, and I am the tenant of the cottage. It's right I should be there.'

'And I'm coming too.' Jon put his arm around her once more. 'I'm not letting you out of my sight again, Kate.'

She looked up at him startled. Then she smiled. Quietly she reached for his hand. She did not see the anger on Greg's face.

LXXII

Anne and Pete watched them from the window as the four figures disappeared into the trees. The house was suddenly very still. Anne bit her lip. 'Hot drink for us?'

Pete nodded. On the sofa, Paddy, tucked up in rugs, was fast asleep. He had cried when Diana told him about his father, as had Kate, but his weariness had been too much for him. As the doctor sat, stethoscope in hand, talking to him, the boy fell soundly asleep. 'Let him be.' Jamieson had stood up, folding the tubing into his pocket. 'Sleep is the best healer of all. He's exhausted and he's sad, but he's a strong chap. He'll be all right.'

Pete and Anne sat facing each other across the kitchen table. 'Rum do.' Pete grinned. His face, weatherchapped and ruddy, broke into a mass of creases when he smiled.

She smiled. 'I keep asking myself what I am doing here.'

He nodded cheerfully. 'Me too. That'll teach us to get involved. All I wanted was to make a few honest bob; one last fare before I knocked off for the night.' He buried his face in his mug and blew off the steam.

'What do you think is going to happen?' she asked after a long silence.

'The police said they'd send a van for Mr Lindsey and the poor chap at the cottage.'

'I meant Marcus.'

He ran his fingers through his hair. 'Marcus has to be dealt with.'

'You can't arrest ghosts.'

Pete gave a slow chuckle. 'I couldn't somehow see that young chap arresting anyone. He looked as though he

484

was still collecting plastic toys from a cornflakes packet.'

'Nice, though.'

'Oh, yes, if you like that sort of thing. Uniforms turn you on, do they?' It was a half-hearted attempt but he was rewarded with a token cuff on the shoulder. As Anne lowered her hand she froze. 'What was that?'

They both listened. 'Shit! I didn't expect him to come back. Not so soon.' Pete stood up. The colour had drained from his face.

They could both hear it clearly now. Footsteps upstairs. Slow, ponderous footsteps.

Quietly, Pete picked up the breadknife from the table. On tiptoe he crossed to the door with a quick glance at Patrick who was still fast asleep.

Anne followed him as, slowly, he crept up the stairs, and peered along the corridor. There was nothing there. Carefully he moved onto the polished boards and pushed open the first bedroom door. Room by room they searched the whole top floor. There was no one there at all. In Patrick's room they stopped and looked at each other. 'Can you smell it?' she said at last. 'Cigarettes.' She bit her lip.

'Not Roman.' Pete gave a short barking laugh. 'Perhaps the lad smokes on the quiet. Or perhaps it's Mr Lindsey,' he went on tentatively. 'Patrolling.'

Anne shivered. 'I'm not sure that that idea comforts me.'

'It should. Come on. Let's go down. This house is bloody cold.' Pete led the way back downstairs. At Patrick's side they stopped, and were both secretly relieved to see that he appeared to be sleeping as soundly as before, his breathing deep and regular, his colour normal.

'"Man never perceives anything fully or comprehends anything completely,"' Anne quoted softly. 'Jung said that. It's something I try to remember when I find my brain getting stressed because I can't make sense of something. It is comforting.' She flung herself down on a chair and closed her eyes. Then she opened them wide.

'I can smell her scent again.' It had been several minutes before it had been strong enough to register.

'Yes.' He had smelt the jasmine too. The tobacco had gone.

'What shall we do?'

He turned, dusting ash and dried lichen from his hands. 'What can we do? We wait.'

LXXIII

All the time it felt less strange. He floated up the beach above the water; he could no longer see the grave where he had lain so long. It didn't matter. Nothing mattered now that his strength was growing. It was the man on the shore, the tall, dark-haired man, the poet, who had given him the energy. Silently, secretly he had drawn it from him as he stooped over the girl, and the man had not even noticed, preoccupied as he was with his own love and his own loss. His beautiful Claudia was here too. Near at hand. Always with him. Her hatred and her curse had given her strength and between them they were going to find justice at last.

Kate was clinging to Jon's arm. Strong, independent, clever Kate, his sparring partner, Lady Muck, was clinging to the effete poet like a stupid bimbo. Greg, limping in front beside Constable Garth, glanced over his shoulder again, amazed by the sudden churning in his stomach. Why had she said it was all over between her and this man if she hadn't meant it? He felt a sudden surge of white hot anger. She was beautiful. Beautiful like Claudia whom he had drawn over and over again without realising it when he was alone at the cottage.

He hunched forward again over his walking stick, trying to control his fury. The wind had dropped completely now, the storm gone as swiftly as it had come. He could feel a new softness in the air. It soothed him a little.

They were unprepared for the sight which greeted them at the cottage. Stopping at the edge of the wood, they peered at what had once been a pretty if overgrown garden and an idyllically sited house. The building stood in a pool of black water which reached halfway up the front door, almost, but not quite, as it had been in the painting which had so upset Kate. Beyond, towards the saltings the sea had encroached on every side, carving new channels through the sand, extending its domain. Already a flock of duck were paddling busily across the muddy water feeding greedily on the debris which floated in slowly spinning mats of vegetation.

'The grave must be under all that,' Greg said soberly. None of them had made a move.

'So. Marcus has won,' Kate was standing beside him now. 'We'll never know what happened.'

Bob Garth was worriedly rubbing the palms of his hands up and down the front of his jacket. 'Where was the deceased when you left?' he said thoughtfully. 'Was he on the ground floor?'

'Oh, no!' Kate buried her face in her hands.

'I'll come with you.' Greg stepped forward. 'Kate, you stay here. There's no need for you to come in.'

The water was swirling around the top of their boots as the two men, followed somewhat reluctantly by Jon, made their way towards the front door. It was several minutes before they reappeared. All three looked grim.

'The water has been in, I'm afraid, Miss Kennedy.' Garth had recovered himself sufficiently by the time he reached her. 'It's made rather a mess in there. I think you should leave it for now. We'll wait for the scene-of-crime officer and forensic to have a look round and then they can remove Mr Norcross's body.'

She nodded. She had no intention of going in.

'Shall we walk out to the grave? The water is not very deep out there and its receding fast.' Greg had followed Garth to her side. His foot, numbed by the cold, ached dully.

She nodded reluctantly. Her own exhaustion had reached such a peak that she wondered if she would be able to walk another step. Gingerly, she stepped into the thick muddy water, feeling the soles of her boots sliding a little on what had once been a lawn. She glanced at the bush of daphne in the corner. The small pink flowers were still there, free now of ice and snow. On the topmost branch she could see a robin.

The tide was still high. They had no way of seeing where the grave was under the choppy, angry waves. Standing calf-deep in water, Kate turned slowly this way and that. The dunes had shifted. She was disorientated. There were no landmarks now to guide her, only a wide expanse of triumphant water.

Bob Garth shook his head. 'If there were bodies in the grave there will need to be a coroners' inquest,' he said doubtfully.

'Just what Marcus didn't want.' Greg was staring at the water.

Garth regarded him dubiously. He could feel it again out here; the strange certainty that all was not right. The feeling that if he were not careful he would hear or see something which he would rather not know about. 'Do you really believe all that stuff about ghosts?' he asked nervously.

Greg threw him a quizzical glance. 'You would rather believe there was a homicidal maniac loose in the woods?'

'We are looking for a murderer, Mr Lindsey.' Garth kept his voice even. 'I'll reserve judgement on who he is, for now.'

Greg did not reply. He had felt it now. The lightest brush, tentative, questing, inside his head. Marcus was still searching for a new source of energy. Angrily, he shrugged it off.

They stood looking down at the water in silence. Greg glanced at Kate. She was frowning. Had she felt it too?

489

She looked up abruptly and caught his eye. He could see the uncertainty there; uncertainty and fear.

'Why don't we go back to the farmhouse?' he said quietly. 'There's nothing more we can do here, is there officer? We've got to wait for the water to go down.'

Garth nodded. 'May as well.' He appeared to notice Kate's white face for the first time. 'You've all had a bad couple of days out here. You wouldn't think people could get cut off like this, not in the nineties, would you?' He began to wade back towards the cottage, relieved to be moving. 'I'm supposed to seal the door before we leave. If you three would like to walk on ahead, I'll only be a minute.'

Kate hauled herself in beside Jon and leaned back, closing her eyes. He touched her hand. 'It'll soon be over.'

She nodded.

'What happened to the book? It's not still in there?'

She gave a weary smile. 'I've got the disk safely. I expect my notes are all right. I left them on the table. Oh, Jon.' With something like a sob she leaned towards him, her head on his shoulder. He put his arm round her, aware again of Greg's baleful glance as he turned to look at them. She gave Greg a weak smile. 'What's going to happen?'

'Nothing. The police enquiries will no doubt draw a blank and that will be that. No one will ever mention Alison's part in this, whatever it was. No one will ever know what happened for sure.'

'Except us.' It was a whisper.

'Except us.'

'And Marcus will rest in peace now the grave has gone.'

Greg gave a short barking laugh. 'You think so?'

'Don't you?' Kate gripped Jon's hand tightly.

'No. I don't. He's still here. I felt him out there.' Greg stopped and closed his eyes with a sigh. Oh yes, he was still there. And so was she. Somewhere. And they were both hunting; hunting for allies, for power, for the life force of a living being to sustain their hatred. The fact that the grave had disappeared meant nothing. He opened his eyes, staring back mutely at the cottage where Bob Garth was screwing a staple and hasp to the front door. There would be no stopping it now. Battle was joined. The question was, whether he was going to fight them, to stand back and watch, or whether he was going to join in. Behind him, Jon had put his arm around Kate. Did they think he couldn't see them? He pulled up his collar and folded his arms. It didn't matter. When it came to rage and jealousy he had a perfect master in Marcus.

LXXIV

Under the water the sand swirled restlessly, turning the encroaching sea the colour of the soil it invaded. The fine suspension danced to the rhythm of the waves, erasing, rearranging, sculpting a new landscape beneath the water. The coast was used to this. The sea was its enemy, ever present, ever waiting, encroaching sometimes millimetres at a time, creeping in snail-like in the soft dawn which succeeded each storm, sometimes leaping angrily on its prey and dragging it out, dismembered, to deposit its spoils on another shore.

As the water seeped deep into the clay, probing, sucking, stirring, the final shreds of leathered skin began to dissolve. Nearby, the golden torc settled more deeply into the silt and came to rest at last upon the tooth of a mammoth, a much earlier victim of the mud of the marsh.

Nion was searching now. Lost. Claudia had gone, following the people and the energy they provided. The beach was deserted. He was lonely again. He felt his anger mount. Was he tied to this place after all? Tied for all eternity? Around him the sea had grown gentle; the water had ceased to attack the land; now it caressed, a lover who had made a long-planned conquest. He had seen them: the woman and the men. The two of them loved her. He had seen the crackle of their hostility, felt its power. So, history repeats itself.

Amused, he waited. They had guessed what had happened here. They knew the Roman's secret. They hated him, but they feared him too. He was powerful,

Marcus Severus Secundus. Powerful and clever, for all his craven terror when he had faced at last the moment of his death.

Anne had made soup when they returned. Cold and shaken they sat around the table gratefully: the taxi driver, the policeman, the poet, the painter, the psychologist and the author. On the sofa Paddy slept on. He had woken once and sat up, putting his head in his hands and rubbing his face. 'Is it true, about Dad? I didn't dream it?' He had looked up pleadingly at Anne.

'I am afraid it is true, Patrick.' She sat down beside him and put her hand on the boy's shoulder, comforting him until he fell asleep again.

'So. What happens next?' Jon looked at Bob Garth.

Ten minutes before, a message had come on the constable's mobile phone that a police car was on its way to pick him up. The young man helped himself to a piece of bread from the basket and spread it thickly with butter. 'As soon as the car comes, I'll go back and report what we found. I can take you with me, Mr Cutler, if you like – and anyone else who wants to leave.' He looked from one to the other.

'You go, Anne,' Kate said quietly. 'You can't afford to be away any longer.'

'I am not leaving you here.' Anne met her eye with determination.

'Don't worry about Kate. I'm going to look after her. She's coming back with me,' Jon said firmly.

Kate shook her head. 'I'm not coming back to London, Jon. Not yet.' She was too muddled, too shocked by everything that had happened to make decisions. 'Or at least, I'll come to Bill's funeral, then I thought I would go to our parents' for a while. I was going there for Christmas anyway.'

'Kate –' Jon looked at her in sudden panic. 'Please –'

'Stay here, Kate.' Greg put in softly. 'At least until the cottage is dried out. It won't take long.'

'She's not going back there!' Jon interrupted. 'After all that's happened. You must be mad –'

'She agreed to take it for six months.' Greg's voice was very calm.

'Things have changed since that agreement,' Kate shook her head. 'I'm sorry, but I can't stay there, Greg. Not now. Not after Bill –'

A sudden imperious crackle from Bob Garth's mobile phone cut through Greg's growing anger. Unclipping it, Garth raised it to his ear. Glancing from face to face he listened to the message intently, then he grinned. 'Well,' he said. 'That's good news. The Farnboroughs are going home. Mrs Farnborough has two cracked ribs and young Susie is suffering from exhaustion, but that's all. Mrs Lindsey is going to stay in hospital with young Alison overnight. They think she is all right, but they are going to do a brain scan just to be sure.' He stood up. 'Well, who is coming with me? Have you made up your minds?' He couldn't wait to be off.

'Go, Anne,' Kate said after a moment's pause. 'I will wait to collect my stuff as soon as they will let me in the cottage, then I'm going to Herefordshire. Allie's gone. The grave's gone. There's no more danger. I'll be all right.' She shook her head ruefully. 'I know you're worried about work – and besides, there's C.J. You go. Only don't get lost this time.' She gave a wan smile.

Anne grimaced. 'If we can be dropped off at the end of the track, Pete has suggested that he drive in front of me, at least on these lanes, to check I don't get lost!' She glanced at the taxi driver mockingly.

'That's right.' He bowed. 'And I'm going to buy her a slap-up meal in Colch to send her on her way thinking a bit better about this part of the world! So don't you worry about us, folks. Just you look after yourselves.'

'I hate to leave you here.' Anne pushed back her chair. She put her hands on Kate's shoulders and hugged her. 'What are you going to do about Greg and Jon?' she asked softly. She could hardly have missed the conflict between them.

Jon did not give Kate the chance to reply. 'She'll be all right, Anne,' he said. 'I'll make sure of it.'

Anne looked him in the eye. For a minute she was silent, then she smiled. 'Make sure you do.'

When the car finally arrived, Patrick went too. He had not argued when Greg suggested that he go to Diana at the hospital and keep her company.

Kate glanced at Jon and Greg as the police vehicle disappeared up the track. Greg had turned away to throw more logs on the fire. Outside, the garden lay very still beneath the thawing snow. She bit her lip. The silence in the house had become suddenly threatening.

Greg straightened. His face was pale and strained. 'You'll have to stay for Dad's funeral, Kate. He would have wanted you to.'

They all glanced towards the door. Someone was coming later to pick up Roger's body and take it to the mortuary.

'I don't know, Greg.' Kate bit her lip. 'Please, give me time to think. Perhaps I can come back just for the day.'

'Just for the day.' Greg's voice was heavy with irony. 'How jolly.' He stiffened suddenly and stared round. The temperature in the room was falling swiftly. 'He's come back,' he said. 'Can you feel him?'

'Marcus?' Jon moved across to put his arm around Kate.

'Marcus,' Greg confirmed. He sounded almost pleased.

Kate shuddered. She looked round. 'Where is he?'

'Here.' Greg could feel the anger; the hatred. But this time the mood was different. It had changed. This time it was accompanied by fear. That was strange. Why should Marcus be afraid? Greg felt himself shiver.

For a moment no one moved, then almost defiantly Greg picked up a candle and limped to the door.

The study was very quiet and cold. His father's body lay on the bed, covered by a clean white sheet. He stood, looking down at it. Was it Roger Marcus feared? Or something – someone – else?

He turned away and picked up his last painting of the woman in blue. Claudia. It had haunted him for so many months, this beautiful enigmatic face. He stared down at the huge oval eyes. They radiated hatred. He could feel it, directed straight at him. He frowned, touching the paint with his little finger then he walked back into the living room, taking the picture with him.

'Well, what do you think?' He propped it on the chair so Jon could see it.

Jon squatted down on his haunches so that he was level with the face. 'Powerful stuff.' He frowned. It was the first time he had smelt it: jasmine. Very strongly, coming from the canvas. He sniffed cautiously. It was heady, overpowering, sexy.

Greg was watching his face. 'At last. He understands.' His voice was very soft.

Kate crouched beside Jon. 'It's a very fine painting. Jon?' She stared at him. 'Are you all right?'

'What?' He looked at her vaguely and then he focussed his gaze once more on the picture.

'The earth is cover'd thick with other clay,
Which her own clay shall cover, heap'd and pent,
Rider and horse, – friend, foe – in one red burial blent'

he quoted softly.

'Jon –'

'Leave him.' Greg's voice was a sneer. 'Poor Kate. You have a rival. You see what she can do? The whore. Her power is infinite.'

'Shut up, Greg!' She rounded on him furiously. 'Jon! Jon, what's the matter?'

Jon looked at her. His eyes looked straight past her; through her. He did not see her.

LXXV

He knew he was dying. Lying on his low bed, his wife sitting at his side, he watched the servants scurrying silently to and fro with coals for the brazier. He was cold, so very cold even though it was still summer. His eyes strayed to the shadows. They were there, waiting. Nion and Claudia. Her dying curse had after all done its work. The web was spun. Already the sticky threads entangling him reached out to the farthest corners of time. But he would evade her; somehow he would evade her – as long as there was no evidence of his crime no man on earth would censure him and, before the gods, he would take his chance like a Roman warrior, wandering the corridors between worlds where she would never find him.

He felt his lungs falter, the breath labouring suddenly in his chest, and a stab of panic went through him. Not yet. He wasn't ready yet. The tablets. He had the wax tablets under his pillow. On them the priest had written the words which would protect him and guide him to places where they would never find him. He had given orders that he be buried without cremation; that would anchor his spirit more closely to the earth. The servants had gone now. The room was empty. Hazily, he could see that his wife was dozing, her head resting on her arm. It must be midnight. The loneliest time. The loneliest place. Through the door, open to allow a draught to stir the heat from the brazier he could hear the water from the fountain in the atrium. It had a pleasant, soothing music to it; a music echoed by the stars he could not see, blazing up there in the midnight sky where, before the dawn began to dim their glory, he too would be wandering, lost in the immensity of time. He tried to move his head a little as on the table beside him the lamp flame flickered and dimmed. Suddenly the room was full of the scent of jasmine. ·

When Kate awoke it was pitch dark outside, but the room was lit by a small lamp on the dressing table. She lay staring round, wondering what had awoken her. Then she realised. It was the engine of a car. She lay listening, trying to summon the strength to stand up and go downstairs to see who it was, but already her eyes were closing again.

When she next opened them it was daylight.

Downstairs the living room was empty. She stared round. It had been tidied. She sniffed. She could smell coffee. Walking over to the pantry door she peered in. Jon was there, rooting around amongst Diana's jars and boxes.

'Hi.'

He jumped, then he smiled. Putting his arms around her he kissed her on the forehead. 'Hi. Did you manage to sleep?'

She nodded. 'I can't believe it but I did.' Yesterday, after he had sat and looked at the picture for what seemed like hours he had retired to the chair by the fire and scarcely spoken again that evening. He had frightened her. Greg, in contrast, had been remarkably cheerful and unthreatening and it was he who had persuaded her at last to go up and get some rest. 'Did I hear a car last night? Who was it?' she asked.

He frowned. 'They came to collect Roger. Greg saw him on his way.'

'Poor Roger. He was such a nice man. I liked him so much.' Kate bit her lip. 'This has all been so terrible, Jon.' She went back to his arms and stood there, her head resting on his shoulder, drawing strength from him. He was himself again now; completely himself. She could feel it, see it. She glanced over his shoulder into the living room. The picture had gone. 'Where's Greg?' She looked up at Jon's face.

'He went out.'

'Did you sleep down here last night?'

He nodded. 'In the chair.'

'And you smelt it: the jasmine.'

He nodded again. 'Her face. It's beautiful.'

'It's beautiful the way Greg painted it; but it's frightening too, don't you think?' She shuddered.

He nodded thoughtfully. 'He moved it. Put it away, I think.' He glanced at her. 'He's a very disturbed man, Kate.'

'Intense; artistic; sad. Not disturbed.'

'Oh yes, disturbed. He's jealous of me to the point of madness. I'm not being paranoid, Kate. I'm serious. He's a threat. A threat to you.'

'Jon –'

He shook his head. 'I know it seems absurd. Perhaps I'm being stupid, but I really believe it. There is something in his eyes – You must come away with me. Today. You know I've paid half the money I owe you into your account, Kate.' He glanced at her. 'The rest will be there by the end of January. You won't let this come between us, will you?'

'Jon, please. Don't push me too fast.' She looked up at his face. 'I'll come back to London. I'll have to anyway to get the train over to my parents.' She grimaced. 'I will have to see about the car insurance and getting a new one. But about us . . .' She wanted to go to him. She loved him, but something held her back. So much had broken in their relationship. It would take time to mend. 'I don't know, Jon. Not yet. Let's take it slowly.'

She sighed. There was an added complication. Greg. She wasn't sure how she felt about Greg. Not yet. 'As soon as they let us into the cottage I'll pack my things and we'll have to think of a way of collecting them. Then we'll go, Jon.'

Perhaps Marcus wouldn't notice that they were leaving. She walked across to the window and stared out with another shiver. 'Jon! Look! The cats.' They were sitting side by side on the wall on the far side of the lawn. 'It must be all right. They've come back. Surely, that must mean it's safe.'

Jon smiled. 'It means they think it's safe out there. You and Anne and your cat lore! I'll have to get used to it again, I can see.' He stood beside her, looking out. A stray patch of sunshine had touched the wall to a warm red, and the cats, true to their kind, had made themselves comfortable exactly in the middle of it.

A movement caught his eye. Greg had been standing on the sea wall looking out across the marsh towards the now half-submerged car. He had turned and was walking slowly and painfully back towards the house, dragging his injured foot. They saw him stop when he saw the cats. He smiled and walked towards them. They stood up, their tails raised in welcome, then suddenly Jon saw first one, then the other stiffen, fur staring. With one bound, both cats had leapt from the wall and fled. Jon glanced at Kate. She bit her lip.

They could both see the anger on Greg's face as he approached the house. It cleared as he saw them. 'Poor old car. It's had it.' He walked in and eased off his boots, wincing at the pain. 'Is there any coffee?'

Kate nodded.

'I saw the police. They've gone on down to the cottage. They've advised us to keep clear for the morning. They're going to take poor Bill away, and when they've finished down there the cleaners are going in. The sea's gone down, apparently.'

'What was wrong with the cats, Greg?' Kate glanced at him as she unhooked three coffee mugs from the dresser.

'They spooked.' Greg shook his head. 'God knows who they thought I was. They'll be back as soon as Ma gets here.' He had felt it at the same moment they had. The sudden anger; the frustrated rage. And now the fear. Marcus. He sipped the black coffee gratefully. 'Are you still determined to leave Redall?'

Kate nodded. 'Today, Greg. I'm going down to my mother's until after Christmas.'

'And then?'

She shook her head. 'Then I'll see.' She sat down opposite him at the kitchen table. 'Who knows, I might come back to write about Boudicca.'

'After Christmas she's coming back to me,' Jon said slowly. 'If I can convince her what an idiot I was to let her go.'

Greg stared at him. It was there again. The rage. He took a deep breath, trying to control himself. That bastard, Marcus. He was so close. It was jealousy. That was it. He was using the jealousy as a lever. He clenched his fists. Pushing back his chair and standing up he half staggered away from the table.

'Greg – ?' Kate was looking at him, frightened.

'It's all right.' He swung away to hide his face. It was like pain. It came in spasms; agonising spasms. This was what had happened to Alison; this was how she had killed Bill. 'You go. Both of you. Go down to the cottage and pack. I'll be all right.'

He pushed through the door into the study and slammed it behind him. The sight of the empty bed with the three blankets neatly folded, brought him up short. He stood still, letting the wave of misery flow over him. Where are you, Dad? He stared up at the ceiling. Help me. Please. He moved across to his father's desk and threw himself down in the chair. For a long time he sat looking at the portrait which lay there, where he had left it the night before, on the blotter. Oh, she was so beautiful, the Lady Claudia. So beautiful. So deceitful. So evil. His eyes blurred with tears.

For a long time he sat there, staring at her face. Then he

stood up. He picked up the picture and slowly he brought it up to his lips. He could smell the jasmine now. The whole room was full of it; beautiful; exotic. Haunting.

He heard Jon and Kate in the hall. They were putting on their boots and coats. His knuckles whitened on the stretcher of the canvas as he listened to their quiet, almost conspiratorial voices. Then the door banged behind them and the house was silent. He looked into her eyes again. Claudia . . .

It took no strength at all to smash the canvas across his knee.

LXXVI

Kate and Jon walked cautiously into the small living room and looked round. Bill's body had gone, so had the police and after them the cleaners who had lifted the rugs, swept out the worst of the mud and opened the windows of the cottage to air. Relieved, Kate sighed. Somehow she had expected something to have remained of the aura — and the smell — of death, but the living room was more or less itself again, tidy and smelling only of damp.

She smiled at Jon. 'I'll go up and pack.' He nodded. He glanced round the room. He had grown very quiet as they neared the cottage; almost brooding, staring at her now and then with a strange thoughtfulness.

It did not take long to pack her clothes and stack her books and papers in boxes. Later they were going to borrow another neighbour's four-wheel drive to take it all back to the farmhouse. She took one last look around the cottage, listening to the silence, sniffing unconsciously for any hint of flowers or peat or Claudia's jasmine scent. There was nothing. The cottage was empty. Reassured she pulled the door closed behind them and heard the lock click home.

The water had sunk slowly back out of the garden leaving a sea of mud. On the north side of the trees and bushes, large lumps of unmelted snow lurked, cushions of white in the damp undergrowth. The south wind after the days of ice-laden easterlies was a balm to the soul — sweet, gentle and almost warm. Jon glanced at Kate. 'Do you want to see the grave before we go?'

She nodded. 'I'd like to see what happened. The sea seems to have gone right back.' Behind them the estuary sparkled in the sunlight covered by flocks of swimming birds.

They walked slowly towards the shore. Where there had been high, sweeping dunes of sand there was now a changed landscape: small, reshaped hillocks; mud; a high, drifted beach and everywhere a covering of tangled black weed, dredged from the bottom of the sea by the ferocious waves. A cloud of gulls rose from the stinking mass as cautiously they picked their way across it towards the spot where the excavations had been. They stood surveying the beach in silence.

'It was about here, wasn't it?' Jon said at last.

Kate looked around. There were no landmarks now; the hump of the dune had gone; the declivity where she and Alison had crouched was no more. The sand all round them was scooped and moulded as though by a giant spoon into a series of smooth, scalloped humps.

She smiled, overwhelmed with relief. 'It's gone. There's no sign of it.'

She had half expected to feel something of Marcus there – resentment, anger, fear – the insidious emotions of another age – but there was nothing. The air was fresh and cool and full of the cries of sea birds and the uneasy shushing of the waves against the sand.

'It's gone,' she said again as he reached across and drew her hand into his.

To her surprise, he laughed. 'No,' he said. 'No, it hasn't gone. Not quite. Look.'

It was a piece of twisted metal, torn from the depths of the sand once again and tossed and tangled with weed. Jon stooped and picked it up. 'A torc. Your torc?' He held it out to her.

She took it reluctantly. 'I thought it had disappeared.'

*　　*　　*

A shadow on the sand, Nion waited, invisible. His torc, the torc Claudia had given to him, which he had flung as a gift to the gods lay, a twisted, corroded half moon of useless metal, in the hand of the living woman. He could feel himself drifting irresistibly towards them, the woman who held his torc and the man who loved her, the man who would give him strength.

Behind them Greg paused on the edge of the beach. Idiots. Couldn't they leave well alone? He clenched his fists. Didn't they understand? This was where it had happened. The Roman woman, Claudia, and her lover. Her British lover. Dead. Together. He narrowed his eyes in the glare off the sea. Two men in love with one woman. A story as old as time itself.

He limped towards them slowly, and almost guiltily, Jon dropped Kate's hand.

'You realise that it was another man who came between them,' Greg said, chattily, as he reached them. 'Why else would Marcus want to kill his beautiful wife?' He took the torc out of Kate's hands and turned it round, staring down at it, picking off the sticky, clinging weed. 'Why do you suppose we haven't heard from him: the lover? Marcus did kill him as well, didn't he?' His eyes strayed from Kate's face to Jon's.

Behind them, shadows in the wind, Nion and Claudia drew closer. Soon they would be together.

'Let's go back, Greg.' Kate stepped away from him towards the sea, feeling the wind pull her hair away from her face. 'The grave itself has gone. There's nothing to see.'

Greg was staring down at the torc in his hand, his grey-green eyes veiled. 'They are here,' he whispered. 'Marcus is here and Claudia, and so is the other, the lover. I can feel them. They are trapped here on this beach together. An eternal triangle.'

'Greg –' Kate interrupted him uneasily. 'Let's go back.'

'Why?' There was open hostility in his gaze.

'Because it's late. Jon and I have to go. We have a long journey back to London.'

'No.' He turned away from them and stared out to sea. 'No, I don't think so. You don't like London, remember?'

Jon frowned, eyeing the other man with caution. Surreptitiously he put his hand on Kate's arm and pulled her away. 'Let's go,' he whispered, his words almost lost in the rush of the sea. Nodding, she turned to follow him, but Greg had noticed. He swung round and his eyes were alight with anger. 'No. You're not going anywhere.'

He could feel Marcus so clearly now. Close. Pushing. Eager.

'Don't be stupid, Greg,' Kate's voice was sharp. 'We are leaving. If you want to stay, that's up to you.' She began to walk inland, turning her back on the place where the excavation had been.

Behind them Greg was staring once more down at the torc. Suddenly his eyes were full of tears. He couldn't fight it much longer. Marcus and Kate. He couldn't cope with both. He stumbled after her. 'You can't go,' he called. 'I won't let you. This was sent here to hold you –'

Jon swung round. He released Kate's arm abruptly, his anger bubbling to the surface at last. 'That is enough, Greg! Kate has told you. She is going. You mean nothing to her.' Angrily he snatched the torc from the other man's hands. 'This has caused enough trouble. Now it is going back where it belongs.' Lifting his arm he flung the torc into the air. As it landed in the heaving greyness of the water, he felt anger sweeping over him uncontrolled.

Terrified, he tried to master it.

It was red, vicious. Blind.

Ecstatic.

He wrestled with it frantically, staggering back from the sea's edge, clutching at his head, hearing nothing but the raging of the waves. He did not see Kate's terror as the swirl of jasmine-scented dust settled over her.

'Jon!' He heard her voice distantly; it was frightened; screaming. 'Greg! Do something! Marcus has got him! Help him! Greg, help him! Help me!'

'No, not Marcus.' Suddenly Greg was laughing. 'Marcus is here. With me! Nion's possessed him.' The name had come to him so easily – the name his wife had screamed into a Beltane dawn. Nion the Druid.

The voices were growing fainter, the sound of the sea louder. Suddenly Greg was afraid. Marcus was there; Marcus was inside him. Turning, he ran towards the water. He could feel the waves icy against his ankles, taking away all the pain. The shock of the cold stunned him.

Fight. He had to fight. The water was deeper now, sucking round his knees. Cold. Clean. Powerful.

Fight. Fight the Roman.

Fight or die.

Where was Roger? He had promised. Dad, help me! Help me fight him. Dad, please. His voice rose in pain and fear and anger.

A wave slammed against his waist and the shock of it stopped him.

He turned and surveyed the beach.

Fight. Jon too was fighting, the battle in his head deafening.

Recite. Fill your head with something else. That's what Anne had said. Don't let him take hold. Recite . . .

Nion must have his revenge.

Marcus is vanquished.

Nion turned his hungry, angry eyes to look for the Roman who had caused his death . . .

Fight. Fight the anger in his head.

Recite.

Byron. She didn't know it, but he had learned Byron for her sake. 'Where'er we tread 'tis haunted, holy ground . . .' Grope for the memory. Fill the mind. 'All tragedies are finish'd by a death.' Was that Byron too . . . ? It didn't matter.

Jon stumbled away from the sea, his hands clawing at his temples. Where was she? Where was Claudia? His love. He shook his head. Kate. Where was Kate –? There was no one there. They had gone. Nion was gaining strength. Marcus? Where was Marcus? Nion had to be rid of Marcus for ever.

Recite. It's the only way. Blank the druid out. Don't let him in. He's not going to win.

Sobbing, he fell on his knees in the wet sand.

> 'She walks in beauty, like the night
> Of cloudless climes and starry skies;
> And all that's best of dark and bright
> Meet in her aspect and her eyes.
> She walks in beauty, like the night . . .'

He repeated the words again and again until he had no strength left and his voice faded in his throat.

Marcus could see them clearly now, through the eyes of the man, Greg. They were there, near him, reaching out to one another.

Nion and Claudia.

Jon and Kate.

Greg groaned as the icy water slapped around his thighs. His eyes weren't working properly. Everything was blurred.

Jon and Kate.

Nion and Claudia.

Slowly he was beginning to understand. Marcus fed on hate and jealousy. Their strength, their love, those were the weapons he needed. Clenching his fists he took a step towards the sand. Then another.

Fight.

Fight the alien inside his head.

Fight him with love. Love that transcends time and space.

Nion and Claudia.

Jon and Kate.

Jon and Kate.

The rage was receding. Greg could feel the anger and hate inside him dwindling. He took another step towards the beach. Marcus was losing. Love would always win over hate.

In the end.

Painfully he shook his head. It was as though he were waking from some hideous nightmare. Far out at sea a stray beam of sunlight had broken through the clouds to touch the sea to silver. He stared at it mesmerized, then slowly and weakly, he began to wade back towards the shore. He had won. Marcus was going. He could feel him shrinking and weakening. He rubbed his eyes. The dream had left him now; it had gone, into the shadows of eternity with its pain.

Kate looked up at Greg as she cradled Jon's head on her knee, her eyes full of tears. The sweet scent of jasmine was all around her.

The hands on his head were gentle. He could feel them clearly, soothing away the pain.

Her voice. It was her voice. She was there. She was with him.

Weeping, Nion the Druid rested his head in the soft blue folds of her gown, and felt himself at peace.

AUTHOR'S NOTE

The name Nion is taken from the Celtic Tree Calendar Beth – Luis – Nion (Birch, Rowan, Ash) depicted by Robert Graves.

This book has many roots: the awe and fear in a little boy's voice many years ago, as we stared together through the window into a midnight garden after a bad dream; a lonely visit to Sutton Hoo on a cold afternoon in winter when the wind screamed through the firs and down across the River Deben; a long, thoughtful visit to the twisted body of Lindow Man in the British Museum and the view from my study window out across fields where Trinovantes and Romans once walked on the edge of the saltings with, in the distance, the icy North Sea, are some of the strongest.

House of
Echoes

Joss Grant's family tree

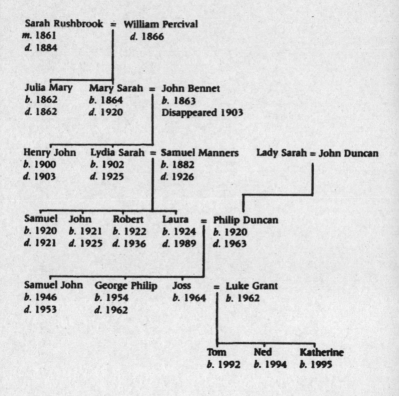

Sarah Rushbrook = William Percival
m. 1861   *d.* 1866
d. 1884

Julia Mary   Mary Sarah = John Bennet
b. 1862   *b.* 1864   *b.* 1863
d. 1862   *d.* 1920   Disappeared 1903

Henry John   Lydia Sarah = Samuel Manners   Lady Sarah = John Duncan
b. 1900   *b.* 1902   *b.* 1882
d. 1903   *d.* 1925   *d.* 1926

Samuel   John   Robert   Laura = Philip Duncan
b. 1920   *b.* 1921   *b.* 1922   *b.* 1924   *b.* 1920
d. 1921   *d.* 1925   *d.* 1936   *d.* 1989   *d.* 1963

Samuel John   George Philip   Joss = Luke Grant
b. 1946   *b.* 1954   *b.* 1964   *b.* 1962
d. 1953   *d.* 1962

Tom   Ned   Katherine
b. 1992   *b.* 1994   *b.* 1995

Prologue

A beam of cold sunshine finds its way through a knot hole in the wood of the shutters and strays across the dusty boards. Laser like, it creeps from right to left until it reaches the flower lying in its path. One by one, in the spotlight, the petals fall open, their thin creamy whiteness already edged with brown.

In the silence the skirt skimming over the boards makes no sound; the footsteps from the past are quiet.

With no ear there to hear them the echoes in the house are silent.

1

ad she really not wanted to know?

Joss put her foot down and accelerated into a bend.

Or had she been afraid of the truth?

'Are you sure you don't want me to come with you?' Before she left home her husband Luke reached in through the open window and put his hand over hers as it rested on the wheel. On the seat beside her was the gazetteer and the file with the copy of her birth and adoption certificates and the note of the address. Belheddon Hall. She had glanced up at him and shaken her head. 'I must do this alone, Luke. Just this first time.'

The gate, hidden behind the yews and laurels, had not been opened for a long while. The wood was damp and swollen and slimy with lichen. It caught on the untrimmed grass as she pushed it back and it hung open behind her as she stepped out onto an overgrown path which appeared to lead into an area of woodland. Pushing her hands down into her pockets she walked cautiously forward, feeling half guilty, half exhilarated as the wind whipped her hair into her eyes. The woods around her smelled of rotting leaves and beech mast, bitter and sharp with early autumn.

Somewhere near her a pheasant crashed out of the undergrowth with an explosion of alarm calls and she stopped, her heart thundering under her ribs, staring round. As the frightened bird flew low through the trees and out of sight the silence returned. Even the cheerful rustling of the leaves overhead died away as the wind dropped. She stared round, straining her ears for some kind of sound. Ahead, the path curved out of sight around a stand of holly trees, their glossy leaves almost black in the dull afternoon light, their berries shocking in their abundant redness.

The holly bears a berry as red as any blood.

The line from the carol floated through her head. She gazed at the trees for a moment, strangely reluctant to walk any further, the hairs on the back of her neck prickling as she became aware suddenly that eyes were watching her from the thicket on her left. Holding her breath she turned her head.

For several seconds she and the fox stared at each other, then he was gone. He made no sound but the space he had filled beneath the old hawthorn bush was empty. She was so relieved she almost laughed out loud. Whatever thoughts had raced through her head at that moment they had not included a fox.

With a lighter heart she stepped forward, aware that the wind was once more blowing strongly in her face and two minutes later she rounded the corner near the holly bushes to find herself on the edge of an overgrown lawn. In front of her stood the house.

It was an old grey building with gabled roofs and mullioned windows, the plastered walls covered in ivy and wisteria and scarlet Virginia creeper. She stood quite still, staring. Belheddon Hall. Her birthplace.

Almost on tiptoe she crept forward. Internal shutters

2

gave the windows which faced her a strangely blind aspect, but for a moment she had the strangest feeling that she was being watched from somewhere behind those shutters. She shivered and turned her attention firmly to the porticoed front door which looked up the long tree lined drive leading out of sight, presumably to the front gates. Where once there had been gravel there were now knee-high thistles and ragwort and wind-blown rose bay.

She sniffed. Emotions she didn't know she had been harbouring seemed to be welling up inside her: loss, grief, loneliness, disappointment, even anger. Abruptly she turned her back on the house and gazed down the drive, rubbing her eyes with the back of her hand.

She spent a long time wandering round the overgrown gardens and lawns, exploring the lake with its perimeter of reeds and bulrushes and weeds, and the stableyard and coach houses which lay through the archway at the side of the house. Her shoulders hunched against the wind she tried the front door and the back, both locked and bolted as she had known they would be, and she stood at last on the terrace at the back of the house looking down towards the lake. It was a wonderful house; wild, deserted, locked in its dreams of yesterday. With a sigh she turned and stared up at the blind windows. It had been her home if only for a few months, and presumably the scene of whatever unhappiness had made her mother give her away. It was in her blood and it had rejected her.

It was for Tom she was doing this she had reflected wryly as she drove through the network of quiet North Essex lanes. Tom. Her baby son. Until she had held him in her arms and gazed into that small, crumpled red face, so like his father's, she had been content to leave her origins a mystery.

3

She had been happy and secure with her adoptive parents. She was special after all; a chosen child. Her day dreams about her real parents had been vague and stereotypical, her mother in turn princess, parlour maid, poet, painter, prostitute. The choices and permutations were endless; harmless fun. One day she would search for the truth but if she were honest she knew she had put off looking for fear that the truth might be dull. It was not until she had looked down at Tom and known what it was like to hold her own baby in her arms that she realised she had to find out not just who her own real mother was, but how and why she had been able to give away her daughter. Between one minute and the next vague curiosity had become burning obsession.

At first it was too easy. Her mother, it appeared from the records, was Laura Catherine Duncan, née Manners, her father Philip George Henry Duncan, deceased. He had died seven months before she was born. She was born at Belheddon Hall, in Essex on 21st June, 1964.

Alice and Joe, her adoptive parents, long prepared for this moment, had tried to persuade her to go to one of the agencies which tracks down families for adopted children but she had said no, this was something she had wanted to do for herself. Even if her mother no longer lived at Belheddon Hall she wanted to see it, to explore the village where she was born; to see if she could feel her roots.

On the map Belheddon featured as a small village on the coast of East Anglia on the border between Suffolk and Essex. Surprisingly remote, it looked north across the broad expanse of water where the Stour Estuary met the North Sea, some five miles from the small town of Manningtree.

She had hoped for something more romantic than Essex, the West Country perhaps, or Scotland, but her brief to herself had been strict. She was not going to prejudge anything or anyone. She was keeping an open mind.

Her mouth was dry with nerves as at last she drove into Belheddon and pulled up outside the single small shop, its window unaesthetically lined with yellowing cellophane paper. Belheddon Post Office and Stores. She had closed her eyes, as she put on the hand brake and turned off the engine, surprised to find that her hands were shaking.

On the cold pavement a scatter of dead leaves cartwheeled past the car. The sign above the door swung violently backwards and forwards in the wind as, climbing stiffly out, Joss glanced round. It had been a long journey. If she had pictured the whole of Essex as a suburban wasteland irrevocably merged into north-east London she couldn't have been more wrong. The drive had taken more than two and a half hours from Kensington, where she and Luke lived, and for at least the last hour it had been through deep country.

Ahead of her the street was empty of both cars and people. Straight at this point, it ran between two lines of pretty cottages before curving away across the village green towards the estuary. It was only a small village – no more perhaps than a couple of dozen houses, a few thatched, two or three timber framed, the last spires of windswept hollyhocks standing sentinel in their gardens. There was no sign of a church.

Taking a deep breath she pushed open the door of the shop which was to her surprise a great deal more sophisticated than she had expected. To her left the window of the small post office was enclosed behind piles of postcards and stationery and racks of sweets; to her right she found herself facing an attractive and well stocked delicatessen counter. The woman serving behind it was small, stocky, perhaps some sixty years old, with wispy white hair and piercing grey eyes. Reaching with

5

a plastic gloved hand into the display for a lump of green cheese she glanced up at Joss and smiled. 'I won't keep you a moment, my dear.'

The woman in front of Joss in the queue succumbed to her curiosity and turned round. Tall, with dark hair escaping from a knotted head scarf, and with a weather-beaten face which spoke of years living within reach of the cold east wind, she gave Joss a friendly grin. 'Sorry, I've been buying up the shop. Won't be two ticks now.'

'That's all right.' Joss smiled. 'I actually came in to ask if you can direct me to Belheddon Hall.'

Both women looked surprised. 'It's up by the church.' The woman in front of her had narrowed her eyes. 'It's all closed up, you know. There's no one there.'

Joss bit her lip, trying to master her disappointment. 'So the Duncans don't live there any more?'

Both women shook their heads. 'It's been empty for years.' The woman behind the counter shivered theatrically. 'Spooky old place.' Wrapping the cheese deftly in some cling film she slipped the parcel into a paper bag. She glanced up at her customer. 'There you are, my dear. That will be four pounds ten pence altogether. My husband and I have only had the shop since '89.' She smiled back at Joss. 'I never knew the people up at the Hall.'

The other woman shook her head. 'Nor I. I believe old Mrs Duncan who used to live at the schoolhouse was a relation. But she died a couple of years back.'

Joss pushed her hands down into her pockets. Her sense of let down was acute. 'Is there anyone who might know what happened to the family?'

The post mistress shook her head. 'I always heard they kept themselves to themselves at the end. Mary Sutton, though. She would remember. She used to work up at the Hall. She sometimes acts a bit ga-ga, but I'm sure she could tell you something.'

'Where could I find her?'

6

'Apple Cottage. On the corner of the green. With the blue gate.'

The gate was stiff and warped. Joss pushed it open and made her way up the narrow path, dodging between overhanging thistles, downy with blown silk. There was no bell or knocker on the door so she rapped with her knuckles. Five minutes later she gave up. There was obviously no one at home.

Standing at the gate she stared round. Now that she had walked a little way out of the village street she could see the church tower partially concealed by trees on the far side of the green. And the Hall was somewhere beside it.

Leaving the car where it was she began to walk across the grass.

'So, do you like our little church? It's thirteenth century, you know.' The voice behind her made her jump as she leaned thoughtfully on the lych gate staring up the path which disappeared round the church.

Behind her a tall, thin man in a dog collar was propping his bicycle against the hedge. He saw her glance at it and shrugged. 'My car's in dock. Something wrong with the brakes. Anyway I enjoy cycling on these lovely autumn afternoons.' He had seen the pensive woman as he turned out of New Barn Road. Coming to a stop he had watched her for several minutes, impressed by her stillness. As she turned now and smiled at him he saw that she was youngish – late twenties or early thirties perhaps – and attractive in a quirky sort of way. Her hair was dark and heavy, cut in a bob with a fringe across her eyes – eyes which were a vivid Siamese cat blue. He watched as his bicycle subsided into the nettles and gave a humorous shrug. 'I was just coming to collect some books I left in the vestry. Would you like to see round before I lock up?'

7

She nodded. 'I was actually looking for the Hall. But I'd love to see the church.'

'You can reach the Hall through the gate over there, behind the yews.' He led the way up the path. 'It's empty, alas. Has been for many years.'

'Did you know the people who lived there?' The intensity of the gaze she fixed on him disarmed him slightly.

'I'm afraid not. It was empty when I came to the parish. It's a shame. We need a family there.'

'Is it for sale then?' She was dismayed.

'No. No, that's the problem. It still belongs to the Duncan family. I believe Mrs Duncan lives in France now.'

Mrs Duncan. Laura Catherine. Her mother.

'You don't have her address, do you?' Joss could hear her voice shaking slightly. 'I'm a sort of relative. That's why I came.'

'I see.' He gave her another quick glance as they reached the church. Taking out a key he unlocked the door in the porch and ushering her into the dim interior he reached for the light switches. 'I'm afraid I don't know where she is, but my predecessor might. He was in the parish for twenty-five years and I think he kept in touch with her when she left. I can give you his address at least.'

'Thank you.' Joss stared round. It was a beautiful small church, plain, with a whitewashed interior which showed off the carved stone of the thirteenth-century windows and the arched doorways and the brasses and plaques with which it was lined. On the south side there was a side aisle where the oak pews gave way to rows of rush seated chairs. The church had been decorated for Harvest Festival and every window sill and shelf and pew end was piled with fruit and vegetables and flowers. 'It's lovely.'

'Isn't it.' He surveyed it with fond pride. 'I'm lucky to

have such a charming church. I have three others of course with three other parishes, but none is as nice as this.'

'Is my –' Joss was looking round. My father, she had been going to say. 'Is Philip Duncan buried here?'

'Indeed he is. Out by the oak tree. You'll see his grave if you walk through to the Hall.'

'Is it all right if I go and look at the house? Is there a caretaker or something?' Joss called after him as he disappeared to collect his books.

'No. I'm sure it will be all right if you go and wander round. There's no one to mind any more, sadly. The gardens used to be beautiful, but they're a wilderness now.' He reappeared from the shadows and closed the vestry door behind him. 'Here, I've scribbled down Edgar Gower's address. I don't know his phone number off hand, I'm afraid. He lives near Aldeburgh.' He pushed a piece of paper into her hand.

She watched from the churchyard as he strode back to his bike, vaulted onto it and rode away, his pile of books heaped in the bicycle basket. Suddenly she felt very lonely.

The grave stone by the oak tree was simple and unadorned.

Philip Duncan
Born 31st January 1920
Died 14th November 1963

Nothing else. No mention of his grieving widow. Or his child. She looked down at it for several minutes. When at last she turned away pulling the collar of her coat up with a shiver against the strengthening wind she found there were tears in her eyes.

It was a long time before she could drag herself away from the old house and walk, thoughtfully, back to the car. Climbing in, savouring the familiar atmosphere of home, she leaned back in her seat and looked round. On the shelf lay one of Tom's socks, pulled off as he sat in his car seat behind her, as a prelude to sucking his toes.

She stayed slumped for several minutes, lost in thought, then suddenly she sat upright and gripped the steering wheel.

In her pocket she had the address of someone who knew her mother; who remembered her; who would know where she was now.

Leaning across the seat she reached for the road atlas. Aldeburgh was not all that far away. She glanced up. The sky was a patchwork of scudding black clouds and brilliant sunshine. Evening was still a long way off.

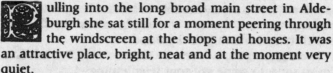

ulling into the long broad main street in Aldeburgh she sat still for a moment peering through the windscreen at the shops and houses. It was an attractive place, bright, neat and at the moment very quiet.

Clutching her piece of paper she climbed out of the car and approached a man who was standing staring into the window of an antique shop. At his feet a Jack Russell terrier strained at the leash anxious to get to the beach. He glanced at her piece of paper. 'Crag Path? Through there. Overlooking the sea.' He smiled. 'A friend of Edgar Gower's are you? Delightful man. Delightful.' Unexpectedly he gave a shout of laughter as he strode away.

Joss found she was smiling herself as, intrigued, she followed the direction of his pointing finger and threaded her way down the side of a fisherman's cottage, crossed a narrow road and found herself on a promenade. On one side stood a line of east-facing houses, on the other, beyond the sea wall, a shingle beach and then a grey, turbulent sea. The wind was very cold here and she shivered as she walked down the road looking for house numbers. Edgar Gower's house was tall and narrow, white painted with a high balcony overlooking the sea. To her relief she could see lights on in the downstairs

11

room and there was a stream of pale wood smoke coming from the chimney.

He opened the door to her himself, a tall, angular man with a ruddy complexion and a startling halo of white hair. His eyes were a brilliant blue.

'Mr Gower?'

Under his piercing gaze Joss suddenly felt extraordinarily self conscious. He did not appear to be gentle or reassuring as his successor at Belheddon had been; this man of the cloth was a complete contrast.

'Who wants me?' The eyes did not appear to have blinked. Although his gaze was fierce his voice was comparatively soft, scarcely audible as behind her the waves, crashing successively onto the beach, rattled the shingle in a shifting deafening background roar.

'I was given your address by the rector at Belheddon. I'm so sorry to come without telephoning –'

'Why have you come?' He cut short her floundering. He had made no move to ask her in and she realised suddenly that he had a coat on over a thick rough knit sweater. He had obviously been on the point of going out.

'I'm sorry. This is obviously not a good time –'

'Perhaps you will allow me to be the judge of that, my dear.' He spoke with ill-concealed though mild irritation. 'Once you have told me the purpose of your visit.'

'I think you know my mother.' She blurted it out without preamble, transfixed by the unblinking eyes.

'Indeed?'

'Laura Duncan.'

For a moment he stared at her in complete silence and she saw that at last she had succeeded in disconcerting him. She held her breath, returning his gaze with difficulty.

'So,' he said at last. 'You are little Lydia.'

12

Suddenly Joss found it difficult to speak. 'Jocelyn,' she whispered. 'Jocelyn Grant.'

'Jocelyn Grant. I see.' He nodded slowly. 'You and I should walk, I think. Come.' Stepping out onto the path he slammed his door behind him and turned right, striding purposefully along the road behind the sea wall without a backward glance to see if she were following.

'How did you find out about your mother?' He spoke loudly against the noise of the wind. His hair was streaming behind him, reminding Joss irresistibly of an Old Testament prophet in full cry.

'I went to St Catherine's House to find my birth certificate. My name is Jocelyn, not Lydia.' She was growing short of breath, trying to keep up with him. 'Jocelyn Mary.'

'Mary was your great grandmother, Lydia your grandmother.'

'Please, is my mother still alive?' She had had to run a few steps to stay beside him.

He stopped. His expression, beaten by the wind into fiery aggressiveness suddenly softened with compassion. Joss's heart sank. 'She's dead?' she whispered.

'I'm afraid so, my dear. Several years ago. In France.' Joss bit her lip. 'I had so hoped –'

'It is as well there is no chance of your meeting, my dear. I doubt if your mother would have wanted it,' he said. The kindness and sympathy in his voice were palpable; she was beginning to suspect that he must have been a very good pastor.

'Why did she give me away?' Her voice was trembling and she felt her tears on her cheeks. Embarrassed she tried to wipe them away.

'Because she loved you. Because she wanted to save your life.'

'Save my life?' Shocked, Joss echoed him numbly.

He looked down at her for a moment, then he reached

13

into his pocket and drew out a handkerchief. Carefully he wiped her cheeks. He smiled, but there was unhappiness in his eyes as he shook his head. 'I prayed you would never come to find me, Jocelyn Grant.'

He turned away from her and took several steps back along the path then he stopped and swung back to face her. 'Are you able to forget that you ever went to Belheddon? Are you able to put it out of your mind forever?'

Joss gasped. Confused she shook her head. 'How can I?'

His shoulders slumped. 'How indeed.' He sighed. 'Come.'

Abruptly he began to retrace his steps and she followed him in silence, her stomach churning uncomfortably.

His narrow front hall, as he closed the door against the roar of wind and sea, was uncannily quiet. Shrugging off his own coat he helped her with her jacket and slung both onto a many branched Victorian hat stand then he headed for the staircase.

The room into which he showed her was a large comfortable study overlooking the sea wall and the white-topped waves. It smelled strongly of pipe smoke and the huge vase of scented viburnum and tobacco flowers mixed with Michaelmas daisies, which stood on a table amidst piles of books. Gesturing her to a deep shabby arm chair he went back to the door and bellowed down the stairs. 'Dot! Tea and sympathy. My study. Twenty minutes!'

'Sympathy?' Joss tried to smile.

He hauled himself onto the edge of his large untidy kneehole desk and looked at her thoughtfully. 'Are you strong, Jocelyn Grant?'

She took a deep breath. 'I think so.'

'Are you married?' His eyes had travelled thoughtfully to her hands and his gaze rested on her wedding ring.

'As you see.'

'And do you have children?'

She glanced up. His gaze was steady. She tried to read it and failed. 'I have a little boy, yes. He's eighteen months old.'

He sighed. Standing up he walked round his desk and went to stand at the window, staring down at the sea. There was a long silence.

'It was after I had Tom that I realised I wanted to find out about my real parents,' she said at last.

'Of course.' He did not turn round.

'Is that my father – the Philip who is buried in the churchyard at Belheddon?' she went on after another silence.

'It is.'

'Did you bury him?'

He nodded slowly.

'What did he die of?'

'He had a riding accident.' He turned. 'I liked Philip very much. He was a kind and courageous man. He adored your mother.'

'Was it because of the accident she gave me away?'

He hesitated. 'Yes, I think that was part of it, certainly.' Sitting down behind his desk he leaned forward on his elbows and rubbed his face wearily. 'Your mother was never very strong physically, although emotionally she was the strongest of us all. After Philip's death she gave up. There had been two other children before you. They both died before they reached their teens. Then there was a long gap and then you came along. She had already planned to leave. I don't think she and Philip wanted any more children . . .' His voice died away thoughtfully. 'I'm sorry, my dear, but you must have been expecting some tale of woe; why else would a woman of Laura's background give away her child?'

'I . . .' Joss cleared her throat and tried again. 'I didn't know anything about her background. Only the address.'

15

He nodded. 'Jocelyn. Once more, can I beg you to forget about all this? For your own sake and the sake of your family don't embroil yourself in the affairs of the Duncans. You have your own life, your own child. Look forward, not backwards. There is too much unhappiness attached to that house.' His face lightened as a quiet tap sounded at the door. 'Come in, Dot!'

The door opened and the corner of a tray emerged, pushing it back. Mr Gower did not stand up. He was frowning. 'Come in, my love and join us for tea. Meet Jocelyn Grant.'

Joss half turned in her chair and smiled at the small, slim woman who had appeared, bent beneath the weight of the tray. Leaping to her feet she reached out to help her. 'It's all right, my dear. I'm stronger than I look!' Dot Gower's voice was not only strong but also melodious. 'Sit down, sit down.' She plonked the tray down in front of her husband where, balanced on top of his papers it sloped alarmingly towards the window. 'So, shall I pour?'

'Dot,' Edgar Gower said slowly. 'Jocelyn is Laura Duncan's child.'

Dot Gower's eyes were, Joss suddenly discovered, as piercing as her husband's. Disconcerted by the woman's stare she subsided back into her chair.

'Poor Laura.' Dot turned after a moment back to her teapot. 'She would have been so proud of you, my dear. You are very beautiful.'

Joss felt suddenly very uncomfortable. 'Thank you. What was she like?'

'Middle height; slim; grey hair, even when she was comparatively young; grey eyes.' Edgar Gower appraised Joss once more. 'You don't have her eyes – or Philip's. But you do have her build, and I should imagine her hair was like yours once. She was kind, intelligent, humorous – but the deaths of the boys – she never got over that and once Philip had gone . . .' He sighed as he reached out to take his tea cup. 'Thank you, my dear. Jocelyn, please. For your own sake, forget Belheddon. They have all gone. There is nothing there for you.'

'Edgar!' Dot straightened from the tray and turned on her husband, her face sharp. 'You promised!'

'Dot. No!'

They were locked for a moment in some intense silent conflict which Joss didn't understand. The atmosphere in the room had become tense. Abruptly Edgar slammed down his cup, slopping tea into the saucer and stood up. He strode over to the fireplace. 'Think, Dot. Think what you are saying . . .'

'Excuse me,' Joss said at last. 'Please. What are you talking about? If this is something to do with me, I think I should know about it.'

'Yes it is.' Dot's voice was very firm. 'Edgar made your mother a solemn promise before she left England and he has to keep it.'

Edgar's face was working furiously, reflecting some inner battle as yet unresolved. 'I promised, but nothing but unhappiness will come of it.'

'Come of what?' Joss stood up. 'Please. I obviously have a right to know.' She was growing afraid. Suddenly she didn't want to know, but it was too late.

Edgar took a deep breath. 'Very well. You are right. I have to abide by Laura's wishes.' He sighed again and then, straightening his shoulders, walked back to his desk. 'In fact, there is nothing very much that I can tell you myself, but I promised her that should you ever come back to Belheddon I would see to it that you were given the address of her solicitors in London. I suspect she has left you something in her will; I know she wrote you a letter the day you were legally adopted. She gave it to John Cornish, her lawyer.' He reached into a bottom drawer of his desk and after a moment or two riffling

17

through the papers produced a card. He pushed it across the desk towards her.

'But why didn't you want me to know about it?' Joss looked at him in confusion. 'Why did you feel I shouldn't know?' A jolt of excitement had shot through her. She clutched the card tightly. A glance had shown her it was a large firm of solicitors in Lincoln's Inn Fields.

'Belheddon Hall is an unhappy house, my dear, that's why. The past is the past. I feel it should be allowed to rest. Your mother felt that way too. That is why she wanted you to have a fresh start.'

'Then why did she write to me?'

'I suspect to comfort herself.'

Joss looked down at the card. 'Can I come and see you again after I have seen the solicitors?'

For a moment she thought he was going to shake his head. A shadow had crossed his face, and something else. Fear. She stared at him aghast, but as quickly as it had appeared the expression had gone. He gave her a grave smile. 'You may come whenever you wish, my dear. Dot and I will help you in every way we can.'

It was not until she was out in the rapidly falling dusk and retracing her steps towards the car that she thought again about that remark and wondered what exactly he had meant. Why should she need help – help was the word he had used – and why was he afraid?

3

t was very late before she drove at last into the narrow mews in Kensington and backed the car into an impossibly small space near the house. Wearily she climbed out and reached for her front door keys.

The light was still on in the kitchen at the back. Luke was sitting wedged into the corner behind the small table, staring down at a cup of cold coffee. His tall frame and broad shoulders dwarfed the narrow room; his elbows, spread over a scattering of papers, supported his chin as though he could scarcely lift his head. His normally ruddy complexion was pale.

'Hi, darling!' She bent and kissed him on the top of the ruffled dark hair. 'I'm sorry it's so late. I had to go all the way up to Aldeburgh. Is Tom asleep?' She was aching to go up and cuddle the little boy.

He nodded. 'Hours ago. How did it go?'

At last noticing his drawn, tired face her bubbling excitement died. 'Luke? What is it? What's wrong?' She slid onto the stool next to him and reached out to touch his hand.

He shook his head slowly. 'Joss, I don't know how to tell you. Henderson and Grant is no more.'

She stared at him in shock. 'But Barry said –'

'Barry has done a bunk, Joss. And he's taken all the money. I thought he was my friend. I thought our partnership was secure. I was wrong. Wrong!' He slammed the table suddenly with his fist. 'I went to the bank and the account had been emptied. I've been with accountants all day and the police. Your sister came and looked after Tom. I didn't know what to do.' He ran his fingers through his dishevelled hair and it dawned on Joss that he was near to tears.

'Oh, Luke –'

'We're going to lose the house, Joss.' He blundered to his feet, sending the stool on which he was sitting sliding across the tiles. Wrenching open the back door which led into their pocket handkerchief sized garden he stepped out onto the dark terrace and stared upwards towards the sky.

Joss hadn't moved. All thoughts of her day had vanished. She was staring at the pale terracotta tiles on the wall above the worktop. It had taken her eighteen months to save up for those tiles, to find them and get someone to put them up for her. It had at long last finished the kitchen, the dream kitchen of their first home.

'Joss.' Luke was standing in the doorway. 'I'm sorry.'

She rose to her feet and went to him, resting her head on his chest as he folded his arms around her. He smelled comfortably of Luke – a mixture of engine oil and aftershave and old wool and – Luke. She snuggled against him, drawing strength from just being near him. 'We'll think of something,' she murmured into his jersey. 'We'll manage.'

He clutched her even tighter. 'Will we?'

'I'll go back to teaching. That will tide us over. Especially if Lyn will look after Tom. I'm lucky to have a sister who likes babies. She gets on with him so well . . .' her voice trailed away.

She had hated teaching towards the end; loathed it, feeling frustrated and confined by the syllabus, not enjoying the challenge of the kids any more. She had been in the wrong job; she knew that, though she was good at it; very good. She was not a born teacher, she was an academic and a romantic. The two did not go well together. Her pregnancy had been a godsend – unplanned, unexpected – and unbelievably, a joy and one of its greatest good points had been the fact that she could finish with teaching forever. She had resigned at the end of the spring term, resisted the blandishments of David Tregarron, the head of department, to change her mind and thrown herself into the joys of approaching motherhood. She sighed. There was a chance the school could have her back. She had only recently heard that her replacement was already leaving. But even if that didn't happen they would certainly give her a good reference. The trouble was she didn't want to teach any more. She wanted to look after Tom.

Taking a deep breath she stood back. The comforting normality of filling the kettle and plugging it in gave her time to gather her wits a little. 'Hot drink and then bed. Neither of us is any good at thinking when we're tired,' she said firmly. 'Tomorrow we will make a plan.'

'Bless you, Joss.' He hugged her quickly. Then guiltily he remembered where she had been. 'So, tell me what happened. How did you get on? Did you find your mother?'

She shook her head, spooning the coffee into the mugs. 'She died several years ago. The house is empty. I don't think there is any family left.'

'Oh, Joss –'

'It doesn't matter, Luke. I've found out about them. She was unhappy and ill and her husband had died. That was why she gave me away. And,' suddenly she brightened, 'apparently she left me a letter. There is a

21

firm of solicitors I've got to contact. Who knows,' she laughed suddenly. 'Perhaps she has left me a fortune.'

'Mrs Grant?' John Cornish appeared at the door of his office and ushered her inside. 'Forgive me for keeping you waiting.' He waved her towards a chair and sat down himself at his desk. A slim plastic file lay on the blotter in front of him. He drew it towards him and then glanced up at her. A man in his early sixties, his dark suit and austere manner belied the kindness in his gentle face. 'You brought your birth and adoption certificates and your wedding certificate? I'm sorry. It's a formality –'

She nodded and pulled them out of her shoulder bag.

'And you got my name from Edgar Gower?'

Joss nodded again.

Cornish shook his head. 'I must say, I have always wondered if you would get in touch. There were only two years to go, you know.'

'Two years?' Joss sat tensely on the edge of the chair, her fingers knotted into the soft leather of her bag.

He nodded. 'It's a strange story. May I give you some coffee before I start?' He gestured towards a tray already standing on the table by the wall.

'Please.' She needed coffee. Her mouth was very dry.

When they were both served John Cornish resumed his seat and sat back in his chair. He did not touch either the file on his desk or the envelope of certificates she had given him.

'Your mother, Laura Catherine Duncan died on 15th February 1989. She moved to France from Belheddon Hall in Essex in the spring of 1984 and since then the house has remained empty. Her husband, your father, Philip Duncan, died in November 1963, his mother, who lived in the village of Belheddon, died three years ago and the two sons of Laura and Philip, your brothers, died in 1953 and 1962 respectively. I am afraid to my knowledge there is no close family extant.'

Joss bit her lip. Dragging her eyes away from his face she stared down into her cup.

'Your mother left two letters for you,' Cornish went on. 'One, I understand, was written at the time of your adoption. The other was entrusted to me before she left the country. It had some rather strange conditions attached to it.'

'Conditions?' Joss cleared her throat nervously.

He smiled. 'I was instructed to give it to you only if you appeared within seven years of her death. I was not to seek you out in any way. It had to be your decision to look for your roots.'

'And if I hadn't contacted you?'

'Then you would not have inherited Belheddon Hall.'

Joss's mouth fell open. 'What did you say?' Her hands had started to shake.

He smiled at her, clearly delighted at the effect of his words. 'The house and its grounds which I believe extend to about ten acres, are yours, my dear. It has been waiting for you. I understand a lot of the contents are still there as well, although some things were sold before Laura left England.'

'What would have happened to it if I hadn't contacted you?' Stunned, Joss frowned. She was still trying to make sense of his words.

'Then the house was to be sold at auction with its contents and the proceeds were to go to charity.' He paused. 'My dear, I should warn you that although enough provision was made for the payment of any inheritance taxes there is no money to go with the bequest. It is possible that you have been left an appallingly large white elephant, and there are conditions and covenants attached to the bequest. You may not turn it down, even though of course you cannot be forced to

23

live there, and, you may not sell the property for a period of seven years starting from the first day you set foot inside the house.' He turned to the file before him and stood up. 'I shall give you her letters and leave you alone for a moment while you read them.' He handed her two envelopes with a smile. 'I shall be in my secretary's office if you need me.'

She sat looking down at the two envelopes for several minutes without moving. One was addressed: To my daughter, Lydia. The other had her name – the name she had taken from her step parents, Jocelyn Davies – and the date April 1984.

She picked up the one addressed to Lydia and slowly ran her finger under the flap.

The single page was embossed with the address: Belheddon Hall, Belheddon, Essex.

> My darling Lydia, One day, I hope you will understand why I have done as I have done. I had no choice. I love you. I shall always love you. Please God you will be happy and safe with your new mother and father. My blessings go with you, my darling baby. God bless you always.

There was no signature. Joss felt her eyes flood with tears. She sniffed frantically, dropping the letter onto the desk. It was several seconds before she tore open the second envelope. It too was headed Belheddon Hall. This letter was longer.

> My dearest Jocelyn. I am not supposed to know your name but there are people who find out these things and once in a while I have had news of you. I hope you have been happy. I have been so proud of you, my darling. Forgive me, Jocelyn, but I can no longer fight your father's wishes, I have no strength left. I am

24

leaving Belheddon with all its blessings and its curses, but he will only let me escape if I give in. He wants Belheddon to be yours and I have to obey. If you read this letter, he will have got his way. God bless you, Jocelyn, and keep you safe.

Laura Duncan.

Joss read the letter again, puzzled. So, it was her father's wish that she inherit the house. She thought of the lone grave beneath the oak tree and shook her head slowly.

It was five minutes later that John Cornish put his head around the door. 'All right?'

She nodded numbly. 'I'm finding it hard to assimilate all this.'

He resumed his chair and gave her a kind smile. 'I can imagine.'

'What happens now?'

He shrugged eloquently. 'I give you a box of keys and you go away and, as our American cousins say, enjoy.'

'And that is all?'

'Bar a few small formalities – papers to sign and so forth – that is all.'

She hesitated. 'My husband's engineering company has just folded. He's been swindled by his partner. There is a chance he is going to be made bankrupt. We've lost our house – I won't lose Belheddon?'

He shook his head. 'I'm so sorry. But this house is yours, not your husband's. Unless you yourself are being made bankrupt, it is safe.'

'And we could go and live there?'

He laughed. 'Indeed you can. Though you should remember it has been closed up a long time. I have no idea what condition it is in.'

'I don't care what condition it's in. It is going to save

25

our lives!' Joss could hardly contain herself. 'Mr Cornish, I don't know how to thank you!'

He beamed at her. 'It is your mother you should thank, Mrs Grant, not I.'

'And my father.' Joss bit her lip. 'I gather it was my father who wanted me to have the house.'

It was several minutes before John Cornish's secretary, on his instructions, appeared in his office carrying a small tin box which she laid reverently on the desk.

'The keys, if I remember, are all neatly labelled.' John Cornish pushed it towards Joss. 'If you have any problems, let me know.'

She stared down at it. 'You mean, that's it?'

He smiled happily. 'That's it.'

'It's my house?'

'It's your house, to do with as you wish, provided you abide by the conditions.' He stood up again, and extended his hand. 'Congratulations, Mrs Grant. I wish you and your husband every happiness with your inheritance.'

4

 don't believe it. Things like that don't happen in real life.' Lyn Davies was sitting opposite her adoptive sister at the small kitchen table, her eyes round with envy.

Joss reached down to Tom, sitting playing by her feet and hoisted him onto her knee. 'I can't believe it's true either. I have to keep pinching myself. It makes up for losing this.' She glanced round her at the little kitchen.

'I'll say. Talk about falling on your feet!' Lyn scowled. 'Have you told Mum and Dad about all this?' Two years younger than Joss, she had been conceived after Joss's adoption, five years after Alice had been told she could never have a child of her own. Totally unlike Joss to look at – she was squarely built, had short, curly blond hair and deep grey eyes. Nobody ever had taken them for sisters.

Joss nodded. 'I rang last night. They think it's like a fairy story. You know, Mum was so worried I'd be disappointed when I wanted to look for my real parents; but she was so good about it.' She glanced at Lyn. 'She didn't mind.'

'Of course she minded!' Lyn reached for the pot and poured herself another mug of thick black coffee. 'She was desperately unhappy about it. She was frightened you might find another family and forget her and Dad.'

Joss was shocked. 'She wasn't! She can't have believed that.' She narrowed her eyes. 'She didn't feel that at all. You're stirring again, Lyn. I wish you wouldn't.' She took a deep breath. 'Look, are you sure you want Tom tomorrow?' She hugged the little boy close. 'Luke and I can take him with us –'

Lyn shook her head. 'No. I'll have him. He'll only get in your way while you're measuring for curtains or whatever.' Catching sight of Joss's face she scowled again. 'All right, sorry. I didn't mean it. I know you can't afford curtains. Go on, you and Luke go and enjoy your day out. It will do him good to get away from all this mess with H & G. Mum and I will love having Tom!'

Luke drove, his handsome square face haggard with worry and loss of sleep. For a second Joss reached over and touched his hand. 'Cheer up. You're going to love it.'

'Am I?' He turned to her and finally he grinned. 'Yes, you're right, I am. If the roof keeps most of the rain out and there is a garden big enough to grow vegetables in, I'm going to love it. I don't care what it looks like.'

The last week had been a nightmare of solicitors, bank managers and police investigators. Meetings with them and with creditors and accountants had filled Luke's every waking hour as he watched the small engineering company which had been his whole life being taken apart and put under the microscope. They were not to be bankrupted at least. But it was no comfort to know that Barry Henderson was being sought by Interpol. The sour taste Barry's betrayal had left in his mouth and the inevitable loss of the mews cottage had detracted badly from his pleasure in Joss's windfall. And from the relief he felt when he realised that for the time at least they would have a roof, however leaky, over their heads whilst they decided what to do with the rest of their lives.

They pulled up at last outside the village shop. 'Are you going to introduce yourself?' Luke smiled at her. 'The new lady of the manor.'

Joss shrugged. 'What do I say?'

'Tell them the truth. You've got to tell them, Joss. They are the post office. They'll be delivering mail pretty soon. Go on. Give the village something to gossip about.' He swung himself out of the car.

The wind was icy, worrying the branches of the ash tree which grew at the road junction opposite like an angry dog, tearing off the remaining leaves. Joss followed him, turning up the collar of her jacket with a shudder as the wind tore at her hair and whipped it into her eyes.

The shop was empty. They stood looking round, savouring the mixed smells of cheese and ham and exotic smoked sausages and the silence after the wind. Moments later the post mistress appeared from a doorway at the back of the counter. She was carrying a cup of coffee. 'Hello, my dears. How can I help you?' She set the cup down. Then she peered at Joss. 'Of course, you were in here the other day, asking about the Hall. Did you manage to find Mary Sutton?'

Joss shook her head. 'There was no one there when I knocked but I met the vicar up at the church and he gave me the address of his predecessor who knew the Duncans.'

'I see.' The woman put her head on one side. 'You've some special interest in the Hall, have you?' Her eyes were bright with curiosity.

Joss heard Luke chuckle. She trod heavily on his toe. Smiling, she held out her hand. 'Perhaps I should introduce myself. I am Joss Grant – this is my husband, Luke. It looks as though we are going to be living there, at least for a while. Laura and Philip Duncan were my parents.

They gave me up for adoption when I was a baby, but it appears that they left the house to me.'

The woman's mouth dropped open. 'Well I never! Oh, my dear! That great place!' Far from being pleased as Joss expected, she appeared to be horrified. 'You're never going to live there! You couldn't possibly.'

Taken aback, Joss frowned. 'Why on earth not? It didn't look to me as though it was in too bad condition.'

'Oh, I didn't mean that.' The woman was immediately embarrassed. 'Take no notice of me! It's a lovely place. You are very lucky. The village will be pleased. The Hall has been empty too long. Much too long.' She shook her head. 'There's me forgetting my manners. I'm Sally Fairchild. My husband Alan is the post master here; I'm the deli counter.' She laughed. 'Alan retired from his accountancy five years back and we thought we'd take over a village shop in our declining years. Thought it would be a nice restful job. Haven't had time to sit down since . . .'

Luke looked across at Joss as they settled themselves back into the car. On the back seat there was a box of supplies – enough for an army for three days at least, Luke had said with a smile, as they selected a picnic for themselves from Sally Fairchild's luxurious counter. 'So. What do you make of all that?'

Joss reached for her seatbelt. 'Nice woman. I had the feeling though, that whatever she said about the village being pleased, they wouldn't be.'

Glancing into the mirror Luke pulled the car away from the kerb. 'Up here? She certainly had reservations, didn't she. Do you still want to stop off and see this Mary Sutton?'

Joss shook her head. 'Let's go to the house first. I can't wait to see what it's like inside.' She reached into the glove compartment and brought out the box of keys, hugging it against her chest. 'We can't expect the locals to accept us just like that. When I rang David Tregarron to tell him our plans he said it would take twenty years for anyone round here to accept a stranger. As I was a blood relation, probably nineteen years eight months.'

Luke laughed.

'Up there now, round the green,' Joss went on. 'I think the drive must lead off the lane beyond the church. He said he would come and see us.' David had been more than just her boss. Confidant, friend, sparring partner, his warmth and genuine regret when she had phoned him a couple of days earlier had touched her deeply. 'There. That must be it.'

The wrought iron gate, standing between two stone gate posts, topped with moss-covered pineapples, was standing half open in the tall hedge. Luke drew the car to a halt. Climbing out he peered up the drive as he tried to force the gate back over the muddy gravel. There was no notice to say this was Belheddon Hall, no sign of the house as the overgrown driveway curved out of sight between the high laurel hedges.

He climbed back into the car. 'OK?' Her excitement was tangible. He reached across and squeezed her hand. 'The return of the prodigal daughter. Let's go.'

The drive was not very long. One sweep past the hedges and they were there, drawing up on the grassy gravel in front of the house. Luke pulled up and cut the engine.

'Joss!' It was all he said. For several seconds they sat in silence, staring through the windscreen.

It was Joss who moved first, opening the door and stepping out into the freezing wind. Silently she stood staring up at the house. It was her birthplace. Her inheritance. Her home.

Behind her Luke stood for a moment watching her. He was intensely proud of his wife; she was beautiful, intelligent, hard working, sexy – sternly he cut short that train of thought – and now an heiress as well! Silently he stepped up behind her and put his hands on her shoulders. 'So, how does it feel to be home?' he said softly. He had read her thoughts exactly.

She smiled, brushing her cheek against his hand. 'Strange. A little frightening.'

'It's a big house, Joss.'

'And we have no money.' She turned and looked up at him. 'You have always liked challenges.' Her eyes were sparkling.

'If we're seriously going to live here for any length of time, we'll need cash from somewhere for taxes, heat, electricity and food. On top of that there will be endless ongoing repairs. Shouldn't be a problem.' He grinned. 'Your mother did leave you a magic lamp, a bag of gold coins and six live-in servants?'

'Of course.'

'Then, as I said, no problem. Come on. Where's the key? Let's go in.'

The keyhole in the front door was two inches high. Joss already knew the contents of the key box by heart; there was nothing in there which would fit. She reached for a couple of yale keys. Both were labelled 'Back door'.

They walked along the front of the house, passing the shuttered lower windows and turned through the stone archway. There a square range of coach houses, garages and stables surrounded a cobbled courtyard one side of which was the east wall of the house. By the back door stood a black iron pump.

'Joss!' Luke stared round. 'You realise what I could do here, don't you! I've had the most brilliant idea! Looking for jobs in London will probably be a dead loss, but I could work here!' In three steps he had reached one of the doors. Pulling it open he peered into an empty garage. 'Cars! I can restore cars. I can start again. My God, there

32

would be room to do it, too. It would give us a living of sorts.' Excitedly he peered into the stable and out-buildings.

Behind him Joss was smiling. The house was working its spell. She could see his depression lifting as she watched. She stood there for a few minutes more, then, unable to resist it any longer she turned alone to the back door.

It was swollen with damp and grated against the York stone flags of a narrow dark hallway. 'Wait for me!' Coming up behind her, Luke caught her hand. 'I think this is somewhere I should carry you over the threshold, don't you?'

Giggling, Joss clung to his neck as he swept her off her feet and he walked with her into the darkness of the first room down the passage. There he set her down, panting. 'My God, woman. What have you been eating? Bricks?'

They stared round in silence. The huge room was shad-owy, a pale, reluctant light filtering around the edge of the shutters. 'It's the kitchen,' Joss whispered. A huge fireplace took up the whole of one wall. In it a double size cooking range slumbered like some great black engine. On it stood an iron kettle. In the centre of the room stood a scrubbed oak table with round it six bentwood chairs. One was pulled out, as though the person seated on it had only a moment before stood up and left the room. To the left a glass-fronted dresser, dusty and hung with spiders' webs, showed the gleam of china.

Silently, hand in hand like two trespassing children, Joss and Luke moved towards the door in the far wall. Over it a board hung with a line of fifteen bells, each controlled by a wire, showed how in days gone by the servants had been summoned from the kitchen quarters to other parts of the house.

Beyond the kitchen they found a bewildering range of

small pantries and sculleries, and at the end of the passage a baize-lined door. They stopped.

'Upstairs and downstairs.' Luke smiled, running his hands over the green door lining. 'Are you ready to go above stairs?'

Joss nodded. She was trembling. Luke pushed the door open and they peered out into a broad corridor. Again it was shadowy, bisected by fine lines of dusty sunlight. Here the scrubbed flags finished and they found themselves walking on broad oak boards which once had carried gleaming polish. Instead of an array of exotic carpets a drift of dried leaves had blown in under the front door and lay scattered over it.

To the right on one side of the front door they found the dining room. A long table stood there in the shuttered darkness, surrounded by – awed, Luke counted out loud – twelve chairs. To the left a large door, much older than anything they had seen so far, Gothic, churchlike, led into an enormous, high ceilinged room. Amazed they stood staring up at the soaring arched beams and the minstrel's gallery, screened by oak panelling, carved into intricate arches. 'My God.' Joss took a few steps forward. 'It's a time warp.' She stared round with a shiver. 'Oh Luke.'

There was very little furniture. Two heavy oak coffer chests stood against the walls and there was a small refectory table in the middle of the floor. The fireplace still held the remains of the last fire that had been lit there.

On the far side of the room an archway hung with a dusty curtain led into a further hallway from which a broad oak staircase curved up out of sight into the darkness. They stood peering up.

'I think we should open some shutters,' Luke said softly. 'What this house needs is some sunlight.' He felt vaguely uneasy. He glanced at Joss. Her face was white in the gloomy darkness and she looked unhappy. 'Come on, Joss, let's let in the sun.'

He strode towards the window and spent several minutes wrestling with the bars which held the shutters closed. Finally he managed to lift them out of their sockets and he threw open the shutters. Sunshine poured in across the dusty boards. 'Better?' He hadn't been imagining it. She was deathly pale.

She nodded. 'I'm stunned.'

'Me too.' He looked round. 'What this room needs is a suit of armour or two. You know, we could run this place as a hotel! Fill it with tourists. Make our fortune.' He strode across the floor to a door beyond the hall and threw it open. 'The library!' he called. 'Come and look! There are enough books here even for you!' He disappeared from sight and she heard the rattle of iron on wood as once again he fought with a set of shutters.

She did not follow him for a moment. Turning round slowly she stared about her at the empty room. The silence of the house was beginning to oppress her. It was as if it were listening, watching, holding its breath.

'Joss! Come and see.' Luke was in the doorway. He was beaming. 'It's wonderful.'

Joss gave herself a small shake. With a shiver she followed him through the doorway and immediately she felt better. 'Luke!' It was, as he had said, wonderful. A small, bright room, full of mellow autumn light, looking down across the back lawns towards the small lake. The walls were lined to the ceiling with books except where an old roll top desk stood, with in front of it a shabby leather chair. Round the fire stood a cluster of three arm chairs, a side table, an overflowing magazine rack and a sewing basket, still with its silks and needles, witness to the last hours of Laura Duncan's occupancy.

Joss stared round, a lump in her throat. 'It is as if she just stood up and walked out. She didn't even take her sewing things – ' She ran her hand over the contents of the basket. There were tears in her eyes.

'Come on.' Luke put his arm around her again. 'Everything was planned. She didn't need her sewing things, that's all. She was looking forward to a life of leisure in France. I bet in her shoes, you wouldn't take your darning needles either.' He squeezed her shoulder. 'The desk is locked. Is the key there, in the box?'

It wasn't. They tried a succession before they gave up and resumed their tour of the house. The only other room on the ground floor was a small sitting room which looked out across the drive. The squeaking shutters opened reluctantly to show their car, already dusted with crisp brown leaves from the chestnut tree on the edge of the front lawn. On the grass a trio of rabbits grazed unconcerned within a few feet of its wheels.

At the foot of the stairs Joss paused. Above them a gracious sweep of oak treads curved around out of sight into the darkness. Aware that Luke was immediately behind her she still hesitated a moment, her hand on the carved newel post.

'What's the matter?'

She shrugged. 'I don't know. I just had the feeling – as if there was someone up there. Waiting.'

Luke rumpled her hair affectionately. 'Perhaps there is. The skeleton in the cupboard. Come on, let Uncle Luke go first.' He took the stairs two at a time, disappearing around the corner and out of sight.

Joss did not move. She heard his footsteps echoing across the floor, the now familiar rattle of shutters and suddenly the stairs above her head were flooded with light. 'Come on. No skeletons.' His footsteps crossed the floor again, growing fainter until she could hear them no more.

'Luke!' Suddenly she was frightened. 'Luke, where are you?' Slowly she began to climb.

The stairs creaked slightly beneath her weight. The polished handrail was smooth and cold under her palm. She looked up, her concentration focused on the upper landing as she rounded the curve towards it. A broad corridor ran crossways in front of her with three doors opening off it. 'Luke?'

There was no reply.

She stepped onto a faded Persian rug and glanced quickly into the doorway on her right. It led into a large bedroom which looked out across the back garden and beyond it, over the hedge towards a huge stubble field and then the estuary. The room was sparsely furnished. A bed, covered by a dust sheet, a Victorian chest of drawers, a mahogany cupboard. There was no sign of Luke. The doorway half way down the landing led into a large, beautiful bedroom dominated by an ornate four poster bed. Joss gasped. In spite of the dust sheets which covered the furniture she could see how exquisite it all was. Stepping forward she pulled at the sheet which lay over the bed to reveal an embroidered bedcover, matching the hangings and tester.

'So, Mrs Grant. What do you think of your bedroom, eh?' Luke appeared behind her so suddenly she let out a little cry of fright. He put his arms around her. 'This is the kind of style to which you would like to be accustomed to live, I suspect?' He was laughing.

Her fear forgotten, Joss smiled. 'I can't believe it. It's like Sleeping Beauty's palace.'

'And Sleeping Beauty needs a kiss from a prince to wake her up and show her she's not dreaming!'

'Luke –' Her squeal of protest as he pulled her onto the high bed and began to kiss her was muffled as he climbed up beside her. 'I think we need to stake our claim on this bed, don't you, Mrs Grant?' He was fumbling for the buttons on her jersey under her jacket.

'Luke, we can't –'

'Why not? It's your house, your bed!'

She gasped as his hands, ice cold from the chill in the house, met the warm flesh of her breasts and pulled away her bra. Her excitement was rising to match his. 'Luke –'

'Shut up.' He dropped his mouth teasing her with his tongue, his hands busy with her skirt and tights. 'Concentrate on your husband, my love,' he smiled down at her.

'I am.' She reached up pulling away his sweater and shirt and pushing them back so that she could kiss his chest, his shoulders, pulling him down towards her, oblivious to everything now but the urgency which was building between them.

In the corner of the room a shadowy figure stood motionless, watching them.

'Yes!' Luke's cry of triumph was muffled by the hangings of the bed. In the ceiling beams the stray sunlight from the garden wavered and died as dark clouds raced in from the east.

Clinging to Luke, Joss opened her eyes, staring up at the embroidered tester above her head. A rosette of pale cream silk, threadbare, cobwebbed, nestled in the centre of the fabric. Stretching, contented as a cat, Joss gazed round, not wanting to move, enjoying Luke's weight, his warmth, his closeness. It was a moment before her eyes registered something in the corner, another fraction of a second before her brain reacted. She blinked, suddenly frightened, but there was nothing there. Just a trick of the light.

Luke raised his head at last and looked down. Joss was crying.

'Sweetheart, what is it?' Contrite he wiped the tears with a gentle hand. 'Did I hurt you?'

She shook her head. 'Take no notice. I'm all right. I don't know why I'm crying.' Sniffing she wriggled away from him and slid off the bed.

Pulling down her skirt she went to retrieve her tights

from the dusty boards. It was as she was putting them on that the sound of a bell pealed through the house.

Luke stood up. Pulling his sweater on over his head he padded across to the front window and looked out. 'There's someone at the front door!' He smothered a laugh. 'How embarrassing! Our first visitor and we're caught in delicto!'

'Not caught!' She pushed her feet into her shoes and smoothed her hair. 'Go on, then. Let them in.'

They couldn't. Of the front door key there was no sign. By dint of shouting through the two inch keyhole, Luke directed their visitor to the back door and it was in the shadowy kitchen that they received their first guest, a tall distinguished-looking woman, dressed in a heavy woollen coat, swathed in a tartan scarf.

'Janet Goodyear. Next door neighbour.' She extended a hand to them both in turn. 'Sally Fairchild told me you were here. My dears, I can't tell you how excited the village will be when they hear you've arrived. Are you seriously going to live here? It's such a God-forsaken pile.' Pulling off her gloves and throwing them on the table she walked over to the range and pulled open the door of one of the ovens. She wrinkled her nose cheerfully. 'This kitchen is going to need at least twenty thou spent on it! I know a brilliant designer if you need one. He would make a really good job of all this.'

Luke and Joss exchanged glances. 'Actually, I want to leave the kitchen as it is,' Joss said. Luke frowned. Her voice was ominously quiet. 'The range will refurbish beautifully.'

Their visitor looked surprised. 'I suppose so. But you'd do much better, you know, to swop it for a decent Aga. And God help you when it comes to the roof. Laura and Philip were always having trouble with the roof.' She turned back from her poking around, her smile all warmth. 'Oh, my dears, I can't tell you how lovely it will

39

be to have neighbours here. I can't wait for you to move in. Now, what I've actually come for is to ask if you'd like to pop over for lunch. We live just across the garden there; in the farmhouse.' She waved a vaguely expansive hand. 'My husband owns most of the land round here.'

Joss opened her mouth to reply, but Luke was ahead of her. 'It's kind of you, Mrs Goodyear, but we've brought our own food. I think on this occasion we'll take a rain check, if you don't mind. We've got a lot of measurements and notes to take while we're here.'

'Twenty thou!' He exploded with laughter when at last they had managed to get rid of her. 'If she knew that we are going to move in here without a penny to our name she would probably have us struck off her Christmas card list before we were ever on it!'

'I don't think she meant to sound so frightening. I quite liked her.' Joss had pulled open one of the tall cupboards. 'She's right in one way, though, Luke. There is a lot to do. The roof – presumably – water, electricity; we don't know if it all works. And the stove. I suppose we could get it going – ' she stared at it doubtfully ' – but it is going to gobble fuel.'

'We'll cope.' He put his arms round her again and gave her a hug. He was, she noticed, looking happy for the first time since he had found out about Barry's treachery. Really happy. 'For a start there was a massive amount of coal in one of the sheds in the courtyard, did you notice?' he said. 'And there will be logs. We'll manage, Joss. Somehow. You'll see.'

5

An empty beer glass had left a wet ring on the pub table which Joss was busy transforming into a figure of eight with variations when David Tregarron fought his way back towards her from the bar carrying two spritzers and a bag of nuts.

The head of the History Department at Dame Felicia's School in Kensington, David was thirty-eight years old, two years divorced and, as house master and second head lived above the job, over four dormitories of unruly little boys, in a Victorian flat with minimal mod cons. His divorce had been an unpleasant messy business, and Joss had been one of his anchor points at the time. She and he might not agree over teaching methods but her loyalty to him as his marriage had unravelled had been unswerving. She had comforted him as his wife took off into the sunset with her new man, propped him up in the staff room with coffee and Alka Seltzer and cheerfully agreed with all his maudlin lamentations over a woman she had never actually met.

When once, some time after the divorce was made absolute, he had grabbed her hand and said, 'Joss, divorce Luke and marry me,' he had realised as soon as he had said it that he was only half joking. He had seen the danger in time and pulled himself together. Being fond of Joss was permissible. Anything more was totally beyond the pale.

'So, how is Luke taking all this new found wealth?' He lowered himself cautiously onto a plush-covered stool and passed her one of the glasses.

Joss gave a wry grin. 'Amazement. Relief. Disbelief. Not necessarily in that order.'

'And you?'

She sighed. 'Roughly the same. I'm still pinching myself. So much has happened to us in the last few weeks, David! I don't think even in my wildest dreams I ever imagined anything like this happening to us!' She sipped thoughtfully from her glass for a moment. 'It was nice of you to call and ask me out. Do you know this is the first break I've had away from the house in days. There has been so much to do. The firm going under has been a complete nightmare.'

David grimaced. 'I was so sorry to hear about it.' He glanced at her. 'Are they making Luke bankrupt?'

Joss shook her head. 'No, thank God! The mews cottage has saved us. Luke's grandfather bought it after the war when it was worth a few hundred pounds. When Luke's father gave it to us as a wedding present he handed us a fortune, bless him.' She gave a sad, fond smile. 'It's going on the market for a lot of money. If I ever get my hands on Barry I'll throttle him personally if Luke or the police don't get to him first. Our lovely little house!'

'That's really tough. But now you have your stately roof in East Anglia to fall back on.'

She gave a wry grin. 'I know. It sounds like a fairy tale. It is a fairy tale! Oh, David, it was so beautiful! And Luke is full of plans. He's going to turn his hand to restoring old cars again. He is a trained engineer after all, and it's what he always loved doing best. I think he was pretty sick of spending all his time on management and paperwork. And they've let him keep some of the machinery and tools from H & G – it's out dated by other people's standards apparently and the buyer didn't want them. He's retrieved lathes and boring and gear cutting equipment and all sorts of stuff. I hope he's right in thinking he can make us some money that way, because we're going to be awfully short of cash. Next summer we can live off the garden, but it's a lousy time of year to be starting out as gardeners! Do you realise we'll be moving in only a few weeks before Christmas!'

'Joss, I've had an idea.' David edged himself out of the way of a crowd of noisy drinkers who were settling around the table next to theirs. 'That's why I persuaded you to come and have this drink.' He paused and gave a theatrical sigh. 'I know you and I didn't always see eye to eye over history and its teaching!'

Joss laughed. 'Always the master of understatement!'

'And we've had the odd tiff.'

'Ditto.' She raised her eyes to his fondly. 'What is this leading to, David? You are not usually so deferential in your suggestions.'

'First, tell me, are you intending to go back to teaching up there in your new home?'

Joss shook her head. 'I doubt it. I expect there's a village school – I don't even know that yet – but I shouldn't think there's any scope locally for the kind of teaching I do. Anyway, I think I've had it with teaching, David, to be honest.'

'You weren't sorry when you handed in your resignation before Tom was born. Even I could see that.'

'And you were probably relieved to see the back of me.' She looked down at her glass.

'You know that's not true.' He hesitated. 'You're a good teacher, Joss. I was desperately sorry to lose you.' He paused. 'In more ways than one.' There was an uncomfortable silence. Pulling himself together with a visible effort he went on. 'You care about the kids, and you inspire them. Something not all history teachers manage by any means. I know we sometimes rowed about your methods, but I was only worried about your ability to stick to the curriculum.' He stopped and shook his head. 'I'm making a mess of this. What I'm trying to say is, that I've a suggestion to make and I don't want you to get hold of the wrong end of the stick. This is not an insult or a sinister plot to undermine your intellectual integrity. And above all I am not criticising your knowledge or interpretation of history, but I think you should give some serious consideration to the idea of turning your hand to writing. Fiction.'

He waited, his eyes fixed on her face.

'Which is more my line than serious history, you mean.' Joss hid a smile.

'I knew you would say that!' He smacked the table with the palm of his hand. 'No, it is not what I mean. All right. You told the kids stories. They loved it. I don't think it was good history but it was good teaching. They wanted more and they missed you like hell when you left. Joss, what I'm saying is that you are a born story teller. You could make money out of it. I'm sure you could. I've read some of your short stories. You even won that competition. I'm being serious. I have a feeling that you could do it. I know one or two people in the publishing business, and if you like, I will show them some of your writing. I don't want to get your hopes up too much because it's a chancy business, but I have a feeling about you.' He smiled at her again. 'A good feeling, Joss.'

She returned his smile. 'You're a nice man, David.' She reached out her hand to his.

'I know.' He left his fingers lying there beneath hers on the table for just a moment too long then reluctantly he withdrew them. 'So, I have your permission to show some stories around?'

'You have my permission. Thanks.'

'And I can come and see you as soon as you're settled?'

'Of course you can. I shall miss you, David.'

He picked up his glass. 'And I you, Joss. And I you.'

Joss was kneeling on the floor packing china when she told Luke of David's idea that evening.

He considered it for a minute, his head on one side, then thoughtfully he nodded. 'You can write and you did win that competition. Joss, it's a brilliant scheme!'

'Winning a competition with a short story is not the same as making a living out of writing, Luke.'

'No, but you could give it a go. And we are going to need money, Joss. Make no mistake about it.'

She frowned, wrapping her arms around her knees as she sat on the floor. 'It's going to be tough at Belheddon, isn't it.'

He nodded. 'Just pray the roof doesn't leak. Your mother and father meant well, leaving the place to you, I'm sure they did, but it's going to take some looking after.'

'We'll manage though. Or you will. I'm glad I married a practical man! And who knows, once we're settled, maybe I'll even write a best seller, too.' She glanced up at him through the dark fringe of her hair. 'It's a dream come true, Luke.'

He slid from his chair and sat down next to her amongst the debris of boxes and partly packed cups and plates. 'I know it is, Joss.' Putting his arm round her shoulders he pulled her to him and kissed her. 'Just remember, we have to keep a tight grip on reality. We are going to have to work our socks off to keep that place going, and it's not going to be easy.'

45

6

As the removal van drove slowly out of the drive and turned out of sight Joss turned to Luke. She caught his hand. 'That's it. Bridges burned. No going back. No regrets?' She looked up at him.

He smiled. 'No Joss, no regrets. This is the start of a big adventure.'

Slowly they walked back into the kitchen. The room had in many ways not changed at all since the first day they had seen it. The range was still there, and to their joy had been found to be fully functional after an overhaul; the plates and cups on the dresser had been washed and were sparkling. The heavy table, decorated now with a scarlet poinsettia, a gift from John Cornish, had been scrubbed almost white by Joss's mother, Alice. The crates of their own china and glass stood piled along the wall. Tom's high chair was pulled up at the head of the table.

Alice was bending over the pan on the stove, stirring something which smelled extremely appetising as they walked in.

'Removal men gone?' Her husband, Joe, was unwrapping saucepans with his small grandson's help, making a huge pile of newspaper in the middle of the room.

'Gone at last, thank God.' Luke threw himself down

46

in one of the chairs. 'That smells wonderful, Alice.'

His mother-in-law smiled. 'You know, I'm really enjoying cooking on this range. I think I'm getting the hang of it at last. This is real cooking!' The range had been one of the urgent things they had had repaired before the move. She glanced at Joss. 'Why don't we all have a glass of wine, while I finish this. Let Lyn take Tom, Joe. She can give him his tea.' Comfortably she stood away from the stove, wiping her hands on the front of her apron.

There were two bottles of wine in a Sainsbury's carrier on the table and a six pack of beer. 'Corkscrew?' Joss extricated the bottles and stood them in line with the poinsettia. After the weeks of worry and packing and organising the move she was so exhausted she could hardly stand.

'On my boy scout knife.' Luke grinned at her. 'Do you remember the removal foreman telling us: "Leave out the kettle and the corkscrew or you'll never find them again after." ' He fished around in the pocket of his jacket and produced a corkscrew which had obviously been nowhere near a boy scout in its life. 'Beer for you, Joe? And I think I'll join you. It's thirsty work, moving house!'

Sitting at the table, watching her sister cut up an apple and put the pieces in front of Tom Joss felt a sudden wave of total contentment. It would probably take them years to sort out the house; months to unpack, but at least they were here properly now. No more London; no more office for Luke as he tried to sort out the last minute details of his former life. And here they had enough room to put up Joe and Alice and Lyn and anyone else who wanted to come and stay for as long as they wanted.

Helping herself to a glass Alice sat down next to her. 'I'll leave that to simmer for a couple of hours. Then we can eat. You look done in, love.' She put her hand over Joss's.

'Done in, but happy.' Joss smiled. 'It's going to work. I know it is.'

47

'Course it is.' Joe had gone back to pushing the crumpled newspaper into a black plastic sack, considerably hampered by Tom who was pulling out the pieces as fast as Joe was putting them in, and tossing them around the room. 'You're all going to be very happy here.' He reached for his beer. 'So, let's drink a toast. To Belheddon Hall and all who sail in her!'

The sound of the back doorbell was almost drowned by their raised voices. It was Luke who, with a groan, levered himself to his feet and went to answer it.

They had met Janet Goodyear several times since she had introduced herself on their first visit to the house almost three months before and Joss was beginning to like her more and more. Her first impression of an interfering and nosy neighbour had been replaced by one of a good-hearted and genuinely kind, if not always tactful, woman, who, far from being pushy was in fact diffident about intruding on her new neighbours. In her basket this time was a bottle of Scotch ('For emergencies, but I can see you've thought of the alcohol bit already',) and, what turned out to be a corn dolly. Accepting a glass of wine from Luke she pulled up a chair next to Joss. 'You'll probably think I'm dotty,' she said cheerfully, 'but I want you to hang this up somewhere in the kitchen here. For luck.'

Joss reached over and picked up the intricately plaited figure. 'It's beautiful. I've seen them of course –'

'This isn't a souvenir shop piece of tweeness,' Janet interrupted. 'Please don't think it is. It was made specially for you. There's an old chap who used to work on the farm – he does some odd gardening jobs for us now – and he made it for you. He asked me to bring it. It's to ward off evil.'

Joss raised her eyes from the plaited straw. 'Evil?'

'Well –' Janet shrugged ' – you have probably gathered by now that the locals are a bit funny about this house.' She laughed uncomfortably. 'I don't believe it. I've always loved it here. It has such a nice atmosphere.'

'What do they say exactly?' Clearing away the remains of his apple, Joss pushed a plate of scrambled egg in front of Tom and put a spoon into his hand.

'I don't know that we want to know, dear,' Alice put in quietly. 'You look at the range, Mrs Goodyear. What do you think of it now?' Joss had told her mother about the estimate of twenty thousand.

'I think it's wonderful.' Still cheerfully unaware of the consternation her initial comments on the state of the house had caused, Janet swung round to inspect it. 'It's so clever of you to get it fixed so quickly.'

'You could join us for supper later,' Joss interrupted. 'Mum has made enough for an army as usual.'

'Thank you but no.' Janet drained her glass and stood up. 'I only came to bring you the dolly. The last thing you all want is a visitor on your first evening. Later, though, I'd love to come. And in the mean time if you need anything at all we are very close. Please, please don't hesitate to ask.' She smiled round at them, then pulling her scarf back over her head, she was gone.

'Nice woman, Janet Goodyear,' Luke said to Joss when they were alone in the great hall later. They had made no attempt to introduce any of their furniture there. The room was too big, too stately, and, they both agreed needed no more than was there already.

The meal had been eaten and the beds made up and Luke's first job, a rusty, shabby 1929 Bentley, had been ushered into the yard on the back of a low loader. It hadn't even required an advertisement in the paper. A card in the shop, and a few words in the pub and the phone had rung three days later. Colonel Maxim, from the next village had owned the car for twelve years and had never got round to working on it himself. Luke could start on it as soon as possible, and when that was done, there was a 1930 Alvis belonging to a friend.

Tom, exhausted by the excitement of the day had gone to bed in his own room without a murmur. The old nurseries led off the main bedroom which was to be Joss and Luke's, and, with the doors open into the short passage which separated the two rooms they would easily be able to hear him if he cried. The nursery complex consisted of three rooms, one of which had been converted into a bathroom. It was a cold, north facing room, and even the string bag full of Tom's colourful bath toys did nothing to cheer it up. 'Curtains, bright rug, wall heater and lots of vivid, warm towels,' Joss dictated as she took the little boy on her knee after his bath and cuddled him dry. Lyn was making a shopping list, sitting on the closed lid of the loo. 'Tom's bathroom and bedroom are a priority.' She shivered in spite of the heat from the gas cylinder heater Luke had put into the room. 'I want him to love this place.'

'At least your four poster will keep the draught out,' Lyn commented. The bedroom she had been allocated off the main staircase, although facing south across the garden, was bitterly cold. In the past it was obvious a fire had been lit in the grate in there. There was a rudimentary central heating system, working off the range, but the heat didn't seem to reach the bedrooms, and they had already decided that they would just have to stay cold. A thousand blankets, hot water bottles and thermal pyjamas were going to be the order of the day from now on.

'How long do you think Joe and Alice will stay?' Joss pulled the fleece lined pyjama top over Tom's curls.

'As long as you like.' Lyn was adding soap, loo paper and cleaning materials to her list. 'Mum doesn't want to get in the way, but she'd really love to stay right up to Christmas. She'd help you get the place straight.'

'I know she would, bless her. And I'd like her to. In fact I'd love you all to stay, if you'd like to.'

*   *   *

'So, what do you think of it all?' Luke put his arm round Joss's shoulders. They had lit a small fire and were standing looking down at it as the dry logs cracked and spat. Lyn and Alice and Joe had all gone to bed, exhausted by their day.

'I suppose it's like a dream come true.' Joss leaned her elbow against the heavy oak bressummer beam that spanned the huge fireplace, looking down into the flames. 'I think we should have the tree in here. A huge one, covered in fairy lights.'

'Sounds good.'

'Tom will be thrilled. He was too young to know what was going on last year.' Joss smiled to herself. 'Did you hear him talking to Dad: "Tom put paper there". He was getting really cross, taking it out of the bag as fast as Dad put it in.'

'Luckily your father loved it.' Luke frowned. 'It must be very strange for them, knowing this house belonged to your real parents.'

'Strange for them!' Joss shook her head hard, as if trying to clear her brain. 'Think what it's like for me. I don't even like to call Dad, Dad. It's as if I feel my other father might be listening.'

Luke nodded. 'I rang my parents while you were upstairs. Just to say we're here.'

Joss smiled fondly. 'How are they? How is life in Chicago?' She knew how much Luke was missing them, especially his father. Geoffrey Grant's sabbatical year in the States seemed to have dragged on for a long, long time.

'They're great. And they're coming home early next summer.' He paused. He and Joss had been planning a trip out to see them. That was not going to happen now, of course. 'They can't wait to see the house, Joss. It's hard to know how to explain all this over the phone.' He gave a snort of laughter.

Joss smiled. 'I suppose it is!' She lapsed into thoughtful silence.

'Have you had another look for the key to the desk in the study yet?' Luke nudged the logs with the toe of his trainer and watched with satisfaction as a curtain of sparks spread out over the sooty bricks at the back of the hearth.

'I haven't been in the study since we arrived this morning.' She stood up straight. 'I'm going to have a tot of Janet Goodyear's present and then I think I might go and have a poke around while you have your bath.'

The room was cold, the windows black reflections of the night. With a shiver Joss set her glass down on one of the little tables and went to close the shutters and pull the heavy brocade curtains. The table lamp threw a subdued light across the rugs on the floor, illuminating the abandoned work basket beside it. Joss stood looking down at it for a long time. There was a lump in her throat at the thought that her mother had used those small, filigree scissors and that the silver thimble must have fitted her finger. Hesitantly Joss reached for it and slipped it on her own finger. It fitted.

There was a key in the bottom of the work basket, lost under the silks and cotton threads – a small ornate key which Joss knew instinctively would fit the keyhole in the desk.

Reaching up she switched on the lamp which rested on the top of the desk, and stared at the array of small pigeon holes which the opened lid revealed. It was tidy but not empty and it was immediately obvious that the desk had been her mother's. Taking a sip from her glass Joss reached for a bundle of letters. With a strange feeling half of guilt, half excitement she pulled off the ribbon which bound them together.

They were all addressed to her mother and they came

from someone called Nancy. She glanced through them, wondering who Nancy was. A close friend and a gossip by the look of it, who had lived in Eastbourne. They told her nothing at all about her mother, but quite a lot about the unknown Nancy. With a tolerant smile she retied the ribbon and tucked them back in their place.

There were pens and a bottle of ink, paper clips, tags, envelopes, all the paraphernalia of a busy person; a drawer of unused headed note paper, and there, in another drawer by itself, a leather bound notebook. Curiously Joss pulled it out and opened it. On the flyleaf, in her mother's hand was written 'For my daughter, Lydia'. Joss shivered. Had her mother been so sure then that she would come to Belheddon; that one day she would sit down on this chair at this desk and pull open the drawers one by one until she found – she flicked it open – not a diary, as she had half expected, just empty pages, undated.

And one short scrawled paragraph, towards the middle of the book:

> He came again today, without warning and without mercy. My fear makes him stronger –

'Joss?' Luke's voice in the doorway made her jump out of her skin. He was dressed in his bathrobe and from where she sat she could smell the musky drift of his aftershave.

She slammed the book shut and took a deep breath.

'What is it? Is something wrong?'

'No. Nothing.' Slotting the notebook back into its drawer she pulled down the flap on the desk, turning the key. 'The desk was my mother's. It seems so strange to read her letters and things –'

My fear makes him stronger

Who, for God's sake? Who was her mother so frightened of and why had she written about him in an other-

53

wise empty notebook which she had left especially for Joss to read?

As she lay in the four poster bed, staring up at the silk decoration in the darkness over her head Joss found it hard to close her eyes. Beside her Luke had fallen into a restless sleep almost as soon as his head had touched the pillow. They were both worn out. After all, the day had started at five in London and now, at midnight, they were at Belheddon, and for better or for worse this was now their home.

Moving her head slightly to left or right Joss could see the squares of starlight which showed the two windows on opposite sides of the room. Divided by stone mullions in the old plaster one looked over the front of the house and down the drive towards the village, the other across the back garden and down towards the lake and beyond it, over the hedge to the river estuary and beyond it the distant North Sea. Initially Luke had closed the curtains when he came upstairs. They were heavy with woollen embroidery, double lined against the cold, luxurious. Looking at them Joss was grateful for their weight against the draughts, but even so, she pulled them open before she climbed into the high bed. 'Too claustrophobic,' she explained to Luke as he lay back beside her. His only answer, minutes later, was a gentle snore. Outside the moon shone onto a garden as bright as day as the frosty sparkle hardened into a skim of ice. Shivering, Joss huddled down under the duvet – a modern concession, the embroidered bed cover carefully folded away for safety – glad of the solid warmth of her sleeping husband. Surreptitiously her hand strayed to his shoulder. As she snuggled up against him in the darkness she did not see the slight movement in the corner of the room.

7

It was still dark when Joss slipped from the bed, tiptoeing across the icy floor in bare feet. Behind her Luke gave a quiet murmur and, punching the pillow turned over and went back to sleep. Switching on the light in the bathroom Joss reached for her clothes, left piled on the chair. Thick trousers, shirt, two sweaters, heavy thermal socks. In the ice cold room her breath came in small clouds. On the window pane, as she held back the curtain and peered out into the darkness she was enchanted and horrified to find the beautiful, lacy designs of Jack Frost on the inside of the glass. With a rueful smile she padded across the floor and glanced through Tom's door. Worn out by the excitement of the day before he was sleeping flat on his back, his arms above his head on the pillow, his cheeks pink with sleep. Tiptoeing to the chest where his night light burned she glanced at the thermometer which Alice had suggested they keep in the room. The temperature was steady. With a fond smile, she tiptoed out of the room and left the door slightly ajar. If he woke, Luke would hear him.

Putting the kettle onto the stove Joss went to the back door and pulled it open. The morning blackness was totally silent. No bird song. No traffic murmur in the distance as there would have been in London; no cheerful clank of milk bottles. Pulling on her heavy coat she stepped out into the courtyard. The bulk of the old Bentley had been pulled into the coach house and the doors closed. There was nothing here now, but their own Citroën, covered in a thick white frost. The gate out into the garden was painfully cold even beneath her gloved hands as she pushed it back and let herself out onto the matted lawn. Above her head the stars were still blazing as though it were full night. Glancing up she could see a faint light shining from behind the curtains in Lyn's room. Was she too unable to sleep in a strange bed?

The grass was spiky, brittle beneath her boots. Almost she could hear the tinkle of broken glass as she walked across it, skirting the skeletal branches of a blackly silhouetted tree, down towards the gleam of water. In the east now, she realised, the stars were dimming. Soon it would begin to grow light.

She stood for several moments, gloved hands in pockets, staring down at the ice as around her the garden began imperceptibly to brighten. She was numb with cold, but through the chill she could feel something else. Apprehension – fear even – for what they had done. They had had no real choice. Even if Luke had found a job working for someone else she doubted if they could have afforded the rent on a flat of a decent size and certainly they couldn't have bought somewhere of their own. They could no longer live in London. But this, this was so different. Another world from the one they had planned together when they had first got married. She frowned, stamping her feet, reluctant as yet to go back inside. A new world, new people, new memories – no, memories wasn't the right word. A history to be learned and assimilated and in some way lived.

Sammy!

The voice, a boy's voice, called suddenly out of the darkness behind her. Joss spun round.

56

Sammy!

It came again, more distant now.

Across the lawn, in the house, a light had appeared in her and Luke's bedroom. The curtains weren't quite closed and a broad vee of light flooded out across the frosted grass.

'Hello?' Joss's voice was a husky intrusion into the intense silence. 'Who's there?' She glanced round. The stars were disappearing fast now. A dull greyness was drifting in amongst the bushes in the shrubbery near her. She frowned. 'Is there someone there?' She called again, more loudly this time, her voice seeming to echo across the water. In the distance a bird called loudly. Then the silence returned.

Turning sharply back to the house she found she was shivering violently as she hurried back in the direction of the kitchen. Pulling off her boots and gloves she ran inside, blowing on her fingers, to find the kettle cheerfully filling the room with steam. When Luke appeared, some ten minutes later, she was sitting at the table, still in her heavy coat, her hands cupped around a mug of tea.

'So, Joss, how is it?' He smiled at her as he found himself a mug on the draining board.

She reached up to kiss him on the mouth. 'Wonderful, strange. Terrifying.'

He laughed, briefly resting his hand over hers. 'We'll cope. Joss.' His face became serious for a moment. 'Are you happy about Alice and Joe staying? You don't want to establish your own territory a bit before they muscle in?' He searched her face seriously. 'I know how much this house means to you, love. I do understand how you must feel about it all. If there is any conflict –'

'There isn't.' She shook her head adamantly. 'I need them here, Luke. I can't explain it, but I need them. It's as though they represent something solid, something to

57

hang on to – a life belt – from my old life. Besides, I love them. They are my parents. Whatever, whoever Laura was, I never knew her.' Pushing back the chair she stood up abruptly. 'I don't want her taking over my life. I don't want her to think she can buy my affection – my love – with all this.' She gestured at the kitchen around them.

'I don't think that's what she intended, Joss.' Luke was watching her, puzzled. Her dark hair had fallen in a curtain across her eyes and she hadn't tossed it back, a habitual gesture of hers which he loved. Instead it hung there, hiding her face, concealing her expression.

'Luke.' She still hadn't looked at him. 'I walked down to the lake while it was still dark. There was someone out there.'

'Out in the garden?' He pulled up a chair and sat opposite her. 'Who?'

'They were calling. For someone called Sammy.'

He laughed. 'Probably a cat. You know how sound travels. On a cold, still night, and near water. It was probably someone in the village.'

At last she had pushed back her hair. She gave him a small lop-sided grin, blowing on her tea. 'Of course. Why didn't I think of that.'

'Because you are an idiot and I love you.' He smiled, still watching her face. She was white with exhaustion. The stress of the last two months had told heavily on her. Preoccupied with the business he had had to leave the organisation of the sale of the house, the packing and the move to her as well as the frequent trips to East Anglia to supervise the opening up of the house and the checks to the plumbing and electricity and although Lyn had from time to time taken Tom off her hands for a few hours to help her, he knew the strain had been enormous. She had lost about a stone and the dark rings under her eyes were gaunt reminders of night after night tossing sleepless beside him as they lay staring up at the

58

ceiling locked in silent thought in the dark before the move.

'First day of the rest of our lives, Joss.' He raised his mug to clink against hers. 'Cheers.'

'Cheers.' She smiled.

Alice and Joe appeared some half hour later as Joss was strapping Tom into his high chair. 'Good morning, sweetheart.' Alice stopped and kissed the little boy on the head. 'Joss, my love, your father and I have been talking and we've decided to go back to town today.'

'But Mum –' Joss stared at her aghast. 'Why? I thought you liked it here –'

'We do, Jossie.' Joe sat down and pulled the teapot towards him. 'And we'll be back. We've things to do at home, and shopping.' He wiggled his eyebrows at Tom, who giggled and banged his spoon on the table in front of him. 'Shopping to do with Father Christmas. We'll be back, love, before you know it. Your mum needs to rest a bit, Joss. She's not really up to doing much at the moment.' He shook his head. 'And I know her. She won't be able to sit still as long as she knows there's work to be done and besides, I think, and your mother agrees with me, that you and Luke need a few days to settle in on your own.'

'But we don't. We've already discussed this, and I want you here.' She knew she sounded like a spoiled child. With a miserable sniff Joss turned towards the stove and reached for the kettle. 'You can't go. Mum needn't do anything heavy. She can rest here –'

'I think maybe they're right, Joss,' Luke said quietly. He glanced over her head at his father-in-law.

'Well, at least Lyn can stay.' Joss took a deep breath. Picking up a jug of milk she reached for Tom's beaker.

'No, love. Lyn is coming with us.' Joe hooked the toast rack towards him. Selecting a piece he buttered it and cut it into strips, putting them down in front of his grandson.

'We've talked it over with her too. She can come back next week if you want her, if she hasn't got another temporary job by then.' He sighed. Uninterested in anything academic Lyn had left school at sixteen and drifted from one unsatisfactory temporary job to another. While Joss had stayed on to do her A levels and followed that with a brilliant career at Bristol University and then a teaching post, Lyn, at the age of twenty-eight, with two failed relationships and an aborted attempt at running her own catering business behind her, had moved back in with her parents and resumed her half-hearted trawl through the agencies. Joe shook his head. 'Then your mum and I will return on the Wednesday after that in plenty of time for Christmas. And we'll all stay as long as you like to help you get straight.'

'They had it all planned!' Standing in the coach house later, with Tom's gloved hand clutched in her own Joss stared at her husband's back as he leaned over the huge rusting engine of the Bentley. 'Why? Was it your idea?'

Luke straightened. 'No, it wasn't. But I had the same feeling they did. You need to be here on your own, Joss. It's important. You need to explore. To get the feel of the place. They know you as well as I do – better, for God's sake. We all know how special places are to you.' He walked over to the bench by the wall where already he had laid out a selection of his tools.

She shook her head. 'Am I so predictable? You can all tell how I feel before I feel it?'

'Fraid so!' He chuckled.

'And what about you? What are you going to feel about this place?'

'Cold mostly.' And uneasy, he was going to say, though he wasn't quite sure why. The same way Joe and Alice had felt. They hadn't said anything, but he could see it in their eyes. No wonder they had wanted to get away. 'So, if you could arrange to have the kettle on in say half an hour, I can come in and thaw out. I want to keep to my plan if I can. Work on the old bus for George Maxim in the mornings, and on the house and garden in the afternoon. That way I can divide my time. Joss –' He looked suddenly concerned. 'We weren't all ganging up on you, love. I promise. Listen, if you think you are going to feel a bit lonely, why don't you ask that Goodyear woman and her husband over for a meal. They are obviously dying to find out about us and we can do some reciprocal pumping about the house.'

'Right, Tom Tom, let's start at the top today for a change.' Two days of unrelenting unpacking and sorting and cleaning later, her phone call made, and her invitation for supper at the end of the week ecstatically accepted by the Goodyears and the Fairchilds at the post office, Joss picked up a duster and broom and made for the stairs, the little boy running purposefully behind her.

In the attics a series of small rooms led out of one another, all empty, all wallpapered in small faded flowers and leaves, all with sloping ceilings and dark, dusty beams. Those facing south were full of bright winter sunshine warm behind the glass of the windows; those which looked out over the front of the house were cold and shadowed. Joss glanced at the little boy. He was staying very close to her, his thumb firmly held in his mouth. 'Nice house, Tom?' She smiled at him encouragingly. They were looking at a pile of old books.

'Tom go down.' He reached out for her long sweater and wound his fingers into it.

'We'll go down in a minute, to make Daddy some coffee –' She broke off. Somewhere nearby she heard a child's laugh. There was a scuffle of feet running, then silence.

'Boy.' Tom informed her hopefully. He peered round her shyly.

61

Joss swallowed. 'There aren't any boys here, Tom Tom.' But of course, there must be. Boys from the village. The house had been empty so long it would have been very strange if no one had found their way in to explore the old place.

'Hello?' she called. 'Who's there?'

There was silence.

'Sammy?' She remembered the name out of nowhere; out of the dark. 'Sammy, are you there?' The silence was intense. It no longer seemed to be the silence of emptiness; it was a listening, enquiring silence.

'Mummy, look.' Tom tugged at her sweater. 'Flutterby!' A ragged peacock butterfly, woken by the heat of the sun on the glass was fluttering feebly against the window, its wings shushing faintly, shedding red-blue dust.

'Poor thing, it's trapped.' Joss looked at it sadly. To let it go out into the cold would mean certain death.

The laughter came from the other end of the attic this time; pealing, joyous, followed again by the sound of feet. Tom laughed. 'See boys,' he cried. 'Me wants to see boys.'

'Mummy wants to see boys too,' Joss agreed. She stooped and picked him up, abandoning the butterfly as she pulled open the door which separated this room from the next. 'They shouldn't be here. We're going to have to tell them to go home for their lunch –' She broke off. The next room, larger than the rest, was the last. Beyond it, out of the high windows she could look down on the stableyard, seeing the doors pulled wide where Luke was standing in the coach house entrance talking to a strange man. Joss swung round. 'Where have those naughty boys gone?'

'Naughty boys gone.' Tom echoed sadly. He too was staring round, tears welling in his eyes. This was where the sound of the children had come from without a doubt, but the room was empty even of the clutter which had stood in some of the others. The boards, sloping with age, were dusty. They showed no foot marks.

'Tom, I think we'll go downstairs.' She was uneasy. 'Let's go and make Daddy his coffee, then you can go and call him for me.' She backed towards the door. Suddenly she didn't want to meet these hidden children after all.

The morning of their first informal supper party three days later Luke pulled open the cellar door and switched on the lights. Tom was asleep upstairs when he had dragged Joss away from her polishing. 'Let's have a real look at that wine. We'll see if we can find something decent to drink tonight.'

Running down the creaking staircase ahead of her he stared round. The cellar was cold and smelled strongly of damp. A preliminary glance a few days earlier had to their excitement told them the cellar contained a great deal of wine; racks of bottles, bins and cases stretched away into the darkness of a second cellar beyond the first. 'Joss?' He turned and looked for her.

Joss was standing at the top of the stairs.

'Joss, come on. Help me choose.'

She shook her head. 'I'm sorry, Luke. No.' She took a step backwards. She couldn't explain her sudden revulsion. 'I'll go and put on the coffee or something.'

He stared up at the doorway. 'Joss? What's wrong?' But she had gone. He shrugged. Turning he stood in front of the first wine rack and stared at it. Joss's father had obviously had a good eye. He recognised some of the vintages, but this would need an expert to look at it one day. Perhaps David Tregarron would advise him when he came down to see them. David's passion for wine, even greater than his love of history had been legendary in Joss's staff room. Luke shivered. It was cold down here – good for the wine of course, but not for people. Reaching out towards the rack he stopped suddenly and turning looked behind him. He thought he had heard something in the corner of the cellar out of sight behind the racks. He listened, his eyes searching the shadows where the light from the single strip light failed to reach. There was no other sound.

Uncomfortably he moved slightly. 'Joss? Are you still up there?' His voice sounded very hollow. There was no reply.

He turned back to the wine rack, trying to concentrate on the bottles, but in spite of himself he was listening, glancing towards the darker corners. Grabbing two bottles at last, more or less at random, he looked round with a shiver and then turning for the stairs, raced up them two at a time. Slamming the cellar door behind him he turned the key with relief. Then he laughed out loud. 'Clot! What did you think was down there!' By the time he had reached the kitchen and put the bottles on the table he had recovered himself completely.

Roy and Janet Goodyear and the Fairchilds arrived together for their first dinner party at exactly eight o'clock, trooping in through the back door and standing staring round in the kitchen with evident delight.

'Well, you've certainly made a fine job of everything,' Roy Goodyear commented thoughtfully when they had all returned to the kitchen after a tour of the house. 'It all looks so nice and lived in, now.' Joss followed his gaze. It did look good. Their china and glass unpacked, the dresser decorated with pretty plates and flowers, the long table laid and the range warming the room to a satisfactory glow. Luke had strung their Christmas cards from the bell wires and a huge bunch of mistletoe hung over the door out into the pantry.

'I'm sorry we're eating in the kitchen.' Joss filled up Janet's glass.

'My dear, we wouldn't want to be anywhere else.

64

You've got it really lovely and cosy here.' Sally Fairchild had seated herself at the table, her elbows spread amongst the knives and forks. Joss could see her gaze going now and then to the corn dolly which Luke had suspended from a length of fishing twine over the table.

'I expect the Duncans were very formal when they lived here.' Luke lifted the heavy casserole from the oven and carried it to the table. 'Sit down, Roy. And you, Alan.'

'They were when Philip was alive.' Roy Goodyear levered his heavy frame into a chair next to his wife. In his late fifties he was taller by a head than Janet, his face weather-beaten to the colour of raw steak, his eyes a strangely light amber under the bushy grey brows. 'Your father was a very formal man, Joss.' Both couples now knew the full story of Joss's parentage. 'But in the sixties people from his background still did observe all the formalities. They wouldn't have known anything else. They kept a staff here of course. Cook and housemaid and two gardeners. When we came to dinner here we always dressed. Philip had a magnificent cellar.' He cocked an eye at Luke. 'I suppose it's too much to hope that it's still there.'

'It is, as a matter of fact.' He glanced at Joss. He had not mentioned his hasty exit from the cellar to her, nor asked her why she had refused to go down there with him. 'We've got a friend in London – Joss's ex boss, in fact – who is a bit of a wine buff. I thought we might ask him to come down and have a look at it.'

Roy had already glanced at the bottle and nodded contentedly. 'Well, if he needs any help or encouragement, don't forget your neighbours across the fields, I would very much like to see what you've got.'

'Apart from the ghost, of course,' Janet put in quietly.

There was a moment's silence. Joss glanced at her sharply. 'I suppose there had to be a ghost.'

'And not just any old ghost either. The village say it is

65

the devil himself who lives here.' Alan Fairchild raised his glass and squinted through it critically. 'Isn't that right, Janet? You are the expert on these matters.' He grinned broadly. Silent until now he was obviously enjoying the sensation his words had caused.

'Alan!' Sally Fairchild blushed pink in the candlelight. 'I told you not to say anything about all that. These poor people! They've got to live here.'

'Well, if he lives in the cellar, I didn't see him.' With a glance at Joss Luke lifted the lid off the casserole for her and handed her the serving ladle, his face veiled in fragrant steam.

Joss was frowning. 'If we're sharing the house, I'd like to know who with,' she said. She smiled at Alan. 'Come on. Spill the beans. Who else lives here? I know we have visits from time to time by village children. I'd quite like that to stop. I don't know how they get in.'

'Kids are the end these days.' Janet reached for a piece of bread. 'No discipline at all. It shouldn't surprise me if they do come here because the house has been empty for so long, but with the legend –' she paused. 'I'd have thought they'd be too scared.'

'The devil you mean?' Joss's voice was light, but Luke could hear the edge to it.

He reached for a plate. 'You're not serious about the devil, I hope.'

'Of course he's not serious.' It was Joss who answered. 'All old houses have legends, and we should be pleased this one is no exception.'

'It's a very old site, of course,' Janet said thoughtfully. 'I believe it goes back to Roman times. Houses with a history as long as that always seem very glamorous. They collect legends. It doesn't mean there is anything to be frightened of. After all Laura lived here for years practically on her own, and I believe her mother did before that, when she was widowed.'

My fear makes him stronger

The words in Joss's head for a moment blotted out all other conversation. Her mother, alone in the house, had been terrified.

'Have the family owned the house for a long time then?' Luke was carrying round the dish of sprouts.

'I should think a hundred years, certainly. Maybe more than that. If you look in the church you'll see memorials to people who have lived at the Hall. But I don't think the same name crops up again and again the way it does in some parishes.' Roy shrugged. 'You want to talk to one of the local history buffs. They'll know all about it. Someone like Gerald Andrews. He lives in Ipswich now, but he had a house in the village here for years, and I think he wrote a booklet about this place. I'll give you his phone number.'

'You said my mother lived here practically on her own,' Joss said thoughtfully. Everyone served at last she sat down and reached for her napkin. 'Did she not have a companion, then?'

He came again today without warning and without mercy

The words had etched themselves into her brain. They conjured for her a picture of a woman alone, victimised. Terrified, in the large, empty house.

'She had several, I believe. I don't think any of them stayed very long and at the end she lived here quite alone, although of course Mary Sutton always stayed in close touch with her. I don't think Laura minded being alone though, do you Janet? She used to walk down to the village every day with her dog, and she had lots of visitors. She wasn't in any sense a recluse. People used to come down from London. And of course there was the Frenchman.'

'The Frenchman?' Luke's eyebrows shot up. 'That sounds definitely intriguing.'

'It was.' Janet smiled. 'My dear, I don't know if it's

true. It was just village gossip, but everyone thought, in the end, that that was where she had gone. She went to live in France and we guessed she'd gone to be with him. She was a very attractive woman.'

'As is her daughter!' Gallantly Roy raised his glass.

Joss smiled at him. 'And the house stayed empty after she left?'

'Completely. The village was devastated. It was – is – after all the heart and soul of the place, together with the church. Have you made contact with Mary Sutton, yet?'

Joss shook her head. 'I've tried every time I've been into the village, but there is never any answer. I wondered if she's gone away or something?'

The four guests glanced at each other. Sally Fairchild shrugged. 'That's strange. She's there. She's not ill or anything. She was in the shop yesterday.' She shook her head. 'Perhaps she's nervous of answering the door to a stranger. I'll have a word next time she comes in. Tell her who you are. You must speak to her. She worked here for years. She would remember your mother as a child.'

'And she would presumably remember the devil if she'd met him face to face.' Joss's words, spoken with a seriousness which she hadn't perhaps intended, were followed by a moment of silence.

'Joss –' Luke warned.

'My dear, I've upset you.' Alan was looking contrite. 'Take no notice of me. It's a silly tale. Suitable for round the fire, late at night, well-into-your-third-brandy sessions. Not to be taken seriously.'

'I know.' Joss forced a smile. 'I'm sorry. I didn't intend to sound so portentous.' She reached for her wine glass and twisted it between her fingers. 'You knew Edgar Gower, presumably, when he was here?' She turned to Roy.

He nodded. 'Great fun, Edgar. What a character! Now he knew your mother very well indeed.'

Joss nodded. 'It was he who put me in touch with the solicitor; it was through him I found out about Belheddon.' She glanced at Luke and then turned back to the Goodyears. 'He tried to dissuade me from following it up. He felt the house was an unhappy place.'

'He was a superstitious old buffer,' Janet snorted fondly. 'He used to encourage Laura to think the house was haunted. It upset her a lot. I got very cross with him.'

'So you didn't believe in the ghosts?'

'No.' The hesitation had been infinitesimal. 'And don't let him get to you, either, Joss. I'm sure the bishop thought he was going a bit dotty at the end and that's why he retired him. Keep away from him, my dear.'

'I wrote to him to say we'd inherited the house. I wanted to thank him, but he never replied.' She had also phoned twice but there had been no answer.

'That's hardly surprising. He's probably too busy having apocalyptic visions!' Roy put in.

'No, that's unfair!' Janet turned on her husband. 'They go off to South Africa every winter since his retirement to spend several months with their daughter. That's why he's not been in touch, Joss.'

'I see.' Joss was astonished for a moment at her disappointment. She had seen Edgar as a strength, there in the background to advise them if ever they should need it. His words returned to her suddenly – words she tried to push to the back of her mind whenever she remembered them; words she had never repeated to Luke. 'I prayed you would never come to find me, Jocelyn Grant.'

The conversation had moved on without her. Vaguely she heard Alan talking about village cricket then Sally laughing at some anecdote about a neighbour. She missed it. Edgar's voice was still there in her ears: 'There is too much unhappiness attached to that house. The past is the past. It should be allowed to rest.' She shook her head abruptly. He had asked her if she had children and when she had told him, he had said nothing; and he had sighed.

Pushing her chair back with a shiver, she stood up suddenly. 'Luke, give everyone second helpings. I'm just going to pop upstairs and make sure Tom is all right.'

The hall was silent, lit by the table lamp in the corner. She paused for a moment, shivering in the draught which swept in under the front door. The kitchen was the only room in the house they had so far managed to heat up to modern standards, thanks to the range.

She needed to think. Staring at the lamp her mind was whirling. Edgar Gower; the house; her mother's fear; there had to be some basis for all the stories. And the devil. Why should people think the devil lived at Belheddon?

Pushing open the heavy door into the great hall she stopped in horror. Tom's piercing screams filled the room, echoing down the stairs from his bedroom.

'Tom!' She took the stairs two at a time. The little boy was standing up in his cot, tears streaming down his face, his hands locked onto the bars. The room was ice cold. In the near darkness of the teddy bear night light in the corner she could see his small face beetroot red in the shadows. Swooping on him she scooped him up into her arms. His pyjamas were soaking wet.

'Tom, what is it, darling.' She nuzzled his hair. He was dripping with sweat.

'Tom go home.' His sobs were heart rending. 'Tom go to Tom's house.'

Joss bit her lip. 'This is Tom's house, darling. Tom's new house.' She cradled his head against her shoulder. 'What happened? Did you have a bad dream?'

70

She held him away from her on her knee, studying his face. 'Tom Tom? What is it?'

'Tom go home.' He was staring over her shoulder towards the window, snuffling pathetically, taking comfort from her arms.

'I tell you what.' She reached to turn on the main light, flooding the room with brightness. 'Let's change your jym-jams, and make you a nice clean, dry bed, then you can come downstairs for a few minutes to Mummy and Daddy's party before going back to sleep. How would that be?'

Holding him on her hip she went through the familiar routine, extracting clean dry clothes and bedding from his chest of drawers, changing him, sponging his face and hands, brushing his hair with the soft baby hairbrush, aware that every few minutes he kept glancing back towards the window. His thumb had been firmly plugged into his mouth as she sat him on the rug and turned to make his bed, stripping off the wet covers, wiping over the rubber sheet.

'Man go away.' He took his thumb out long enough to speak and then plugged it in again.

Joss turned. 'What man?' Her voice was sharper than she intended, and she saw the little boy's eyes fill with tears. Desperately he held out his arms to her. Stooping she hauled him off the ground. 'What man, Tom Tom? Did you dream about a nasty man?' In spite of herself she followed his gaze to the corner of the room. She had found some pretty ready made curtains for his window. They showed clowns somersaulting through hoops and balloons and ribbons. Those and the soft colourful rugs had turned the nursery into one of the brightest rooms in the house. But in the shadows of the little night light, had there been anything there to cast a shadow and frighten him? She bit her lip.

'Tell me about the man, Tom,' she said gently.

71

'Tin man.' Tom reached for the locket on a chain round her neck and pulled it experimentally. She smiled, firmly extricating it from his grasp. 'A tin man? From one of your books?' That explained it. She sighed with relief. Lyn must have been reading him *The Wizard of Oz* before she left. With a glance round the room she hugged him close. 'Come on, Tom Tom, let's take you down to meet the neighbours.'

She knew from experience that within ten minutes, sitting on Luke's knee in a warm kitchen, the little boy would be fast asleep and tomorrow before anything else she would buy a baby alarm so that never again would the little boy scream unheard in his distant bedroom. With a final glance round she carried him out into the darkened main bedroom. It was very cold in there. The undrawn curtains allowed frosty moonlight to spill across the floor, reflecting a soft gleam on the polished oak boards, throwing the shadow from the four poster bed as thick bars over the rug in front of her feet. She stopped, cradling Tom's head against her shoulder, staring suddenly into the far corner. It was deep in shadow. Her jacket, hanging from the wardrobe handle, was a wedge of blackness against the black. Her arms tightened around the little boy protectively.

Katherine

It was a whisper in the silence. Tom raised his head. 'Daddy?' he said. He craned round her shoulder to see.

Joss shook her head slightly. It was nothing. Her imagination. Luke was in the kitchen. 'No, darling. There's no one there.' She kissed his head. 'Daddy's downstairs. Let's go and find him.'

'Tin man.' The thumb was drawn out of the mouth long enough for Tom to point over her shoulder into the darkness of the corner. 'Tin man there.' His face crumpled and a small sob escaped him before he buried his face in her shoulder again.

72

'No, darling. No tin man. Just shadows.' Joss made for the door. She almost ran along the corridor and down the stairs.

'Hey, who is this?' Roy stood up and held out his arms to Tom. 'How come you've been missing the party, old chap?'

'Joss?' Luke had spotted Joss's white face. 'What is it. What was wrong?'

She shook her head. 'Nothing. He was crying and we didn't hear him. I expect he had a bad dream.'

A dream about a tin man who skulked in dark corners.

he drawers of the desk were full of papers and letters, the general detritus of a life time, dealt with, filed, and forgotten. Sitting on the floor with them spread out around her a couple of evenings later Joss could find nothing to explain or even relate to her mother's mysterious notebook. She had studied it again and again. No pages had been torn out. No entries eradicated in any way. It was as if, having carefully inscribed the flyleaf for Joss, her mother had once, and once only, grabbed the empty notebook in desperation and scribbled those two lone sentences in it. They haunted Joss. They were a plea for help, a despairing scream. What had happened? Who could have upset her so much? Could it have been the Frenchman who the village thought had come to woo her?

She had said nothing to Luke about the notebook. It was as if her mother had whispered a secret to her and she did not want to betray the confidence. This was something she had to find out on her own. Putting down the notebook she reached for the coffee mug standing on the carpet next to her and sipped thoughtfully, staring out of the French doors across the lawn. There had been another heavy frost in the night and the grass was still white in the shelter of the tall hedge beyond the stables. Above it the sky was a clear brilliant blue. In the silence, through the window she could hear the clear ring of metal on metal. Luke was well into his work on the Bentley.

A robin hopped across the York stone terrace outside the window and stood head to one side staring down at the ground. Joss smiled. Earlier she had thrown out the breakfast crumbs, but there was little left now after the flock of sparrows and blackbirds had descended on them from the trees.

The house was very silent. Tom was asleep and for now at least she had the place to herself. Lightly she touched the back of the notebook with her finger. 'Mother.' The word hovered in the air. The room was very cold. Joss shivered. She had two thick sweaters on over her jeans and a long silk scarf wound round and round her neck against the insidious draughts which permeated the house but even so her hands were frozen. In a moment she would go back to the kitchen to warm up and replenish her coffee. In a moment. She sat still, staring round, trying to feel her mother's presence. The room had been Laura's special, favourite place, of that she had no doubt. Her mother's books, her sewing, her desk, her letters – and yet nothing remained. There was no scent in the cushions, no warmth of contact as her hand brushed the place where her mother's hand had been, no vibrations which still held the vital essence of the woman who had borne her.

The envelope with the French stamp had slipped between some old bills in a faded green cardboard wallet. Joss stared down at it for a moment, registering the slanted handwriting, the faded violet ink. The post mark, she noted was Paris and the year it was posted 1979. Inside was one flimsy sheet of paper.

'Ma chère Laura – As you see I did not reach home yesterday as I intended. My appointment was postponed until tomorrow. I shall ring you afterwards. Take care of yourself, my dear lady. My prayers are with you.'

Joss squinted at the paper more closely. The signature was an indecipherable squiggle. Screwing up her eyes she tried to make out the first letter. P? B? Sighing, she laid the paper down. There was no address.

'So, what are you up to?' Luke had come into the room so quietly she had not heard him.

Startled she looked up. 'Sorting through the desk.'

He was dressed like her in several old sweaters; over them the stained overalls and the woollen scarf did nothing to hide how cold he was. He rubbed his oily hands together. 'Feel like some coffee? I need to thaw out.'

'Yes please.' She was pushing the papers together in a heap on the carpet in front of her when the telephone rang. 'Mrs Grant?' The voice was unfamiliar; female; elderly. 'I understand you have been trying to reach me. My name is Mary Sutton.'

Joss felt a leap of excitement. 'That's right, Mrs Sutton –'

'Miss, dear. Miss Sutton.' The voice the other end was suddenly prim. 'I do not answer my door to strangers, you understand. But now I know who you are you may come and see me. I have something which may interest you.'

'Now?' Joss was taken aback.

'That's right. It is here, now.'

'Right. I'll come over now.' Joss shrugged as she hung up. 'A somewhat peremptory Miss Sutton wishes to see me now. I'll take a rain check on the coffee, Luke, and go before she changes her mind. She says she has something for me. Will you watch Tom Tom?'

'OK.' Luke leaned across and kissed her cheek. 'See you later then.'

This time when Joss knocked at the cottage door on the green it opened almost immediately. Mary Sutton was a small wizened woman with wispy white hair, caught back in a knot on the top of her head. Her narrow, birdlike face was framed by heavy tortoiseshell spectacles.

Joss was shown into a small neat front room which smelled strongly of old baking and long dead flowers. A heavy brown oil cloth covered the table on which was a small notebook. It was identical to the one Joss had found in her mother's desk. Her eyes were glued to it as she took the proffered seat on an upright chair near the window.

After several long seconds of silent scrutiny the solemn face before her broke suddenly into a huge beam. 'You may call me Mary, my dear, as your mother did.' Mary turned away and began to pour out tea which had been laid ready on a tray on the sideboard. 'I looked after you when you were very small. It was I who gave you to the adoption people when they came to collect you.' She blinked hard through her pebble lenses. 'Your mother could not bring herself to be there. She walked in the fields down by the river until you had gone.'

Joss stared at her aghast, trapped into silence by the lump in her throat. Behind the glasses the old lady's eyes, magnified into huge half globes, were brimming with tears.

'Why did she give me away?' It was several minutes before Joss could bring herself to ask. She accepted the tea cup with shaking hands and put it down hastily on the edge of the table. Her eyes had returned from Mary's face to the notebook.

'It was not because she didn't love you, my dear. On the contrary, she did it because she loved you so much.' Mary sat down and pulled her skirt tightly over her knees, tucking the voluminous fabric under her bony legs. 'The others had died, you see. She thought if you stayed at Belheddon, you would die too.'

'The others?' Joss's mouth was dry.

'Sammy and George. Your brothers.'

'Sammy?' Joss stared at her. She had gone cold all over.

'What dear?' Mary frowned. 'What did you say?'

77

'You looked after them? My brothers?' Joss whispered.

Mary nodded. 'Since they were born.' She gave a wistful little smile. 'Little rascals they were, both of them. So like their father. Your mother adored them. It nearly broke her when she lost them. First Sammy, then Georgie. It was too much for any woman to bear.'

'How old were they when they died?' Joss's fingers were clenched in her lap.

'Sammy was seven, near as makes no difference. Georgie was born a year after that, in 1954, and he died on his eighth birthday, bless him.'

'How?' Joss's whisper was almost inaudible.

'Terrible. Both of them. Sammy had been collecting tadpoles. They found him in the lake.' There was a long silence. 'When Georgie died it was nearly the end of your mother.'

Joss stared at her speechlessly as, shaking her head, Mary sipped at her tea. 'They found him at the bottom of the cellar steps, you see. He knew he was never allowed down there, and Mr Philip, he had the cellar keys. They were still there, locked in his desk.' She sighed. 'Sorrows long gone, my dear. You must not grieve over them. Your mother would not have wanted that.' She reached for the notebook and took it off the table, holding it on her lap with little gentle stroking movements of her fingers. 'I've kept this all these years. It's right you should have them. Your mother's poems.' Still she didn't release the volume, holding it close as if she could not bear to part with it.

'You must have loved her very much,' Joss said at last. She found there were tears in her eyes.

Mary made no response, continuing to stroke the notebook quietly.

'Did you – did you know the French gentleman who came here?' She studied the old lady's face. There was a slight pursing of the lips, no more.

'I knew him.'

'What was he like?'

'Your mother was fond of him.'

'I don't even know his name.'

Mary looked up at last. This at least was something she seemed able to divulge without reservation. 'Paul Deauville. He was an art dealer. He travelled the world I understand.'

'Did he live in Paris?'

'He did.'

'And my mother went to live with him?'

A definite frisson – almost a shudder. 'He took your mother away from Belheddon.'

'Do you think he made her happy?'

Mary met Joss's eye and held it steady through the grotesquely magnifying lenses of her glasses. 'I hope so, my dear. I never heard from her again after she left.'

As if she were afraid she had said too much Mary clamped her lips shut, and after several more perfunctory attempts at questioning her Joss rose to leave. It was only as she turned to walk through the front door into the blinding frosty sunlight that Mary at last relinquished the notebook.

'Take care of it. There is so little of her left.' The old lady caught her arm.

'I will.' Joss hesitated. 'Mary, will you come and see us? I should like you to meet my little boy, Tom.'

'No.' Mary shook her head. 'No, my dear. I'll not come to the house if you don't mind. Best not.' With that she stepped back into the shadows of her narrow front hall and closed the door almost in Joss's face.

The graves were there, beyond her father's. Quite over-grown now, she hadn't seen the two small white cross headstones side by side in the nettles under the tree. She stood looking down at them for a long time. Samuel John and George Philip. Someone had left a small bowl of white chrysanthemums on each. Joss smiled through her tears. Mary at least had never forgotten them.

Luke and Tom were busy in the coach house when she got home. With one look at their happy oily faces she left them to their mechanical endeavours and clutching the notebook retreated to the study. The sunshine through the window had warmed the room, and she smiled a little to herself as she stooped and throwing on some logs, coaxed the fire back into life. In a few moments it would be almost bearable. Curling up on the arm chair in the corner she opened the notebook at the first page. *Laura Manners – Commonplace Book.* The inscription in the flyleaf of this notebook was in the same flamboyant hand as that in the other. She glanced at the first few pages and felt a sharp pang of disappointment. She had assumed her mother would have written the poems herself, but these were bits and pieces copied out from many authors – a collection obviously of her favourite poems and pieces of prose. There was Keats's ode *To Autumn*, a couple of Shakespeare sonnets, some Byron, Gray's *Elegy*.

Slowly, page after page she leafed through, reading a few lines here and there, trying to form a picture of her mother's taste and education from the words on the page. Romantic; eclectic, occasionally obscure. There were lines from Racine and Dante in the original French and Italian, a small verse from Schiller. She was something of a linguist then. There were even Latin epigrams. Then suddenly the mood of the book changed. Stuck between two pages was a single sheet, old and torn, very frail, held in place by tape which had discoloured badly. It was an India paper page, torn, Joss guessed from a Roman Missal. On it, in English and in Latin, was a prayer for the blessing of Holy Water.

> ... I do this that the evil spirit may be driven
> away from thee, and that thou mayest banish
> the enemy's power entirely, uprooting and cast-
> ing out the enemy himself with all his rebel
> angels . . .
>
> ... so that whatsoever in the homes of the
> faithful or elsewhere shall have been sprinkled
> with it may be delivered from everything
> unclean and hurtful. Let no breath of contagion
> hover there, no taint of corruption. May all the
> wiles of the lurking enemy come to nothing,
> and may anything that threatens the safety or
> peace of those who dwell there be put to flight
> by the sprinkling of this water . . .

Joss stared round, letting the book fall into her lap,
realising she had been reading the words out loud. The
house was very silent.

Exorcizo te, in nomine Dei † *Patris omnipotentis, et in nomine
Jesu* † *Christi Filii ejus, Domine nostri, et in virtute Spiritus* †
Sancti . . .

The devil himself lives here . . .

Alan Fairchild's words echoed through her head.

For several minutes she sat staring into space then,
closing the notebook she stood up and going to the desk,
she reached for the phone.

David Tregarron was in the staff room marking test papers
when her call was put through.

'So, how is life in the outback, Jocelyn?' His booming
voice seemed to echo round the room.

'Quite a strain actually.' She frowned. The words had
come spontaneously, accurately, instead of the easier
platitude she had framed in her head. 'I hope you can
come and see us soon.' She sounded so much more desperate than she had intended. 'David, would you do me a

81

favour? When you are next in the British Library reading room would you look up Belheddon for me and see if you can find anything about its history.'

There was a slight pause as he tried to interpret her tone. 'Of course I will. From what you said before it sounds like a wonderful old place. I'm looking forward to my first visit.'

'So am I.' She heard the fervour in her voice with surprise. 'I'd like to know what the name means.'

'Belheddon? That sounds fairly straightforward. Bel – beautiful, of course, or if the name is much older it might come from a Celtic derivation, like the Irish, which if I remember it rightly, has much the same meaning as Aber in Wales or Scotland – the mouth of a river. Or it could come from the old gods Bel, you remember Beltane, or Baal from the Bible who came to represent the devil himself. Then I think heddon means heather – or a temple on a heathery hill or some such –'

'What did you say?' Joss's voice was sharp.

'A temple –'

'No, before that. About the devil.'

'Well, it's just a possibility I suppose. Rather romantic really. Perhaps the original site housed a temple.'

'There's a local legend, David, that the devil lives here.' Her voice was strangely thin and harsh.

'And you sound afraid rather than amused. Oh, come on Joss. You're not letting the credulous yokels get to you, are you?' The jovial manner had dropped away abruptly. 'You don't believe in any of this, surely?'

'Of course not.' She laughed. 'I'd just like to know why the house has this reputation. It is a bit sort of dramatic!'

'Well, I suppose it is on dark nights with the wind howling round. I must say, I can't wait to come and see it.' There was a pause. 'I don't suppose I could look in this weekend, could I? I know it's getting awfully near

Christmas but term's practically over. I can look a few things up for you; find a few books, perhaps?'

She laughed, extraordinarily pleased. 'Of course you can come! That would be wonderful. One thing we are not short of is space, providing you pack enough warm clothes. It's like the Arctic here.'

When Luke came in, carrying a filthy small boy, both of them cold and terribly pleased with themselves Joss was smiling to herself as she stirred a huge pan of soup. 'David's coming up the day after tomorrow.'

'Great.' Luke held Tom under one arm over the sink and reached for the Swarfega. 'It will be nice to see him. He'll bring news no doubt of dear old London and civilisation.' He chuckled, smearing green goo all over his small son's hands as Tom crowed with delight. Luke glanced at her over the sticky curls. 'He's not going to make you feel you're missing out, is he? Rural stagnation instead of academia.'

She shook her head. 'Nope. If I want to get back into it, I can always start some kind of research project with the prospect of a book in about a thousand years' time. Or something less academic and more lucrative. The book David suggested I have a go at, perhaps. I might just have a chat to him about that.' The idea had in fact been growing on her.

Reaching for the pepper mill she ground it over the soup, stirred, put down the wooden spoon and sat down at the kitchen table. 'You haven't asked how I got on with Mary Sutton.'

Luke raised an eyebrow. 'I could see it was good and bad when you came back. Want to tell me now?'

'Both my little brothers died here, Luke. In accidents.'

She was looking at Tom, suddenly aching to hold him. How could her mother have borne to lose two boys?

'Nothing will happen to Tom Tom, Joss.' Luke could always read her mind. He changed the subject adroitly.

83

'Listen, talking about Tom Tom and your writing what do you think of the idea of asking Lyn if she'd like to come and help you look after him. As a sort of proper job.' Drying Tom's hands he posted the little boy in Joss's direction with a gentle slap on the behind.

Joss held out her arms. 'While she's out of work, you mean? She's certainly good with Tom and we could do with some help, though we could only pay her pocket money. It would give me time to get on with the house.' She smiled. 'And write my best seller.'

'No joking, Joss. We need the money. You've had stuff published in the past. I'm sure you could do it.'

'In the past it was in academic magazines, Luke. They don't exactly pay megabucks. And just those few short stories.'

He smiled. 'Mini bucks would do, love. I do think you should give it a go. Anything to help. Keep us in bread and spuds until next year when we start our own vegetable patch, vineyard, bed and breakfast business, vintage car restoration workshop – with small business grant –' he had all the papers spread out over the dining room table – 'herb nursery, play group and counterfeit money press.'

She laughed. 'I'm glad we're not contemplating anything too ambitious. Pour me a glass of wine to celebrate and we'll drink to Grant, Grant and Davies Industries.' She hauled Tom onto her lap and dropped a kiss onto his hair, screwing up her face at the smell of oil and hand cleaner and dirt. 'You need a bath young man.'

Tom wriggled round to smile dazzlingly up at her. 'Tom go swim in the water outside,' he said.

Joss froze. Her arms tightened round him as suddenly the image of another small boy rose before her eyes, a small boy collecting tadpoles from the lake.

'No, Tom,' she whispered. 'Not outside. You don't swim outside. Not ever.'

9

uke?'

'Mmm.'

Luke was poring over some papers, sitting at her mother's desk in the study. They had had supper and had brought the last of the bottle of wine, eked out from lunch, to drink by the fire. Joss was sitting on the rug, feeding twigs to the hungry crackling flames. Outside the curtains a deep penetrating frost had settled over the silent garden.

'I suppose with a cellar full of wine, we could afford to open another bottle, couldn't we?' Beside her sat a box of letters and papers, extricated from beneath some old silk curtains in the bottom drawer of the chest in her bedroom. It was still tied with a piece of string. The label on the box said Bourne and Hollingsworth. It was post marked September 23 1937 and addressed to John Duncan Esq, Belheddon Hall, Essex.

'We could. But one of us would have to fetch it.'

'Bags you do.'

He laughed. 'Bags we both do. It means we'd have to go down there.'

'Ah.' She bit her lip.

'It's not so scary, Joss. There's electric light and hundreds and hundreds of wonderful bottles. No rats.'

85

'I'm not scared of rats!' She was scornful.

'Right then.' He threw down his pen and stood up. 'Come on.'

'Why don't I fetch the corkscrew from the kitchen?'

'Joss.'

She gave an awkward shrug. 'It's just – Luke, one of my brothers died falling down the cellar stairs.'

He sat down again abruptly. 'Oh, Joss. Why didn't you tell me?'

'I only found out this morning from Mary Sutton. But last time, when you went down – I felt it. Something strange – something frightening.'

'Only the smell of cold and damp, Joss.' His voice was very gentle. 'Surely there would be nothing frightening about a little boy's death. Sad, yes. Very sad. But a long time ago. We are here now, to bring happiness to the house.'

'Do you think so?'

'Why else did your mother give it to you?'

'I'm not sure.' She hugged her knees, gazing into the flames. 'She gave it to me because my father wanted me to have it.' She shook her head. 'It's strange. He seems such a shadowy figure. No one talks about him. No one seems to remember him.'

'He died a long time before your mother, didn't he? That's probably why.' He stood up again. 'Come on.' Stooping he caught her hand and hauled her to her feet. 'We'll find a bottle of Philip's best and get gloriously uninhibited, while Tom's asleep and we've still got the house to ourselves. Sound good?'

'Sounds good.' She reached up and kissed him.

The key was in the door. Turning it, Luke reached round into the dark for the light switch and clicked it on, looking down the wooden stairs towards the small underground vaults and the wine racks. Dust lay over the bottles. The cellar was very cold. Cautiously he padded down the steps ahead of Joss and waited for her at the bottom. 'OK?'

She nodded. The air was a curious combination of stale and fresh – the stillness and silence of a tomb and yet, through the mustiness, the clear freshness of the frosted garden outside.

'See.' Luke pointed to the top of the wall. 'Gratings which lead out to the flower beds outside the front walls of the house. The air gets in, but for some reason the temperature never varies much. Perfect for wine.' He turned his attention to the rack nearest them. 'Some of these newer ones are probably best. I'd hate to drink something worth hundreds, just in order to seduce my wife!'

'Thanks very much!'

There was nothing frightening down here now. Just stillness and, perhaps, memories. She tried not to think of an eight year old boy, excited, happy, on his birthday, opening the door and peering down into the dark . . . The thought could not be tolerated. Angrily she pushed it away. 'Just grab something and let's go. It's cold down here.'

'OK. Here goes. We don't tell David, right? We'll dispose of the evidence in the bottle bank before he gets here.' He pulled two bottles from the rack. 'Come on then.'

The cellar door safely locked, the corkscrew retrieved from the kitchen, Tom Tom checked – the baby alarm switched on – they settled back by the fire. 'So, let's see what we've got.' Luke scrutinised the label. 'Clos Vougeout 1945. Joss, this is old after all! I suspect this ought to breathe before we drink it.'

'Draw the cork and put it by the fire for a bit.' Joss reached for the box of letters. Anything to take her mind off the child, peering through the door into forbidden territory, full of excitement, on his birthday . . .

Belheddon Hall,
Belheddon,
Essex

29th September, 1920

Dear John,
Samuel and I were so pleased to see you
here yesterday, and to hear that you are once
more to settle at Pilgrim Hall. And so you are to
marry! Lady Sarah is a lovely and gentle person.
I know she will make you so very happy. As we
told you, my confinement is expected within a
few weeks but as soon as possible after that I
hope we may entertain you both at Belheddon.
My Samuel is hoping next year to resume tennis
parties here at the Hall. It would be such fun if
you could both come.
Your ever affectionate cousin, Lydia Manners.

Lydia Manners. Joss turned the sheet of paper over in
her hand. The grandmother after whom her mother had
named her when she was born. She pulled another small
bundle of letters out of the Bourne and Hollingsworth
box. Tied with pale blue ribbon they were labelled,
'Father's letters'. It was not Laura's writing. Joss frowned
as she leafed through them. Different handwriting, different dates, different addresses, addresses which meant
nothing to her. Then another, from Belheddon Hall. It
was short and to the point:

Our son little Samuel was born safely on 30th
November. Please thank Lady Sarah for her
note. I will write more soon.
Yr affectionate Cousin, Lydia.

The envelope was addressed to John Duncan at Pilgrim
Hall. So, John was John Duncan, a relative of Philip's.
Perhaps his father and so her own grandfather? Putting

down the letters Joss stared into the fire thoughtfully, listening to the voices echoing in her head, voices from her unknown past.

'How about some wine now?' Luke had been watching her for some time as she sorted through the box. Pushing aside his invoices with relief, he flung himself down beside her on the floor and put his arm around her. 'You are looking too serious.'

She smiled, nestling up against him. 'Not at all. Just learning some more about the past. My father's family this time.' She watched as Luke poured two glasses. The wine was delicious. It was dark brown and smoky, like a wood in November. She could feel the rich warmth of it running through her veins. After only a few sips she was feeling extraordinarily sexy. 'Is it the wine, or just the suggestion,' she whispered.

'What suggestion?' Luke tightened his arm around her, leaning back against the arm chair. His hand drooped lazily over her shoulder and fondled her breast through the heavy wool of her sweater.

'That one.' She pushed the box of papers aside with her foot and took another sip. 'This wine seems very strong.'

Luke chuckled. 'I suspect it was worth a fortune, but who cares, if we get our money's worth? Shall we go upstairs?' He was nuzzling her ear, gently nibbling the lobe.

'Not yet. Another glass first. Luke –' She turned to him, suddenly serious. 'I wouldn't dare ask you this if I were entirely sober. You don't regret coming here do you?'

'Regret it! Certainly not.' He inserted his hand under the collar of her sweater.

'You are sure. We've no income to speak of –'

'Then we won't speak of it.' As he would never speak to her of his nightmares about the business; the creditors lurking in the woodwork, the waves of depression which

89

sometimes swept over him when he thought about Barry and what he had done to them. What was the point? That was all in the past. Putting his glass down he leaned across, pressing his lips against hers. 'Come on. It's time we went upstairs.'

Sammy! Sammy, where are you?

The snow had melted; already snowdrops were pushing up through the frozen ground. The little boy ducked under the graceful boughs of the old fir tree and disappeared out of sight. When he reappeared, he was running down the lawn towards the lake.

'Stop!' Joss screamed. 'Stop. Don't go down there, please –'

Someone was in her way. Pushing against him she struggled to get past . . .

'Hey! Stop it!' Luke wriggled out of reach of her flailing fists. 'Joss, stop it! What's the matter?'

'Sammy!' She was battling up out of a fog of sleep, her mouth sour, her head thudding like a steam hammer. 'Sammy!'

'Wake up, Joss. You're dreaming.' Luke caught her hand as it struggled free of the entangling duvet. 'Joss! Wake up!'

She was naked, her clothes trailed across the floor; her shoulders, bare above the duvet ached with cold. The moonlight, streaming across the floor showed the overturned glass on the floor beside the bed, the empty bottle on the table by the lamp. Dragging herself back to the present she turned her head on the pillow, still disoriented. 'Sammy –'

'No Sammy. No such person, Joss. It's Luke, your husband. Remember?' He stroked her shoulder, wincing at the ice cold feel of her skin, and drew the duvet higher to cover her.

'Tom –'

'Tom's OK. Not a peep out of him. Go back to sleep. It will soon be morning.' He tucked her up tenderly and remained, propped on his elbow looking at her for a few moments, studying her face in the strangely ethereal moonlight. Her eyes had closed. She had never really awoken. It had all been some frightening dream. Too much wine. He glanced ruefully at the bottle. He already had the beginnings of a headache. By morning it would have turned into something approaching a hangover. Stupid. He threw himself back on the pillow, staring up at the embroidered bed hangings while beside him Joss's breathing slowed and settled back into deep sleep.

The shadow in the corner, ever watchful, stirred slightly, scarcely more than a flicker of the moonlight on the curtains, and a shiver of lust curled into the darkness.

10

avid had leapt at the idea of a weekend in East Anglia before he sat down and thought out the consequences. Peering now through the windscreen of his eight-year-old Vauxhall at the ancient, creeper-covered façade of Belheddon Hall he felt a pang of something near terminal jealousy. Then his better nature asserted itself firmly. If anyone deserved the fairy tale romance which had handed her this pile on a plate, it was Joss. He thought again of the few rough notes he had scribbled down for her and he smiled to himself. The house was far far older even than the architecture visible from where he sat implied, and it had an enviably romantic history.

Climbing stiffly out of the car he straightened to stretch the exquisite agony of cramp out of his bones before diving head first back in to withdraw suitcase, box of goodies from Harrods food hall and briefcase.

'See here.' He tapped a page of notes with his finger as they sat an hour later at the lunch table. 'The church was built in 1249. I don't know for sure, but I would think the foundations of this house go back that far at least. I'm no expert of course, but that glorious room of yours with the gallery looks fifteenth century if not earlier. Why haven't you contacted this local historian chappy yet?'

'We haven't had time.' Joss whisked off Tom's bib and wiped his face with it while David watched with horrified disgust. 'Wait while I put this young man down for his rest, then we'll talk some more. Put the coffee on, Luke.' She hauled the child out of his high chair and straddled him across her hip. 'You don't know how glad I am to see you, David.' She rested a hand lightly on his shoulder as she passed. 'I need to know about the house.'

David frowned as she disappeared through the door. 'Need to know is rather a strong term.'

'It's weird for her, living here.' Luke filled the kettle and put it on the hot plate. 'Imagine it. Generations of her ancestors and yet she knows almost nothing even about her mother.' Sitting down he leaned forward and cut himself a generous lump of cheese. 'She's been having a lot of nightmares. Some tactless old biddy who lives locally told her that both her elder brothers died here in accidents. She's got a bit obsessed by the thought.'

David raised an eyebrow. 'I can hardly blame her for that.' He shivered. 'How dreadful. Well, the more distant past seems to have been more cheerful. A junior branch of the De Vere family lived here for a couple of hundred years. One of them got his head chopped off in the Tower.'

Luke laughed, reaching for the wine. 'And you find that more cheerful?'

'I'm a historian; it fills me with morbid delight.' David chuckled contentedly. 'History is a moving staircase. Characters step onto the bottom, rise slowly. They get to the top, they descend. Occasionally something goes wrong and they fall off or get a foot trapped. They face forwards, looking up at the heights or they face backwards, looking down.' He smiled, pleased with his metaphor. 'In the end it makes no difference. One disappears, one leaves no trace and already another queue of figures crowds behind one all rising and falling in just the same way.'

'Chateau-bottled philosophy.' Luke topped up Joss's glass as she reappeared. She had combed her hair and removed from her cheek the imprint of Tom's gravy-covered fingers. 'This has been a house of substance for hundreds of years, my love. You should be very proud to be its chatelaine.'

'I am.' Switching on the baby alarm which stood on the dresser, Joss sat down contentedly. 'I'll take you over to the church later, David. It's very beautiful. They were doing the Christmas decorations and flowers earlier.' She smiled. 'Janet said I would be let off helping this year, as we've only just arrived.'

'Imagine!' Luke shook his head in wonder. 'Joss, do you remember the old joke about the flower ladies hanging in the porch? Another few weeks and you'll be a pillar of the church.'

David was scrutinising Joss's face. She had lost a lot of weight since he had seen her last; there were dark rings under her eyes and in spite of the laughter he sensed a tenseness about her which worried him. It was two hours before he had the chance to talk to her alone, when she put Tom in his buggy and they pushed him across the drive and down the narrow overgrown path towards the churchyard gate.

'That's my father's grave.' She pointed down at the headstone.

'Poor Joss.' David pushed his hands deep into his pockets against the cold. 'It must have been disappointing to find neither he nor your mother were still alive.'

'To put it mildly.' She pushed Tom on a few feet and stopped as the little boy pointed at a robin which had alighted on a headstone only a few feet from them. 'Did you find out anything else about the name?'

'Belheddon.' He chewed his lip. 'The name goes back a very long way. Multitudes of spellings, of course, like most old English place names, but basically the same in the Domesday Book. That takes you back to about 1087. How far did you want me to go?' He grinned at her, blowing out a cloud of condensed air to make Tom laugh.

'You mentioned Celtic. Iron Age? Bronze Age?'

'That was guesswork, Joss, and I'm afraid I haven't made any more progress on the definitions. There was a possibility of it coming from *belwe* which means bellow in middle English. Heddon does seem most likely to mean heather hill. Perhaps they grazed noisy cattle up here once! But we're really talking archaeology here. There are recognised sites around here – I noticed in one of the county histories that there are several very close to the house – but who knows when it comes to names? I don't know yet if there is anything Roman.'

'Why would the devil live here, David?'

She had her back to him, watching the robin. He frowned. There was a strange tone to her voice – a forced jocularity.

'I very much doubt if he does.' She turned and he met her eye. 'What is frightening you, Joss?'

She shrugged, fussing with Tom's harness. The little boy had started to whine. 'I don't know. I'm usually quite sane. And I adore the house. It's just that somehow, something is not right here.'

'But not the devil.' It was his most school masterly tone, stern with just a hint of mocking reproach.

'No. No, of course not.' Comforting the child, she sounded far from sure.

'Joss. If the devil chose anywhere to live on Earth, I doubt that, even as his country residence, he would choose Belheddon.' He smiled, the corners of his eyes creasing deeply. 'For one thing it's far too cold.'

She laughed. 'And I'm keeping you hanging around. Let's go into the church.'

The iron latch was icy, even through her gloves.

Turning the ring handle with an effort she humped the buggy through the doors and down into the shadowy aisle.

'It's a lovely old church.' David stared round him.

She nodded. 'I've even been to one or two services. I've always loved evensong.' She led the way towards the far wall. 'Look, there are several memorials and brass plaques to people from the Hall. None with the same names, though. It's as if a dozen families have lived here. It's so frustrating. I don't know who, if any, are my relations.' She stood staring up at a worn stone memorial by the pulpit. 'Look. Sarah, beloved wife of William Percival, late of Belheddon Hall, died the 4th day of December, 1884. Then, much later, there was Lydia Manners, my grandmother, then my parents' name was Duncan. All different families.'

'Have you found the family Bible?' He had wandered up into the chancel. 'Ah, here are some De Veres. 1456 and 1453, both of Belheddon Hall. Perhaps they were your ancestors too.'

Joss pushed the buggy after him. 'I hadn't thought to look for a Bible. What a good idea!'

'Well if there is one and it is sufficiently huge you ought to be able to find it quite easily. I'll help you look when we get back to the house. But Joss –' he put his arm round her gravely, 'I very much doubt if you are descended from the devil!'

'It would be an interesting thought, wouldn't it.' She stood in front of the altar rail and stared up at the stained glass window. 'I suspect if I was there would have been a smell of scorching by now, if not whirling winds and screaming demons flocking round my head.'

Katherine

The sound in the echoing chancel arch above her was no more than a whisper of the wind. Neither of them heard it.

David sat down in one of the pews. 'Joss, about the writing. I gave your short story *Son of the Sword*, to my friend Robert Cassie at Hibberds. It intrigued me so much when I read it. That mystery thriller angle set in the past: I thought it worked really well and I was always sad it was a short story. I thought it would make a good novel then, and I still do.' He glanced up at her under his eyelashes. 'Bob agreed with me. I don't know if that particular idea appeals, but if you thought you could expand it into a full length novel, he would be interested to hear your ideas on how to do it; perhaps write some character sketches, a few chapters, that sort of thing.'

She stood stock still, looking down at him. 'Was he serious?'

David nodded. 'I told you you could do it, Joss. He liked the characters; he loved the mystery – and of course, in the story, it's never solved.' He raised an eyebrow. 'Do you know what happened at the end yourself?'

Joss laughed. 'Of course I do.'

'Well then. All you have to do is tell the story.'

They found the family Bible that evening. The huge, leather-covered tome was stored sideways in the bottom of the bookshelf behind her mother's chair in the study. 'Bookworm.' David fingered the crumbling edges to the pages. 'And probably mice. And there you are. Dozens of entries written on the end papers. Fascinating! Let's take it through to the kitchen and we can put it on the table under the bright light.'

Luke was scrubbing oil off his hands at the sink when they carried in their find in triumph and laid it reverently down. 'Now what have you found.' He grinned at them tolerantly. 'You are like a couple of school kids, you two. Such excitement!'

David opened the book with careful fingers. 'Here we are. The first entry is dated 1694.'

'And the last?' Joss craned over his shoulder.

He turned the heavy handmade page. 'Samuel John Duncan, born 10th September 1946.'

'Sammy.' Joss swallowed hard. Neither Georgie nor she, the rejected member of the Duncan family, were there.

David stood back from the table, half diffident, half reluctant to relinquish his treasure. 'Go on, have a look.'

Joss sat down, leaning forward, her finger on the page. 'There she is,' she said, 'the Sarah in the church. Sarah Rushbrook married William Percival 1st May 1861. Then Julia Mary born 10th April 1862, died 17th June 1862 – she only lived two months.'

'It was a cruel time. Infant mortality was appalling, Joss. Remember your statistics,' David put in sternly. He was suddenly strangely uncomfortable with this close encounter with the past.

Joss went on. '"Mary Sarah, born 2nd July 1864. Married John Bennet spring 1893. Our firstborn, Henry John was born the 12th October 1900" – she must have written that. "Our daughter Lydia" – I suppose that's my grandmother – "was born in 1902" and then, oh no –' she stopped for a moment. 'Little Henry John died in 1903. He was only three years old. That entry is in a different handwriting. The next entry is dated 24th June, 1919. "In the year 1903, three months after the death of our son Henry, my husband John Bennet disappeared. I no longer expect his return. This day my daughter, Lydia Sarah, married Samuel Manners who has come to Belheddon in his turn."'

'That sounds a bit cryptic.' Luke was sitting opposite her, his attention suddenly caught. 'What's next?'

'"Our son, Samuel, was born on 30th November, 1920. Three days later my mother, Mary Sarah Bennet, died of the influenza."'

'Incredible.' David shook his head. 'It's a social history

in miniature. I wonder if she caught the tail end of the great flu epidemic which spread round the world after the First World War. Poor woman. So she probably never saw her grandson.'

'I wonder what happened to poor old John Bennet?' Thoughtfully Luke sat back in his chair.

'There is a letter in the study,' Joss said slowly, reverting to a previous thought. 'A note from Lydia to her cousin John Duncan telling him about her son's birth. She must have written it straight away, before she realised her mother was dying.' She glanced back at the page. 'She had three more children, John, Robert and Laura, my mother, each born two years apart and then –' she paused. 'Look, she herself died the year after Laura's birth. She was only twenty-three years old!'

'How sad.' Luke reached out and touched her hand. 'It was all a long time ago, Joss. You mustn't get depressed about it, you know.'

She smiled. 'I'm not really. It's just so strange. Reading her letter, holding it in my hand. It brings her so close.'

'I expect the house is full of letters and documents about the family,' David put in. 'The fact that your mother obviously left everything just as it was is wonderful from the historian's point of view. Just wonderful. There must be pictures of these people. Portraits, photos, daguerreotypes.' He rocked back on his chair, balancing against the table with his finger tips. 'You must draw up a family tree.'

Joss smiled. 'It would be interesting. Especially for Tom Tom when he's big.' She shook her head slowly, turning back to the endpapers where the scrawled Italic inscriptions, faded to brown, raced across the page. The first four generations, she realised, had been filled in by the same hand – a catching up job in the front of the new Bible perhaps. After that, year after year, generation after generation, each new branch of the family was recorded by a different pen, a different name. 'If I copy these out, I can take the list over to the church and find out how many of them were buried there,' she said. 'I wonder what did happen to John Bennet. There is no further mention of him. It would be interesting to see if he was buried here. Do you think he had an accident?'

'Perhaps he was murdered.' Luke chuckled. 'Not every name in this book can have died a gentle natural death . . .'

'Luke –' Joss's protest was interrupted by a sudden indignant wail from the baby alarm.

'I'll go.' Luke was already on his feet. 'You two put away that Bible and start to think about supper.'

Joss stood up and closed the heavy book, frowning at the echoing crescendo of sobs. 'I should go –'

'Luke can deal with it.' David put his hand on her arm. He left it there just a moment too long and moved it hastily. 'Joss. Don't push Luke out with all this, will you. The family. The history. The house. It's a lot for him to take on board.'

'It's a lot for me to take on board!' She thumped the heavy book down on the dresser as over the intercom they heard the sound of a door opening, and then Luke's voice, sharp with fear. 'Tom! What have you done?'

Joss glanced at David, then she turned and ran for the door. When she arrived in the nursery, with David close on her heels, Tom was in Luke's arms. The cot was over by the window.

'It's OK. He's all right.' He surrendered the screaming child. 'He must have rocked the cot across the floor. It is a bit sloping up here. Then he woke up in a different place and had a bit of a fright, didn't you old son?'

He ruffled the little boy's hair.

Joss clutched Tom close, feeling the small body trembling violently against her own. 'Silly sausage. What happened? Did you rock the cot so much it moved?'

Tom snuffled. Already his eyes were closing. 'It might have been a dream,' Luke whispered. 'For all that noise, he's barely awake, you know.'

Joss nodded. She waited while he pushed the cot back into the corner and turned back the coverings. 'Tom Tom go back to bed now,' she murmured gently. The little boy said nothing, the long honey blond eyelashes already heavy against his cheeks.

'Clever invention, that alarm,' David commented when they were once more back in the kitchen. 'Does he often do that?'

Joss shook her head. 'Not very. Moving has unsettled him a bit, that's all. And he's excited about Christmas. Alice and Joe and Lyn will soon be back. Lyn has agreed to come and help me look after him as a part time nanny. And on top of all that Luke has promised him we will do the tree tomorrow.' She was laying the table, her careless movements quick and imprecise. David leaned across and neatened the knives and forks, meticulously uncrossing two knife blades with a shake of his head. 'The devil apart, do you think this house is haunted?' he asked suddenly, squaring the cutlery with neat precision.

'Why?' Luke turned from the stove, wooden spoon in hand and stared at him. 'Have you seen something?'

'Seen, no.' David sat down slowly.

'Heard then?' Joss met his eye. The voices. The little boys' voices. Had he too heard them?

David shrugged. 'No. Nothing precise. Just a feeling.'

The feeling had been in Tom's bedroom, but he was not going to say so. It was strange. A coldness which was not physical cold – the Dimplex had seen to that. More a cold of – he caught himself with something like a suppressed laugh. He was going to describe it to himself as a cold of the soul.

resents, food, blankets, hot water bottles. I'm like a Red Cross relief van!' Lyn had driven into the courtyard next morning, her old blue Mini groaning under the weight of luggage and parcels. 'Mum and Dad are coming back on Wednesday, but I thought I'd give you a hand.' She smiled shyly at David. 'I'm going to be Tom's nanny so Joss can write world-shaking best sellers!'

'I'm glad to hear it.' David grinned. He had only met Joss's younger sister on a couple of occasions, and had thought her hard and, he had to admit, a little boring. For sisters the two had had little in common. Now, of course, he knew why. They weren't sisters at all.

It was eleven before he managed to cajole Joss away from the house on the pretext of hunting up some of the names from the Bible in the church. They started in front of Sarah Percival. 'I noticed her because the memorial was so ornate. There must be older ones,' she whispered. She wandered away from him down the aisle. 'Here we are, Mary Sarah Bennet died in 1920. It just says of Belheddon Hall. No mention of her disappearing husband.'

'Perhaps she didn't want him buried with her.' David was staring absently up into the shadows near the north door. 'There's a lovely little brass here. To the memory of Katherine –' he screwed up his eyes, 'it's been polished so often I can't make out the second name. We need more light.' He stepped closer, reaching up the wall to trace the letters with his finger. 'She died in 14-something.'

Katherine

In the silence of the old church Joss flinched as though she had been hit. She was standing on the chancel steps, staring at a small plaque on the wall behind the lectern. At David's words she turned, to see him stroking his fingers lightly over the small, highly polished brass. 'Don't touch it, David – 'she cried out before she had time to think.

He stepped back guiltily. 'Why on earth not? It's not like walking on them –'

'Did you hear?' She pressed her fingers against her temples.

'Hear what?' He stepped away from the pulpit and came to stand next to her. 'Joss? What is it?'

'Katherine,' she whispered.

He had been riding – riding through the summer heat, trying to reach her . . .

'That was me, Joss. I read out her name. Look. Up there on the wall. A little brass. There are some dead flowers on the shelf in front of it.'

Riding – riding – the messenger had taken two days to reach him – already it might be too late –

In the cut glass bowl the water was green and slimy. Joss stared down at it. 'We must renew the flowers. Poor

103

things, they've been dead so long. Nobody cares –'

Foam flew from his horse's mouth, flecking his mantle with white . . .

'There aren't any flowers at this time of year unless you go to a shop,' David commented. He wandered away towards the choir stalls once more. 'Did you bring a notebook? Let's copy some of these names down.'

Joss had picked up the vase. She stared at it vacantly. 'There are always flowers in the country, if you know where to look,' she said slowly. 'I'll bring some over later.'

He glanced at her over his shoulder. She seemed strangely preoccupied. 'Shouldn't you leave it to the flower ladies?' he said after a moment.

She shrugged. 'They don't seem to have bothered. No one has noticed. The vase was hidden there, in the shadows. Poor Katherine –'

Katherine!

Furiously he bent lower over the animal's neck, urging it even faster, conscious of the thud of hooves on the sunbaked ground, knowing in some reasoning part of himself that his best mount would be lamed for life if he kept up the pace any longer.

'David!'

The pounding in Joss's skull was like the thud of a horse's hooves, on and on and on, one two three, one two three, over the hard, unrelenting ground. Everything was spinning . . .

'Joss?' As she collapsed onto the narrow oak pew David was beside her. 'Joss? What is it?' He took her hand and rubbed it. It was ice cold. 'Joss, you're white as a sheet! Can you stand? Come on, let's take you home.'

Behind him, far behind, a scattering of men, the messenger amongst them, tried to keep up with him; soon they would have fallen out of sight.

In the silent bedroom Joss lay on the bed. Sitting beside her was their new doctor, Simon Fraser, summoned by Luke. His hand was cool and firm as he held her wrist, his eyes on his watch. At last he put her hand down. He had already listened to her chest and pressed her stomach experimentally. 'Mrs Grant,' he looked up at last, his eyes a pale clear blue beneath his gold rimmed glasses. 'When did you last have a period?'

Joss sat up, relieved to find her head had stopped spinning. She opened her mouth to answer and then hesitated. 'What with the move and everything, I've sort of lost track –' Her smile faded. 'You don't mean –'

He nodded. 'My guess is you are about three months pregnant.' He tucked his stethoscope into his case and clicked the locks shut. 'Let's get you down to the hospital for a scan and we'll find out just how far along you are.' He stood up and smiled down at her. 'Was it planned?'

Katherine

It was there again, the sound in her head. She strained to hear the words, but they were too far away.

Katherine: my love; wait for me . . .

'Mrs Grant? Joss?' Simon Fraser was staring at her intently. 'Are you all right?'

Joss focused on him, frowning.

'I asked if the baby was planned,' he repeated patiently. She shrugged. 'No. Yes. I suppose so. We wanted

105

another to keep Tom company. Perhaps not quite so soon. There's so much to do –' It had gone. The voice had faded.

'Well, you are not going to be the one doing it.' He lifted his case. 'I'm going to be stern, Mrs Grant. That turn you had this morning is probably quite normal – hormones leaping about and rearranging themselves – but I've seen too many women wear themselves out in the early months of pregnancy and then regret it later. Just take it easy. The house, the boxes, the unpacking – none of it will go away by itself, but at the same time, none of it is so urgent you need to risk yourself or your baby. Understood?' He grinned, a sudden boyish smile which lit his face. 'I've always wanted to come and see this house – it's so beautiful – but I don't want to be coming up here at all hours because the new lady squire is overtaxing herself. Right?'

Joss sat up and swung her legs over the side of the bed. 'It sounds to me as though you've been got at. Luke must have talked to you before you came up here, doctor.'

He laughed. 'Maybe. Maybe not, but I'm a fairly good judge of human nature.'

Luke's hug, in the kitchen later, swept her off her feet. 'Clever, clever darling! Let's have some champagne! David, are you prepared to brave the cellar? There is some there.'

'Luke –' Protesting, Joss subsided into a chair. 'I shouldn't have champagne. Besides, shouldn't we wait until I've had the proper tests?' She still felt a little odd – disorientated, as though she had woken too suddenly from a dream.

'No chance.' Luke was glowing with excitement. 'We'll have another bottle then. Besides there's no doubt is there? He said he could feel it! I'm sure, and you are too, aren't you –' he paused for a moment on his way to

106

collect four glasses and looked at her shrewdly. 'A woman always knows.'

Raising her fingers to her forehead Joss pressed distractedly against her brow. 'I don't know. I suppose there have been signs.' Queasiness in the mornings for one. In the rush to get Tom up and dressed she hadn't taken much notice. Her tiredness she had put down to the fact that she was doing much too much. 'So nanny – ' she looked at Lyn, 'you'll have another charge soon, it seems.'

Lyn's eyes were sparkling. 'You'll have to pay me more to look after two.'

'Oh great. Thanks!'

'At least writing your book will keep you sitting still. You've got no excuse not to start, now,' Luke said firmly. He put the glasses down on the table and then dropped a kiss on the top of her head. 'I'll go and help David find a bottle.'

David was standing in the cellar in front of the wine racks as Luke walked slowly down the steps. 'It's bloody cold down here. This is all vintage, you know. And some of it is still in really good nick.' He glanced at Luke and lowered his voice. 'If you need money you could do worse than sell some of this. There are some very valuable wines here. Look at this! Haut-Brion '49 – and look Chateau d'Yquem!'

'What sort of money are we talking about?' Luke reached for a bottle and extracted it carefully from the rack. 'This is – ' he squinted '– 1948.'

'Don't shake it whatever you do! That's about 350 quids' worth you've got in your hand. You are looking at thousands, Luke. Ten. Twenty. Maybe more.'

'You know, I did wonder. That's why I wanted you to have a look at them.'

David nodded. 'I can give you the name of someone at the wine auction house at Sotheby's who would come and value it and catalogue it. It would be a tragedy in a way to get rid of it, but I know you're strapped for cash, and with another kid on the way, you could do worse than raise some like this. Besides, you're just as happy with plonk, aren't you, you ignoramus!' He chuckled.

'I think I'd better put this back –' Luke glanced at the bottle in his hand.

'You'd better! Come on. Let's find some champagne for the baby.' David selected a bottle from the rack and studied the label, 'Pommery Brut 1945. Not bad!'

'Just twenty or thirty quid a bottle, I suppose?' Luke groaned.

'More like fifty! It's a strange life you lead here, isn't it.' David shook his head slowly. 'All the trappings of grandeur, yet a bit short of cash.'

'A bit!' Luke grinned. He was not going to let himself think about Barry and H & G's money. 'We were planning to live off the land here. Literally. The money I can make from doing up cars is peanuts. It's a mug's game – so slow – but at least it will bring in enough hopefully for electricity bills and community charge, that sort of thing. Joss would never hear of selling anything out of the house – she is so obsessed with the history of it all, but wine is not quite the same, is it? I'm sure she wouldn't mind about that. It could make the difference between hell and a hard place for us, David.' He cradled the bottle in his arms. 'Tell me something. Do you think Joss really could make any money out of writing?'

David grimaced. 'She can write. She has a wonderful imagination. I've told her that I've taken the liberty of showing some of her stuff to a publisher friend of mine. He particularly liked one of her short stories. He's keen to see more, and he wouldn't say that unless he meant it. But beyond that it's in the lap of the gods.' He gave a sudden shiver. 'Come on, old chap. Let's get out of here. It's so bloody cold. A hot meal is what we all need, I think!'

It wasn't until quite a bit later that Joss managed to go back to the church alone. She had in her hand a small bunch of holly mixed with red dead nettle, and winter jasmine and shiny green sprigs of ivy covered in flowers.

The church was almost dark when she found the key in its hiding place and pushed open the heavy door to make her way up the dim nave. The vase was clean and full of fresh water as she stood it gently on the shelf in front of the little brass. 'There you are, Katherine,' she whispered. 'New flowers for Christmas. Katherine?' She paused, almost expecting there to be a response, a repeat of the strange reverberation in her head, but there was none. The church was silent. With a wry smile she turned away.

The kitchen was empty. For a moment she stood in front of the stove, warming her hands. The others were all out, all occupied. She should be unpacking boxes or packing presents; there was no time to stand and do nothing. On the other hand now would be the perfect time, alone and undisturbed, to turn once more to the box of letters in her mother's study. And the doctor did tell her to rest . . .

The great hall was already taking on the look of Christmas. Luke and David had brought in the seven foot tree they had cut in the copse behind the lake that morning and the whole room smelled of the fresh spicy boughs. It was standing near the window, firmly wedged into a huge urn filled with earth. Lyn had found the boxes of decorations, and they stood on the floor near the tree. They had promised Tom that he could help decorate the tree after his supper and before he went to bed. She smiled. The little boy's face as the tree was dragged in had been a sight to behold.

She had filled a huge silver bowl with holly and ivy and yellow jasmine and it stood in the centre of the table, a blaze of colour in the dark of the room.

Joss frowned. There was a strange electric tingle in the air, a crackle of static as though a storm were about to break. It was there again: the echo at the back of her head – the voice she could not quite hear.

As he thundered into the courtyard the house lay quiet under the blazing sun. His horse's breath was whistling in its throat as he dragged it to a halt. There was no sign of servants, even the dogs were silent.

Puzzled, Joss shook her head. She was staring hard at the bowl of flowers. The silver, still dull where her quick rub with a duster had failed to remove the years of tarnish gleamed softly in the dull light from the lamp near the table. As she watched a yellow petal from the jasmine fell onto the gleaming black oak.

Throwing himself from the saddle he left the sweating trembling horse and ran inside. The great hall, dim after the sunlight, was equally empty. In five strides he was across it and on the stairs which led up to her solar.

The smell of resin from the newly cut fir tree was over powering. Joss could feel the pain tightening in a band around her forehead.

'Katherine!' His voice was hoarse with dust and fear. 'Katherine!'

'Joss!' The cry echoed through the open doorway. 'Joss, where are you?'

Luke was carrying a great bunch of mistletoe. 'Joss. Come here. Look what I've found!' In quick strides he crossed the room to her side and held the huge pale green silvery bouquet above her head. 'A kiss, my love. Now!' His eyes narrowed with laughter. 'Come on, before we decide where to put it!'

Katherine!

Joss stared at Luke sightlessly, her mind focused inwards, trying to catch the sounds as they came, seemingly from endless distances away.

'Joss?' Luke stared at her. He lowered the mistletoe. 'Joss? What's wrong?' His voice grew sharp. 'Joss, can you hear me?'

Katherine!

It was growing fainter; muffled; distant.

'Joss!'

She smiled suddenly, reaching out to touch the mistletoe berries. They were cold and waxy from the old orchard where lichen-covered apple trees tangled with greengage and plum.

In the end they put one bunch in the kitchen and one in the great hall hanging from the gallery. Before he left to return home David gave Joss a lingering kiss under the bunch in the kitchen. 'If I find out any more about the house I'll stick it in the post. And in the mean time, you get a couple of chapters under your belt to send to my friend Bob Cassie. I have a good feeling about your writing.'

'And so do I, Joss.' After he had gone Luke and Joss were discussing it in the study. 'It makes perfect sense. Lyn is here to help you with Tom and the baby when it's born. You can write, we all know that. And we do need the money.' He didn't dare count on the wine yet.

'I know.'

'Have you got any ideas?' He glanced at her sideways.

She laughed. 'You know I have, you idiot! And you know I've already made some notes on how to expand that story. I'm going to take it back to when my hero is

111

a boy living in a house a bit like this one. He's a page, learning to be a gentleman, and then he gets mixed up in the wars between the white rose and the red.'

'Great stuff.' Luke dropped a kiss on her head. 'Perhaps they'll televise it and make us millionaires!'

Laughing she pushed him away. 'It's got to be written and published first, so why don't you go out and play cars while I make a start right now.'

She had found an empty notebook of her mother's in one of the drawers. Sitting down at the desk she opened it at the first page and picked up a felt tipped pen. The rest of the story was there, hovering at the edge of her mind. She could see her hero so clearly as a boy. He would be about fourteen at the beginning of the novel. He was tall, with sandy hair and a spattering of freckles across his nose. He wore a velvet cap with a jaunty feather and he worked for the lord of Belheddon.

She stared out of the window. She could see a robin sitting on the bare branches of the climbing rose outside. It seemed to be staring in, its bright eyes black and intent. He was called Richard, her hero, and the daughter of the house, the heroine of her short story, his age exactly, was called Anne.

Georgie!

She shook her head slightly. The robin had hopped onto the window sill. It was pecking at something in the soft moss which grew around the stone of the mullions.

Georgie!

The voice was calling in the distance. The robin heard it. She saw it stand suddenly still then with a bob of its head it turned and flew off. Joss's fingers tightened round her pen. Richard was of course in love with Anne, even at the beginning, but it was a sweet innocent adolescent love that only later was to be dragged into adventure and war as opposing sides brought tension and dissent and murder to the house.

She wrote tentatively, sketching in the first scene, twice glancing at the window, and once at the door as she thought she heard the scuffle of feet. In the fireplace the logs shifted and spat companionably, once filling the room with sweet-smelling smoke as a gust of wind outside blew back down the chimney.

Georgie! Where are you?

The voice this time was exasperated. It was right outside the door. Joss stood up, her heart pounding, as she went to pull it open. The hallway outside was empty, the cellar door closed and locked.

Shutting the study door she leaned with her back against it, biting her lip. It was her imagination, of course. Nothing more. Stupid. Idiot. The silence of the empty house was getting to her. Wearily she pushed herself away from the door and went back to the desk.

On her notebook lay a rose.

She stared at it in astonishment. 'Luke?' She glanced round the room, puzzled. 'Luke, where are you?'

A log fell with a crackle in the fire basket and a shower of sparks illuminated the soot-stained brickwork of the chimney.

'Luke, where are you, you idiot?' She picked up the flower and held it to her nose. The white petals were ice cold and without scent. She shivered and laid it down. 'Luke?' Her voice was sharper. 'I know you're there.' She strode across to the window and pulled the curtain away from the wall. There was no sign of him.

'Luke!' She ran towards the door and tugged it open. 'Luke, where are you?'

There was no answering shout.

'Luke!' The scent of resinous pine was stronger than ever as she ran towards the kitchen.

Luke was standing over the sink scrubbing his hands. 'Hello. I wondered where you were –' He broke off as she threw her arms around his neck. Reaching for the towel on the draining board he dried his hands and then gently he pushed her away. 'Joss? What is it? What's happened?'

'Nothing.' She clung to him again. 'I'm being neurotic and hormonal. It's allowed, remember?'

'You're not going to let me forget, love.' He guided her to the table and pushed her into the arm chair at the end of it. 'Now. Tell me.'

'The rose. You put a rose on my desk . . .' her voice trailed away. 'You did, didn't you.'

Luke frowned, puzzled. With a quick glance at her he sat down next to her. 'I've been out working on the car, Joss. It seemed a good idea before it got too dark. The lights in the coach house are not good and it's freezing out there. Lyn is still out with Tom. They went to collect some fir cones but they'll be back at any moment, unless they came past me without my noticing. Now what's this about a rose?'

'It appeared on my desk.'

'And that frightened you? You cuckoo, David must have left it.'

'I suppose so.' She sniffed sheepishly. 'I thought I heard –' she broke off. She had been about to say, 'Someone calling Georgie,' but she stopped herself in time. If she had she was going mad. It was her imagination, working overtime in a shadowy too-silent house.

'Where is this rose? Let's fetch it in.' Luke suddenly stood up. 'Come on, then I'll help you put the supper on for the infant prodigy. He's going to refuse to go to bed until he's had his money's worth of the Christmas tree this evening.'

The fire in the study had died to ashes. Stooping Luke threw on a couple more logs as Joss walked over to the desk. Her pen lay on the page, a long dash of ink witness to the haste with which she had thrown it down. Next to it lay a dried rose bud, the petals curled and brown,

114

thin and crackly as paper. She picked it up and stared at it. 'It was fresh – cold.' She touched it with the tip of her finger. The petals felt like tissue; a crisped curled margin of the leaf crumbling to nothing as she touched it.

Luke glanced at her. 'Imagination, old thing. I expect it fell out of one of those pigeon holes. You said they were full of your mother's rubbish.' Gently he took the rose out of her hand. Walking over to the fire he tossed it into the flames and in a fraction of a second it had blazed up and disappeared.

12

 ydia's notebook fell open at the marker, a large dried leaf which smelled faintly and softly of peppermint.

16th March, 1925. He has returned. My fear grows hourly. I have sent Polly to the Rectory for Simms and I have despatched the children with nanny to Pilgrim Hall with a note to Lady Sarah beseeching her to keep them all overnight. Apart from the servants I am alone.

Joss looked up, her eyes drawn to the dusty attic window. The sun was slanting directly into the room, lighting the beige daisies which were all that was still visible on a wall paper faded by the years. In spite of the warmth of the sun behind the glass she found she was shivering, conscious of the echoing rooms of the empty house below her.

The rest of the page was empty. She turned it and then the next and the next after that. All were blank. The next entry was dated April 12th, nearly a month after the first.

And now it is Easter. The garden is full of daffodils and I have gathered baskets of them to decorate every room. The slime from their stems stained my gown – a reprimand perhaps for my attempts to climb from the pit of despair. The best of the flowers I have saved for my little one's grave.

April 14th. Samuel has taken the children to his mama. Without Nanny I cannot look after them.

April 15th. Polly has left. She was the last. Now I am truly alone. Except for it.

April 16th. Simms came again. He begged me to leave the house empty. He brought more Holy Water to sprinkle, but I suspect like all the perfumes of Arabia, even jugs full of the miraculous liquid cannot wipe away the blood. I cannot go to the Rectory. In the end I sent him away . . .

'Joss!'

Luke's voice at the foot of the attic stairs was loud and sudden. 'Tom's crying.'

'I'm coming.' She put the diary back in the drawer of the old dressing table and turned the key. There were only two more entries in the book and suddenly she was afraid to read them. She could hear Tom's voice now, quite clearly. How could she not have heard it before?

Which of Lydia's children had died? Who amongst her lively, much-loved brood occupied the grave in the churchyard which she had decorated with Easter daffodils?

Two at a time she fled down the steep stairs and along the corridor to the nursery. At every step the fretful wails grew louder.

He was standing up in his cot, his face screwed up, wet with anger and misery. As he saw her he stretched out his little arms.

'Tom!' She scooped him up and cuddled him close. 'What is it, darling?' Her face was in his soft hair. It smelled of raspberries from his jelly at lunch.

How could Lydia have borne to lose a child: one of her beloved brood?

She hugged Tom closer, aware that his bottom was damp. Already the sobs were turning to snuffles as he snuggled against her.

'Is he OK?' Luke put his head round the door.

Joss nodded. For a moment she couldn't speak for the lump in her throat. 'I'll change him and bring him down. It's almost time for his tea. Where's Lyn?'

Luke shrugged. Striding into the room he threw the little boy a pretend punch. 'You OK soldier?' He glanced at Joss. 'You too?' He raised a finger to her cheek. 'Still feeling bad?'

Joss forced a smile. 'Just a bit tired, that's all.'

Tom changed and smart in a new pair of dungarees and a striped sweater his grandmother had knitted him, Joss carried him into the study. Putting him down on the floor she gave him the pot of pencils to play with, then she sat down at the desk and reached for her notebook. On the table nearby sat Luke's Amstrad. The file headed *Son of the Sword* already contained several pages of character studies and the beginning of her synopsis. She looked at her notebook, staring down sightlessly at the pages, then back at the blank screen of the computer. She wanted to get on with her story, but her eye had been caught by the family Bible, lying on its shelf in the corner. With a sigh of resignation she closed the notebook. She knew she could not concentrate on it until she had spent just a bit longer on the story unfolding on the flyleaves of that huge old tome. Heaving it up off its shelf she laid it on the desk and opened it.

Lydia Sarah Bennet married Samuel Manners in 1919. They had four children. Baby Samuel who died three months after his birth in 1920, John, who was born the following year and died aged four in 1925, Robert, born in 1922 who died at the age of fourteen, and Laura, her mother who was born in 1924 and died in 1989, aged sixty-five. Lydia herself had died in 1925. Joss bit her lip.

The diary entries must have been written only a few months before she herself was dead.

She swallowed, looking down at the page in front of her. The faded ink was blurred and in places the pen which had made the entries had blotted the page with a smattering of little stains. Slowly she closed the book.

'Mummy. Tom's tea.' The anxious voice from the carpet caught her attention. He was sitting on the hearth rug looking up at her. His face was covered in purple ink.

'Oh, Tom!' Exasperated she bent to pick him up. 'You dreadful child. Where did you find the pen?'

'Tom's colours,' he said firmly. 'Me draw pictures.' His fist was clamped around a narrow fountain pen which Joss could see at once was very old. It couldn't have still had ink in it so the lubrication for the nib had appeared when the little boy had sucked it. Shaking her head, she slung him onto her hip. . . . *Except for it* . . . the phrase was running round and round in her head. *Except for it. . . . . . My fear makes him stronger* . . . Words written by two women in their diaries more than half a century apart, two women driven to extreme fear by something which came to them in the house. Two women who had resorted to the church and to Holy Water to try to protect themselves, but to no avail.

As she carried Tom through the great hall she glanced at the Christmas tree. Covered now in silver balls and long glittering swathes of silver cobwebs and decorated with dozens of small coloured lights it stood in the corner of the room like a talisman. Already she and Luke had placed a pile of parcels under it including one for each of them from David. Tomorrow Alice and Joe would arrive and with them lots more presents. 'Me see tree.' At the sight of it Tom began to struggle in her arms. 'Me walk.' As she set him on his feet he was already running towards the corner, his chubby hand pointing at the top of the tree. 'Tom's angel!'

'Tom's angel, to keep us safe,' Joss agreed. Luke had lifted the little boy up so he could put the finishing touch, the beautiful little doll, made by Lyn, with its sparkling feathered wings. 'Please,' she murmured under her breath as she watched the little boy standing open mouthed below the sweeping branches, 'let it keep us safe.'

They were half way through an early supper when the front doorbell pealed through the house and almost at once they heard the raised voices from the front drive.

'Carol singers!' Lyn was first on her feet.

The group stayed twenty minutes, standing round the tree while they had a glass of wine each and sang carols. Joss watched from the oak high-backed chair in the corner. For how many hundreds of years had just such groups of singers brought wassail to the house? Through narrowed eyes she could picture them as Anne and Richard in her story would have seen them, clustered in front of the huge fireplace, muffled against the cold, in boots and scarves, with red noses, and chapped hands. Their lanterns were standing in a semi circle on the table, and Lyn had lit the candles in the old sconces and turned out the lights, so there was no electric light save for the little coloured balls of glass upon the tree. Even the carols would have been the same – from *This Endris Night* they had launched into *Adam lay ybounden*. She let the words sweep over her, filling the room, resonating around the walls. Katherine might have heard these songs five hundred years ago on just such an icy night. She shivered. She could picture her so easily – long dark hair, hidden by the neat head-dress, her deep sapphire eyes sparkling with happiness, her gown sweeping across the floor as she raised a goblet of wine in toast to her lord . . .

Sweetheart! He had first met her at the Yule tide feast, his eyes following the graceful figure as she danced and played with her cousins. The music had brought a sparkle to her eyes, her cheeks glowed from the heat of the fire.

Joss shuddered so violently that Lyn noticed. 'Joss, are you all right?' She was there beside her, putting her arm around her shoulders. 'What's wrong?'

Joss shook her head, staring down at her feet in the candlelight. 'Nothing. Just a bit cold.' The singers hadn't noticed. They sang on, reaching effortlessly for the high notes, their voices curling into the beams. But it was their last carol. They had to move on to the Goodyears' farm and then to the Rectory itself. Scarves were rewound, gloves pulled on, change found for their collecting bag.

The silence when they had gone was strangely profound. As if reluctant to lose the mood they sat on by the fire staring into the embers.

Katherine, my love, wait for me!

They were so nearly audible, the words, like a half remembered dream, slipping away before it is grasped. With a sigh Joss shook her head.

'The carols were beautiful. You know, it's strange, you would expect there to be a feeling of evil in this house if the devil lived here. But there isn't.'

'Of course there isn't.' Luke dropped a kiss on her head. 'I wish you would forget about the devil. This is a fabulous, happy house, full of good memories.' He ruffled her hair affectionately. 'The devil would hate it!'

He was asleep when Joss climbed up into the high bed later. She had lain for a long time in the bath, trying to soak the chill out of her bones in water that was not quite hot enough to do the trick, and she had found she was pressing herself against the warm enamel, trying to extricate the last hint of heat from the rapidly cooling bath. When she finally dragged herself out onto the mat and wrapped the towel around her she realised that the

121

heating system such as it was, fired from the range in the kitchen, had long ago turned itself off for the night with its usual ticking and groaning. There would be no more hot water and no more barely warm radiators until next morning when, with more ticking and groaning, the system would, God-willing, drag itself once more back into life. Shivering she looked in on Tom. He was pink and warm, tucked securely under his cellular blankets and fast asleep. Leaving his door a fraction ajar she crept into her room and reluctantly taking off her dressing gown slid in beside Luke.

Outside, the moon was a hard silver against a star flecked sky. Frost had whitened the garden and it was almost as bright as day. Luke hadn't quite drawn the curtains over the back window and she could see the brilliance of the night through the crack. Moonlight spilled across the floor and onto the quilt.

They were all there, in the shadowy room: the servants, the family, the priest. White faces turned towards him as he burst in, his spurs ringing on the boards and catching in the soft sweet hay which had been spread everywhere to muffle the noise.

'Katherine?' He stopped a few feet from the high bed, his breath rasping in his throat, his heart thudding with fear. Her face was beautiful and completely calm.

There was no sign of pain. Her glorious dark hair, free of its coif, lay spread across the pillow; her eyelashes were thick upon the alabaster cheeks.

'KATHERINE!' He heard his own voice as a scream and at last someone moved. The woman who had so often shown him up to this very room and brought him wine, stepped forward, a small bundle in her arms.

'You have a son, my lord. At least you have a son!'

Uneasily Joss turned to Luke and snuggled against his back.

The moonlight disturbed her. It was relentless, hard, accentuating the cold. Shivering she pulled the covers higher, burying her head in the pillow beside that of her husband, feeling his warmth, his solidity, reassuring beside her.

Frozen with horror he stared down at the woman on the bed.
'Katherine.'
This time the word was a sob; a prayer.
Throwing himself across the body he took her in his arms and wept.

With a sigh Joss slept at last, uneasily, her dreams uncomfortable and unremembered, unaware of the shadow which drifted across the moon throwing a dark swathe across the bed. She did not feel the chill in the room deepen, nor the brush of cold fingers across her hair.

Katherine, Katherine, Katherine!
The name rose into the darkest corners of the room and was lost in the shadows of the roof beyond the beams, weaving, writhing with pain, sinking into the fabric of the house.
His face wet with tears he looked up. 'Leave me,' he cried. 'Leave me with her.'
He turned to the servant, and his mouth was twisted with hate. 'Take that child away. He killed her. He killed my love, God curse him. He killed the sweetest, gentlest woman in the world!'

When she woke it was with a splitting headache, and only seconds later the realisation that she was going to be sick. Not pausing to grab her dressing gown she threw herself out of bed and ran for the bathroom, falling on her knees in front of the lavatory. It was Luke, gently stroking her head while she vomited, who wrapped something round her shoulders and later brought her a cup of tea.

r Robert Simms was rector of the church at Belheddon from 1914 until 1926. Standing in front of the stained glass window which had been erected to his memory in the church Joss wondered just how much he had been able to comfort Lydia in her last months. Had he sprinkled Holy Water around the house? Had he buried her son? Presumably he had buried her. The grave out in the churchyard was overgrown now with nettles and covered in ivy but, scraping away the moss she had found the inscription:

Samuel Manners, born 1882, died 1926
also his wife
Lydia Sarah Manners, born 1902, died 1925
also their children
Samuel, born 1920, died 1921
John, born 1921, died 1925
Robert, born 1922, died 1936

What happened to the sons of this house that they died so young? Walking back slowly up the path from the church towards the gate into the garden Joss stopped for a minute beside her brothers' graves. Luke had cut the nettles now, and she had scraped away some of the moss and planted bulbs in the cold earth between them.

She shivered. Edgar Gower's words kept returning to her: 'Don't embroil yourself in the affairs of the Duncans; Belheddon Hall is an unhappy house, my dear. The past is the past; it should be allowed to rest.' Was there something terribly wrong at Belheddon? And if there was, why did she feel so happy here? Why did Luke love it so much? Why had they not felt the evil which had so terrified Lydia and Laura?

Luke was lying under the Bentley, a spanner in his hand when she walked into the courtyard. 'Hi there!' His voice came from the shadows beneath the chassis. 'Lyn has taken Tom into Colchester. Are you feeling better after your walk?'

'A bit.' She leaned against the coach house wall, hands in pockets, staring down at his feet. 'Luke, do you want a coffee? There's something I want to ask you.'

'Why not.' He scooted himself out from beneath the car and grinned. There was a patch of oil on his forehead and his hands as always now were ingrained with black.

'So?' Blowing on the hot mug he sat at the kitchen table. 'What's the problem?'

'There's something wrong, Luke. Terribly wrong. Can't you feel it?' She sat opposite him. The smell of the coffee was making her feel sick again.

His face sobered. 'In what way wrong? Not the baby?'

'No, not the baby. Luke, I've found letters and diaries and things, written by my mother and grandmother.'

'I know. I've seen you engrossed in them.' He reached for the biscuit tin and levered off the lid. 'I thought they interested you.' He poured some more coffee into his mug.

'They both talk about something dreadful, something terrifying in the house.'

'Oh Joss.' He shook his head. 'Not that again. Not the devil himself, living in the cellar? For goodness sake!' He heaved himself to his feet, grabbing another biscuit.

'Listen love, I've got to go back to work. I need to try and sort out that carburettor by lunch time if I can.' He bent over her and kissed the top of her head. 'Don't look for problems where there aren't any. We are damn lucky to have this place. We're happy here. It's given us the chance of a new start, and it's given you a second family to research and get to know. But keep your imagination for your book, Joss. This was real life. Real people living in real times. It wasn't fiction. Maybe your grandmother and your mother were neurotic. You don't know. Maybe they were both incipient novelists – perhaps that's where you get it from. We don't know. All we know is that this is a fabulous, happy house. Alice and Joe will be here tomorrow, it's Christmas in three days and our own family is the one that you should be thinking about.'

He had been right, of course. Every time over Christmas when her thoughts returned to the tragedy of her brothers' deaths, or her mother or her grandmother's fears Joss firmly brought them back to the realities of running a house full of people, cooking on an antiquated stove, thinking about the book and scribbling notes on the pad she kept in the pocket of her jeans and keeping Tom's excitement within bounds all while hiding as much as possible her lingering morning sickness and exhaustion. Alice was not fooled for a moment but she went along with the deception in spite of Joe's protests that she must not do too much herself, calmly and firmly taking as much as possible out of Joss's hands and slowly, to her surprise Joss found that she was indeed beginning to relax. With people in it the house did not seem so large. The silences had gone; every room was full of family, whispering, wrapping presents, hiding parcels. The silver glitter on the tree was the only thing that moved in the shadows and the voices were silent. Twice she went out onto the lawn late at night to look up at the stars alone. Awed by their frosty beauty she stood quite still, her hands pushed down into the pockets of her jacket, imagining the ethereal beauty of the music of the spheres ringing through the silence of the garden. But in reality she could hear nothing but the distant piping of the pewits under the moon on the fields and the quick urgent hunting calls of the little owl as it quartered the old gardens beyond the lake.

'Sammy? Georgie?' Her call was tentative, making her feel a little foolish. She knew there was no one there. Probably she had imagined it all.

She smiled to herself as she turned back towards the courtyard. It was going to be a good Christmas and they were all going to enjoy Belheddon and be very very happy there.

Three weeks after Christmas, Joe came and found Joss dozing by the fire in the study, her notebooks on her knee, a pen lying slack between her fingers. 'Your mother's not well, Joss. The doctor said she mustn't tire herself out and that's just what she's been doing these last few weeks. I'm taking her home so she can rest. And Lyn will still be here to help. She's a good girl, and she's loving the country life.' His face creased into a network of deep wrinkles as he smiled at her fondly.

'Dad.' Joss reached out for his hand. She had been dreaming, she realised, about Richard, happily living inside the plot of her book, walking around an earlier, more primitive but sun-filled Belheddon. 'I had no idea Mum was ill! Why didn't she tell me?'

'She didn't want anyone to know. And there's nothing rest and a bit of TLC from her old husband can't put right. Don't you go worrying yourself now. Just let us go home quietly.'

Sitting in her bedroom later Joss looked up at Lyn who

was standing by the window. 'She wouldn't tell me what was wrong.'

'Nor me.' Lyn bit her lip. 'You know what she's like. She never makes a fuss.' There were tears brimming in her eyes. She turned to Joss. 'If she gets worse I'll have to go back. I can't leave them on their own.'

'Of course you can't. Lyn, why won't they stay here? We could both look after them.'

Lyn shook her head. 'Come on, Joss. This is your home. Your real parents' home. However lovely it is here, this is not Mum and Dad's scene. It's not really mine, though I'm prepared to make a big sacrifice.' She gave a wan smile. 'They're not really happy out of London, you know that. All their friends are there. The rest of the family is there. This is fantasy land. They are pleased for you – really pleased – but they don't belong.'

'I suppose so.' Joss leaned back on the bed with a sigh. 'Why do things have to change, Lyn? Why do people get old and ill. It seems so unfair.'

'It's life.' Lyn headed for the door. 'Some people get old, others have babies. I'm not a philosopher like you, but even I can see that's the way it works. I expect every new generation puts up a fight as it sees old age coming, then it gives up and accepts the inevitable. You rest now. You look washed out too. You know the doctor told you not to do too much. I'll take Tom for a walk and we'll have a cup of tea later, OK? Once it gets dark and Luke's indoors.'

Shivering, Joss pulled the counterpane up over herself. Outside the garden was very still. A sprinkling of snow that morning had melted and everything was dank and dripping. She smiled as she heard Tom's voice, shrill and excited, outside the window, then it faded as Lyn took him down the drive towards the village and the room sank back into silence. After a while she dozed, drifting in and out of sleep. The room grew darker. Shivering she wriggled down further into the bed, her eyes shut.

The hand on her forehead was cool; gentle. It seemed to soothe her.

Katherine, my clever love.

'Luke?' she murmured, barely awake. His hand had moved down to her breast and languidly, still half asleep, she moved beneath the gentle fingers. 'I'll come down, soon.' She slept again.

When she woke it was dark. She lay still for a moment, still wrapped in her dream, her body glowing, sleepily aware of the hands which had caressed her breasts as she slept. Groping for the light switch she looked at her watch. It was nearly five. With a groan she heaved herself off the bed and stood up. The house was still silent. Probably Lyn had put the television on in the kitchen to keep Tom quiet while she made his tea, the routine they had fallen into so Joss could keep the afternoons for writing. She had almost two complete chapters finished now as well as a sheaf of notes and a chronology of the Wars of the Roses. Luke would be in by now. The house downstairs would be warm and busy and welcoming. She shivered, reaching for a thick sweater and pulling it over her head. All she had to do was go downstairs.

The last two entries in the diary had been short. Her grandmother had written:

> I feel strangely weak. The doctor came again this morning and said it was the result of being tired. I shall get up when the rain stops and the sun returns. How I crave the sun.

Four days later she wrote:

> The loneliness becomes worse. I do not let them know I am alone. The effort of going downstairs for some beef tea is too much. Perhaps tomorrow.

129

That was all. The rest of the book was empty. Four days later she was dead.

Shivering Joss put the diary back into the bedside drawer. She wished she had not read that. The thought of the woman alone in the house, completely alone and dying, was intolerable. She stood up, conscious of a slight cramp in her leg and went to look down into the garden. It was very black. Rain slanted down across the grass dissolving the last remaining patches of snow.

'Joss!'

It was Lyn calling up the staircase. 'Phone call for you.'

Shaking herself Joss turned away from the darkness and ran downstairs. In the study Lyn had thrown several logs onto the fire and the room was almost hot. 'David.' She nodded towards the phone which lay on the desk. 'He sounds excited.'

'David?' Joss put the receiver to her ear.

'Joss. Only a week until school starts. Can I come up and see you?' He sounded almost breathless.

'Of course. You know we've got room.' Joss sat down at the desk, pressing the phone to her ear unaware that her voice was seductively husky with sleep. Her hands were, she realised suddenly, shaking. 'Any special reason?'

'Wait and see. I'll be down tomorrow if that's all right. And you will never guess who I met at a dinner yesterday. A chap called Gerald Andrews who is your friendly local historian. He and I belong to the same club, it seems. Listen, we had quite a talk about Belheddon. I gave him your phone number and he is going to get in touch. And Joss. I am having lunch next week with Robert Cassie. If you have got some stuff ready for our book I could deliver it in person and if that's not an incentive, I don't know what is! See you tomorrow.'

'He's coming down.' Joss put the phone down and

came to join Lyn by the fire. 'He seems to have found out some more about the house.'

'You and your bloody house!' Lyn shook her head. 'Can't you think of anything else?'

Joss flinched. 'I'm sorry. Am I being boring?'

'You certainly are.' Lyn reached for the poker and stabbed ferociously at the fire. 'Still I'm glad David is coming down. He seems to be our only remaining link with civilisation.'

'The country is getting to you.' Joss smiled, determined not to be goaded.

'Well even you can't like it in this bloody weather. No doubt it will improve when spring comes,' Lyn relented a little. 'The vicar came while you were asleep. He brought the parish magazine, a piece of paper asking for jumble and a packet for you from someone called Mary Sutton.'

Joss stared at her. 'Why didn't you tell me that before? Where is it?'

'In the kitchen. Joss –'

As Joss scrambled to her feet she was brought up short by the anguish in Lyn's voice. 'You do realise Ma might be dying, don't you?'

Joss froze. 'She's not dying, Lyn. She's tired. Not very well –'

'She's got to have lots of tests, Joss. Dad told me on the phone. She doesn't want you to know. She thinks it might upset you.' Lyn's voice was suddenly harsh. 'Apparently they don't mind upsetting me.'

'Oh, Lyn.' Joss knelt and put her arm around her sister's shoulders. 'You know Mum and Dad. It's because of the baby. They come from a generation who thought any old thing could upset a baby on the way. They've told you because they want your comfort.'

'I wanted to go to be with them. They don't want me. They want me to stay here.'

131

'Then stay here.' Joss's arms tightened round her. 'When they need you they will tell you.'

'You think so?' Lyn's eyes were full of tears.

'Of course.'

For a while they sat together in front of the fire, lost in thought, then at last Joss climbed stiffly to her feet. 'Come on. Let's make a cup of tea.'

Lyn nodded. She sniffed. 'I'll get the young lord and master up from his rest. You go and put the kettle on.'

The packet from Mary Sutton was a large envelope. Lyn had left it on the kitchen table with the parish magazine, a flimsy pamphlet with a lurid purple cover. Eyeing the package Joss filled the kettle and put it on the hot plate. Only then did she allow herself to open it. It contained another notebook – by now Joss was familiar with her mother's jottings; she must have bought a whole stack of them in a job lot somewhere – and a few more letters and some photographs. She glanced at the photos. Sammy and Georgie. She didn't need the pencilled names on the back to identify them. They were black and white school photos, she guessed, both wearing the same school uniform in spite of the eight year gap between them. Sammy was very dark – she could see the resemblance to herself – with a thin, intense face and round light coloured eyes, perhaps blue like her own. Georgie was fairer, chubbier, more mischievous. Both had been about six when the photos were taken. She stared down at them for a long time before she saw the note scribbled by Mary. 'I thought you could have the photos of my boys. The other things I found the other day. You may as well have them too.'

The notebook was full of loosely scribbled writing. Poems, recipes, and again diary entries, seemingly carelessly and unchronologically scattered. Her mother, she was beginning to think, had a butterfly mind, leaping from here to there, from thought to thought, idea to idea, and from self conscious musing to the need to confide somewhere, if only to an inanimate diary.

The two letters were addressed to Mary. Joss picked them up, touched that Mary should part with them. One was dated 1956.

> Take care of my little one, Mary dear. Remember the doctor's advice about his tummy aches. Kiss him for me and look after him. I'm so much happier to know he is there with you in your mother's cottage.

Joss looked up. The letter was headed Belheddon Hall. Why had Laura thought it necessary for Georgie to go and stay with Mary in the village?

She smiled at Lyn and Tom as they appeared in the doorway. 'Tea is nearly ready.'

Next morning, almost before they were up, David had appeared with an extra belated Christmas present for Tom – a furry, hideously green, hippopotamus with which the little boy fell instantly in love and christened for some obscure reason, Joseph. 'Arimathea or Carpenter?' David asked mischievously and the little boy answered solemnly, 'Hittopomatus.'

In the laughter which followed David glanced at Joss. Pregnancy seemed to be agreeing with her. She seemed to be growing more attractive every time he saw her. Sternly he reined in his thoughts. 'So, have you written enough for me to take to Bob?'

She nodded. 'Two chapters, like you said. I printed them up yesterday.'

He grinned. 'Great. Well, here's your reward. More stuff about the house.' He put a folder down on the table in front of her. 'I've found out who Katherine is. Or was.' He smiled. 'Katherine de Vere was the eldest daughter of the Robert de Vere who lived here in the mid-fifteenth century. She was betrothed to the son of a local earl.

*Handsome and light hearted, the young man rode to Belheddon
daily and Katherine's father laughed out loud in delight.*

*'We have a love match here,' he guffawed to all who would
listen and when he saw the debonair Richard tuck his daughter's favour in his cap he slapped him on the back and planned
the wedding.*

*She had eyes for no one but this young neighbour. Whilst
she curtseyed to the king and served him with wine she did not
look up and see his face.*

To her he was old.

David turned the page in his folder and went on: 'I'm
not sure whether or not she actually married him. The
records are a bit cryptic about that, I thought. Anyway
only a year later in 1482 poor Katherine died, and she's
in the church as Katherine de Vere. She was only seventeen or eighteen. When her father died Belheddon Hall
passed to an Edward, presumably her younger brother.
He too died at the age of eighteen, but had time to marry
and have a daughter. By that time we are in the reign
of Henry VII. The strange thing is – ' he paused and looked
round – 'that already, by the end of the sixteenth century
the house had a reputation for being haunted.' He
grinned at Joss. 'Do you want to know this?'

'No!' 'Yes!' Luke and Joss spoke simultaneously.

David shrugged. He reached for a page out of the file.

' "The beauteous house of Belheddon Hall,
though well-favoured, did not boast many
tenants. Men and dogs alike fled in terror from
the wails of an apparition which inhabited its
lofty chambers."

'That was written in the late seventeenth century
by a diarist called James Cope who stayed here – only
once.

134

' "For more than a hundred years the house has been inhabited by this creature whose unhappiness is distressing to the ear and frightening to the eye." '

David laughed. 'He then adds:

' "Though I stayed three nights it did not, to my sorrow appear and has not been seen these last forty years." '

'He doesn't mention the devil, though, does he,' Luke put in tartly. 'That's interesting. An old gossip like that would have put that snippet in if he had heard it.'

David nodded. 'Interestingly though there is a mention of the devil in an account written only fifty years later by James Fosset, an antiquarian who spent several months collecting stories and history in the district. His theory seems to me to be on the right lines. Listen.

' "Belheddon Hall, one of the most beautiful of the local houses was built on a much earlier site. Some say it goes back to the dawn of time. The name derives from the old English *bealu*, meaning evil or calamity, and *heddon* meaning a heather-covered hill and would appear to point to the site having been used in pagan times as a site of worship and perhaps of sacrifice. Superstition and fear cling to the site and as little as a hundred years ago a witch was taken and hanged after having concourse with the devil in the grounds of the house."

'Do you see a pattern beginning to form? The hauntings, the pagan site, some poor old woman taken as a witch – slowly the pieces are falling into place. Somehow over the ages the two have got amalgamated and the result is a wonderful legend that it is the devil who haunts, or inhabits, the house. There. Your problem is solved. Andrews was a fascinating man. He knew most of this, I suspect, though he hadn't come across the Fosset references. He says Edward IV actually came to the house on several occasions. That was when the de Vere family lived here. In fact he may have given them the house as at an earlier date the manor was in royal domain. After their day he thinks a whole host of different families lived here – none seems to have stayed more than a few generations, if that, although he thinks on several occasions the house passed down through the female line, so of course the surnames would have been different, just as it is now of course, with you.' He looked up at Joss and smiled. 'I hope you are pleased with my humble efforts?'

Joss nodded slowly. Her head was buzzing.

'The king! The king is coming!'

The excitement in the house was reaching fever pitch.

Katherine scowled as her mother reached for the brush and dragged it through her tangled curls.

'Be sweet to him, child.' The cold lips were very close to Katherine's ear.

The earl's son was a good catch, but the king was better.

'Be loving. Whatever your king desires, remember, it is his to command!'

'There is so much to take in.' Joss gave a little half laugh. 'It's fascinating. I especially like the link with Edward IV. As my book is set during the Wars of the Roses, I can do my research right here.' She shook her head again. Briefly she wondered if David too had heard the strange echo which seemed to fill the spaces of the house.

14

n the kitchen Tom was whining crossly, pulling at Lyn's long checked skirt. 'Pick me up!' When she ignored him he stamped his small foot and wailed even louder.

Joss frowned. Her arms full of dirty washing she had pushed open the kitchen door and come in to find Lyn on the phone. 'Lyn?'

Tom's wails grew louder.

Lyn turned away from him in irritation, clapping her free hand over the ear that was not pressed to the receiver. 'Listen, I can come up any time,' she said into the phone, 'you know I can. I want to.' She pushed Tom none too gently towards his toys and his wails doubled in volume.

Joss dropped the clothes she was carrying onto the floor in front of the washing machine and went to Tom, squatting down to give him a hug. 'Leave Aunty Lyn while she's on the phone.' She looked up at Lyn. 'Is that Mum you're talking to?' she whispered.

Lyn nodded.

'How is she? Can I speak to her?'

But Lyn was already hanging up. 'She's OK.'

'But she's not! I wanted to speak to her.'

'Then ring her back.' Lyn scowled. 'Tom was making such a racket I couldn't hear myself think.'

137

Joss shook her head. 'You know he doesn't like us talking on the phone. He just wants attention and hates us being distracted from him. It's a phase they all go through.'

'Well, I hope it's not a long one!' Lyn stared at the washing in distaste. 'I suppose you want me to put that lot in the machine.'

Joss narrowed her eyes. Lyn's voice was full of resentment.

'No, I can do it. What's wrong, Lyn?'

'You don't care about Mum at all. You haven't given her a thought. When did you last ring her? She said she hasn't spoken to you in days!'

'Lyn –'

'No. You don't care anymore, do you. You're just going to forget them. Your new family is so much more exciting. We were never good enough for you, were we!' Lyn stormed across to the window and stood, arms folded, staring out.

'That's not true! For goodness' sake, what's the matter with you?' Joss had to raise her voice as, upset by Lyn's tone, Tom started to scream in earnest. Stooping, Joss picked him up and swung him onto her hip. 'Lyn, what is it? Did Mum say something? Does she know what's wrong with her?'

Lyn shook her head without speaking.

'Is it cancer, Lyn?' Joss put her hand on her sister's shoulder.

Lyn shrugged miserably.

'You must go, if you want to.' Joss's voice was gentler. 'You don't have to stay here, you know.'

Lyn sniffed. 'You need me.'

'I know I do. And Luke and I love having you here, Lyn. But if you're not happy –'

'I love Tom.'

Joss smiled. 'I know that too. And I love Mum and

Dad. I always have and I always will. You mustn't believe for a minute that I don't. If I didn't ring Mum yesterday, it was only that I was too busy –'

'Too busy to pick up the phone for two minutes?' Lyn was still staring out of the window.

'It didn't mean I stopped loving her, Lyn.'

'That's what she thinks.'

'She does not!' Joss was angry suddenly. 'And you know it.' She turned away and unceremoniously dumped Tom on the floor in front of a pile of coloured bricks. Scooping up the heap of clothes she pushed them into the machine and reached for the detergent.

'She's going into hospital tomorrow, Joss.' Lyn's gaze was fixed unseeing on the window catch as she scratched at the flaking paint with her nail. Her voice was leaden.

Joss sat down at the kitchen table. 'Why didn't you say so?'

'She's going to die.'

'Lyn –'

'I can't bear it if she dies.' There were tears running down Lyn's cheeks.

'She won't die.' Joss put her head in her hands and took a deep unsteady breath. 'She won't, Lyn. She's going to be all right. I'm sure she is.' She had to be. She couldn't cope, she realised suddenly, if her mum, the woman who had been her mother all her remembered life, was not there in the background to support her. She looked down at Tom. Suddenly engrossed in his toys his wails had ceased as he examined a large yellow beaker and she was overwhelmed by a sudden rush of love for him. It was love that made everyone so vulnerable, in the end. She sighed again. That was what made families such a joy and such a heart-break.

Gerald Andrews drew his cup towards him and raised it with difficulty in arthritic fingers. He beamed at Joss however as he got it at last to his lips. 'My dear, it was good of you to ask me to tea. You don't know how much I have longed to come to see this house. It seems extraordinary that I should have written a history of it and yet never set foot across the threshold.'

The history in question, a slim booklet in pale buff cardboard covers, lay between them on the kitchen table. On the front an eighteenth century woodcut showed the front of the house with the beech tree perhaps half as big as it now was.

'I couldn't believe my luck when I found myself talking to David Tregarron and he said he knew you!' He picked up a biscuit.

'It's lucky for me too.' Joss was dying to look through the book. 'I have so much catching up to do. I know so little of my family.'

He nodded. 'I wrote to your mother several times asking if I might come and see her when I was writing that, but I understand she had not been well. Miss Sutton wrote back and each time said it was not convenient. Then your mother left and it was too late.'

'You lived in the area a long time?' Unable to resist it any longer Joss picked up the pamphlet and opened it. The first chapter was called *Early Days*.

'About ten years. I compiled some half dozen of these little books. All on the notable houses of the district. The Old Rectory, Pilgrim Hall, Pickersticks House . . .'

'Pilgrim Hall?' Joss looked up. 'My father's home?'

'Your grandfather's home. John Duncan was appointed guardian to your mother and her brother Robert when their mother and father died – I suppose it was inevitable that his son should fall in love with Laura – he kept both houses going for a while, then after Robert died he took Laura back to live at Pilgrim Hall with them. This place was practically derelict for a bit, but of course it was Laura's inheritance and they couldn't sell. John Duncan came into a lot of money, late in life – an inheritance as far as I remember from some relative who had lived in the Far East. He was a strange man, John. He hated Belheddon and Pilgrim Hall with equal loathing. He settled money on the two children, Philip and his ward, Laura, and went to live abroad. His wife, Lady Sarah, stayed on for several years, until the children got married, then she sold Pilgrim Hall which is much smaller than this, and went off to join him. He never came back, not even for the wedding. It was a frightful scandal at the time. People locally though he'd gone off with a dusky lady,' he gave a delighted chuckle. 'I don't somehow think Lady Sarah would have stood for that. She would have beaten any rivals to death with her umbrella. Powerful lady, your grandmother on the Duncan side.'

Joss smiled. 'They died abroad, did they?'

'John did, I believe. He had vowed never to come back to England. I never found out why. Some kind of quarrel with the family, I suppose. After he died, Lady Sarah came home. She even tried to buy back Pilgrim Hall. That must have been in the sixties, but by then they had built a huge annex and turned it into a country house hotel. I met her once, because I had already published the booklet on Pilgrim Hall. She wanted a copy for herself. It must have been the mid to late sixties because your father, Philip, was already dead – that dreadful accident with the horse – so sad – but I expect you know all about that. She suggested that I write about Belheddon. She was very scathing about the place. Thought it was cursed. She thought Laura was mad to stay here, but Laura seemed to be unable to tear herself away. I can remember her telling me that she was fixated on the house. She would walk about on her own, even at night, for hours, sometimes talking to herself.' He glanced at Joss. 'She thought Laura had finally lost her mind when she gave you up for adoption. The whole village took it very badly. Your mother was virtually ostracised afterwards. Lady Sarah said she would never speak to her again, and not long after that she moved somewhere up north.' He hesitated. 'It was her theory that the house was cursed which attracted my attention. I don't normally believe in these things,' he smiled almost apologetically, 'but this place has had more than its share of tragedy by any standards.'

'So many of the children die.' Unconsciously Joss put her hands protectively over her stomach.

He frowned. 'You shouldn't perhaps read too much into infants' deaths. Such high mortality is profoundly shocking, but remember, in every age but our own such things were normal.'

'I suppose so.' She was staring at the booklet in her hands:

> *Four major rivers find their sources in Belheddon Ridge, a sandy, gravel escarpment which cuts across the clays of East Anglia in an east west slash through the landscape, visible for miles,* she read. *Such a place was an obvious candidate for early settlement and indeed there is archaeological evidence of an iron age camp under what is now the west lawn of the house ...*

She turned the pages eagerly. 'There never seems to have been one family in the house for any length of time,' she said at last. She glanced up at him. 'From the letters and diaries I've been studying and the family Bible there seem to be so many names, although they are related.'

'Female descent.' Andrews reached for another biscuit. 'It happens. If you look you will find the house was nearly always inherited by daughters, so of course the surname changes generation after generation. Not every time. There were years when it stood empty and when it had tenants, but it seems always to have come back in the end to some relation or other. It's had a longer history in one family than you might think.'

'Really?' She looked up at him eagerly. 'We're not descended from the de Veres?'

'Oh almost certainly. That was something which intrigued me, as I was telling Dr Tregarron. The trouble is I didn't have enough time to follow it through in detail – you could get a genealogist to do it, I suppose, if you were interested. Matrilineal descent is a fascinating phenomenon. Strange to us but a matter of course to some people. In this case obviously it wasn't a policy decision, it just worked out that way. No sons.' He stuffed his biscuit into his mouth and glanced at his watch. 'I hate to seem too eager, Mrs Grant, but you said I might glance at some of the main rooms.'

'Of course.' Reluctantly Joss put down the book. 'I'll show you round.'

In the course of the next hour Joss was given a potted, breathless and ecstatic history of the English manor house, taking in pargetting, chamfering, stopping, plasterwork, the art of the fresco ('Almost certainly, under this panelling. The panelling would protect it, you know,') staircases, solars, bedchambers and the great hall as centre of the house. Her head reeling, Joss followed in his wake, wishing again and again she had a tape recorder with her to take down this man's encyclopaedic knowledge. He laughed when she told him as much. 'I'll come again, if you let me. We can make notes. Now, the cellar.' They were standing at the foot of the main staircase and his nose was quivering like a dog's scenting a rabbit. 'There we may see traces of early vaulting.'

Joss pointed at the door. 'Down there. Do you mind if I don't come down? I get claustrophobia.' She laughed deprecatingly, aware of his sudden shrewd gaze.

'Am I tiring you, Mrs Grant? I know I go on and on. I used to drive my wife mad. The trouble is I get so excited

143

about things.' Already he had fumbled awkwardly with the key, swung open the door and found the light switch. She watched as he disappeared, hampered by his stiffness, down the steep stairs, then she turned away into the study. She waited by the window, staring out across the lawn. Hours seemed to pass. Frowning she glanced at her watch. Wafting across the great hall from the kitchen she could smell onions and garlic. Lyn must be putting on the lunch while Tom would be watching *Sesame Street* on the TV. There was no sound from the cellar. She walked across to the door and peered down the stairs anxiously. 'Mr Andrews?' There was no answer. 'Mr Andrews?' There was a sudden tightness in her chest. 'Are you all right?'

She could feel the cold air rising. It smelled musty and damp and somehow very old. With a shiver she put her hand on the splintery banister and leaned forward, trying to see into the first cellar. 'Mr Andrews?' The stairs were very steep, the old worn wood split and pitted. Reluctantly she put her foot on the first step. 'Mr Andrews are you all right?' The unshaded bulb was very bright. It threw the shadows of the winebins, black wedges across the floor. 'Mr Andrews?' Her voice was shaking now, threaded with panic. Clutching the rail she crept down another two steps. This was where Georgie had fallen, his small body hurtling down the steps to lie in a crumpled heap at the bottom. Shaking the thought out of her head she stepped down again, forcing herself down the steps one by one. There was a sudden movement on the wall near her. She froze with terror, staring, and her eyes focused at last on a small brown lizard, clinging to the stone. It stared back at her and then with a flick of its tail it ran up the wall and disappeared through a crack into the darkness behind the wall.

'Mrs Grant, look at this!' The voice, so loud and excited, right behind her, made Joss jump round with a small cry. 'Oh, my dear, I'm sorry. Did I startle you?' Gerald Andrews appeared through the arch which led into the next cellar. 'Come and see. There is the most perfect medieval vaulting through here. Very early. Oh, I wish I'd known about this when I wrote the book. It takes the date of the original house back I should say to the thirteenth or fourteenth century . . .' Already he had disappeared through the arch again, beckoning her to follow.

Taking a deep breath Joss made her way past the gleaming ranks of bottles, awaiting the visit and tasting next week from the wine expert from Sotheby's, and found herself staring up at the stone arches of the second cellar.

'You see, under the great hall. A flint undercroft, built of the same stuff as the church.' He was spluttering with excitement. 'And the carving, here, on the key stone and the corbels, see?' He beamed at her. 'You have a treasure here, Mrs Grant, a real treasure. This vault has been here if I'm right for six or seven hundred years.'

'Seven hundred?' Joss stared at him, her fear subsiding as his enthusiasm increased. She hugged herself against the chill.

He nodded, patting the wall. 'May I bring a colleague to see this? And someone from the Historic Buildings department? It is quite wonderful. And here, all along!'

She smiled. 'Of course you may. How exciting. You may have to bring out a new edition of your book.'

He laughed. 'How accurately you read my thoughts, my dear. I'm a silly old fool, I know. I get so carried away, but it is so exciting. It's suddenly seeing history before you – the bones of history – the actual fabric within which events took place.'

'Would this have been a cellar then?' Joss glanced over her shoulder.

'Maybe. An undercroft, a storeroom, even a well chamber.' He laughed, staring round. 'But no well.'

'The well is in the courtyard.' She was edging back

towards the stairs, trying to draw him away from his wall. 'Why don't we go up, Mr Andrews. It's so cold down here. You can always come back.'

He was stricken. 'How selfish of me. I'm sorry, my dear. You do look cold. Of course we must go.' He cast one last longing glance back at his vaulting and followed her to the staircase.

Lyn and Tom were still deeply engrossed in cooking supper when at last she waved Gerald Andrews down the drive, so, reaching for her coat, Joss opened the back door and went out into the dusk. Beyond the lake a small gate in the hedge led out into the lane. A few hundred yards' walk led up to the back of the field from where she could look down on the estuary and out towards the dark sea. She stood for several minutes, her hands in her pockets, looking down at the water then with a shiver she turned back into the lane, which with its thickly tangled hedges was more sheltered. Slowly she walked back, savouring the sweetness of the smell of spring flowers and wet earth and sodden bark after the salt sharp tang nearer the sea. From here she could see the silhouette of the church tower, and now and then, from a higher point on the bank the roofs of the Hall. In the deep shade between the hedge banks it was cold and damp and she shivered again, hurrying to get back.

As she let herself in through the wicket gate by the rowan tree she saw a boy standing by the lake. He had his back to her and he seemed to be standing staring down into the water. 'Sammy?' Her whisper was choked with fear. 'Sammy!' This time it was a shout. The boy did not turn. He did not seem to hear her. Running now, she crossed the lawn, round thickets of elder and winter dead hawthorn shrouded in ivy, and burst out on the bank of the lake near the little landing stage.

There was no one to be seen.

'Sammy!' Her cry put up a heron which had been

146

standing motionless in the shallows on the far side of the water. With an angry harsh cry it lifted laboriously into the evening sky and skimmed the hedge out of sight.

'Sammy,' she whispered again. But he was gone. If a real child had been playing by the water the heron would have flown away long before she arrived on the scene.

She put her hand to her side with a small grimace. Her desperate run across the grass had given her a stitch. Frowning with pain she doubled over for a minute, then slowly she began to walk back towards the house.

Lyn and Tom were in the kitchen. Tom's face, covered in chocolate, betrayed the fact that they had now reached the stage of preparing the pudding.

'You OK?' Lyn glanced at Joss as Tom ran to her and gave her knees a sticky hug.

Joss grimaced. 'A bit of a stitch. Silly.'

'Go and sit down by the fire. I'll bring you another cup of tea.' Lyn slid her baking tins into the oven. 'Go on. Off with you.'

The fire in the study was almost out. Bending down wearily Joss threw on some logs and a shovel of coal, then she picked up David's notes and sat down in the old arm chair. Her back was aching now too and she felt inordinately tired.

When Lyn came in half an hour later with a cup of tea she was fast asleep. For a minute Lyn stood staring down at her, then with a shrug she turned away. She did not leave the tea.

'Luke!' Joss's cry turned into a gasp as a violent cramp tore her out of her sleep. 'Luke, the baby! Something's wrong.' Miserably hugging her stomach she slipped to her knees on the carpet. 'Luke!'

There was a hand on her shoulder. Gentle, caressing, he was there. Sobbing she reached up to grip his knuckles. The lightest touch across her back, fingers rubbing her shoulders. She could smell roses. Where had Luke found roses at this time of year? Her hand groped for his. There was no one there. Shocked, she stared round, another kind of fear flooding icily through her as she realised the room was empty. 'Luke!' Her voice rose to a shriek.

'Joss? Were you calling?' The door was pushed open and Lyn put her head round it. 'Joss? Oh God! What's the matter?'

Luke drove her to the hospital. His face was white and Joss kept noticing the smear of oil across his left cheek. She smiled fondly. Poor Luke. He was always being dragged away from his precious car.

The pains had stopped now. All she felt was a strangely overwhelming tiredness. She could hardly move. She couldn't keep her eyes open. Even her fear for the baby couldn't keep her awake.

She was vaguely aware of being wheeled in a chair from the car to a lift, and of being put into bed then she was lost in velvety blackness. Twice she woke up. The first time Simon Fraser was there, sitting at her bedside, holding her wrist. He smiled, his sandy hair flopping round his face, his glasses reflecting distorted images of the side ward where they had put her. 'Hello there.' He leaned forward. 'Welcome back to planet Earth. How are you feeling?'

'My baby – ?'

'Still there.' He grinned. 'You're going up for a scan a bit later, just to make sure all is well. Rest now, Joss.'

When she woke again Luke was there. The smear was gone from his face and he was wearing a clean shirt, but he was as pale and strained as before. 'Joss, darling. How are you feeling?'

'Is the baby all right?' Her mouth felt like sandpaper. Her voice was husky.

'Yes, it's fine.' He leaned forward and kissed her on the lips. 'What happened? Did you fall?'

She shook her head slowly, feeling the coarse cotton of the pillow slip abrading her hair. 'No. I was asleep.' She had run across the lawn, she remembered that. It had given her a stitch. Then someone had been there, in the study with her. Someone had touched her. Not Luke. Not Lyn. The touch had not been frightening; it was as if someone had been trying to comfort her, to help. She drew her brows together, trying desperately to remember but already she was feeling sleepy again. 'I can't stay awake.' Her mouth refused to form the words properly.

Luke's face was swimming, suddenly huge, close to hers. 'I'll leave you now. You must sleep. I'll come back later.' She felt the touch of his lips, but already she was slipping back into the dark.

Later they took her to another ward. Someone smeared her stomach with jelly and ran something cold and hard across it.

'There you are. Can you see the screen, dear? There. The little mite is all safe, curled up out of harm's way. See?'

Joss peered obediently at the flickering blurred screen beside the bed. She could not make out anything, but her relief at the radiographer's words was enormous. 'Is it all right? Can you tell?'

'It's fine. Absolutely fine.' The woman was wiping her stomach with tissues and pulling down her gown. 'You're going to have a beautiful June baby.'

Already they were pulling back the curtains, wheeling her away, bringing in the next patient.

Simon Fraser was waiting for her when they brought her back to her bed. 'I had to visit another couple of patients, so I thought I'd look in on you again. How are you feeling?'

'Better.' Joss eased herself up on her pillows.

'Good.' He put his head on one side. 'Home, then rest for a couple of weeks. I've spoken to your sister. She says she can cope with everything. Is that right?'

Joss laughed weakly. 'She's very good at coping.'

'Good. You've got to make up your mind to rest, Joss. I mean that.'

When she got home she found that the whole family had been suborned. She was firmly escorted to bed and there, she discovered, she had to stay even when Sotheby's came to collect the wine from the cellar for the auction.

They told her about it that evening. 'You should have seen the care they took packing it all up. It was treated like gold dust. They said the labels and capsules had to be kept in as good condition as possible. I hardly dared breathe as I watched them.' Luke sat down on the bed after he and Lyn and Tom came up when the van had finally left. 'It could be our bail money, Joss. When he examined it the man from Sotheby's said it looked good. The cellar conditions are perfect. So, here's hoping the auction goes well.'

It was something to distract her. And so was the return of David a few days later.

'Books. Articles. A letter from your new publisher!' He tipped an armful of things onto the bed and then hauled himself up onto the counterpane next to her.

'My new publisher?' She stared at him, hardly daring to hope.

He nodded, clearly delighted. 'He liked your outline and the chapters you sent him. I think he's given you a few suggestions in the letter and made one or two notes which he thinks will be helpful. And he's prepared to give you a contract and a small advance. No –' He raised his hand to forestall her excitement. 'It won't be enough to retile the roof, but it is a start. And it means you have a perfect excuse to lie here in bed composing wonderful

150

prose and be waited on hand and foot by Luke and Lyn while that baby of yours gets bigger.'

Joss laughed. 'Well, I hope he gets bigger soon. At the moment I'm flat as a pancake. If I hadn't seen that scan I might have wondered if he was still there.'

'He is a *he*, is he?'

'I don't know. That was a figure of speech. And a dreadfully sexist one at that.' She smiled. 'Sister thought it would be a boy, though. She said boys always give more trouble than girls, the way they mean to go on.'

'And that's not sexist, I suppose?'

'No. That's observation.' She was opening the letter David had dropped on the bed. The one with the Hibberds' colophon.

'It's from Robert Cassie himself,' David put in, watching her face. 'He was enormously intrigued to hear you were going to set it in this house.'

'Three thousand pounds, David! He's going to pay me three thousand pounds!' She waved the letter at him. 'You say that's not much? It's a fortune! Lyn! Look at this!' Her sister had just appeared in the doorway with a tea tray.

Tom had scrambled after her. He ran across the room and tried to climb up onto the high bed. 'Mummy carry Tom,' he announced, wriggling down amongst her books and papers, and bouncing on the duvet.

'You mind your little brother, old son,' David said. He picked up the child and sat him on his knee. 'Or sister, though heaven forbid that a girl should be so unprincipled as to threaten to arrive early.' He laughed as Joss leaned forward to smack him.

Joss lay back on the pillows after they had all gone downstairs, Robert Cassie's letter in her hand, and reread it for the tenth time. A contract. An advance against royalties and an option on her next book; her next book when she had hardly started this one!

Her eyes strayed to the Amstrad which Luke had carried upstairs for her and set up on the table by the window. She had made a lot of progress on the book, her enforced bedrest giving her all the time she needed to get the story down. It was galloping through her brain so quickly she couldn't keep up with it, the adventures coming thick and fast. Later she would get up and put on her dressing gown and sit at the table in the window watching the dusk creep in across the garden whilst beneath her fingers Richard hid in the newly built haystack beneath a huge summer moon.

When Luke looked in, half an hour later, she was asleep, the letter still in her hand. He took it gently and read it with a smile then quietly he sat down next to the bed looking at her. Her face, still thin and tired, but rested by sleep, was extraordinarily beautiful, even sexy in the shaded lamp light. He bent forward and kissed her lightly, so as not to wake her.

Behind him outside the window, a bird flapped suddenly against the glass, tossed by the wind, and as suddenly it had gone. The curtain blew inwards and he shivered as he felt the cold draught penetrating deep into the room. Standing up he went and peered out. It was black outside and all he could see was the reflection of the lamp behind him. With a shudder he pulled the curtains across.

He stood for a moment looking down at Joss. There was a slight smile on her face now and her cheeks had flushed with a little colour. On the pillow beside her lay a rose bud. It was white, the petals slightly tinged with pink. He stared at it. Why hadn't he noticed it before? Leaning across he picked it up and looked at it. It felt very cold, as though it had just been brought in from the garden. David. David must have brought it for her. He frowned angrily then, throwing it down on the bedside table, he walked purposefully out of the room.

15

ow can he have gone back to London?' Joss sat up in bed, her elbow on the pillow, and stared at Lyn. 'Why?'

Lyn shrugged. 'I think he and Luke had words about something.' She was stacking coffee cups onto her tray.

'What do you mean they had words?' Joss frowned, shocked. 'What about?'

'Can't you guess?' Lyn stood looking down at her. 'He thinks David fancies you.'

Joss opened her mouth to protest. Then she shut it again. 'That's silly.'

'Is it?'

'You know it is. David and I were colleagues. Yes, he's fond of me and I of him, but that's all it is. Luke can't think anything else. It's crazy. Damn it all, I'm pregnant!'

'He thinks David has been giving you flowers.'

'Flowers!' Joss was astonished. 'Of course he hasn't given me flowers. And even if he did, what's wrong with that? Guests often bring their hostesses flowers.'

Lyn shrugged. 'Ask Luke.'

Joss lay back on the pillows with a deep sigh. 'Lyn.' She ran her fingers gently over the bed cover. 'What kind of flowers does he think David gave me?'

Lyn gave a small laugh. 'Does it matter?'

153

'Yes, I think it does.'

'Well, you'll have to ask Luke. I don't know.'

'I will. He can't order our friends out like that!'

'I don't think he ordered him out. He just went. It's a shame. I like David. We need visitors here to cheer us up.'

Her voice was light, casual, but Joss frowned distracted for a moment from her own worries. 'Is it too lonely for you, Lyn? Are you missing London?'

'No. 'Course not. I've told you before.' Lyn picked up the tray.

'I feel so guilty that you've got to do so much while I'm stuck here in bed.' Joss reached out and put her hand on Lyn's arm. 'We'd be lost without you, you know.'

'I know.' Lyn softened the abruptness of her answer with a grin. 'Don't worry. I'm tough. Looking after this house is a doddle and you know how much I love Tom.' She paused. 'Dad just rang, Joss. The last set of results were good.'

'Thank God!' Joss smiled. 'You must go up and see her again, Lyn. Whenever.'

'I shall.'

'I would go if I could, you know that.'

Lyn gave a tight smile. 'Of course you would,' she said. She hitched the door open with her elbow, the heavy tray balanced in her hands. 'Simon is coming later. He said not to tell you or you'll get your blood pressure up!' She grinned again. 'Yoga breathing and meditation for you, madam, and then if you are sufficiently calm and laid back, maybe he'll let you come downstairs.'

He did in the end. Gentle walking. No housework, and don't try to carry Tom. Those were the instructions.

The first moment she had on her own in the study she picked up the phone and rang David. 'Why did you go like that – not even saying good-bye?' Luke had driven over to Cambridge for the rest of the day in pursuit of spares. She couldn't ask him.

154

She heard the hesitation in his voice. 'Joss, I think maybe I had come down once too often to see you.'

'What do you mean?' Joss frowned. 'Lyn thinks you had a row with Luke. You can't have. No one rows with Luke.'

'No?' He paused. 'Let's just say that Luke and I had a small disagreement over something. Nothing serious. I just thought maybe it was time to come home and do some preparation for the new term. No sweat.'

'What did you have words about?' She glanced at the door. The house was silent. Lyn and Tom had gone for a walk.

'He feels maybe I am encouraging you too much in your obsession with the house.' He did not mention Luke's sudden strange hostility. The accusation, sudden and frenzied, about the rose.

Joss was silent.

'Joss, are you still there?'

'Yes, I'm here. I didn't think he minded.'

'He doesn't mind your interest. He's interested himself. He just doesn't want you to get things out of proportion.'

When Luke got back she pounced on him. 'What on earth do you mean, quarrelling with David and sending him away like that? If you have a problem with him doing research on the house tell me, not him. I asked him to do it!'

'Joss, you're becoming obsessed –'

'If I am, it has nothing to do with David!'

'I think it has.' Luke tightened his lips.

'No. Besides, it's more than that, isn't it. You've got some crazy idea that he's in love with me.'

'I don't think that's crazy, Joss. It's obvious to everyone, including you.' He sounded very bleak. 'You can't deny it.'

She was silent for a moment. 'He's fond of me, I know. And I of him.' She met Luke's eye defiantly. 'That doesn't mean we're planning a raging affair, Luke. You're the man I love. You're the man I married, the father of my children.' She rested her hand on her stomach for a moment. 'Luke.' She hesitated. 'Did this start off as a row over some flowers?'

Luke shrugged. 'A rose is usually a love token, I believe.'

'A rose.' She went cold all over.

'He left a rose on your pillow.' Luke's face was set with anger. 'Come on, Joss, even you can see the significance of that.'

She swallowed. The rose, when she had found it on her bedside table had been cold and dead. She knew it had not come from David.

For a long time she said nothing else about the house or the family, reading her mother's diaries in private and, between stints of writing, climbing to the attics only when Luke was out or safely ensconced beneath the car. David did not come again that term, nor did he send her any more cuttings or notes gleaned from his research.

Taking advantage of Lyn's baby sitting and making visits to Mothercare and research for the book her excuse, Joss made one or two trips to Ipswich and Colchester. She went to libraries, looking at books on local history, borrowing tomes on medieval costume and food and fifteenth century politics. Given the all clear by Simon, on the condition she rested whenever she felt tired she drove around the countryside, astonished to find that, away from the house and the strained atmosphere with Lyn, she felt happier and more positive than she had for months.

Coming home exhilarated and inspired she wrote and wrote, hearing the story inside her head almost as if it were being dictated to her by Richard himself. She began to think that the story was like a charm. As long as she thought about it and stopped thinking about the family into which she had been born, the house remained gentle and benign, content to sleep with its memories, content perhaps, she sometimes wondered, that she was weaving its story into her novel and exorcising its legends by putting so much of it down on paper.

Sometimes, when it was her turn to do the lighter chores she was still allowed she would straighten up from sorting clothes or dusting or washing up and listen intently, but the voices in her head were only those of her own imagination. Perhaps the ghosts had gone. Perhaps, they had never been there at all.

A few weeks later Gerald Andrews came. On the back seat of his car was a pile of books. 'I thought I would leave them for you. Just for when you have time. No rush to give them back.' He shrugged. 'I am hoping to go into hospital next month. When that's all over may I come again and bring my friends? I so want to be there when they see the vaulting.' He smiled conspiratorially and she said she would look forward to seeing him. She put the books in the study, in a pile behind the chair. Luke would never notice a few more amongst so many.

For several days she ignored them, then she realised they could be fruitful sources for her novel. One by one she brought them out when she wasn't writing and scoured the pages for information.

It was all there – especially in the Victorian guide books to East Anglia. The legends, the rumours, the ghost stories. Belheddon Hall had had a reputation as long as it had stood.

Outside, a short grey February leached into March. Her stomach had at last rounded a little as though acknowledging that spring was on the way. There were golden whips on the willow trees, hazel catkins in the hedge. Snowdrops and primroses gave way to daffodils. Hidden under her steadily growing manuscript was her family tree. She had filled in details covering more than a hundred years now – births, marriages and deaths. So many deaths. It was compulsive. She pushed the pile of paper aside and read about the house again. Her excursions became fewer, and as she moved around the house with dustpan and brush or piles of clean clothes and towels for the various cupboards and drawers or took her turn – less often because she hated cooking as much as Lyn loved it – at the hot stove in the kitchen, she found she was again listening for voices.

Climbing to the attics, almost against her will, when Lyn or Luke and Tom were all out in the stableyard she moved slowly through the empty rooms, listening intently. But all she could hear was the wind, soughing gently in the gables and she would go back down to the bedroom or to the study with a sigh.

She was mad, she knew that. To want to hear the voices again was idiotic. But they were the voices of her little brothers; her only contact with a family that had gone forever. She began to ignore her writing, deliberately challenging her theory that the intensity of her concentration on the book had driven Georgie and Sammy away, but without her writing there was an empty space inside her – that thought made her smile wryly as she patted her steadily swelling stomach – an empty space which left her feeling frustrated and unfulfilled.

Luke noticed her restlessness and tried to help. 'Lyn wondered if it would be fun to take Tom to the zoo. He's had so few excursions since we moved here. Shall we make a day trip of it? All of us go? It'll get you out of the house.' He had noticed that her own private excursions had stopped.

She felt her spirits rise. 'I'd like that. It would be fun. Tom will love it!'

They settled on the following Wednesday and Joss began to look forward to the trip. Her aimless visits to the attic stopped and she helped Lyn prepare Tom for the animals, looking at pictures of elephants and lions and tigers and telling him stories about the other animals they thought they would see there.

On Tuesday night Tom was sleepless with excitement. 'It's our own fault.' Wearily Joss stood up. They were sitting at the kitchen table finishing supper when the baby alarm had crackled into life for the second time that evening. 'It's my turn. I'll go and see to him.'

She let herself into the great hall, hearing Tom's cries for real now, not through the plastic alarm on the kitchen dresser. Hurrying to the foot of the stairs she peered up into the dark and reached for the light switch.

The shadow on the wall at the angle of the stairs was clearly that of a man. Hunched towards her menacingly it hovered above her as she clutched at the banister. Paralysed with fear she stood for a moment staring up towards it, Tom's screams echoing in her ears.

'Tom!' Her whisper was anguished as she put her foot on the bottom step, forcing herself to move towards it. 'Tom!'

One of its arms was moving slightly, beckoning her onwards. She froze, willing herself upwards, craning her neck towards the landing. Luke's waterproof jacket was hanging jauntily from the carved acorn knob at the top of the stairs. What she had seen was its shadow.

That night she had a nightmare which woke her shivering and sweating. In her dream a huge metal drum on legs had walked slowly towards her across the room. On top of it a jaunty tricorn hat belied the evil expression in its two press-stud eyes. Its arms like giant linked paper clips were stretched out towards her, its method of propulsion hidden by the gleaming aluminium of its body. She awoke with a start and lay there, too afraid to move, her heart thundering in her chest. Beside her Luke stirred and groaned. She listened intently. Beyond his gentle snores there was silence. No sounds from Tom. No sounds from the house. There did not seem to be a breath of wind outside in the garden.

When she awoke at last it was with a splitting headache. She sat up and groped for the alarm clock and then fell back on the pillow with a groan. She could hear Lyn talking cheerfully to Tom as she got him up. The little boy was giggling happily. Of Luke there was no sign.

By the time the others had had breakfast she knew she couldn't go with them to the zoo. Her head was spinning and she was so tired she could barely move.

'We'll put it off; go another day.' Luke bent over her, concerned.

'No.' She shook her head. 'No, you can't disappoint Tom. You go. I'll go back to bed and sleep the rest of the morning. Then I'll do some work on the book. Honestly. I'll be fine.'

She waved them off, torn by Tom's tears when he found his mummy wasn't coming too, and then, her head throbbing she turned back towards the house.

It was after two when she awoke. The morning sun had gone and the sky was overcast and sullen. As she made her way downstairs she could hear the wind in the huge chimney.

Making herself a cup of tea and a Marmite sandwich she sat for a long time at the kitchen table before at last reaching for her jacket.

At the edge of the lake she stopped, her hands in her pockets, watching the gusty wind blow sheets of black ripples across the water. Staring down into its depths she hunched her shoulders against the cold, deliberately fending off the thought of a little boy with his jam jar of tadpoles bending towards the water on the slippery bank.

She tensed at a sound behind her. Turning she surveyed the lawn. There was no one there. She listened, straining her ears to separate sounds from the roar of the wind in her ears, but there was nothing.

160

Turning she began to walk slowly back towards the house. Another cup of tea and she would go back to the book. She had wasted too much time day dreaming; she had a novel to write.

Sammy!

One hand on the mouse the other on the keyboard she looked up, listening. Someone was running down the stairs.

Sammy! Play with me!

Holding her breath she stood up slowly and tiptoed towards the door.

'Hello? Who's there?' Reaching out to the doorknob she turned it slowly. 'Hello?' Peering out into the hall she squinted up the staircase into the shadows. 'Is there someone there? Sammy? Georgie?'

The silence was electric; as if someone else too were holding their breath and waiting.

'Sammy? Georgie?' She was clutching the doorknob as though her life depended on it, a thin film of perspiration icing her shoulder blades.

She forced herself to take a step out into the hall, and then, slowly, she began to climb the stairs.

'You know better than to ask me for sleeping pills.' Simon sat on the chair next to her in the study. He was watching her closely. 'Come on now. What is it? You're not afraid of the birth?'

'A little. What woman isn't.' Joss hauled herself up from her chair and went to stand at the window with her back to him, wanting to hide her face. Outside, Lyn and Tom were playing football on the grass. Not too near the water, she wanted to shout. Don't go too near. But of course Lyn wouldn't let him go too near. Even if she did there was a solid wall of vegetation round the lake now – dead nettles, brambles, a tangle of old man's beard.

Sammy

The voice calling, was loud in the room. It was the third time she had heard it that morning. She swung round and stared at the doctor. 'Did you hear that?'

Simon frowned. 'What? Sorry?'

'Someone calling. Didn't you hear?'

He shook his head. 'Come and sit down Joss.'

She hesitated, then she went and perched on the low chair opposite him. 'I must be hearing things.' She forced herself to smile.

'Maybe.' He paused. 'How often do you hear "things", Joss?'

'Not often.' She gave an embarrassed smile. 'When we first moved here I began to hear the boys – shouting – playing – and Katherine – the voice calling out for Katherine.' She shrugged, finding it difficult to go on. 'I don't want you to think I'm ready for the men in white coats. I'm not mad. I'm not imagining it –' she paused again. 'At least I don't think so.'

'Are we talking about ghosts?' He raised an eyebrow. Leaning forward, his elbows on his knees, he was watching her intently, studying her face.

She looked away, unable to meet his gaze. 'I suppose we are.'

There was a long silence. He was waiting for her to say something else. She gave a nervous laugh. 'Women grow fanciful in pregnancy don't they? And, thinking about it, I've been pregnant since we moved in.'

'Do you think that is what it is?' He leaned back in the chair, crossing one leg over the other, almost too deliberately casual.

'You tell me. You're the doctor.'

He took a deep breath. 'I don't believe in ghosts, Joss.'

'So I'm going mad.'

'I didn't say that. I think you have been physically and mentally exhausted since you moved into the house. I

162

think you have allowed the romance and history and emptiness of the place to play upon your mind.' He sighed. 'I suppose if I told you to take a holiday you would say it was out of the question?'

'You know Luke can't go away. He's got three cars to work on now.' They were even discussing his taking on some help.

'And it's out of the question that you go away without him?' He was still studying her face. She was too thin. Too pale.

'Out of the question.' She smiled.

Why did he get the distinct impression that her answer had, in fact, nothing at all to do with Luke. He shook his head. 'Then you must be firm with yourself, Joss. More rest. Real rest. More company. I know that sounds a contradiction, but you have a real treasure here in Lyn. I know she would welcome visitors and take the strain off you. You need distraction and laughter and, not to put too fine a point on it, noise.'

She laughed properly this time. 'Simon, if you knew how awful that sounds! I'm not lonely. I'm not suffering from the quiet and I'm sure I'm not having delusions.'

'So you believe in ghosts.'

'Yes.' One word, half defiant, half apologetic.

'When I hear or see something myself, then I'll believe you.' He stretched, groaned, then stood up. 'Well, I'm afraid I can't help with the sleeplessness. Gentle walks in the fresh air, cocoa or Horlicks before bed and an easy conscience, that's the best prescription a doctor can give.' He turned to the door and reached for the handle, then he stopped. 'I hope you're not afraid of the ghosts, Joss?'

'No.' She smiled reassuringly. 'I'm not afraid.'

The attic was full of bright sunshine. It showed up the marks of rain and dust on the window, and made the air dance with sunbeams. It would make the perfect setting for one of the scenes in her book – just like this – the hot sun, the smell of centuries, old oak, the dust, the absolute silence. Puffing slightly after the steep stairs Joss went straight to the trunk by the wall and threw back the heavy lid. She had only managed to open the padlock a few days before. Not wanting to ask Luke to cut it off for her she had sat there for an hour with a hair pin and suddenly, easily, the lock had clicked back and the hasp swung open. Elated she had lifted the heavy lid and stared inside. Books, letters, papers – and an old bunch of dried flowers. She had picked them up and stared at them. Roses. Old dried roses, colourless with time, tied with silk ribbons. Laying them gently on the floor beside her she began to look through the paper. From the depths of the chest drifted a musty smell of cedar and old brittle paper.

In the bottom of the box she had found John Bennet's diary – the John Bennet who had married her great grandmother in 1893 and nine years later, in 1903, had disappeared without trace.

The last entry in the diary which seemed to cover, on and off, about five years, was dated April 29th 1903. The writing was shaky, scrawled across the page.

> So, he claims yet another victim. The boy is dead. Next it will be me. Why can't she see what is happening? I have asked that the sacrament be celebrated here in the house and she refuses. Dear sweet Jesus save us.

That was all.

Joss sat on the closed trunk, the book open in her lap staring out of the dusty window. The sky beyond was a dazzling ice blue. *Dear sweet Jesus save us*. The words echoed through her head. What had happened to him? Had he run away, or had he, as he feared, died? She looked down at the book again, leafing through the pages. Until the last few entries the handwriting had been

164

strong, decisive, the subject matter on the whole impersonal – to do with the farm and the village. She had
found the entry for little Henry John's birth.

> Mary had an easy delivery and the child was
> born at eight o'clock this morning. He has red
> hair and looks much like Mary's father.

Joss smiled, wondering if that was a touch of humour.
If it was, the reason for it had long gone.

Further back she found the entry where his marriage to
Mary Sarah in the spring of 1893 was similarly laconically
described:

> Today Mary and I were married in the church
> at Belheddon. It rained, but the party was I think
> a merry one. We have waited so long for this
> marriage I pray that it may be joyous and fruitful
> and that happiness will come now to Belheddon
> Hall.

Joss chewed her lip. So, even then, he knew. Where
had John Bennet come from? How had he and Mary
met? It was all there. His father was a clergyman in
Ipswich; his mother had died some time before. He himself had trained for the law, and for several years he
seemed to have been a partner in a firm of solicitors
in Bury. When he married he gave up the partnership,
presumably to manage Belheddon which had been at
that time a large and prosperous estate, with farms and
cottages and hundreds of acres.

The diary fell in her lap and she leaned back against
the wall, staring at the shadows on the far side of the
attic. The hot sunshine, the heavy carved mullions, the
arched roof beams: the combination sent a network of
dark shadow over the wall paper, shadow that looked –
almost – like the figure of a man. She frowned, trying to
focus, conscious suddenly that her heart was beating fas-

ter than normal. Her palms had grown moist. She pressed them hard on the lid of the trunk on which she was sitting, taking comfort from its solidity and glanced at the doorway. It seemed a hundred miles away. The attics were unnaturally quiet. The usual creaks and groans of the timbers, the soft soughing of the April wind, all had faded to silence.

'Who are you?' Her whisper seemed crude and violent in the emptiness. 'Who *are* you?'

There was no answer. The shadows had rearranged themselves, back into a criss-cross of architectural shapes.

Swallowing nervously she pushed herself up until she was standing upright. The diary fell unnoticed to the floor, and lay, face down, the pages splayed at her feet.

'In the name of Jesus Christ, go!' Her voice tremulous, she found her hand tracing the age old pattern from head to heart, from shoulder to shoulder, the protecting, blessing cross. Slowly, step by step she sidled towards the doorway, her eyes fixed on the wall where she had seen – thought she had seen – the shape of a man. Her back to the wall she edged out of the attic, then she ran. She ran through the attics, down the steep stairs, down the main staircase, through the great hall and into the kitchen. There, panting, she threw herself into a chair and buried her head in her arms on the table.

Slowly her panic subsided and her breathing calmed. She pressed the heels of her hands into her eyes. Then reflexively she cradled her arms around her stomach. She was still sitting there when Lyn came in with Tom in his buggy.

'Joss?' Lyn abandoned the pushchair and ran to the table. 'Joss, what is it? What's happened? Are you all right?' She put her arms around Joss's shoulders. 'Is it the baby? Are you in pain?'

Joss smiled weakly and shook her head. 'No, no. I'm

fine. I just had a bit of headache, that's all. I thought I'd make a cup of tea, and I felt a bit dizzy.'

'I'll call Simon.'

'No.' Joss shouted the word in a panic. Then more gently she repeated it, 'No. Don't fuss, Lyn. I'm OK. Honestly. I was sitting down and I stood up too suddenly, that's all.' She dragged herself to her feet and went over to Tom, releasing his harness and humping him to his feet. 'There, Tom Tom. Did you have a nice walk?'

The things she had heard, children's voices, the voices of her own brothers, they had nothing to do with whatever had scared generation after generation of grown men and women in the house. Georgie and Sammy had been born long after their grandparents and great grandparents had died. John Bennet, Lydia Manners – they could not have heard the laughter of Georgie and Sammy in the attics. Controlling herself with an effort she picked up the kettle and carried it to the tap. No one else had heard anything. No one else seemed worried. Perhaps Simon was right. She had got herself into a silly neurotic state as a direct result of her pregnancy. Perhaps all the pregnant women in her family had the same wild fancies. The idea struck her suddenly as ludicrous and she found as she turned with the filled kettle to put it on the hot plate that she was smiling.

Lyn noticed and smiled back. 'Before I went out David rang,' she said abruptly. 'I said we wanted him to come down. I said I thought it would cheer you up. He was a bit iffy about it but he said he would. Next weekend. Is that all right?'

'Of course it is.'

'I told Luke.'

'Good.' Joss glanced at Lyn. 'How did he take it?'

'OK. I told him it wasn't just you who liked David. And not all of us are married.' Lyn's face had coloured slightly, and Joss found herself studying her sister with sudden perception. The normally colourless complexion, the slightly surly demeanour had been replaced by a sparkle which Joss had never seen there before. She sighed. Poor Lyn. Sophisticated, intellectual and well-read, David would never fancy her in a million years.

At first the weekend went well. David arrived loaded with wine for Luke, ('Now that so much of yours has been taken away I reckoned a donation to help top up the cellars would be appreciated – when is the auction, by the way?') books for Joss, a pretty porcelain vase for Lyn and a massive black teddy bear dressed in a crocheted lace jumper for Tom. He insisted on helping Lyn cook lunch, admired the latest car in the coach house, met Luke's new part time assistant, Jimbo, a twenty-year-old apprentice mechanic from the village and, Joss felt, avoided her as much as possible.

Determined not to show how hurt she felt she declined the offer of a walk with the others after lunch and climbed instead to the bedroom where she flung herself down on the bed. Exhausted she was asleep in seconds.

In her dream she seemed to be looking down upon herself as she slept. The figure standing near the bed was more defined now. It was tall, broad shouldered, clearly a man, or all that was left of the spirit of what had once been a man. It moved closer, looking down at her, stooping slightly to rest a hand as transparent and light as gossamer on her shoulder under the cover. Gently, imperceptibly, the hand moved down to rest on the hump of her stomach, almost caressing the baby which nestled there in the safe darkness of her womb. The room was unnaturally cold, the atmosphere electric. Joss groaned slightly, and moved in her sleep to ease the discomfort in her back. The figure did not move. It bent closer. The icy fingers brushed lightly across her hair, her face, tracing the line of her cheekbone. With a cry of fear Joss awoke and lay staring up at the tester of the bed. She was perspiring slightly and yet she felt desperately cold. Shivering she pulled the covers round her more closely. The shadow had gone.

It was early evening before she had a chance to speak to David alone. Luke had gone over to see the Goodyears and it was Lyn's turn to put Tom to bed. Sitting opposite Joss in the study, his legs stretched out to the fire, a glass of whisky in his hand, David scrutinised her appreciatively for a moment, then he grinned. 'So, how is authorship?'

'Fine. Good fun. Hard work.'

He took a sip from his glass. 'I had lunch with Gerald Andrews last week. I don't know if he told you but he's about to go in for a hip operation, poor man. He's very frustrated. He won't be able to help us with our research after all. We talked about you quite a bit.'

'And?'

'And –' he paused in mid-breath as though changing his mind about what he was going to say. 'Joss, have you ever thought about selling Belheddon?'

'No.' She said it uncompromisingly, without even a moment taken for thought. For a moment neither of them said anything, then she looked him in the eye. 'Why?'

Uncomfortably he put down his whisky glass. Rising he went over to the French doors and stared out across the moonlit lawn. It was very bright out there, and cold. There were still traces of the previous night's frost lying in the shade of the hedge.

'We felt that maybe the stories about the house might be depressing you a bit,' he said after a moment.

'Did you mention this to Luke?'

'No.'

'Well please don't. I'm not in the slightest bit depressed. Why should I be? It is in the nature of history that most of the players are dead.'

169

His face cracked into a smile almost against his wishes. 'I couldn't have put that better myself.'

'David. What about you and Luke? Is it all right?' She looked away from him, a little embarrassed.

'It's fine. I wouldn't be here otherwise.' He did not turn round. There was a long silence and at last she stood up. Coming over to stand next to him at the window she decided to change the subject.

'Something Gerald said stuck in my mind. He noticed that Belheddon nearly always passed down through the female line. That is why everyone has different surnames even though they are related. Matrilineal descent, he called it. I checked up on it afterwards on the family tree I've been drawing up. It's true. No son has ever lived to inherit Belheddon Hall. Not once. Ever.'

She did not look at him as she spoke. Her eyes seemed to be focused on a distant point on the water of the lake, where the moon glittered on the grey surface, turning it into a diamanté cloak.

'We hoped you wouldn't notice.'

'No exhortations to ignore it; to believe it is just coincidence?'

'What else could it be?' His voice was bleak.

'What else indeed.' Her voice was flat. She went back to her chair and threw herself into it.

'Have you told Luke about this, Joss?' David followed her to the fire. He stood with his back to it, looking down on her.

She shook her head. 'I tried telling him about the diaries, the letters. He didn't want to know. It was you who told me not to ram my inheritance down his throat. How can I tell him that this house is cursed?'

'It isn't. I'm sure it isn't.' In spite of himself he shivered.

'Isn't it? Do you know how many accidents have happened here over the years? Over the centuries? And never to a woman. Never. Only to men. My brothers,

170

my father, my grandfather – only my great grandfather escaped, and you know why? Because he saw it coming. He wrote in his diary that it – it – was going to get him next.' Her voice had risen. She slumped back in the chair suddenly. 'Perhaps it did get him. All we know is that he disappeared. We will never know whether he ran away, or did something awful happen to him? Perhaps he was cornered in the woods or the lanes, or in the garden and his body was never found.'

'Joss, stop it.' David sat down on the arm of her chair and reached for her hand. 'This is ridiculous. It is coincidence. It has to be coincidence.'

'Then why did you want me to sell up?'

He smiled ruefully. 'Because in each of us, however down to earth and boring, there is a tiny treacherous bit of superstition.'

'And that bit believes the devil lives at Belheddon.' Her voice was very small.

David laughed. 'Oh no, I didn't say that. No not the devil. I don't believe in the devil.'

'That, if you don't mind me saying so, hardly proves that he doesn't exist.'

'True. But I'm happy with the theory. No, whatever happened here, it is a mixture of things. Tragic accidents, like your brothers and your father – all things that could happen in any family, Joss, and probably have. In the past, maybe there was some other factor at work. Maybe the water was contaminated and the germs affected boys more than girls; maybe there was a sex-linked gene in the family which made the male children weaker – susceptible to something.'

'A sex-linked gene making the male children more susceptible to falling into the pond?' Joss forced a smile. 'Not very convincing, David.'

'No, but as likely as any other theory.'

Behind them the door opened, and Luke looked in.

171

His eyes immediately went to the arm of the chair where David's hand rested on Joss's. 'I see I'm interrupting.' His voice was cold.

'No, Luke. No.' Joss levered herself from the chair as David moved away. 'Listen. There is something I must tell you. Please – listen.'

Coming in, he closed the door behind him. His face was white. 'I'm not sure I want to hear this.'

'Well, I want you to listen. There is something you must know. I've tried to tell you, but – ' she shook her head and looked helplessly at David. 'It's to do with the house. We – I – think there is a curse on it.'

'Oh please.' Luke pushed her away. 'Not that again. I have never heard such crap. A curse! That's all we need. In case you've forgotten, we have to live here. You can't sell. That was a condition of your mother's will. If you want to leave, we lose the house. We have no money, no job. Here I can work. You can write your stories. Lyn and your parents can come if they want. There is room even for your friends.' He glared at David. 'I must say, David, I'm surprised you've been encouraging her in all this. I thought you had more sense.'

'I do think there is something in what she says, Luke, old boy.' David looked distinctly uncomfortable. 'You should listen to her. I don't think the house is cursed. Maybe it is just an accumulation of old stories and circumstances, I agree, but it does seem strange – too strange to be entirely coincidence – that so many things have happened here over the centuries.'

'And you think the devil lives here? Satan himself, complete with pitch fork and furnace in the cellar?'

'No. Not that. Of course, not that.'

'I should bloody well think not. Have more sense, David. Joss is pregnant. The last thing she needs is someone winding her up and encouraging her in all this stupidity. Simon Fraser had a word with me. He says she's got herself in a state. She's supposed to keep calm. And I find you holding her hand, discussing with her the possibility that our son will die.'

There was a sudden total silence. Joss went white. 'I never said that,' she whispered. 'I never mentioned Tom.'

'Well, that's what this is all about isn't it? The sons of the house dying. The voices in the dark. Little boys in the cellar.' Luke rammed his hands deep into the pockets of his old cords. 'I'm sorry, Joss. I just want you to realise how preposterous this sounds. Your family are dead. They are all dead. Like all families some of them died young and some in old age. Obviously the further back you go the more likely they are to have died unexplained and unsatisfactory deaths – that is the nature of those days. They had no medicine, no surgery. Children died all the time, that is why Victorians had so many children – to try and up the ante a bit. Luckily we are living in a more enlightened and scientific age. End of problem. Now, if you will excuse me, I'll go and finish up in the coach house. Then I suggest we all have supper and forget this whole sorry rigmarole.'

The door shook as he closed it. Joss and David looked at one another. 'Not an easy man to convince,' David said quietly, after a minute. 'Besides, Joss, I do think that he is in many ways right. Relax. Try and put it all out of your mind, but maybe be a little on your guard as well.'

'On my guard against what?' With a shiver she stood closer to the fire. 'In the diaries he is described as he or it. Something or someone who terrified sane, rational, educated women.'

And killed little boys. She did not speak the words out loud.

'And you, who are also sane, rational and educated, have seen nothing. And you have heard nothing – nothing but some voices, trapped like echoes within the fabric of the house.' He smiled. 'Come on, Joss. You know the sign against the evil eye, don't you.' He raised his two forefingers and crossed them in front of her face. 'Be ready if he or it ever manifests. Otherwise forget it. Tom loves it here. It's a great place. All houses have dangers. Cellar stairs and ponds are obvious dangers and an unsupervised youngster could fall foul of them any time in history or today. You take precautions, you watch him, Lyn clucks round him like a mother hen. No one could do more.'

'I suppose not.'

So, he claims yet another victim. The boy is dead. Next it will be me. Why can't she see what is happening . . .

Could so many people have imagined the same thing? Had they all read each other's diaries, perhaps sitting in this very room, taking comfort from the fire as their hair stood on end and their toes curled with terror in the darkness of long gone winter nights? Somehow that didn't seem likely.

The kitchen was deliciously warm and bright and sane. Lyn glanced at them as they walked in. She had just put a cake in the oven and her face was shiny with the heat of the stove. On the floor in the corner, Tom was playing with his Duplo, building a castle with some very questionable symmetry. Self consciously she rubbed her face on her sleeve. 'Luke just went out muttering,' she said. 'I gather he thinks you two are round the bend.'

'Something like that.' Joss forced a smile. 'Anyway we have been well and truly reprimanded, and full of repentance we are going to help you set the tea things.' She was gazing at Tom, needing suddenly to hold him in her arms.

'Great.' Lyn did not seem that enthusiastic. 'He says you think the house is cursed.' She frowned. 'You don't really think that, do you, Joss?'

'No of course she doesn't.' David hauled himself up

onto the table beside her. 'Now, what can I do to help. I feel a cookery lesson coming on.'

Lyn glanced at him archly. 'I suppose I could make some biscuits.' She blushed.

The magic word had an immediate electrifying effect on Tom. Scattering brightly coloured plastic bricks all over the floor he scrambled to his feet, dodged effectively past Joss's outstretched hand and ran towards them. 'Me cook bickies,' he announced firmly, and standing on tiptoe he grabbed a wooden spoon from the table.

Joss watched them for several minutes. Her back ached and she was feeling peculiarly tired. Lyn was flirting openly with David and after an initial show of reluctance he had obviously decided to humour her. When Joss finally wandered out of the kitchen and back to the study no one noticed her go. David and Lyn, covered in biscuit mixture as much as Tom, were laughing too much to hear the sound of the softly latching door.

In the great hall she stopped and looked round. Lyn had put a huge vase of daffodil buds on the table and in the comparative warmth of the house they had opened. The glorious scent filled the room. It was a happy smell, one that reminded her of spring and optimism and rebirth. She stood for a while looking down at the flowers then she went through into the study. On the chair where she had been sitting lay a rose bud. She stared at it. David would not have put it there. He would not have done anything so stupid! Putting out her hand she touched it. It was ice cold; frosted; already growing limp in the heat of the room, the white petals falling open, it was collapsing as she watched. Distastefully she picked it up and looked at it closely. There was something sad and decadent about it – something unpleasant that she couldn't quite put her finger on. She looked at it for a moment longer, then with a shiver she threw it on the fire.

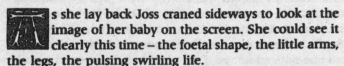

s she lay back Joss craned sideways to look at the image of her baby on the screen. She could see it clearly this time – the foetal shape, the little arms, the legs, the pulsing swirling life.

'Can you tell if it's a boy or a girl?' she asked. The question had been seething inside her all morning.

'If I can, I'm not allowed to tell.' The radiographer calmly went on with the scan.

'I need to know.' Joss's voice was tense. 'Please. I do need to know.'

'Oh come on, Joss.' Luke was with her, sitting on a chair nearby, peering in some confusion at the strange blobs and swirls which showed his child. 'It's more fun not to know. It's not as though we mind, either way, as long as he or she is healthy.'

'I need to know, Luke.' Her voice was fierce. 'Please. Can't you tell me? I shan't breathe a word.'

The woman stepped back from the bed. 'It's the hospital's policy not to tell mothers.' She pulled a wad of tissues from a box and began to rub away the gel from Joss's skin. 'But in fact, my dear, I don't know. Not the way your baby is lying. So you must wait and see. Not long now. Twenty-eight weeks and as far as I can tell the little one is absolutely fine. No trouble there at all.' She smiled as she covered Joss up. 'Now, you get up in your own time while I fill in the form, and you can have a picture to take home.' Sitting down she scooted her chair across the floor to her desk.

'Luke. Make her tell me.' Joss's eyes filled with tears.

Luke stared at her. 'Joss! What on earth is the matter? We agreed we don't mind what it is.'

'Well I do mind. I want to know.'

The radiographer had put on a pair of wire-rimmed spectacles. She turned and peered over them at Joss. 'Mrs Grant. I told you I couldn't tell you, even if I wanted to.' She frowned as she stood up and threw the glasses onto her desk. 'Now, you mustn't get yourself in a state. That's not good for you. Not good at all.'

In the car going home Luke said nothing until they had reached the outskirts of the town. 'Come on, Joss. What is it? She said the baby was fine.'

'I need to know, Luke. They'd tell me in London, I'm sure they would. Don't you see? If it's a boy, it's in danger –'

'No!' Luke slammed on the brakes. 'Joss that is enough! I will not listen to any more of this. It's crazy. Tom is not in danger. That baby, boy or girl, is not in danger. You are not in danger. I am not in danger.' Behind them a car hooted and edged past them. The driver lifted the middle finger of his hand as he passed. 'You are not to worry. Listen. I am going to ask the rector to come in and talk to you. Would you feel better if he blessed the house, or exorcised it or something? Would that put your mind at rest?'

Exorcizo te, in nomine Dei † Patris omnipotentis, et in nomine Jesu † Christi Filii ejus, Domine nostri, et in virtute Spiritus † Sancti . . .

With a sigh Joss leaned back in her seat and slowly

she shook her head. What was the point? It had already been tried.

Luke called him anyway in the end three weeks later. James Wood sat on the edge of his chair and listened politely to Joss and then again to Luke as the May sunshine poured in through the windows. Then he smiled. 'I am always prepared to bless a house. I usually do it when people first move in. I pray for their happiness in the house and that it should be a sanctuary and a home.' He shook his head slowly. 'But I normally pass ghosts over to a colleague who specialises in such things.'

Joss forced herself to smile. She liked the rector and had enjoyed going occasionally to his services in the church, but his reaction to their request did not inspire her with any confidence. 'Your blessing would be wonderful, rector. Thank you.' She glanced at Luke. He was looking away from her, seemingly studying the fire and she could not see his face.

They both sat, heads bowed, there in the study while he prayed over them, then they stood in the great hall while he said another short prayer, presumably designed to cover the rest of the house. It was as he was leaving that he turned to Joss. 'My dear. You told me I think that you had visited Edgar Gower? Have you spoken to him about your troubles?'

She shook her head. 'He's still away.' She had tried to ring him almost every day over the last month or two, hoping he might be back from South Africa.

'I see.' He sighed. 'He would be the man to help you, I feel sure. He knows Belheddon. He knew your mother and father. And he is more sympathetic than I to the ideas you are putting forward.' He looked shame faced for a moment. 'I have never seen a ghost or experienced anything remotely supernatural outside my own religious experience. I find it hard to understand.'

Joss put her hand on his arm. 'It doesn't matter. You have done your best.'

The trouble was, his best might not be good enough.

For several weeks she thought it had worked. The weather had grown steadily warmer; Luke's vegetable garden was beginning to take shape.

In the middle of the month Luke went up to London for the wine auction.

'I wish you had come with me, Joss.' He was full of excitement. 'It was amazing! We're rich!' He seized her hands and whirled her round. 'Even after they've taken their cut we will have about £27,000! No more worries for a bit. Oh Joss!'

Joss, buoyed up with energy and optimism threw herself into her writing again. Working with Lyn in the house, cooking, helping Luke with his accounts she tried very hard to put her worries out of her head. The house was at peace. The atmosphere had lost its tension. The spring sun had swept away the shadows.

Then about an hour after he had been put to bed on Friday night Tom had another nightmare. The adults had just sat down around the kitchen table when his screams rang out from the baby alarm. All three jumped to their feet. Joss, in spite of her increasing bulk was there first.

The cot had once more moved across the nursery floor to the corner near the window. Tom was standing up, his face red, tears streaming down his cheeks, his eyes tight shut. 'Tin man,' he bellowed. 'Me see the tin man. Me don't like him!'

'Don't pick him up, love, he's too heavy for you now.' Luke's admonition came too late as Joss swung him up out of the cot and hugged the little boy to her, feeling his legs straddling her rib cage, his small arms tightly clinging round her neck. 'What is it? What tin man.' She buried her face in his hot little neck. 'Sweetheart, don't

179

cry. You've had a bad dream, that's all. There is no one here. Look Daddy is going to put your bed back where it belongs.'

Luke was looking at the floor. 'I had wedged those castors so they couldn't move. I can't think how he's managing to rock himself across the room like that. He must be remarkably strong.' He straightened the bed, still miraculously dry, and reached out his arms for his son. 'Come on, sausage. Let Daddy carry you.'.

'Who is this tin man he sees?' Joss was looking at Lyn. 'I thought I asked you not to ever read him *The Wizard of Oz* again! It's upsetting him.'

Lyn shook her head impatiently. 'I haven't, Joss. As far as I know we haven't even got a copy. We are reading Babar books, aren't we Tom –' She broke off as Luke tried to lower Tom into the bed. The child's scream was piercing. 'He'll have to come down. Let him fall asleep with us. I'll bring him up later.' Fussing she followed Luke as he carried the little boy downstairs, bringing with her his comfort blanket and his black teddy bear. In the doorway she paused. 'Joss? Are you coming?'

'In a second.' Joss was staring round the room. 'Let me just look. Maybe it's a shadow or something that he sees.'

She heard their footsteps cross her and Luke's bedroom, then clump across the landing. In a moment they had walked downstairs and she was alone. She looked round the room. Behind the thick curtains it was still daylight outside, but the room was brightly lit now from the centre light, the floor a litter of Tom's larger toys, the small ones neatly put away in his playbox. In the corner his chest of drawers stood between the door and the wall, on it the shaded night lamp. There was nothing there that could possibly frighten him. Aware that her own heart beat was thudding uncomfortably fast in her ears, Joss went to the door and switched off the main light then she walked back and stood by the cot, looking round. The shaded bulb hardly penetrated the murky corners of the room. Standing beside the cot she could see the huge multi-coloured plastic ball the Goodyears had given him, the bright rag rug and the toy box itself, cardboard, but covered by Lyn with thick sticky-backed scarlet and blue paper, almost in the corner of the room, the heaped toys spilling out of the top. The curtains were pulled tightly across the window. She frowned. The curtains were moving, sucked in and blown out as though by a strong draught. Nervously, she stepped towards them.

'Who's there?'

Of course there was no one. How could there be? But the window was shut. It was very cold. Outside one of the late frosts that so often blight an English May was turning the garden silver, and she had shut it herself when she kissed Tom good night earlier. So why were the curtains moving? Her heart in her mouth, she was there in two steps, flinging back the multi-coloured curtains to expose the windows behind. The reflection of the lamp shone back at her, somewhere behind her shoulder. There was no stirring from the fabric now except that which she had caused by her own impetuous movement. She shivered.

Katherine. Katherine, sweet child, won't you talk to your king?
   His eyes followed the girl as she flitted through the house. From behind the heavy curtain of rippling, dark-coloured hair, she flirted with eyes the colour of speedwells, her laughter echoing through the rooms.

It was intensely cold over here by the window. Far colder than the rest of the room. Quickly Joss dragged the curtains closed again and turned.

It was standing right behind her, a shadow between

181

her and the lamp. Between one second and the next it was there, blocking out the light, towering over her and then it was gone.

'Oh.' Her involuntary gasp seemed a pathetically small sound in the dimly lit room. She stared round frantically, but there was nothing there, nothing at all. She had imagined it.

Lyn glanced up at her as she entered the kitchen. Luke was cuddling Tom, sitting on the rocking chair by the range and already the little boy's eyes were closed. 'Come and sit down, Joss. I'm just rewarming supper. He'll be asleep in a minute and we'll snuggle him up in a blanket on the chair.'

'I don't think we should let him sleep alone in that room any more.' Joss flung herself down at the table and put her head in her hands. 'I'd rather he slept in with us. We can move his cot into our bedroom.'

'No, Joss.' Luke frowned over Tom's head. 'You know as well as I do that that is the thin end of the wedge. He'll never go back on his own if we let him sleep with us now. Besides with the baby coming so soon you need your rest. Let him stay where he is.'

'He'll be all right, Joss. Honestly. All kids have nightmares from time to time.' Lyn was watching as Luke stood up carefully and lowered the little boy onto the chair where he had been sitting. Tucking him up with his blanket, he slipped the teddy bear in next to him and stood for a moment looking down at his son's slightly flushed cheeks, listening to his regular breathing.

'I suppose so.' Joss stared at her son, her heart aching with love.

'I know what you're thinking, sweetheart.' Luke came over to her and dropped a kiss on the top of her head. 'All those children who have gone before. Don't. It's stupid and it's morbid. That was then. Now is now.'

*　　*　　*

In her sleep Joss stirred. A smile touched the corners of her mouth and she gave a small moan. Gently, not waking her, the bed covers were slowly eased back and her night shirt fell open, exposing her breasts to the starlight.

She woke heavy eyed while it was still dark. She stared up at the ceiling for a moment, disorientated and then reached across with a groan to find the alarm clock. It was half past four. What had woken her? She listened. Tom had not woken the night before when at last Luke had carried him upstairs, snuggling down at once with his teddy and turning over with his back to them, his arms around the furry creature's body, but even though there was no sound from Tom's room, she knew already that she would have to get up and see that he was all right.

Heaving herself carefully out of bed she stopped for a moment, looking back towards Luke's humped form. She could barely see him – just the outline in the light from the landing which streamed through the half closed door. He did not stir. Reaching for her bathrobe she padded on bare feet through to Tom's room and pushed open the door. The room was cold. Far colder than the rest of the house. Frowning she went to the radiator and checked the switch and thermostat which had been left on in case the weather should suddenly revert to winter. It was hot beneath her hand. Shivering she went over to the window. It was open only a crack. Her own reflection as she peered out into the darkness of the garden was dim – a silhouette, back lit by the night light. As she peered she could see the dull gleam of water far away at the end of the lawn, reflected in the starlight.

If you look you will find the house was nearly always inherited by daughters.

Gerald Andrews' words ran suddenly through her head as the baby kicked beneath her ribs. It would be a boy.

She knew it with absolute certainty. A brother for Tom and they were both in terrible danger. Closing her eyes she took a deep breath, trying to stifle the cry of anguish which seemed to be rising inside her from the very depths of her soul. No!

No! Surely to God it was not possible. It could not be possible. Her hands cradled over her stomach, she turned slowly, her whole body clammy with fear, expecting it to be there again – the tall, broad figure between her and the cot. There was nothing.

For a long time she sat, her arms wrapped around her knees, uncomfortably plumped on Tom's bean bag, her eyes fixed on the sleeping form, hunched under his quilt. From time to time the little boy snuffled and smacked his lips, but otherwise he slept undisturbed. Slowly her lids dropped.

As her head fell forward she jerked awake. In the semi-darkness she felt a moment of confusion. She couldn't see Tom any more. The cot, black with shadow, stood empty. Scrambling desperately to her feet she staggered towards him, realising only after she half fell, that her legs had gone to sleep.

He was there, almost invisible in the pool of shadow, but still safe, still asleep. With a small sob she turned away. Hesitating in the doorway she glanced back. The room was warm again now. It seemed snug and safe and almost happy; she was overwhelmed suddenly by a longing for Luke.

Rubbing her eyes she made her way back to her own bed. The wedge of light was still shining through the door from the landing and for several minutes she stood staring down at him. He was curled up in the same position as his son, his face slightly flushed, relaxed and happy in sleep. Instead of a teddy bear he was cuddling a pillow. Smiling, she reached for the knot securing her bathrobe. As she slipped it off and threw it across the foot of the bed she glanced back at the landing. It was empty. Quiet. Nodding to herself, reassured, she pulled back the covers, ready to climb into bed. On her pillow lay another rose.

Backing away she stared at it in horror. 'Luke!' It came out as a strangled whisper. 'Luke, did you –' put it there, she was going to ask, but already she knew he had not. None of the roses had come from Luke.

Staring down at it in horrible fascination, she crossed her arms over her breasts. She felt sick and degraded. It was on her bed, her pillow, where earlier her head had lain, defenceless, asleep. For all she knew, he – it – had been standing there, watching her.

Shuddering, she backed away from the bed. 'Luke!' She reached for the light switch. 'Luke!'

'What is it?' With a groan he turned over and peered at her, his eyes gummed with sleep, his hair tousled. Like this he looked more like Tom than ever.

'Look.' With a shaking hand she pointed at the pillow.

'What?' Groaning, he sat up. 'What is the matter with you? Is it a spider?' He peered round myopically. She had never been afraid of spiders.

'Look at the pillow!' she whispered.

Luke stared at the pillow. He shook his head. 'Can't see it. It must have gone. For God's sake, Joss, it's the middle of the night!'

'There. There!' She pointed.

'What?' Wearily he climbed out of bed and pulled the covers right back, exposing the pale green sheets. 'What is it? What are we looking for?'

'There, on the pillow.' She couldn't bring herself to come any closer. From where she stood she couldn't see it, but it was there.

Without touching it she knew how it would feel. Ice cold, waxy.

Dead.

185

'There is nothing here, Joss. Look.' His voice had lost its grumpiness as sleep left him and suddenly he was gentle. 'You must have dreamed it, darling. Look. Nothing. What did you think was here?'

She took a step closer peering at the pillow. 'It was there. In the middle. A flower. A white flower.' Her voice was shaking.

Luke looked at her hard. 'A flower? All this panic for a flower?' Suddenly he was cross again. 'Flowers don't just appear in the middle of the night. They don't drop onto your pillow from nowhere.'

She flared up defensively, 'For God's sake. Do you think I would be afraid of a real flower?'

'What sort of flower was it then?'

'Dead.'

He sighed. For a moment he seemed at a loss what to say, then slowly, almost resignedly, he started pulling the covers back across the bed. 'Well, what ever it was, it's not there now. You dreamed it Joss. You must have done. There is nothing there. Look. Smooth sheet. Smooth duvet. Smooth, clean, fresh pillows. And I for one am getting into them and going to sleep. I am tired.'

She gave a small humourless smile. 'I'm not going mad, Luke. It was there. I know it was there.'

'Of course it was there.' Irritated he thumped the mattress beside him. 'Are you coming to bed, or do you want to go and sleep in the spare room?'

'No. I'm coming.' Tears of anger and humiliation and exhaustion welled up in her eyes. Quickly, not giving herself time to think, she made for the bed and climbed in. Luke's energetic stripping of the linen had left the bed cold and pristine. It no longer felt cosy. Reluctantly she lay back and stared up at the tester as he leaned across and switched off the light. 'Now, please let us get some sleep.' He hunched the pillow round his shoulders. As he fell asleep he remembered only briefly the rose he had found on her pillow once before. The rose he had accused David Tregarron of leaving there.

Miserably she turned away from him.

Beneath her cheek the hard stem of the flower was cold and very sharp, the petals like soft wax.

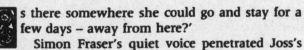

s there somewhere she could go and stay for a few days – away from here?'

Simon Fraser's quiet voice penetrated Joss's brain at last. It was two weeks later.

'No, I can't go. I mustn't. I have to stay here.'

'Why, exactly, Joss?' The doctor was sitting on her bed holding her hand. The clock on the bedside table said it was ten minutes to four. Outside it was slowly growing light.

She shook her head. 'I just want to be here. I have to be here. This is my home.' Her desperate need to stay in the house was irrational, she knew, but she could not fight it.

'Your home seems to be giving you nightmares at the moment. This is the second time in two weeks, that Luke has called me out. You are tired and over stressed.' Simon smiled at her patiently. 'Come on, Joss. Be sensible. Just for a few days so that you can have a good rest, be pampered, stop worrying about Tom and the baby.'

'I'm not worrying –' she could feel the house listening, pleading with her to stay.

'You are. And it's understandable. You are perfectly normal, you know. You have probably been sleeping badly and when you do sleep, you dream violently. The weather has suddenly grown hot and the baby is lying heavy on your stomach, as my old grandmother used to say. After all, there's not long to go now. What are you? Thirty-six weeks? There is nothing wrong with you – or the house – but just at the moment I think it would be a good thing if you were separated. Luke will look after things here, and Lyn will take care of Tom. There is nothing for you to worry about. Lyn has told me it might be nice if you were to go up to London to see your parents. I know things there were not exactly ideal, with your mother ill, but I understand from Lyn that all the tests have been reassuring and she is on the mend and they would be happy to have you, so I think that is a good idea. An ideal solution.'

'Luke?' Joss stared at him. 'Tell him I can't go.'

'You can go, Joss. I think you should. Just to give you a bit of a change.'

'No!' It came out as an undignified shriek. She struggled to get out of bed, pushing past Simon, who stood up and began to pack his bag. 'I will not go. I won't. I'm sorry, but this is my home and I am staying here.' Barefoot, she rushed past Luke and into the bathroom where she slammed the door. She was hot and shaking, a pain somewhere up under her ribs. Stooping over the basin she splashed cold water onto her face and then stared up into the mirror. Her cheeks were flushed, her eyes bright, tears still clinging to the spikes of her eyelashes. 'They can't make me leave.' She spoke out loud to her reflection. 'They can't force me to go.'

She could still hear her own screams ringing in her ears and feel the waxy imprint of the rose against her cheek – the rose which was never there when she awoke.

'Joss?' There was a soft knock at the door. 'Come out. Simon is leaving.'

She took a deep breath. Pushing her hair out of her eyes she turned and unlocked the door. 'I'm sorry,

Simon.' She gave him a determined smile. 'I'm a bit tired and overwrought, I admit it. All I need is some more sleep. I am so sorry Luke called you out again.'

'That's OK.' Simon lifted his bag from the bed. 'As long as you are all right.' He gave her one more beetly look from beneath his bushy eyebrows. 'Keep calm, Joss, please. For the sake of the baby. Stay here, if that is what you want, but don't let the place get to you, and,' he gave her a stern look, 'I think we should consider the idea that you might have the baby in hospital after all. Just a thought!' He gave a sudden beaming smile. 'Now, I'm for my own bed, and if you are sensible that's what you two will do as well. No more alarums and excursions please. No, Luke, don't show me out. I know my way by now.' He lifted his hand and disappeared towards the stairs, leaving Luke staring at his wife.

'Joss.' Suddenly he seemed incapable of saying anything else. He shrugged. 'Do you want a cold drink or something?'

She shook her head. She sat down on the edge of the bed, sheepishly. 'I'm sorry, Luke. I really am. I don't know what came over me. I suppose I was dreaming. But you shouldn't have called Simon, you really shouldn't. The poor man has enough to do with people who are really ill.' She hauled herself up onto the high mattress and lay back against the pillows. 'It felt so real, I thought I really did feel something, you know. Another of those dead roses.' She shuddered.

He sighed. 'I know, Joss. I know.'

She found it impossible to sleep again. The lights out, the sheet, which was all she could bear over her in the hot room rearranged, she tried to get herself comfortable beside Luke. But sleep eluded her. The house was completely silent, the room still shadowy, but outside as the sun rose out of the sea behind the field she could hear the chorus of birds. She stared at the windows, watching the morning star fading between the mullions behind the half drawn curtains. Beside her Luke grunted and sighed and almost at once began to breathe deeply and evenly. His body, heavy and hot, seemed to mould itself into the mattress, secure, safe, reassuring, while she lay, rigid and afraid, every part of her body aching and uncomfortable. She shut her eyes, screwing them up tightly, trying to focus on sleep.

In the corner of the room the shadow that was never very far away stirred and seemed to shiver, an insubstantial wraith. Near it a spider tensed and fled beneath the coffer which stood in front of the window.

When Luke awoke, to the not very tuneful singing of his small son from the nursery, Joss was fast asleep. The room was full of bright sunshine, and he could hear a pigeon cooing soothingly in the tree outside the window. The first days of June had brought a heat wave and it was already very hot. He looked down at Joss for a moment. Her face was still flushed, pressed against the pillow. There was a frown between her eyes and she looked as though she had been crying in her sleep. With a sigh he slid out of bed, careful not to wake her and padded across towards the little boy's bedroom.

She was still asleep an hour later when he brought her a cup of tea and the post. Putting the cup down gently on the bedside table he went to stand looking down on the garden. Behind him the shadow in the corner stirred. It moved away from the corner and hovered in the centre of the room. There was no question now that it was anything other than a man. A tall man.

Joss stirred and turned over to face it, but she did not open her eyes. In her sleep her hand went protectively to her stomach and rested there. Luke did not move. With a sigh he rested his forehead against the glass, savouring the coolness of it. His head ached. His eyes were gritty with lack of sleep. When he turned back towards the door he did not see the shadow which had drawn near his wife. Rubbing his face with the palms of his hands he reached for the handle and let himself out onto the landing, closing the door behind him. In the bedroom the shadow bent over the bed. The slight indentation on the sheet was the only sign of where it touched her.

Joss had tried the number four times that week. Once again this morning it rang with no reply. Putting down the phone she put her head in her hands and stared down at the desk top without seeing it. Her sleep after the doctor had gone had been shallow and troubled; she had woken herself twice with her own whimpering, staring up at the bed hangings above her head. When she got up she felt stiff and uncomfortable, unable to eat any breakfast. All she could think about was the need to speak to Edgar Gower. With a shaking hand she dialled his number and at last there was a reply.

'It's Joss Grant. You remember? Laura Duncan's daughter.'

Was it her imagination or was the pause the other end longer and more uncomfortable than it ought to have been.

'Of course. Jocelyn. How are you?'

In her anxiety she ignored his question. 'I need to see you. Can I come up to Aldeburgh today?'

Again the pause. Then a sigh. 'May I ask what you want to see me about?'

'Belheddon.'

'I see. So. It has started again.' He sounded resigned and a little cross.

'You have to help me.' She was pleading.

'Of course. I'll do everything I can. Come now.' He paused. 'Are you ringing from Belheddon, my dear?'

'Yes.'

192

There was a moment's silence. 'Then be very careful. I will see you as soon as you can get here.'

The coach house was empty and locked. Luke was nowhere to be seen and there was no sign of Jimbo. The Citroën had gone. Joss stared at the place it was usually parked in dismay. There had been a heavy thundery shower an hour before and she could see the dry patch on the gravel where it had stood. Going back into the kitchen she shouted for Lyn. There was no reply. There was no sign of her or of Tom. Running to the back door she looked at the hooks where the coats usually hung. Lyn's mac had gone. So had Tom's and so had his little red gumboots. They had gone out with Luke without telling her; without saying good-bye or coming upstairs to see if she were all right.

For a moment she was panic stricken.

She had to go now. She needed to see Edgar Gower without delay. Lyn's car. Puffing she ran out to the coach house. Lyn's car stood in one of the open coach bays. It was locked. 'Oh, please. Let the keys be here.' Turning she sped back into the house. The keys were not on the shelf by the back door where Lyn sometimes threw them. They were not on the dresser or the kitchen table. Setting her teeth grimly Joss walked through the house to the stairs. Her hand on the rail she looked up towards the landing, suddenly reluctant to go up there. There was no one there. Nothing could hurt her. Her mouth dry she put her foot on the bottom step and began slowly and quietly to climb.

In her bedroom the shadow stirred. It drifted slowly towards the door.

Katherine, I love you!

Half way up the stairs Joss stopped, dizzy. Gritting her teeth, hanging on to the banister, she pulled herself up step by step, increasingly weary and turned towards Lyn's door. Pulling it open she stepped into the room.

Lyn's room was as always spotlessly tidy. The bed was made, the cupboard closed. No clothes lay strewn about, no books or papers. Her belongings, on the dressing table and the high Victorian chest of drawers were meticulously arranged in small piles. The car keys were there, next to the hairbrush and comb.

Grabbing them Joss turned to the door. It was closed. She stared at it, her stomach churning suddenly. She had not closed it and there had been no draught. Although Lyn's window was open the curtains were not moving at all. Taking a step towards it she was conscious suddenly of how quiet the house was. There were no sounds anywhere.

The door was not locked. Pulling it open she stared across the landing towards her own bedroom. The skin on the back of her neck was prickling. There was someone there, she could sense it; someone watching; someone pleading with her to stay. Closing her eyes for a moment she took a deep breath, trying to steady herself.

'Who is it?' Her voice sounded very odd in the silence. Defiant and frightened. 'Luke? Lyn, are you home?' There was no sound.

She had to look. Slowly, plucking up her courage she forced herself to move towards the doorway. She was torn. She needed to escape; she wanted to stay; she wanted to surrender to that languid ecstasy which had overwhelmed her disguised as dreams as she lay on her bed. She could feel it pulling her, soothing, gentle. Hesitantly she took two more steps towards the room and looked in. There was no one there. It was completely empty.

_____

18

Her hand shook so much she could not get the key into the lock of the Mini. Desperately she tried again, glancing over her shoulder across the courtyard towards the house. The back door was closed. She had slammed it behind her but not paused to double lock it. Too bad. She was not going back now. Closing her eyes she took a deep breath and tried to steady herself before bringing the key towards the lock again. It clicked against the car's paint work, slid towards the slot and at last engaged. She turned it and wrenched the door open. Diving head first into the seat she wedged herself behind the wheel, pulled the door closed behind her and pushed down the locks, then she sat for a moment, her head resting against the steering wheel. When she looked up the courtyard was still empty; the back door still shut. Huge swathes of blue sky were spreading now between the thundery clouds.

A note. She should have left a note. Oh God! They would wonder where she was. She looked beside her to the passenger seat where her shoulder bag should be lying, chucked there as she got in. It wasn't there. It was still lying on the kitchen table together with her house keys. Almost as soon as she thought of it she knew she was going to do nothing about it. They would guess when they saw Lyn's car was gone that she had driven some-where and she could phone them once she got to the Gowers.

In the drive she pulled up and for a moment sat staring over her shoulder at the front of the house as she tried to steady her breathing. The windows were all blank. There were no faces looking down at her from her bed-room window.

The roads were almost empty. She made good time as far as Woodbridge and was setting off northwards when she happened to glance at the petrol gauge. It was hover-ing over empty. She had been driving fast, concentrating on putting as much space between her and Belheddon as possible, thinking about Edgar Gower and what she was going to say to him when she got there.

If she got there.

Without a handbag she had no money.

'Shit!' She didn't often swear, and certainly not alone, out loud. 'Shit shit shit!' She banged the steering wheel. 'Oh please, let there be enough to get me there.'

Leaning across, she pulled open the glove compartment and rummaged through the tapes and sweets which Lyn had left there. She found a couple of fifty pence pieces, her fingers sorting through the contents while her eyes were still fixed on the road ahead of her. All she needed was another pound and she could perhaps get a gallon – enough to get her there. A garage loomed ahead, its ugly neon sign bright in the rain-swept landscape and she pulled in, avoiding the pumps, drawing up near the air and water. With both hands now and the help of her eyes she began to ransack the glove compartment. Sweet papers, tapes, shopping lists tumbled to the floor. How strange that Lyn, so meticulous at home, should be so messy in her car. She smiled as she realised that most of the sweet papers related to Tom and then she frowned, wondering just how many sweets Lyn gave him. Her fingers closed over another coin. Five pence. Please, please, let there be some more money there.

In the end she found three pounds in scattered coins around the car – one coin under the floor mat, one down the side of the seat, another on the shelf under Lyn's sunglasses. Relieved she backed the car up to a pump, put in the petrol and at last was on her way again.

She drew into Aldeburgh as a heavy thundery shower of rain began to fall. It was very hot. Pulling into the square she climbed stiffly out and ran, awkwardly because of her bulk, towards the Gowers' house. The door had opened before she got there. 'I saw you from the window, my dear.' Dot pulled her in. 'Are you soaked? You should have brought an umbrella, you foolish child!'

In no time at all, it seemed to her, she had been dried, reassured, settled into a comfortable chair in Edgar's study and given a glass of iced lemonade. Edgar had waited behind his desk whilst his wife fussed around Joss and only when she too had at last settled onto the sofa by the window did he come forward and sit down.

His face was very serious as he reached for his own drink. Then he glanced at Dot. 'She is expecting a baby,' he said with a slow shake of the head. 'I should have guessed.'

'We can all see that.' Dot sounded impatient.

He gave a deep sigh. 'So, Joss. What can I do for you?'

'What do you mean? Why is it significant that I'm expecting a baby?' She needed to hear him tell her why.

Edgar Gower shrugged. 'Perhaps you should tell me first why you wanted my help.'

'You know about Belheddon. You know what it was that haunted my mother and grandmother. You know what happened to my brothers. You know about the roses.'

He frowned. 'I know a certain amount, my dear. Not

perhaps as much as you might be hoping. Tell me what has happened. From the beginning.'

'I went to see John Cornish after you gave me his name last year. I tried again and again to ring you and thank you. It turned out that I had been left the house in my mother's will. She said if I turned up within seven years of her death I was to inherit it. As you know, I did. It came at the right moment for us. My husband lost his job and we were penniless. We moved in, even though it was fairly run down and we are living there now. Myself and my husband and my sister – my adopted sister, that is – and my son, Tom.' She scarcely noticed as Dot leaned forward and took the empty glass out of her hands. 'I found diaries and letters in the house. My mother and my grandmother seem to have been haunted by something. They were very afraid. And now –'

She couldn't go on. Afraid that she was going to cry she reached for a handkerchief and found a wad of crumpled tissues in the pocket of her skirt.

'And now it is your turn to be afraid.' Edgar's voice was matter of fact, unemotional. 'My dear, I received your letter. I'm sorry. I hadn't got round to replying as yet. Perhaps I wasn't sure what to say. You have made me feel very guilty. Can you tell me what has happened since you arrived in the house?'

'Roses.' She found the laugh she was going to give came out as a sob. 'It sounds so silly. To be haunted by roses.'

'In what way are you being haunted by roses?' Unseen by Joss Edgar gave his wife a quick worried glance. She was sitting, lips pursed, Joss's glass still in her hand.

'Just that. They keep appearing. Dried roses – no, not always dried. Sometimes fresh and cold – almost slimy –' she shuddered. 'On my desk. On the table, on my pillow –'

Edgar sighed once again. 'At least roses are unthreatening. You have never seen anything else?'

She shook her head and then shrugged. 'I don't know. I don't think so. But I sometimes wonder if Tom has.'

'Tom is your son?'

She nodded. 'He's only two. He doesn't understand. But something frightens him. He has bad dreams. I'm sorry. I really am. I can't sleep any more. I'm so afraid. They want me to leave the house. To go away until the baby is born, but I don't want to do that. It's my home. My family home. And I've been part of the family for such a short time.'

He nodded. 'I can understand that, my dear. But nevertheless I'm not sure that they're not right.'

'There must be something else I can do. Something you can do. Is it the devil? Does he really live at Belheddon?'

She expected him to laugh, to shrug; to deny it absolutely but instead he frowned. 'There have been exorcisms at Belheddon. Several, I think. I know your mother had one carried out before I came to the parish, and I myself blessed the house and celebrated holy communion there on one occasion. Your grandmother too may have done the same. There was a history going back many centuries of reports of ghosts and even of devils, though I don't myself believe it is the devil or even one of his minions.' At last he permitted himself a little smile. 'No, I think there is an unhappy spirit in the house. And I think it finds itself attracted to women. I don't think you yourself are in any danger, Joss. None at all.'

'But what about the others?'

He looked up and met her eye. For several seconds he said nothing. 'I think you should be aware that it is possible that it is in some way more hostile towards men. And boys.'

'So hostile that no boy has ever lived to grow up in the house.'

He shrugged unhappily. 'Your brothers' deaths were recorded as accidental, Joss. Both seemed terribly, terribly sad accidents, the kind of thing that can happen any-where in any period. I really don't know if there was anything sinister about them. I was with your mother after the deaths of both boys, and she never for a moment seemed to suspect anything else. She would have told me if she had, I'm sure of it. And yet –' he stood up, shaking his head uncomfortably and went to stand at the window, looking down at the sea which was black and oily beneath the thunder clouds. Running his finger round the inside of his collar he turned at last. Perspiration was standing out on his forehead. 'Joss. I do not want to alarm you, but I am not happy about you and your family staying in that house. Why not go away for a few weeks. When is the baby due? Surely you could stay with friends or family until then.'

'You could even come here, my dear,' Dot put in. 'We'd be happy to have you. All of you.'

Joss shook her head slowly. 'I don't know. I don't want to go away. Belheddon is my home now. I love it so much.' She shrugged. 'And the others don't feel any-thing. Luke loves it there too. It's perfect for him. He can run his business from the courtyard, and he's doing really well. He would think it a tragedy to leave now, just when it's all coming together. And I . . . I'm happy there.'

'What about your son?' Dot's voice was sharp.

'Dot!' Her husband rounded on her. 'Young Tom will be fine. Joss is a different woman from her mother. She can cope. She can keep them all safe, I'm sure she can.'

Joss stared at him. 'What exactly does that mean?' Her own voice had suddenly become hard with suspicion.

'It means that your mother became nervous and lonely after your father and brothers died. And who can blame her. She was not a strong woman at the best of times and she became a little neurotic. I think she imagined a great deal of what she thought went on in the house.'

'What sort of things did she imagine?' Joss was watching him intently.

He did not meet her eye. 'She imagined she heard things; saw people. She thought things were being moved about. Towards the end she was hallucinating – of that there is no doubt. When her French friend suggested she move away from Belheddon, for a long time she was too afraid to go. She seemed to feel that someone was keeping her there. We – that is the village quack and I – thought it was the memory of the boys – and of course your father. Nothing could have been more understandable. Less hard to understand was her resolve to give you away. No one understood that. No one.' He shook his head.

'She did it to save me.' Joss was twisting her fingers into the cotton of her voluminous shirt. 'She wrote me two letters which John Cornish gave me. One said she hoped one day I would understand why she had given me away; the other said that it was my father's idea that I should be allowed to inherit Belheddon and that she could not leave until she had arranged that I should, even though it was not what she wanted. My father died before I was born, so presumably he left some kind of will which included his unborn child.' She shrugged. 'He must have loved me.'

Neither of the Gowers reacted to the illogicality of this remark. Edgar merely slowly shook his head. 'They both loved you, my dear. Your father was so pleased your mother was going to have another baby after all the unhappiness in the house. His accident was the most dreadful tragedy. My hope is that the happiness of having a young family in the house again will wipe out all the sadness once and for all.'

'And the unhappy spirit you were talking about?'

He glanced at his wife. 'I think what I will do is have a talk to one or two colleagues who know more about these things than I do. I have an idea what we should do, but I need to consult. Will you trust me?' He smiled. 'And above all be brave. Remember prayer will act as a shield and a strength. I will come and see you as soon as I have worked out what to do. And now –' he took a deep breath, 'I think what we are going to do is give you a decent lunch to fortify you before you go home.'

Home! She hadn't rung. They would be wondering what on earth had become of her.

When she finally got through Lyn was furious. 'Who said you could take my car? I was going home this afternoon and Luke needs the Citroën. What were you thinking about? For God's sake, Joss, you could have guessed we were only down in the village. What the hell is the matter with you?' The angry voice echoed round the Gowers' living room. Joss's hosts had withdrawn tactfully to rummage in the kitchen and begin to make lunch.

Joss looked out of the window towards the sea. 'I'm sorry, Lyn. I really am. It was urgent.'

'And what am I supposed to do? Isn't it bad enough having to look after your bloody family every second of the day, without you taking my only means of escape!'

There was a long silence. Joss's attention had come back sharply to the phone. 'Lyn –'

'Yes, Lyn! What would you do without Lyn?' The voice had grown more shrill. 'I'm sorry, Joss. But it is too bad. I am fed up with it all. I know you can't do much at the moment, but why should it all fall on me?'

'Lyn, I am so sorry. I thought we'd talked it through. I had no idea you still felt like that.'

'No. You have no idea about a lot of things.' The resentment in the voice was unabated. 'You live in your own happy little world, Joss, and see nothing of what is going on around you. That's always been your trouble and now it's ten times worse. I don't know what this bloody house has done to you, but it is not good.'

'Look I'll come back straight away –'

'Don't bother. Luke is going to drive me to the station. And now I've got to go and get Tom's lunch. You'd better see you're back in time for his tea because Luke is going to be in charge all afternoon!'

Joss sat staring at the receiver in her hand for several minutes after Lyn had banged down the phone. Lyn was right. She had been so involved with the house and the book she had not noticed that Lyn was unhappy and restless again. She did take Lyn for granted. Lyn would look after things. She always had.

Wearily she stood up and made her way towards the kitchen. It was a small room, warm and cheerful, full of flowers and scarlet French cooking pans, decorated with Provençal pottery. It made the kitchen at Belheddon look very dark and Edwardian in contrast. She took the chair that Edgar Gower proffered and sat down heavily, her elbows on the small littered kitchen table.

'My sister is furious. I pinched her car without asking.' She tried to make it sound like a joke, but her exhaustion and worry were beginning to wear her down. 'It sounds as though she's had enough of us.'

Dot sat down opposite her. 'Come here to stay, Joss. Bring your little boy. I would love to look after him. It would be no trouble. It would give your sister a rest and I am sure your husband wouldn't mind being on his own if he has a business to run. Ask Edgar. I am a sucker for children and our grandchildren live so far away I can only indulge myself once a year. You would be doing me a kindness.' She reached across the table and took Joss's hand. 'Stop trying to take it all on your own shoulders, Joss. Let other people help.'

Joss rubbed her hands up and down her cheeks wearily. 'I feel tempted. It would be nice to get away – just for a few days.'

She meant it, she realised, suddenly. No more listening for children's voices. No more glances over her shoulder into the dark shadows of her bedroom. No more stomach turning fear each time Tom awoke screaming from a nightmare.

'Good. Then that's settled.' Pushing back her chair, Dot stood up. 'Go home this afternoon and pack up some things, put Tom in your own car this time, and bring him to us. This afternoon I shall get the rooms ready. We have a couple of lovely spare rooms in the attic. A bit of a climb, I'm afraid –' she paused, eyeing Joss's figure. 'If it's too much then Edgar and I will move up there and you can have our room. The trouble with this house is it's tall and thin. Everything on top of each other.' She beamed happily. 'Now, let me make us a salad and we can all get on.'

The salad was delicious with home-made dressing, whitebait, fresh from the beach and home-made bread, followed by strawberries and cream. At the end of the meal Joss felt calmer, and it was with something like optimism that she walked back to the car, with borrowed money in her pocket for petrol, amid promises to return with Tom the next morning.

Tom and Luke were in the kitchen when she arrived home. Tom was filthy – still covered, obviously, in his lunch, together with a great deal of black motor oil. Luke's mood was as black as his son's hands and face.

'Were you out of your mind, taking Lyn's car like that? Couldn't you have left a note? Anything? That woman has given me complete hell, thanks to you, and it wouldn't surprise me at all if she didn't come back. Then where will we be?'

'Don't be silly, Luke.' Extricating herself from Tom's ecstatic welcome at seeing his mummy again, Joss was reluctant to abandon her good mood. She went to the sink and squeezed out a sponge. Kneeling down she began to wash the little boy energetically. 'Of course she'll

204

come back. I'm sorry I upset her, I really am. She was only miffed with me because she had an arrangement this afternoon. But there was no need for her to behave like that. I know Lyn. She'll be terribly sorry once she's cooled down. You'll see.' She sat Tom down and gave him one of his books. 'Lyn has a self esteem problem. If she doesn't think people are acknowledging her full worth she gets really shirty. But it doesn't last. I shall grovel all over the place when she comes back. And,' she hesitated. 'Luke, I've arranged to go away for a few days with Tom. That will give her a break. And you.'

'You've arranged to go away for a few days!' Luke echoed. He was standing hands on hips watching her. 'You have arranged to go away for a few days! And were you going to tell me about this or is this a spontaneous decision too?'

'Don't be silly.' She didn't look up. 'I am telling you now. I went to see the Gowers in Aldeburgh and they have suggested that I go and stay with them for a few days to give everyone here a rest. Dot says she will look after Tom. She loves children.'

'I see. And who exactly are these people?'

'The Gowers. You remember. It was Edgar Gower who gave me John Cornish's address right at the beginning. He was my parents' rector here.'

'And why, may I ask, did you find it so urgent to go and see them this morning that you had to drop everything, leaving the radio on, half the lights, no message, doors unlocked! Can you imagine what we thought when we got home and found the house abandoned?'

Joss bit her lip. 'Oh, Luke. I am sorry. I was going to leave a note, but then –' she stopped abruptly. She couldn't explain to Luke her wildly swinging emotions, her longing, and then the fear and terror she had felt; she couldn't tell him about the panic as she sat in the little car groping for the ignition. How could she? 'I forgot.

I'm sorry,' she finished lamely. 'I really am sorry. I didn't mean to frighten everyone. Blame it on my sleepless night. I don't think my brain was functioning very well this morning.'

Throwing the sticky sponge on the table she went to him and put her arms round his neck. 'Please, don't be cross. I was hoping you might drive Tom and me up there tomorrow. Then you can meet the Gowers and bring the car back for when you need it. I'll make it up to Lyn, don't worry. She needs this job as much as we need her, so I don't think she's going to quit just like that.'

'Don't you be so sure.' Disengaging himself from her arms Luke turned away. 'And don't forget if, God forbid, your mother does get worse, Joe won't be able to look after her on his own. He's going to need help.'

'Oh, Luke.' Joss slumped miserably on a chair, confused and guilty that for a moment she had been going to correct him. Adopted mother. Not mother. Never real mother.

He stood looking down at her for a moment, then his face softened. 'Well, let's hope that doesn't happen for ages yet. I'm sure it won't. Not before the baby comes anyway. And you're right. Lyn will come round. So, we'd better get ourselves organised. Maybe I can take a couple of hours off tomorrow to take you up there, if it's what you want. Simon certainly said you should get away for a bit, so perhaps this is a good idea after all.'

Katherine! Sweet Jesus, Katherine, don't leave me

Neither of them heard the voice from the echoes. In the silence of the kitchen, only Tom looked up. 'Tin man sad,' he said conversationally. He picked up his colouring book and then threw it down on the floor.

Luke had taken the chair opposite Joss. 'You look very tired, old thing,' he said gently. 'I'm sorry I snapped. Only Lyn can talk like a cheese grater at times.'

Joss smiled. 'I know. She's my sister.'

206

Adopted sister.

Wearily she got to her feet and went to put the kettle onto the hot plate. When she turned round Luke had scooped the little boy off the floor. 'Come on, Tom Tom, let's get Mummy settled in the study, and then we'll go and work in the garden for a bit so that she can sit and have her cup of tea in peace.'

Joss smiled. Slowly she followed them through into the great hall. Half way across it she stopped. The room was very cold after the sultry heat everywhere else. The stormy bronzed sunlight barely seemed to filter across the grey flagstones. She must put some new flowers on the table, bring in a few more lamps to brighten the room up.

Katherine. Sweet Katherine. I need you

Uncomfortably she looked round. Something was wrong in the room. There was a resonance in the air, a movement, as though someone or something had spoken. She shook her head, aware that the small hairs on the back of her neck were beginning to move.

'Luke!'

Her voice sounded raw and out of place in the room. In the distance, from behind the study door she could hear Tom's giggle and then his father's deep laugh. They were tidying the room, playing, making a game of it, waiting for her. So why could she not move?

'Luke!' It was more urgent this time. Louder. But still they did not hear her.

Katherine, I can't live without you. Don't leave me . . .

There were words in her head, hurtling round her brain, but she could not hear them properly. Confused, she turned round, her hands to her face.

'Luke!'

Katherine

'Luke, help me.'

She groped for the chair by the empty fireplace and

207

sat down, her head spinning, her breath painful, concentrating on a patch of brilliant sunlight which had appeared on the floor near her. A prism of green and blue and indigo floated over the cool flags and then was gone. She looked up at the window. The sky was leaden again, heavy with purple cloud and the garden appeared to be growing dark.

She took a deep breath. It was easier this time. And another. He – it – had gone.

'Joss? Are you OK? What are you doing there?' Luke appeared in the doorway.

She smiled at him. 'Just a bit tired suddenly. I was watching the sunlight on the floor.' She levered herself out of the chair. 'I'm coming.'

'It's all ready for you. Come and sit down.' He was studying her exhausted face. The strain was more than just physical. He could see the fear in her eyes.

'Joss –'

'A cup of tea, Luke. It solves everything. Then tomorrow I'll go away for a bit, just to rest. That's all. I'll come back. Soon.'

She was not talking to him, and they both knew it. Luke glanced round the room. As he put his arm round his wife's shoulders and led her into the study he swore under his breath.

19

wave of pain took her and carried her in the warm sea water, brushing against the soft green weed. She flailed with her arms and splashed desperately, trying to reach the land, but the swell, inexorable, powerful, had her in its grip and pulled her onwards towards the horizon. Someone was standing there on the shore, waving at her. She could see his distress as he reached out towards her. It wasn't Luke. It was a tall man, fair, broad-shouldered and she could feel his pain mingling with her own. Again she tried to call out to him, but the warm sea water washed into her mouth and she felt her cry smothered before it had left her lips. He was growing smaller now, more distant, standing up to his thighs in the waves, gesticulating desperately in her direction but a new momentum of pain had taken her and she turned her back on him, curling up in the water to become one with her agony.

Surfacing, blinking the salt drops from her eyes she looked back at last. She could hardly see the beach now; his figure was all but invisible against the glare of sunlight but she could feel his love, like a tangible web which enfolded her and drew her slowly back. The pain was there again, hovering on the edge of consciousness, deep inside her, part of her, drawing her bones and muscles apart, with pitiless, torturing fingers. As she curled her body into another crest of anguish the figure disappeared and the line of the beach vanished below the horizon.

Thunder rumbled in the distance and a flash of lightning illuminated the sky. She opened her eyes and saw that darkness had come to the sky save where the storm flickered and rumbled on the horizon. A zigzag of light tore the sky apart suddenly and the thunder reverberated closer, vibrating through the water. She trod the waves, trying to get her bearings and it was then she saw the flowers. Roses, their white petals floating and slowly disintegrating on the tide all around her. She reached towards them feeling their flesh as cold and slimy and dead and at last she opened her mouth to scream.

'Joss! Joss, wake up!'

Luke sat up and bent over her, shaking her shoulder gently. 'Joss, you're having another bad dream.'

With a groan Joss turned towards him, wrenching her eyes open. Lightning flickered at the bedroom window and she could hear the rumble of thunder in the room. So, it had not been a dream at all – she stared into the darkness, confused, her head aching with exhaustion, clinging to the last remnants of sleep as once again the pain began to build.

'Luke.' With a groan she curled around her stomach. 'Oh, God, I think it's the baby. Contractions! Can you phone Simon.' She was fully awake now, clenching every muscle against the building pain. Relax. Go with it. Breathe. 'Oh, God! They're coming quickly. I think you'd better call an ambulance.' She gritted her teeth as Luke shot out of the bed and, turning on the light, made for the door. Relax. Let it come. Ride with it. Breathe.

Oh Christ, she had to get out of the house!

Waiting for the peak of the pain to pass she sat up. A flash of lightning lit the window for a blinding moment and in the brightness which filled the room she saw the figure clearly, standing in the corner. It was the man from the beach – tall, fair haired, broad-shouldered.

'No!' Joss pushed herself up off the bed and backed away, blinded in the sudden total darkness, putting the bed between her and the corner as another flash of lightning followed the first. He had gone. There was no one there. She clutched the bedpost as another wave of pain began to build. Oh God, this is what bedposts were for! In the old days. The days she was writing about in the book. She braced herself against it desperately. Luke! Where was Luke. She had to get out of the house. Away from him – from it – away to a nice bright, noisy, safe hospital where she would be surrounded by people and technology and there would be no shadows at all.

'Luke!' She raised her voice at last. 'Luke, where are you?' She had to pack, to try and get dressed. There was no time for an ambulance. Luke would have to drive her to the hospital – ring them to say she was on her way. Oh God, it was coming again, the pain, inexorable, building like a great monster inside her, pulling her body this way and that as she clutched the bedpost, pressing her face against the old black wood.

Another flash of lightning tore through the room and she opened her eyes, fixing her gaze on the corner. It was empty. There was no one there. Only the shadow of the cupboard across the floor. Outside, through the open window she could hear the sudden downpour of rain, a hiss on the canopy of leaves, a drumming on the grass of the lawn. The sweet smell of wet earth flooded up into the room and at last Tom began to cry.

'Tom Tom! I'm coming!' She staggered towards the door. 'Luke! Luke where are you?'

The corridor was dark, and the door to Tom's bedroom almost shut. She pushed it open and stared into the room. Tom was sitting huddled in the corner of his cot, his hands to his eyes. As she pushed the door further open he began to scream, long high pitched, mindless screams of pure terror.

'Sweetheart, don't be afraid. It's only a silly old storm.' As she hurried across the floor towards him the pain began again. Gritting her teeth she grabbed the little boy from his cot and held him against her, conscious of the wet nappy and damp pyjamas pressed against her breast.

His little arms were around her neck and he was sobbing convulsively as she stood breathing deeply, trying to control the pain, feeling his weight dragging her down.

'Tom Tom, I'm going to have to put you down for a minute, darling –' she could hardly speak. Desperately she tried to disengage herself, but the more she tried to loosen his grip, the more tightly he clung, terrified by her frantic efforts to dislodge him.

'Joss? Where are you?' Luke appeared in the doorway suddenly. 'Oh Joss, darling. Here, let me take him.' She was kneeling by the cot, her arms round the child, panting as the wave of pain receded once again. 'Oh Christ, how can this happen? Why does it have to be now, when Lyn's away?' He tried to loosen Tom's grip but the little boy was screaming hysterically, beyond all reason as another sizzling flash seemed to cut through the room.

'That's struck something awfully close.' Luke disengaged the child's arms by force and dragged him from Joss's neck. 'Come on sweetheart. Can you walk? I think we should go downstairs. You can lie on the sofa in the study.'

As he swung Tom up into his arms the night light on the table in the corner went out.

'No! Oh please, no!' Joss climbed to her feet, hauling herself up on the bars of the cot. 'Have they all gone out? Luke? Are you there? I can't see you!'

Panic was rising in her voice.

'It's all right, Joss. Don't move. Stay where you are

212

and I'll get a torch. There's one by our bed. Don't worry, I've got Tom Tom. He's all right.'

The child's screams receded slightly as Luke groped his way out of the room and along the corridor leaving Joss alone.

'Luke!' Her own cry echoed in the silence. 'Luke, don't leave me! Is the ambulance coming? Luke, please.' Darkness pressed against her eyeballs like a physical blindfold. She could feel the heavy velvet blackness of it all around her. Holding her hands out in front of her she groped towards the cot, sobbing. She could hear nothing but the blanketing silence round her, see nothing. Then she heard Tom crying. His little footsteps in the hall. 'Mummy. Find Mummy.' He was sobbing so hard his breath was coming in little hiccoughs.

'Tom Tom,' she called out to him, facing the door in the darkness. A brilliant flash of lightning showed the door opening and the small face peering round it. 'Mummy!' He ran to her and threw his arms around her legs.

'Where's Daddy? Tom Tom.' The dull ache in her back was growing stronger again.

'Daddy find matches.' The small face was buried in her night shirt.

'Oh God.' The pain was swelling round her. She took a staggered step round Tom towards the cot, and gripped the rail, gritting her teeth.

From the doorway a pale flickering light appeared, throwing immense shadows as Luke appeared down the passage, a candle in his hand.

'Luke, thank God. Is the ambulance coming?' Her knuckles whitened on the cot rail as the contraction began to build. Feeling her pain with her Tom began to scream again. In an instant Luke was beside her, an arm around her shoulders, holding her as her beleaguered muscles tensed again.

'How long?' She spoke through clenched teeth. 'How long till it gets here?'

'I can't get through, Joss.' He caught both her hands in his. 'The phone is dead. It must be the storm. I'm going to drive over to Simon's –'

'No!' Her cry of alarm ended as a sob. 'Don't leave me.'

'Then I'd better drive you to hospital myself. Let's grab your dressing gown and we'll go straight there. We can do it in forty minutes. It's all right, love. We'll make it.' He squeezed her hand harder. 'Come on. There'll be someone there who can take care of Tom Tom as well.'

Even as he said it he knew that it was too long.

'No!' This time it was a cry of real anguish. 'Luke, I don't think there's time. They're coming too quickly.' Perspiration beaded her upper lip and ran down her neck. It streamed between her breasts as the pain spread across her back like a tightening vice. 'Luke, I don't know what to do.'

'Of course you do. You've done it before.'

She shook her head. 'Luke, you're going to have to deliver him. Oh, God!' With a groan she fell to her knees, her arms clutched across her stomach in an attempt to ward off the new pain.

'Tom? Tom Tom, come to Daddy.' Desperately Luke tried to disengage the little boy from his mother as he clung more and more tightly to her. 'Come on, old chap. Let's get Mummy back to her bed. She's not feeling well. She's got a tummy ache and we're going to have to look after her for a bit. Are you going to help me?' He was resorting to force now, unclasping the child's fingers from Joss's night shirt, pulling him away. 'Can you walk, Joss? Can you get back to our room?' He was shouting to make himself heard above the screams of the child. 'Tom. Please. Let go.'

'Let him be, Luke.' Joss was panting. 'You're frightening him more. Tom Tom.' She put her arm round the little boy as the contraction passed and hugged him against her. 'You've got to be very brave and very grown up. Mummy's all right. She's going to be fine.' Was he too little to tell him what was happening? They had hardly mentioned to him yet the possibility of a new brother or sister. The baby wasn't due for two or three weeks. Dear God, and there was no one to help. She bit back tears of panic and frustration, gritting her teeth as a new contraction built while she felt the little boy's grip relaxing a little. 'Stay with him here, Luke, while I get back to bed. See if you can calm him down and get him to sleep.' She pulled herself upright on the bars of the cot and turned towards the door.

'Mummy!' Tom's little hands reached out after her.

'Take him, Luke.' She couldn't hide the pain much longer.

Luke grabbed the child and lifted him into his cot. Tom's screams doubled in intensity.

'Oh sweetheart, don't!' Joss held out her hand towards him, then as the pain seized her she stepped back and doubled over with a groan. Relax. Go with the pain. She gasped as she felt her bones beginning to wrench themselves apart.

'Go, Joss. Go to bed!' Luke was trying to force Tom to lie down. 'Go on. He'll calm down once you've gone.'

The pain was receding, her body resting momentarily, gathering itself for the next battle. She turned and closing her ears to the screams she headed back towards the bedroom.

The bed. She must put something on the bed to protect that deep old mattress – a mattress which must have seen dozens of births in its time. Desperately she tried to keep her mind on the practicalities. What was it they say in films about home births? Hot water and towels. Lots of hot water and towels. Hot water, she was sure someone had said was just to keep the husband occupied. Towels were in the linen cupboard, a huge old oak press on the landing outside the bathroom. A million miles away.

'Oh God!' She couldn't bite back her cry of pain. Surely it was going to happen any moment.

She could see the bed, its posts and draperies illumined suddenly in a lightning flash; it seemed an insubstantial thing, a wavering oasis with its crewel work embroidery hangings, flowers of fantastic mossy green and dull reds and ochres entwined with tortured stems and tendrils climbing the bedposts in sinuous undulating spirals. The curtains were moving, fading, swelling, one moment diaphanous, as transparent as mist, the next growing heavy and thick, the ribs of woollen stitching as thick and corded as a man's wrist. Joss let out a sob. It was too far away. She couldn't move. In the intense darkness which followed every flash the great black bulk of the bed had moved away. It was out of reach, beyond some invisible barrier which she couldn't penetrate. Luke. Where was Luke? Dear God, help me, please.

Then he was there – a hand on her arm, a pressure at her shoulder, comforting, guiding, pushing her gently across the room. Another flash of lightning; she could see nothing now but the imprint of the window mullions, thick scarlet brands on her retina.

Groping, she reached for the bed, dragging off the heavy counterpane with its thick stitching, and throwing it to the floor.

'Luke – find something to put under me.'

She could see a flickering light appearing in the passage now. Luke was there, the candlestick in his hand. 'It's all right, love. I've thought of that. I've got something.' His voice came from the doorway. The spare waterproof sheet from Tom's chest of drawers, then some towels, then he was helping her up into the cool soft sheets. 'Hang on, sweetheart.' His hand on her forehead was hot, nervous, unlike the other hand, the cool hand which had guided her to the bed. Her eyes flew open. Luke had put the candle down beside her. He had only just come into the room . . .

She turned on her side with a groan as the pain hit her again, curling herself around it, conscious with some distant part of her mind that she could smell roses in the air.

'Luke!'

'I'm here, darling. Pant. Remember, they told you to pant.' He was pulling the sheet over her.

'You're going to have to deliver it.'

'I'd already worked that out for myself.' She could hear the wry tone in his voice.

'Tom!'

'Tom's asleep. He was completely worn out. Once you'd gone he was settled in seconds, the poor little mite.' He reached for her hand and clasped it tightly. 'So, tell me what to do.'

'Boil some water to sterilise some thread and scissors. Then find the baby clothes. They're stored in the bottom of Tom's chest. The blankets are there too. Don't wake him.' She groaned, clutching his hand. 'You were there when Tom was born. You saw what went on. I was up the other end, remember?' She managed a laugh, which ended as a sob.

'I remember.' Luke scowled. 'There was a doctor and two midwives and I closed my eyes at the crucial moment.'

'Go. Luke. Get the water going.' She was drifting away from him again, into a sea of pain.

She had no idea how long he was gone. It seemed like a month of agony, a few seconds respite – then he was there again with the saucepan and more towels, a pile of shawls and tiny white garments. She turned her head towards the window. It was growing less dark. There hadn't been a rumble of thunder for a while now and the flashes of lightning were growing less intense, just flickering faintly on the horizon out to sea.

The smell of the roses was stronger now as Luke moved round the bed to rub her back. She lay still, staring up into the darkness of the shadowy tester, her body relaxed, pain free for a few blessed seconds.

And then it began to build again. She didn't remember screaming in the hospital, but then they had given her an epidural.

The pain, the fear, the awful voice in her head.

Katherine!

He was there in the shadows, in his usual place near the window, the tall man with the sad eyes. She hadn't seen him before. Not so clearly. Not for sure. She reached out her hand to him and smiled. 'I'll be all right.' She mouthed the words, but no sound came out. Not until she screamed again.

'Joss!' Luke's voice was suddenly excited, full of awe. 'I can see its head.'

It was a boy. Holding him, dried and warmly wrapped, in her arms, Joss looked down at the small head and nestled him against her chin. She looked up at Luke and smiled. 'Congratulations, doc.'

He grinned. 'He looks OK, doesn't he?'

'He's fine.' The baby was making small contented snuffling noises, his face very red against the white of the blankets. Outside it was full daylight now, the garden cool and cleansed by the rain, lying silent beneath a pall of white mist. Exhausted Joss lay back and closed her eyes. The silence was total. Luke had checked that Tom was all right and found the little boy sleeping peacefully, his thumb in his mouth. With the lights and phone still disconnected he had tiptoed off through the shadows of the early morning house to put the kettle on again – this time for tea.

The slight pressure on the blanket was so gentle that she hardly noticed it. Smiling as she drifted off to sleep she eased her aching body into a more comfortable angle round the crooked elbow which held her new son and pushed her head deeper into the pillow.

She was jerked awake by the baby's sudden squeal.

'What is it? Little one?' Sitting up she peered down at the tiny face, screwed up now into screams of unhappiness. 'Oh sweetheart, quiet.' She stared round the room. The cold had come back. The terrible, all-encompassing cold which was the cold of the tomb. 'Luke?' Her voice was lost in the ceiling beams, panic-stricken. 'Luke?'

He was there. Somewhere.

Desperately she held the baby to her. 'Luke!'

A boy. Oh sweet Jesus, why couldn't it have been a girl? She realised suddenly that she was crying. Deep, body shaking sobs of exhaustion and fear.

She was still crying when Luke came back with the tray of tea things. 'Joss, what is it, love? Is something wrong?'

'He's a boy.' She was holding the baby tightly against her.

'Of course he's a boy.' Luke sat on the bed. 'Come on, sweetheart. There's nothing wrong. Jimbo will be here in an hour. I'll send him straight off for Simon and he can come and give you both a check up. Come on, love, there's nothing to cry about.' He leaned forward and touched the baby's tiny hand. 'So, what are we going to call him?'

Joss looked up at him. Her cheeks were still damp with tears, her eyes reddened, her face pale with exhaustion. 'I'd like to call him Philip.'

Luke frowned. 'After your father? Won't that upset Joe?'

She nodded miserably.

'Then let's think of another name to go first. A name

that has no complications – then he can have Philip and Joe as his second and third names.' He smiled.

'Ever the diplomat.' She regarded him wanly. 'So. Think of a name.'

'We don't have to decide at once.' He looked down at the sleeping infant. 'Why don't you rest. Later, when you're feeling stronger we'll do some brain storming, OK?'

He had found the little crib basket, and lined it with sheets. Taking the baby gently from her he laid him in the basket and tucked the blankets round him. 'There. Rest now, Joss. Everything's all right. When the phones are back on I will ring Lyn, and Alice and Joe. They'll all be so excited.' He stooped and kissed her forehead. Then he tiptoed out of the room.

In the shadows the anger and fear had begun to build once more.

ell, you both seem extremely well, considering.'
Simon put away his stethoscope and tucked the
baby's little shirt back down under the blankets.
He had examined Joss and the baby and inspected the
afterbirth. 'I suppose I should have expected some kind
of rebellious move like this!' He grinned. 'Didn't like the
idea of a high tech birth, you said, if I remember?'

Joss laughed. She was sitting on the edge of the bed,
fully dressed, drinking a cup of tea.

Simon reached for his own cup.

'I don't think we need send you to hospital. As far as
I can see everything is fine. As I said before if I remember,
take it easy don't do too much and I will ask the midwife
to call later this morning.' He glanced at the lamp by the
bed. 'Have you got your electricity back yet up here?'

Joss shook her head. 'No electricity and no phone. I'm
pursuing the primitive birth thing to its ultimate conclusion.'

'I see.' Simon stood up. 'You modern women never
cease to amaze me. Well. I must go on my rounds. Don't
hesitate to send for me if there are any problems, no
matter how small.'

After he had gone Joss lay back, exhausted, on the
pillows. Outside the mist had lifted to leave a beautiful

hot day. A sky the colour of cornflowers arched above the garden, reflecting in the lake at the end of the lawn. The house was very quiet. Luke had driven over to Janet Goodyear with Tom, hoping she would look after him for a few hours and hoping even more that the Goodyears' phone was working. If ever they had needed Lyn it was now. Stretching, Joss stared up at the tester, then slowly she moved her head on the pillow to look towards the front window. The room was full of sunshine. There was nothing there to frighten her. Luke had thrown open the casement and she could hear the birds and smell the wet freshness of the earth and the grass, mixed with honeysuckle.

Edgar! She sat bolt upright. Edgar was expecting her. Damn the phone. Sliding off the high bed with a surge of sudden energy she went to the baby's basket which was standing on the chaise longue near the back window and peered in. He was asleep, the small lids, blue veined, a fringe of dark lashes on the soft cheeks. He had thick dark hair, like her and Luke, and it stood up on the top of his head with every appearance of having the same wild individuality as his father's. She smiled. Tom had taken one quick look at his new brother and seemingly lost interest. As far as she could see he was none the worse for the traumas of the night. In fact he seemed remarkably cheerful – the more so at the thought of visiting Janet and the basket of kittens at present occupying the prime spot in front of her Aga.

Slowly and a little painfully Joss made her way downstairs and through the great hall towards the kitchen. Luke had left the post unopened on the kitchen table. Pulling the kettle onto the hot plate Joss opened her first letter while she was waiting for it to boil. It was from David. 'A few more pieces of the jigsaw,' he had written in his neat small script. 'I've found a wonderful old book which mentions Belheddon several times.' Folded into the envelope was a thick wad of photocopied pages. Joss looked up as the kettle began to steam. Putting the letter down she made herself a cup of tea and then, feeling shaky and suddenly very tired she sat down, picking it up again. David went on:

> It was published in 1921 and tells some half dozen stories of mystery and mayhem all set in East Anglia. I remember your telling me about John Bennet who disappeared some time at the beginning of the century. Well, the author of this book has the story. It's weird. Are you sitting comfortably? Then read on . . .
>
> David.

Joss put down the letter and extricated the folded pages. David had photocopied about six and spreading them out in front of her she began to read.

One of the many legends attached to beautiful Belheddon Hall, an ancient manor house set in lovely rolling parkland on the edge of the sea, concerns the family who lived there within very recent times. Mary Percival inherited the house on the death of her mother in 1884 when she was just twenty years old. A determined and resourceful young woman by all accounts, she resolved to run the huge estate single handed, rejecting all offers for her hand, offers of which as may be imagined, there were many.

As far as we can gather Mary was an attractive and popular member of the community and when at last she gave her heart it was to the handsome son of a Suffolk clergyman who was practising as a lawyer in Bury, a town some miles from Belheddon. John Bennet was a year her senior and on their marriage abandoned the law in order to help Mary look after the estate. This heavy responsibility he took over completely within a few months as Mary waited for the birth of her first child. Henry John Bennet was born in October 1900 and two years later his sister Lydia Sarah followed.

223

As far as is known all was contentment within the Bennet household and the first sign of a problem in the house was noted by the local rector. In his memoirs there are several references to Belheddon Hall and he was called to perform a Service of Exorcism in the house on at least two occasions. He was called to the Hall in the winter of 1902 after servants reported sightings of an apparition, variously described as a knight in armour, a Martian and astonishingly a 'tripod' (this was four years after the appearance of the War of the Worlds *by Mr H. G. Wells) and a monster foretelling the end of the world. In the course of the next year the Bennets found it impossible to keep servants at the Hall. One after another they left and their replacements departed in similar short order. Only a few months later, in the spring of 1903, tragedy struck the family. Little Henry John died as the result of a terrible accident.*

This is where the mystery begins. There is no record of how or why he died. It was presumably no ordinary childhood malady which carried him off. The shock and horror throughout the county precludes that.

Joss laid down the sheets of paper and reached for her tea cup thoughtfully. She gazed into the depths of the tea, remembering. She was sitting in the attic, the brilliant blue sky outside the windows, with John Bennet's diary lying in her lap. The words sprang out at her as they had then.

So, he claims yet another victim. The boy is dead. Next it will be me.

She was not at all sure she wanted to go on reading this. Folding the pages she stood up and pushed them into the pocket of her trousers, then picking up the cup she made her way through to the great hall. The room was bright, sunshine flooding in through the rain smudged windows and casting moted beams across the floor. The flowers she had put on the refectory table only yesterday had shed petals all over the black polished oak and there was a dusting of sticky pollen round the silver bowl. With a shiver she glanced around the room and then she headed for the staircase.

She realised as she looked down into the crib that her heart was thudding with fear. What had she expected? To find something awful had happened to her baby? She gave a smile. He was awake, his little fists waving aimlessly free of his shawl.

'Hello, stranger,' she whispered. Stooping she scooped him up into her arms. Carrying him over to the chair by the window she settled herself comfortably so she could look out over the garden, and slowly she began to unbutton her blouse.

Ned. The name came to her out of nowhere. Edward. There were no Edwards in her family as far as she could remember. Frowning she tried to picture the family Bible downstairs in the study. And there were certainly none in the Davies family. 'Edward Philip Joseph Grant.' She repeated the names to herself out loud. 'Not a bad handle for a very small chap.' She dropped a kiss on the fuzz of dark hair.

When he was once more asleep she went over to sit on the window seat and only then did she pull the photocopied pages from her pocket once more.

Stories continued to circulate throughout the next few months and must have distressed the bereaved family enormously. Mr and Mrs Bennet became increasingly unsettled and the rector was repeatedly sent for to the Hall. Then at the end of June in that year John Bennet disappeared and despite country-wide attempts to locate him was nowhere to be found.

No trace of him was ever discovered at the time, but some fifteen years later rumours began to circulate around the Essex-Suffolk borders as to what had really happened.

An elderly man was reported to have been seen in several different hostelries, claiming to be the missing John Bennet. He looked like a man in his eighties (John Bennet would by now have been about fifty-five, a year older than his wife) with white hair, vacant eyes and a severe nervous twitch. Word of his presence on the Suffolk border of course reached Mary Sarah, living still at Belheddon Hall with her only surviving child, Lydia, now a young lady of sixteen. The demons of Belheddon had, it seemed, been laid to rest after the disappearance of the master of the house. Mary Sarah, it is reported, denounced the man as an impostor and refused to see him. He on his part refused to go to Belheddon Hall and when asked about his life in the intervening years became vague and troubled.

Nothing more would have been heard of him perhaps, had he not been discovered unconscious on the steps of the church in the village of Lawford. The rector had him carried into the rectory and there he was nursed back to a semblance of life. The story he told the rector was never divulged officially but a housemaid in the rectory said that on several occasions her duties took her into the rector's study to stoke the fire while the two men were talking. The story the visitor was unravelling filled her with horror.

John Bennet — so the story went, and so he claimed to be — was walking in the garden at Belheddon one evening as dusk was falling when he was confronted by something which had the appearance of a man encased in the armour of yesteryear. The figure, at least seven feet tall, strode towards him, its hands outstretched.

In turning to flee his foot slipped in the mud at the edge of the lake and he fell awkwardly upon his back. To his terror the apparition stooped over him and proceeded to lift him in the air. Before he knew it he found himself hurled into the water.

When he surfaced and looked round trying to see his assailant there was no sign of him. The banks of the lake were empty and there was nothing to be seen in the darkness but the outlines of the nearby trees. Swimming to the far bank Bennet, if indeed it was he, climbed out, but his sanity, already unhinged by the death of his only son, had completely deserted him. Instead of making his way to the house and safety, he remembered fumbling for the latch on the gate into a back lane, and running, still dripping with ice cold water into the coming darkness. It was the last thing, or so he claimed, that he remembered, before waking up in the rectory fifteen years later.

What happened to the man who told this story no one knows. He remained in the rectory for several days, then one night he let himself out into the darkness from which he had emerged and was never seen again.

Joss let the pages fall into her lap. From where she was sitting she could see the lake across the grass, concentric circles forming on its glassy surface amongst the lilies as fish came up for flies.

A man in medieval armour? The tin man? She closed her eyes against the glare of the sunlight on the water.

She was awakened by Luke's hand on her shoulder.

'Hi. How are you?' He had brought her a cup of tea which he set down on the small table beside her.

She stared at him blankly for a moment, then she sat up, leaning towards the crib. 'Is Ned OK?'

'Ned?' For a moment Luke paused, head to one side. 'Yes, I think I like that. Edward Grant. He's fine.' Luke stood looking down at the baby fondly.

'And Tom?'

'Tom is happy as a sandboy. I've left him with Janet for the day. And their phone was working, so I've rung your Edgar Gower and he and his wife are going to drive over tomorrow to see you. I've rung Lyn and she is coming back immediately and some good news: she said Alice's tests are encouraging. The biopsy showed no malignancy. So, sweetheart, you don't have a single thing to worry about in the entire world! And another piece of good news. My parents are back. I rang them in Oxford just in case and they got home last night! They send all their love and congratulations and they're longing to see their new grandson!'

Joss smiled. On the floor, the photocopied pages which

227

had slipped from her knee were scattered around her feet. 'So, all that and a perfect husband and a cup of tea as well.'

'All that!' He sat down on the window seat. 'Oh, and Jimbo has brought you a box of chocolates!'

Janet brought Tom back while Luke was collecting Lyn from the station that evening. Stooping over the baby she examined the sleeping child with the same dispassionate eye she had turned on their cooking range. 'Bit small, I suppose, but very pretty,' she announced. 'Well done you!' She straightened and turned her back on the baby, the inspection complete. 'A bit dramatic, even for Belheddon, wasn't it? Giving birth in a thunderstorm like that!'

'I suppose so.' Joss lifted the baby out of his basket. 'The midwife has been twice and so has Simon, so I'm being kept a strict eye on!' She glanced up at Janet. 'You and Roy were here when Edgar Gower was rector, weren't you.'

Janet nodded. 'He'd been here years when we bought the farm.'

'What did you make of him?'

Sitting down she unbuttoned her shirt and put the baby to the breast. Janet looked the other way but Tom, fascinated, leaned against her knees and poked at the small ear with his finger.

'A man of fire and steel – so different from dear gentle James Wood. Come here, Tom.' She hauled the little boy onto her knee. 'Luke rang him, you know, from our place. He wanted to come over now, today, straight away. He sounded terribly worried.' She eyed Joss for a moment. Joss's face was hidden by her curtain of hair as she looked down at the baby in her arms. 'Joss –' she paused. 'Listen, I know we've all made a bit of a drama out of the stories about this house. One does. It's –' she hesitated, ' – it's fun, I suppose. Dramatic, spooky. Everyone loves a good ghost story. But you mustn't take it too seriously. Edgar was a bit –' she stopped, searching for the right word. 'Superstitious, I suppose. A mystic. Some people might have said a bit of a nutter. Some members of the PCC used to have terrible doubts, you know. Not quite the thing at all in a conservative parish. The thing was, he and Laura used to wind each other up. Nothing really out of the ordinary happened here, you know. Just a series of terrible tragedies. Laura just couldn't accept that they were accidents. She needed to believe there was more to it than that. But these things do happen. Families have the most rotten runs of luck and then it changes suddenly.' On her knee Tom, his fingers wound into her pearls, had closed his eyes. She hugged him gently. 'He's exhausted poor lamb. A new brother and the promise of his very own kitten when it's old enough to leave its mother. You don't mind, do you?'

Joss looked up at last. 'Of course not. We need a cat. That would be lovely.'

'And you won't worry any more?'

'Not if the cat is black.' Joss managed a smile.

Janet shook her head. 'They're all splodgy. Calico cats. But just as lucky.'

She stood up carefully, holding the sleeping child. 'What shall I do with him?'

'Can you put him in his cot? Through there, on the left.' She sighed as Janet disappeared with Tom. Was that what it was? Imagination. A superstitious man and a hysterical woman in a hot house environment: isolated, bored, lonely.

She cocked her head suddenly at a noise above her head. Mice playing in the attics, or children?

Dead children.

Generations of little boys, their shouts and laughter still echoing in the roof timbers of the house.

*   *   *

229

'Lyn!' Joss threw her arms round her sister and hugged her. 'I'm so sorry about the car.'

Lyn smiled. 'All forgotten. You were obviously under stress.' She looked round as she dropped her bags on the floor. 'So, where is the latest little Grant?'

'Upstairs. They're both asleep. Oh Lyn, I don't know how we would ever manage without you!'

'You can't. It's as simple as that.' Lyn looked at her for a moment before turning away and heading towards the door. 'So, are you going to show me?'

They stood for several minutes by the crib, staring down at the sleeping baby. Gently Lyn reached in and touched the little hands. Her face softened. 'He's gorgeous. You haven't asked me about Mum.' She was still concentrating on the baby.

'Luke told me. It's not malignant.'

'You might have rung her!' Lyn looked up at last. 'You might have told her about the baby!'

'Lyn, I couldn't!' Stung, Joss spoke more loudly than she intended and the baby stirred. 'The phones have been out of order since the storm. Luke must have told you. That was why we were stuck here on our own, for God's sake!'

She stooped as Ned let out a wail of anguish and she scooped him out of the cot.

'OK. I'm sorry. Of course you couldn't. Here, let me hold him.' Lyn reached out her arms. 'But ring as soon as you can, Joss. It would mean so much to her. He is her grandson, remember.' She said it with a note of defiance in her voice.

Joss frowned. Laura's grandson. A son of Belheddon.

'Of course.'

Joss woke at the first sound of a whimper from Ned. She lay for a moment in the darkness staring towards the window where the garden was as bright as day in the moonlight. In the silence she heard the sharp yip yip of a little owl and again Ned gave a little cry. Sitting up, trying not to disturb Luke, she pushed her feet over the side of the bed and reached for her cotton bathrobe. The room was cold. Too cold. She glanced round with a shiver. Was he there, lurking in the shadows, Tom's tin man? The man without a heart. The alien intruder. The devil of Belheddon.

The moonlight was flooding the small basket bed as she crept over to it and stared in. Ned's face, turned away from the brightness, was alert. He appeared to see her at once, and she saw a small fist appear from beneath the swaddling, waving in the air. She stood looking down at him, overwhelmed by such a flood of love and emotion that she was incapable for a moment of doing anything. Then at last she picked him up; kissing him she carried him to the seat by the window. Before she sat down she stood for a moment staring out into the garden. The central casement between the mullions was open a crack. She pushed it slightly, surprised to find that the sweet night air which flooded in was considerably warmer than the air in the bedroom. For a moment the balmy beauty of the night overwhelmed her. Then the distracted crying of the baby in her arms brought her back to the present. Pushing her night shirt off her shoulders she put the baby to her breast still staring into the distance towards the lake. A cloud shadow drifted across the grass. She frowned. The night was very silent. She stood there for several minutes, lulled by the gentle rhythmic sucking of the baby, conscious of the gentle snores of her husband in the bed behind her then, tired, she lowered herself at last into the chair. It was as she was preparing to move the baby to the other breast that she heard the nightingale. Entranced she stared up at the window. The pure notes poured on and on, coming she supposed from the woods behind the church. The sound filled the room. Standing

231

up again she walked back to the window and looked out. Two children were playing in the moonlight near the lake. She stiffened. 'Georgie? Sammy?'

Sensing the change in her mood at once Ned stopped sucking and turned his head away, screwing up his little face to cry. Her mouth had gone dry. 'Sammy?' she breathed the name again. 'Sammy?'

'Joss?' Luke stirred and turned towards her. 'Everything all right?'

'Everything is fine.' Shushing the child she rocked him against her gently, realising suddenly that the nightingale had stopped singing. And the figures in the moonlit shadows had disappeared.

'Come back to bed.'

'I'm coming. As soon as he's asleep again.'

Tucking Ned back into his little crib at last, Joss straightened wearily and stretched her arms. She could hear the nightingale again now, more distant, echoing in the silence of the garden. 'Can you hear it?' she whispered to Luke. 'Isn't it beautiful.'

There was no answer.

Turning she stared at the bed. Luke's face lay in shadow, the heavy drapes of the bed curtains half pulled across by his head as though warding off the moonlight. With a smile she turned back to the window. On the sill, silver in the moonlight, lay a white rose.

She stared at it for several seconds, feeling the scream mounting in her throat. No. She must be imagining it. It wasn't there. It could not be real! Taking a deep breath she shut her eyes, her fists clenched, and counted slowly to ten, hearing the clear liquid notes of bird song louder and louder in her brain. Then at last she opened them again and stared down at the stone sill.

The rose had gone.

21

eading the way into the sun-filled study next morning Joss set her tray of coffee and biscuits down on the desk. The midwife had gone as the Gowers arrived. They stood just inside the doorway now staring round the room.

'Why, it hasn't changed at all since your mother was here,' Dot said in evident delight. 'Oh, Joss, dear, this is such a lovely room. And is this the little one? May I see?' Ned was sleeping in his crib beside the open window. She stood looking down at him for several seconds, then she turned and smiled. 'Edgar? Come and look. I think this house is blessed. I think all the unhappiness has gone.'

Her husband stood looking down into the crib as she had, then his face too relaxed into a smile. He glanced up at Joss. 'My dear, the last time I came into this house I performed a service of blessing and exorcism for your mother. I think it worked. Dot is right. The atmosphere has changed completely. I will never forget the anguish and fear and hatred which seemed to pervade the very walls on that occasion. I felt as though I were wrestling with the devil himself. But now . . .' he shook his head wonderingly. 'This place is full of joy and light.' Turning to the fireplace he stood for a moment with his back to it, then he lowered himself into an arm chair. 'May I suggest something?'

Joss gestured Dot towards the other chair and then turned to pour out the coffee. 'Of course.'

'I think it would be nice to baptise the little one as soon as possible. Would you allow me to do it? Unless of course you have already made plans in that direction.'

'Well, no, we hadn't.' Joss passed him a cup. 'I must discuss it with Luke, but I think that would be wonderful. Tom Tom was christened in London.'

'Soon.' Edgar's brilliant blue eyes were fixed on her face.

Joss frowned. 'You are still worried.'

'No. But I believe in taking no chances. I know that to many people the baptism is merely a social occasion – a marker to place the child in the community – but it has a far more important purpose than that: to save and protect the child in Christ's name. You do not need to send out invitations.'

Joss sat down, suddenly very weary. 'You mean you want to do it now.'

'It would be best.'

'Here. In the house.'

'In the church.'

'Would James Wood mind?'

'I shall ring him first, of course.' Edgar sat back in his chair and sipped his coffee. 'My dear, I'm sorry. I don't mean to railroad you into this. You need time to think and discuss it with your husband, of course you do. I can always come back. Or Wood can do it.' He smiled, pushing the shock of white hair back out of his eyes. 'There is no need for an indecent hurry. I was filled with such unease about this place, but it was not necessary. I can sense that. I think the problems have gone. Perhaps your poor mother, God rest her soul, brought them on with her unhappiness.' Putting down his cup he stood up restlessly and went back to the window, glancing down at the sleeping baby as he did so. Then he swung round. 'May I wander round a little? Forgive me. Call it professional interest.'

Joss forced a smile. 'Of course.'

He nodded. 'Stay and talk to Dot. She'll tell you what an insufferable boor I am, and you can moan about my ideas as much as you like!'

In the hall he stood still, gazing up the staircase. For a moment he did not move, then slowly he reached into his pocket for his crucifix.

The staircase was dark. Groping on the wall he found the light switch and flicked it down. The lights were dim – a bulb had gone half way up at the corner of the stairs and the flight wound up into the shadows. Taking a deep breath he put a foot on the bottom step.

Ignoring Lyn's room he made his way at once into the master bedroom and looked round. The four poster was the same, the heavy cupboard by the window, the rugs, the chairs. The only differences came from the clothes scattered around, the books piled on the window sills, the flowers in vases on the chest of drawers and the shelf by the chimney breast and the small crib by the back window with its trail of white shawls, the attendant piles of small garments, the garish plastic changing mat and huge bag of disposable nappies.

Standing in the middle of the room he listened intently.

Katherine

Was that a voice in the echoes? He remembered from last time the anguish, the pain that permeated the very plaster of the walls of this room, the conviction that if he tried harder he would be able to hear the voice that seemed to scream its agony beneath this roof.

A pox on you priests. Why could your prayers not save her?

With a sigh he turned round, then taking a deep breath

and squaring his shoulders he knelt on the rug at the end of the bed and began to pray.

When he returned to the study. Dot and Joss had been joined by Lyn and Tom. 'I was telling Lyn that we thought we might have the christening early,' Joss said slowly as Edgar appeared. She was tight lipped. 'She doesn't feel it would be right.'

'Of course it's not right.' Lyn was clearly angry. 'You can't do it without Mum and Dad. They would be desperately hurt.' She turned on Joss. 'I don't know what's the matter with you! Doesn't the past mean anything to you at all? All the years they have treated you as their daughter, loved you, cared for you! Now this bloody house comes into the picture and dear old Joe and Alice are so much rubbish you'd rather forget about!'

'Lyn!' Joss stared at her. 'That's not true. That's absolute nonsense and you know it! We're not talking about a christening to thwart Mum and Dad's chances of a nice party, we're talking about saving a baby who might have a terrible accident at any moment!'

There was a shocked silence.

'Joss, dear.' Dot put her hand on Joss's arm. 'I am sure there is absolutely no danger of little Ned having any kind of an accident. Edgar had no business frightening you like that. And I don't think we should discuss it any more at the moment. Edgar, a christening is a family occasion and it's important that Joss's parents have a chance to be here. A few days or even weeks are going to make no difference whatsoever.' She sounded really cross.

Edgar shrugged. 'I'm sure you're right, dear.' His eyes contradicted the meekness of his tone. They were plainly angry. 'Very well, may I suggest we leave the discussion now. Should you wish me to baptise little Ned I shall do so of course. Otherwise fix it up with James Wood, but

I beg you to do it as soon as possible.' He cleared his throat. 'Dot, I think we should be going. Jocelyn has only just had a baby and she must be very tired.' He smiled suddenly. 'He is a beautiful child, my dear. Congratulations. Don't let my wittering on frighten you. Enjoy the baby and enjoy the house. It needs happiness – the best exorcism of all.'

As soon as the Gowers' car had disappeared up the drive Joss turned on Lyn. 'What on earth is the matter with you? How dare you think I am trying to cut out Alice and Joe. That's an outrageous thought. What kind of person do you think I am?'

Lyn was unrepentant. 'I am beginning to wonder. I think all your new found grandeur has gone to your head.'

'Lyn!'

'Take a look at yourself, Joss.' Lyn scooped Tom up into her arms. 'Now, I'm going to get lunch. May I suggest you rest or something as the lady of the house should!'

Joss stared after her as the door closed. Then, miserably she turned towards the pram. Picking Ned up she cuddled him for a while before carrying him to the chair and sitting down. Closing her eyes she tried to relax. It was natural for Lyn to be jealous. She had every reason. Joss had a husband, children, a beautiful house – it must seem like untold riches to Lyn, who had failed to find a job at all for the last year, and had until Joss and Luke had offered her this one, been unemployed. Joss dropped a kiss on Ned's little head.

In her arms the baby slept. Closing her own eyes Joss, worn out, let her head rest against the chair back and drifted into sleep.

She was awoken by screams as Ned suddenly slipped from her arms.

'Ned! Oh God!' She grabbed at him in time to stop him

237

falling to the floor and clutched him against her. She was shaking. 'Oh my little love, are you all right?' Ned was crying hard, small high pitched screams of distress which tore at her heart.

'Ned! Ned, little one, hush.' She cradled him to her, cursing herself for falling asleep.

'Joss?' It was later. Luke put his head round the door and then came in.

Joss was sitting by the window, the baby at her breast, listening to the tape of Chopin nocturnes which had been her favourite listening for the last week. 'How is he?'

'OK.' She bit her lip.

'Lunch is nearly ready. I hear the Gowers were here.'

She nodded. 'I suppose Lyn has told you.'

'She's very upset. You know, Joss, you're not handling her very tactfully.' He sat down opposite her, watching fondly the cameo before him of mother and child. 'I've warned you. We have to be careful. We don't want to lose her. Don't forget, you have a job to do. That publisher was serious about his contract. You're not just playing at the hobby of writing now. It's for real. With real money. You can't risk losing Lyn.'

Joss nodded. 'I know. And I didn't mean to upset her. Or you. It was Edgar who thought it so important that Ned be baptised.'

'And he will be. Just as soon as we've got a date organised when Alice and Joe can get here. And my parents too, Joss. Don't forget them. They haven't even seen the house yet.'

'She's going to neglect Tom, you know.' Lyn turned from the range where she was stirring a saucepan of soup as Luke came in.

'Nonsense.' Luke sat down at the table with a four pack of Fosters he had taken from the fridge. 'Here, like one?'

'No thanks. She is.' She turned back to her soup. 'Poor little Tom Tom really was the Davies's grandson. Ned – you're not really going to call him that, are you? – is the Belheddon child.' Her voice stressed the last two words with heavy sarcasm. 'Believe me, Luke, I know her.'

'No, Lyn, you're wrong.' Luke shook his head adamantly. 'Terribly wrong.'

'Am I?' She flung down her spoon and turned to face him. 'I hope so. But I want you to know I love little Tom as if he were my own. While I'm here he will never be second best.'

'He will never be second best with Joss or me either, Lyn.' Luke kept his voice steady with difficulty. 'Where is Joss now?'

'With the baby, I don't doubt.'

'That goes without saying, Lyn.' Luke took a deep swig from his can. 'The baby is two days old, for God's sake!' Unable to contain his irritation with her any longer he turned and walked out of the kitchen. In the courtyard he stood still for a minute staring up at the sky, taking deep breaths to calm himself. Silly bitch. Stirring it. The rivalry and antagonism which had always been so close to the surface between the sisters was beginning to get to him. He took several more gulps of lager as a thin brown face, creased with anxiety appeared round the coach house door. 'Luke, that you? Can you come a minute?'

'Sure, Jimbo. On my way.' Putting his thoughts about Lyn firmly out of his head Luke tucked the empty can into the dustbin as he passed and disappeared into the oil smelling interior of his domain.

Lying awake, staring towards the window, Joss could feel every muscle in her body tense. There was no sound from either of the children; the house was silent. Her eyes were gritty with sleep. She moved uncomfortably, trying not to disturb Luke, totally alert suddenly. Something was wrong. Swinging her legs over the side of the bed she padded across to the crib to look down at little Ned. She had been feeding him every couple of hours during the day, but now he was fast asleep at last, his little eyes tight shut in the shaded light of the lamp.

On bare feet she passed through to Tom's room and gently pushed open the door. Holding her breath she tiptoed in and stood for a moment looking down at him. He was sleeping peacefully, his cheeks pink, his hair tousled, his covers for once pulled up around him. Smiling she gently touched his cheek with her finger. Her love was so intense it was like a pain squeezing round her heart. She could not bear it if anything happened to either of them.

She glanced towards the window. There was no wind tonight. No draught touched the curtains. There were no shadows in the dark.

Silently she pulled the door half closed behind her and went back to her bedroom. Luke had moved in his sleep, sprawled across the bed, his arm outflung on the pillow. Beside his hand she could see something lying in the dip where her head had been. Her stomach lurched with fear. For a moment she was too scared to move. Her throat clamped shut and she felt the cold trickle of sweat between her shoulder blades. Then Luke moved. With a mutter he turned over, humping the duvet over him and she saw the mark on the pillowcase flatten and stretch and vanish. It had been no more than a crease in the cool pink cotton.

The christening was fixed for ten days later – a Saturday – which gave the Davieses and the Grants, the godparents and other guests time to assemble at Belheddon. It was a thundery day, reminiscent of the night of Ned's birth, and the humid air was heavy with the scents of the wet garden. The night before Janet had helped Joss with the flowers in the church.

'You look tired, love.' Deftly Janet slit the stem of a rose bud and inserted it into her vase. 'Look, aren't these lovely? I thought we'd put them round the base of the font.' She had produced a basket of white roses from her garden, their tightly furled buds still glistening with rain drops, the tips of their petals blushing slightly to a gentle pink.

'Roses. Bring her roses. Cover her with roses.'

He could not stop his tears. Slowly, gently, he brought his lips to the cold forehead. He knelt beside her while they brought the flowers. White roses in heaps, their fragrant petals covering her like soft snow.

Joss stared down at the basket. 'Oh, Janet.' She felt a sudden churning of fear in her stomach.

'Whatever is it?' Janet dropped the basket at her feet and reached out a concerned hand. 'Joss. Aren't you feeling well?' Joss had gone as white as the flowers.

Shaking her head, Joss moved away and sat down at the end of the back pew. 'No. No, I'm fine.' She shook her head. 'Just a bit tired. I've been trying to make some headway with my writing and I'm feeding Ned about every two hours, even at night.' She forced herself to smile, but her eyes were drawn back again and again to the roses. 'Janet, do you mind. Can we put them somewhere else. Perhaps over there, by the choir stalls. I know they're lovely. It's just –'

'Just what?' Janet frowned. She came and sat beside Joss, putting her hand firmly over Joss's as they clutched the back of the pew in front. 'Come on. Tell. What is it? They're only roses, for goodness' sake. The best I could find in the rose garden for my new little godson.' With

Lyn already Tom's godmother it had been an easy and unanimous choice for Joss and Luke to pick Janet as one of Ned's three godparents.

'I know. I'm being silly.'

'So. Explain.'

Joss shook her head. 'Just a silly phobia. Thorns. You know. Round the font. Everyone will catch their dresses. And Edgar will rip his surplice.' She laughed unsteadily. 'Please, Janet. Don't be hurt. They're beautiful. Exquisite. Just put it down to post partum neurosis or something like that.'

Janet stared at her for a moment, then she shrugged. She stood up. 'OK. Roses on the window sill up there. And what round the font? How about these?' She gestured at a bucket full of lupins and delphiniums and marguerites.

Joss took a deep breath. 'Lovely. Perfect. Just what the doctor ordered. Here, let me help.'

It was late by the time they had finished, locked the church, hidden the key and gone back inside the house for a quick drink before Janet made her way home. Lyn had long since put Tom to bed and pushed supper onto the back of the stove. 'Luke and I have eaten,' she said from the sink as Joss walked in. 'If you want yours it's there, keeping warm.'

Joss sighed. 'Thanks. Any sign of David?' Against strenuous disapproval from Luke she had asked David to be one of Ned's godfathers. The other was to be Luke's brother, Matthew.

Lyn shook her head. 'He rang to say he'd be late leaving London and not to wait supper. He probably won't be here till ten or eleven.'

'And Mum and Dad?'

'They should be here any minute. They rang too. They stopped for tea with the Sharps and they were coming on after that. Their rooms are all ready.' Lyn had been

242

dusting and sweeping and polishing in the attics, making beds and arranging flowers for the last two days. 'No one else is coming tonight. Luke's family are going to be here for lunch tomorrow, which is for family and godparents only, then everyone else will arrive for the christening itself and stay on to tea afterwards.' She was obviously still ticking off items mentally as she stared round the kitchen.

'You've been a brick Lyn. You've done everything.' Joss opened the cupboard and rummaged for the bottle of Scotch. She found two glasses and poured herself and Janet a small drink.

Lyn stared at her. 'You're not going to drink that?'

'Why not?' Sitting down at the table, Joss picked up the glass.

'Because of your milk of course.'

There was a moment's silence, then Joss took a sip of the whisky. 'I'm sure Ned wouldn't begrudge me this,' she said firmly. 'And he may as well start as I'm sure he will go on. If he gets hiccoughs in church it's too bad.'

'Right. Well, I can see it's none of my business.' Lyn, tight lipped, made for the door. 'I'll see you later.'

'Oh dear.' Janet raised her glass at Joss and smiled. 'Are you behaving badly, my dear?'

Joss nodded. She took another sip from the glass. 'It's not as though she's had any kids of her own!' she burst out suddenly. 'She acts as though she knows the lot.'

'She is their nanny, isn't she?' Janet leaned back in her chair, her eyes on Joss's face. 'She probably feels it's part of her brief. Besides, she's had training for it, hasn't she?'

'She's had training for absolutely nothing except cooking.' Joss stood up restlessly and walked round the table to the stove. She pulled the saucepan forward and peered into it. 'She's done a bit of temping, and she's the kind of person who can clean and organise a house naturally.'

'That doesn't make her less intelligent or less sensitive, Joss,' Janet put in gently.

'Oh, I know.' Joss came back to the table and sat down. 'Oh Janet, that sounded so awful of me. It's not as though I'm not grateful. We couldn't survive without Lyn. It's just that she makes me feel –' she spread her hands helplessly, 'so inadequate. In my own house. I take ages to sort something out and polish it. She comes in and does it in thirty seconds. But she does it in such a cold, efficient way. She doesn't feel anything –' she shrugged. 'It's hard to explain.'

Janet smiled. 'No it's not. You are just two very different personalities. And that has nothing to do with being adopted sisters. My sisters and I can't get on either and one of them is my twin. Accept that you're different, Joss. Martha and Mary, if you like. You should complement each other. But you are both, I think, feeling threatened by each other at the moment and that's silly. Forgive a comparative outsider commenting, but perhaps I can see it. You're too close. Lyn is feeling very insecure. After all, you hold all the trump cards. It's your house, your children, your family, and you are the one who has a burgeoning career as a writer. All that.' She reached for the bottle and poured herself another Scotch. 'I won't give you one, in deference to Ned's hiccoughs. As his godmother I'm probably the one he'll be sick over in church.' She laughed loudly, one of her great guffaws. 'Come on, love. Too much stress and not enough fun makes everyone miserable. Probably you and Lyn should leave Luke in charge one day and take yourselves out on a day off. That would sort it.'

Joss smiled wearily. 'Would it? I wonder.' She sighed. 'Yes, you're probably right.'

When Alice and Joe arrived Joss flung herself into her mother's arms. 'I was so worried! All those tests! Half the time Lyn didn't tell me until it was too late, what was happening.'

Alice held her at arm's length and studied her face. 'I don't need to see you every day to know you care, you silly child.' She pulled Joss back into her arms and gave her a hug. 'You're a clever, clever girl. Another beautiful grandson is the best medicine I could possibly have! And a christening party is the best celebration. I'm going to enjoy myself here, Joss. And I want to see you doing the same.'

Lunch was a great success. Lyn had laid the table in the dining room, loading the sideboard with cold meats and salads, whole grain bread, cheeses and fruit and white wine from the bottles remaining in the Belheddon cellar. Tea was already prepared and ready in the great hall, the refectory table with its huge bowl of gladioli groaning under plates and cups and a vast array of cling film-covered sandwiches and cakes and biscuits. The pièce de resistance, the christening cake, made and iced by Lyn was standing by itself on a table near the window and beside it stood a dozen bottles of champagne, a contribution from Geoffrey and Elizabeth Grant, who had driven over from Oxford.

It was Joss who had taken them on a quick tour of the house before lunch. 'My dear, it's more beautiful than I ever dreamed!' Geoffrey put his arm round her shoulders and gave her a hug. 'You and my son have the luck of the devil.'

He did not notice the look she gave him as she led the way through into the great hall. 'Nothing here is to be touched until later or Lyn will kill us,' she said, staring round at the feast already spread before them.

'That girl must have worked so hard.' Elizabeth went over and examined the cake. 'What a treasure. Why on earth hasn't some man snapped her up?'

Joss shrugged. 'I just hope they don't. At least not for a while. I can't live without her at the moment.' She glanced round the room, frowning. It felt fine. Happy. There was no atmosphere; there were no shadows, no echoes in her head. She was beginning to wonder if she had imagined the whole thing.

Smiling she turned to Geoffrey. 'You can stay a few days, can't you? I'm afraid our facilities are a bit primitive, whatever it may look like on the surface, but we'd like it so much if you can. And Matthew. Luke misses him so much, you know, now he's got the job in Scotland.'

Geoffrey nodded. 'They were always close those two. Never mind. Life goes on. It makes occasions like this even more special, my dear. And this is the most special we've had for a long time.'

22

n spite of the distant rumbles of thunder and the darkness outside the stained glass windows of the church, the christening service was full of charm. Cuddling Ned to her Joss looked round at the twenty or so guests clustered around the font and felt a tremendous elation, which increased as she passed the baby to Edgar Gower.

She glanced from Edgar to James Wood, who stood beside him. Lucky baby to have two vicars at his christening. A double blessing. A double safety net. She glanced at David and found him watching her with a slightly absent frown on his face. Was he thinking the same thing, she wondered? Was this belt and braces christening enough to ward off the horror which had sent John Bennet fleeing forever from his home? She looked up in spite of herself at the window where Janet had placed the huge foaming bowl of white roses and she shuddered.

There was a touch on her shoulder. Luke. He was looking down at her with an expression of such tenderness that she felt a lump in her throat. She reached for his hand and together they heard their son named Edward Philip Joseph before the world.

*   *   *

David managed to manoeuvre Joss into a corner half way through tea. Around them guests were devouring cake and drinking champagne or tea with equal enthusiasm. Tom, covered in cake and icing and melted chocolate, worn out with the excitement had curled up on one of the sofas and was fast asleep, whilst the star of the show, sleeping equally peacefully, was in his pram in the study where it was quieter.

The great hall rang with shouts and laughter. Wine flowed and the boards groaned beneath their load of food.

Katherine and Richard, hand in hand, led the dancing and their faces glowed in the candlelight.

The king's gift of heavy silver filled with white roses stood in the place of honour on the high table.

With it came his love.

'So. It's going well.' David raised his glass. 'Well done. A wonderful spread.'

'Thanks to Lyn.' Joss, clutching a tea cup was longing to sit down; she was wobbly with exhaustion.

'You read the photocopies I sent you?' David reached over to the table and helped himself to a couple of egg sandwiches.

She nodded. 'Let's not talk about it now, David.' Even the thought of the contents of those few sheets of flimsy paper sent a shiver down her spine. 'Edgar thinks this – all this –' she waved her hand behind her as the crescendo of conversation steadily increased, 'will help to make the house a happy place again. No more shadows.'

David shrugged. 'Good. There's more to discover, though, you know. Going right back into the past, there is something or someone at the root of all this and I want to find out what or who it is.'

Joss looked up at him, half amused, half irritated.

'What if I don't want you to? What if I tell you I want to stop the research.'

He looked shocked. 'Joss, you can't mean that. You can't not want to know!'

She shook her head, and shrugged. 'I don't know what to think. I'm confused. If it were somebody else's house, David. Someone else's problem. But I live here.' She gazed round the room as though looking for some clue which would tell her what to do. 'Supposing the truth is too awful, David? Supposing it is insupportable?' She held his gaze for several seconds, then slowly she turned away.

It was very late before everyone went to bed that night, Luke's parents and Matthew in the two attic rooms which had been made hospitable, David in the spare room where he usually stayed. It was an airless muggy night, the occasional flicker on the horizon and the almost inaudible grumbles of thunder betraying the fact that storms were still prowling around.

Exhausted, Joss threw herself on the bed, still fully dressed. 'I don't think I have the strength to have a bath.'

Luke sat down beside her. He gave a great contented sigh, stretching his arms above his head. 'I really enjoyed today, Joss. It's so nice having Ma and Pa and Mat here. They love the house, did they tell you?' He smiled, reaching over to kiss her. 'Come on, sleepy head. Climb out of your dress. It'll get spoiled if you sleep in it. I'll go and check on Tom and Ned.'

Ned had been allocated his own small bedroom, opposite Tom's. A cot, a pine chest of drawers and now lots of shiny christening presents adorned the room which Lyn had papered in a pattern of teddy bears and balloons. Luke peered in. The baby was fast asleep his little hands lying half clenched above his head, his face pink. Above him hung a mobile of small red fire engines, a present from his godfather, Mat. 'He needs something he can use now,' Mat had said cheerfully. 'The mug is boring. He won't need it till he's about twenty. I wasn't sure what babies like when they're this big – or,' he had peered into the pram doubtfully, 'to put it another way, small.' The mobile was perfect. Already Ned had spent a happy half hour seemingly gazing at it before he drifted off to sleep.

Tom was fast asleep too, lying on his tummy, his bed-clothes tumbled at the end of the bed. Luke left them.

Even with the windows thrown open it was too hot to breathe. He stood for a while in the bathroom sluicing cold water over his face and head then at last he climbed into bed and lay staring into the darkness.

He was woken much later, by a piercing scream from Tom.

'Christ! Joss, what's that?' He was out of bed before he was properly awake and before he realised that Joss wasn't there. Scrabbling for the light switch Luke ran into Tom's room. The little boy was lying on the floor beside his cot amidst a tangle of sheets, sobbing his heart out.

'Tom? Tom, my God, what happened old chap?' Scooping him up into his arms Luke was trying to comfort the little boy as Joss appeared in the doorway. In her white cotton night-dress she looked almost ethereal for a moment as she peered in. 'What's wrong?' She looked odd to Luke. Vague. Spaced out.

'Where on earth have you been?' he shouted. 'Didn't you hear Tom crying? He fell out of bed!'

Joss frowned. 'Tom?' She stared round. 'He can't have. The cot side is up.' She took a step into the room. 'I was feeding Ned.' She reached to touch Tom's head with her finger tips then she stooped and picked up the tangled sheets. 'He must have climbed out. I'll remake his bed and you can settle him down again.'

Shaking out the small white cotton sheets she

smoothed them over the mattress, tucking them in. 'OK? Do you want to put him down now?'

'He won't go, Joss. He's too upset.' The little boy was clinging to his father's neck, his face red with screaming, tears pouring down his cheeks and nose.

Suddenly Joss too was near to tears. 'Luke – I can't cope. I'm too tired. You'll have to deal with him.' She was white and strained. 'Do you mind?'

Luke stared at her then his face softened. 'Of course not, sweetheart. Off you go. Go to bed.'

It was a long time before he climbed back in beside her.

It was Joss who moved first. 'What's the time?'

'About three, I think. Sorry. Did I wake you?'

She grimaced. 'I couldn't sleep. Too tired. Is Tom OK? I can't think why he didn't wake everyone.'

'He's settled now. Poor little chap. Joss –' he turned to her and propped his head on his arm. 'Joss, when I changed him – he was covered in bruises.'

'But he was all right.'

'Yes, he was all right.'

'He must have got them falling out of bed.' Her voice was blurred with exhaustion. 'Don't worry. He'll be OK.'

The next morning the storms had cleared away out to sea and the air was fresh and bright.

Matthew was entranced by everything he saw. Standing next to his brother on the terrace at the back of the house he took a deep breath and beamed. The same height and colouring as Luke with dark hair and hazel eyes, he had inherited a crop of freckles from his mother which gave him a carefree, unruly appearance that made him irresistible to women. 'I'm going to say it again, brother. You're a lucky, lucky sod!' Mat clouted Luke affectionately across the shoulders. He raised his hands above his head and took a deep breath of the sweet air.

'It's a heavenly place for kids to grow up. I heard young Tom playing in the attics behind my bedroom this morning. God, I wish you and I had had somewhere like this when we were kids!'

'You heard Tom in the attic?' Luke stared at his brother, surprised. 'Well, that's somewhere he shouldn't have been. He's too young to go off up there on his own. I expect he was looking for you or Ma.'

'Georgie. He was calling someone called Georgie.' Mat stepped onto the lawn. 'Come on. I want to see your fish. Are there carp in that lake?' He set off over the grass, leaving Luke staring at him thoughtfully.

'You know Tom's covered in bruises.' Lyn had come up behind him, her bare feet silent on the warm York stone terrace.

'I know. He fell out of his cot.'

'When?' Lyn stared at him in horror.

'Last night.'

'And where was Joss. Why didn't you call me?'

Luke shook his head. 'Joss was feeding the baby. I didn't call you because there wasn't any need. I coped.' He smiled. 'Come on. Let's go and find a carp for Mat.'

David was watching them from the study window. He stepped back as Joss came in behind him and he felt his heart turn over. Her exhaustion had forged her dark beauty into something ethereal. He closed his eyes, willing himself to put all his lustful thoughts out of his head and with a supreme effort kept his voice steady. 'Kids OK?'

She nodded wearily. 'Two grannies baby sitting. I thought I'd have a sit down for a minute.' She glanced out of the window where Luke and Mat and Lyn were strolling down across the grass towards the water.

'Poor old Joss. But sorry old thing. No time for resting.

252

I want you to come with me back to the church. There's something I want to check.'

'No, David.' She threw herself into a chair. 'I told you, I don't want to think about all that now. I really don't.'

'You do, Joss, if it puts your mind at rest.' He squatted down in front of her and reached for her hand. 'I had a long talk to your rector yesterday – the old one with the white wild hair – and I put one or two thoughts I'd been having to him for his views.' He stared up into her face. 'I think he and I may have similar theories on this one, Joss, and I think that whereas he is coming at it from an intuitive angle, I as a historian have the edge. I know where to look for the proof.'

'Proof?' She rested her head against the back of the chair, her eyes on his face. 'What sort of proof?'

'Evidence. Gossip. Chronicles. Records. Letters. Not proof perhaps that would stand up in a court of law, but nevertheless something to substantiate and explain what has happened here in the past.'

'And stop it happening again?' She looked at him wearily.

'Until we know what it really is, we won't know how to fight it, Joss.'

'And the answer is in the church?'

'Maybe.' He stood up and held out his hand again. 'Come on. Take the opportunity, while the grandmas are here and on call and still delighted with their new grandson. Take advantage of the chance. It probably won't last.'

'All right.' She grasped his fingers and let him pull her to her feet. 'Let's go and look.'

The path to the church, cut back neatly for the christening, was lined with pink roses, cascading in heavy curtains from the wild rose bushes, nestling between hedgerow trees and curtains of ivy. Under foot the soft moss, greened by the thundery rain, allowed them to

253

walk silently as far as the door. Reaching for the handle Joss swung it open and they stepped down into the dim cool interior.

'Don't the flowers look nice.' David pulled the heavy door closed behind them.

'We didn't come to see the flowers.' She averted her eyes from the window with the white roses. One of them had blown and she could see the petals on the floor, drifting over a grating.

'Up here.' He headed towards the chancel steps. 'Gower said to look under the carpet.'

They stood looking down at the faded Persian runner which lay between the choir stalls. Even in the dim light they could see the richness that had once been there. David crouched and flicked back one corner of the rug. 'Good Lord. Look. He's right. There's a beautiful brass under here.' He dragged the carpet back revealing the exquisitely elaborate detail of an inlaid brass about six feet long.

'It's a woman,' Joss said after a moment. She grimaced. What else would it be at Belheddon.

'A beautiful rich woman.' David stood with his back to the altar so he could see her the right way up. 'Gower said this was only uncovered in 1965 when they took the floorboards up because of dry rot. The original stone floor had been covered to raise it at some point.'

'Who is she, do we know?' Joss joined him with her back to the altar.

'Margaret de Vere. See.' He pointed to the ornate lettering: *'Hic jacet ... Margaret ... uxor ... Robert de Vere ... morete in anno domine 1485.'* He glanced at Joss. 'This is Katherine's mother!'

Katherine!

She had seen the king's gaze following the girl around the hall and she had long ago sensed his lust.

'Husbands can be disposed of, my lord.' Her eyes narrowed as she smiled.

He frowned and shook his head.

The presence of the woman made his flesh crawl. But still his whole body ached to have the girl.

Squatting by the elegant pointed feet of the woman on the floor before them David leaned forward and touched the cold brass with a tentative finger. 'Margaret de Vere was accused of sorcery and fortune telling, which was their way of saying witchcraft,' he whispered. 'It was even rumoured that she had brought about the king of England's death. The king being Edward IV – the king who came to Belheddon.'

There was a long silence. Joss's first reaction, incredulous disbelief, wavered. At Belheddon anything was possible.

'What happened to her? Was she burned or did they hang her?' Joss stared down at the aquiline features beneath the ornate head-dress.

'Neither. Nothing was ever proved. She died at home in her bed.'

'At Belheddon.'

'At Belheddon.'

They both stared down at the floor.

'Do you think she was a witch?' Joss asked at last.

David shook his head thoughtfully. 'I don't know. I wondered if we would find a clue. Some kind of symbol on the brass perhaps. You know, the way you can tell whether a crusader reached Jerusalem or not by whether or not his feet are crossed. I've always wondered if that is true or not!'

Joss managed a smile. 'You mean we're looking for a heraldic broomstick?'

He shook his head. 'Witchcraft wasn't so much a cottage industry then. It was a far more aristocratic pastime at this period, don't forget. The court was riddled with accusations. There were rumours about Elizabeth Woodville, Edward IV's queen, and the Duchess of Bedford, her mother, and at least one of his mistresses, Jane Shore –'

'Surely a lot of those accusations were part of Richard III's propaganda against the princes who were Elizabeth's sons.' Joss sat down in the front choir stall, still staring down at the brass.

'But not all. Accusations had been made against Elizabeth Woodville from the start, because no one at court could understand why King Edward married her. There was this young, tall, handsome, romantic king, and he meets this widow, who is a Lancastrian, has two children already, is not even particularly beautiful, in the middle of a forest and within days and against everybody's advice he's married her! Perhaps she did bewitch him.' He smiled. 'And there lies our problem. No historian worth his solid, scientific salt, would believe it. It must have been something else. Something dynastic.'

'Or just her beautiful blue eyes?' Joss smiled.

He scowled. 'Or was there no smoke without fire? Did these women and others like her – the Duchess of Bedford or Margaret de Vere here, actually find a means of summoning the devil to help them achieve their ends?'

The atmosphere in the church appeared to have dropped several degrees.

Joss shivered. Did he really believe that? 'You're talking about Satanism, David, not witchcraft,' she said at last.

'Devil worship.' He glanced at her. 'Don't tell me you're one of these women who believe that witchcraft was some kind of goody goody, never hurt a fly, paganism which does no harm to anyone and is the feminist answer to the patriarchal, misogynist church!'

Joss smiled. 'Something like that, perhaps.' She found

herself staring into the shadowy nave. 'But not in this case. Here, I think you may be right.'

Almost unwillingly she looked down at the brass at her feet, picking out one by one the details from the ornate curlicues of the surround. Were there hidden symbols there, clues she could not see or recognise?

'You believe that she,' she gestured at the floor, 'conjured the devil here, at Belheddon.'

'I think maybe she did something rather strange. Enough to make people suspicious. I've a few more sources to look up before I try and formulate a theory.'

'I think it will be very hard to find proof, David.' Joss gave him a tolerant grin. 'We're dealing with a field here which is not amenable to the kind of reductionist study you are used to.'

He stooped again and began dragging the carpet over the brass. 'That won't stop me trying, old girl,' he said cheerfully. 'Not now I've got my teeth into it.'

She stared down for one last time as he pulled the rug across the cold haughty face of the woman on the floor and she shuddered. 'It would be wonderful if you could find a way to end all the unhappiness.'

'We'll find a way, Joss. You'll see.' He reached out for her hand. 'Come on, let's go back to the house.' Did she realise, he wondered, just how beautiful she was looking – more so every time he came to visit the house – every time he set eyes on her.

23

lice was alone in the study reading one of the pile of copies of *Good Housekeeping* which she had brought for Joss and Lyn. She looked up as Joss walked in and put it down with a smile. 'Hello, love. How are you? I've seen hardly anything of you, you've been so busy.'

Joss sat down near her and reaching forward took Alice's hand. 'I'm sorry. What with the christening and everything. How are you, Mum?'

'I'm fine. Just fine. Still a bit tired, but better every day for knowing there's nothing terrible wrong with my insides.' Alice scanned Joss's face carefully. 'Don't do too much, Joss. Let Lyn help you as much as she can, won't you.'

Joss gave a wry smile. 'I think Lyn feels she's doing enough already.'

'Rubbish.' Alice sounded suddenly brisk. 'That young lady has more energy than she knows what to do with. And she's worried about you, Joss. You've not long ago had a frightening birth and on top of that there's this big house to look after.' She stared round the room with pursed lips. 'I can see it's a joy for you, but it's a big responsibility as well. You let Lyn help. And your Dad and I will too, if you'll let us. You've only got to ask.

Joe,' she took a deep breath. 'Joe feels you might be a bit reluctant to have us here, dear, seeing as it's your real mum's house, but I told him you would never, never feel such a thing. I'm right, aren't I?'

Joss slipped to her knees beside the sofa and put her arms round Alice. 'How could he even think such a thing? You've been more to me than real parents ever could, you know that. You always used to tell me I was special because I was the chosen baby. I really believed it.' And Lyn, who had once heard her father say it to Joss when no one knew she was there, had never forgotten or forgiven the fact that she was not chosen. She just arrived. She hoped Alice and Joe would never find out that little source of some of Lyn's bitterness.

'Right, dear.' Alice pushed her away gently and edged herself forward so she could climb off the sofa. 'Now that's settled, let's go and find the others. I let Elizabeth and Geoffrey take that baby out in its pram, and I reckon it's time this set of grandparents had a go, don't you?' She chuckled. 'So, where's little Tom got to?'

Joss shrugged. 'There are so many people looking after him I've lost track. He's having the time of his life with so much attention.'

'Yes, well. Don't let him get spoiled.' Alice pursed her lips as she opened the door. 'And Joss, remember what I said. Rest. You're looking peaky.'

Mat was standing in the great hall looking up at the picture over the fireplace. He grinned at Alice and then caught Joss's hand. 'A word before you rush off, sister-in-law.'

She looked up at him in surprise. 'I am popular today.'

'Popular, and as your mother said, peaky. Luke's worried about you, you know, Joss.'

Joss shook her head. 'Why on earth is everyone so concerned suddenly?'

Mat looked down at her, his dark eyes, so like his

brother's, deeply troubled. 'David Tregarron has no business worrying you about the house. Luke says he's winding you up, frightening you deliberately.'

'That's not true!' Joss was indignant.

'Luke thinks it is. Being Luke he's not about to say anything, Joss. At least not to you. He knows you value David's friendship, and he knows you'd resent him interfering.' He paused. 'David's in love with you, isn't he?'

'That's none of your business, Mat.'

'Oh, I think it is. Be careful. Don't hurt Luke.'

'Mat –'

'No, Joss. Let big brother speak.' Mat gave his slow, intimate smile. 'He's worried sick and not just about David. He says you're hearing voices, seeing things, scaring yourself witless, and all that is not good, especially when you have a new baby in the house. Thinking there is some kind of a threat to the baby is crazy, Joss. You must get that idea right out of your head. You do see that, don't you?'

Joss was silent for a moment. 'I appreciate your talking to me, Mat,' she said at last, firmly. 'But there is nothing wrong with me. You must tell Luke I'm OK. I'm not imagining things, and I'm not letting David wind me up. I promise.' She glanced at Mat and smiled. 'And Luke knows that whatever he feels for me, I'm not in love with him. I promise.'

'You've no business complaining to Mat about me!' Joss cornered Luke alone in the coach house. 'All you are doing is worrying him and your parents absolutely unnecessarily. What on earth were you telling him, anyway?'

'Only that I was worried about you. And I did not complain to him. He had no business speaking to you.' Luke looked at her wearily. 'Joss, I don't think you realise how much strain you are under.'

'I realise perfectly well, thank you. And there is nothing wrong about it. I gave birth only a couple of weeks ago! Ned cries a lot. I am feeding him myself. I am missing a lot of sleep. What is so odd about me feeling strained?'

'Nothing.' Luke put down the spanner he had in his hands and came towards her, wiping his fingers on the seat of his overalls. 'Come here, you gorgeous, clever lady and let me give you a kiss.'

He put his wrists on her shoulders, drawing her towards him, dangling his oily hands behind her head so as not to touch her with his fingers. 'Don't take it wrong that I worry, Joss. It's because I love you so much.' He looked into her eyes. 'Now, I've got some good news for you. This old bus is just about finished. She'll be off home next week, if all goes well, and I've had two new enquiries, one of which is a definite, for full restoration jobs.'

Joss laughed. 'That's brilliant!'

'And what about you? How is the book going? Are you getting any work done at all with both our families encamped in the place?'

'No. Of course not.' She gave him a playful cuff on the side of the head. 'But I think I'm allowed a few days off while my favourite parents and in-laws are in residence. Plenty of time to write again once they've gone.'

He grinned. 'The trouble is we might not get them to go away. They love it here so much.'

'I'm glad.' Walking back to the door she stared out into the yard where Jimbo was industriously polishing two great disembodied head lamps. 'He's a godsend, isn't he.'

'Certainly is. Who knows. Next year I might just look for another one like him.'

Joss frowned. 'With all this talk about me, no one has said anything about you looking tired, Luke.' She reached up and touched his face. He was pale and thin, his eyes

261

reddened from lack of sleep. 'No one sympathises with the father, do they. It's tough.'

'Very.' He nodded vigorously. 'Don't you worry. I'm playing for all the sympathy I can get from my mummy and daddy right now.' He laughed. 'It's nice having them here.'

In the yard, as though sensing their eyes upon him Jimbo had turned and looked at them. He raised a hand and Joss waved back. 'I'd better go and find Tom. No one seems to know who's looking after him.'

'He's loving all the attention.' Luke shook his head fondly. 'We'll have trouble when they all go.' He hesitated. 'Have you heard when David is leaving?'

Why – can't you wait to get rid of him? Joss was about to reply, but she swallowed the comment. David was going anyway. 'He's driving up to town this evening. It's still term time, don't forget.'

'Well, as long as he doesn't decide to come down here for the whole summer.' He softened the words with a smile.

'He won't.' She reached out and touched his hand. 'It's you I love. Never forget that, Luke.'

There was no sign of anyone indoors. She hurried through the rooms, calling, but the house was deserted. From the study window she could see Elizabeth and Alice strolling across the lawn. Elizabeth was pushing the pram, an expression of intense concentration on her face while Alice was talking nineteen to the dozen, gesticulating as she walked. Joss smiled fondly and turned away from the window. Tom could be with Mat or with Lyn or Geoffrey or Joe or even David. Someone would be keeping an eye on him. So why was she so uneasy? She knew why. Because they could all so easily be thinking the same thing.

'Tom!' she whispered his name. Then, 'Tom!' louder. Heading for the staircase she ran up into his bedroom. It was deserted and tidy, as was Ned's. There was no one in her room or Lyn's or David's. She stood at the bottom of the attic stairs and stared up. The Grants' bedrooms were there, and little Tom had plodded up at least twice to find them.

Slowly she climbed the flight and stood on the landing listening. The attics were very hot; they smelled strongly of rich, dry wood and dust, and they were quite silent.

'Tom?'

Her voice sounded indecently loud.

'Tom? Are you up here?'

She went into Elizabeth and Geoffrey's room. It was strewn with clothes; the small chest of drawers was littered with items of make up and Elizabeth's strings of beads and Geoffrey's tie, torn off as soon as possible after the christening guests had left the day before and not replaced. The bed was a low divan – nowhere under it to hide. There was no sign of Tom. He wasn't in Mat's room either. She stood in the middle of the floor looking round, listening to the scuffling from behind the far door, the door which led into the empty attics which stretched the rest of the length of the house.

There were footsteps, the sound of a piece of furniture being moved, a suppressed giggle.

'Tom?' Why was she whispering?

'Tom?' She tried a little louder.

Silence.

'Georgie? Sam?'

The silence was so intense she could feel someone listening to her, holding their breath. Slowly, almost as though she were sleep walking she moved towards the far door. She put out her hand to the key and turned it. The silence deepened. As she pushed open the door it became something tangible, opaque, heavy with threat.

'Tom!' This time her shout was loud, high pitched, bordering on panic. 'Tom, are you there?'

Pushing the door back against the wall she stepped into the empty room and looked round. The light was shadowy, full of dust motes. A bee, trapped against the glass of the window, buzzed frantically, yearning for the sunlight and flowers of the garden. Another door on the far side of the room stood half open. Beyond it the shadows were thick and warm.

'Tom?' Her voice was shaking now, the panic heavy in her throat. 'Tom, where are you darling? Don't hide.'

The giggle was quite near this time; a child's giggle, half stifled, very close. She swung round. 'Tom?'

There was no one there. Almost running she dived back into Mat's bedroom and looked round. 'Tom!' This time it was a sob. Retracing her steps at a run she plunged through the first two empty attics to the third and last, the one with an end window overlooking the courtyard. 'Tom!' But there was no one there and no answer save the single panicked sound of the bee against the window. Walking slowly back through the empty shadowy rooms she went over to the small window and forced it open, watching the bee soar with sudden palpable joy up into the sunshine. There were tears on her cheeks, she realised, tears pouring down her face. Her throat was tight and her heart thudded unevenly under her ribs. 'Georgie, is that you? Where are you? Sammy? Is it you?'

Unsteadily she made her way back through the Grants' bedroom to the top of the staircase, peering down, trying to see through her tears. 'Tom? Where are you?' Sobbing she sat down on the top step as her strength drained from her. She was shaking, exhausted and terribly afraid.

'Joss?' It was Mat, peering up from the landing. 'Is that you?' He took the stairs two at a time. 'Joss, what is it? What's the matter?'

'Tom.' She was shaking so much she could hardly speak.

'Tom?' He frowned. 'What about Tom? He's down in the kitchen with Lyn.'

Joss was clasping her knees; raising her head she stared at him. 'He's all right?'

'He's all right, Joss.' He stared at her, searching her face for a clue to her behaviour. Sitting down on the step next to her he put his arm round her shoulders. 'What is it, Joss?'

She shook her head, sniffing. 'I couldn't find him –'

'He's OK. Honestly.' He hugged her then he stood up and reached down for her hand. 'Come on, we'll go and see him.'

She looked up at him, pushing her hair out of her eyes, aware suddenly of how she must look. 'I'm sorry, Mat. I'm so tired –'

'I know.' His grin was so like Luke's it tugged at her heart strings. 'That's babies for you, I guess. Not enough sleep.'

She nodded, climbing wearily to her feet. 'Don't say anything. Please.'

'Scout's honour.' He raised two parallel fingers to his forehead. 'On one condition. You have a sleep this afternoon. A proper one, letting us take care of the kids so there is nothing to wake you, nothing to worry you. Agreed?'

'Agreed.' She let him take her hand and guide her down the stairs, feeling a little foolish as, following him into the kitchen she found a room full of people, noise and laughter and at the centre of all the activity an unconcerned Tom, kneeling up on a kitchen chair drawing with large plastic crayons on a huge sheet of paper.

'There you are, Joss.' Lyn looked up from the work top where she was chopping onions. Her eyes were streaming. Pushing her hair out of her eyes with the back of her wrist she grinned. 'We couldn't think where you'd got to.'

She looked too cheerful, almost frenetic.

'Where's Luke?' Joss asked. He was the only one missing from the cheerful gathering.

'He went out to have a word with Jimbo,' Lyn said turning back to her onions. 'Then he's coming in for lunch. Are you going to feed Ned first?'

Joss nodded. She could see the baby asleep in the pram by the dresser. He seemed able to sleep through any amount of noise at the moment and for that fact she gave a quiet vote of thanks. 'Sit down, Joss.' Mat guided her by the shoulders to a chair. 'I was just telling Joss that she needs to rest,' he said firmly as she collapsed into it. 'I think this afternoon the doting grandparents and uncles and godfathers should remove the junior Grants from the premises and allow their mum to have a really good sleep.'

'First rate idea.' Geoffrey smiled. 'You do look washed out, Joss my dear.'

Washed out, she thought much later as she climbed the stairs to the bedroom. I suppose that's one word for it. She felt almost sorry for the others. In spite of the heat they felt duty bound she suspected to go for that one last walk before setting off in their various directions. The Grants to Oxford – Mat was spending another couple of days with his parents before setting off back north – David and her parents to London. In some ways she was glad they were going. Having so many people in the house was exhausting; but in other ways she was sorry. While they were there, there were people to keep an eye on the children, people to create noise – critical mass – within a large house, drowning out the other sounds, the sounds that came from the silence.

Sitting on the edge of the bed she kicked off her sandals and lay back on the pillow. She had drawn the curtains against the sun and the room was shadowy, the heat stifling. She could feel her eyes closing. Relaxing on top of the duvet she could feel some of the aching tension easing out of her bones, the heat and the darkness behind her eyelids like a warm bath of peace. Sleep. That was all she needed to soothe away her fears. Sleep, undisturbed by a crying baby or the restless, hot body of her husband next to her in the bed. Poor Luke. He was out in the coach house with Jimbo working amongst the smells of oil and petrol and the heat of sun-warmed metal.

The weight on the side of the bed was so slight she barely noticed it. For a moment she lay there, eyes still firmly shut, resisting the lurking flutters of fear, then slowly, reluctantly, she opened them and looked around. Nothing. The room was still. There was nothing near the bed which could have caused the slight frisson of movement in the air, the almost unnoticeable depression of the bedclothes near her feet – nothing beyond the stirring of the bed curtain in a stray breeze from the window. Feeling her mouth dry and uncomfortable she swallowed and closed her eyes again. Nothing to worry about. Nothing to be afraid of. But the moment of relaxation had gone. She could feel the uncomfortable trickle of adrenaline into her system, nothing dramatic, nothing startling, just a premonitory priming of the nerves. 'No.' Her whisper was long drawn out, anguished. 'Please, leave me alone.'

There was nothing there. No shadow in the corner, no strange half heard echoes in her head which seemed to come from some unrecognised aural receptor which had nothing to do with her ears, nothing but a shred of instinct which was telling her that all was not well.

Pushing herself up on her elbow, she could feel a trickle of perspiration running down her face. Her hair was sticky; it needed washing. More than anything, she realised suddenly she would love a long, cold bath, somewhere she could wallow sleepily with the door locked, and the humid heat of the afternoon kept at bay.

Swinging her feet to the floor she dragged herself off the bed, realising at once that she was still dizzy and aching with exhaustion. Padding on bare feet across the cool boards she headed for the bathroom and putting the plug in the bath turned on the taps – mostly cold – and tipped in a little scented oil. Her face, as she examined it in the mirror was white, damp, and even to herself exhausted. There were dark rings over as well as under her eyes, where the lids were sunken and drawn, and her body, as she peeled off her thin cotton shirt and blouse and underwear was ugly – still swollen, her breasts huge and blue veined, damp with sweat. She scowled at herself, tempted for a moment to veil the mirror with a towel. The idea made her smile as she stooped to turn off the tap and step gingerly into the cool water.

The bath was definitely an improvement on the bed. A huge old-fashioned bath with ornate iron legs she smiled to herself every time she climbed into it at the thought that such things were now the height of expensive fashion. Cool, supporting to her back, it felt solid and somehow secure. She lay back until the water lapped around her breasts, her head against the rim, and closed her eyes.

She wasn't sure how long she had slept but she woke to find herself shivering. Chilled she sat up with a groan and hauled herself out of the water. She had left her watch on the shelf above the wash basin. Grabbing it she looked at it. Nearly four. The others would be back from their walk soon, and Ned would be wanting a feed. Snatching her cotton robe from behind the door she went back into the bedroom. It was just as before – hot and airless. Pulling back the curtains she stared down into the garden. It was empty.

Reaching for her hair brush from the dressing table Joss began to brush her hair vigorously, feeling the residual tension from her forehead and the back of her neck receding with every stroke. Throwing it down she was reaching into the drawer for fresh crisp clothes when she glanced up at the mirror and felt her stomach drop. For a split second she didn't recognise the face before her. Her brain refused to interpret the image. She could see eyes, nose, mouth, like gaping holes in a waxen mask – then, as shock-driven adrenaline flooded through her system, the images regrouped, cleared and she found herself looking at a frightened facsimile of herself – eyes, huge; skin, damp; hair, dishevelled, her bathrobe hanging open to display the heavy breasts, breasts which for a fraction of a second had felt the touch of a cold hand on the hot fevered skin.

'No!' She shook her head violently. 'No!'

Clothes. Quickly. Quickly. Bra. Shirt. Panties. Jeans. A protection. Armour. Outside. She must get outside.

The kitchen was empty. Throwing open the back door she looked out into the courtyard. 'Luke?'

The Bentley had been pulled out of the coach house. It stood gleaming gently in the sunlight, strangely blind without the two huge headlights which still stood on a trestle table just inside the open double door of the coach house.

'Luke!' She ran across the cobbles and stared in. 'Where are you?'

'He's gone out for a walk with the others, Mrs Grant.' Jimbo appeared suddenly from the shadows. 'With his Ma and Pa being here and that, he thought he'd take the chance.'

'Of course.' Joss forced a smile. 'I should have thought of that.' She was conscious suddenly of how hard Jimbo was staring at her. The young man's face had fascinated her when she first saw it. Thin, brown, with strangely sleepy slanted eyes, the planes of the cheeks and brow bones were flattened into Slavic features of startling dramatic cast. She could never see him without picturing him on a pony, a rag tied round his head, a gun brandished in one hand as he galloped over the plain. It had been something of a disappointment when, unable to resist it, she had asked him if he could ride and he had looked at her askance with the unequivocal answer, no way.

'You all right, Mrs Grant?' The soft local vowels did not fit the hard features. Nor, she had to admit, did the eyes: the strange all-seeing eyes.

'Yes. Thank you.' She began to turn away.

'You look tired, Mrs Grant.'

'I am.' She stopped.

'The boys been keeping you awake, have they? I heard them when I stayed at yours with my mum when I was a lad. She says they always come back when there are folk in the house.'

Joss turned and stared at him. 'Boys?' she repeated in a whisper. He wasn't talking about Tom and Ned.

'All the lost boys.' He shook his head slowly. 'Like Pe'er Pan. I didn't like the house. My dad said I might get taken too, but Mam had to caretake here some times for Mrs Duncan before she packed up and went to live in Paris, and I had to come too then.'

Joss's mouth was dry. She wanted to turn and run, but, pinned by his sly gaze, she was suddenly rooted to the spot.

'Did you ever see them?' she managed to whisper at last.

He shook his head. 'Our Nat saw them though.'

'Nat?' Joss could feel the tightness in her throat increasing.

'My sister. She liked it up here. Mam used to clean for Mrs D and she often brought us to play in the garden while she was working. Nat would play with the boys.' His face darkened. 'She thought I was a wimp because I didn't want to. I thought she was loopy. I wouldn't stay.

270

I'd go and hide in the kitchen and get under Mam's feet or if she got cross I'd nip through the hedge and go home. No matter how often she tanned my backside I wouldn't stay.'

He looked remarkably cheerful about it now.

'But your sister liked it here?'

He nodded. 'Well, she would, wouldn't she,' he said cryptically. He reached for a soft cloth and began buffing the huge head lamps.

'You don't mind working here now, though?' Joss said thoughtfully.

He grinned. 'Na, I don't believe in that stuff any more.'

'But you think I do?'

He winked. 'I heard them talking about you. I didn't think it was fair. After all, it's not just you, is it. Loads of people have seen the boys.'

And the tin man without a heart?

Joss wiped the palms of her hands across the front of her shirt. 'Does your sister still live in the village, Jim?'

He shook his head. 'She got a job in Cambridge.'

She felt a sharp pang of disappointment. 'But she comes back? On visits?'

He didn't look too sure. With a shrug he rubbed at an almost invisible speck of rust. 'Not often.'

'And your mother?'

He shook his head. 'When Mam and Dad split up, Mam went to live in Kesgrave.'

'Does your Dad remember this house in my mother's time?'

Jim shrugged. 'I doubt it. He wouldn't set foot in the place.' He looked up at her and again she saw the narrow, calculating look. 'He didn't want me to take this job.'

'I see.' She supposed she didn't need to ask why. Too many local tradesmen had explained with a shudder why they would not want to live here themselves.

She sighed. 'Well Jimbo, if you see Luke tell him I was looking for him, OK?'

'OK, Mrs Grant.' He was smiling. As she turned away she felt rather than saw him straighten up from the lamp and stand watching her as she retraced her steps across the courtyard.

The French doors in the study were open onto the terrace. Standing just outside on the cool stone she surveyed the rather motley collection of garden furniture they had assembled from the outhouses round the courtyard. There were two Edwardian recliners – a little rotten, but remarkably solid considering their age. Two wicker chairs, chewed by mice, but again just about serviceable, and a couple of decidedly dodgy deck chairs both within days of the ultimate split which would deposit their occupiers unceremoniously onto the ground with total lack of dignity. She smiled involuntarily as she always did when she looked at them. Enough to make the owner of an upmarket garden centre go prematurely grey. To sit at this moment in one of those long, Edwardian recliners, which smelled of damp and age and lichen, even though they had cooked for weeks now on the terrace would be heaven. With a cup of tea. Just for a few minutes. Till the others came back.

She turned back into the study. She ought to take the opportunity to write, while the house was quiet. She looked guiltily at the pile of neatly printed pages on the desk. It was nearly three weeks since she had touched it. Picking up the last few pages she glanced at them. Richard – the hero of her story, the son of the house whose tale came so easily to her pen that she wondered sometimes if it were being dictated to her – had he been one of the lost boys? Were there generations of boys like George and Sam haunting the attics of the house? She shuddered. Had Richard in real life not survived his adventures to live happily ever after as he was going to in her story, but fallen prey like her brothers to another of the accidents and illnesses which plagued the sons of Belheddon? 'Please, God, keep Tom and Ned safe.' Throwing down the pages she went back to the doors. Geoffrey and Elizabeth had appeared on the far side of the lawn. Behind them she could see Joe and Alice with the pram just coming through the gate. They must have all walked across the fields and down to the low red cliffs above the estuary. Mat had appeared now, with Tom Tom sitting on his shoulders, and Lyn beside him and last of all, Luke. They were all laughing and talking and for a moment she felt a wave of utter loneliness, strangely excluded from the group, even though they were of all the people in the world those closest to her.

She watched as they approached her across the grass. 'Did you sleep well?' Luke greeted her with a kiss.

She nodded. She stooped and lifted Ned from the pram. He was fast asleep, oblivious to the world. Hugging him against her she felt the ache in her breasts, the need to feed him. She glanced at Lyn. 'Shall we have tea soon?'

'Sure.' Lyn was relaxed and smiling. Her tee-shirt had slipped off one tanned shoulder; her legs, long and slim, were dusted with sand beneath the frayed, cut-off jeans.

'You all went on the beach?' she asked.

Lyn nodded. 'Mat and I took Tom down to make sand castles. It's glorious there today.' She stretched her arms languidly above her head. Joss saw Mat's eyes go involuntarily to Lyn's breasts, outlined so clearly under the thin blue tee-shirt. He was looking remarkably cheerful.

'I'll take Ned up and change him.' Joss headed for the stairs as the others trooped, talking loudly, towards the kitchen.

She glanced warily around her bedroom. The sun had moved round slightly and the room was cooler. In her arms the baby had opened his eyes.

He was gazing up into her face with unwavering

concentration. She dropped a kiss on the end of his nose, overwhelmed with love for him. No one. No one was ever even to think of harming him or she would not be answerable for her actions. Sitting down in the low chair by the window, she gazed down at him, overcome with love as he dozed off again, seemingly not ready yet to be fed. Breathing in the heavy scent of mown grass and roses from the climber outside the window she felt herself grow drowsy and as her eyelids became increasingly heavy her arms began to loosen the hold on the baby, almost as if someone was gently taking him from her . . .

'Joss? Joss, what the hell are you doing?' Lyn's shriek brought her back to the present with a jerk of terror. Snatching Ned from her, Lyn had turned on her with the ferocity of a spitting cat. 'You stupid idiot! You could have killed him! What were you doing?'

'What – ?' Joss stared at her blankly.

'His shawl! You had his shawl over his face.'

'I didn't.' Joss looked round, confused. 'He didn't have a shawl. It was too hot.'

But it was there, still wrapped round him, covering his head and face and trailing from Lyn's arms as the baby began to scream.

'Give him to me.' Joss snatched Ned from her sister. 'He's hungry. I was just going to feed him, that's all. He's all right. He's just hungry.'

She cuddled the baby to her, unbuttoning her shirt. 'Go and make tea! I'll be down soon.'

She watched as Lyn backed away towards the door. Lyn's face was preoccupied and uneasy as she let herself out onto the landing.

'Silly Aunty Lyn.' Joss guided Ned's mouth towards her nipple with her little finger. 'As if I would hurt you, sweetheart.' Lowering herself back onto the chair near the window she gazed out at the garden as Ned suckled, relaxing back against the embroidered tapestry cushion which Elizabeth had brought as a house-warming present.

On the bed, the rose which lay on her pillow wilted in the last rays of the sun as it moved across the window into the western sky and one by one the petals fell, small white patches on the rich colours of the crewel-work bed cover.

he house was very quiet after the departure of the family. As each stifling airless day followed the one before Luke and Joss and Lyn found themselves growing increasingly listless. Even Tom was subdued, missing the posse of adoring grandparents. Each morning after feeding Ned and putting him down to sleep Joss disappeared into the study where, with the French windows opened wide, she would sit in front of the Amstrad, wrestling with Richard and the climax of her story.

Twice David phoned, the last time before he set off to spend the summer in Greece. 'Just to see how you are. Is the book going well?' He did not mention his researches into the house any more and she did not ask.

Out in the courtyard the Bentley went to be replaced by a 1936 SS and then a Lagonda. In the shadowy coach house, the coolest place in Belheddon save for the cellar, Jimbo and Luke worked early in the morning and late in the afternoon, saving the hot midday for a swim in the sea, sandwich lunch and then a siesta under the trees. During the long evenings Luke and sometimes Jimbo too would work in the garden until dark.

Lyn, ignoring all warnings about the sun, stretched out

on one of the old chairs, firmly plugged into her Walkman, while the children slept in their bedrooms. Twice she had written to Mat. He had not replied.

At her desk, Joss stared out at her sister and frowned. In spite of the liberal application of sun oil Lyn's legs were peeling; pink flaky patches appearing through the brown. Lyn was constantly watching her. Ever since that afternoon where she had snatched Ned from Joss's arms she had the feeling she was being checked on. She shook her head wearily and stretched her arms above her head, easing the cramp from her muscles. Tom and Ned were both growing fast, seemingly thriving in spite of the heat. Were it not for Tom's nightmares all would have been peaceful. Simon, called in at last at Lyn's insistence, gave Tom a complete check up and blamed the heat. 'He'll settle down once it's cooler, you'll see.' The arrival of two kittens from the Goodyears' farm, christened with due ceremony by Tom Kit and Kat cheered him up enormously, but did not stop the dreams. If they were dreams. Getting up, night after night to feed Ned, and see to Tom, Joss was growing more and more tired and her tiredness was beginning to show. The book was going badly. The story wouldn't progress and Lyn was getting on her nerves. Often now, when she picked him up Ned would start to scream. She would hug him and comfort him but as though sensing her exhaustion and her distress he would cry all the harder. And every time he cried Lyn would be there, reaching out for him, trying to take him, looking at her accusingly.

'You see! When I hold him he stops.' She would croon over the baby and then look up in triumph.

'It's normal, Joss,' Simon said gently. 'Babies often cry when their mums pick them up because they want her milk. It's frustration and hunger because they can smell it so close. Lyn has nothing Ned wants, so he doesn't bother.'

Lyn was not convinced.

The hot weather broke at last at the beginning of September. Torrential rain hurtled across the gardens, and the roof began to leak. Wearily Joss and Lyn trudged up and down to the attics with buckets and washing up bowls and Tom caught a violent cold. Wiping his nose for the hundredth time as they all huddled in the kitchen Joss had sent him off to play before going out to the door to collect the post. Glancing through the handful of letters she paused, looking at one particular envelope, then she threw the whole pile on the table. 'Bills,' she said casually. 'Bills and more bills.'

'In that case I'm going out to the cars.' Luke stood up, stuffing the last piece of his toast into his mouth. 'Like to bring us out some coffee at about eleven? That would be nice.' He glanced at Lyn and then at Joss. 'Please?' he wheedled.

They both laughed. 'We'll toss for it,' Lyn said. She stood up and began to stack the dishes.

It was Joss who carried out the two steaming mugs and a pile of home-made cookies later, leaving Lyn with the washing. Her raincoat collar pulled up against the cold wind and streaming rain she ducked into the coach house and put them down on the bench amid a pile of brake drums and shoes and old spanners.

'Where is he, Jimbo?'

'Under the car.' Jimbo jerked with his thumb towards the chassis blocked up in the middle of the coach house.

Joss crouched down. 'Grub's up!' She peered down to see Luke lying on his back, groping above his head in the car's intestines. 'Great.' His voice was muffled. 'Thanks.' He began to push himself out. As his face appeared, black and grinning from beneath the wing the car with no warning lurched suddenly sideways. 'Luke!' Joss's scream brought Jimbo leaping to her side.

'Watch out. The axle stands are slipping.' Jimbo's

warning shout as Luke rolled clear was drowned by the crash as the car body slid down onto the ground.

Luke stood up shakily. 'Close one!' He wiped his forehead on the back of his hand.

'Luke. You were nearly killed.' Joss had gone white.

'Fraid so. Never mind. I wasn't.' He turned to Jimbo who was picking up the stands. 'What happened?'

Jimbo was ashen. He shook his head. 'Must have been knocked, I reckon.'

'Knocked?' Joss looked from one to the other. 'By me? It must have been me?' She was distraught. 'Oh God, I'm so tired these days I can't see what I'm doing.'

Luke shook his head. He came and put his arm round her. 'You weren't anywhere near the car, Joss. Anyway, it doesn't matter, love. No harm done. These things happen.'

'Oh, Luke.' Her knees had begun to shake. 'It was me! Luke, I could have killed you.'

'Take more than that to kill your husband, my dear.' Luke grinned. He reached for one of Lyn's biscuits. 'Go on. Forget it. I'm OK.'

The rain clouds had blown themselves out by lunch time and the afternoon was crisp and glorious. Leaves scattered across the lake, and the lily pads slapped playfully on the water. Standing side by side Luke and Joss were silent as they watched a heron take off on the far side of the lake and fly laboriously over the hedge with indignant raucous squawks of complaint. One of the kittens, half hidden in the undergrowth had been stalking it with exaggerated care. As the huge bird lifted above its head the small cat turned and fled towards the house. 'Are you OK?' Luke glanced at her sideways. 'You're not still worrying about that silly accident with the car are you?' Joss's face was pale and strained. There were dark circles under her eyes.

She gave a wan smile. 'Not really.' In her shock at what had happened she still couldn't believe the fact that she had been nowhere near it when the car began to move. In theory she knew perfectly well that the accident had not been her fault, but deep down inside she wasn't certain.

'Are you sure?' He was studying her face. Something was wrong. More than just the tiredness. He turned back to look at the water, screwing up his eyes against the glare from the sun on the dancing ripples. 'Have you heard from David recently?' he asked. He kept his voice casual.

For a moment she didn't answer. Then she shook her head. 'Not for ages. Why?'

'I just wondered.'

He rammed his hands into his pockets with a shiver. The autumn wind was growing cold. He had seen the envelope lying in the pile on the kitchen table and he had recognised the writing, just as she must have. It had been bulky and sealed with Sellotape. The stab of rage he had felt when he saw it was irrational and violent. Why hadn't he thrown the thing on the stove? Why hadn't he opened it and read it? After all he could guess what was in it: more about the bloody house. At first she had ignored it – left it on the table to be lost in a swirl of newspapers and shopping lists – then at lunch time he saw that it had disappeared. Tear it up, he thought. Please, Joss, tear it up.

He took a step or two nearer the steep bank, staring down into the water to where goldfish and tench flitted amongst the roots of the lilies, faint shadows in the water – water which was deceptively deep.

'Luke.' Joss's voice came from further away now.

Luke swung round. He frowned. He couldn't see her. A raft of ripples crossed the water, rocking the floating leaves. Near the far bank a moorhen ran lightly across the lily pads, scarcely rocking them, giving sharp croaks of alarm.

'Joss? Where are you?'

There was no warning, no sound of steps, just the sudden firm, violent push from two hands squarely planted in the small of his back as with a shout of surprise and fear he felt himself hurtling down the steep bank and into the water. No longer glittering gold, it was brown, sandy, cold and very very deep. His eyes open, he found himself staring round the murky depths of the lake, then, arms flailing he fought his way to the surface, choking, feeling the weed and lily stems clutching at his legs, pulling him back. As his head broke the surface he took great gulps of air, clawing at the leaves around him. 'Christ Almighty, Joss, what did you do that for?' He was apoplectic with anger and fright. 'You could have drowned me!'

'Luke? Luke, what happened?' Joss was standing a few yards away. Her face was white. 'Here, catch my hand.' She stepped gingerly down towards the water and stooped towards him.

He grabbed her fingers and hauled himself dripping onto the bank. 'I suppose you think that was funny?' He glared at her, shaking himself like a dog. 'For pity's sake, Joss!'

'I don't think it was funny at all,' she retaliated. Then her mouth twitched very slightly at the corners. 'Oh Luke, but you did look funny, suddenly hurling yourself into the water. What on earth made you do it? Did you slip?'

'Slip? You know bloody well I didn't slip. You pushed me.'

'I didn't.' Her face was a picture of injured innocence. 'How could you think such a thing?'

He was taking deep breaths, trying to catch his breath. In the cold wind, he was suddenly shivering violently.

'Well, I'm not going to argue the toss now. If I stand here much longer I'll get pneumonia.' He turned towards the house and strode away up the lawn. Joss stood still, looking after him. Her sudden hilarity had gone as swiftly as it had come. She hadn't pushed him. She had been standing several yards away from him when he had suddenly given the surprised shout and hurtled forward into the water. He hadn't slipped; he hadn't jumped. He looked as if he had been pushed. But if she hadn't done it, who had?

She shuddered, looking round. The moorhen had disappeared. The bright autumnal sun had vanished behind a cloud and the garden was suddenly very bleak and cold.

She watched as Luke disappeared round the side of the house towards the kitchen, then she turned and looked back at the dull black surface of the lake, the lake where Sammy had died and she shuddered violently. Dear sweet God, it was starting.

Lyn was in the kitchen making pastry when Joss made her way in through the back door and hung up her jacket in the hall. She glanced up at Joss over the rolling pin and raised an eyebrow. 'Luke is pretty pissed off with you,' she said. Beside her, Tom, his sleeves rolled up was kneeling on a kitchen chair rolling out his own small piece of dough. He was covered in flour. 'What on earth made you do it?'

'I didn't do it, Lyn.' Joss went to the stove and lifted the kettle. She reached for a mug. 'I wasn't anywhere near him.'

'So he jumped in by himself?'

'He must have slipped. Do you want some coffee?'

Lyn shook her head.

'Daddy all wet,' Tom observed. He stuck his thumb into his dough and made two eyes. Then he gouged out a smiling mouth.

'I'll take him up a hot drink.' Joss spooned coffee into

282

two mugs and stirred the hot water. She added milk. 'I didn't do it, Lyn,' she repeated firmly. 'Really I didn't.'

Luke was running a bath. He was tearing off his sodden clothes as Joss came into the bathroom. 'Here,' she said. 'Coffee, to thaw you out. Are you all right?' There was a long bleeding scratch on his leg.

'Yes, I'm fine.' He lowered himself into the hot water and reached for the mug. 'Sorry to be so cross, but it wasn't my idea of a joke, Joss.'

'Nor mine.' She sat down on the lid of the lavatory. 'I didn't do it, Luke. Honest. You must have slipped. I was miles away from you. I saw you just take off suddenly.'

He leaned back and closed his eyes, sipping at the hot drink. 'If you say so.'

'Luke, I think we should leave Belheddon.'

'Joss.' He opened his eyes and looked at her. 'We've discussed this before. I'm sorry, but it's impossible. Even with the money from the wine. You must see that. The terms of your mother's will say we can't sell it; we still need to earn a living, and our only chance is to persevere with my restoration and with your writing. Well, I suppose you can do your writing anywhere, but the cars, no. I need space for that. Space and covered accommodation, and now I need Jimbo. That lad is worth his weight in gold. He has a real feel for old cars. And here I can put the fiasco of Barry and H & G behind me. They're never going to catch the bastard. It's no use me thinking they will. I needed a new life, Joss. And here we have room for Lyn too. It's perfect in every way.' Putting down his coffee he reached for the soap and began lazily to lather his arms. 'I know you're nervous about the stories about this house, but they are so much crap, you must know that at heart. You mustn't let people wind you up. People like David.' He glanced at her again searching it for any reaction and his face relaxed into a smile. 'I'm glad in a way you thought it funny, watching your husband hurtle into fifteen feet of ice cold water. I haven't seen you laugh for a long time.'

'I didn't laugh.'

'Well, smile, then. Joss, I know it hasn't been easy, love. Coming here, with all the memories and stories about your family. I do understand.'

'Do you?' She stared at him thoughtfully.

'Yes, I do.' He sat up, the water coursing off his shoulders and arms and reached towards the towels. She took one and passed it to him. 'I also understand it's not easy seeing Lyn spending so much time with the little boys, when you have to lock yourself away in the study writing.'

'I'm terrified the story won't be any good when it's finished.'

'It will. After all they've seen a chunk of it, and they know what's going to happen. It will be fine.'

'Do you think so?' She hugged her arms around herself.

'I know so.' He stood up and wrapping himself in the towel, put his arm round her and she found herself enveloped in a warm steamy hug that smelled of soap and Radox. 'Forget the ghosts, love. They don't exist. Not in real life. Wonderful for novelists and historians and old biddies in the village, and even retired vicars looking for jobs as exorcists, but not for real. No way. OK?'

She gave a tight smile. 'OK.'

'So, let me get dressed and we'll go down and drink to Belheddon enterprises, and confusion to the ghosts of yesteryear. Agreed?'

'Agreed.'

Tom's first scream brought Joss to her knees on the bed as she was dragged violently out of her dreams. She was out of bed in a flash. Behind her Lyn appeared in the doorway dragging on her dressing gown.

Tom was standing in the middle of the floor. Joss reached him first and picked him up.

The child clung to her sobbing. 'Tom Tom fall. Tom Tom fall on the floor.' He buried his head in her neck, nestling into her curtain of hair.

Lyn let down the side of the cot. 'For goodness sake, Joss. Look. You didn't fasten the side properly. The poor child could have been badly hurt.' Crossly she began to remake the tangled bed.

'Of course I fastened the side properly. I always check.' Joss glared at her over Tom's head.

Lyn sniffed. 'If you say so.' She smoothed the sheets efficiently down and turned back the blankets. 'Come on Tom Tom, let's see if you need changing before I put you down.' She reached for him and Joss felt the child relinquish his tight grip on her neck and transfer it to Lyn's. She clutched at him. 'Tom Tom, stay with Mummy,' she said firmly. 'I'll do it. You go to bed, Lyn.'

Lyn stared at her. 'Why? I'm offering.'

'I know you're offering and I'm grateful, but I want to do it myself.'

Lyn relaxed her hold on Tom and stood back. 'OK, please yourself. Shall I check on Ned?'

Joss shook her head. 'No. I'll go to him when I've done this. He'll be ready for his night feed soon. Go to bed, Lyn.'

She sat the little boy down on his changing mat and began to unbutton his pyjamas. He was still sniffling miserably as she laid him back and eased off his trousers, conscious that Lyn was hovering in the doorway. Half hidden by the plastic toddler's nappy a huge black bruise was developing on Tom's leg. Undoing the plastic tabs she took off the nappy and gasped. The bruise covered his whole hip.

Lyn had seen it too. 'Dear God, how did he do that?' She came and peered at the little boy.

Joss stared at it, horrified. 'Tom Tom, sweetheart! Oh you poor little lamb!' She ran her fingers gently over the bruise. 'How did you do it? Let Mummy see. I'll put some arnica cream on it. He must have done it falling out of the cot.' She rolled up the wet nappy and putting it into the bucket under the table she reached for the talcum powder and a dry nappy from the packet.

'He didn't fall.' Lyn suddenly bent closer. 'Look. Those bruises on his leg. The marks of fingers.' She stood back suddenly and stared at Joss. 'You must have done it. You!'

Joss, having smoothed on some soothing cream was easing the little boy's hips onto the fresh pad folding it over, sealing the sticky strips. She looked up at Lyn furiously. 'How could you say such a thing!'

'Luke. Look.' Lyn swung round to Luke who was standing by the wall watching. 'For Christ's sake, Luke, say something. She's hurt him. Her own child.'

'Lyn!' Joss repeated angrily. 'Luke, don't listen to her!'

'You know that's not possible, Lyn,' Luke said quietly. 'You're being silly. Joss would never hurt Tom. Never.'

'No, I wouldn't! How dare you!' Joss took a deep breath. 'Go to bed, Lyn,' she repeated. 'You're obviously tired. Let me get on with settling Tom down.' She was keeping her temper with difficulty. 'I would never hurt him in a million years, and you know it. The poor little boy has had a horrid fall out of his cot, and he's bruised, but that's all. He's fine now, aren't you, Tom Tom?' She pulled on his pyjama bottoms and buttoned them back to the tops. Then she sat him up. 'OK, soldier, let's pop you back to bed.'

'Tin man gone?' Tom refused to lie down. He stood in the bed, holding onto the bars, staring past her into the corner of the nursery.

Joss bit her lip. She could feel a small worm of panic beginning in her stomach. 'No tin man, Tom. That's your bad dream. He's gone. Silly tin man. He didn't want to frighten you. He's gone away now.' She saw Luke and Lyn exchange glances over her head. 'Come on. Let's tuck you up.'

The night feed was the only one she was still giving Ned from the breast. It had seemed to make sense to wean him slowly onto the bottle so Lyn could take over more of the feeds herself, but this last one, in the quiet depths of the night she had been reluctant to relinquish, even though it added to her exhaustion. As she sat with the baby cradled in her arms she knew she would hang on to this precious moment each night as long as she could, when Ned was hers and hers alone.

It had been a long time before she could persuade Luke and Lyn to go to bed and leave her to settle Tom. When at last they had gone she had sat down beside his cot and read him a story and soon, very soon, his eyes had closed. Kissing him she had self consciously made the sign of the cross over him before tucking in his blankets and tip-toeing out of the room.

As she sat, with the baby cradled in her arms she found her thoughts going back to Lyn. It was as though her sister didn't trust her. Or was it just that she was jealous, without babies of her own? She frowned, picturing the bruises on Tom. It was not the first time the little boy had fallen and been bruised, and she was sure that Lyn must have seen those bruises too. Bruises from falls. They must be. After all, he was growing more adventurous now, banging his head on the corner of the kitchen table, nearly tipping over his high chair. Bruises were normal in a toddler. But what about nightmares? His nightmares about the tin man.

She sighed. They were not nightmares. She had seen him, sensed him, too, in the corner of the room, Tom's room, her own bedroom and the great hall, watching from the shadows, no more than a shadow himself, yet always there, waiting. Waiting for what? Even the kittens had sensed him, she was sure of it. Neither of them liked the great hall, avoiding it where possible, or if intent on finding her in the study scampering through with huge eyes and flattened ears. She shivered, her arms tightening round the baby and Ned stopped sucking. He gave a resentful whimper and opened his eyes to look up into her face. She smiled at him and dropped a kiss on the dark hair. 'Sorry, little one.'

Her thoughts went back to David's letter. After she had picked the envelope up off the breakfast table she had put it on her desk in the study unopened. David's letters were no longer seized and torn open with eager anticipation. Now she dreaded them, although she didn't have the will-power to ask him to stop writing. She had sat down at the desk and drawn her mug of coffee to her, cupping her hands around it, staring sightlessly out of the window. In front of her the pile of manuscript was very little higher than it had been a month before. Her long sessions in the study were more and more unproductive. Sitting at the desk, her ears straining for sounds from the depths of the house – a whimper from Ned, a cry from Tom – she could not concentrate on the story unfolding before her. And always there was the fear that she would hear the others – the lost boys.

Reaching for the computer switch she had watched the screen as her program came up, sipping at the steaming coffee. Then her eye had fallen again on the envelope. With a sigh she reached for it and slipped her finger under the flap.

No photocopies this time, just several pages of David's closely typed script. She pictured his old battered portable – sometimes to be seen on the staff room table, more often lying tossed and abandoned in the back of his car, the case covered in torn travel labels. He typed with two fingers, often crossed as he explained to anyone who came face to face with his efforts – but there was no sign here of the rows of xs which so often littered his work. Where he had hit wrong keys he had left the results uncorrected.

Dear Joss

Hope my godson flourishes. Give him a kiss from me.

Re: the tin man. I think I know who/what he is!!!! Maybe!!! I've been following up on Katherine de Vere and her witchy mother. There are some wonderful records of court proceedings extant. They didn't entirely get away with it, you know. Margaret was actually arrested in 1482. She was taken from Belheddon to London but before she could be brought before the court she demanded to see the king – Edward IV. He interviewed her in the Tower. It is not recorded what she said but the charges were immediately dropped and she left London laden with gifts. It's my guess that she had something on him, as they say, and that that something was to do with her daughter Katherine. King Edward had visited Belheddon four times the previous year and on each occasion he stayed several days – once for ten days which was comparatively unheard of. What was the attraction? The place was hardly a political centre in any sense and taking time off from the war/ruling the country was not a particularly expedient action at that time. One contemporary source says Margaret bewitched him to fall in love with her daughter. The idea was that Elizabeth Woodville would die and he would then marry Katherine de Vere.

The Belheddon de Veres were close kin of the

Earls of Oxford, and the political implications
were enormous if they could net the king and
ally themselves by marriage to the white rose . . .

Joss put the letter down and rubbed her eyes wearily.
The white rose. It seemed almost corny, but did King
Edward present white roses to his girl-friends? Is that
where they came from? Or did Margaret de Vere use
them in her magic spells to conjure the love of a king for
the daughter of a minor noble who lived at the east-
ernmost edges of his kingdom. She shuddered. Leaning
forward she pulled open a small drawer. She had put one
of the roses in there, at the beginning, before they had
begun to fill her with such dread.

She poked around amongst the pencils and stamps and
sticks of sealing wax, but there was no sign of it now.
Not even the crumbs of brittle petal in the bottom. The
drawer, when she pulled it right out and held it up to
her nose smelled of camphor and dust, nothing more.
She took a deep breath, sliding the drawer back into
place, and picked up the letter again.

Of course, we will never know how much of all
this was malicious gossip and rumour, and how
much if any was based on fact.

Fact: Elizabeth Woodville outlived her
husband.

Fact: Katherine de Vere married a man who
died in mysterious circumstances only six
months later.

Fact: Katherine herself died a month after
that, probably in childbirth.

The king died seven months after that in 1483
at the age of forty. He died suddenly and
unexpectedly at Westminster. The death was
considered suspicious by many and at that point
all the accusations of witchcraft resurfaced and

various people were accused of procuring his death. Amongst them was Margaret de Vere who was rearrested. Apparently she counter claimed against the king, blaming him for Katherine's death. Why? My suspicion is that King Edward was the father of the child that killed her. I'm leaping to conclusions here, Joss, as you will immediately point out, and being shockingly unscientific and even romantic in my deductions, but perhaps some of this makes sense? What do you think? Could our ghost be King Edward – a tin man in armour?

Must go. Have got to teach lower fifth ladies about Disraeli and Gladstone, God help me. If I could talk about Dizzie's racy novels and Glad's girls they'd pay attention. To the Irish question – not a hope! See you all soon. Regards to Luke and Lyn.

D.

Slowly Joss refolded the sheets of paper and reinserted them into the envelope which she stuck into one of the pigeon holes of the desk. Then she had sat for a long time staring out of the window, lost in thought.

whole picture were somehow an illusion for
bushes covered them more thoroughly or were
nearer. Nervously, distractedly, she counted
It must happen this way. Reaching into her
bucket of chalk, away up the steps of the
long low cupboard where the rest of the box
failed her, panic gripped her into immobility.
The door was immediately in front and beyond
that the wall and over the wall something in
darkness, but something like a pair of dim-
......What to ride about I shall never know,
King Edward......

he barometer in the dining room was falling
steadily. As the winds increased the following
day, rattling the windows and howling around
the chimneys, the family congregated in the kitchen. By
four o'clock Luke had sent Jimbo home and he too was
sitting at the kitchen table, a dismantled carburettor
spread out before him on a newspaper. He glanced up at
Joss, unable to contain his curiosity any longer. 'Was that
a letter from David yesterday morning?'

Joss was cutting up pieces of fruit for Tom's tea. She
glanced up at him, knife raised. 'It was. He sends you
both his regards.'

'And has he found out any more history about the
house?' He held the housing from one of the twin carbs
of the SS up to his mouth and breathing on it heavily he
rubbed the gleaming aluminium with a duster.

'A bit. Apparently King Edward IV visited here on several occasions. David thinks he fancied one of the daughters of the house.' She scooped pieces of chopped apple
and banana onto a saucer and put it in front of Tom.
There was no way they could see that she was holding
her breath, straining her ears towards the hall, wondering
if someone was there, listening, someone who might
resent her light, almost flippant tone.

Lyn was studying a recipe book with a frown, pencil in hand as she noted down ingredients on her shopping list. 'Of course, it would be a king,' she observed quietly. 'No lesser mortal would dare to chat up a Belheddonist.'

Luke raised an eyebrow. He caught Joss's eye and grinned. 'Not bad. A Belheddonist. I like that.'

Joss laughed uncomfortably. 'Is that what we are too?'

'Lotus eaters, one and all.' He began stacking the pieces of metal back into an old cardboard box. Standing up he walked over to the sink to wash his hands under the tap. 'So, shall I put on the kettle?'

Joss nodded. 'Then I'd better get back to work. I don't seem to be making much progress at the moment.' Her deadline was not very far off and twice now she had had letters from Robert Cassie asking her if she thought she would complete the book on time. They had only added to her guilt.

It wasn't until Joss had retreated to her study, cup of tea in hand, and Lyn had set Tom drawing pictures at the table with a box full of crayons that Lyn sat down opposite Luke. 'What really happened yesterday?'

'Yesterday?'

'You know what I mean, Luke. The lake.'

'I fell in.'

'Fell?'

'Yes, fell.' He looked up and met her gaze. 'Leave it, Lyn. I've told you before. This is between Joss and me.'

'Is it? And is it between you and her when she hurts the children? You don't think those bruises on Tom came from the fall, do you? There were finger marks, for God's sake. And Ned. How many accidents has he had now? Little ones, admittedly. A knock here and there, a blanket over the face. What about the things we don't know about? What is it going to take for you to pay attention, Luke?' She stood up and paced up and down the floor a couple of times. 'Can't you see what's under your nose?

293

Joss can't cope. She's depressed. It's all getting too much for her. I think she's hurting them. She's doing it. It's a plea for help, Luke, but who knows how far it will go? You have to do something.'

'Lyn, you don't know what you're saying!' Angrily Luke thumped the table with his fist. 'You're her sister, for God's sake –'

'No. No, Luke, I'm not her sister. Not any more. That's been made perfectly clear. But I still love her like a sister.' She pushed her hair out of her eyes angrily. 'And I can see what's happening. This house, the family, even these bloody ghosts she thinks are here – everything is combining to make her depressed. She's not writing, you know. I've looked at that manuscript on her mother's precious desk. She had got to page 147 three or four weeks ago and she's written nothing since. She just sits there, brooding.'

'Lyn, it may have escaped your notice but she's trying to do a lot of the housework as well as feed Ned and write a book. And why is she doing housework? Because you feel you're being asked to do too much! She's tired, Lyn.'

'Yes, she's tired. I'm tired. We're all tired. But we don't go around hurting the children.'

She became aware suddenly that Tom had put down his crayons and was staring at her and Luke solemnly, eyes huge, thumb in mouth. 'Oh, Tom, darling.' She ran to him and picked him up, swinging him onto her hip. 'Aunty Lyn is going to look after you, sweetheart, I promise.'

'Lyn.' Luke controlled his temper with difficulty. 'Please, don't ever say things like that again. It's not true. Joss would never, never hurt the children.'

'No?' She glared at him. 'Why don't we ask Tom?'

'No!' He stood up, sending the chair shooting backwards across the floor. 'No, Lyn that's enough. Have some common sense, please!'

Angrier than he had been for a long time, he slammed

out of the kitchen and into the hall, aware of Tom's gaze, thoughtful somehow beyond his years, fixed unwaveringly on his back.

In the great hall he stopped in the middle of the floor and took a deep breath. He was letting Lyn get to him and it was crazy. He could see what she was up to – undermining Joss, trying to win him and the children away from her, planting seeds of doubt. Damn it, she almost had him believing it was Joss who had pushed him into the lake.

Around him the room seemed suddenly very silent. Ramming his hands down into the pockets of his cords he shivered, staring down at the empty hearth. A mound of cold ash lay between the fire dogs, a scattering of small twigs around it. The room was very cold. He could feel the chill striking up from the flag stones into his bones. He was conscious suddenly of the sound of the wind in the great chimney. It was moaning gently and every now and then as a stronger gust shook the house the sound changed and took on a strange resemblance to laughter – children's laughter.

'Joss!' He turned abruptly and strode towards the study.

She was standing staring out of the French windows at the dark garden. The computer, he noticed, was not even switched on.

'Joss, what are you doing?' He saw her guilty jump and the way she reached for the curtains, pulling them quickly across to shut out the darkness almost as though she didn't want him to see what it was she had been watching. He also saw the surreptitious gesture she made to wipe away the tears on her cheeks.

'Joss, what is it? Why are you crying?'

She shrugged, still not looking at him.

'Joss, come here.' He drew her into his arms and held her against him. 'Tell me.'

Wordlessly she shrugged again. How could she tell him her fears? They sounded crazy. They were crazy! The images which haunted her dreams and her waking hours were no more than that – images which derived from some archetypal nightmare world where Luke was being threatened on every side and Ned and Tom were in danger of their lives and other people, people she didn't know, were running, fearful, through the house.

The young man writhed in pain, spittle frothing at the corners of his mouth, his hands clutching at hers.

'Katherine! Sweet wife! Hold me.'

'Richard!' She pressed her lips against his hot sweating forehead and soothed him gently.

'I'm done for, sweetheart.' He retched again, his body contorted. 'Remember me.'

'How could I forget,' she whispered. 'But you will get well. I know you will get well.' She was crying so hard she could hardly see his face.

He shook his head. He had read his doom in his mother-in-law's eyes. 'No, my love, no. I have to leave you.'

He too was crying as he died.

'Is it the book? Are you having trouble with the book?' He was talking softly, his mouth pressed against her hair. 'Joss, you mustn't let things get out of proportion, love. It doesn't matter. Nothing matters so much that you let it make you ill.'

His arms round her were strong. Within their embrace she felt completely safe, and yet John Bennet had been strong; her own real father had presumably been strong and what had happened to them? With a violent shudder she pushed Luke away. 'Take no notice of me. I'm being silly. It's lack of sleep, that's all.'

'Joss, you know Lyn has offered –'

'Oh, I know she has offered.' The emotion in Joss's response astonished her as much as Luke. 'I don't want her taking over Ned's life. I don't want her doing every single thing for him. I don't want him to think she is his mother. I want him myself, Luke. I want to look after him! She's stealing him from me.'

'Of course she isn't, Joss –'

'No? Take a look at things.' She tore herself out of his grip and went to stand in front of the computer. The screen was a reproachful blank.

'You take a look at things, Joss.' Luke kept his voice deliberately even. 'You and I are employing Lyn to be the children's nanny. We are giving her board and lodging and a small wage to do a job. That was supposed to help both of you. She needed a job and I suspect a home away from Alice and Joe for a bit to give her some independence, and you wanted space to write a book and get on with doing up Belheddon and researching its history. After Tom was born you felt the restrictions of looking after a small child very badly if you remember. Having Lyn here wasn't a plot to deprive you of the boys, Joss. It was to help you. If it's not working, we'll tell her to go.'

Sitting down at her desk, Joss put her head in her hands. Wearily she rubbed her temples. 'Oh, Luke. I'm sorry. I've been feeling as though my life has been running away with me. As if it is living me instead of me living it!'

He laughed. 'Silly old Joss. If ever there was a lady in charge of her own destiny, it's you.'

Joss put both children to bed while Lyn was making the supper and they were sitting round the table in the kitchen when Janet arrived. Shedding her Barbour in the back porch she came in, her cheeks whipped pink by the wind, her hair wet and tangled. 'I've got something for my godson in the car.' She accepted the offer of a cup of coffee with alacrity. 'It's so gorgeous I had to bring it straight over. Until he's old enough I thought his brother would adore it too.'

'Janet, you spoil them. First Kit and Kat, and now – what is it?'

Janet beamed. 'All right. I can't wait. I'm no good at building suspense. Come and help me, Luke. It's in the back of the car.'

They disappeared outside the door, letting in a waft of wet night air.

Joss glanced at Lyn. 'Have we got enough to offer her supper? Roy is still away at some conference or other so she's on her own.'

'Of course we have.' Lyn nodded vehemently. 'You know I always make enough for two or three meals.'

'Great,' Joss nodded. 'Lyn – I'm sorry I've been a bit of a bear.'

Lyn turned to the stove so that Joss couldn't see her face. 'That's OK.' She was going to add something else when the door reopened and Luke staggered in carrying a wooden rocking horse.

'Janet!' Joss's squeal was one of genuine pleasure. 'It's the most beautiful thing I've ever seen!'

Hand carved in painted dapple grey, the horse had a rippling black mane and tail and a red leather bridle and saddle, studded with brass headed nails.

'Tom is going to adore it.' She stroked the shining mane as Luke set it down on the floor by the dresser.

'I always thought there should be a rocking horse at Belheddon.' Janet picked up her mug and warmed her hands on it. 'I was so sure there must be one hidden away somewhere that I sent your brother, Luke, on a secret mission to all the old attics and outbuildings when he was here for the christening.'

'He never said.' Joss stared at her, amused.

Janet shook her head. 'No sign of a rocking horse, he said. It was originally going to be a christening present, but then I realised how long it was going to take to make. There's a waiting list with this chap near Sudbury who makes them.'

She chuckled as Kit and Kat, climbing languidly from their basket by the stove crept up to the horse and feigning indifference inspected it from a safe distance before pouncing at the long tail.

'Another of your wonderful craftsmen.' Luke put his arm around Janet's shoulders and gave her a hug. 'Clever girl. I had no idea old Mat was poking round in the attics. He did that very discreetly.' He glanced at Joss, but her attention appeared to be fully on the horse. 'Shall we see if Tom is still awake? If he is he can come down to see it while Janet's here? As it's a very special occasion.'

Janet nodded. 'Oh please. Would you? Just this once? I know it was a silly time to bring it, but I only collected it this afternoon, and I couldn't wait.'

'I'll get him.' Luke strode towards the door. 'It's the sort of surprise he'll probably remember all his life.'

The kitchen was warm, full of succulent smells from the cooker. Kit and Kat, having examined the new acquisition in great detail were curled up once more, safe in their basket, when there was a click and then a crackle from the baby alarm standing on the dresser. 'Joss!' Luke's voice was tinny, distant, but sharp with anxiety. 'Where is he, Joss?'

Joss stared at the dresser. 'What do you mean, where is he?' But he couldn't hear her. Her frantic question shouted into the speaker of a one way system was lost in the silence of the kitchen.

'Christ!' Lyn pushed away the bottle she was opening so violently it fell over and rolled to the edge of the table, splashing wine onto the flags. 'What's happened now?'

She looked at Joss for a fraction of a second before she made for the door.

The three women ran for the staircase and found Luke standing in Tom's bedroom. The bed was neat and appeared unslept in. 'The baby alarm was switched off. Where is he, Joss? Where did you put Tom?' His voice was shaking as he caught her arm.

'What do you mean where did I put him?' Joss stared down at the little bed in disbelief. 'He was here. I tucked him in, he had his teddy.' A cold lump of something like stone seemed to have settled in her stomach as she stared round wildly. 'He was here. He was fine. I read him a chapter of Dr Seuss – look, here's the book.' It was lying face down on his chest of drawers near the night light. She stared down at the new candle in the holder. 'I lit it. I remember lighting it . . .' The electric lamp had been too bright.

'Where is he, Joss?' Luke's grip tightened on her arm. She shook her head. 'He was here.'

'For God's sake, she's obviously not going to tell us. We've got to look.' Lyn's voice was shaking. She turned back out of the room and crossed the narrow corridor into Ned's. The baby was fast asleep. There was no sign of Tom in there.

'He's in the attic,' Joss whispered suddenly. 'I think he's in the attic with the boys.' She didn't know how she knew.

The others stared at her for a moment and she was the one to run first towards the attic stairs. 'Tom –' her scream echoed round the house. 'Tom, where are you?'

He was sitting contentedly in the middle of the double bed in the attic room which had been occupied by Elizabeth and Geoffrey Grant. Before him, on the middle of the eiderdown was a box of wooden animals. At the sight of the faces in the doorway he beamed at them contentedly.

'Georgie's toys,' he said happily. 'Tom play with Georgie's toys.'

'How many times do I have to tell you, I put him to bed.' Joss sat down at the table and put her head in her hands. 'He was all right. I read him a story. I tucked him in. I put the side of the cot up and checked it. I lit the night light and I turned on the baby alarm.'

Tom had gone back to his bed with only a token protest, after twenty minutes ecstatic rocking on the horse, asleep almost as soon as his head touched the pillow. Making sure the alarm was on this time, they left him and came back down to the kitchen.

Luke was watching her soberly. 'Perhaps you ought to see Simon, Joss,' he said tentatively. 'Honestly, it might be the best. I'm sure it's no more than lapse of concentration or something because of your tiredness.'

'There is nothing wrong with me.' Joss rubbed the palms of her hands up and down her face several times, hard. 'For God's sake, why will no one believe me?'

She was conscious of Lyn and Luke exchanging glances. It was Janet who came up to her and gave her a hug. 'I believe you, Joss. I think there's something funny in this house. And I think you should all leave. Come and stay with me. We've plenty of room. I'd love to have you.' She glanced at them all again. 'Please.'

'That's kind of you, Janet.' Luke spoke firmly before Joss had a chance to reply. 'But there is no need. There is nothing odd about the house which isn't in my wife's imagination. She has been scared by a lot of silly stories and the sooner we admit that, the better. I'm sure she's fine. All she needs is to rest. I'll get Simon to come over tomorrow and prescribe something.'

'Luke!' Joss stared at him. 'How dare you! It's me you're talking about. You sound like a Victorian patriarch! I am not imagining things, and I did not take Tom

301

upstairs and leave him in the ice cold attics to gratify my lurid imagination. And where did those toys come from, is any one going to tell me that? I've never seen them before. If they were Georgie's, how did Tom Tom know? Oh, Luke, how could you think that I would terrify my own child like that!'

'He wasn't terrified, Joss,' Janet said quietly. 'Whatever happened and however he got up there, he wasn't terrified. He was having a good time with those toys, and that's the main thing, surely. There is no harm done.'

'There's a great deal of harm done.' Lyn's hands were shaking. Sitting down abruptly, she chewed her lip, trying to stop herself sobbing out loud. 'When will someone realise that the children are in danger?'

'I agree.' Joss met her eye steadily. 'The children are in danger. But not, for God's sake, from me!'

'There is no danger.' Luke gave a deep dramatic sigh. 'My God, this is what happens when you have a house full of hysterical women. For heaven's sake pull yourselves together. This is the twentieth century. The nineteen nineties. Lyn, let's have supper. Please! We'll forget all this for now. Tom Tom is asleep and safe and the alarm is on, so there is nothing for us to fret about for now.'

There was a moment's silence as all four of them looked towards the dresser where the small white plastic box of the baby alarm sat between a bowl of fruit and the coffee jug. From it came the sound of gentle snuffling snores.

302

26

om Tom, are you awake?' Joss lowered the side of the cot gently and touched the little boy's cheek with a cautious finger. 'Tom Tom, can you hear Mummy?'

He mumbled and stirred slightly in his sleep.

'Tom Tom, who was it that took you upstairs to play with Georgie's toys?' she whispered.

There was no reply. The little boy began to breathe deeply and evenly again, his eyes tight shut, his thumb in his mouth. Joss watched him for a few minutes in silence. Across the passageway Ned, fed and changed had snuggled back into his own small crib and both rooms, lit by the gentle glow of night lights were warm and safe. The sound of the wind playing amongst the gables of the house emphasised the silence and the gentle breathing of the sleeping child.

With a sigh she turned away from the cot. Lying on the chest of drawers, just within the pool of light thrown by the night light lay a white rose.

She stared at it, feeling suddenly sick. It had not been there when she walked into the room.

Don't scream.

Don't wake them.

Taking a deep breath she clenched her fists, then slowly

303

she turned round to face the window. There was always a pool of deep shadow there, where the faint candle light never reached. The room felt the same as usual. It wasn't especially cold; there was no strange half echo in her head. A stronger than usual gust of wind blew and she saw the curtains move slightly. Her palms were sweating. Stepping closer to the cot she gripped the rail on the side. 'Go away,' she mouthed silently. 'Go away. Leave us alone.' She was aware suddenly that Tom's eyes had opened. He was watching her, his thumb still in his mouth. He caught her eye and gave her a big smile. Withdrawing the thumb he held out his arms. 'Kiss Mummy good night.'

She smiled at him and bent over the cot, stroking his hair. 'Good night little chap.'

'Tin man take Tom to play with Georgie's toys,' he murmured sleepily. Already his eyes were closing.

Joss felt her heart do a somersault with fear. Stepping away from the cot she studied the room again. There was no one there. Even the shadows were empty.

The rose was fresh, velvet to the touch and sweetly scented. It did not fall to pieces. She carried it into the bathroom, and for a moment she was tempted to try and flush it down the lavatory. Instead she threw open the window, and leaned out into the wind. As she dropped it, it vanished out of sight into the darkness like a puff of thistledown. When she closed the window again she found her finger was bleeding where she had caught it on one of the thorns.

'Joss? What time did you get up?' Luke came into the study, rubbing his eyes at about six thirty. 'Ned's crying. You said you wanted to do his morning feed.' He groaned, running his fingers through his hair. 'God, it's cold in here. Why on earth haven't you lit the fire?'

She stared at the hearth blankly. It had been about

half past two when she gave up all attempts to fall asleep and, careful not to wake Luke, had crept out of bed and come downstairs. She had lit the fire then and wrapped in a rug, had curled up in the arm chair, cradling Kit on her knee and gazing into the flames. Obviously she had fallen asleep in the end. The room was freezing.

With a groan she tried to straighten her legs. 'I couldn't sleep and I didn't want to disturb you. Can you make us a cup of tea while I get his bottle ready?'

He nodded. 'Of course. Five minutes.'

Joss tucked Ned inside her dressing gown and, sitting down, abandoned herself to the silence of the early morning and the gentle rhythm of the baby's sucking as she gave him his bottle. When the door opened and Lyn appeared she was almost asleep.

'Joss! What are you doing?' She too was carrying a newly warmed feeding bottle.

Joss opened her eyes. 'I'm giving my son his breakfast.'

'But that's my job!' Lyn was fully dressed, her hair neatly brushed.

'Didn't you see Luke in the kitchen? He's making tea. He should have told you I was doing it. I'm sorry, Lyn. Could you get Tom up?'

Lyn swallowed a retort and banging down the bottle on the table turned on her heel. 'Perhaps next time you want to do it, you'll let me know so I don't have to get up at dawn.'

'Oh Lyn, I'm sorry –'

'No. That's OK. I'm just reminding you.'

Already she had gone. With a sigh Joss dropped a kiss on Ned's head, listening as Lyn's voice changed from nagging sarcasm to bright and cheerful. 'Good morning Tom Tom. Time to get up, sweetheart. Tom Tom?' The tone abruptly turned sharp with fear. 'Oh God, Tom!'

'Lyn? What is it?' Joss stood up. Dropping Ned into his

305

cot she ran towards Tom's room, pulling her dressing gown around her. 'Lyn, what's happened?' Behind her the baby was screaming with indignation.

Lyn had lifted Tom from his cot. 'Quick, he's choking on something. He's turning blue.'

'Push his tummy – quickly –' Joss grabbed the little boy, folding him across her arm. With two desperate gasps Tom coughed up a tiny wooden bird, vomited a trail of bloody spit and began to cry in short rasping sobs.

'Tom!' Joss hugged him. 'Tom, darling –'

'Sweet Jesus, why did you give him these? You must have known he'd put them in his mouth!' Lyn had picked up a handful of the tiny birds which were scattered all over his bed.

'I didn't give them to him.' Joss was trying to soothe the sobbing child.

'Hush, darling, please. Tom – please stop crying. It's all right now. Everything's all right now.'

'Blood! Joss, there's blood all over the bed!' Lyn pulled back the covers. 'Oh God, Tom. Where's he bleeding?'

'He's not bleeding.' Joss was managing to soothe him at last. 'He's OK. Just very frightened, that's all.'

'I'm going to call Simon. Look at the blood round his mouth –'

'It's only a tiny bit, Lyn. He's all right –' Joss was calming down far more quickly than Lyn now that the initial panic was over.

'He's not all right. Where did the blood on his sheets come from?'

'I expect from me. I pricked my finger last night. It wouldn't stop bleeding.'

'So you were in here last night. It was you who gave him the toys.' Lyn's voice was a mixture of accusation and triumph at catching her out.

'I am allowed in my own child's bedroom, Lyn,' Joss's

temper suddenly snapped, 'and I never gave him those animals. I told you. I wouldn't be so stupid!'

'Well then, who did? Tell me that. Luke?'

'No, of course not Luke.'

'Then who? Go on, Joss, as you know so much. Who?'

'I don't know who.' Joss cradled Tom's head against her shoulder.

'Look Lyn, go and ring Simon. Perhaps he could look in on the way to the surgery. Go on,' she repeated as Lyn hesitated.

Reluctantly Lyn went through to the bedroom. Behind her, Joss carried Tom through to Ned's room. 'Will you stand close to Mummy while I see if your little brother needs a burp before I change his nappy?' She set Tom down on the floor, disengaging herself from his arms with difficulty. He had stopped crying at last. Hanging on to her dressing gown with one hand the thumb of the other had found its way back into his mouth. Stooping over the screaming Ned she picked him up and held him against her shoulder.

'Who gave you those little birds, Tom Tom?' Joss kept her voice as casual as she could as she gently rubbed Ned's back. He was quiet at last.

'Georgie.' The thumb came out long enough for the one word.

Joss took a deep breath trying to steady the sudden jolting of her heart. 'I know they're Georgie's toys, but who put them in your cot?'

'Georgie.' He reached for her sash and began to swing the ends of it backwards and forwards..

'Tom,' she moved Ned to the other shoulder and crouched down to put her free hand round Tom's shoulders, 'darling, what does Georgie look like?'

'Boy.'

She swallowed hard. Her mouth had gone dry. 'What sort of boy?'

'Nice boy.'

Ned was already asleep when she tucked him back into his crib. Then she squatted down in front of Tom once more and took his hands in hers. 'Tell me about him. Is he bigger than you?'

Tom nodded.

'And what colour is his hair? Is it like yours?' She fingered Tom's curls.

He nodded. 'Like Mummy's hair.'

'I see.' There was a lump in her throat which would not go away. 'And the tin man, Tom. Was he there too?'

Tom nodded.

'Did he play with the toys?' Her breath felt as though it were being squeezed between ribs of steel. She couldn't breathe properly.

Tom nodded again.

'And you're not frightened of him any more?'

Tom nodded a third time.

'You mean you are frightened?'

Tom's eyes filled with tears. 'Don't like tin man.'

'Tom –' she hesitated. 'Tom, has he ever given you a rose to play with?' He looked at her uncomprehendingly. 'A flower – a white flower with prickles . . .' The other roses hadn't had thorns – none of them had had thorns.

Shaking his head Tom poked at her skirts with his finger.

'Why are you frightened of him, Tom?'

He stared at her with huge eyes. 'Tom go see horse.'

Joss smiled. 'You liked the horse, Tom?'

He nodded vehemently.

'Right then, let's go and see him. You can have a ride while Aunty Lyn and I get breakfast.'

The doctor was in the kitchen with Luke when Joss and Tom arrived downstairs. The two men were seated at the table over cups of coffee, talking in subdued tones which ceased the moment she appeared. Joss felt a moment's unease as she caught Simon's speculative gaze on her but she smiled and greeted him amicably. 'So, Luke, what happened to my cup of tea? I was waiting for it with my tongue hanging out.' Tom had released her hand and run straight to the rocking horse.

'Sorry, I got delayed.' Luke stood up and went to lift him onto it. 'Jimbo wanted the keys to the coach house. He got here early.'

Simon, relaxed, in an open-necked shirt and heavy sweater took another sip of his coffee. 'So, it doesn't look to me as though there's much wrong with that young man of yours.'

'There isn't.' Joss picked up the teapot and shook it experimentally. 'You managed to get here very quickly, Simon.'

'Lyn caught me on the car phone. I was on my way back from the Fords. Their fifth was born in the early hours.' He grinned wryly. 'Someone needs to tell Bill Ford to tie a knot in it or they'll end up with fifteen in as many years.' He chuckled. 'Forget I said that. Most unprofessional. So, young Master Grant, I gather you've got a bit of a sore throat this morning. Didn't your Mummy ever tell you not to put things into your mouth?' He opened his bag and produced torch and spatula.

'What were you thinking about, Joss, to leave such small toys in his cot?' Luke stopped pushing the horse and stood back out of Simon's way.

Joss took a deep breath. 'I did not give them to him. I am not a complete fool!'

'Then who did? It wasn't Lyn or me.'

'I asked Tom who gave them to him.' Joss had poured her own tea. Turning away from them she stood for a moment looking through the window out into the court-yard. The doors of the coach house were open and the light poured out into the still dusky yard.

'And what did Tom say, eh?' Simon's voice was carefully neutral as he peered at Tom's throat.

Tom pushed the spatula away. 'Georgie gave Tom toys,' he said helpfully.

'Georgie?' Simon switched off the torch. 'And who is Georgie?'

There was a silence. 'Georgie does not exist.' Luke's voice was suddenly repressive.

'I see.' Simon went back to the table and picked up his cup. 'An imaginary friend.'

'No.' Joss spoke sharply from the window. She did not turn round. 'Not imaginary. If he was, how could he give Tom the toys?'

'Right.' Simon glanced at Luke, who shrugged. 'Luke, would you mind?' He gestured towards the door with his head. He waited until Luke had let himself out into the courtyard before standing up again. 'Why don't I give you a bit of a push, old chap.' He went back to the horse.

'There's no problem here, Joss. Just a fright. A bit of bruising locally, nothing more. So,' he glanced at her, noting the tense shoulders. 'Tell me how you are.'

'I'm fine.' Her voice was still tight.

'Really fine?' He was still gently pushing the horse's glossy dappled rump.

Joss turned. 'What has Luke been saying to you?'

'He's worried. He thinks you're doing too much.'

'He thinks I'm going round the bend.'

'Do you?'

He expected her to flare up at the question. Instead she left the window and sat down at the table, her cup in front of her. 'I think I'm beginning to wonder.'

'So. Who is Georgie?'

'My brother.'

'Your brother?' He looked astonished. 'I didn't realise you had one.'

'I don't.' She looked up. 'He died in 1962, two years before I was born.'

'Ah.' There was only the slightest hesitation in the rhythm of his pushing as he noticed Tom's sudden tension. Releasing his vice-like grip on the red leather reins with one of his hands, the child's thumb crept up to his mouth. Simon frowned. 'Where's Lyn?'

Joss shrugged. 'Listening at the door?'

'Oh, Joss, hey, come on.' Simon walked over to it and opened it. The hall was empty. 'I'd like Lyn to come and give Tom here his breakfast before he starves so much he turns into a little tiny frog, and I want you and me to have a little talk. Lyn?' His shout was surprisingly loud.

They both heard the slap of her exercise sandals on the stone flags as she answered the call. She had not been far away.

'So, tell me what's going on.' In the study, Simon took up a stance in front of the fire. Lyn had already made it up, Joss noted. It was burning merrily, filling the room with the sweet smell of fruit wood.

'What did Luke tell you?'

'That he thought you might be suffering from post natal depression.'

'And do you think I am?'

'I think it unlikely. Maybe you're tired and maybe you're a bit depressed – show me a new mother who isn't – that doesn't mean it's anything serious. How are you sleeping these days?'

'All right.' It was a lie and they both knew it.

'And you're still breast feeding?'

She nodded. 'Just one feed a day.'

'I'd better take a look at that young man while I'm here, too.'

'Simon.' She walked restlessly over to the desk. 'I did not make Georgie up. You heard yourself that Tom has seen him.'

311

'I heard. So tell me about it.'

'If it were just me, Simon, I'd wonder if I needed putting in a straitjacket, but it's not.' She shook her head. 'Other people have seen them too.'

'Them?'

She sat down. 'Are you taught that irritating, unflappable tone of voice at medical school?'

He smiled. 'On day one. If you can't do it, they kick you out straight away.'

'So you can sound as if nothing in the whole wide world can surprise or shock you.'

'Nothing can, Joss, believe me.'

'So, if I say the house is haunted, you won't turn a hair?'

'Not even one of my grey ones.'

'I've heard Georgie and Sammy, my other brother, and there's something else.' She couldn't hide the slight quaver in her voice.

'Something else?'

'Tom calls him the tin man. I think maybe he's wearing armour.'

There wasn't a trace of a smile on her face. Simon noted the dark shadows, the pale skin, the trapped dull look behind her eyes.

'What particularly interests me is how Tom came by these toys. You and he think Georgie gave them to him. Does that mean that a ghost is capable of carrying things? The toys were clearly themselves real.'

'I don't think they have any trouble carrying things at all.' She was thinking of the roses.

'And that includes people? I gather Tom was taken up to the attic and has also fallen or been thrown from his cot.'

She bit her lip, nodding.

'Have you asked him who took him up to the attic himself?'

'He says it was the tin man.'

'Who you think is a man wearing armour. Do you believe him?'

'Who else could have done it? Luke and Lyn were in the kitchen.'

'Joss, you haven't been suffering from any headaches lately? Dizzy spells? Lapses of memory?'

'Oh I see. You mean I did it. Of course, we had to come to that didn't we.'

'I have to check every possibility. You must see that.'

'Right. Well, you've checked. Have you asked Lyn and Luke the same question? After all, either of them could have slipped out of the kitchen. Either of them could be lying too.'

For the first time he looked uncomfortable.

'I thought not. I assure you, Simon, I am perfectly sane.'

'And the bruises, Joss. On Tom. Did Georgie do that? Or the tin man?'

Her eyes flashed dangerously. 'He fell from his cot!'

'And you're sure of that?'

She hesitated. 'What else *can* I think? Simon, it wasn't *me.*'

He looked at her for several seconds then he shook his head. 'No, I don't think it was. Joss, if you are unhappy here, would it be possible for you to go away for a bit – with the children? To stay with friends, or family. Just to give you all a change of scene.'

She shook her head. 'Luke won't go.'

'I'm not suggesting Luke goes too. Just you and the children.'

'Not Lyn?'

He put his head on one side slightly. 'Do you want Lyn to go with you?'

She shrugged. The idea of going away without Lyn suddenly seemed very inviting. She looked up at him. 'I

313

sometimes think it would be lovely to have the boys to myself.'

'That is not something you need be ashamed of, Joss. It's perfectly natural to want your babies to yourself. Lyn is an extremely efficient lady, I can see that. Someone you would be very thankful for under normal circumstances, but maybe she has taken just a bit too much on herself and you are feeling a bit left out?'

Joss sniffed. 'Now you're playing the psychiatrist.'

He laughed. 'That's day two of being a medical student.' He gave a deep sigh. 'Listen, I have to go home and have a bath and grab some breakfast before going off to surgery. Think about a holiday, Joss. Give yourself a bit of a break. I think this house and its memories have got on top of you a bit.' He moved away from the fire reluctantly and Joss followed him back towards the kitchen. Lyn was tidying up when they walked in and Joss caught the look of enquiry she threw towards Simon.

'I'm afraid they're not going to section me, yet, Lyn,' she said.

Lyn shook her head. 'Of course they're not. I hope you've ticked her off, Simon, and told her to rest more.'

'Indeed I have.' Simon grabbed his jacket. 'Farewell ladies. I'll let myself out.'

Straight across the yard to the coach house and Luke, Joss noted, as she watched him from the window. She turned to face Lyn. 'I'm sane, sober and exonerated,' she said softly. 'Please don't suggest anything else in future.'

Lyn raised an eyebrow. 'If there was no need, I wouldn't dream of it.'

'Good. We could manage without you, you know.'

Lyn flushed a deep red. 'That's up to you.'

'Yes.' Joss looked at her thoughtfully. 'Yes, it is.'

uke's office was an old suitcase in which he kept all his paperwork, to be produced once in a while and spread across the kitchen table, held in place by a cup of coffee, an apple and a plate of bread and cheese. An office day was not to be interrupted by any one, but on this occasion Lyn ignored the warning frown he gave her as she walked in. 'Luke, I have to talk to you. Now, while Joss has taken the children out.'

'Oh, Lyn, not again.' With a groan Luke pushed back a pile of bills and reached for his glass.

'Yes, again. How many times do I have to warn you? Something awful is going to happen and it will be your fault. You can't see what's happening in front of your nose.'

'I can see, Lyn. There is nothing happening. Joss is coping very well. The children are happy – partly thanks to you, partly thanks to their mother who adores them. They are in no danger from her or from anyone else. If you would just let this stupid idea go and let us all relax and get on with life I should be a lot happier.'

Lyn closed her eyes and took a deep breath. 'There were bruises on Tom's arm again this morning.'

Luke frowned. 'I helped bath him last night, Lyn. The bruises are what's left from his fall.'

'New ones. Luke, for pity's sake, please, you have to believe me. It's a plea for help. That's what they always say when a mother starts knocking her kids around.'

'Joss is not knocking the kids around, Lyn.' Luke stood up abruptly. 'I don't want to hear any of this, do you understand? I can't believe you would say all this about your sister.'

'She's not my sister, Luke. That's the point.' Lyn's voice was suddenly bleak. 'She has made it very clear. She is the la-di-da lady of the manor, I'm just an uneducated girl who is no better than a nursery maid in her eyes.'

Luke stared at her shocked. 'Lyn! You know that's rubbish! Joss doesn't think that at all. How could you even imagine it?'

With a little half laugh Lyn shrugged. 'Quite easy, under the circumstances. You may as well know, Luke, I'm only staying because I love little Ned and Tom so much and I think they need me. Otherwise I would tell her to stick her job!'

He stared at the door open mouthed as she went out, slamming it behind her.

'Lyn –' His cry of protest hung unheard in the air.

'My goodness you've walked a long way!' Janet pulled Joss into the hall of the farmhouse and helped her negotiate the double buggy round the corner into her own kitchen. 'You idiot. In this weather too.' The afternoon had degenerated into a cold, blustery grey laced with spinning leaves and icy needles of rain. 'I'll run you back when you've had a cup of tea.' She smiled as Tom, cheeks scarlet from the wind, ran to throw his arms around the neck of the old labrador who had risen from beside the Aga to meet him with wildly wagging tail. 'Joss?' Sharp eyed she caught sight of the tears on Joss's cheeks before her guest bent to release the baby from the cocoon of blankets which kept him warm. 'What is it? What's happened?'

'Nothing.' Holding Ned close Joss shrugged. 'Lyn thinks I'm hurting them, Janet.'

'She what?'

'She thinks I'm battering the children.' She sniffed hard. 'Look at Tom's arm.'

Janet stared at her for a moment, then she went across to Tom and the dog. 'Here Tom Tom, let me take your coat off, then we'll find the bicky tin.' Pulling off the little boy's jacket and gloves, she pushed up his sleeves. On his left arm was a series of bruises which looked exactly like finger prints. She swallowed hard. Pulling down the sleeve she straightened and went to find him a biscuit. 'Most for you and only a tiny tiny bit for Sim, Tom. He's getting so fat.' She handed the boy a piece of shortbread, then she glanced at Joss. 'That wasn't an accident.'

'No.' Joss spoke in a whisper.

'If it wasn't you, who could it have been?'

'Not Luke.'

'Of course not Luke.'

'Not Lyn. Oh, Janet, she adores him.'

'Then who? And don't tell me that a ghost did that, because I won't believe it. That was done by a real person, Joss. Come on, think. He must have been playing with someone. What about that Jimbo boy who helps Luke? His mother and sister were both a bit strange. Have you ever left Tom with him?'

Joss shook her head. 'That happened last night, Janet. Luke helped me bath him. Those marks weren't there then. And when Lyn dressed him this morning, there they were.'

'And she thought you'd done it?'

'I'm the only one who goes to the children at night.'

'Joss –' Janet plonked the biscuits down in front of her

on the table and caught Joss's two hands in a warm firm grip. 'Is there any possibility you could be sleep walking?'

Joss stared at her. For a moment she hesitated. 'No. No, of course not.'

'You don't sound entirely certain.'

'Well, how can I be? But surely, Luke would have heard me? He'd know.'

'Yes, I suppose he would.' Climbing to her feet again Janet went to lift the heavy kettle off the stove. 'OK. Let's think of something else.' She poured boiling water into the teapot. 'What does Tom say?'

Joss shrugged.

Janet looked at her sharply. 'You have asked him?'

'Not this time.'

'Oh come on, darling, you can't not ask.' Janet went down on her knees in front of the little boy who was gamely trying to save some of his biscuit, now a soggy remnant of crumbs from the labrador's enthusiastic lick. 'Go on, give it to Sim. You'll have to have another one. You can't eat it after he's woofed it!'

Tom giggled. 'Sim's woofed it!' He was delighted with the word.

'And you can woof the next one. So, Tom Grant, you look as if you've been fighting a war. Who did this to you then?' She pulled the little boy's sleeve back again gently.

Tom half glanced at it, his attention still on the dog. 'The tin man.'

Behind them Janet heard Joss make a strangled sound that was half gasp and half sob.

'And when did this nasty old tin man do this?' she asked cheerfully.

'At bed time.'

'Why didn't you call your mummy and daddy when he came?'

'Did.'

Tom pulled another biscuit from the tin she was holding and broke it in half.

'But they didn't come?'

'No.' He shook his head.

'Why not?'

'Don't know.'

'What did the tin man do?'

'Hurt Tom.'

Janet bit her lip. 'Did he try to pick you up?'

Tom nodded.

'But you didn't want to go?'

Tom shook his head.

'Why not?'

'Don't like him.'

'Tom, what does he look like? Is he big and tall like Daddy?'

Tom thought for a moment and the dog, taking its chance neatly removed the biscuit from Tom's grasp. Tom smiled impishly at Janet. 'Sim wants 'nother one.'

'Sim's a greedy pig. Tell me about the tin man, Tom.'

'Like Daddy.'

'And what does the tin man look like?'

'Cat food.'

'A cat food tin?' Janet stared at him then she looked up at Joss, suppressing a giggle with difficulty. 'Are we talking a bed time story here?'

Joss shrugged. She was smiling but her face was very white. 'Tom, tell Aunty Janet about the tin man's face. What does he look like? Has he got a beard like the milkman?' Their milkman's beard fascinated Tom who took every opportunity – of which there were mercifully few – to tug it.

Tom shook his head.

'Does he wear a hat? A big tin hat?'

Tom shook his head again.

'Once he gave you some of Georgie's toys. Has he ever given you anything else?'

Tom nodded. 'Flowers. Prickly flowers. Tom pricked myself.'

'Joss, what is it?' Pushing the tin of biscuits into Tom's arms, Janet climbed to her feet and went to Joss who had sat down abruptly at the kitchen table and put her head into her arms.

'Roses. White roses.'

'Right.' Janet was suddenly brisk. 'I don't believe what you're telling me, but whatever it is, I don't like it one bit. You are not going back to that house. I want you to stay here. All of you. There's loads of room. We'll go and collect some stuff when you've got this cup of tea inside you, and then we're all coming back here. Understand?'

Joss nodded weakly.

'Would you like that, Tom?' Janet gave him a hug. 'Come and stay with Sim?'

Tom nodded. He glanced at Joss. 'Tom have Sim's puppy?' he said hopefully.

Janet laughed. 'Not a chance, old son. Poor old Sim is not the puppy-bearing type.' She glanced back at Joss. 'Drink.'

here was no sign of Luke as the two women entered the kitchen at Belheddon. In the courtyard, where they had left Janet's Audi, the coach house was locked and in darkness.

Joss frowned. Normally by now Lyn would be cooking supper, but there was no sign of any preparation. 'I'll go and see where they are.' She pushed Ned into Janet's arms. 'Tom, you stay here. Show Aunty Janet how well you can ride your horse.'

The great hall was in darkness.

'Luke? Lyn?' Joss's call seemed indecently loud to her own ears. 'Where are you?'

The house felt empty. One of the bulbs in the wall light by the door had gone out and the other one gave a weak light which scarcely reached the far wall as she switched it on. The wind was moaning gently in the chimney as she reached the bottom of the stairs and peered up into the darkness.

'Katherine!' He drew her towards him gently. 'My little love. Come, I won't hurt you.' He cupped his hands around her breasts and kissed the nape of her neck, then expertly he began to undo the lacings of her gown.

Naked she turned to him, her body young and firm, her skin as white as milk. She did not shrink as he pulled her nakedness against him; her eyes were strangely blank.

As he kissed and groaned and sweated she gazed slit-eyed into the distance.

She was listening to the echoes.

Joss could feel the small hairs on her forearms pricking. 'Lyn? Are you up there?'

Her voice sharpened. 'Lyn?' She groped for the light switch and turned it on.

He was there. She could feel him, and this time he was not alone.

Immobile, with one hand on the banister, she waited a few more seconds, trying to force herself to put her foot on the bottom step – then she turned and ran.

In the courtyard she stood taking deep breaths of the frosty air, trying to steady the panic churning inside her.

'Joss?' Janet's voice from the doorway was sharp with alarm. 'Joss, what is it?'

She shook her head, not trusting herself to speak, hearing Janet run towards her, feeling Janet's arms round her shoulders, shivering so much she could not think as she turned and buried her face in Janet's coat.

The headlights of Lyn's car cut a swathe across the darkness before it turned through the archway and came to rest, focused full on them.

'Joss, where the hell have you been?' Lyn threw herself out of the car. 'Luke and I have been frantic. Where are the boys?'

Joss stood transfixed by the beam of the headlight unable for a moment to speak and it was Janet who answered. 'The boys are here. They're fine.' The calmness of her voice cut through the icy wind. 'Nothing is wrong. We wondered where you were.'

'I told you I was taking them for a walk, Lyn.' Joss moved at last, stepping out of the lights. From the darkness she stared round, no longer blinded. 'Where's Luke?'

'He went across the fields after you.'

'But why? You knew where I was going.'

'I knew you were going for a walk. Hours ago. In broad daylight. Joss, for God's sake, you had two tiny children with you!'

'I told you I was going to Janet's,' Joss interrupted firmly.

'No. No, Joss, you didn't. You said you were going for a walk along the cliff. A walk in the sun. Couldn't you have rung from Janet's when you found yourself there? It was too much trouble, wasn't it! And now I see Janet had to bring you home.' Leaning into the Mini to turn off the engine and the lights she could see for the first time Janet's car parked in the darkness.

There was an awkward silence. Janet frowned uncomfortably then she cleared her throat. 'I offered to bring them back if Joss stayed to have a cup of tea with me, Lyn. If you want to blame anyone, then blame me. Where is Luke now, by the way?' Behind her Tom appeared in the doorway. He stood for a moment on the step and then jumped off it, running to Janet and sliding his hand into hers.

'He went after her.' Lyn slammed the car door.

'When?' Joss swung round, and stared out through the courtyard arch into the dark gardens.

'Hours ago.'

'So, where is he now?'

'I don't know.' Lyn shook her head wearily. 'He never came back. Why do you think I got in the car and started driving round? I've been up the cliff lane and down to the village. There's no sign of him.'

'Was it daylight when he left?' Joss grabbed her sister by the shoulders. 'It's dark now, Lyn. I went over to

Janet's hours ago. So where is he now?' She could feel a sour churning in her stomach.

The only light now came from the lamp in the back hall, spilling out in a pale wedge into the thick darkness. Silhouetted in the light were Janet and Tom, hand in hand, their shadows, one small, one tall, stretching over the cobbles almost to Joss's feet.

'Come in, Joss.' Janet's voice was clear in the silence. 'And you Lyn. There's no point in standing out here and freezing. I'm sure Luke's OK. He's probably arrived at the farm by now and is trying to work out where we all are. Come on.'

After a moment's hesitation Lyn turned away from Joss. Stooping she swept Tom up into her arms, detaching him from Janet and disappearing into the house.

Janet waited. 'Joss?'

'He's out there, Janet. In the dark.' Joss couldn't keep the terror out of her voice. Quotes from David's letter kept nudging into her head 'John Bennet . . . walking in the garden at Belheddon . . . was confronted by something . . . his sanity, already unhinged by the death of his son, completely deserted him . . . he remembered running into the darkness . . . Something . . . a figure, at least seven feet tall . . .'

Janet reached out and put her arm around her again. 'Joss –'

'He's out there, Janet. Can't you feel it? In the darkness. Watching us?'

'Luke, you mean?' Janet followed her gaze, but could see nothing.

'No not Luke. Him. The devil. The monster that haunts Belheddon.'

With a sigh Janet shook her head. 'No, I can't feel him. I can't feel anything. I'm too cold. Come in and have a cup of tea –'

'He's looking for Katherine.'

'Who's Katherine?' Janet's voice sharpened. 'Joss, for goodness' sake!'

'He kills everyone who stands in his way.' Her stomach churning, her legs unsteady, Joss clutched at Janet's hand. 'We have to find Luke. Janet, you have to help me.'

The latch on the gate was jammed. Frantically she scrabbled at the ice cold metal, trying to lift it. 'Janet!'

'Joss, I don't think this is a good idea.' Janet was beginning to feel the fear. It was contagious. She looked round as a sudden icy wind ruffled her hair, listening to it swirling through the branches of the chestnut trees, and wishing, just for a moment that it would stop so that she could listen in the silence. 'Joss, let's go inside. It's silly to go out there. We don't know where he is and we'd never find him in the dark.'

The latch had lifted at last with a metallic click and the gate swung open. Above them the half moon swam high behind a veil of streaming cloud. It gave enough light to see the leaf strewn lawn as a paler grey in a monochrome world. Running onto the grass Joss stared round – beyond the moon dusk the shadows were black and unyielding, hiding everything and nothing.

Janet stepped beside her and caught her arm again. 'Come inside, Joss.' She spoke more urgently than she intended. 'Please.'

'He's out there, Janet.'

'No he isn't.' Janet wasn't sure whether they were talking about Luke or – or who? She felt another cold wash of fear drench her shoulder blades. 'Joss, the children need you. You must be there for them. You have to pack and come back with me. Now. I have a feeling that we'll find Luke waiting at the farm when we get there.'

'I suppose so.' Joss was still hesitating. As she stared out into the shadows there was a movement near them and she tensed feeling her heart flip somewhere under her ribs. For a moment she could see nothing, aware that Janet was staring at the same spot, then suddenly Janet's cheerful laugh broke the silence. 'It's Kit and Kat, look!'

The two small cats hurtled out of the darkness, tails at right angles to their bodies, intent on a fast and furious game of chase culminating in a huge leap which took both animals high in the air before they disappeared into the wintry rose beds on the far side of the lawn.

The tension was broken. Without a word Joss followed Janet back into the courtyard and watched as she fastened the gate behind them. Seconds later they were in the house.

Janet flung herself down at the table and put her head in her hands. 'If you offered me a black coffee I'd probably say yes.'

Without a word, Joss went to put the kettle on.

Janet rubbed her face with her hands. 'What was that all about, Joss?'

'I told you.'

Janet looked at her searchingly for a moment then she stood up and went to the phone. 'I'll call the farm. Maybe Luke is there. He knows where I hide the key.'

She let it ring for a couple of minutes before hanging up. 'Of course, he may not have gone in when he found we weren't there.'

'He isn't there, Janet.' Joss stared down at her hands, aware that they were shaking. 'He's out there, somewhere.'

Like John Bennet. Like her father.

'Get the children's things, Joss.' Janet stood behind her, giving her shoulders a quick massage, a firm reassuring pressure.

Nodding, Joss stood up, ignoring her strange reluctance to leave the house which clung to her like a sticky, entrapping net. 'Lyn must have taken the boys upstairs. I'll pack a case. Do you want to wait here?'

Janet shook her head. 'Perhaps I'll come too. Give you a hand.'

The kitchen, always so warm and welcoming, seemed very safe as they opened the door into the hall. The draught, sweeping under the front door was icy.

The two women hurried across the great hall towards the staircase and, not giving herself time to think Joss led the way up. Lyn was in Ned's room, changing his nappy. Tom, in his own room across the narrow passage had tipped his playbox on the floor and was happily stirring the resulting mess.

'Lyn, I'm taking the children over to Janet's for a couple of days.' Joss bent to pick up a small jumper from the floor. It was there again; the reluctance to leave; the certainty that it would be easier to stay.

'You're welcome to come too, Lyn,' Janet smiled at her as Lyn looked up from the baby, a tin of talcum in her hand.

'It would be nice if you would come,' Joss went on without enthusiasm. 'Or if you want to take a couple of days' break so you can go and see Mum and Dad, I know they'd love that.'

Lyn went back to her task, deftly folding and taping before replacing Ned's jumpsuit and sitting him up. 'Is Luke back then?' She swung the baby onto her shoulder.

Joss shook her head. 'There's no sign of him.' She bit her lip. 'Lyn, exactly what time did he go out?'

'About an hour after you.'

'And you haven't heard anything from him since at all?'

Lyn shook her head. 'He probably got thoroughly pissed off looking and went down to the Swan.'

Joss gave a faint smile. 'I wish I believed that.' She glanced at Janet. 'I can't go till I know he's safe. I'm going after him. Watch the children, Lyn. Don't let them out of your sight.' She reached over and planted a kiss on Ned's head then she turned and ran out of the door.

'Joss!' Janet called after her. 'Wait. I'll come with you!'

'No. Stay and watch with Lyn. Don't leave the boys.' The words floated over her shoulder as she took the stairs two at a time and disappeared.

Lyn looked at Janet and pursed her lips. 'She needs a rest badly.'

Janet nodded. 'It will be good for her to have a bit of a break. This house is getting to her.' She glanced round with a shudder. 'Do you think there really is something here?' Her voice had dropped to a whisper.

Lyn smiled. 'Of course not. Simon says it's a touch of post natal depression. He seems to think she's doing too much. He obviously doesn't realise who does all the work round here. If anyone needs a rest it's me.' Her voice was tart. She laid Ned in his cot and tucked the blanket over him.

'You're going to leave him up here on his own?' Janet stood back out of the way as Lyn whisked round the room, tidying powder and nappies into neat piles.

'I'll put on the baby alarm. He'll be all right. If he cries we'll hear him, and Tom Tom can come downstairs for his tea now. She'll probably be hours, then she'll be even more worn out when she gets back.' Lyn gave a deep sigh. 'It's not easy to work for your own sister, Janet –' she paused. 'Adopted sister, I should say. We are not allowed to forget our station.' She banged a drawer shut.

Janet frowned. 'You know, I think you do her an injustice if I may say so. She loves you like a sister.' She gave a sudden snort. 'I should know. I've got three and we all fight like cat and dog half the time. But that doesn't mean we don't love each other dearly. All for one and one for all if anyone comes between us. Don't underestimate the strain all this has been on her, Lyn. Finding her family and this house have been an enormous emotional shock. You and your parents are probably doubly precious to her. You are there for her, and always have been. Her real mother ·is something out of a dream which has, I suspect some pretty nightmarish qualities.'

Besides, there is something frightening about this house. She stopped herself saying it out loud in time. 'Come on. Let's feed this young man, then when Joss comes back we can pop them all in the car and I'll take them back to the farm for a few days.'

She glanced back through the door into Ned's bedroom. He was lying in his cot gurgling happily. She could see his arms waving in the air. Air which had grown suddenly strangely cold.

The beam of torch light was very thin as Joss ran across the lawn towards the gate. To her right the black water of the lake reflected the frosty starlight, glittering between the darker patches which was where the water lilies, soggy and submerged with the heavy autumn rains barely broke the still surface. As she walked silently through the frosted grass a squawk and sudden rush of wings and water showed where she had disturbed a roosting duck.

The gate was swollen and hard to open. Pushing it with all her strength she let herself out into the lane and stopped, flashing the torch in front of her. The hedges, newly slashed by a hedge trimmer, showed raw torn spikes of white wood. In the distance an owl gave a series of sharp quick cries as it floated on silent wings over the field.

She swallowed, gripping the torch more tightly. Luke would have assumed that she would go down the lane as far as the footpath towards the cliffs and then follow it across the short rabbit cropped turf to where the land dropped sharply towards the beach. It was one of her

329

favourite walks, easy to manage, even with the buggy, and led round in a wide circle either back to the house or if one took another path across the newly planted winter wheat to the back of the farm. The whole walk was, she supposed, about three miles. She shivered. It was bitterly cold and the night seemed very quiet. Gritting her teeth she began to walk briskly forward, shining the torch to right and to left into the hedges and down into the deep ditches which lined the lane.

'Luke!' Her voice was thin and lacked strength in the immensity of the silence. 'Luke, are you there?' He could have fallen, twisted his ankle – or worse. He could be anywhere along the route. She stopped, shining the torch down into the ditch where it widened between the angle of two fields. Drainage pipes deep beneath the black newly ploughed soil were pouring water beneath the mat of nettles and bramble making the ditch sound like a fiercely running river. As she walked slowly on, the torch light picking out the coral pink berries of a spindle bush at the corner of the lane, she heard the indignant metallic shout of a disturbed moorhen on its roost.

'Luke!'

Her boots were uncomfortable on the frosted ridges of the lane. 'Luke, where are you?'

She swung round suddenly, flashing the torch behind her. Her heart had started thumping wildly. But there was nothing there.

How far from the house would he – it – travel? She swallowed, standing still for a moment, listening carefully.

'Luke?' It came out as a whisper now.

Suddenly she was running, the torch light flailing in front of her as she slid and stumbled, turning onto the footpath across the grass.

She was panting violently when she reached the edge of the cliff. Standing still she stood staring down at the sea. The tide was high. In the patchy moonlight she could see the water, a slate-coloured heaving mass, silently shifting immediately below her. There was no beach to be seen. The tide was as high as she had ever seen it. Raising her eyes she looked out towards the horizon. She could see the lights, a long way off, of a huge North Sea ferry moving purposefully and at surprising speed towards Harwich. For a moment she was comforted at the thought of the huge vessel, with its crowds of passengers and steadily beating engine, then she became aware once more of the immense expanse of the sea around it and she found herself shivering violently again.

The path was so easy to see on the cliff top that she switched off the torch, walking quickly on the short grass. She could see a long way and there was no sign of another human being. Or anything else. She was conscious of a sudden soreness on her lips and she realised she had been biting them in the cold wind. She could taste the sharp salt of blood on her tongue. 'Luke!' The call was fruitless. Stupid. A waste of her voice, but the sound of it comforted her as she trudged on.

She switched the torch on again when she came to the mid field path, following the frozen mud track over the newly sprouted winter wheat, on up the hedgerow and towards the old orchard at the back of the farm. She was miles from Belheddon Hall here. Surely there could be no danger. No danger other than the normal hazards of the track. The torch wasn't so bright now. She flashed it ahead into the grey tangle of old apple boughs.

'Luke!' Hoarse with exhaustion she felt hot tears well up suddenly in her eyes and splash down onto her cheeks. 'Luke? Are you here?'

There was no reply. Behind her, on the field a flock of pewits called to each other, gossiping in the starlight which was suddenly as bright as day as the clouds rolled back.

ith Tom settled in his chair with a plate of Marmite sandwiches, Lyn sat down at the kitchen table opposite Janet.

'Lyn, don't underestimate Joss's worries about the children.' Janet hesitated. 'Not all her concerns are imaginary, you know.'

'The ghosts, you mean.'

Janet nodded. 'This house has a reputation for strange happenings – a reputation which goes back hundreds of years. I don't think they should be completely written off.' She smiled, half apologetically. 'There are more things in heaven and earth and all that.'

Lyn raised an eyebrow. 'I think it's all rubbish. I don't believe in ghosts and I never have. What you see is what you get in this world. And this world is it. Nothing else afterwards.' She got up and going to the tap drew herself a glass of cold water.

'And you can see no possibility that you might be wrong?' Janet spoke mildly, hoping her rising antagonism didn't show.

Lyn shrugged. 'I may not be as well educated as Joss, but I know enough to realise that religion is no more than glorified crowd control. It's brainwashing on a vast scale. Wishful thinking. Man is so arrogant he can't believe he can just stop being.' She sat down and put her glass down in front of her. 'You will have gathered that I'm a bit of a cynic.'

Janet gave a wry smile. 'Just a bit.'

'Joss, besides being over educated in my view, is also a bit hysterical.' Lyn sighed. 'Something which is obviously hereditary judging by all this stuff her family have put in their letters and diaries. And of course the village believed them. Everyone loves a good ghost story. So do I, as long as one remembers that that is all it is. A story.'

'So, you're not worried about Luke.'

Lyn shrugged. 'I'm a little worried I suppose in that he has been gone a hell of a long time. But I don't think he's been attacked by ghosts and demons. And I don't think Joss will be either. I would hardly have let her go off on her own if I thought there would be any danger out there.'

'No, I don't suppose you would.' Janet's voice was a little bleak. 'Obviously a few days' change of scene will benefit Joss and the boys, though, don't you agree?'

Lyn shrugged. 'I suppose so. Anyway, I'd be glad of a break, to be honest. It all gets a bit incestuous round here – the atmosphere is dreadful sometimes.'

'The atmosphere between Luke and Joss?'

Lyn shook her head. 'Not exactly. Just Joss and her theories, I suppose. She believes it all so passionately I sometimes think she could make it happen by sheer will power.' She glanced up suddenly, her head to one side. 'Is that someone at the door?'

Janet felt a small shiver of apprehension. She glanced over her shoulder. An icy draught swept through the kitchen and then stopped as suddenly as it had come as the outer door was banged shut.

'Lyn, has she appeared yet?' Luke stood in the door-way, still in his jacket. His gaze took in Janet and then Tom, earnestly stuffing bread and Marmite into his mouth and his expression softened. 'I see she has. Was she with you, Janet?'

Janet nodded. 'I'm sorry. It all seems to have been a misunderstanding.'

'And where is she now.' He stripped off his jacket.

'She's gone to look for you.' Lyn stood up, automatically reaching for the kettle. 'She thinks the ghost has got you.'

'Oh my God, not that again.' Sitting down he gave a deep sigh.

'Luke,' Janet leaned forward on her elbows. 'Listen, please don't dismiss everything Joss is saying out of hand –'

'The trouble is, you encourage her!' Luke shook his head. 'The last thing she needs if you don't mind me saying so, is local gossip egging her on in these wild fantasies of hers. There is nothing wrong in this house. There is no danger to the children and there never has been. It's all in her head. A story. Make believe. A romantic fiction she's concocted, with herself as the lead heroine. Don't you see, Janet? It's all part of her background. Adopted. A dreamer, bless her. Suddenly fact seems to be even better than any fiction she ever dared invent for herself and it's all got out of hand. Just leave her alone and she'll get over it.'

'She was thinking of taking the children over to Janet's for a few days, Luke,' Lyn put in quietly. 'To get away from the atmosphere here.'

'No!' Luke banged his fist on the table. 'No, Janet, it's kind of you, but absolutely not. I'd be grateful if you'd just leave her alone.'

'It's for her to decide, Luke, surely.' Janet spoke as calmly as she could.

'No. It isn't. Not in this case. This is a matter between her and me.'

'But –'

'Janet,' he stood up abruptly. 'Please, don't think me rude, but I'd be grateful if you could leave us now. It's time for Tom to go to bed. Please allow Joss and me to work this out for ourselves.'

Janet stared at him open mouthed. Slowly she pushed back her chair. She took a deep breath. 'Very well. If that's the way you want it. Poor Joss.' She glanced at Lyn who had gone very pink. 'Take care of them all. Tell Joss I'm there if she needs me.'

No one spoke until she had gone. 'That was very rude, Luke,' Lyn said mildly. 'She's a nice woman.'

'She is sometimes an interfering busybody.' He stood up. 'I'm going out to check the garages are all locked up for the night.'

Lyn sat for several minutes after he had gone, then with a sigh she stood up and turned to Tom. 'Ready for your drink, young man?'

Pulling the carriage house door open Luke stood staring at the bonnet of the Lagonda. In the light of the fluorescent strip which ran down the ceiling of the garage the pale blue paintwork gleamed softly. Folding his arms across his chest, he sank into deep thought, listening as the sound of Janet's Audi died away in the distance.

'Luke?' Joss's voice was hesitant. 'Luke, is that you?' She had appeared at the gate of the courtyard.

He sighed. 'It's me.'

'And you're all right?' Her chilled hands fumbling with the latch she pushed the gate open and came towards him. 'Oh, thank God! Luke, I thought something awful had happened to you!'

'Which is exactly what I thought about you earlier.' He put his arms round her and held her close. She was shivering violently. 'Why on earth didn't you say you were going out for the entire afternoon?'

'I did. I'm sure I did.'

He smiled ruefully. 'Well, never mind. You're all back

and safe now.' He pushed her away gently. 'Come on, let's go back indoors. Lyn will be getting the supper on.'

'Where's Janet's car?' Wearily Joss looked round.

'She's gone.'

'Gone? But I was going over there. I was taking the boys –'

'I told her it was a bad time, Joss. I need you here.' He took her hand.

'Luke!' She pulled away from him. 'You don't understand. I have to get them away from here. I have to.' The net was closing; she could feel the lethargy, the reluctance, the pull of the house like a huge magnet, holding her close.

'No, darling. You don't. I think it's time we got this quite straight, don't you. An awful lot of what has been going on has been totally in your imagination. You have to admit it. Lyn and I are here to help you. There is no threat – none at all – to the boys. This ghost business is just so much hysterical rubbish on the part of people like David and, let's face it, Janet herself. Come on. Let's go indoors. We'll talk about it after supper.'

'Luke –'

'Later, Joss. Come on. It's bloody cold out here. Let's go in.'

He pulled the carriage house door shut and clicked the padlock into place then he held out his hand. Reluctantly she took it.

The kitchen was very warm after the frost outside. Tom, surrounded by toys was playing on a rug in front of the television, half heartedly watching Pingu whilst Lyn was peeling potatoes. She glanced up as they appeared. 'At last. The whole family together. If you're going upstairs, Joss, you might look in on Ned. He sounds a bit restless.' She dug her peeler energetically into a deep eye.

336

Joss stared at her. Then she turned and ran from the room.

There was a single lamp on in their bedroom. Tearing off her jacket she threw it down on the bed before hurrying towards Ned's little nursery. There was no sound from him now, just the soughing of the wind in the bare branches of the creeper outside the windows. She pushed open the door.

'Ned?' she whispered. She crept towards the cot. 'Ned?'

He was lying on his stomach, his small fists clenched on either side of his head.

'Ned?' She bent over him. He was very still. In sudden panic she pulled back the covers. 'Ned!'

Her sharp cry woke him with a start and he jumped. As she gathered him up into her arms he was screaming indignantly.

Lyn was in the room in seconds, with Luke just behind her. 'Joss, what is it? Is he all right? We heard you on the baby alarm.'

'He's fine.' Joss cradled him gently in her arms, soothing him. 'I didn't realise he was asleep, that's all and I woke him up, poor little darling.' She was shaking like a leaf.

Lyn noticed. She glanced at Luke, then she held out her arms for the baby. 'Come on, Joss. You're cold and tired. Why not have a hot bath while I get supper? I'll take this young man and put him back to bed.' She took Ned and gave a grimace. 'I'll change him quickly first. Go on. No arguments. Have a nice bath. Get Luke to bring you up a drink.'

Laying the baby down on his changing mat she began to strip off his pyjamas. Joss was just leaving the room when she heard Lyn's sharp intake of breath, hastily swallowed. She stopped and turned, in time to see Lyn pointing to Ned's arm. 'What is it? What's wrong?'

'Nothing, love. Ned's had a bit of a bash, that's all. I

337

expect he's knocked his arm against the cot.' Lyn was frowning.

'Let me see.' She was frantic.

'No need. Nothing to worry about. Hardly a mark.' She pushed her gently out of the room and Joss found herself staring at the closed door.

Exhausted, defeated and cold she was suddenly too tired to argue. Walking slowly back into their bedroom she kicked off her wet shoes and began to unfasten her jeans. Running hot water into the huge old fashioned bath she tipped in some bath oil and stood in front of the swiftly steaming mirror, slowly brushing her hair. How had Ned got bruised? Had she done it, when she pulled him out of the cot? It was quite possible. She had been in such a panic. Or had something else been near him. Something, or someone. Her knuckles whitened on the hairbrush. Putting it down she unbuttoned her shirt and pulled it off. Then her bra. Her breasts were still heavy and blue veined; she surveyed them miserably through the condensation before turning to bend over the bath, stirring the water with a hand which still tingled with cold.

Katherine

The sound had mingled with the rush of water in her head. For a moment she didn't react. Then slowly, she turned off the taps. The skin of her back was crawling. Not looking round she groped behind her for the towel on the rail, her fingers flailing in the air till at last they connected with it. Grabbing it she pulled it off the rail and whisked it round her.

Katherine

It was louder this time, easy to hear above the drips from the taps. She backed away from the bath. Wraiths of steam hung in the air, condensing on the walls. The water was growing cooler already as she stood with her back to the wall.

It was stronger again. No possibility of it being her imagination. She stared round wildly, clutching the towel round her breasts.

'You give her to me, but she does not love me!' The king stared in anger at the woman who stood so arrogantly before him. 'I did not want a whore, madam. You promised me love in exchange for my adoration! I take her to my bed and she lies like a wax doll in my arms!'

Turning to pick up the goblet of hot wine he did not see the woman tense at his words, nor the expression of feral cunning which flitted across the strangely golden eyes.

'Joss? Can I come in?' It was Luke's voice that brought her out of her panic-stricken daze. She flung herself at the door and slid back the bolt.

'Why on earth did you lock it?' He had a couple of glasses with him. 'Come on. I thought I'd talk to you while you have a soak. Lyn's getting supper and Ned is fast asleep.' He grinned at her then, as he noticed her white face his smile died. 'What's wrong?'

'Nothing.' She shook her head. She was trying desperately to get a grip on herself. 'Nothing's the matter. I'm just much tireder and colder than I thought.' She took the glass, sipping at the white wine gratefully. 'Sit yourself down and talk to me.'

With him there she would be safe. Glancing round in spite of herself, she dropped the towel and hopped into the bath, lowering herself with a groan into the steaming water.

'Better?' Luke was watching her carefully. He could see clearly the signs of strain and agitation. Closing the lid of the loo he sat down on it and leaned forward, elbows on knees, studying his wife. She was still very beautiful, her body already more or less recovered from the birth; the only sign was a wonderful voluptuousness of breasts and belly which he found a great turn on. Leaning forward he put a hand gently on her breast. 'Nice.'

She smiled sleepily, submerging beneath the viscous bubbles, feeling the water and Luke's presence comforting, reassuring. Closing her eyes she reached up to touch his hand. 'You're sure Ned was OK?'

'He was OK.' His voice was calm but he frowned suddenly. The bruises on Ned's arm had definitely been the marks of fingers. 'Here.' He lifted her glass and passed it to her. 'Drink.' Slipping onto his knees beside the bath he pulled up his sleeve and putting his hand into the water he ran his fingers down and over and round her breasts, feeling the slipperiness of the bath oil on her skin, gently massaging and rubbing, sliding his hands on down over her belly.

She took a sip of wine, giving a quiet groan of pleasure. 'Does it matter if we're late for supper?'

He smiled. 'Not in the least. Lyn is putting Tom to bed. I said you'd look in later and say good night, but we both know he'll be asleep by then.' His hand was still moving rhythmically over her breasts making little choppy waves in the bath water.

'Luke –'

'Sssh.' He bent over and kissed her on the lips. 'Am I going to get in there with you?'

She giggled. 'We'd never fit.'

'Then you'd better get out.'

'I don't want to. It's cold out there.'

He laughed. Standing up he pulled the heap of towels from the towel rail and spread them on the floor. 'Come on. You won't feel cold with your husband to keep you warm.' He was pulling at his belt, sliding it through the loops, unzipping his jeans, then suddenly he swooped and she felt his arms slide under her. 'Luke, you'll strain something!' She smothered another giggle as he heaved her out of the bath and laid her dripping on the heaped towels. Kneeling astride her he leaned forward and pressed his lips on hers.

Katherine gazed up at him and smiled. Her arms went round his neck and her lips, soft and sweet as cherries, seized greedily on his.

'My love,' she murmured. 'My king.'

With a groan he caught her to him, his hands running over every inch of her body, his tongue greedily questing over her face, her neck, her breasts, glorying in her heat and in her passion.

His cry of triumph and possession hung in the rafters above the bed and rang around the shadowy spaces of the house.

Contentedly Joss put her wet arms round Luke's neck, pulling him closer. 'Love you,' she whispered. She opened her eyes sleepily, revelling in his warmth, running her tongue over the roughness of his cheek, gazing unfocused into his eyes. 'Luke, I want to take the children away tomorrow,' she whispered. 'Just for a few days. Please.'

He frowned. She felt his body tense. 'Joss –'

'Luke. Please. Humour me.' He was on the same side as the house, wanting to keep her there – not wanting her to go. She reached up to nibble his ear. It had she realised become suddenly very cold in the bathroom. She had begun to shiver in spite of the warmth of his body above hers.

He had lifted his head to look down at her and she saw the anger in his eyes. 'Joss –'

'Please, Luke.'

She reached across him to pull at one of the towels,

trying to cover her legs. 'I'm getting cold, Luke.' She was shivering so violently her teeth had begun to chatter. Suddenly she found it difficult to breathe. His weight on her was intolerable, pressing on her chest. Panicking, she pushed at him violently. There was something over her face, pushing over her nose and mouth, an invisible weight, pushing her into the floor. With a violent wrench she threw Luke off her and staggered to her feet. Running over to the window she threw it open, leaning out into the icy wind and taking deep gasping breaths of air.

'Joss?' Luke's voice behind her was sharp with concern. 'Joss, what on earth is it? What's wrong?'

She couldn't speak. The stone of the mullions was freezing against the skin of her breasts, her fingers were locked onto the ivy-covered sill. She gave a great wheezing gasp, followed by another. 'I'm sorry . . . couldn't breathe . . . I need a drink, Luke . . . water . . .' It was pressing in behind her now – the sense of someone close to her – breathing down her neck, closer, pressing against her. Luke had grabbed her glass of wine from the rim of the bath. Chucking the contents into the foamy water he ran to put it under the tap and brought it to her. Wrapping her dressing gown round her naked shoulders he pushed the glass into her hand. 'Here. Drink this.'

She turned and took it in shaking hands. The figure standing behind Luke was absolutely distinct. A man – taller than Luke, and older, a man with anguished blue eyes and greying fair hair, a man with fury and pain etched into every angle of his face. As she met his eye he raised his hand towards her, then as she watched he dissolved into the steam of the bathroom and in a few seconds he had gone.

The wine glass slipped from her fingers and crashed to the floor. Slivers of glass scattered round her bare feet but she didn't notice them. She stared over Luke's shoulder for several seconds in shocked disbelief.

'Joss? Joss, what is it?' Luke swung round to look where she was staring. 'What is it? What's wrong? Are you ill?'

She couldn't speak. He had been so real. So clear. The figure that had been only shadow and a sense of oppression to her before had shown himself clearly in all his pain and anguish and she had made eye contact with him. He had been real. For those few brief seconds he had been as real to her as Luke was now. Blinking hard she stared round, aware for the first time of the icy wind blowing in through the opened casement.

Somewhere outside the shriek of a fox rang out of the darkness. Luke leaned past her and pulled the window closed. 'Come on, Joss. Into the bedroom. Let's get you warm. Mind your feet, there's glass everywhere.'

He pulled the towel round her again, and put his arm round her shoulders.

'We have to go, Luke. Now. I have to take the children away.' She grabbed his shirt and made him face her. 'Luke, you have to understand. The children are in danger.' She pushed past him and ran through into the bedroom, treading on a piece of glass which sliced diagonally into her toe. Grabbing at her dressing gown she pulled it on properly. 'Call Lyn. Tell her to help us. We'll take them over to Janet now. Luke. Don't look at me like that, for God's sake! Do it!' She slid her bleeding foot into a slipper and pushed her hair back off her face. 'Quickly. Don't you understand? He has become strong enough for me to see him! The boys are in danger.'

She ran through into the hall and stood outside Tom's room, staring in. The little boy was asleep, the night light burning steadily on the table by the window. 'Let him sleep, Joss.' Luke came up behind her and peered through the door. He put his hands on her shoulders. 'Come on, love, you're overwrought. Let it be. Come to bed and I'll get you some supper.'

The shadow was there again – by the window in its usual place. Her mouth went dry; she stared, not daring to take her eyes off it. It was moving. Moving towards the child's cot. She could see the shape distinctly now – a man's shape, a tall, broad-shouldered man, his figure bulked grotesquely by some kind of breast plate beneath the flowing cloak.

'The tin man!' She didn't realise she had spoken out loud. She turned and caught at Luke's arm. 'Look! You don't believe me? Look, for God's sake! Get him. Get Tom before it's too late!'.

Luke put his hands on her arms. 'Joss –'

The shadow was closer now, nearly at the cot. It was bending – reaching out . . .

With a scream Joss flung herself into the room. She could feel it – a solid presence between her and Tom. Frantically she reached into the cot and grabbed the small boy by the arm. Hauling him out bodily she flailed out at the figure behind her. 'Go away! Leave us alone! *Luke*!'

Above Tom's screams she could hear Luke's voice, but she couldn't reach him. The figure was between her and the door. In her arms, Tom's cries were piercing. Across the landing she could hear Ned crying too.

Clutching Tom against her chest she tried to run towards the door. Something was holding her back. Something was trying to snatch Tom from her.

'Joss!' Lyn's voice reached her through the screams. 'Joss, give him to me!'

Lyn was there somewhere. Lyn was trying to help.

She stared round frantically fighting her way through the blue folds of the swirling cloak, feeling a mailed hand on her arm, the fingers biting into her flesh as she clung to the screaming child.

She was losing him; she could feel her hold slipping. The strength of the man was too much for her. 'Luke!' Her frantic sob was drowned by Tom's screams as he was

344

wrenched from her arms, and then suddenly it was all over. The figure had gone.

Joss collapsed on the floor sobbing. 'Tom . . .'

'I've got him, Joss.' Lyn's voice was tight with fear.

'Take Tom downstairs, Lyn, and get in the car. Now.' Luke was standing over Joss. He pulled her to her feet. 'What the hell were you playing at? You nearly killed that child! I saw you do it! I *saw* you! What the hell is the matter with you, Joss? You should be in hospital. You're not fit to look after the children.' His voice was shaking. 'Lyn's right. I should have listened to her weeks ago. I'm sorry, darling, but I'm not taking any more risks. I'm taking the children. Now. Do you understand? Are you listening to me, Joss?' He caught her arms and dragged her round to face him. 'I'm sorry, darling. I know you're not yourself. But I can't risk this happening again.'

'Luke?' She was staring at him. 'Luke, what are you talking about –'

He stared at her, then with a sigh he let her go. 'I suggest you have a good night's sleep. Then if you've any sense you'll ring Simon in the morning and get him to sort you out. Once I've got the children away safely I'll come back and we'll decide what to do.'

He strode out of the nursery and across into Ned's little bedroom. Scooping a pile of clothes and nappies into a bag he lifted the screaming baby out of his bed. 'Go to sleep, Joss. Have some rest. We'll sort this out tomorrow.'

'Luke!' She was standing staring at him in bewilderment. 'Luke, what are you doing?'

'I'm taking the children away, Joss. Now. Before you hurt one of them really badly. I didn't believe Lyn. I wouldn't let her ring Simon. But she was right. It was you all along.'

'Luke –' Her knees had turned to cotton wool. She couldn't run after him. All the strength had drained out of her. 'Luke, wait –'

For a moment his face softened. 'I'll come back, Joss. Later. When we've taken the boys to Janet's. I promise, darling.'

Then he had gone. She heard his footsteps, running down the stairs and then there was silence.

'Luke.' It was a whisper. She stared round the empty nursery, the silence somehow more shocking after the noise of the children's screams. The flame of the night light flickered a little and steadied. Her own shadow, humped and grotesque in the candlelight crouched against the wall near the cot, huge and menacing. She stared at it in confusion, hugging her dressing gown round her. In her left slipper the blood from her cut foot oozed steadily through the soft sheepskin, staining it red.

'Luke?' The small, querulous cry of protest had no strength. 'Luke, don't leave me.'

She heard the sound of the car clearly. Outside in the drive the headlights arced across the frosted trees for a moment and then they disappeared in the direction of the village.

Tom's favourite teddy bear was still lying discarded in the cot. He would never get to sleep without it. Picking it up Joss stared down at the silky brown fur and small beady eyes. It was wearing a yellow knitted jumper. Hugging it to her she sank to her knees and began to cry.

It was some time later that the pain of the stiffness in her legs made her move. Staring round the room she realised the night light was flickering, the wick only a fragment in the last liquid drops of translucent wax. Still clutching the teddy bear she dragged herself to her feet and made her way back into the bedroom. The house was bitterly cold. She could hear the wind now, knocking the creeper against the windows. There was a hollow moaning from the chimney. Outside, the clouds were building and it was beginning to sleet. Her slipper was

346

stiff with dried blood and her foot hurt. Making her way towards the door she went out onto the landing.

At the top of the stairs she stopped and looked down. They had turned the lights off; the great hall was in darkness. She swallowed, her right hand clinging to the newel post at the top of the banisters, listening to the wind howling in the huge chimney. It was very cold downstairs. They hadn't lit a fire in the vast fireplace for days and the chill of the autumn nights had penetrated deep into the room. She took a deep breath and put one tentative foot on the stairs, hearing the protesting creak of the oak. Her heart was thudding so loudly she could feel it in her ears. It made her feel dizzy, disorientated. She took another step down, the landing light throwing her shadow down before her. There was something lying on the stairs a few steps down in the shadows. She frowned. The others must have dropped something in their hurry. She took another step, staring at the soft glow of the polished wood on the step. It was white. A rose bud. She stood still, clinging to the banisters, staring at it, bile rising in her throat.

'Leave me alone,' she whimpered into the darkness. 'Do you hear me? Leave me alone. What have I done to *you*?'

There was no reply.

She took another step down, still holding onto the wooden hand rail as though her life depended on it, and stepped carefully round the rose. Its scent was sweet and delicate, reminding her of early summer. She took another step, sliding away from it warily, and then another and another. A gust of wind hit the house and she felt the chimney shudder with the strength of it. Another two steps and she would be able to reach the light switch, illuminating the great hall, throwing gaunt reflections back from the glass, cold behind undrawn curtains.

Katherine. I'm here, Katherine

One more step. Her hand reached out, the fingers grasping for the switch.

Katherine. Sweet lady, don't die. Wait for me, Katherine. Why did your mother not send for me, Katherine? A pox on her for her hatred and her scheming

The light came on with a sharp click and she stood, her back pressed against the wall, staring out into the room. A dusting of ash had blown out of the hearth, scattering across the stone flags. On the polished table the chrysanthemums which Lyn had picked a week earlier in the garden had wilted, their petals showering in a ring of sticky pollen.

I curse the child that killed you, Katherine. Would that it had died instead of you. Come back to me, Katherine, love of my life and my destiny . . .

'Stop it!' Joss shook her head, pressing her hands to her ears. 'Stop it!' The words were there, hammering inside her skull, echoing strangely without form. 'Stop it! Leave me alone!'

She took a step out into the room, shivering violently, her hands crossed tightly across her chest. Opposite her the door into the main hall seemed a life time away. She took another step, afraid to run as though it might provoke some kind of pursuit. Another gust of wind; a movement in the hearth caught her eye, and she stopped again, staring at it as a shower of white rose petals floated gently into the room from the chimney and settled on the flags. In the kitchen the two cats, cuddled together in their basket awoke suddenly, their fur on end, and fled as one across the kitchen floor and out of the cat flap into the wind and icy rain.

'No.' She bit her lip. 'No, please.' Only another few steps and she would be through the door down the hall and into the kitchen, then out of the house. She took another step, her eyes straining into the corners of the room, then at a sound behind her she whirled round.

The door of the study had slipped off its latch and swung open as with a violent crash the French windows, not properly shut last time they had been used, flew open onto the garden. Wind and rain lashed through the room as the doors were hurled back against the wall. Running back she stared round in despair. Sleet was pouring into the room, soaking the carpet. She raced to the window and wrestled the doors shut, then switching on the desk light she locked them and pulled the curtains closed, out of breath with the effort. The papers from her desk were scattered across the room. She surveyed them miserably – the manuscript of the book, notes, letters, some of her mother's things – all strewn across the carpet, some of them near the window, soaking wet. She left them. Running back to the door she stopped dead.

The figure was standing in the doorway to the great hall, huge and clear as he had been in the bathroom. There was no armour now. He was dressed in black and purple, his dark blue cloak swinging from his shoulders as he raised a hand towards her.

Her reaction was reflexive. She turned and wrenching open the nearest door, that of the cellar, she dived through it, taking the steps three at a time into the darkness. Sobbing she fled across the first cellar out of the diagonal light thrown down the steps from the hall and into the total darkness of the second. Crawling behind the empty wine bins she pressed herself against the cold damp bricks and held her breath.

The cellar steps creaked. Moaning, she crouched smaller, hiding her head in her knees, her arms clutched round her. She could feel him near her, his presence like an electric charge in the darkness.

Katherine. Come to me

'No.' She had stopped breathing. She could smell the roses – their scent filled the air round her.

He was close to her now, having no difficulty finding her in the darkness, seeing not a strange woman hiding amongst the wine bins of a twentieth century cellar but the love of his life, lifeless on a bier – lifeless until he could breathe life into her with his love and tear the child from her, the child that had stolen her life.

Katherine

He put out his hand to touch her hair, scattering around her the rose petals they had used to pack her coffin. She was moving. She was alive, the wraith he had seen flitting through the house, the woman who was so like his dead Katherine that he had grown confused. One more time. Make love to her one more time and waken her with the sheer force of his passion.

With a groan he gathered her against his chest, pressing his cold lips against hers.

Katherine!

She could feel the strength of his arms around her, the enveloping, stifling softness of the velvet wrapped around her, pinioning her arms, sapping the last of her resistance.

Katherine!

His breath on her cheek was icy, his fingers as they began to open her dressing gown felt like those of a frost-rimed statue in the centre of a winter fountain.

'No.' Joss's pitiful whisper was no more now than an exhalation of breath. Katherine was there; Katherine was inside her head. Her stomach knotted with fear and lust, she was looking out of Katherine's eyes.

'Edward! My lord!'

His hands were on her breast now, his kisses raining on her throat, her breasts, her belly. *'Sweet child, you are alive.'*

She couldn't move. Paralysed at first with fear, she could feel tremors of excitement coursing up her legs and into the muscles of her belly. Her breath was coming in short, shallow gasps. Her dressing gown had fallen completely open and now there was nothing between them: the soft velvet and the brocade and the silk had all gone. All she could feel was the hard urgency of his flesh.

Looking down into Katherine's eyes, Edward of England smiled. Gentleness was forgotten. This was his sweetheart, his woman, the mother of his child, the love promised and paid for in a pact with darkness.

Holding her wrists tightly in his massive fists he kissed her again, enjoying her feeble struggles, knowing the fear in those brilliant blue eyes would turn soon to a lust and passion to match his own.

Katherine!

With a shout of triumph he entered her warm flesh and sank his face, sobbing, into the dark silken halo of her hair.

30

'Joss?' Luke walked into the kitchen and stared round. The room was silent. Kit and Kat were curled up on the rocking chair near the range, a mass of black and white and orange fur. He sighed. She must have gone to bed. He had left Lyn and the children at Janet's, and from there he had phoned Simon, then he had climbed once more into the car and driven back through the lashing sleet.

With a sigh he reached for the whisky bottle out of the cupboard and poured himself a small measure which he drank straight down neat. Putting down the glass he walked through into the great hall. Behind him Kit and Kat, scampering down the hall after him stopped in the doorway. Their game forgotten in an instant they turned and fled, their fur on end, their tails bushed. The light was on and Luke stared round. There was ash all over the floor where the wind had blown back down the chimney.

'Joss?' He strode across towards the door and looked out into the hall at the foot of the stairs where the lights were on as well. The door into the study was closed. Pushing it open he stared in. The room was a mess with paper all over the floor and the desk, the carpet soaked. He walked across to the window and pulling back the curtain stared out through the glass. The door had obviously been opened. Was Joss out there? But the key was in the lock on the inside. Turning he surveyed the mess again for a minute, then he ran out of the room and raced upstairs, two at a time. 'Joss? Where are you?'

On the rug in Tom's bedroom he could see slight traces of blood. Was she hurt? His stomach turning over with fear he stared round, but there was no other sign of Joss; nor in either of the boys' bedrooms. He did a quick search through Lyn's and then on up to the attic. She was nowhere to be seen.

Cursing himself for leaving her alone he walked back downstairs and into the study once more. It was only then that he spotted the teddy bear, lying on the floor behind the door. She must have dropped it. He knew they hadn't taken it with them – it had been a matter of extreme distress to Tom when he found Ted had been left at home.

'Joss?' He felt the stirrings of unease again. 'Joss, where are you?'

He walked out again to the foot of the stairs. It was very cold there. He shivered, glancing round again. In the great hall, in the shadow of the minstrel's gallery it was very dark. He could hear the wind in the chimney. For some reason the house felt strangely sinister. No wonder Joss was afraid. He sighed. Turning he looked back upstairs.

If she wasn't in the house that left the gardens and – his mind shied away from the idea – the lake. It was as he was turning to walk away that his eye caught the cellar door. Surely earlier that day it had been closed and locked? They were so careful about locking it.

The door was slightly open, the cold draught playing round his ankles in the hall undoubtedly coming up from the cellar stairs. 'Joss?' There was a tight knot of fear in his stomach as he pushed the door wide. 'Joss, are you down there?' He leaned in and clicked on the electric light, peering down the staircase. It was very cold; he could see the dull gleam of condensation on the bottles nearest to him. Reluctantly he put his foot on the first step. 'Joss?' It was too silent.

He stopped, about to turn back, then on second thoughts he went on down. She was not in the first cellar. He ducked through the arch into the second one, remembering the fear he had felt the first time he had set foot down here. He could hear something now. It sounded like someone laughing. He swung round. 'Joss?'

The laughter stopped suddenly, as though cut off by a knife.

'Joss? Where are you?' It hadn't been her voice, he was sure of that. It sounded more like children. 'Joss?'

The silence was tangible. He could feel the small hairs on the back of his neck stirring. 'Who's there? Come out. I know you're here somewhere!'

He stepped further into the cellar, firmly trying to push the thought of Joss's little dead brother out of his mind. 'Joss! Is that you?'

It was shadowy in here. The single bulb, suspended from the vaulted ceiling did little to illuminate the end of the wine racks and the bins on the far wall.

Slowly he moved towards them and his gaze was suddenly caught by a dark shadow on the floor in the corner. 'Joss? Joss, oh my God!'

She was there, wedged between two of the bins and she was still wearing her dressing gown. It had pulled open and he could see her white breasts, her bare legs, her slipper half off, encrusted with dried blood.

'Joss!'

She did not move.

'Joss? Dear God, are you all right?' He was beside her on his knees, feeling for a pulse. Her skin was ice cold and she appeared to be deeply unconscious; the pulse when he found it was faint and irregular, fluttering beneath his finger like some tiny thing which could die at any moment. 'Joss! Hang on, my love.' He didn't dare move her. Pulling off his jacket he laid it over her, then he ran for the cellar steps.

He nearly collided with Simon in the great hall.

'Sorry. I did ring the back doorbell, but no one heard so I came in.'

'Simon. Down here. In the cellar. She's unconscious. Oh God, I shouldn't have left her! I was so stupid! I just wanted to get the boys away from her –'

Simon frowned as he followed Luke down the stairs. 'Did she fall down the stairs, do you think?'

'I don't know. If she did, she managed to crawl a long way before she collapsed. Look, she's through here.'

Simon pushed past him. Like Luke he felt for her pulse, then gently he ran his fingers down her neck and arms, feeling her bones. 'I don't think anything's broken. There is just this massive bruise on her forehead. It looks as though she caught it on the corner of the wine rack here, do you see?' He continued his examination. 'I don't think she's had a fall, Luke. It looks more as though she was trying to hide here – see how her hand is clasped round the side of this bin?' He loosened her fingers with some difficulty. 'Just to be on the safe side I won't try and move her. I'll call an ambulance.' He glanced up. 'Run up and get some blankets so we can keep her warm until it gets here.' He reached into his pocket for his mobile phone. 'Go on, man. Hurry.'

'Luke?' Joss opened her eyes slowly. 'Luke, where am I?'

He was sitting by her bed in the small, darkened room off the main ward. The only light came from a lamp on the table in the corner.

'You're in hospital, love.' He stood up and came to her. 'How are you feeling?'

She frowned, screwing up her eyes. 'I've got a headache.'

'I'm not surprised. You've got an awful bump on the head. Do you remember how it happened?'

She lay for a minute, staring at the opposite wall, her concentration fixed on a small print which showed a bluebell wood in spring, then at last she shook her head. Her mind was a total blank.

'I think you fell down the stairs.' He took her hand and pressed it, drawing up a chair near her with his foot. 'We found you unconscious. Oh, Joss, I'm so sorry. We shouldn't have left you alone. I feel dreadful about it.'

'The boys?' She gave a deep sigh, her eyes still closed. 'Are they OK?'

'They're fine. Lyn is with them at Janet's.'

She smiled. 'Good.'

'Joss?' He paused, looking down at her exhausted face. 'Do you remember anything about what happened this evening?'

For a moment there was no response, then she gave a small groan.

'Does that mean no?' He squeezed her hand.

'That means no.' It was a whisper.

'Do you want to go to sleep, Joss?'

There was no reply. When Simon looked in some twenty minutes later Luke was still sitting by the bed, holding her hand. He looked up.

'She came to for a few minutes, then she fell asleep.'

'Did you call the nurse?'

Luke shook his head. 'There wasn't time.'

'Was she lucid?'

'Sleepy. She didn't seem to remember what had happened.'

Simon nodded. He reached for her hand and took her pulse again. 'There is bound to be some concussion after a bang like that on the temple. Luke, can I suggest you go home and get some sleep yourself. I doubt she'll wake again before morning now, and if she does the hospital will take care of her. Come again tomorrow. Not too early, OK? Provided there's no real structural damage to that poor old head of hers – and we're pretty sure there isn't, the duty psychiatrist will pop in to see her tomorrow morning. We need to find out what she was doing in the cellar – why she fell – if she did. And we have to get to the root of the other problem with the children. It's far more common than you may realise in women who have given birth reasonably recently – there is a tremendous strain, you know, and if the hormonal system is not quite running as it should it can just tip someone over into doing things they would never in a million years do under normal circumstances. As the boys have you and Lyn to look after them, I'm quite sure that at this stage we can sort this out in the family. So, don't worry.' He walked over to the window and looked out across the darkened car park towards the sleeping roofs of the town. 'I might suggest, Luke, that you find somewhere Lyn could take Tom for a while so that Joss can have a complete rest. Joss has more or less stopped breast feeding now; she's told me that Ned has begun to sleep through the night, so she might consider letting him go too. I don't want to separate her from him, of course, unless she agrees, but we'll have to take the advice of the psychiatrist.' He turned. 'Is there somewhere Lyn could go? Grandparents perhaps?'

Luke nodded. 'Both sets would have them like a shot. But Joss –'

'Joss may need a complete rest, Luke. I'd like her to get away from that house for a bit. From what you've told me, it is the root of her problems. She's had a tremendous emotional shock, you know, inheriting that place and all the history that goes with it – and with the birth so soon after you moved, she hasn't really had time to adjust. I

357

think a couple of weeks in the sun might do the trick. Any chance you could arrange that?'

Luke looked gloomy. 'Money's a bit tight. I could probably manage something.'

'Well.' Simon folded his stethoscope. 'Just give it some thought. We can all discuss it tomorrow when we see how she is.'

The psychiatrist, bearded, grey haired, and gentle, sat on her bed, sharing her grapes as he talked. He pulled no punches. 'A touch of what we call puerperal psychosis, I think.' His calm voice was strangely comforting in spite of the intimidating words. 'From what your husband and your GP say and from your own story, I'd say that's the problem. It can make you imagine all kinds of very frightening things.' He glanced at her from under bushy eyebrows. 'Very frightening.' He paused. 'You are sure you can't remember what happened to make you go down into the cellar?'

Joss shook her head. There was a wall in her mind – a wall of impenetrable blackness – a wall behind which she did not want to look.

He waited, watching her thoughtfully, the silence drawing out between them.

'No.' She shook her head again, as she spoke at last. 'No, I can't remember.'

He nodded. 'Well, as I said, I've spoken to your GP and your husband and they both feel very strongly that what you need is a bit of time away from everything.' He thought for a minute. 'I'm going to give you some tablets and I'm going to let you go away for a few days with your husband.' He paused and then went on carefully, 'I think your doctor mentioned to you the possibility of leaving the children behind. How do you feel about that?'

Joss shook her head. 'Not happy. Of course, not happy, but Lyn would look after them, I suppose. I . . .' she hesitated. 'I do want to rest. To sleep.' To feel safe. She didn't say it out loud, but the fear was there, lurking; the fear in the house. She closed her eyes, letting her head fall back onto the pillow.

He was watching her closely. He couldn't decide whether she was suppressing the memory of what had happened to her consciously or not. Or was it just that she didn't want to tell him. On the whole he thought it was a genuine amnesia, induced by shock. The interesting thing would be to find out exactly what had caused it.

He stood up, tweaking the bedcover straight behind him. 'So, enjoy your break. And I shall need to see you as soon as you get back. Just to see how you are.'

'Paris?' Luke stared at her in astonishment.

He had expected protests at the thought of leaving Tom and Ned, refusal to leave the house, not this sudden almost feverish desire to cross the Channel.

'We needn't go for very long. The doctors are right. It's just what I need.' She had been reluctant to leave Ned and Tom with Lyn, but the suggestion that Lyn take the boys to Oxford to stay with the Grants had mollified her. She knew how much Tom adored his Granny Liz and their big house could easily absorb three visitors and two small cats, where the small terraced house in London where the Davieses lived would have bulged uncomfortably however much Alice and Joe would have loved to have them.

'I suppose we could afford it with the wine money.' Luke smiled. 'The only real problem is time. We've promised the Lagonda by the end of next month and there's a little Austin Seven coming in next month too but if I can persuade Jimbo to keep things ticking over while we were away I reckon we could do it. Yes. Why not? It would be fun.'

31

Putting down the telephone David sighed. He had been trying to phone Belheddon for three days. Where were they all? He paced up and down his small study once more, glancing at the piles of books and notes on his desk. There was so much information here. So much to tell Joss. Frustrated, he stared down at the notes he had been making that morning. He had planned to go down to Belheddon over half term and now he couldn't raise them. Time was so precious when you were tied to a job like his.

He made up his mind in the time it took to pace towards the door and back to the window – four large steps, that was all. He would go down there anyway. Joss had to know what he had discovered. She had to know it as soon as possible.

The coach house door was standing open when he turned under the arch and brought the car to a rest near the kitchen door. He could see the lights on and hear from somewhere deep inside the raucous beat of heavy metal being played on something the tone of which left a lot to be desired. Rather apt, he thought with a wry grin as he climbed out of his car and made his way towards the noise. 'Hello? Luke? Anyone at home?'

The radio was switched off abruptly and Jimbo appeared from the back of the garage, wiping oil off his meaty forearms. 'Hello Mr Tregarron.' He gave a grin.

'Jimbo. Where are Luke and Joss?'

'They've gone to France.'

'France?' David stared at him in shock. It had not crossed his mind that they might not be there at all.

'Went two days ago. Joss had a bit of a fall. She hadn't been well so they thought they'd get her away for a break.'

David was shocked. 'What happened? Is she all right? My God, I didn't know!'

'She's OK. They'll be back at the end of the week.'

'I see.' David felt deflated. His shoulders slumped. He hadn't realised just how much he had been looking forward to seeing Joss again. 'And Lyn and the children? Are they still here?'

Jimbo shook his head. 'They've taken the cats with them and gone off to stay with Mr and Mrs Grant. Somewhere near Oxford, I heard.'

'That's a bit of a blow. I was hoping to stay a couple of days.'

'I've got the keys if you want. Don't s'pose they'd mind if you use the house.' Jimbo turned to the work bench which ran down the side of the coach house and rummaged amongst his tools. He produced a bunch of keys. 'Wouldn't do no harm for the place to have some heat on. They asked me to keep an eye on things, but I haven't been in.' He folded his arms with a gesture of finality.

'I see.' David hesitated. 'You don't have a phone number for them, I suppose?'

Jimbo shrugged. 'I was told if there was a problem to get in touch with Mr Goodyear at the farm.'

'Right.' David glanced over his shoulder towards the back door. He felt strangely reluctant to go in on his own.

'Supposing I have a brew up. Would you like to come in and get some coffee?'

Jimbo shook his head. 'I'd as soon stay out here.'

'Right,' David said again. 'Fair enough. I'll go in and have a look round then.'

He put his hand out for the keys. As he turned towards the back door he felt Jimbo's eyes following him. The young man's expression was far from reassuring.

The kitchen was ice cold. The range was out and the room was unusually tidy. He flicked on all the lights, wondering if they had an electric kettle. If they didn't he would have to fire up the stove and wait while the heavy iron kettle boiled. He scowled. The weekend was not turning out quite as he had hoped.

By the time he had made the coffee and carried a mug out to the coach house Jimbo had gone. He stared at the padlocked doors in disbelief then reluctantly he turned back towards the house.

He established a base camp in Joss's study, clearing her notes and manuscript into meticulously arranged piles on the floor under the table, well out of the way and spreading out his own material in its place. He had had only a brief struggle with his conscience about whether he ought to stay in the house uninvited as he was. But he had been given the keys by Jimbo who was, it seemed, in charge, however unlikely that appeared to be, and he was after all Ned's godfather which made him almost a relation, and he was certain had Joss been there that he would have been made welcome. Whether Luke would have been quite so welcoming he did not consider quite so closely.

He sat down at Joss's desk and began to read through his notes. First thing in the morning he was planning to visit the church. There were several things he wanted to check against the brasses and plaques, but until then he wanted to get a feel of the house.

362

He glanced up at the fire which had been left ready laid. It was crackling merrily, already throwing warmth into the room. His researches seemed to prove that the original house had been built on the site of a Roman villa; the building as it stood was certainly a substantial manor house in its own right by the early fifteenth century, probably a hundred years before that. It was the fifteenth century he was interested in, however. And in particular the reign of King Edward IV.

He ran through the dates again in his head. Three times, Edward had come to East Anglia in 1482. On two of those occasions Belheddon was mentioned by name and on the third by implication. David had made a chart of the king's movements. It was exactly nine months after his last visit that Katherine de Vere had died. For two weeks in the month of her death he had visited Castle Hedingham. In the previous year he had spent several weeks at Belheddon and in the year before that two visits of a week each. Katherine's marriage he was prepared to bet had been arranged by the king's command to give the king's bastard a father. The poor young man had not lived to enjoy his rather dubious honour; within months he had died. Of natural causes, or at the hand of a jealous man who could not bear to see his mistress as another man's wife? Probably they would never know.

David sat for a moment, staring out of the window. All those facts were, near enough, just that: fact. He had guessed perhaps at motive, and he had certainly guessed that the child that had killed Katherine was the king's but the rest was the stuff of record. The remainder of his researches had moved well beyond the realms of what was acceptable to a serious historian. He found himself smiling, alone as he was, in something like embarrassment. This was the matter of Margaret de Vere and her witchcraft. That she was accused was fact. That she had been arrested twice was fact. That she and the women accused with her were guilty as charged was something dismissed as rubbish by historians. The women had been framed by the supporters of Edward's brother, Richard. But. He ran over the facts again. The first time Margaret was arrested, it was by Edward's orders, shortly after a visit by him, to Belheddon Hall. There was no question then of her being framed by anyone – unless it was by Edward himself and why would he want to frame (and by implication get rid of) his hostess, the mother of the young woman he loved? Unless she opposed him. But surely it made no sense at all to oppose a match, even one on the wrong side of the blanket, with the king himself? No ambitious woman of the period would do that if she were in her right mind.

Unless she really was a witch.

He had trouble with this. Big trouble. Witchcraft could not be real. Or could it? Feminists always thought accusations of witchcraft were macho-male-misogynist politically inspired, didn't they? Witchcraft either did not exist at all and was drummed up as a charge by these fearsome women haters, or, it was a harmless, indeed benevolent remnant of some pre Christian paganism dating from a Golden Age which had never existed, but which antagonised a male-macho-etc Christian hierarchy.

Supposing neither was true? Supposing the witchcraft as practised by Margaret de Vere was real, effective and as malevolent as popular myth described it?

He gazed into the warm, cheerful depths of the fire and wished Joss were here. He would like to argue this out with her. Without her acerbic comments to keep him in line, he was floundering deeper and deeper into a mire. Could Margaret have killed and/or cursed King Edward IV? and could that curse, effective five hundred years later, still be blighting the house where she had uttered it? The thought which haunted him, one that had arrived unbidden as he lay sleepless one night in his London flat mulling over the problem was a simple one. Did Margaret de Vere kill her daughter's baby by the king? And had the curse, raging out of control, threatened every boy baby to be born in the house ever since?

He shuddered. Not the best thing to think about if he was going to spend the night alone in the place. Not the best thing at all.

He stood up and went to stand near the fire, stooping absent-mindedly to throw on a log. It was very quiet without the others there. He stared down into the flames, watching them lick greedily over the wood. Quiet and somehow brooding. He gave himself a mental shake. He did not believe in ghosts, nor the power of the occult. It was an intriguing theory, but one based solely on the superstition and gullibility of its audience. It might – would – have worked in the fifteenth century. It could still work presumably in the twentieth but only by association; it relied on rumour and fear and ignorance to give it energy. He turned his back on the fire, massaging his backside in the warmth. Yet Joss believed it. She was neither ignorant nor gullible, nor, as far as he could remember, superstitious. He frowned. She was, though, a woman with two small children and through them desperately vulnerable.

The sound of scuffling in the hall was very small. He hardly heard it above the crackle and hiss of the fire. Stiffening, he listened, every ounce of his attention fixed, not conscious before just how twitchy he had been. He felt the sweat start out on the palms of his hands. It couldn't be the cats. It was his imagination – or at worst, mice.

Cautiously he tiptoed away from the fire towards the door, listening as hard as he could, cursing the fact that the dry log he had thrown on was crackling and spitting merrily and noisily behind him. He put his hand on the doorknob and waited, his ear to the panelling. Nothing. There was no sound. He stood there for a couple of minutes before gently beginning to turn the knob.

The hallway outside was in darkness. He frowned. Had he forgotten to turn on the light? Of course, it had not been dark when he came into the study. The early dusk of November had fallen swiftly and like a blanket across the garden. Pushing the door wide so the light from the study fell across the floor he took a step forward, his hand raised towards the light switch.

The scuffling came from above him this time, on the broad staircase, where it swept round out of sight into the darkness. It took all his resolution not to dive back into the study and slam the door. Instead he took another step forward and turned on the light then he looked up. Silence. His back to the wall he listened, frowning. He had the very strong impression that there was someone up there, sitting on the stairs, just out of sight.

'Who's there?' His voice sounded shockingly loud. 'Come on. I can see you.'

There was a suppressed gurgle of laughter – a child's laughter and then he heard the thud of footsteps as someone ran on up the stairs. He swallowed hard. Children from the village? Or Joss's ghosts. He licked his dry lips, not moving. 'Sam? Georgie?' This was ridiculous. All he was proving was that he was as superstitious and gullible as the next man when it came to spending a night alone in a haunted house. 'Come on, Tregarron. Pull yourself together.' He spoke under his breath. 'You've got to go up there. You've got to search the place. Supposing they're thieves. Or vandals!' He did not move. His limbs seemed anchored to the spot. Behind him the study was warm and welcoming. His coffee was getting cold. Cautiously, a step at a time he retreated into the study, leaving the lights on, and pulled the door closed. Mug in hand he went sheepishly to the telephone and picked it up. The Goodyears were in the phone book.

'I didn't realise that Joss and Luke were away. I feel a bit of a fool – here on my own – I wondered if I could ask you both over for a drink. I'm sure they won't mind.' He glanced at the windows, seeing his own reflection, upright, tense, on the edge of the chair, staring back at himself in the glass. He should have drawn the curtains at once, before he phoned.

'Oh, I see.' He tried to keep the disappointment and fear out of his voice as Roy explained that they were going out. Laughing, he brushed off Roy's apology. 'Not to worry. Next time perhaps. No, no. I'm going back to town early tomorrow. Good night.' He replaced the receiver with a shaking hand. Getting up he went to the curtains and pulled them across, then he wandered over to the desk and stood looking down at his meticulously written notes.

Georgie!

He looked up at the door, shocked. The voice had been so close. So clear.

Georgie!

He clenched his fists. They're only children. They can't hurt me.

What am I saying. They don't exist.

His mind was whirling into activity now. Superstitious nonsense. Idiot. Ignoramus. I don't believe this.

Slamming his notes into a pile he strode towards the door and threw it open. There was no one there. Moving swiftly towards the stairs he ran up them two at a time and reached for the landing light. 'Where are you?' His voice was stronger now. 'Come on. I want you out of here.' He strode into Joss and Luke's bedroom. It was tidy, strangely impersonal without them there, and empty. Swiftly he headed for the door, searching Ned's little room, then Tom's. Both were empty. He went into Lyn's

367

next, then not giving himself time to think he ran on up towards the attics, searching the two spare rooms, then pausing at last before the door which led through into the empty rooms. Surely there was no need to search those? Too right there is, he lectured himself furiously. Don't be a fool. Pulling open the door he hesitated, staring into the darkness. There appeared to be no light switch here. Perhaps there were no lights. He could smell the slightly damp, cold smell of emptiness and disuse, and at last he conceded defeat. He closed the door again and turned back to the stairs.

A small painted wooden car lay discarded on its side on the top step of the staircase. He stared down at it, his arms and back crawling with fear. It had not been there a few moments before. If it had been he could hardly have avoided seeing it. He would have fallen over it. He stared down at it in horror, then overcome by curiosity he bent and picked it up. It was about four inches long, and two inches high, crudely made and painted a bright blue, though the paint was worn and chipped. He turned it over in his hands, then slipping it in the pocket of his jeans he ran on down the stairs, leaving all the lights on behind him.

In the kitchen the stove had heated up enough to put something in the oven. He rummaged through the freezer and found a foil wrapped package labelled steak and kidney pie. Heaven knows how one was supposed to cook it, but he supposed if he stuck it in the oven until it was done it would be all right. He put the whole thing, foil and all into a baking tin, put it in the oven and reached for Luke's whisky on the dresser. Then he pulled out the car. Standing alone on the kitchen table it looked shabby and forlorn – and distinctly old. Toys these days were made of plastic or metal; they were brightly coloured and non toxic. This looked as though it would be eminently toxic. The paint was flaking off even as he touched it. He frowned. Ghosts didn't have toys. Or did they, if they were little boys, trapped in a house where they would never grow up? He frowned, taking a deep swig of Scotch, hoping that Margaret de Vere, if she was guilty of witchcraft as charged, was having a really bad time in hell.

One of the books he had brought with him to show Joss was a history of magic in the middle ages. He had left it on her desk in the study. Putting down his glass he went to fetch it, gathering up an armful of books while he was there to bring back to the comparative warmth of the kitchen. It felt more comfortable there. He would read while he was waiting for his foil wrapped package to cook or self destruct depending on which happened first. Pouring another drink and slopping in some water he spread the books out and opened the book on magic.

Twice he looked up, listening. It was strange how the silence at this end of the house was companionable; not threatening. He felt safe here, even content, as slowly the smell of cooking steak and rich gravy began to permeate the room.

Procuring people's deaths by magic was a common enough charge in the Middle Ages; any sudden death was immediately suspect. With minimal medical knowledge and even less forensic what else was there to fall back on? He sighed, flicking through the book. He was right, wasn't he, in dismissing magic as nonsense? His gaze strayed to the little car on the table near him. Supposing Margaret de Vere had real power? Had she caused the king to fall in love with her daughter? Had she gone on, when her scheme had gone tragically wrong, to bring about the downfall of both king and bastard child? Was it possible? If so where had she got the knowledge from? Picking up the car, he turned it over and over in his hands as though seeking inspiration from the small wooden toy.

369

The legends of the devil at Belheddon went back into the mists of time. They seemed to predate Christianity. She must have known about them too. Was that where she had found her power?

He gave an involuntary shudder. Putting down the car he got up and went to the oven, pulling the baking tray out with hands padded with dish cloths. He examined his supper. Inside the foil there was a solidly frozen amorphous lump inside a gloriously rich mess of gravy and meat. The pastry appeared to have disintegrated into a soggy mess. He shrugged, pushing the whole lot back in the oven again. No doubt it would taste nice, whatever it looked like.

Did she conjure the devil? Did she swop her eternal soul for power? He wished he had paid more attention to the stories and legends which he had always dismissed as philosophical hogwash. He was beginning to feel grave doubts about all this.

On a sudden impulse he went to the dresser and pulled the phone book out from its position under the telephone. Edgar Gower's Aldeburgh number was listed.

The clergyman listened carefully as David spoke. He was sitting at his desk overlooking the blackness of the sea, twiddling a pencil in his hand. From time to time he made notes, frowning. 'Mr Tregarron, I think you and I should meet.' He shifted in his seat slightly so the reflections moved in the window. He was watching the lights of a fishing boat far out at sea, moving slowly up the coast. 'When will you next be coming up to East Anglia?'

'I'm here. Now.' David carried the phone to the table and sat down. The smell of steak and kidney was getting stronger and more mouth watering.

'Here?' The voice at the other end of the line had sharpened.

'I came up this morning. I'm at Belheddon.' He reached

370

out and put his finger on the roof of the little car, running it up and down the table.

'I see.' There was a long pause. 'You're there alone, I gather?'

'Luke and Joss have gone to Paris.'

'And the children?'

'I understand they're with their grandmother.'

'But not at Belheddon.'

'No. Not at Belheddon.' There was a moment's silence as both men had the same thought: Thank God.

'Mr Tregarron.' Edgar could no longer see the ship. 'A thought has struck me. If you would like to drive to Aldeburgh, we are only about an hour's drive away. It would be good to talk this over, and – ' he added casually, ' – you might like to stay the night here.'

David closed his eyes, overwhelmed by a rush of relief. 'That's good of you. Very good.'

The urge to abandon everything and leap into his car was very strong. It was his pride which stopped him. He would eat his supper, collect his books and papers and then check the house and turn off the lights before he left. He glared at the whisky bottle. He had probably had too much of the damn stuff to drive without some food inside him anyway.

The pie, though messy and in some parts disintegrated, was good. He ate it swiftly, with relish, straight out of the foil. Washing up his fork and glass he banked up the stove and then turned towards the door.

He forced himself to go upstairs first, turning off the lights, closing doors. The house was quiet, even benign. Checking Joss and Luke's room though was different. He stood for a moment in the centre of the floor, listening intently. The silence was heavy; almost tangible. There had been some sort of shift in the atmosphere. It was as if someone or something was watching him. He swallowed hard, heading for the door and clicking off the light he went out onto the landing. He could feel it there too: a brooding resentment, a chill which had nothing to do with the physical cold in the house.

Ignore it. Collect the books and go. He put his hand on the top of the banisters and looked down. In the bright cold light of the hall he could see the toys lying all over the floor. Cars, like the one he had left on the kitchen table; pieces of meccano, a pencil box . . .

'OK,' he spoke out loud, his lips dry. 'Point taken. I'm on my way.' It took an enormous amount of willpower to walk down the stairs, to step over the scattered toys, and go into the study. He looked round, expecting to see something in there as well, but the room seemed much as he had left it. The fire had died down and it was cold, but otherwise the room felt friendly, almost safe. He prodded the fire flat and put the guard in front of it to be doubly safe, then heaped his papers and books together into his arms. One quick glance round and he was ready. Switching off the light he closed the door behind him.

In the hall he hesitated for a moment, then stooping, he scooped some pieces of meccano and a car into his pocket. 'I'll bring them back, lads,' he said out loud. 'Just want to check something.'

The giggle behind him came from the staircase out of sight beyond the curve. He glanced up. He was not going to go up or run away. They were only kids. Kids teasing. They couldn't hurt him.

Could they?

Hesitating he glanced up again. 'So long, boys,' he said softly. 'God bless.'

Pulling the back door shut behind him he heard the dead lock click. He threw his books into the car and climbed in. It was only as he slammed the locks down that he realised he was shaking all over. It was several seconds before he could get his key into the ignition. As the car shot through the courtyard arch and out into the drive he glanced once into the rear-view mirror. The windows of the house were all once more blazing with light. Putting his foot on the accelerator he skidded down the drive and out into the road.

Mary Sutton stopped as she walked across the village green in the dark, returning home late after the bus had dropped her at Belheddon Cross, and she watched the car screech out of the gates of the Hall scattering mud and stones behind it as it turned west through the village. She gazed at its retreating tail lights until it was out of sight then she turned and thoughtfully studied the drive-way. The Grants had gone away, Fred Cotting, young Jimbo's dad, had told her that. The house was supposed to be empty.

It was a clear cold night and as she stood in the entrance gateway she could see the house in the starlight. The windows were dark now and uncurtained, the glass black; unreflective.

She hesitated, gripping the top of her capacious hand-bag very tightly with both hands. Little Lolly would have wanted her to keep an eye on the place. That was what Laura's brother Robert had called his little sister. Robert who had died, aged fourteen, falling out of that great chestnut tree which guarded the front of the house. She hadn't told Laura's daughter about those two boys, Laura's brothers. She could see that Jocelyn could barely cope with the idea of her own brothers' deaths.

Mary pursed her lips. Slowly she began to walk up the drive. She did not think the car which had left in such a hurry could have been a burglar's. No one in its entire history had burgled Belheddon Hall. No one dared. So, who had it been?

She stood on the front gravel staring up at the house, feeling the waves of emotion coming off it: the fear, the hate, the love, the happiness; feeling the blessing woven by little boys' laughter and behind it all the ice cold venomous evil which poisoned the very air itself.

Gripping her bag even more tightly she began to walk around the house. Every door and every window was locked, and at each she muttered a few words and traced the sign of the sealing, pointed star. Her powers were long unused, weak compared to those of Margaret de Vere, but her loyalty to little Lolly and her daughter was absolute. They would have whatever strength was left to her.

hey had picked up a taxi at Les Invalides two days earlier after an easy flight from Stansted to Orly and gone straight to their hotel near the Étoile. Joss was very quiet. Each time Luke looked at her she seemed more withdrawn and pale. By the time they had paid off the driver and found their room she looked as though she were about to collapse.

'Do you want to ring Mother and see how the boys are?' He sat down next to her on the bed. Outside the traffic was roaring down the street, tyres rattling over the pavé. They could smell coffee and garlic and wine from the café across the road opposite their window as their net curtains blew inwards on a strong draught. He stood up and went to close the window, then he sat down next to her again.

'So, what are we going to do?' He took her hand after she had made the call. 'They're well. They're happy, and they're absolutely safe so you have nothing to worry about except how we are going to amuse ourselves!'

Joss took a deep breath and as she let it out she could feel her tension dropping away. She was safe. The children were safe. Luke was safe. Outside the roar of traffic down the road, only slightly muffled by the closed window and its swathe of white net curtain was a comforting balm. Unexpectedly she threw herself back on the bed and stretched her arms luxuriously above her head. Later she would think about her mother's Frenchman, but now, just for a while, she needed to relax. For the moment Belheddon was very far away. She had escaped.

Luke looked down at her and smiled. 'Paris seems to be doing you good already.'

'It is.' She reached up to him. 'I think you and I should have a little rest and then, this afternoon do you know what I would like? To go on a *bateau mouche*. I haven't been on one since I was a child.'

Luke laughed. He leaned over her, kissing her forehead and her cheeks and then her lips. 'I think that sounds like an excellent plan.'

As his fingers moved expertly down the row of buttons on her blouse she tensed for a moment, but the black wall in her mind held firm and relaxing again she put her arms around his neck and abandoned herself to his attentions.

'It's strange how much better things feel in daylight.' David had produced the back door key and inserted it in the lock.

Behind them the coach houses were still shut fast. There was no sign of Jimbo, though it was nearly eleven in the morning.

'Darkness doth make cowards of us all,' Edgar commented tersely. In his hand was a black briefcase. 'I can't tell you how glad I am you came to us last night. It's strange but the subject of black magic and witchcraft has never really surfaced here before. Poor Laura and I never looked beyond the actual presence of malign influences. I know she was very conscious of the tragedy of Katherine but as far as I know she never suspected her or her mother of any influence on the house.'

He followed David into the kitchen which was warm and welcoming, the stove still banked from the night before.

Turning on all the lights David reached for the kettle. 'So, what happens now?'

Edgar frowned. He put his briefcase down on the table. 'While you make us a cup of coffee each I think I will have a walk through the house. Just get the feel of things a little.' He gave a grim smile. 'What Margaret de Vere did was probably not done openly and in public. It would have been done surreptitiously, in secret, without witnesses other than her accomplices if she had any. I may be able to tell where it happened.'

'She must have known she would be sentenced to death if she had been caught.' David reached into the fridge for a jar of ready ground coffee.

'Indeed. But I suspect she was confident in her allies. The devil is a powerful friend.'

David shivered. 'Let's hope the church is stronger,' he muttered. His fervent plea went unheard as Edgar disappeared into the passage.

Their meeting the night before had lasted long into the night after David's arrival in Aldeburgh. His books and papers were spread all over Edgar's desk in the window of his study, and as the night cleared and the stars appeared they glanced from time to time up at the uncurtained window to see the luminous blackness of the sea with its trails of silver and white as small uneven waves criss crossed the incoming tide. It was half past four before Dot had at last managed to chase them to bed, David in the attic bedroom which too looked out to sea, and only five hours later when she had woken them with cups of tea and toast. In twenty minutes they were on the road back to Belheddon. In Edgar's case was Holy Water, wine and bread, a crucifix and a Bible.

*　　*　　*

The great hall was very cold when Edgar walked into it. He stared round, shivering. Outside there was brilliant sunshine, and the low November sun was slanting in at the windows, throwing patches of warm light on the flag stones. He saw the dead flowers and frowned. Bad vibes. He grinned to himself. There were things that even his New Age dotty daughter could teach him and vibes was one of them. Vibes mattered. He walked through to the study, stepping over the scattering of toys on the floor at the foot of the stairs and pushed open the door. Sunlight filled the room. It was warm and welcoming. He felt a quick surge of anger. This was such a beautiful house. A home. A family home for hundreds of years and yet it was blighted – blighted by the spite and greed of one woman if David's theory was to be believed. A woman who had used her daughter to lure a king, who had conspired to have the king sleep with that daughter and who, when she found he was not prepared to abandon his wife to marry the girl, used her evil arts to cause her death and probably his as well.

He stood thoughtfully in front of the fire. She had been very powerful, Margaret de Vere, if they were right. She had enlisted the help of the devil, and somehow her viciousness had survived the centuries to threaten the occupants of the house to this very day. He went over in his mind the things he would do. The rite of exorcism was powerful. He had done it here before when he had been licensed by the bishop to perform the service, and he had come here with Holy Water to cleanse the house on more than one occasion both before and since. Why had that not worked? Why had nothing worked? Was it that he was not powerful enough?

He swallowed his doubts quickly, gazing round the room again. On each previous occasion he had addressed his exorcism to some unspecified evil – probably male – not identifying his quarry. This time it would be different.

He intended to address Margaret de Vere by name and banish her forever from the house.

He found David opening a biscuit tin. 'All right?' David sounded anxious. He had been gone longer than he realised.

'All right.' Edgar wished he felt stronger. He sat down at the table and helped himself to one of the blue earthenware mugs. 'We'll do it in the great hall, I think. It's the centre of the house, and wherever she cast her spells and wove her charms, it is the whole house that needs to be freed from her.'

'And can you release the boys?'

Edgar shrugged. 'I hope so.'

David grimaced. 'I feel as though I'm taking part in some fairy story written by the brothers Grimm. Magic. Witches. Trapped enchanted children. It's grotesque.'

'It is.' Edgar put down his mug. Suddenly he could not face coffee or biscuit. 'Come on. Let's get on with it, shall we? The sooner the better.'

Picking up his briefcase he led the way through into the great hall once more. The sunlight had gone. In the short space of time while he had been in the kitchen the skies had greyed and the room was filled with gloom. 'Can you get rid of those flowers, old chap. I'll spread my stuff out here on the table.' He unpacked the cross and stood it before him.

Georgie

The voice from the stairs was loud and quite clear.

The vase of flowers slipped from David's hand and crashed to the floor, spilling slimy green water and dead flowers over his feet and onto the flags. 'Christ! Sorry.' The stench from the water was overpowering.

'That's all right. I'll help you clear it up. Careful, don't cut yourself.' Edgar stooped down next to David, picking up slivers of broken glass. 'I should have warned you. There may well be manifestations.'

'What sort of manifestations?'

Edgar shrugged, his hands full of glass and flower stems. 'Noises. Lights. Banging and crashing. Evil doesn't like to be dispossessed.'

David took a deep breath. 'I'm trying to think of this as historical research.'

'Don't,' Edgar spoke sharply. 'Bring this all through to the kitchen and we'll find something to mop up the water. This is not an experiment for your amusement. This is serious beyond words.' He threw the mess in his hands into the bin and reached for a floor cloth, wringing it out in the sink. 'I want that room spotless. Foul water is not something we want in there.'

Obediently David helped him clean the floor, and finish it off with a spray of disinfectant from the bottle under the sink. Only when order was completely restored would Edgar, his hands washed and dried, go back to his unpacking. David stood close to him, wishing the sun would come out again. He was finding the darkness of the room oppressive in spite of the lights. 'Shall I find some candles?' He had expected to find them part of Edgar's kit.

The other man nodded. 'It would be helpful.'

They were, David remembered, in the cupboard under the gallery. He walked over to it and pulled open the door. A toy car fell out at his feet. He stared down at it, feeling suddenly rather sick.

Sammy

The call was from the opposite doorway. He swung round.

'Take no notice.' Edgar's voice was calm and steady. 'Bring the candles over here.'

'I can't. There aren't any.'

'Look in the kitchen then. I saw some candlesticks on the dresser.'

David walked towards the doorway where the voice

had come from. To his shame he was feeling a little unsteady. He took a deep breath and went out into the long passage which led from the front door back to the kitchen. It was very cold, the draught from the door as bad as ever. The kitchen was a haven of warmth and brightness. He collected the two candlesticks from the dresser, and rummaging in the drawers, found two new blue candles. Putting them in place he carried them back to the great hall.

Edgar frowned. 'Were there no white ones? It's stupid of me. I should have brought them. I usually keep them in my case.'

'They're the only ones I could find.' David put them reverently on either side of the cross. 'What now?'

'I'm going to bless the house and cleanse it with Holy Water. Then I'm going to pray for the banishment of evil and I'm going to celebrate communion here at this table.'

Sammy! Come and play! Sammy? Where are you?

The plaintive voice was very clear. The scuffle of feet on the stairs and the giggle as if someone was running away echoed across the room. 'Take no notice,' Edgar repeated calmly. He was lighting the two candles. 'They are just what they seem. Two innocent mischievous children.' He shook his head. 'I conducted their funeral services. Both of them.' He took a deep breath. 'Sweet Jesus, bless this place. Look on us now and give us your strength to vanquish all evil from this house. Release and bless the souls of the children who have died in this house. Remove and cleanse the evil and the hatred which have trapped them here.' He opened a leather case which proved to contain a set of small bottles and silver topped pots. 'What Dot calls my travelling picnic kit,' he said quietly. 'Oil. Water. Wine. Salt and wafers.'

There was a resounding crash upstairs. David looked up. His mouth had gone dry with fear. 'Should we go and look?' he whispered.

Edgar shook his head. He had opened his prayer book. 'Concentrate on the prayers. Stand here. Close beside me.'

Somewhere a child had started crying. David clutched at Edgar's sleeve. 'We ought to go and look.'

'We know there is no one there, man.' Edgar's fingers had tightened on his prayer book convulsively. 'Concentrate.'

The candle flames were flickering wildly; as David watched a splattering of blue wax fell across the table. 'They should be white,' he was muttering to himself. 'You're right. The candles should be white.' He found he was shivering violently.

Edgar frowned. He was having difficulty finding the right page. 'Our Father,' he began, 'which art in Heaven. Hallowed be Thy name –'

Another crash, this time from directly overhead. In the hearth the ash was blowing about, a fine mist above the fire dogs. With a puff of wind a cloud blew out into the room, scattering across the floor to their feet. Edgar gave up trying to turn the fine India pages of his prayer book and put it down. His fear was making him angry. 'Enough!' he suddenly bellowed. 'Get thee hence! Out of this house, do you hear me? In the name of Jesus Christ Our Lord, leave this place. Now! Take your evil doings and your malice and your hatred out of this house and leave the people who live here in peace.' He raised his hand and made the sign of the cross in the air. 'Out!' Seizing his bottle of water he tucked it into his arm. Taking one of his small pots he struggled to remove the lid. 'In the name of the Lord!' he cried through gritted teeth. The lid flew off and salt spilled all over the table. David stood back, shocked, tempted to dive forward and throw some over his shoulder, but Edgar had already scooped some up into his palm, and was putting it into the water, blessing it with the ancient words: *Commixtio salis et aquae pariter fiat, in nomine Patris et Filii et Spiritus Sancti,'* words which seemed to him more fitting for their purpose than the plain English he had been about to use.

Upstairs the little boy was crying. Involuntarily David took a step away from the table, unable to stop himself, his heart wrung by the misery of the sound. Edgar, without taking his eyes off the ritual he was performing shot out a hand and grabbed David's jacket. 'Don't move,' he muttered. 'Stay right here. There's nothing up there, I promise you. She's playing with us. We can defeat her. If only we believe hard enough.'

He lifted up the cross. 'Here. Carry this and follow me.'

Slowly they processed around the room, Edgar in front, flicking the Holy Water into every corner, David behind clutching the cross. For all his fear David could not help giving his own small prayer of gratitude that his head master could not see him at this moment, and unbelievably a small gurgle of laughter rose in his throat. Edgar stopped and turned. His face was white with anger. 'You find this funny? After all we have discussed? After all you have heard here, you find this funny?' He was almost shouting with fury.

'No. I'm sorry.' David bit his lip, holding the cross higher, in front of his face. 'Put it down to hysteria. I'm not used to this sort of thing –'

'Thank God you are not!' Edgar stared at him for a long moment. 'I just hope that our witch has not got to you as well. Perhaps it would be better if you waited outside.'

'No.' The thought that he might have been bewitched was so frightening David felt the cold sweat drenching his shoulders. 'No, Edgar, I'm sorry. Please. I'll help you.' He glanced up at the beams of the high ceiling as they both heard clearly the sound of running feet. 'Don't forget the king, Edgar. If the king is here too –'

'First things first,' Edgar snapped. His hands had begun

to shake. He tossed a shower of water into the dark corners beneath the gallery. *'Ab insidiis diaboli, libera nos, Domine. Ab ira, et odio, et omni, libera nos Domine!* This way.' He turned towards the door. *'. . . ubicumque fuerit aspersa, per invocationem sancti nominis tui, omnis infestatio immundi spiritus abigator, terrorque venenosi serpentis procul pellatur . . .'*

'Mr Tregarron? Are you there?' The loud voice echoing suddenly through the room stopped him dead. 'Mr Tregarron, are you all right?'

David closed his eyes. He wiped his face with the back of his arm. 'It's Jimbo; Luke's mechanic,' he whispered. His hands were shaking so much he had to clutch the cross against his chest.

'Mr Tregarron?' The voice sounded less certain now.

'Keep quiet. He'll go away,' Edgar commanded in a whisper.

'Mr Tregarron? The back door was open.' The voice was closer suddenly. 'I thought I'd better check.'

'Speak to him.' Edgar slumped forward, crossing his arms across his solar plexus, all the energy draining suddenly out of him. 'Speak to him. Send him away.'

David put the cross down on the table and made for the door. 'Jim?' His voice was croaky. 'Jim, it's all right. I'm here.' He walked out into the kitchen, taking deep breaths, feeling as though he had been let out of prison. With a huge, body shaking sigh he leaned his arms on the kitchen table, his head in his hands.

'Are you sure you're all right, Mr Tregarron?' Jimbo had been standing in the doorway. He moved forward, his face creased with concern. 'You look white as a sheet, mate. What's happened?'

David forced himself upright. 'Just a bit tired. Sorry, I didn't mean to give you a fright. I didn't realise I'd left the door open.'

'No problem. As long as everything's OK.' Jimbo hesitated. 'There's nothing wrong through there, is there?'

David shook his head.

'I'll go on back to work then. I had to go into Ipswich this morning to collect some parts.' He still hadn't moved. 'Shall I put the kettle on for you? You look as though you could do with something hot.'

David shook his head wearily. 'No. Thanks Jimbo. I'm fine. Perhaps I'll make some later.' He forced himself to smile. 'I'm going back to London today. I'll look in on you before I go and give you back the key.'

He stood watching as the young man at last turned to go. As the door closed behind him he had a tremendous urge to call him, but somehow he resisted it.

He had to go back.

33

uke, I have to visit the place where my mother lived.'

'Oh, Joss!' Luke sat up and stared at her. 'We came here to leave all that behind.'

'I can't leave it behind, Luke.' She shook her head. 'All I need to do is look. See where she stayed. I've got the address. I need to know she was happy here in Paris.'

'And how will you know that?' He took a deep breath. 'Joss, she's been dead for years. I don't suppose anyone is even going to remember her.'

'They might.' She clenched her fists. 'It's not so long. Please, Luke. I'll go alone if I have to.'

He sighed. 'You know I won't let you do that.'

She gave him a shaky smile. 'Thank you.'

'All right. I give in. Let's get something to eat then we'll go and find it. Then, please, can we relax and enjoy ourselves again? For our last few days?'

She pushed back the bedclothes. 'Of course. I promise.'

Rue Aumont-Thiéville was in the 17th arrondissement. Their taxi driver dropped them off in a short street of what looked like purpose built *ateliers*. Looking up at the huge studio windows Joss took a deep breath. 'It was here. Here that she lived with Paul after she went to join him.'

'Are you going to knock?'

She bit her lip. 'Doesn't one look for the concièrge? Or don't they exist any more? I seem to remember that they are supposed to know everything about every one of their tenants in Paris.'

Luke grinned. 'They're dragons. Direct descendants of the *tricoteuses* who sat at the foot of the guillotine knitting, counting heads as they fell into the basket!'

'You're trying to put me off.'

'Not really. I know nothing will do that.' He put his arm round her shoulders. 'Go on. Ring the bell.'

The young woman who opened the door to them looked nothing like a *tricoteuse*. She was smart, well made up, and spoke fluent English. 'Monsieur Deauville? Yes, he still lives here, Madame.'

Joss glanced at Luke, then she turned back to the young woman. 'Perhaps you remember my – that is, his . . .' she floundered to a stop. It had suddenly dawned on her that she did not know if her mother had remarried or not. 'Madame Deauville,' she went on hastily. 'She died about six years ago.'

The young woman made a face. 'Pardon, Madame. My mother was here then. I've only been here two years. All I can say is that there is no Madame Deauville now.' She shrugged. 'Do you wish to go upstairs?'

Joss nodded. She glanced at Luke. 'Do you want to come or would you rather go for a walk or something?'

'Don't be silly.' He stepped inside after her. 'Of course I want to come.'

The lift was wrought iron, small, ornate and terrifying. It carried them with unbelievable slowness up to the third floor where they heaved back the gate and stepped out onto the bare scrubbed landing. It took several minutes for the door to be answered. Paul Deauville was, Joss guessed, in his eighties, tall, white haired, astonishingly good looking and full of charm. His smile was immediately welcoming. 'Monsieur? Madame?' He looked from one to the other in enquiry.

Joss took a deep breath. 'Monsieur Deauville? Do you speak English?'

His smile broadened. 'Of course.'

He was dressed in an open necked shirt and heavy wool sweater. There were tell tale paint stains on his sleeve.

'Monsieur, I am Laura's daughter.' She stared at him anxiously, half expecting a rejection as a look of shock then astonishment and then at last delight played across his expressive features. 'Jocelyn?'

He knew her name.

Her face relaxed into a smile of relief as she nodded. 'Jocelyn,' she confirmed.

'Oh, *ma chérie!*' He put out his arms and pulled her to him, planting a kiss on each cheek. 'At last. Oh, how long we waited, Laura and I, for this moment.' He drew back suddenly. 'You knew – forgive me – you knew she was dead?'

Joss nodded.

He echoed her nod, then he seized her hand. 'Please. Come in. Come in. This is your husband, no?' He released her to give Luke's hand an equally warm squeeze.

Joss nodded. 'I am sorry to come without warning.'

'That does not matter! What matters is that you come at last! Come in, come in. I will put on the coffee. No, we need something better than that. Something special to celebrate. Sit down. Sit down.' He had ushered them into a huge studio room. The walls of the ground floor area were lined with paintings. There were two easels both with canvases standing near the vast window; behind them a small area served as the sitting room; three comfortable chairs, covered in woollen throws, a coffee table, a television with all round it piles of books and papers. To one side of the studio an open plan staircase

– almost a ladder – ran up to a gallery where presumably he had his bedroom. The old man had disappeared into the kitchen area. As Joss and Luke stood in front of one of the canvases, looking in delight at the riot of colour in the painting, he reappeared with a tray carrying three glasses and a bottle of wine. '*Voilà*! To drink a toast!' He put the tray down on a low table in front of the chairs. 'Look, have you seen? The portraits of your mama? Here? And here?'

There were several of them. Huge, reflecting his style of large solid blocks of colour, pure emotion, warmth and vibrancy and yet at the same time all managing to capture something of the delicacy of the woman they portrayed. Her hair – in two dark, streaked with white, in the last grey and white and wild, a gypsy's hair. She was swathed in bright shawls, yet her skin had the fine luminous texture of the English aristocrat; her eyes remained wistful behind their teasing. Joss stood a long time in front of the last.

'I painted that after we knew she was ill.' Paul came to stand beside her. 'She was twenty years younger than me. It was very cruel that she should be taken so soon after we had found each other.'

'Will you tell me about her?' Joss found there were tears in her eyes.

'Of course.' He led her back to the chairs. 'Come, sit down. I will give you some wine then I will tell you everything you want to know.' He began to pour. 'You have of course found Belheddon.' He did not look up from the glasses.

She nodded. 'That is how I knew how to find you.' She took one from him. 'Did you ever go there?' She had gone back to look at the picture again.

He nodded, passing Luke his wine, and then sitting down himself, his long legs, encased in old denims, stretched out in front of him. 'And are you pleased with your inheritance?' The question was posed cautiously as he took a sip of his wine.

Joss shrugged. 'There are problems.'

Paul nodded slowly. 'There are always problems with old houses.'

'Why?' Joss turned away from the picture and looked at him hard. 'Why did she leave it to me when she was so afraid of it herself? Why, if she knew there was danger there? I don't understand.'

Paul met her gaze for several seconds then he put down his glass. With a shrug he climbed awkwardly to his feet and went over to the huge window. The greyness of the afternoon had lightened a little and a few streaks of brightness illuminated the sky above the houses opposite. His back to her he put his hands into the pockets of his jeans, his shoulders hunched. 'She was in torment, Jocelyn. Torn this way and that. I had known her, I suppose, ten years. I met her a long time after your father died. She told me, of course, about your brothers and about you. She talked about you a lot.' He was staring up, over the house roofs opposite into the sky, as though his gaze could recall the past.

'I asked her to marry me then,' he went on, 'but she refused. She was a prisoner of that house.' His voice took on a bitter tone. 'She hated it. But also she loved it.' There was another long silence. 'You have asked yourself, of course, why she had you adopted?' Still he did not turn round.

Joss nodded. She found she couldn't answer.

He took her silence for assent. 'I did not know her then, of course. I can a little imagine her pain after your father died. She adored him all her life.' He gave a self deprecating smile. 'I was only ever a poor second best for her. But even then I could not imagine how she could give you, her last link with him, away to a stranger. Once or twice only, in all the time I knew her she tried to explain a little to me, but that part of her life she guarded. I think – ' he paused, choosing his words carefully, 'I think she felt that if you stayed at Belheddon, you too would be harmed, as her sons had been harmed. The only reason that would make her give away the little *bébé* she loved, was to save your life.' He turned round at last with an expressive gesture of the hands. 'Do not be angry with her, Jocelyn. She did it to save you. The act brought her only unhappiness.'

'Then why,' Joss cleared her throat. It was hard to speak. 'Why then did she leave the house to me?'

'I think it was the only way she could escape herself.' He went back to his chair and sat down, running his hands through his thick white hair. 'She found you, you know. I don't know how, but she found who had adopted you and somehow she kept an eye on you. I remember her saying,' he gave a wry smile, ' "The girl is being brought up very solidly. They are good people and they have no imagination." I was very cross with her. I said, "You mean you don't want your daughter to have imagination, the most precious thing in the world?" and she said, "No, I don't want her to have imagination. I want her to be down to earth. Solid. Happy. That way she will never look for her roots." '

Joss bit her lip. She couldn't speak. It was Luke who turned to Paul. 'You mean she never intended Joss to have the house?'

Paul shrugged. 'She was a very complicated woman. I think she was trying to fool herself. If she left the house to Jocelyn she would appease some spirit of the place which would then let her go. But when she made the will she made it sufficiently complicated, no?' He glanced at Joss again. 'So that it was unlikely that she would inherit. It had to be Jocelyn's free choice. If she made that choice, then,' he lifted his hands helplessly, 'she would have brought whatever fate brought to her upon

391

herself. She was if you like being deliberately self deluding.'

'She said, in the letter she left me, that it was my father's wish that I inherit the house,' Joss said slowly.

'Your father?' Paul looked shocked. 'I find that very hard to believe. Your father hated the house, I understand. He begged and begged her to sell it, she told me.'

'How did you make her leave, in the end?' Luke reached for the bottle of wine and poured himself a second glass.

'It was the will.' He shrugged. 'I don't know who persuaded her to leave the house to you, but as soon as she had done that it was as if the locks had been unfastened and suddenly she was free.'

'I don't know why, but that thought leaves rather a nasty taste in my mouth,' Luke said softly. He was watching Joss. 'You know, the terms of her will forbid us to sell it for a set number of years.'

Paul frowned. 'But you don't have to live there.'

There was a silence. He sighed. 'It is perhaps already too late. The trap has closed. That is, of course, why you are here.'

Joss sat down at last. Her face was pale and strained as she looked at him.

He found himself biting his lip. She was so like her mother – her mother as she had been when he first met her, before that last cruel illness had struck.

'Did she tell you about the ghosts?' she asked at last.

Paul's face grew wary. 'The little boys upstairs? I did not believe her. It was the imaginings of a grieving woman.'

'They weren't imaginings,' Joss's voice was very quiet. 'We've all heard them too.' She looked at Luke, then back to Paul. 'There is something else there. The devil himself.'

Paul laughed, '*Le bon diable*? I don't think so. She would have told me that.'

'She never told you about the tin man?'

'Tin man?' Paul shook his head.

'Or Katherine?'

He looked suddenly wary again. 'Katherine who is buried in the little church?'

Joss nodded slowly.

'Yes. She told me of the sorrow that still haunts the house. She told me that, like in a fairy story, there needs to be a deliverance. To break the spell.'

Joss stared at him a sudden flash of hope in her eyes. 'Did she tell you what that deliverance would have to be?'

He shook his head slowly. 'She did not know, Jocelyn. Otherwise she would have done it. Once, when she came to Paris for the weekend we went to Montmartre where I have many friends. That day we went to the Sacré Coeur together. There she bought in the shop a cross. She asked the priest to bless it for her, and she wore it round her neck until she died. That day we lit a candle to bring peace to the children at Belheddon, and to Katrine,' he pronounced it the French way. 'She was very superstitious, your mother, though she was so intelligent a woman. We quarrelled about that.' He gave a sudden mischievous smile. 'We often quarrelled. But there was much love between us.'

'I'm glad she was happy here.' Joss's eyes strayed back to the painting.

Paul followed her gaze. 'The pictures of her will be yours one day. To take back to Belheddon. And,' he levered himself to his feet once more, 'there are some things of hers here, which you should have. I will fetch them.'

They watched as he climbed the stairs to the gallery and they heard the sound of drawers being pulled in and out, then he appeared once more, negotiating the ladderlike contraption without any difficulty in spite of

393

his age. Under his arm he had wedged a small carved box. 'Her pieces of jewellery. They should be yours.' He pushed it at her.

Joss took the box with shaking hands and lifted the lid. Inside was a tangle of beads and pearls, two or three brooches, some rings. She looked down into the box, shaken by the emotion which had suddenly swept over her.

Paul was watching her. 'Do not be sad, Jocelyn. She would not have wanted that.'

'Is the cross here? The one she had specially blessed.'

He shook his head. 'She took that to her grave. With her wedding ring.'

'You and she were married?' It was Luke who asked.

He nodded. 'I could never persuade her at the beginning. We lived in sin for years.' He grinned. 'You are shocked?'

Joss shook her head. 'Of course not.'

'I think the people of Belheddon would have been. No matter. This is Paris. We lived *une vie bohème*. She liked that. It was part of the escape. We married in the end just before she died.' He hesitated. 'I can take you to see her grave if you wish? Tomorrow, perhaps? She is buried in a village outside Paris. Our real home, where I still go to paint in the summer. She loved it there. It was there that she died.'

'I'd like that.' Joss smiled. 'You've been very kind.'

He bent to hug her. 'I wish she could have known you, Jocelyn. It would have given her so much pleasure. A pleasure she denied herself to save you.' He sighed. 'I hope the fact that you have gone to Belheddon has not made that sacrifice a vain one. It seems the fate of your family is very strong. The tie to the house is like a binding chain.'

Luke frowned. 'It is a beautiful house.'

'I think that is its tragedy. Katrine died for it. And so many others.'

They both stared at him. 'You know something you haven't told us?'

He shook his head. 'I know so little. Your mother would not talk about it once she came to Paris. The curse of the house goes back a long way. Yet it can be broken. She was so sure of that.' He put his hands on Joss's shoulders. 'You are like the daughter I never had. *Ma fille.* I like that. I want to help you. If you wish, perhaps you should go as she did to the Sacré Coeur. Buy a crucifix. Have the blessing of a priest. Believe. Believe that God and Our Lady will protect you. They protected her. She said it was the prayers of Rome which reached out across the years as the prayers of her English church could not. She wanted Our Lady's blessing on Katrine.'

'Codswallop!' Luke's muttered imprecation was clearly heard by both of them. Paul frowned at him. 'You are not a believer. Nor am I. But for those who believe, the prayers work. Perhaps Katrine believes.'

'Katherine has been dead for five hundred years,' Joss said sharply.

'Your mother told me that she was a *sorcière*; a witch. She cannot rest without prayers.'

'Oh, come on.' Luke rammed his hands into his pockets.

'Is it not worth a try? Especially if one day you have children. Then perhaps you will understand why it is important – why they have to be protected.'

'We have children!' Joss interrupted. 'We have two little boys.'

Paul stared at her. '*Mon Dieu* – forgive me. I had not realised.' He sat down abruptly. 'That is why you are here, of course. Where are they?'

'In England. With their grandparents.'

'Not at Belheddon?'

'No.'

'That is good.' He sighed. 'Forgive me. I am tired. Tomorrow we will go out together. I will borrow a car. I will show you Laura's grave. Take her things. Go through them carefully. There are more at the house that you should have.'

The interior of the cathedral of the Sacré Coeur was very dark. Luke looked through the door and gave a shudder. 'Not my scene, Joss. You go on in. I'll wait here.' He sat down on the steps, staring out across the panoramic view of Paris that was laid out in front of him. She glanced down at him and shrugged then she stepped inside the huge domed church. The shop was packed with devotional aids – pictures, crosses and crucifixes, rosaries, statues. They lined the walls, crowded the counter, hung from the ceiling. Staring round she wished she had asked Paul what kind of cross her mother had bought. It was silly. Silly to come here; superstitious, as he had said. And yet something in his words had struck a chord. Perhaps he was right. Perhaps it needed the trappings and the blessings of the Church of Rome to reach out to England's pre Reformation past.

She chose a small silver crucifix and the least kitsch most graceful little carved statue of the Virgin and carefully counted out her francs. Then she went in search of a priest. His blessing was perfunctory and in French, not Latin which bothered her. She wanted to call him back, but already he had turned to others and so clutching her purchases she wandered deeper into the church. For two francs she bought a candle and lit it from its neighbour, then she knelt before the blazing ranks of flame and gazed up at the statue of the Virgin and Child, strangely certain that this was the same spot where her mother had prayed.

* * *

396

At Belheddon, in the ice cold darkness of the locked church, a new spray of white rose buds lay on the stone step before the memorial plaque to Katherine de Vere.

34

_____

'Edgar?' David pushed open the door into the passage. 'Edgar?'

He could hear someone laughing. It sounded like a woman. 'Edgar? Where are you?' He stood in the doorway looking round the great hall. The cross and candles on the table had been knocked over. A pool of blue wax had spread across the dark oak and spilled onto the stone floor. 'Edgar?' His voice sharpened. 'Edgar, where are you? Are you all right?' He stepped into the room, his mouth dry with fear and stared round. 'Edgar?' His voice rose. The room was very silent – too silent. It was as if someone was listening to him. He took a huge gulp of breath, feeling his shoulders rise and holding them there, somewhere around his ears. 'Edgar!' This time it wasn't so loud. Slowly he turned on his heel, staring into the dark corners of the room, looking at the chairs, the chests, his eyes going almost involuntarily to the dark shadows behind the curtains where someone – anyone – could hide.

There was no one there. He stepped closer to the hearth and his eye was caught suddenly by something lying amongst the ash. He stooped and picked it up. It was one of the small silver-lidded pots from Edgar's briefcase.

Spinning round he strode towards the stairs and stood

at the bottom looking up. 'Edgar? Are you there?'

He put his hand on the newel post, clutching it tightly. 'Edgar!'

The silence was unnerving. He glanced round, searching for a light switch. The well of the staircase was dark and he could see nothing beyond the bend where it turned out of sight. 'Edgar?' Taking a deep breath he put his foot on the bottom step.

The sound of laughter came from behind him this time. He spun round and ran back into the great hall. 'Who's there? Who is it? Edgar, where are you? Answer me, for God's sake!'

It was a melodious laugh, attractive, husky, the laugh of a woman who once had known herself to be beautiful. He swallowed, clenching his fists inside his pockets as he stared round, fighting his panic. 'What have you done with him?' he shouted suddenly. 'What have you done with him, you bitch?'

Silence. Intense; pregnant; listening.

He whirled round. In two steps he was back in the hallway at the foot of the stairs. He threw open the study door and then the dining room. There was no one in either room. Then his eye was caught by the cellar door. He frowned. The key was in the lock and the door was an inch or two open. 'Edgar!' Pushing the door open he groped for the light switch.

Edgar was lying crumpled at the bottom of the steps. 'Oh Christ!' David ran down two at a time. The old man was alive. He could hear his forced noisy breathing, see the livid colour of his face. 'Edgar? What happened? Listen old chap, I'm going for help.'

He scrambled back up the stairs and ran through towards the kitchen. It took only seconds to dial 999, then he threw open the door and ran out into the yard. 'Jimbo?' Please God let him still be here. 'Jimbo? Quickly!'

Jimbo appeared at the door of the coach house, wiping oil off his hands onto a filthy old towel. 'Problem?'

'Quickly. There's been an accident. I've dialled 999. Come and help!'

He didn't wait to see if Jimbo was following. Turning back inside the house he ran into the kitchen.

Jimbo was right behind him. 'Did you ring the doctor? He's much closer than an ambulance.'

'Can you do it? I don't know his number. Then come and help. In the cellar.'

Grabbing a couple of coats from the rack as he passed he ran back through the house and down the stairs. 'Edgar? Edgar, can you hear me?' He didn't like to touch the man's head which lay at an awkward angle. Resisting the urge to put something comfortable under it, he spread the two coats over him and gently touched his hand. 'There's an ambulance on its way, and the doctor. Hang on in there. It's going to be all right.' He saw a flicker beneath the old man's eyelids. He was trying to speak.

'No fool –' Edgar was gasping for breath, ' – like old fool. I thought I knew enough; thought I was strong enough. She's too good for me.' He gave a rasping painful cough and David saw him wince with pain. 'Don't stay here. Don't let them come back. Not yet. I must –' he took a deep harsh breath, ' – must talk to bishop –'

'This cellar should be walled up.' The doctor's voice above them made David jump. 'Dear God, how many more people are going to fall down these stairs?' Bag in hand he ran down lightly and knelt beside Edgar. 'Well Mr Gower. I thought you had more sense! A man your age running up and down and playing hide and seek in the cellars!' His hands were running gently over Edgar's head and neck, then on down his body, checking his arms and legs. 'The paramedics are not going to believe this, you know.' He was frowning, but his voice was cheerful as he went on. 'I suppose you were pushed by the ghost as well?' He raised an eyebrow as he turned to his bag and opening it drew out his stethoscope. 'Here, let's make you a bit more comfortable. You haven't broken your neck as far as I can see. Tough old codgers, you clergymen!' He lifted Edgar's head and gently pulled some of the jacket under it to cushion it then he glanced at David. 'Do you want to run upstairs and keep a look out for the ambulance? It should be here about now.'

Jimbo was waiting in the kitchen. 'What's happened?'

'You didn't think to come and look and perhaps help?' David rounded on him.

'You shouldn't have meddled.' Jimbo backed away from him. 'I'm not going through there. No way. Is he dead?'

'No, he's not dead. What do you mean, we shouldn't have meddled.'

'You were trying to exorcise him, weren't you. You were trying to chase him away from Belheddon. Well you can't. There's dozens have tried and they've all failed. They've died or they've gone mad. I told Joss. I told her not to meddle, but she wouldn't listen. He won't hurt her. He never hurts women.'

'It was a woman we were trying to exorcise. A witch.' David thrust his hands deep into the pockets of his jeans. 'She's at the root of all this trouble.'

Jimbo stared at him. 'What do you mean, a witch? It's Bael; the devil; old Nick. That's who lives here.'

'Maybe. But it was a witch who we were after. She's at the root of all this trouble.' David shuddered. 'Did you hear a siren? That will be the ambulance. I'll go and see.'

In the silence broken only by the electronic bleeps in the ward Edgar opened his eyes suddenly. He clutched David's sleeve. 'You have to go back to the house. Collect all my stuff. Don't leave it there. You must not leave it there, do you understand?' Beside him Dot, white with fear, was clutching his other hand.

David stared at him. 'You want me to go back to Belheddon?' He glanced involuntarily at the window. It was dark outside now.

'You have to.' Edgar was breathing with difficulty, his chest heaving. Beside him a battery of monitors measured every step of his battle for life. Only his extreme agitation had forced the doctors in the intensive care unit to allow David in to stand now, helplessly, at his bedside. 'Believe me, I wouldn't ask you to do it if it weren't important.' His voice was very weak. 'Don't stay. Don't do anything. Ignore everything else. Just collect the wine and the bread and the other things. They use them, you see. Use them for evil.'

David nodded slowly. 'I see.'

'Please. You don't have to come back here. Keep them in your car. Just as long as I know they're not in the house.' He was tiring. His face was draining of colour as his eyes closed.

'Please.' Dot took David's hand and led him away from the bed. 'You'll be safe. Take this.' She fumbled at her neck and produced a small gold cross. 'Here. Let me put it on you.' She reached up and fastened the chain round his neck, tucking the cross down out of sight under his shirt, then she smiled. 'It'll keep you safe. Ring me from London and tell me you've done it. He won't rest till he knows.' She turned back to the bed and David saw her lean over to plant a gentle kiss on the old man's forehead. He opened his eyes and gave a faint smile. 'She was too strong for me, Dot. My faith wasn't strong enough.' David could just hear the agonised whisper. 'I've failed.'

'Edgar –' Dot bent closer to the bed. 'Edgar, you haven't failed.'

'Fraid so.' The silence in the room as his fingers fell away, cold, beneath hers, was broken by the sudden strident alarm from the monitor by the bed as his heart slowed, faltered and finally stopped.

As David drove slowly through the darkness away from the hospital some time later there were tears on his cheeks. The end had been so undignified, so panic-stricken, doctors and nurses pushing Dot out of the way, the electric paddles in a nurse's hands, and then the swinging door blocking everything from his view. He had offered to drive her home, but she had shaken her head. 'Go. Do as he asked. Go back to Belheddon. Rescue the sacrament.' Reluctantly he had left her to wait for Edgar's brother, and set off into the dark, consumed with misery and guilt.

And now as he drew closer and closer to Belheddon he was growing more and more scared. He was not sure he would be able to enter the house.

He swung the car into the village and drove slowly down the row of small houses looking for the one where Jimbo lived. It was a pink half timbered cottage two doors up from the post office. Drawing to a halt he sat still for a moment staring out of the windscreen, hoping that Jimbo would be out. Without the key he could not get into the Hall.

The lights were on in the cottage and he had a feeling that the strong smell of chips on the air came from behind its closed, brightly lit windows.

Mr Cotting opened the door which led straight into the small living room, dominated by a large television. Jimbo lay sprawled on the sofa, his feet over the arm, a can of lager in his hand. His gaze switched from the screen to David with an effort.

David gave him an unhappy grin. 'It seems that I need the key to the Hall. Mr Gower left some things there.'

Jimbo's eyes widened. 'You're going back there? Tonight?'

David nodded. 'I don't suppose I could persuade you to come with me?'

'No way, mate.' Jimbo stretched out even further on the sofa and took another swig from his can. 'Dad, get Mr Tregarron a drink. I reckon he's going to need one. How is the old boy?'

David lowered himself gingerly onto a chair opposite the television. 'I'm afraid he died.'

'Died!' Jimbo echoed him in disbelief.

David nodded unhappily.

'Oh my Lor'.' Jimbo sat up and swung his legs to the floor.

'Here.' Fred Cotting handed David a can of lager. 'Get that inside you. I reckon you need it.'

'You can't go back in that house.' Jimbo's face was pale beneath his tan. 'You can't!'

'I've got to. I promised. Then I'm going on back to London.'

'Pity young Jim's sister's not here,' Fred Cotting observed slowly. He sat down on the edge of the table. 'She'd go with you. She's never been afraid of that place. I tell you what, why don't you get the vicar to go with you? That's his job, isn't it? To chase out evil.'

'Mr Wood doesn't believe in that sort of thing, Da,' Jimbo pointed out uncomfortably. 'Anyway, I told Mr Tregarron, it can't be done. Loads of people have tried to get rid of old Nick from the Hall. It's never worked. Never will.'

David put down his can unopened and stood up. 'I'm sorry, I don't think I want this after all. If you can give me the key . . .'

Jimbo climbed to his feet – a giant in the small room, and went over to the sideboard. He picked up the key and tossed it to David. 'Bung it through the letter box on your way back, mate. Good luck.'

David grimaced. 'Thanks.'

'If I were you, I'd go and get Mr Wood anyway,' Fred Cotting put in as he opened the door. He put his hand on David's arm. 'You don't want to go up there on your own. Not now.'

David nodded. He did not need to be reminded.

'Go on. The Rectory is up there. On the left. Past the street light. You see it?' He had stepped outside onto the path in his slippers.

David nodded. 'Thanks. Perhaps I will.'

David watched as Jimbo's father went inside and closed the door, throwing the small front garden into darkness.

In his hand the back door key of Belheddon Hall felt very heavy. He held it out, looking down at it then he turned away from his car and began to walk swiftly up the road. They were right. It was the rector's job.

rom her window Mary Sutton had seen the doctor's car and then the ambulance. For a long time after they had gone she stood staring across the green towards the Hall then slowly she turned to her telephone and picked up the receiver. It rang for a long time unanswered and in the end she put it down. She walked through to her kitchen and there she pulled open the drawer in the table. Sorting through the kitchen knives and spoons, the ladles, the old flat grater, the used corks, the skewers and the peelers she found what she was looking for at last. A key. A large old-fashioned key. The key to the front door of Belheddon Hall. It was leaden in her hand and ice cold. She held it for several minutes, deep in thought, then at last with a sigh she put it in the pocket of her skirt and went out into the hall. Reaching down her winter coat and her scarf from the pegs she pulled them on and let herself out of her front door.

The lock had rusted and the key was hard to turn, but at last she managed it, using both hands to force it round, and summoning every ounce of strength she had to push back the great oak door.

The atmosphere in the house was strange. She stood still, scenting the air like a dog. It was sulphurous; blood-stained, heavy with evil.

'Georgie, Sam?' Her voice quavered as she called. 'Robert? Children, are you there?'

The answering silence was suddenly attentive, full of tension.

'Boys? It's Mary. Protect me, boys.' Squaring her shoulders she walked firmly towards the door into the great hall, a small determined figure in her ankle length skirt and thick stockings. In the doorway she reached up and clicked on the light, looking round.

So, they had tried another exorcism. Was that the priest they had taken away in the ambulance to die? She had no doubt he was dead. She could smell death, like a miasma over the room.

Walking across to the table she stared at the cross, the candlesticks, the splashes of blue wax and slowly she shook her head. The power was there in the holy things, if only they knew how to summon it; their God was all-mighty, it was his servants who were weak.

Once she might have taken the things herself – the bread and wine – and used them, not for evil exactly, never for evil, but to weave her own quiet spells, but not now. She had done with all that.

Glancing round she listened carefully. The house was silent. They were watching to see what she would do next.

There was very little Holy Water left in the flask. Picking it up she dribbled it in a circle around the table and then stepped inside the circle – protective, powerful, as safe as a stone wall. Picking up the discarded briefcase she quickly packed the cross, the candlesticks, the empty pots. The wafers and salt she put inside her clean handkerchief and tucked inside her pocket. The wine in one of the flasks she put under her coat, and the briefcase she slid under a coffer. Then she stood upright again.

'So, madam, you shall not have these to play with! You've done enough damage today, I think.' Her voice was steady, ringing strongly through the room. 'Leave the Grants alone. They know nothing of the past!'

Safe in her circle she looked round, listening.

There was no reply. Shaking her head she stepped out of it, leaving it where it was to dry upon the flags and she walked slowly to the door.

Reaching for the light switch she turned and glanced back into the room. Nothing had changed; there was no sound.

Locking the front door behind her she switched on her small torch and began to walk swiftly across the gravel. Turning into the path which led to the church she stopped once and glanced over her shoulder, listening, then she hurried on.

The key to the church was where it always had been, hidden near the porch. Inserting it into the lock she pushed open the door and paused. It was ice cold inside and very black. She hesitated then, reaching for the bundle in her handkerchief and the small flask she stepped in and strode quickly up the aisle, her torch beam faintly lighting her footsteps.

On the rug between the choir stalls she paused. Perspiration had begun to stand out on her forehead. The handkerchief crumpled in her hand felt very hot.

With a last effort of will she almost ran the last few steps to the altar rails and stooped looking for the latch to open the little gate, her fingers scrabbling amongst the intricate wooden carvings to reach the hidden bolt. She found it at last and tore it back; pushing the gate she stepped up to the altar and put down the bread and wine, in front of the cross. 'There!' She was panting. 'Safe! You can't touch it there, my lady!'

Turning she flashed her fading torch down the aisle in triumph.

At the far end she could see something moving between her and the door. She narrowed her eyes, peering through her thick glasses and her throat constricted in fear.

Behind her was the God she had rejected in her youth. Was it too late to ask His help now? In front of her the twisting spiral of light was growing larger. With a gasp of terror she plunged blindly down the chancel steps and ran into the side aisle, dodging behind the pillars, trying desperately to reach the door.

'Let me just get this straight.' James Wood looked at David with a troubled frown between his eyes. 'You and Edgar Gower went to the Hall with a view to performing an exorcism of the ghosts there?'

David nodded. He felt a small surge of irritation. 'All I want is for you to come up with me and take charge of Edgar's kit. His Holy Water and stuff. He was worried that –' he hesitated. 'That it might fall into the wrong hands.'

'The hands of the ghosts, presumably.' Wood tightened his lips. 'Of course I'll come with you. Poor Edgar. I'm so very sorry.' He glanced at David. 'You mustn't blame yourself, David. It wasn't your fault, you know.'

'No? I brought him here. If it wasn't for me –'

'Accidents happen. They are no one's fault. Edgar was always obsessed with that house; no one could have kept him away. And if he had heart trouble anyway –'

'They don't know that.' David sighed.

'They are doing a post mortem, you say? I suppose they have to.' Shaking his head sadly James Wood reached up to the coat rack in his hall for a thick jacket and dragged it on then he opened the drawer of a table by the front door and took out a serviceable looking torch. 'I will drive across to see poor Dot. It must have been such a shock for her. Well, come on. We'll go over there now. I'll be back in twenty minutes, dear,' he bellowed over his shoulder towards the kitchen from where David's nose

409

had been picking up the wonderful smells of frying garlic and onions. Banging the door behind them he set off on foot up the road.

'I've a car by the post office –.' David protested.

'No need. It's only ten minutes' walk.' Wood was striding out in front of him, the beam of the torch playing across the frosty tarmac. 'It will give us a chance to calm ourselves down.'

David raised an eyebrow. There was no sign that James Wood was anything but calm. 'You don't believe in ghosts, I think you said,' he commented as they walked shoulder to shoulder across the green.

Wood gave a throaty chuckle. 'Not when it comes to Belheddon Hall. I don't think I've ever come across such a case of mass hysteria. It's the house. Old, beautiful, full of history, probably a lack of modern bright lighting which floodlights the whole place at the flick of a switch and a tendency to be especially cold. I'm always being told about cold spots. People forget they are used to modern houses with central heating and double glazing. The slightest draught and they put it down to a malign spirit wafting across the room.' He laughed quietly. 'What has happened to Edgar is a dreadful, sad accident, David. You must not be taken in by all this ghost business. I know Edgar was much involved with it when the Duncans lived here. He encouraged them. Poor things, they had a very unhappy life, but in my view he was very very wrong to take all this talk of ghosts seriously.'

'I thought the church did take it seriously,' David put in thoughtfully. 'Edgar told me there was a special department within each diocese to deal with exorcism.'

There was a moment's silence. 'There are some very out dated aspects in the Church of England still. Not in my view healthy ones.'

'I see.' David raised an eyebrow. In front of them the entrance to the drive loomed out of the hedgerow and

410

they turned into it. The shrubs were very black in the darkness, and the frost had set the gravel hard, cutting out the usual welcome crunching from beneath their feet as they made their way silently up to the front door.

'I've the key to the back,' David whispered as they stood looking up at the house front. In the starlight they could see clearly the angles of the gables and the tall chimneys and the dark uncurtained windows. He shivered, remembering the blazing lights which had shone from every floor when he had driven away only twenty-four hours earlier.

Leading the way round the corner he walked through the archway into the stableyard and paused, looking round. The doors of the coach houses were all locked fast. The courtyard was very silent. Groping in his pocket for the key he walked slowly towards the back door.

The kitchen was still warm as they made their way in and turned on the lights. David glanced round, relieved to see that nothing appeared to have been moved. He gave James Wood a determined grin as the latter switched off his torch and rammed it into his jacket pocket. 'This way. In the great hall.'

Pushing open the door into the passage he paused, listening. The house was very quiet. Resisting the urge to tiptoe he strode down the passage to the great hall, gratefully aware that Wood was very close behind him. Groping for the switch on the wall he turned on the lights and looked round. The room looked normal. Stepping out onto the flagstones he walked across to the oak refectory table and stared down. A pool of solid blue wax showed where the candles had stood and then been knocked over. Otherwise the table was bare. He turned round slowly. Edgar's briefcase had sat on a chair by the hearth; the bottles of wine and oil and water had been on the table. One small pot with a silver top, containing the salt for the exorcism had been on the table, near the cross.

'I don't understand.' He walked across to the hearth and poked around in the ash with his foot. 'It's all gone.'

'What's gone?' Hands in pockets, James Wood was staring up at the portrait over the fireplace.

'Edgar's stuff. The cross. The candles. The sacrament.' He ran his fingers over the cold wax on the table. 'Here. See? This is where he was working. His case was here, on the chair.' He turned round slowly, probing the shadows.

Wood frowned. 'I'm sure there is a perfectly reasonable explanation. Young Jimbo Cotting for instance. Do you think he cleared up after you had left for the hospital?'

David shook his head. 'It was me who locked the door. He wouldn't come through here; he won't come into the house beyond the kitchen. I turned out the lights and locked up while they were loading poor Edgar into the ambulance, then I gave Jimbo the key and followed them in my car. He wouldn't have come back in, I'm sure of it. He's terrified of the place.'

Wood pursed his lips. 'It is possible you tidied up yourself? In the stress of the accident and everything maybe you forgot you'd done it.'

'No. Believe me, I'd have remembered.' David could feel a small knot of anger and fear forming somewhere in the base of his stomach. 'Perhaps we should search the place.' He walked across to the hallway at the foot of the stairs. He had locked the cellar door, he remembered that clearly, and thrown the keys onto the desk in the study. Pushing open the door he went in and stared down at the desk. The bunch of keys still lay there where he had tossed them on the blotter, next to the neat pile of Joss's manuscript. Aware that Wood was watching him from the doorway he turned round slowly, scanning the room for the battered black leather briefcase but there was no sign of it.

412

'Shall we go upstairs?' He bit his lip.

Wood nodded. 'We'd better have a good look round now we're here and make sure there have been no intruders. It's been known, you know. People follow ambulances and when the family rush off after them to hospital, often not locking up properly in their panic, they nip into the house and clean it out.' He shook his head. 'It's a very sad, cynical world.'

David scowled. 'But in this case I did lock up.'

'Of course.' James Wood turned off the light and closed the door. He turned his attention to the cellar. 'Should we check in there?'

'I suppose we should check everywhere.' David picked up the keys. Poor Edgar. Pushing open the door and clicking on the lights he hesitated for a moment, then he led the way down the uneven steps and stood at the bottom looking round. 'No sign of anything unusual down here.'

They both listened for a moment in silence. 'I wonder why he came down here?' James Wood was frowning as he stepped through into the further cellar. 'It does seem a rather odd thing to do.' His voice echoed slightly as he moved out of sight.

David shrugged.

'Of course, one of the children died in here, didn't he.' The disembodied voice drew further away. 'These cellars go on for miles. I'd no idea they were so big.'

David frowned. 'They're not that big! Mr Wood? James?' In a sudden panic he sprinted towards the archway and peered through.

James was standing by the wine bins, peering into the darkened corner. 'Someone has left some toys down here. What a shame, they'll get ruined in the damp. Look.' He had picked up an old woven rush basket. In the harsh light of the electric bulb they could clearly see the green mould growing on the handle. Inside were a half dozen or so of the same little wooden cars which David had seen earlier, and a rusty toy gun and beneath them a penknife and a red painted yo-yo.

'I think they must have belonged to one of the boys who died,' David said slowly. He reached out and touched the yo-yo with a finger. 'They're not Tom's.'

He shivered, unable to stop himself glancing over his shoulder. 'There's nothing else down here. Shall we go back up?' At least it was marginally less cold upstairs. All he wanted now was to get the hell out of here as soon as possible.

James nodded. He put down the basket. 'So sad,' he murmured. 'So sad.' He frowned. 'What was that?'

'What?' David's nerves were raw. He spun round, listening.

'I thought I heard something. A voice.'

'A woman laughing?' Swallowing, David faced the staircase.

'No.' James looked confused. 'I'm not sure. Probably the water pipes or something.'

'Let's get out of here.' David moved swiftly towards the stairs. 'Come on. I don't like cellars.'

'Nor I.' With a rueful smile James followed him. 'I must confess I see your point about this house. The atmosphere leaves a lot to be desired when it's empty like this. But we mustn't be foolish. Our rational minds tell us there is nothing to fear.'

Emerging on the landing they stood for a moment both looking towards the great hall. Reaching behind him David turned off the cellar light and pulled the door closed. Locking it carefully he withdrew the keys and went with them into the study. 'Tell me, James, how does your rational mind cope with a belief in God if it rejects all other aspects of the supernatural?' he called over his shoulder. He was about to throw the keys down on the desk once more when his eye was caught by

414

something lying on the manuscript of Joss's book. A dried flower. He was sure it hadn't been there before. Frowning he dropped the keys and picked it up. A rose; an old dried rose, its petals, once white, now the colour and texture of soft chamois leather. He stared at it thoughtfully, aware that the small hairs on the back of his forearms were stirring uncomfortably.

Roses. He dropped it and turned towards the door.

'James?'

There was no reply.

He took a deep breath. It couldn't happen again. Forcing himself to move slowly and calmly he went through into the great hall and stopped dead. James was standing by the table staring down at it in disbelief, Edgar's briefcase open before him.

David went to stand beside the other man and looked down in silence. 'They're empty,' James said after a moment. He nodded towards the vessels. 'All of them. The rest of it's here: the cross, the candlesticks. It was under the chest here. Someone must have hidden it all.'

David shook his head. 'There's no one else in the house, James.'

'There must be.' The rector sounded desperate. 'There has to be some logical explanation. Children perhaps; children from the village. I remember Joss saying she thought there were children hiding in the house.'

'There are.' David was aware how bleak his voice sounded. 'But not children from the village.'

James looked at him in silence for a moment, then slowly he closed the lid of the case. Neither of them had noticed the faint outline on the flags where the salt water had dried in a perfect circle.

'What do you suppose has happened to the contents?' David asked soberly.

'Very desirable in some quarters. They use them for

415

Satanic rites; witchcraft; that sort of thing.' James's previous hearty tone had gone. It had been replaced with weary disillusion.

'So we were too late.'

James nodded. 'It looks like it.' He gave a deep sigh. 'The Grants are all away, you said?'

David nodded.

'Then there's no danger to the family in the immediate future.' James stared round the room thoughtfully. 'I can't feel anything, you know. Nothing at all. I wish I could, then I'd be more use in knowing how to deal with it.'

David shook his head. 'Just be thankful you can't feel anything! I don't think it can be very nice to be psychic. Not very nice at all.'

He did not mention the rose. Waiting for James to pick up the case he walked back to the wall to switch off the lights. There was someone up there in the gallery, watching, he was sure of it. He could even feel the suppressed triumph.

He did not look up. Walking back into the room he hustled James out in front of him. The laughter he thought he could hear behind him was not that of a child. It was a woman.

In the churchyard Mary lay on her back in the long grass, staring up at the sky. One by one the stars had disappeared as the clouds rolled in from the sea and the sky was totally black now. She closed her eyes, pleased the pain had gone away at last. Slowly her legs were growing numb.

Her shoe was still caught on the wrought iron kerb around the old grave where she had tripped. In the dark she couldn't see the blood from her trapped foot seeping inexorably into the grass.

Somewhere in the distance she heard a door slam.

416

'Here! I'm here!' she called, but her voice was barely more than a whisper and no one heard.

She should have known the evil was in the church now; she should have been able to feel it, realise that something had awakened it, but she was getting old. Too old. Too weak. She must warn Jocelyn. Slowly her eyes closed again and her head fell back onto the soft pillow of dead grass. Another short rest and she would try and move again, but suddenly she was so very tired.

'Georgie? Sam?' Her whisper was very faint. 'Help me, boys. I need you.'

hen Mat arrived in Oxford unannounced, hugging his parents and the children before giving her a brotherly kiss on the cheek Lyn was as surprised and pleased as they were.

'You might have let us know, Matthew!' Elizabeth Grant feigned annoyance. 'It's typical. You just arrive, assuming there will be room for you!'

'Of course there's room.' His put his arms around his mother again and squeezed her hard. 'There's oceans of room! I only knew yesterday that I could wangle five days in the south before starting on the new project so I thought I'd grab the chance and I did. I didn't think I'd need to book.'

'I'm afraid the boys and I are filling up the house a bit.' Lyn felt suddenly shy as she smiled at the handsome, cheerful, carefree face.

'Nonsense.' Elizabeth and Mat spoke at the same moment and then both dissolved into laughter.

'There's room for all of you,' Elizabeth went on firmly. 'I was only teasing!'

It wasn't until the evening that Lyn found herself alone in the sitting room with Mat after the children had been put to bed. He poured her a sherry and sat down opposite her, his long legs loosely crossed at the ankle as he sipped at his own. He gave her an amiable grin. 'So, how are Joss and Luke really?'

'Fine.' She looked at him fiercely for a minute. 'You never answered my letters.'

'I know. I'm sorry.' He seemed embarrassed. 'I meant to. It's just – you know how things are.'

'No. Supposing you tell me.'

He looked distressed. Standing up he put his glass down carefully and moved across the room to stand at the French doors looking down towards the bottom of the garden where the River Cherwell ran between banks of lush willow. 'I live in Scotland, Lyn. I have a life up there.'

'I see.' She could not hide the bleakness in her voice. 'How stupid of me to think you'd have time to write a few lines on a postcard!'

He swung round. 'Please try and understand. You're a very attractive woman –'

'No.' She stood up slopping her sherry onto her skirt as she slammed the delicate cut glass down onto the coffee table. 'Please don't make it worse.' Her face was scarlet. 'I have to go and check on the boys if you'll excuse me. Then I'll help your mother with the supper.'

By the morning she had made up her mind.

'But Lyn, why don't you stay a bit longer, my dear! You know how much we love having the children.' Elizabeth removed Tom's bib and helped him down from his breakfast chair. 'There, sweetheart, take a chocky out of Granny's tin and then go and play while Aunty Lyn and I have a talk.'

Lyn gave a tight smile. 'It's very nice of you, Mrs Grant, but honestly, I'd rather have them in their own home. Their routine is getting badly unsettled by the break and it's time we got back. Tom was due to start playgroup for an hour or two this week.' With dismay she watched Tom helping himself to a fistful of chocolate toffees.

'But this is so sudden and Luke was so insistent we look after you all, my dear. And it's been such fun.'

419

Elizabeth got up and went to the sink. 'You know, I don't think you ought to go back without checking with them, I really don't.' Squeezing a flannel out under the hot tap she went in pursuit of her grandson before he managed to spread the mess on his fingers to her gingham table cloth.

Lyn hid a scowl. 'It has been fun here,' she said as sincerely as she could. 'But I think Luke and Joss would want him to go to the playgroup. There is such a waiting list. We were very lucky to get him in.'

Elizabeth looked up. Then she shrugged unhappily. 'I hope it's nothing to do with Matthew coming.' She glanced at Lyn shrewdly and noted the sudden defensive look in her eyes. She sighed. Wretched boy! Another heart broken. She shook her head, too tactful to say any more. 'Well, you're in charge of the little ones, I suppose. Perhaps you're right,' she added after a minute. She looked down at the revolting cloth in her hand and gave a rueful laugh. 'Yes, perhaps you are right. Short visits, and often – that's always supposed to be the best, isn't it? But do try and ring Luke and Joss, my dear. They left the hotel number. Just check it's all right to go back, won't you?'

When Lyn turned the Mini under the arch into the court-yard a light rain was falling from a leaden sky. She glanced at the open garages; obviously Jimbo was around somewhere, but to her relief she couldn't see him. She was not comfortable in his company. Each time she had seen him when Luke was not around he had leered at her suggestively, and the awful thing was she did find him and his strange eyes extremely attractive, and that made her think about Mat again with a sharp pang of regret.

Pulling Luke's keys from her pocket she climbed out of the car. Unstrapping Tom she lifted him out, then she turned to Ned. 'Come on, baby. Let's have you. It'll soon be time for your lunch and I'll bet the house is freezing cold. We'll have to put the fire on in your bedroom before you can go upstairs.' His harness was awkward to undo. Swearing to herself, she pulled at the small square buckles and at last managed to extricate him from the back seat. Standing upright, the child in her arms, she turned round to lift out the cat basket – Kit and Kat were anxiously squeaking for their release after their long journey – then she looked round for Tom.

'Tom! Tom, where are you?' He had vanished. 'Tom?' She turned round crossly, flicking the rain out of her eyes. 'Come on, you're getting wet.' The little brat had obviously made a bee line for the open carriage house door. Damn. The last thing she wanted to do was have a long conversation with Jimbo. 'Tom, come here quickly. I want to get lunch.'

She could hear him giggling. 'Tom! Where are you hiding, you horror?' His footsteps rang out behind her, running over the cobbles. She spun round, Ned in her arms. 'Tom!'

'You're back then.' Jimbo had appeared in the doorway to the garage, a spanner in his hand. He was dressed as always in filthy oily overalls, his unkempt hair knotted back on his neck with an elastic band. He ran his eye up and down her as though she were wearing a skimpy bikini instead of an old pair of jeans and a bright blue anorak. She could feel herself growing hot in spite of the icy rain trickling down her neck.

'As you see. Is Tom in there?'

'Tom?' He stared round his feet as though the child might be hiding behind his legs. 'No, I don't think so.'

'Can you look, please? In the garage. I want to get him inside. The rain is getting worse.' She was trying to shelter Ned with the flap of her anorak.

Jimbo ducked out of sight. There was a transistor radio

playing softly somewhere inside, Lyn realised suddenly. To her surprise this time it appeared to be playing some sort of classical music. She took a step closer. 'Is he there?'

'No, he's not here. I didn't think he was. I'd have seen him. The little monkey gave you the slip did he?'

'He did.' Lyn tightened her lips.

'Tell you what. You take the baby inside and I'll look for him.' Jimbo stopped in his tracks, a frown slowly spreading across his face. 'Does Joss know you've brought them back?'

'I'm going to ring them tonight. I tried their hotel last night but they were out.' She hesitated. 'I can't think where Tom's got to.'

'I don't think you ought to have brought them back, you know.' Jimbo rubbed the back of his neck with an oily hand. 'They shouldn't be in the house.'

'Oh for goodness sake, not you as well!' Lyn spun round and began walking quickly towards the back door. She was not about to tell him that it was Joss herself who had hurt the children and imagined all the stories about the house. If anyone was going to explain anything to him, it would have to be Luke. 'Please, Jimbo, find him quickly. He's going to get so wet out here in the rain.'

Still looking round for him she juggled the baby over her shoulder and fished in her pocket for the keys. The back door swung open onto a house that was surprisingly warm. She paused thoughtfully, then she went on into the kitchen. Sure enough the range, although nearly out, had been stoked in the last twenty-four hours. She had done it enough times herself to know exactly how long it would have lasted. There were two glasses on the kitchen table, and Luke's whisky bottle, nearly empty, together with a wooden toy car.

Setting Ned down in the chair she propped him up against the cushions and began to pull off his waterproof jacket and trousers. His small bouncy chair was where they had left it behind the rocking horse in the corner. Strapping him in near the range she gave him a gentle shove to make it swing, then she turned back to the door.

'Jimbo, who's been in here? Was it you?'

For a moment she couldn't see him, then she caught sight of a movement in the bushes in the far corner of the yard. 'Is he there? Oh, thank God!'

Jimbo had appeared carrying the small boy. Tom was crying.

'What is it? What's happened?' Grabbing him from Jimbo Lyn turned towards the kitchen. With a slight hesitation Jimbo followed her and stood in the doorway watching as she tried to console the boy.

'You shouldn't have brought him back.'

'Why not?' She turned on him furiously. 'Look, you've frightened him.'

'It wasn't me frightened him.' Jimbo set his mouth in a tight line.

'What did then?'

'You'd best ask him, hadn't you.' He sniffed loudly. 'And no, it wasn't me sitting in here drinking when I should have been working, so there's no need to think it. Mr Tregarron was up here with the Reverend Gower. There was an accident. The reverend's dead. He had a heart attack, I heard.'

Lyn stared at him in horror. 'When was this?'

'Night before last.'

'And where's Mr Tregarron now?'

'Back to London. He wouldn't have liked you bringing the boys back.'

'No, I bet he wouldn't.' Lyn scowled. 'OK, Jimbo, thanks. I'd better get these two fed and let them have a rest. They've had a tiring journey.' For a moment she thought he wasn't going to go.

423

He hesitated just too long on the threshold and then with a shrug he turned away. No need to tell her yet about poor Mary. She'd been dead for hours when they found her, and no one knew even now what she'd been doing in the church in the dark. She'd left the door open when she left, and fallen amongst the old graves under the yews.

'You call me if you need me,' he shouted over his shoulder as he ran down the steps. 'But if I were you, I'd spend the night with Mrs Goodyear. Don't let the boys stay here.'

Lyn stared after him for a moment then she turned to Tom, scolding, as she pulled off his jacket. He had spotted the car on the table and stood on tiptoe to reach up and get it. 'That's Georgie's toy,' he said conversationally as she straightened his jumper and reached it over for him before she turned towards the kitchen range. 'Tom play with Georgie's car.'

'We must ring your parents later, Luke.' Joss was sitting with him at the huge scrubbed table in the farmhouse which had been her mother's last home. They had eaten a wonderful meal, cooked by Paul, washed down with a rough, thick country wine and they were both feeling sleepy and more rested than they had for a long time.

'I am glad that I persuaded you to leave your hotel and come here to stay.' He was spooning thick coffee grounds into the cafetière. 'You both look better already.' He gave his slow, charming smile. 'Of course, you may ring whoever you like. I wish you had the children with you.' He shook his head. 'How Laura would have loved to know that she had grandchildren. Now, while you drink your coffee I shall bring for you Laura's things.' He hesitated. 'I do not want you to be sad, Jocelyn. Are you sure you want these things?'

She was peeling an apple with a small fruit knife. 'I

would love to have them, Paul.' She smiled wistfully. 'It sounds strange when I already have so much that was my mother's at Belheddon, but none of it seems personal; it consists of all the stuff she didn't want; the things she was prepared to abandon. Apart from a work basket and the things in her desk there is nothing that was close to her.'

He frowned. 'What is a work basket?'

'Sewing.'

'Ah, I see.' He let out a guffaw of laughter. 'She hated sewing. Not even a button. I did all the buttons! I'm surprised she didn't put it in the garbage!'

'So.' Joss shrugged her shoulders and raised her hands in an unconscious imitation of his wonderful Gallic gestures. 'What did she love?'

'She loved books. She read and read. She loved poetry. She loved art. That was of course how we met. But there were things she hated. Strange things.' He shook his head. 'She hated flowers – especially roses –'

'Roses?' Joss tensed.

'Roses.' He did not notice the sharpening of her tone. 'She detested roses. She said the *greniers* – the attics – at Belheddon always smelled of roses. I could not understand why she disliked them so much. Roses are beautiful things; their smell is –' he searched visibly for a word and found it with a kiss of his finger tips, *'incroyable.'*

Joss glanced at Luke. 'I can understand. The roses at Belheddon are not like other people's roses.' She gave a small sad smile. 'Poor Mother.'

The men left her with the suitcase full of letters and books and the leather box full of more of Laura's jewellery, planning to walk across the fields and down to the river. Settling down alone on the hearth rug in front of a gentle, sweet smelling fire of apple logs Joss sat for a long time gazing into the flames, hugging her legs, her chin resting on her knees. She felt closer to her mother

425

here than she had at any time at Belheddon. It was a nice feeling; warm, protective. Safe.

It was almost with reluctance that at last she reached into the box and began to sort through the papers. There were loads of letters – all from strangers – none of special interest though all showed how much her mother was loved – and several demonstrated how she was missed by friends back in England. None however came from the village of Belheddon, she noticed, remembering how Mary Sutton had complained how Laura had never written; no one mentioned the life she had abandoned in East Anglia.

At the bottom of the box she found two notebooks she did recognise. The same make that Laura had used for her diaries and commonplace books at home. They were full of closely written notes. The same mixture as before. Poems, interesting snippets and diary entries. She settled herself more comfortably, leaning back against one of the chairs and pulling a cushion down behind her head as she started to read.

> I had a dream last night about the old days. I woke in a cold sweat and lay there shaking, praying I had not awakened Paul. Then I wished I had. I snuggled against him for comfort, but he did not stir. Bless him, he needs his sleep. An earthquake would not awaken him.

And two days later.

> The dream came again. He is looking for me. I could see him searching the house, slowly, unhappily. He is lost and lonely. Dear sweet God, am I never to be free of this? I thought of speaking to Monsieur le curé, but I don't want to breath His name aloud out here. This is too special a place and surely he can't reach me any more. Not in France!

Joss looked up for a moment. So He – *it* – had a name. She read on; at the beginning of the second book came a revelation.

> I wonder whether I should write to John Cornish and ask him to tear up the will; to leave the house straight to charity. How would anyone at Belheddon know what I had done? Here he can only reach me in my dreams and I cannot tolerate the thought of Jocelyn learning of her good fortune and going in all innocence into the trap. There will be no danger to her, of course. He will love her. But should she ever have children. What then? If only I could talk to Paul but I want nothing to spoil our relationship, not even the mention of the name . . .

Joss put the book down, tears in her eyes. She shivered. So her mother had known only too well the nature of the dangers at Belheddon and had felt guilty enough after all, about leaving the house to her, to have thought of changing the will. She sighed. But if she had done that, there would have been no story, no family, no home; once Luke's business had folded, no cars, no money. She frowned, brushing away the tears. There was so much that was wonderful at Belheddon.

Surely – surely there must be a way of removing the danger. She sighed. At least the children were safe. There was no possibility of them going back to Belheddon until the problems had been resolved.

She picked up the diary again, turning almost fearfully to the last pages.

> The pain grows worse each day. Soon I shall not be able to hide it from Paul and I shall have to stop my writing. I must burn this and all the rest before I grow too weak or silly to do it.

427

Joss paused. So, she had never meant anyone to read all this. For a moment she felt guilty, but she read on.

> One of my fears is that he – Edward – will be waiting for me when I die. But, how can he if he is earthbound? Will Philip be there, and my boys? Or are they too trapped at Belheddon?

So, had she and David been right? It was Edward. Was it Edward IV of England, and had she inadvertently named her younger son after him? Shuddering, Joss skipped on. There were several more pages of closely written script, the writing growing more and more illegible as the days passed. Then came the last page.

> So. I am accepted into the Catholic church and Paul and I are married at last. I have done all I can for the safety of my soul.

There was a trail of ink across the page as though her hand was too tired to hold the pen properly any more, then the writing resumed.

> I was so sure she could not cross water.
> Katherine
> my nemesis . . .

That was all. Joss rested the book on her knee and stared into the flames.

Katherine.

The name that echoed through her head and through the history of the house. *I was so sure she could not cross water*. What did that mean? That she had come to France? Followed Laura here?

What was the significance of crossing water? Witches couldn't cross water; wasn't that a part of the tradition? But it was Katherine's mother who was the witch. And why should Katherine come here? What was Laura to her?

Her head was throbbing. She rested it wearily on her

knees as the book slid to the floor and lay face down on the carpet. She could hear the ticking of the long case clock in the hall, slow, hypnotic; reassuring. In the hearth the logs burned with an occasional quiet hiss throwing a wonderful fragrant warmth around her. Closing her eyes she laid her head back against the cushions.

Come back to me, Katherine, love of my life and my destiny . . .

The cry wrenched her back from sleep with a leap of fear. It had been too loud; too desperate.

It was a dream; nothing more. A nightmare sparked off by reading the diaries. She picked up the book and clutched it against her chest. Poor Laura. Did she have any peace at all before she died? She had died here, in this house, Paul had said, attended by a full-time nurse over the last few days. The end had been quiet, he said, although she had said she wanted no more drugs. He had been sitting with her, her hand in his, and she had smiled at him, perfectly lucid, before closing her eyes for the last time. If she had cried out the names of any strangers he had not mentioned it.

Trying to shake off her melancholy she drew the small leather jewel box towards her and opened the latch on the flap which fastened it. Inside cushioned in faded blue velvet lay several very beautiful pieces – a string of pearls, some lapis beads, several brooches and half a dozen rings.

It was growing dark when Paul and Luke returned, hearty, glowing with cold and eager they had already laughingly agreed for an English cup of tea. Standing in the doorway Paul looked down at Joss near the fire. He could hardly see her in the dusk of the room. 'Ma chère Jocelyn, I'm sorry. Were you asleep?'

For a moment she closed her eyes, trying to compose herself then with a smile she scrambled to her feet. 'No. Only dreaming and perhaps a little sad.'

'Ah. Perhaps we should have given you longer to look

at your treasures.' He came over and put his arm round her, giving her shoulder a squeeze. 'Laura would not have wanted you to be sad, Jocelyn. She was happy in France.'

'Was she?' Joss hadn't meant it to come out that way – as an accusation. 'Are you sure? Are you sure she didn't bring her demons with her?' She brushed her eyes with the back of her hand.

'Demons?' he echoed.

She gestured at the notebook on the carpet. 'Did you read her diaries?'

For a moment he looked shocked then slowly he sat down. 'Jocelyn, it may surprise you to know that I never did. Laura asked me to burn them, and I meant to. I put all her things in that box to take them outside to the garden and put them on the fire, but I couldn't bear to do it. In the end I put the whole box away – perhaps in a strange way to wait for you to make the decision if you ever came,' he shrugged, 'I don't know. But for whatever reason the things were there for you. But they were not mine to read.'

'But you were her husband.'

'Yes.' He gave a grave smile.

Joss looked up at him. 'You were only married at the very end.'

He nodded. 'So, she wrote about that.'

'And that she had converted to Catholicism.'

Sighing he leaned back in the chair and stared up at the ceiling. Behind him Joss was conscious of Luke standing silently by the window. No one had turned on the lights and the only illumination came from the dying fire and the slight tinge of pale light still showing in the sky out of the window. 'I am not a religious man. I did not encourage her in this – either the marriage or the lessons with the *curé* – this came from inside her. I asked her to marry me of course, when she came to France, but she

430

did not want it and here no one minded – no one asked. We were both free – I think, as I told you, that perhaps she enjoyed the – how you call – naughtiness of it? She had been for so long a respectable lady in England.' He gave a huge warm smile, his eyes focusing on a distant memory. 'Then at the end, when she became ill, I think she became a little afraid.' He frowned. 'Do not misunderstand. She was very brave, your mother. So brave. When the pain came she did not complain ever. But there was something – something out there –' he gestured towards the sky outside the window. 'Something which had always haunted her; the thing she had fought with her visit to Sacré Coeur. For a while it was held at bay. She did not think of it. Then one day, I came home and found her sitting by the fire in the dark, much as you were doing just now. And she was crying and she told me that the ghosts had followed her to France. That first they had come in her dreams, and that now she thought they were growing stronger.'

'No.' Luke stepped forward suddenly. 'I'm sorry, Paul, but I think we've had enough of these ghosts. They were the reason we came to France in the first place.'

Paul turned in his seat. 'Put on the lights my friend. Pull the curtains. Let us see what we are doing.' He turned back to Joss. 'Do you wish to talk of this now?'

She nodded. 'Luke. It's important. Paul, I have to know. Did she say who was haunting her?'

'The ghost of her lover.'

Joss stared at him, completely shocked. 'Her lover?'

'That is what she said.'

'She had a lover!'

'Why not. She was a beautiful woman.'

'But I thought –' she shook her head as though trying to dislodge her thoughts. 'I thought that it was a ghost. A real ghost. From the past.'

He smiled again. 'All ghosts are from the past, Jocelyn.'

Her thoughts were whirling. 'Did she mention anyone else to you? Anyone else who came here. A woman called Katherine?'

He nodded. 'At the end. It upset her very much. I do not know how she came in – the nurse said she had opened the door to no one, but somehow she came to see Laura.'

'Did you see her?'

'*Non.*'

'Who was she, do you know?'

'She had been this man's lover too. And he had left her, that much I understood. She was very bitter that Laura had stolen him. I was so angry when Laura told me. Not about the lover, although she had never told me about him either,' he shrugged gallantly, 'but this woman was apparently young and beautiful, and my Laura was so ravaged by the disease. It was an obscenity for this Katherine to come here. It was only a day or so later that your mother died.'

Katherine

The word seemed to fill the silence in the room.

Luke came and sat down near Joss. 'That's a terrible story. What happened to her? Did she ever come back?'

Paul shrugged. 'No. If she had she would have regretted it. All my rage and misery and grief was directed at that woman. To come to a dying woman and taunt her with her own beauty. Laura kept talking about her beautiful, long dark hair. And then she brought some roses. The roses which Laura hated most in the whole world.'

'White roses,' Joss whispered.

'*Exactement*! White roses. I threw them from the window. It was as if she knew, Laura said, that it would kill her to bring them here.'

'How did she know where Laura was?' Joss was still frowning, trying to rearrange her thoughts.

Paul shrugged once more. 'Who knows? She probably

hired a detective. I do not make a secret of my home. I have this house for thirty years. Everyone knows me. We had nothing to hide.'

There were several seconds of silence, then Luke cleared his throat. 'Why don't I go and put on the kettle.'

When he returned with a tray and three mugs of tea and a saucer full of lemon slices for Paul, they were both still sitting there, staring at the fire, each preoccupied with his own thoughts.

'Were there two Katherines then?' Joss said at last. 'The Katherine who died in 1482, whose presence fills the house at home; and now this other. I never thought – I never ever guessed, that mother had a lover.'

Paul got up to throw a log onto the fire. 'She had me!'

'I know.' Joss smiled fondly. 'But that was different. One expects everything to do with the French to be decadent and shocking.' She was teasing now. 'The thought that my mother had a lover – an English lover – at Belheddon – that is somehow wrong.'

Paul clicked his teeth. 'You English are not logical. Not at all. Ever.'

'I know.'

'Your father died over thirty years ago, Jocelyn. Would you expect your mother to be without love for so long? Surely you would not have condemned her to that.'

Joss shook her head. 'No. Of course I wouldn't. No one should have to live without love.' She held out her hand towards Luke, who came and took it. He put his arm round her.

'It is all a little bewildering for us, Paul,' he said slowly. 'We have been imagining the house full of ghosts from the past – the distant past – and now it seems that they come as well from the living present.'

'But not the children,' Joss whispered. 'The children came from the past.'

'That house is not good for children,' Paul said thoughtfully. 'You should be careful. Laura was full of superstition about it. Coincidence is strange. It attracts more coincidence. The expectation of people is liable to be fulfilled. Once the expectation changes, then slowly the mood will change and the coincidences will no longer be there.'

'You sound very wise.'

He let out a crack of laughter. 'That is probably the only good thing about being as old as me. Age gives a spurious sense of experience and wisdom. Now,' with a groan he levered himself to his feet. 'I shall stop being pompous and I shall go and look for a bottle of wine while you ring *grand-mère* and check that your babies are well. When you have done that we can all relax and talk of what we shall do tomorrow.'

Luke waited until he had left the room before he spoke. 'What an incredibly nice man. Your mother was so lucky to have found him.'

'Wasn't she.' Joss curled up on the sofa, hugging a cushion. 'I'm so confused, Luke.'

'But happier, I hope.'

'I think so.' As he reached for the phone and began to dial she rubbed her eyes wearily.

Katherine

A medieval Katherine with long wild hair and flowing gowns. And a modern Katherine. A Katherine in high heels with soignée artfully tumbled hair and red lipstick; a Katherine who could fly to Orly just as they had, not on a broomstick but on a plane. Were they different women or the same? She would never know now.

Katherine

The echo in her head would not go away; it was an echo from the past, an echo that was tinged with laughter . . .

Luke had, she realised, put down the phone. He looked

434

thoughtful. 'Lyn took the boys back to Belheddon yesterday,' he said slowly.

Joss went white. 'Why?'

He took a deep breath. 'Mum says she was getting more and more resentful and possessive; she didn't want any help or advice and contradicted everything they tried to do.' He raised an eyebrow.

Joss scowled. 'That sounds familiar. The stupid, stupid girl! How dare she! Luke, what are we going to do?'

'Ring her presumably. No –' he raised his hand. 'Let me. You'll rush in and make things worse.'

'She can't stay there, Luke. She's got to take them out of the house. Tell her to go to Janet. She won't mind –'

'Let me speak to her, first.' He was dialling, lifting the receiver to his ear.

Katherine

The echo in her ears was louder; the laughter wilder; a medieval Katherine and a modern Katherine. Two women with the same eyes, the same red lips, the same wild hair, two women out for revenge.

Scrambling to her feet Joss went to stand beside Luke. She could hear the phone ringing on and on. No one answered.

Behind them Paul appeared with a small tray. He stood for a moment in the doorway, then he put down the tray. 'What is wrong? Can't you get through?'

'Lyn has taken the boys back to Belheddon,' Joss was biting her lip hard. 'There's no reply.'

Paul frowned. 'Is there a neighbour you can ring? I am sure there is no need to worry.' He put his arm round Joss's shoulders.

'Janet. Ring Janet.' Joss dug Luke in the ribs.

'OK. OK. Wait.' He put the receiver down and picked it up again.

In Janet's house too, the phone rang on and on unanswered.

uddled up on the end of Lyn's bed Kat stood up. Staring with huge eyes towards the half open door she arched her back and spat in terror. In a fraction of a second she had leaped from the bed and disappeared through the door and down the stairs in a blur of yellow, black and white fur.

Lyn woke very suddenly and lay staring at the ceiling, her heart thudding beneath her ribs. She listened hard, focusing on the doorway. Had one of the children stirred? She had left all the doors between them open a little so that if one of them cried she would wake up.

The house was very silent. Her gaze went to the window. She had left a crack open between the curtains and beyond them she could see the sky, bright with moonlight. There must be a heavy frost out there; there didn't appear to be a breath of wind. For several moments longer she lay still then, reluctantly she pushed her feet out of the warm bed and reached for her dressing gown.

She had left the landing light on. Padding across it she went through Joss and Luke's empty room. The curtains there were open and moonlight flooded across the floor. Standing still for a moment she stared round, half expecting to see something out of place. But there was nothing wrong that she could see. Pulling her belt a little tighter around her waist she tiptoed through towards Tom's room. He was asleep, his thumb in his mouth, having kicked off all his bedclothes. He seemed warm enough though, his small face pink and relaxed in the glow of the night light near him. Pulling his covers up Lyn tucked them in, careful not to disturb him, then she turned towards Ned's room.

The cot was empty.

She stared at it for several seconds, her stomach tying itself in knots, then she flew back across to Tom's room.

'Tom? Tom wake up! Tom what have you done with your brother?' Oh please God let him be all right! She was shaking like a leaf. 'Tom, wake up!'

The little boy opened his eyes slowly and stared up at her sleepily, his eyes blank.

'Tom!'

There was no recognition in his gaze.

'Tom, wake up!' She shook him. 'Where's Ned?'

He was looking at her vacantly, his body awake but his mind still lost in some dream far away. 'Oh please God, let him be all right!' She couldn't hear the baby crying. If he was cold or hungry he would cry as loudly as he could, unless – she did not let herself pursue that thought. 'Tom, darling, I want you to wake up and help me.' She took the little boy's shoulders and pulled him into the sitting position. 'Can you hear me, sweetheart? I need you to help me.'

He was beginning to move at last. Puzzled, he blinked several times and at last the thumb went back into his mouth. She smiled at him, trying to keep her voice gentle. 'Now. Were you playing with little Ned?'

Tom nodded.

'Do you know where he is now?'

The little boy shook his head.

'Try and think, Tom. Where were you both playing?

437

It's important. Ned is cold and frightened all by himself. He wants us to go and find him.'

'Tom show Lyn.' He scrambled to his feet.

Lifting him out of the cot she put him down on the floor and pulled on his small pale blue dressing gown. 'That's it. Now slippers.' Her hands were shaking so much she was finding it difficult to dress him. 'Now, Tom, show me where he is.'

Tom took her hand and skipped confidently out into his parents' bedroom. From there he led the way across to the landing and on up the attic stairs. Lyn was trembling. It was bitterly cold up there. No heating relieved the iciness as they walked through into the first attic.

'What were you doing up here, Tom?' she asked as he led the way across the floor towards the door in the far wall. 'It's dark and cold.'

'The moon.' He gestured towards the window. 'Georgie wants us to play in the moon.'

Lyn swallowed. Opening the door she peered into the darkness of the passage and then at the doors opening off it. Moonlight flooded across the dusty floor boards. 'Where's Ned, darling? Show me quickly.'

Tom seemed less confident now. He hung back. 'Don't like it.'

'I know. It's cold. But Ned is cold too. Let's fetch him and then we can all go back downstairs to the warm.'

Still unwilling to move, Tom pointed ahead of them. 'He's there.'

'There? In the next attic?' She ran towards the door, leaving Tom standing in the middle of the room. He had begun to cry.

The door was locked. 'Oh no. Please God this can't be happening. It can't.' She spun round. 'Tom, where's the key?'

He shook his head, tears running down his cheeks.

'Darling, please, try and remember. We have to have

438

the key. Poor Ned is very cold. We must find him quickly.'

'It's Georgie's key.'

Lyn took a deep breath. 'Georgie is imaginary, Tom. He's not really there. He can't have a key. Tom has got the key. Where is it?' Her voice was beginning to shake.

'Georgie put it on the door.' He pointed above the doorway. She stared up at the pale, worm-eaten beams which framed the room, then she reached up, feeling on the dry, splintered wood. A heavy iron key, dislodged by her groping fingers fell down with a clatter and lay at her feet. Grabbing it she tried it in the lock. It was very stiff, but at last it turned and she managed to force the door open. There was what seemed a cruelly small bundle of blankets lying on the floor in the far corner.

'Ned?' Icy with terror she ran towards it and fell on her knees. For a moment she thought he was dead. He lay quite still in her arms, his eyes shut, then as she clutched him against her they fluttered open and he stared at her. For several moments he did not move then at last he gave a big smile of recognition.

'Oh thank God! Thank God! Thank God!' She was crying now in earnest.

Behind her Tom crept into the room and came over to her. His hand clutched at her dressing gown. 'Is Ned happy now?'

'Yes, darling. Ned is happy now. Come on, let's go downstairs and get warm.'

She took them both down to the kitchen. Warming milk on the stove she was thinking very hard. Of course, he must have fetched a chair to put the key so high; but why? Why should the little boy want to get rid of his brother. She glanced at Tom who was sitting half asleep on the rocking chair, cuddling Kit. Ned, in his bouncy chair was watching her alertly, obviously pleased with the idea of a warm night time drink – something he had finally relinquished as a regular activity weeks before. Of course hostility was common in elder children when their siblings arrived; very common; it wasn't really surprising. It was only odd that Tom had shown no sign of it before.

As if conscious of her gaze Tom looked at her suddenly. He gave her a sleepy smile. 'Georgie likes Ned,' he said slowly.

'Everything OK?' Jimbo was standing in the doorway next morning watching as she cooked breakfast.

'Fine. Why shouldn't it be?' Astonishingly, she felt pleased to see him. She took two pieces of toast from the toaster and put them in the rack. 'Would you like some coffee?'

He hesitated, then slowly nodded. 'All right then. Thanks.'

'Sit down.' Lyn spread the pieces of toast and cut them into fingers. 'Is something wrong?' He was still standing by the door.

'No. No, I suppose not. Thanks.'

He moved into the room awkwardly, half shy, half nervous and inserted himself without pulling it out onto a chair which was drawn up close to the table.

Lyn smiled to herself. Putting a large cup of coffee down in front of him she turned back to the dresser. 'Do you want some toast now you're here?'

'Might as well. Thanks.'

'Help yourself to milk and sugar.' She paused. 'Jimbo, what is it? I'm not going to bite you.'

He blushed scarlet. 'I know that. It's just . . . it's just I reckon I don't like this house, that's all. It don't feel right. I don't know how you could stay here by yourself.'

'There's nothing to be afraid of here.' She sat down with her own cup. 'Nothing at all. It's a lovely house.'

'Look at what happened to Reverend Gower.'

'A heart attack can happen to anyone.'

'I suppose so.' He shook his head. 'And Mary Sutton.

440

What about Mary Sutton?' He had finally told her about Mary's death the evening before. He shrugged. 'I reckon that had something to do with this house an' all. You heard when Joss and Luke are coming back?'

Lyn shook her head. 'There's no hurry. They need the break. There's nothing wrong in the work shop, is there?'

'No. That's all fine. You'll be staying on here on your own then, until they get back?'

Lyn nodded. 'Try and look a bit more pleased about it.'

He gave a tight little laugh. 'I'm very pleased. I don't like being up here, even outside, on my own. I was just thinking about those kids.' He gestured towards Tom with his head. 'I don't like to think of them up here. Things happen to kids in this house.'

'Oh please. Not that again.' Lyn stopped. The night before, after giving them their drinks she had put the boys back to bed. Then she had switched on the baby alarm in Ned's room, and threading the wire under the door had put the speaker in her own. She had not liked locking the door on the baby, but the key was not going to leave her person. She had threaded it on a piece of ribbon and hung it round her own neck. The rest of the night had been peaceful, but this morning – she chewed her lip again at the memory – this morning when she let herself into the room to the contented sound of Ned's gurgling away to himself in his cot, she had found him playing with a small wooden elephant that she did not remember ever having seen before in her life.

'Something wrong?' Ever alert, Jimbo had noticed her sudden silence.

She shook her head.

'Right.' He plainly wasn't going to press her. Standing up he drained his mug. 'I'd best be getting on.'

'What about your toast?'

'I'll take it with me, if that's all right.' He scraped some honey onto it and turned towards the door, stopping at the last moment to turn back to her for a second. 'You sure you're all right?'

'I told you!'

'Yes. Right.'

She stood silently for several seconds after he had gone, then she shrugged and shook her head.

Tom looked up at her for a moment and stopped chewing. He wondered why Aunty Lyn hadn't noticed the woman standing behind her; it was the woman who had carried Ned up to the attic and then beckoned him to follow. She hadn't seen the tin man last night either. He took another solemn bite out of his toast finger. If she wasn't frightened he supposed it must be all right.

'You don't usually come home dinner time. What's the matter boy?' Jimbo's father was reading the *Mirror* at the kitchen table amid a litter of take-away containers from the night before.

'I want to talk to Nat. You got her number?'

'You leave your sister alone, Jim. She doesn't need you ringing her at work.'

'She said I could any time. And this is important. They've got problems up at the Hall, and I reckon she should come over and speak to them.'

'Oh no. Now you keep your nose out of all that. If I think you mean what I think you mean –'

'Dad. Listen. It's bad. Those kids are in danger. That Lyn doesn't have a clue. She wouldn't see a tractor if it drove through her kitchen wall and ploughed up her breakfast dishes. With Luke and Joss away, it's up to me.'

'Luke and Joss, is it.' His father put on a la-di-da voice. 'They say you could call them that?'

'Course. Shut up, Dad. Just tell me where the number is.' Jimbo was riffling through the pile of old newspapers and notes on the kitchen counter beside the phone.

442

'Up there. Pinned on the wall.'

'Right.' His face grim, Jimbo began to dial.

'Nat, that you? Can you talk? It's important.' He glared at his father who was lounging back in his chair listening. 'Listen, I reckon you need to come back here and talk to the Grants up at the Hall. Things are bad there again.'

He listened intently for a few seconds. 'Yes. Joss has seen him; and the little boy. Reverend Gower came back to try and do something and he ended up dead. It's only a matter of time before someone else gets killed. I reckon you're the only one who can help.'

He scowled at his father who was shaking his head, looking up at the ceiling. 'Yes. Joss will listen to you. She's really nice. Luke doesn't believe what's in front of his nose and that Lyn who looks after the kids is as thick as two planks. It's up to you. Reckon you can come home this weekend? Great!' He beamed at the phone. 'See you then.'

'Your sister's got better things to do than come back here and interfere with things that don't concern her.'

'No she ain't. She's pleased to help. You should be proud of her, Dad, not ashamed.'

'I'm not ashamed.'

'You are. And you called her a witch. That's stupid. And sexist.' Jim grinned. 'Even I know that. Now, what you got for dinner? I'm starving.'

Janet had seen Lyn walking towards the village with the children in the double buggy as she was making her way up to the church to do the flowers. She frowned. She hadn't realised they were back. Lyn looked very tired, and little Tom, she could see from the car as she drove past waving, was fast asleep. Neither of them saw her. Intent on her own thoughts Lyn was pushing the buggy across the village green, her head down, her steps weary, plodding in the direction of the village shop. She could

443

catch them there after she had checked the church and topped up the vases with water.

Janet hesitated near the church door, gazing across the quiet churchyard to the spot where they had found Mary Sutton's body. The village was still shocked at the tragedy and whispers were flying from door to door about what she had been doing out there in the dark and cold alone. The rector had rung Roy who was one of the church-wardens about what they had found in the church – the bread and wine on the altar, almost certainly that used in the exorcism at the Hall – and there had been an emergency meeting at the rectory. Roy did not tell her what they had discussed, but it seemed there would be no funeral in the church. Mary had always said that she wished to be cremated and her ashes scattered in the sea.

Letting herself into the shadowy nave Janet groped for the light switches and made her way towards the vestry. The church was looking good; Michaelmas daisies lasted well, and there were huge displays of them in the chancel and in front of the pulpit. She picked up the heavy brass water jug and began to tour each arrangement. In front of the small brass plaque to Katherine she stopped. Some-one had left a bunch of white roses on the ground in front of it. She stared down at it thoughtfully. The church was open for visitors during the day. Anyone could have done it – so why did she feel suddenly so wary. She eyed the flowers then slowly she backed away.

Between one moment and the next the church had become uncomfortable; there was a strange feeling of hostility where usually she felt nothing but an all encompassing peace and security. Hastily, with a glance over her shoulder she retraced her steps to the vestry and set the jug on its shelf. Coming out she pulled the door shut and made her accustomed small bow to the altar before walking quickly back down the aisle towards the door at the rear of the church. Four pews from the end she stopped. There was something between her and the door. She blinked. It was a trick of the light, a patch of sunlight thrown unexpectedly through the south windows out of the gloom of the morning onto the old flag stones. It looked like a mist, a slowly spinning mist. She caught hold of the pew end near her and shook her head, disorientated and slightly dizzy. It was moving almost imperceptibly away from the door across the back of the church towards the font, then as she watched it stopped, seemed to hesitate and then changed direction. It was moving east now, up the centre of the aisle towards her.

She took a step backwards and then another, her legs shaking so much they would barely support her. The church seemed very empty, the lights high on the roof beams directed up into the vaulted ceiling, the chancel still in comparative darkness where she hadn't switched on the other lights. She glanced over her shoulder towards the altar and then turned and ran, skipping round the front of the pews and into the side aisle. The spinning mist seemed to hesitate then it moved on towards the chancel steps. Janet ran on tiptoe down the small side chapel, dodged round the pillar and reached the door.

Grabbing the ring she tried to open it. For a moment in her panic she thought it was locked, wrestling with it desperately, then at last the latch clicked up and she hauled the heavy door open, throwing herself out into the porch. Slamming the door behind her she ran out into the churchyard, taking deep breaths of the cold air.

There was no sunshine. The sky was heavy with cloud. She glanced over her shoulder, almost expecting to see the door opening, but the porch was still; the door remained closed. Head down, walking as quickly as she could she hurried down the path to her car and climbed in. Slamming down the locks she tried with shaking hand to insert the key in the ignition. After a couple of attempts she managed it and turned it on, revving the engine before shooting the car out onto the road.

Lyn was choosing some cold meats from the delicatessen counter when Janet walked into the shop. She glanced up as the door banged shut and smiled. 'Tom says he's hungry enough to eat that horse you gave him.'

'That hungry, eh?' Janet ruffled Tom's hair. Her hand was shaking and she found she was shivering violently. Behind the counter Sally Fairchild glanced up from the meat slicer. 'You look peaky, Janet. Something wrong?' She was peeling the ham from the blade onto her polythened palm with a rhythmic hissing sound which had Tom mesmerised.

Janet shook her head. 'I was up in the church. The door banged. Gave me a fright, that's all.'

Sally stopped slicing and gave her a long appraising look. 'Since when did a door banging make you shake like a leaf?'

Janet shrugged. 'Nerves. Probably too much coffee this morning.' She gave an unconvincing laugh.

'You're getting like Joss.' Lyn did not make the remark sound like a compliment. 'You'll be seeing ghosts round every corner next.' She turned back to her purchases. 'That's plenty, Sal, thanks. And some sausages please. A pound will do.'

'Where is Joss?' Janet tried to steady herself with an effort.

'Still in Paris as far as I know.'

'Are you up at the house alone?'

The question sounded too urgent.

Lyn frowned. 'Of course. Why not?'

'No reason.' Janet shrugged. 'I just thought – Lyn, you will be careful, won't you.'

Lyn turned to face her. 'Listen. There is nothing wrong with that house now that Joss isn't there. Do you understand me? Nothing goes wrong. Nothing sinister happens –' she broke off suddenly, remembering her panic of the night before.

Sally glanced up from the bag into which she was inserting Lyn's purchases. She caught Janet's eye.

Janet shrugged. 'OK. I'm sorry. Just remember I'm there if you need me.' She turned towards the door.

'Janet, wait.' Lyn fumbled in her purse for some money. 'Look, that was rude of me. But there isn't anything wrong.'

'Good.' Janet stood for a moment, her hands wedged in her pockets looking into Lyn's eyes. Then she turned to leave. 'Just remember where I am if you get fed up with your own company.'

Sally was ringing up Lyn's purchases on the till. She stopped as soon as the door had shut behind Janet. 'She looked really ragged.'

Lyn nodded. 'I wonder what happened up there.'

'Something strange, I'll be bound. Maybe old Mary is haunting the place already!' She gave an ostentatious shiver. 'You are sure you are all right up there, my dear? Nothing would make most of the locals sleep alone in that house, you know, never mind with small children.'

'No. So I keep being told.' Lyn packed the shopping into her haversack. 'Thanks Sally. I'll probably be back tomorrow.'

The buggy seemed heavier on the way back, or perhaps it was that she was tired. Lyn regretted for a moment that she hadn't begged a lift from Janet, then she remembered why. Janet would have lectured and hectored her and tried to put on the pressure to bring the boys to stay at the farm, when all Lyn wanted was to have them to herself while she had the chance. Plodding on she glanced up at the sky. The clouds were becoming heavier and more threatening; she would be lucky if it didn't rain before she got home. She glanced down at her charges.

447

Both warmly wrapped and tucked beneath their blankets they were sound asleep.

The first rain drops were beginning to fall as she reached the gate and began the last haul up the drive.

The house seemed very dark as she came round the corner. Puffing along behind the buggy, forcing the wheels through the muddy gravel, she glanced up at the rain-streaked windows. There was a face at the attic window above the front door. She stopped and stared. Was Joss home? Squinting, she shook the ice cold drops of sleet off her eyelashes, trying to make out who it was for several seconds longer, then she headed for the back of the house and the kitchen. The courtyard was empty. Jimbo appeared to have closed up and gone – for lunch she supposed. There were no other cars there. She frowned. Who on earth was it then at the window? Groping in her pocket with ice cold fingers for the key she pushed the door open and bent to lift Tom out. 'Come on, sausage. You know I can't lift you both up. You'll have to run inside for Aunty Lyn and open the kitchen door. Shall we try and do it without waking the tornado?' That was their private name for Ned.

Tom giggled and pushed himself out of the chair, rushing ahead of her into the kitchen. Turning she bumped the buggy up the back steps and manoeuvred it past the coats and into the kitchen before stopping to unbutton her own jacket. 'Tom? Come and take your coat off.'

There was silence.

'Oh Tom, not again. Come on.' She sighed, turning to hang up her coat and shake and fold the damp blankets onto the rail in front of the stove to dry. 'Tom? Come on, then you can help me get lunch.'

The door to the hall was open. With a glance at Ned who was still asleep Lyn left him in the buggy and ran into the corridor and through into the great hall. 'Tom? Come on. Where are you?' She stopped, staring at the

448

fireplace. A fire was burning in the grate. She could see the logs, neatly heaped into a pyramid, the blown ash swept up, the room warm and filled with the sweet rich smell of burning oak.

'Joss? Luke? When did you get back?' She went to the study door and peered round it. 'Where's the car? I didn't see it?'

The study was deserted, the curtains still half drawn as she had left them that morning.

'Joss? Luke? Where are you?' Lyn stood for a minute at the bottom of the stairs. Then she began to climb.

uke neatened all the small empty pots and containers and lined up the knives and forks on the tray in front of him with precision and pushed it to one side. He glanced at Joss. 'Not long now. We'll be landing in about fifteen minutes I should think.' The stewardesses were trundling their carts along the plane, collecting all the rubbish. He looked down at Joss's meal. She had barely touched anything. 'They'll be all right. Lyn's just been out that's all.'

'Out late at night, with two small children? Out again first thing in the morning?' She shook her head in despair. 'We should have rung the police, Luke. Supposing something's happened to them.'

'Nothing's happened to them, Joss.' He gave a deep sigh. 'Look we'll try and phone again from the air terminal, and if we can't get through to Lyn we'll try Janet again. There's always the chance of course that they've gone off on a spree together. Don't forget they're not expecting us yet.' He reached for her tray and passed it with his own to the flight attendant. 'Come on. Cheer up. We don't want to undo all the good the rest has done you.'

'I know.' She nodded wearily. 'I did enjoy it. I did like Paul.'

She fell silent. Paul had arranged the flights – getting them on the plane at short notice by pulling one or two strings with someone he knew – and he had insisted on driving them back to Orly. There had been tears in his eyes as well as Joss's when they finally embraced at the check in. 'Come and see us,' she had whispered. 'If it doesn't make you unhappy to come there without her, come and see us.'

'Of course.' He kissed her on both cheeks. 'And you will come back to stay with me in the summer and you will bring your little boys with you.'

There had been a moment's silence as they had both thought the unthinkable and he squeezed her shoulders again. 'They will be all right,' he said, watching as Luke pushed their passports over the counter. 'You will see. They will be just fine.'

In the phone booth in the high airy terminal building at Stansted Joss stood listening to the line ringing. There was no reply. She glanced at her watch. The boys should be resting by now after their lunch. With a glance at Luke who was standing only three feet away watching their luggage she dialled Janet. This time there was an answer.

A few minutes later she hung up. When she turned to face Luke she was smiling. 'Janet saw them all in the shop this morning. She says they're fine. The phone must be out of order or I've rung each time when Lyn has been out. She saw them on their way home too.'

'Good.' Luke stooped to swing their cases up and he began to walk towards the doors. 'Then perhaps you can stop worrying while we find the car and sort ourselves out.' He was heading towards the bus which would take them out to the distant car park. Outside the huge ever-circling door he stopped and waited for her. 'Joss. You're going to be sensible from now on; no overdoing it. No arguing with Lyn. No worrying about ghosts and noises

451

and silliness where there is no need for it. Remember, you've got to see that doctor again.'

Joss stared at him. 'I haven't been making any of it up, Luke. Why do you think we've come stampeding back like this! For goodness sake. Paul believed me. He knew. He had seen my mother go through it –'

'Your mother was being persecuted by a real woman, Joss. Not a ghost. A real flesh and blood woman.' He swung the cases onto the bus and they found some seats. 'Her Katherine wasn't a ghost.'

'Wasn't she?' Joss seemed to be looking right through him. 'We'll see.'

Pulling the car up in the courtyard next to Lyn's Mini Janet peered through the windscreen at the house.

For a moment she didn't move, then, almost reluctantly she opened the door and climbed out.

The back door of the house was unlocked. After a couple of knocks she pushed it open and walked through the lobby into the kitchen. It was empty. The buggy stood near the window, and the neatly folded blankets were hanging on the rail in front of the range. She touched them; they were completely dry and warm. There was no sign of anything cooking. In the corner the rocking horse stood abandoned, its rein hanging to the floor. She frowned. For a moment she had thought it was rocking gently by itself as though pushed by an unseen hand. She stared at it. It was her imagination of course. It had to be. Walking to the door she peered through.

'Lyn? Where are you?'

Her voice echoed in the silence.

'Lyn? It's Janet. Are you there?'

She took a few steps into the great hall and looked around. The place was in shadow, the remains of a fire smouldering in the hearth. Although the room was quite warm she found she was shivering as she walked through

452

towards the study. It was empty, so she went back and peered up the staircase. 'Lyn?' she called softly. If the boys were asleep she didn't want to wake them. 'Lyn, where are you?'

Tiptoeing up she paused on the landing outside Lyn's room. The door was shut and she tapped on it gently. 'Lyn? Can I come in?'

There was no answer. She hesitated a moment, not liking to open it in case Lyn was asleep, then she took her courage in both hands and pushed it. The room was empty and somehow very bare. There was no sign that Lyn had been there recently at all.

She was on her way to the boys' bedrooms when she heard a faint knocking in the distance. She stopped, listening. There it was again – a distinct hammering sound from somewhere upstairs. She eyed the ceiling suspiciously, then she turned and went out to the stairs again.

The attics were very cold. Nervously she peered into the first. It was furnished as a spare bedroom, but there was no sign of anyone there. Beyond it the rest of the top floor was empty – a long string of low-ceilinged rooms leading out of each other the length of the house. 'Lyn?' she shouted. 'Are you up here?' The sound of her voice was somehow shocking in the intense silence. It was as she was standing listening for a response that she heard the knocking once again, louder this time, and more frenzied. 'Lyn? Are you there?' Ducking through the door she made her way into the next room. That too was empty, dusty and smelling of cold and damp. 'Lyn, where are you?'

The door at the furthest end of the line of attics was closed. The banging was coming from behind it. 'Lyn, is that you?' Janet put her ear to the wood panelling. 'Lyn?' She put her hand on the latch and rattled it. The door appeared to be locked.

'Let me out. For God's sake let me out!' Lyn's voice from behind the door was completely hysterical. 'I've been here for hours. Are the boys all right?'

Janet grimaced. 'I haven't seen the boys. Hold on. I'll try and find the key.' She looked round frantically. The room in which she was standing was empty. There was nowhere a key could be hidden.

'Feel on the beam over the door,' Lyn instructed, her voice muffled by the thickness of the wood. 'That's where it was last time.'

Janet looked up. Cautiously she put her hand above her head and ran her fingers over the studs and cross beams which made the partition wall. It was several seconds before she connected with cold metal. 'Here it is. Found it!' She grabbed it and inserted it into the large key hole.

A second later the door swung open. Lyn was white faced, her hair dishevelled, her clothes filthy. 'Thank God you came. I was afraid I'd be there forever.'

'Who locked you in?' Janet was running after her back towards the stairs.

'Tom. It must have been. The little devil.'

'It can't have been. That beam was far too high for Tom.'

'He must have fetched a chair or something.' Lyn brushed the tears out of her eyes with the back of her hand. 'For pity's sake hurry. There's no knowing what he may have done.'

She hurtled down the staircase and through towards his bedroom. It was empty. 'Tom? Tom where are you? Don't hide from me.' She pushed open the door to Ned's little bedroom. That too was empty.

'Oh God!' It was a sob. 'Janet, where is he?'

Janet bit her lip. 'Where were they when you last saw them? Tom presumably upstairs and Ned? Where was Ned?'

'Ned should be in his buggy in the kitchen.'

Janet shook her head. 'No, I've just come from there. The buggy's empty.'

'He was still fast asleep, so I left him. He was strapped in. There was no danger. It was only for a minute.' Lyn burst into tears again. 'Oh God!' She wiped her face with her sleeve. 'Tom ran away and hid and I heard noises up there in the attic. Giggling. Running about. It was Tom. It had to be, so I ran up to find him. He's not allowed to play up there on his own, and anyway I wanted to get lunch.' She sniffed. 'I looked everywhere for him. I could hear him. He was hiding somewhere up there. When I was in that far attic the door banged and I heard the key turn then there was complete silence. I begged him. I promised him all sorts of things if he would open it, but there was total silence. No more running about, no more giggles. I knelt down to look through the key hole at once – did you see how big it was – I could see the whole attic. He wasn't there, Janet. Nowhere. And there was no chair. I'd have heard if he'd dragged a chair across the floor. He's only a little boy. He couldn't have lifted it by himself.'

Janet put her arm round her shoulders. 'Try and keep calm, Lyn. We've got to work this out. We must search the house again, carefully. You know how children love hiding. Tom has probably hidden himself somewhere and he's having a good laugh.'

'With Ned?' It was a whisper.

Janet shrugged. 'I expect he's tucked Ned up somewhere and left him; he's too young to play with properly.' Her voice died away. After a second's silence she went on. 'We know he's not in the attic. Let's search this floor then we'll go on down. We must be systematic.'

They were. They searched each room in turn, looking under beds, behind curtains and in cupboards, then, certain neither child was there they went down to the study.

'No sign.' Janet had even looked in the drawers of the desk.

'The cellar,' Lyn whispered. 'We must check the cellar.'

The door was locked and there was no sign of the key.

'They can't be down there.' Janet was eyeing the door dubiously.

'They might be. I'll fetch the key.' Lyn disappeared for a moment and then reappeared with it in her hand. She inserted it into the lock with a shaking hand and pushed open the door.

The cellar was in darkness. 'There's no one here.' Janet's voice echoed slightly as she reached past Lyn and switched on the lights. 'It doesn't look as if anyone has been here for weeks. Do you want us to go down to look?'

Lyn nodded. 'We have to look everywhere.' She was feeling very sick.

'OK.' After a moment's hesitation Janet led the way down the steps.

At the bottom they both stopped and listened. 'He's not down here,' Lyn whispered. 'He can't be.'

'We'd better look properly.' Janet was feeling distinctly uneasy. 'Where is his favourite hiding place? Does he have one?'

'He does seem to like the attic. I've never known him come down here. But he's not allowed to. It's always kept locked and the key was where it's supposed to be – so how could he be down here?'

Janet shrugged. 'We had to check. After what happened to Edgar.'

Lyn stared at her. 'But that was a heart attack.'

'I know. But why was he down here? No one seems to know.'

They stood for a moment looking round then Lyn walked through and stood in the second cellar. There was no sign of anything and nowhere to hide. Closing her eyes with a deep sigh of relief she turned. 'We'd better go on looking upstairs.'

The great hall, dining room, morning room, passages, pantries and sculleries behind the kitchen – each one was subjected to a careful and thorough search. When they were once more in the kitchen Janet reached for her jacket. 'Come on. We're going to have to look outside. I wonder if Jim is back yet. He can give us a hand.'

But the courtyard was empty, the garages and coach houses all padlocked. 'At least we know they can't be there.' Lyn rattled one of the locks. She was feeling more and more afraid.

The gardens were bleak, the November light failing as they let themselves through the gate onto the lawn. 'We've got to check the lake.' Lyn's hands were shaking. 'Oh, Janet, why? What was Tom thinking of?' Suddenly she was crying again.

'We don't know anything's wrong.' Janet gave her a quick hug. 'Come on. It's a childish prank, that's all. I'm sure they're perfectly safe.' Her voice lacked conviction.

Walking down the lawn towards the still water of the lake both women were silent. After a few steps Lyn broke into a run. On the bank she stared round, scanning the reeds and lilies. A moorhen broke cover near her and paddled furiously towards the far bank with a sharp cry of distress and a heron, which had been feeding on the island in the centre of the water lumbered awkwardly into the air croaking with indignation.

'I can't see anything.' Lyn dashed the tears out of her eyes as Janet caught up with her, panting.

'Nor can I. You go that way and I'll go this way. I'll meet you round the other side. That way we can be sure.' She squeezed Lyn's arm and set off, her shoes squelching in the damp muddy grass. The air felt very cold and she shivered as she hurried on, her eyes scanning the water, dreading the thought that she might actually see something there, but the lake and its surroundings were empty of any signs of the small boy or the baby. When she caught up with Lyn she was smiling. 'Thank God they're not here. I couldn't have borne it. Where else can we look?'

Lyn stared round desperately. 'Tom's only little. He can't have got far. Not on his own.' She bit her lip. 'You don't think – you don't think they've been taken away?'

'Who on earth by?' Janet shook her head. 'They were in the house. You'd have known if there was someone else there.'

'Someone locked me in, Janet.'

They stared at each other for a moment. 'I think we'd better call the police,' Lyn said at last. 'Let's go back inside.'

As they walked they were both scanning the garden for any signs. 'You know he could just be hiding – in a hedge or a bush or something. We should be calling.' Janet stopped and turning round cupped her hands round her mouth. 'Tom! Tom Tom, where are you?'

'Tom!' Lyn echoed. She ran towards the shrubbery at the edge of the lawn. 'Tom Tom! Come on. It's lunch time.'

By the time they had worked their way round to the front of the house they were both exhausted, hoarse with shouting and filthy from peering into the muddy places under bushes and trees.

'It's no good. It will have to be the police. The woods go for miles. We can't search them on our own.' Lyn was white as a sheet.

'No.' Janet eased her frozen hands into her pockets. 'No, you're right. We'd better go in and phone.'

They walked across the gravel in front of the house, and ducked through the arch into the courtyard. Luke's car was parked by the back door.

'Oh no.' Lyn stopped. She had gone white. 'What am I going to tell them?'

'The truth, love. Come on. The sooner we've done that, the sooner we can call the police.' Janet put her arm round Lyn's shoulders again.

Together they went into the back hall and pushed open the kitchen door.

Luke and Joss were standing by the table laughing. Tom was between them, holding Joss's hand. In the other he was clutching a model of the Eiffel Tower.

'Tom?' Lyn's cry made them all turn round. 'Tom, where have you been? Where's Ned?'

'Lyn! Janet! What on earth is the matter?' Joss stared at them in horror. 'Ned's here. Asleep. In the buggy. What's wrong? Why are you both so wet?'

Lyn walked slowly round the table and stood in front of the buggy for a full minute staring down at the sleeping baby, then slowly she knelt down and began to undo the harness which held him safely in; the harness which had clips far too stiff for Tom's small fingers to undo. Around him was tucked one of the soft blankets which she remembered hanging on the front of the range.

She felt it carefully. It was bone dry. Tears running down her cheeks she stared up at Joss who had come to stand behind her.

'What happened, Lyn?' Joss was frowning.

'I thought I'd lost them.' Lifting Ned out, Lyn kissed the top of his head. Climbing to her feet she pushed him into Joss's arms. 'I thought we'd lost them. I thought . . . I thought . . .' Sitting down at the table she put her head in her arms and burst into sobs.

Luke frowned at Joss. 'It looks as though it's a good thing we came back. Hey, old thing, come on. Cheer up. Everyone is all right.' He patted Lyn's head awkwardly then he looked at Janet. 'You both look as though you've been dragged through a hedge backwards. Do you mind telling me exactly what's been going on here?'

'Wait. First let me ask Tom something.' Janet knelt down before the little boy and gave him a hug. 'OK, sausage. I want you to tell Aunty Janet where you and Ned were hiding.' She gave him an encouraging smile. 'You were hiding, weren't you.'

Tom nodded vigorously.

'So. Where were you? Aunty Lyn and I looked and looked and we couldn't find you.'

'We were playing with Georgie.'

'Now, why don't I find that surprising,' Janet said softly. She raised her hand sharply to forestall Joss's cry of alarm. 'So, where do you go to play with Georgie, Tom?'

'Upstairs.'

'Right upstairs? In the attic?'

He nodded.

'And was it you that locked Aunty Lyn in the attic?'

He stared at her for a moment. 'That was Georgie.'

'I see. You knew that was naughty of him, didn't you.'

Tom looked shame faced. He peeked at Lyn and then buried his face in Janet's sweater. She looked up at Joss over the little boy's head. 'Please, bring them back to me. Don't keep them here.'

'Janet –'

Luke's protest was cut short by Lyn. 'Please, Luke. Until we've sorted out what happened.'

'But you don't believe in all this rubbish about ghosts!' Luke stared at her.

'I don't know what I believe any more. I think we should all go to Janet's. If she'll have us. Just till we find out what's happening.'

'I'd love to have you all, Luke.'

Suddenly he caved in. 'OK. You girls go, and the kids. But I'm staying here.'

'No; remember what Paul said.'

'Joss, I am not afraid of a jumble of legends and stories. I live here. My job is here. I like this house and I'm not afraid of it.' He gave a sober smile. 'Honestly. I'll be all right. You two take Tom and Ned to Janet's because I know you won't get a wink of sleep unless you do, but then tomorrow we're going to have to work something out. We can't go on like this.'

In the end they persuaded him to come back to the farm for supper at least, but later, after they had all eaten, and checked on the children, asleep and safe upstairs in the long low-ceilinged bedroom Luke eventually got up and stretched his arms above his head. Lyn had gone to bed half an hour before. 'I don't know about you, Joss, but I'm feeling a bit jet lagged.' He grinned at his own joke. 'I think I'm off home now.'

'No.' Joss clutched at his hand. 'Stay here. Just tonight.'

He shook his head. 'Joss, my love. I must go back. I am not going to be chased out of our own house. That is ridiculous. And tomorrow we've got to find a way of reassuring you and Lyn.' He turned to Janet and gave her a kiss on the cheek. 'Thanks for a wonderful meal. You look after them and keep the hysteria levels down, OK? I think perhaps what we'll do is get the family to rally round. The christening contingent. Your mum and dad, Lyn and my mum and dad and perhaps Mat as well. And David and Uncle Tom Cobbleigh and anyone else who wants to come. We'll have a pre Christmas wassail.' He grinned. 'No ghost would dare show its face in a house that full, would it?' He gave Joss a hug. 'Now, no more worry, OK? And remember, if Janet doesn't mind, you promised you'd ring Paul and tell him everything was all right.'

In a moment he was gone. Janet sighed. 'Men. They won't be told. Isn't he scared at all?'

Joss shook her head sadly. 'I think he's as scared as hell. He just won't admit it. Not even to himself.'

Paul was reassuring. 'He'll be all right, Jocelyn. He is strong, your husband. But if you want more reinforcement call me and I will come too.' She could hear his laughter and his affection down the phone.

'Bless you, Paul, I will.' When she had hung up she turned to Janet who had picked up her needlepoint and was working by the light of a lamp near the fire. 'Can I ring David? I want to find out what happened here when he came.'

'Of course.' Janet bit off a thread. 'Get him up here as well.'

'I don't think I can. It's term time still.' She pulled the phone down off the table and sat in front of the fire near Janet with the instrument on her knee.

David was marking a pile of essays on the Education Act. Nemesis, he thought ruefully as he sat staring at them, listening to a soft background Sibelius. He was far from displeased when the phone rang even though it was after eleven.

'David? It's Joss.'

'Joss?' His heart leaped at the sound of her voice. 'Where are you? Are you home?'

'The boys and I are with Janet.'

'Thank God you're not in that house. I suppose you heard what happened.'

'Some.' She was conscious of Janet staring at her. 'Can you tell me exactly what happened?'

It was several minutes before she spoke again.

'Can you come, David? Can you come, so we can talk?'

He hesitated. His flat was warm and comfortable and above all safe. Staring down at the pile of essays he was tempted to say no, but the edge of panic in Joss's voice had reached him. Her dumbo husband still did not seem to have caught on about what was happening. She needed someone who understood.

'OK. I'm free after fifth period tomorrow. I'll come

462

up then.' There was a moment's silence as he mentally questioned his own sanity. 'Can you stay away till I come?'

'No, David. Of course I can't stay away.'

'Then keep the children away and you be careful. Please.'

She sat for a long time after she had rung off staring into the flames, aware that Janet had put down her embroidery and was watching her carefully.

She looked up at last. 'So, supposing you tell me what really happened this afternoon. You and Lyn seemed determined to keep it quiet.'

'We didn't want to frighten you.'

'So, frighten me now they're safe.' She turned a speculative gaze on Janet.

It did not take long to tell the story.

Joss turned back to the fire. She did not want Janet to see her fear.

'It can't have been Tom,' Janet repeated. 'He couldn't have reached the key and he couldn't undo the baby harness in the buggy.'

'But you don't think it was a real person.'

'Jimbo?' Janet shrugged. 'I gather he has a key, but somehow I doubt it. Who else is there?' She began to fold her work away into her sewing basket. 'I'll tell you one thing, Joss. I wish Luke hadn't gone back there, I really do.'

uke turned off the kitchen light and made his way slowly towards the stairs. In the great hall he stopped and stared round. The room was still warm, though the fire had long ago died, and it smelled nice – wood smoke and flowers and old lavender polish. He stood savouring the moment, his hand on the light switch. It was good to be home again, though he had enjoyed the trip to France; he had liked Paul enormously, as had Joss, and he hoped to see him again. Sighing he turned off the switch and began to climb the stairs.

Flicking on their bedroom light he was pulling off his jacket when he noticed the bed. He stared for a minute, hardly able to believe his eyes, then slowly he walked across to it and bent down to run his hand over it. It was covered in white rose petals. His mouth fell open. They were ice cold, like snow flakes, scattered thickly over the whole area of the crewel work cover.

Lyn or Janet? A practical joke – and not a very kind one – aimed at Joss. Angrily he swept them off the bed, watching as they scattered all over the floor.

In the corner of the room, in the far shadows, the slumbering silence stirred and one of the shadows detached itself and moved a little closer to the bed.

Luke was pulling the cover back, shaking it and folding

it onto the chair in the corner. He turned, surveying the floor, and decided it was too late to bother with sweeping it. Time enough for that tomorrow before Joss came home. Hauling his sweater up over his head he walked through into the bathroom and began to run the hot water.

Whistling to himself under his breath he peered at his reflection in the mirror as he reached for the toothpaste, noting the bags under his eyes with a scowl then he stopped what he was doing suddenly and held his breath; he was listening, he realised, straining his ears above the sound of running water. Impatiently he turned off the tap, wrenching at it as the water flow continued for a few seconds. Then came the drips plopping seemingly unstoppably into the bath with the sound of stones rattling in a dustbin and then at last silence. Tiptoeing to the door he turned the handle soundlessly and eased it open, peering out into the hallway. The house was silent.

Reaching for his dressing gown he pulled it on, belting it over his jeans and took a step out onto the landing. Cautiously he peered over the banisters and down into the stairwell. He wasn't sure now what he had heard, but he could feel rather than hear that there was something – or someone – there.

'Joss?' It was a whisper. 'Joss?' he tried louder. The silence seemed to deepen. He wished he had some kind of a weapon to hand. Looking round desperately he spotted the pewter candlestick on the coffer between the doors to the bedrooms. Stealthily he crossed over and taking out the candle he hefted the heavy lump of metal into his hand before turning once more to the stairs.

'Joss? Who's there?' His voice was stronger this time. 'Come on, I can hear you.'

It wasn't true; the silence was so intense it was almost tangible.

'Joss?' He put a foot on the first step down. 'Joss? Lyn?'

He was half way down the stairs when he heard a movement behind him. Spinning round he looked up onto the landing, peering through the turned wooden posts of the banisters and caught sight of something as it fled into his bedroom. Not Kit or Kat. A woman.

'Joss? That is you, isn't it? Come on. Stop playing the fool. I nearly hit you with the candlestick.' Two at a time he retraced his steps and pushed open the door.

She was lying on the bed under the covers – an indistinct shape in the dim light of the bedside lamp. He smiled, relief flooding through him. 'My God, you had me going there; I thought it must be your ghost.' Putting down the candlestick he walked across to the bed. 'Joss? Come on. No need to hide.' Reaching down he pulled back the covers.

There was no one there.

'Joss?' His voice slid up the register. 'Joss, for Christ's sake, stop messing about.'

He peered behind the hangings and then stooped to look under the bed.

'Joss, where are you?' Spinning round, he peered into every corner of the room. 'Joss!' The palms of his hands were sweating. 'That's enough. You've had your little joke.' He backed away from the bed towards the door. With one last glance over his shoulder he turned and fled down the stairs.

In the kitchen he threw himself into the chair at the head of the table and put his head in his hands. What in God's name was the matter with him? He was going neurotic; he was going mad; he rubbed his face with his hands and for a moment he sat still, just staring at the door, half expecting someone to appear through it at any moment.

It was several seconds before he stood up again and went to the stove. Pulling open the door to the fire box he peered in. The coals were glowing nicely and for a

466

minute he stood, his hands outstretched to the warmth. There was no way he was going back to Janet's! He was not going to be chased out of the house by the girls having a joke on him, or by anything else.

He frowned for a moment, not wanting to think about what else it might be. Joss's terror and Paul's very real warning hovered for a moment at the corners of his mind, but he pushed them back angrily. This was complete nonsense. He had allowed them to get to him, that's all. And it wasn't going to go on. He was going to stay in the house and that was that.

For a moment he was tempted to retrace his steps to the great hall, stand up and make an announcement to that effect to any ghosts or spirits or demons who might be lurking, but he thought better of it. A good night's sleep – or at least what was left of the night – he looked at his watch and realised suddenly that it was well after one – was a more sensible plan of action and in the morning the others would be back.

Sitting at the kitchen table, a mug of hot chocolate in front of him, he cupped his hands round the comforting warmth of the pottery and stared blankly ahead, aware that his eyes were closing. Slowly his head began to nod. Once or twice he jerked it up and resolved to stand up and go back upstairs, but each time he leaned back, sipped the chocolate and decided to wait a few more minutes by the warmth of the stove.

He was awakened by the phone ringing. Staring round, confused, he found he was still in the kitchen and it was – he peered at the wall clock – nearly seven o'clock. Outside it was still pitch dark. Fumbling for the phone he picked up the receiver.

'Mr Grant?' The voice was unfamiliar. A woman with a soft local accent.

He grunted assent, running stiff fingers through his hair. The inside of his mouth felt like old mouldy felt.

'Mr Grant, I'm Natalie Cotting. Jim's sister.'

'Jim?' For a moment Luke was confused. 'Oh, Jimbo.'

There was an amused snort from the other end of the line. 'Jimbo. Right. Did he tell you he'd been on to me?'

'No. He didn't. Did you want to speak to him?'

'No. No. I'm sorry to ring so early, but I've been thinking and I reckon I should come over today if I can get the day off. Is your wife there, Mr Grant?'

'Joss? No.' He was shaking his head, confused. 'She spent the night with a neighbour.'

'Ah.' There was a moment's silence. 'And your children. They're with her, right?'

'Yes.'

'Good.' The relief at the other end of the line was palpable.

'Look –' Luke took a deep breath trying to clear his mind. 'I'm sorry. Perhaps I'm being obtuse. You want to speak to Joss, right?'

'Right.' He could hear the amusement in her voice. 'If I set off now, I should be with you in an hour and a half, or thereabouts. Can you tell Jim – that is Jimbo,' she snorted once more, 'that I'm coming, please. And tell Mrs Grant to stay away until I get there, OK?'

'What do you mean, stay away –' Luke was indignant. 'Hello? Are you still there?' He knew she wasn't. He had heard the click as she hung up.

Washed and shaved and in a fresh shirt he felt a new man. It was only as he walked through into the bedroom and rummaged in the chest of drawers for a thick sweater that he noticed the bed. Staring, he walked towards it and stood looking down. It was neatly made, the covers in place, not a dent or wrinkle anywhere and around it the floor was spotless. There was no sign anywhere of a single white petal.

* * *

Jimbo arrived at eight thirty as usual. He was unlocking the carriage house when Luke walked out of the back door and joined him, looking down at the shining chassis on the blocks before them. 'Nearly finished.' Jimbo's voice was filled with pride. 'I got a lot done while you were away.'

'You did indeed.' Luke glanced at him. 'Jimbo, your sister rang this morning. She said to tell you she was coming over.'

'Nat? She's coming? That's good.' Jimbo avoided his eyes. 'I thought she should talk to Joss.'

'So she said. May I ask what about?'

Jim took a deep breath. 'Ghosts. She knows a lot about ghosts. She can talk to them. They never frighten her.'

'And they frighten you?' Luke's hands were rammed down in his jeans pockets. He felt less confident than he had before.

'I'll say. No way will I go into that house.' Jim smiled sheepishly. 'I never liked it, and now –' his voice trailed away.

'And you think Joss and the children are in danger.'

'Not Joss. No. Joss has never been in danger.' Jim shifted his feet uncomfortably. Then he glanced up. 'I think you should watch it, though.' He shrugged, embarrassed. 'Not keen on men, the ghosts in this house. Look at what happened to the Reverend Gower.'

'He had a heart attack, Jimbo. It could have happened anywhere.'

'It didn't though, did it. It happened here.' Jimbo turned to the work bench and reached for a spanner. 'That Lyn, she's over at the Goodyears' too, is she?' he asked casually.

'Yes,' Luke nodded. 'They're all over there.'

'That's good.' Jimbo turned back, the spanner in his hand. 'You just think what happened to old Mr Duncan, and his two boys. I thought Nat should know Joss says it's all happening again.'

469

'So, how can Nat – Natalie – help?'

Jimbo shrugged his shoulders. 'She always said she could. When she was little. No one would listen to her then, of course. But now – well, she knows about these things. She's a psychic, you see.'

'Oh.' Luke raised an eyebrow. 'I see.'

He wasn't at all sure what he was expecting a psychic to look like – shawls, beads and big hooped ear rings, at least – certainly not the neat young woman in a business suit who turned in under the archway some forty minutes later, driving a Golf GTi.

'Sorry.' She reached out to shake Luke's hand. 'I couldn't leave at once after all. I had to look in at the office first. Is Joss here?'

Luke shook his head. 'My wife is still over at the Good-years' with the children.'

'Good.' Natalie glanced over her shoulder at the house. 'May I go in and wander round? There's no need for you to come in too.'

Luke hesitated.

'That's a bit rich, Nat. He doesn't know you're not a burglar,' Jim put in. 'He doesn't know you from Adam.'

Luke laughed. 'I'll take a risk. Yes, please, go on in.'

He stood and watched as she walked over the cobbles towards the back door, noting absent-mindedly that she had extremely good legs beneath her short executive skirt.

'What sort of job does she do, Jim?' he asked as he turned back to the work bench.

'She works in a solicitors' office.' Jim grinned at him over an oily carburettor. 'She inherited all the brains of the family. None left for me.' He sniffed good-naturedly. 'Can't think where she got them from. Not my dad, bless him, that's for sure.'

*　　*　　*

'Are you going over to the house, later?' Lyn had finished clearing away the children's breakfast and returned Janet's kitchen to a pristine neatness. She glanced over at Joss who was sitting at the table over a cup of coffee. 'You haven't eaten anything, you know. You must have something.'

Joss shook her head. 'I'm feeling a bit queasy to tell you the truth. I'll get something later. This will do. I thought I'd go and have a chat with Luke a bit later, yes. If you don't mind keeping the boys here.' She smiled fondly at Tom who was playing on the mat with the brother of Kit and Kat who was still firmly resident at the farm.

'Have you rung Luke?'

Joss shook her head. 'I've been trying not to since five o'clock this morning. I'm sure he's OK.'

Lyn raised an eyebrow. 'Sure he is.' She scrutinised Joss for a moment. 'You are looking lousy. Why not go back to bed for a bit. Janet won't mind. As soon as she comes in from her hens or wherever she is she suggested she and I take the boys shopping. Tom would enjoy it and Ned can come in his pram. It'll give you the chance to rest.'

I've been resting. For days. Joss could feel the words hovering on her lips, but she didn't say them. She did feel lousy, and she would like nothing more than to go back to bed, but she had to go over to the house. She had to talk to Luke. And above all she did not want the boys there. Not ever again.

She waited until they had gone before letting herself out of the back door and walking swiftly across the garden towards the orchard. The morning was dull and cold; occasional showers of drips cascaded from the bare branches of the tall old apple trees as she walked past, and above through the network of twigs she could see the rain waiting in the bellying clouds. Shivering she walked more quickly, feeling the wet grass and mud slippery beneath her shoes as she turned out of the orchard and onto the footpath. In the distance she could see the roofs of Belheddon Hall huddling in the mist on the crest of the ridge.

The garden seemed very silent as she let herself in by the gate and walked slowly around the lake. A duck was paddling on the far side, dipping its beak from time to time into the weed and she stood for a moment, staring at the pattern of rings spreading out from it across the water.

The shutters in the study were still closed. She could see the blank windows from here. Standing still she studied the house and surreptitiously her hand went up to the crucifix on the chain around her neck.

No one saw her approach. Leaving a trail of darker footprints in the wet grass she stepped onto the terrace, shivering with cold and walked towards the windows. Peering into the great hall she could see the room in the dim morning light. There was no fire and on the table she could see a vase of dead flowers, petals scattered around on the dusty surface. Her scalp was tingling and she rammed her fingers down into her pockets. They were ordinary flowers. Chrysanthemums and autumn daisies, but why had Lyn left them to die?

With heavy steps she walked round towards the gate into the courtyard and stopped. The coach house doors were open and the lights were on, brilliant strips of fluorescent tubing, and she could hear the cheerful banging of a hammer on metal. Someone – Jimbo – was whistling.

It was like looking at a stage from a darkened auditorium; a world that was separate and unreal was displayed before her – a world of noise and bright lights and happiness and laughter while she, on the outside, peering through the bars of the gate was in some strange limbo where time stood still and shadows lurked in the darkness.

There was a tightness in her chest and in her pockets the palms of her hands were beginning to sweat. Quietly she unlatched the gate and pushed it open. Passing the garage without announcing herself she let herself into the kitchen and stopped in astonishment. A stranger was standing near the kitchen table.

'Joss?' The young woman held out her hand. 'I'm Natalie Cotting, Jim's sister. I've come to help.'

---

his was always one of the centres of activity.'
They were standing in the great hall in front
of the fireplace. 'Here and the large bedroom
upstairs.' Natalie stood for a long moment in complete
silence, her eyes on the floor a few inches in front of her
feet. Joss watched her, standing a yard or so from her.
She could feel a tight knot of tension somewhere below
her ribs. It was interfering with her breathing.

Slowly Natalie nodded. Without saying a word she
moved towards the staircase where she stopped for a
moment. 'There never used to be any trouble in the
study. Is it still happy in there?'

Joss nodded.

'Good. Let's go upstairs then.'

They toured the house slowly, room by room, then
found themselves back once more in the kitchen. There
too Natalie stood in silence, her head bowed until at last
she looked up and caught Joss's eye. 'Sorry. You must
think I'm loopy.'

Joss smiled. 'No. Tell me what you've been doing.'

'Just having a feel around.' Natalie slipped into the
chair at the head of the table and leaned forward earnestly, her chin cupped in her hands. She looked as if she
were about to address a board of directors. 'I used to

come here a lot when I was little. I would play with the boys, Georgie and Sam. Georgie died about ten years before I was born and Sam I think about ten years before that. They must have been your brothers, I suppose?' She waited for Joss's nod. 'Of course they didn't know each other in life, but where they are now, in whatever dimension it is, they are a pair of tearaways.' She smiled affectionately.

'My son Tom talks about them. He's found some of their toys. And – ' Joss hesitated, 'I've heard them calling to each other.'

Natalie nodded. 'Monkeys. There are other children here too of course – the boys who have been lost. There's Robert. He was your mum's brother. And little John. He's only a wee thing of about three, with golden curls and big blue eyes.'

Joss gasped. 'You can see them?'

Natalie nodded. 'Inside my head. Not always. Not today. I'm not seeing today.' She frowned. 'There's a lot of other things here today. Unpleasant things.' She clenched her fists. 'People have been meddling. The Reverend Gower – Jim told me. He always made things worse because he didn't understand what he's dealing with here. Exorcism works when the priests understand. So many don't. Often they are dealing with people – people like you and me – not demons. Other times they are dealing with evil far worse than they can conceive and their faith in what they are doing lets them down. They aren't strong enough.'

'And what are we dealing with here?' whispered Joss. Her eyes were fixed on Natalie's.

'I'm not sure yet. When I came as a child I was always welcome. I could talk to Sam or Georgie or Robert. But they're not there. They're hiding. There's something else.' She stood up, her movements restless and quick. Looking out of the window she shook her head. 'There's too much here now. It's confused. I'm going to need some time. Let's go back to the great hall.'

A few minutes later standing in front of the fireplace she shook her head again. 'I can feel so much anger and so much pain.' She put her hands to her temples. 'It's filling my head. I can't sort out the voices.'

Joss shivered. There was something in her own head as well – an echo, nothing more; an echo she couldn't quite hear.

Katherine

It was the name from the shadows.

'Katherine,' she whispered. 'Is she a part of this?'

Natalie frowned. She half raised a hand to silence Joss, still listening hard to something Joss could not hear.

Katherine, my love. You were meant to be mine forever
Katherine! Where are you?

Natalie was nodding. 'Katherine is part of the grief. His mourning is trapped in every stone and timber and tile of this house.'

'Whose mourning?' Joss whispered. 'Is it the king?'

Natalie's eyes focused sharply. 'So you know? You've seen him?'

Joss shrugged helplessly. The shutter had suddenly come down in her mind again; the black wall she could not penetrate. 'I think so. Yes. My little boy calls him the tin man because of his armour.'

Natalie gave a small puzzled smile and nodded. 'It is odd, isn't it, to wear armour in his lover's house.'

'That's what I thought. But he's an angry, bitter man. Why else should he kill?'

'Ssh.' Natalie lifted her hand sharply. 'Perhaps we can get him to speak to us. But not now.' She shook her head. 'Let's go outside. Do you mind?'

There was no sign of Jimbo or Luke in the coach house as they walked out and into the garden, Natalie wearing

476

a pair of Lyn's boots and an old jacket of Joss's over her smart office clothes.

Once on the grass she shook her neat, glossy hair out in the wind and took a couple of small childish skips across the grass.

'Sorry. The atmosphere in there was so oppressive I couldn't think straight. I could feel them listening all round me. Better to talk out here and decide what to do in private as it were.'

'Tom and Ned are in danger, aren't they.' Joss was walking beside her slowly, her hands in her pockets as they headed towards the lake.

'I think if the past history of this place is anything to go by, you must assume so, yes.'

'But why? Why does he hurt the boys?' She paused for a moment then she looked up. 'Did you mean it? Can you get him to speak to us?'

Natalie shrugged. 'I can try.' She sighed. 'I wish I wasn't feeling so tired. I feel as though I'm being drained.'

They had reached the lake. She stood staring down into the water. 'You know, I said in there I couldn't sort out the voices. There were more than I expected. Not the children's voices, not the lost boys or the men who have died. Other voices, powerful voices.'

'Men's voices or women's!' Joss was watching the moorhen scurrying back and forth between the water lily leaves.

'That's the strange thing. I'm not sure. I can hear snatches of words – powerful words, but I can't make them out. It's like fiddling with the dial on a radio. One flashes backwards and forwards through the stations – some are loud, some faint and there is lots of static – then occasionally – just occasionally – one finds a station where one can understand the language and the reception is good and for a while one can tune in, then something happens – perhaps the wind changes or the antennae in my head move slightly and it's gone and I can't find it again.'

There was a long silence. Joss was shivering. 'You can hear them, but can they hear you?'

'Why do you think I came out here?'

'You think they're trapped within the walls of the house; that they can't travel?'

Natalie shrugged. 'I don't know.' She gave a grimace. 'But I feel safer out here.'

Joss pulled up the collar of her jacket. 'Luke and I have just returned from France. We went over there to see Paul Deauville, my mother's second husband. He gave me her last diaries. She mentioned Edward by name. She said she dreamed that he was looking everywhere for her here. He couldn't reach her in France. Then she made a strange entry: she said, "I was so sure she could not cross water".'

'She?'

'What kind of person can't cross water? A vampire? A dead person?'

'A witch?' Natalie's voice was very thoughtful.

'Margaret de Vere was accused of witchcraft; accused of trying to kill the king,' Joss went on slowly. 'She was Katherine's mother; Katherine, who we think was the king's lover. Here.' The moorhen took flight suddenly. Flapping its wings wildly it ran across the top of the lilies until it was airborne and dived out of sight behind the hedge. 'While we were in France I found out that Katherine – a Katherine no one except my mother saw – visited her when she was dying. She took my mother white roses. Paul says that a Katherine had been the mistress of the man who became my mother's lover here at Belheddon, and that her rage and jealousy were so great she hunted my mother down across the water.' She was staring sightlessly down at the slowly spreading ripples beneath a wind spun leaf. 'I'm trying to work this out,

478

and it makes no sense. Are we saying that King Edward of England, a man who had been dead for five hundred years, was my mother's lover?' She looked up and held Natalie's gaze. 'That is what we're saying, aren't we? But it can't be. It can't.'

'They were both lonely, Joss. Your father had died. And he, Edward, had lost his Katherine.'

'But he was dead!' Joss was revolted.

'He's an earthbound spirit who still has earthly emotions,' Natalie said gently. 'He still feels anger and fear and bitterness – those are the things which I suspect anchor him here – but perhaps he also feels loneliness and even love. We don't understand these things, Joss, so we must use our intuition. It's all we have.'

Joss was staring down at the water again. A memory had surfaced out of nowhere. The cellar; a face; a pair of arms . . .

'Joss? Joss, what is it? What's wrong?' Natalie's arm was round her shoulders. 'Joss, you're white as a sheet. Come on, it's cold out here. We ought to go in.'

'No.' Joss shook her off. She was trying to think, to remember, to grasp at a sliding mirage, a chimera at the edge of her mind, but already it had gone and the wall was once more firmly back in place, leaving nothing but the sour aftertaste of blinding panic.

Natalie was watching her carefully. She could see the fear and the revulsion like a cloak around the other woman and suddenly she began to understand. 'Dear God,' she whispered. 'He's made love to you too.'

'No!' Joss shook her head violently. 'No, of course he hasn't. How could he? That's disgusting. It's not possible! No!' She was growing increasingly agitated. Running a few steps along the bank she stopped. Under the warm layers of jacket and sweater and shirt her skin was ice cold and she could feel crawling shivers of disgust. Another memory flashed before her. Eyes. Blue, warm eyes, close

479

to her face and a swirl of soft dark velvet then they were gone again and she was standing by the lake with Natalie under the lowering November clouds.

There was another long silence, then, 'Are you all right?' Natalie said softly. She had followed her and her eyes met Joss's sympathetically.

Joss gave a weak smile. 'Let's go back in.'

'All right. If that's what you want.' Natalie hesitated. 'I could try and speak to him on my own, but –' she paused, 'it would be better if you were with me. You belong to the house, you see. You're part of it all.'

Joss nodded. Walking slowly back up the lawn she stared at the house in front of her. It looked strangely blank, the study windows shuttered, her bedroom curtains only half open, the glass deadened and unreflective beneath the heavy sky. 'David Tregarron is coming up sometime this afternoon,' she said at last. 'He's a friend of ours – Ned's godfather. He was with Edgar Gower when he had his heart attack. He's been studying the history of the house. He's the one who found out about Margaret de Vere.'

Natalie stopped dead. 'Does he see?'

Joss shook her head. 'Not that I know of. He loves the history and romance of it all. And the mystery, of course.'

'Of course.' It was said somewhat dryly.

'I asked him to come so I could find out what really happened that night with Edgar and also because he believes it all. Unlike my husband, who questions my sanity. He believes Margaret de Vere really was a witch. Not a poor silly misguided old woman, but an educated clever practitioner of some kind of black magic. There's a brass to her in the floor of the church here, did you know?'

Natalie stopped in her tracks. 'A brass? In the church?'

'Under that old rug in the chancel.'

'She can't be buried there. It must be just a monument.'

480

'Why not? Why can't she be buried here?'

'Not if she was a witch.'

'Of course not.' Joss hesitated. 'Do you want to come and see the brass?'

'Now?'

'Why not.' Joss gestured towards the church. She shuddered. It would at least put off for a while the need to go back inside the house.

A few cold drops of rain were beginning to fall as Joss grasped the iron ring to lift the latch and pushed open the door. The church was very dark. Behind her, Natalie hesitated. 'Wait, I'll switch on the lights.' Joss moved ahead, and a few seconds later those in the nave and the chancel came on, illuminating the vaulted roof.

'It's over here. See?' Joss was standing near the rug. 'Natalie?' Natalie was still hesitating in the doorway. 'What's wrong?' She stooped to lift the corner of the rug.

'Don't touch it!' Natalie called sharply. Slowly she stepped away from the door and began walking up the aisle between the pews. She could feel the thick miasma of hatred coming from the spot where Joss was standing. It was like a tangible object in the centre of the floor.

By the time she was beside her she could feel the sweat standing out on the palms of her hands. 'She is buried here, and whoever did it, did so against the wishes of the church and with her they buried the tools of her trade,' she whispered. 'They must have been very powerful or very influential to have managed to do that.'

'They were a powerful family,' Joss murmured back. 'In with the king.'

'Indeed,' Natalie replied grimly. She hooked her foot under the corner of the rug and nudged it backwards, exposing a little of the beautiful filigree metalwork in the stone. 'I don't remember ever seeing this before; ever feeling anything before. Something has awoken the evil.'

Joss grimaced. She gave a small shudder. 'There's another brass over there – a tiny one let into the wall, to her daughter, Katherine.'

Natalie glanced at her. She too shivered. The church was cold.

'Margaret was accused of bewitching the king to win him for Katherine, but then she died. Natalie?' Her voice sharpened suddenly. 'What's that? It smells like smoke.'

'It is smoke.' Natalie was staring down the church towards the door through which they had just come. A column of smoke, wispy, smelling of autumn bonfires, was slowly revolving in the back of the church.

Joss caught her arm. 'What is it?' she whispered.

Natalie gave Joss a small push. 'I don't think we're going to wait to debate about it. Let's get out of here.'

'We need to turn off the lights –'

'Forget the lights! Come on, quickly.' She dragged Joss down towards the side aisle as the column of smoke began to move towards them. In thirty seconds they were out, pulling the door shut with a crash.

'What was it?' Joss was panting as they made their way swiftly up the path. She was feeling sick with fear.

'Some kind of energy. Black energy.'

'It wasn't a person?'

'No, it wasn't a person.'

Joss stopped, clutching her side. 'I'm sorry, I've got a stitch. I can't go on. Are we safe here? I thought churches were safe, sacred places, Natalie!'

'They are usually, but this one was desecrated by the burial of someone who practised the black arts, right in front of the altar. Who knows what it might have done to the church?' Natalie took a deep breath, more unnerved than she liked to admit even to herself. 'As I said, I've never felt anything before here – but then,' she gave a tight smile, 'I never came here much. Something has happened here recently –' she paused. 'Mary Sutton.

Jim told me she died here. Maybe it was her. Maybe it was you coming back to the Hall with small children; there haven't been any children here in years. I don't know.' She shook her head. 'There used to be stories about the church – there was a booklet, my mum had it. Maybe I'll ask her. I think we should go back to the house.'

'But the house –'

'I know.' Natalie gave a grim laugh. 'The house is frightening too. But at least I know what I'm dealing with there.'

'I hope you're right.' Joss had doubled up, trying to ease the pain in her side, overcome by a wave of dizziness.

Natalie did not appear to have noticed. She was frowning back at the church. 'Joss, did you see where that energy came from?'

'Near the door.'

'It started in front of Katherine's brass.'

Katherine

The word reverberated in the silence.

This time they both heard it.

'Is she buried near that brass or is it just a memorial?'

Joss shrugged. Slowly she straightened. She leaned back against the old chestnut tree near the gate and took deep slow breaths, trying to calm the lurching in her stomach. Nearby, the grave of her father lay in deep shadow. Beyond it she could just see the small white crosses which showed her where Georgie and Sam were buried.

Almost without realising it, Joss reached out for Natalie's hand. 'I'm scared,' she whispered. 'Terribly scared.'

avid was standing in the courtyard with Luke when they emerged from the path. He kissed Joss and shook hands with Natalie and led the way into the kitchen. Jimbo after giving his sister a perfunctory slap on the back preferred to stay with the car he was working on.

'I found someone to look after my classes for me this afternoon, so I could get away.' David was carrying his hold all and an arm full of books and papers which he dropped onto the kitchen table. 'Lots more about Belheddon and the families that lived here and the de Veres and Edward IV and Richard III.' Neither he nor Luke appeared to have noticed the women's white faces or their silence.

Acutely aware that her hands were shaking, Joss reached for the books, staring curiously in spite of herself, at the top one.

'It was dreadful – the accident. Quite dreadful. I still feel so guilty.' David met Joss's eye at last. 'I should never have rung him; never have let him come here. I'm so sorry.'

'It wasn't your fault, David.' Joss put down the books and took his hand. 'You mustn't blame yourself.'

His fingers closed over hers and for a moment he felt he

was drowning in her gaze. Beautiful, bewitching woman. Abruptly he remembered where he was and let go of her hand. Luke hadn't noticed. He was talking to Natalie.

He glanced at the newcomer again. She too was a very attractive woman, he noticed, and smartly dressed now that she had taken off that horrendous old jacket. He wondered how she fitted in.

As if she had heard his question she fixed her large grey eyes on his. 'You are asking yourself what I am doing here. Let me introduce myself. Visiting psychic, medium, nutter and according to my father, witch.' She smiled in, he thought, an extremely sane fashion. 'I'm here to try to help.' She glanced at Joss and gave her a reassuring nod. Neither of them for the moment, were going to mention what had happened in the church.

'That's good to hear.' David smiled back. His nervousness about returning to the house had gone. It was all right, here in the warm kitchen, with three other people in broad daylight. He looked at Luke. 'The boys are staying with the Goodyears, you say? Don't let them come back until this is sorted out.'

Luke tightened his lips. 'I think that has already been agreed. So, what are you going to do? I take it that you have come to help too.' His gaze rested on David's face for a few seconds longer than was necessary. Then he looked from David to Natalie and back.

David shrugged. 'I leave it up to the expert.'

Natalie grimaced. 'Who is, at the moment, a little at a loss.' She pushed back her chair and stood up. 'Can I suggest you wait in here? Make some coffee or something and let me go for another wander round on my own. There are things I need to understand.'

They watched in silence as she let herself out of the kitchen and the sound of her heels on the flags in the hall died away.

'Brave lady,' David commented quietly. 'Especially in

view of some of the things I've read in here. One interesting snippet of history. Katherine's child, whether he was the son of her husband or of the king survived the birth that killed her. He lived until 1500, and although he was only eighteen when he died he had had time to marry and father a daughter, a daughter named for his mother, Katherine.' He patted his pile of books. 'Otherwise these are more to do with witchcraft and magic. They were into some really sophisticated evil in those days.'

'Do you think Natalie's really a witch?' Luke raised an eyebrow. 'Not quite my image of what a witch should be. I can see her commuting on the 7.40 to the City far more easily than I could see her dancing naked round a bonfire with a broomstick!'

'Sounds to me, old boy, as if you're guilty of some fairly serious stereotyping, if not chauvinistic and politically incorrect something or other there!' David put in amiably. He winked at Joss. 'What do you think? Can she sort it all out?'

Joss shrugged. 'I hope so for all our sakes.'

'I'm going to see what she's up to.' Luke headed for the door.

'Luke! No!' Joss called.

'Let him go for a minute, Joss.' David caught Joss's hand. 'A word quickly, while we're on our own.' His tone was serious.

She raised an eyebrow. 'What is it?'

'Joss, I wanted to tell you. I've decided to leave Dame Felicia's at the end of next year.' It sounded so easy, so matter of fact. She would never guess the sadness behind those words; the loneliness. 'I've accepted a post, teaching in Paris.' He forced a grin. 'A complete change is always good, as you know. After all, my research fellowship with Belheddon Enterprises will be over soon. When we know all there is to know, then what will I do with my spare time?'

'David – '

'No, Joss. My mind is made up. Don't worry I won't lose touch. After all, I have to keep an eye on my godson. And you'll be coming to Paris more often too now you've discovered Paul.' He grimaced. 'Pastures new, Joss. Always a good idea.' He held her eye for a moment then looked away. Did she, he wondered, even suspect how fond he had become of her? He hoped not.

'We'll miss you, David.' Her voice was very quiet.

He nodded, unable to trust himself to speak for a moment. 'Well, you'll see plenty of me before I leave, I promise. I'm not going for months yet.' He gave her hand a squeeze. 'And now, back to the fray. Let's call old Luke back before our witch spots him and turns him into a toad!'

In the great hall Natalie was standing in front of the fireplace once again. She could see it clearly now. The power which was surging around her – uncontrolled, random power – coming up from beneath the cold flags. She frowned, holding out her hands, palm down, allowing herself to sense its origin. There was something there, deep beneath the ground.

Frowning with concentration she moved slowly across the floor towards the hall and the staircase and put her hand on the door to the cellar. It was locked. She shook the handle. Before, the feelings from the cellar had been negative, unhappy but gentle. The grief which had surrounded the small crumpled body of a little boy had permeated the walls, but that had disappeared. Even through the door she could feel something else.

Making up her mind she turned on her heel and marched back to the kitchen. 'I need the key to the cellar, please.'

'The cellar,' Joss echoed. 'Again?'

'Please. There's something down there. No,' she raised

a hand as Joss stood up. 'Please, stay in here. All of you. Just tell me where the key is.'

With it in her hand at last she stood for a minute in the middle of the study, taking slow deep breaths, feeling herself centred and strong, surrounding herself with an armour of light. Pushing the small niggling core of fear which was worming its way into her stomach firmly to one side, she moved resolutely back to the cellar door and put the key into the lock.

The blast of cold air which rose from the damp darkness was the same as before. Switching on the lights she stepped through the door, onto the top step.

And began to walk down.

At the bottom of the stairs she stood still every sense alert. She was not seeing the wine racks, or the dust or the festooned pipes and electric cables which the twentieth century had introduced. Her eyes were focused on medieval vaulting, and in the farthest corner of the cellar, beneath the great hall, the shadows cast by long dead candles.

Silently she stepped closer. She could feel it more strongly now: a feral, sweat-sharp scent of danger and excitement.

Joss shivered. 'I can't stand it any more. I've got to go and see what she's doing.'

'She's told you not to, Joss.' Luke shook his head. He was uncomfortably tense, every nerve in his body stretched.

'I have to. This is my house, Luke. I have to be there.' She said it gently without challenge, but both he and David heard the steel in the tone.

'Be careful, Joss.'

Her smile was absent-minded. 'I will.'

She paused at the top of the cellar stairs and looked down. The lights were on but the first cellar was empty.

Biting back a shout to Natalie she carefully and silently began to descend the stairs into the cold, holding her breath as she strained her ears for any sound. The silence was intense; solid. At the bottom of the stairs she waited a moment, looking round. 'Natalie?' The call under her breath was barely more than a whisper. 'Where are you?'

There was no reply.

Cautiously she stepped towards the archway which led into the second cellar. Natalie was standing near the far wall, staring at the stone. She appeared to be listening intently.

Silently Joss stepped up beside her. Natalie gave no indication that she knew she was there. Her eyes were focused on the wall, her hands out in front of her, fingers spread as if searching for something she could not see.

'It's here,' she murmured. 'The focus. Can you feel it?'

Joss stepped a little closer to her. She could feel every nerve and muscle in her body clenched.

'What is it?' she breathed.

'I don't know.' Natalie was shaking her head. 'There's a lot of energy under ground here. I think a dowser might tell you there was an underground river or spring or perhaps just earth energy. But it's been tapped. Someone has used it, and they've used it wrongly.'

Joss swallowed hard. She could feel her skin prickling. 'Can you do anything?'

'I'm not sure yet.' Natalie took a step closer to the wall and rested her hands on the cold stones and as Joss watched her she ran her fingers down the wall, almost to the floor.

'It's behind here. Whatever it is.' She turned to Joss. 'I think we need to look. I'm sorry, but we've got to do it.'

'You mean we have to take the wall down?'

Natalie nodded. 'Not all of it. I think it's here. I can feel it through the stone.' Her hand was pressed for a moment on one of the roughly shaped blocks. Gripping the edges as best she could with her nails she gave a tug but nothing happened.

'It's been cemented in. Look.' Joss leaned over her shoulder and pointed at the crumbling mortar.

Natalie nodded. 'We need a crowbar.'

'I'll go and fetch the others.' Joss hesitated. 'Do you want to come with me? Don't wait down here.'

Natalie gave a grim smile. 'Don't worry. I'm all right. Just fetch something to lever this out with and bring your friend David down. Not Luke. Not at the moment. Not till we know what we're dealing with.'

Joss stared at her, then she nodded. Without a word she retraced her steps up into the hall. Staring at the dead flowers on the oak table she shuddered violently and almost without realising it her fingers went to the small cross at her throat.

'No, I can't stand it. I'm not staying away!' Luke had found a crowbar in the coach house. 'For God's sake, Joss! If it's dangerous do you think I'd let you go down there? Either I come or neither of us goes.'

'You could stay here with me, Luke.' Jimbo was wiping his hands on an oily rag. 'If Nat says you shouldn't be there, you shouldn't. She knows what she's talking about.'

'I'm sure she does, but it's my house and what goes on in it is my business.'

'It might be woman's business, Luke.' Jimbo shifted uncomfortably.

'Then they wouldn't want David.' Luke hefted the crowbar into one hand and brought the handle down with a smack onto the palm of the other. 'You come or stay, whichever you like, but I'm going down there now.'

David and Joss exchanged glances and Joss gave a rueful shrug. 'OK. Come on. Let's see what Natalie says.'

Natalie was standing where Joss had left her when they trooped silently back down the stairs. She didn't look round. 'Joss, you wear a crucifix. Give it to Luke. Put it round his neck.'

The other three looked at one another. Natalie had not taken her eyes off the wall; the cross was hidden beneath Joss's clothes. As far as Joss knew Natalie had not seen it at any time since she had arrived. Reaching up obediently she unclasped the chain. To her surprise Luke made no fuss when she put it round his neck and she thought she knew why; the atmosphere in the cellar had thickened perceptibly.

Without a word David took the crowbar out of Luke's hand and stepped forward. 'What do you want me to do,' he whispered.

'Here. I think it's here.' Natalie pointed. 'See if you can loosen this stone.'

Cautiously David inserted the end of the crowbar. 'It's old lime mortar. Look. It's very soft.' He wiggled it back and forth, pushing the wedge-shaped point further in. 'There. It's coming. Everything is so crumbly down here.' Panting with exertion he gave one last push and levered the stone out. It fell with a loud crash onto the flags.

There was a long silence as, putting down the crowbar, David felt in his pocket for the torch he had picked up from the dresser as they left the kitchen. He shone it into the cavity. 'There's quite a hole in here.'

'You'd better give it to me.' Natalie's voice was husky. She could feel waves of emotion coming out of the wall at her; sour, malevolent tides of anger and hatred and spite as, reluctantly she took the torch from David's hand. She glanced at the others. 'You all all right?'

They could all feel it to some degree, she could see, even Luke. Joss's face was grey and drawn with pain.

Stepping forward she shone the torch into the hole.

At first she thought there was nothing there then as

her hand steadied the shaking beam she slowly began to make out the shapes in the cavity behind the wall. It was far smaller than she had expected, perhaps three feet by two. No room for the body or bodies she had half expected to find immured there. With an inward sigh of relief she shone the light round the dark space again and only then did she notice, lying amongst the rubble in what was little more than a hidden cupboard, the small wrapped package.

'That's it.' She was talking to herself, although she spoke out loud. 'That's where the energy is coming from.'

Her skin crawling with revulsion she reached into the hole and picked the packet up with her finger tips.

'What is it?' Joss breathed. They were all staring down at the object on Natalie's palm. It was about three inches long, perhaps a little less wide, covered in dust and cobwebs and crumbs of mortar.

'It's wrapped in some kind of material,' David said slowly. He reached out to touch it, then changed his mind and drew back. He looked at Natalie's face. 'What is it?'

Slowly she shook her head.

'We have to look.' It was Luke. He took a deep breath. 'Do you want me to open it?'

'No.' Natalie shook her head again. 'I think we need to be very careful with this.' She could feel the power in it, the weight, the cold. With a shudder she had to restrain herself from hurling it as far away from her as she could. 'I think we should take it upstairs – outside.' She had begun to feel sick. Her fear and distaste were gripping her with a violence she couldn't control. Her hand was beginning to shake.

'Natalie –'

'Out of my way.' Gritting her teeth she closed her fingers over the object in her hand and headed for the stairs. She had to get outside. Now. Quickly. Before the evil closed over them all.

go te baptiso – '

*She stopped suddenly and held her breath, the only
sound in the darkened church the beating of her own
heart. Above her head the sanctuary lamp flickered wildly and
she heard the squeak of the chains on which it hung.*

*'Ego te baptiso in nomine Patris, et Filii, et Spiritus Sancti – '
she started again.*

*'Edward – ' Her fingers traced the sign of the cross over the
little wax figure in her hand.*

'Edward of York, King of England – '

*She smiled, stroking the doll's head with its little roughly
shaped crown of wire. Her finger tip moved down across its
shoulders, down the chest and rested for a moment at the top
of its legs where a small lump depicted its manhood.*

*Setting the doll down on the altar she reached into the tass-
elled purse hanging at her girdle for a second doll as crude as
the first, meant, from the small swellings on its chest, to be a
woman.*

'I baptise thee, Katherine . . .'

Katherine!

The name reverberated through the shadows of the church.

*'And now,' she breathed, 'I bring you together, together here
in the house of your God!'*

Holding both figures up before the crucifix high above the altar she smiled and slowly she pressed them together, feeling the beeswax grow soft in the heat of her hand. The sweet stickiness of honey was all around her as she bound the two little dolls face to face with a scarlet thread of silk.

'In the name of God, I pronounce you man and wife.' She smiled. 'Not in the porch but here before the altar of God, and now the act of union will be sanctified by the holy mass itself.'

She glanced over her shoulder, uncertain of the shadows, never sure that eyes weren't watching, that the priest might not be there, somewhere behind the carved screen.

Lifting the embroidered altar cloth in an act which was somehow as indecent as the act she had perpetrated on the dolls she tucked them out of sight and then with a smile she let the cloth fall. Soon the priest would come to celebrate the mass and the union of the dolls, sanctified by his act, would be complete. Indissoluble for all eternity.

She wiped her hands on the heavy brocade of her skirts and stepped away from the altar.

Only then did she smile.

Edward and Katherine.

Nothing now could keep them apart and nothing could prevent Katherine from conceiving a child.

Nothing.

'Bring it out here. Put it on the table.' They were outside on the terrace in the wind and rain, standing round the grey, lichen encrusted garden table.

Joss put her hand on Natalie's shoulder. 'Are you OK?'

Natalie nodded. She felt better now they were outside; the oppression and the anger were less. The rain was growing heavier and she raised her face to it, feeling it fresh and clean, sweeping back across her face and into her hair. Taking a deep breath she laid her hand on the table palm up and opened her fingers.

'Wait, I'll put up the umbrella.' Luke had grabbed it as they went out.

'No.' Natalie shook her head. 'Let it get wet.'

The wrapping was silk – old and grey and fragmented, disintegrating beneath her fingers in the rain. As she cautiously peeled it back they stared down at what lay within.

Two pale sausage shaped objects, pressed close together, with fragments of nearly black thread around the middle lay before them on the wet table.

'What is it?' Joss breathed.

'I think you'll find it's what are they.' Natalie stood back, looking down as the rain battered down on the object on the table.

'It's wax.' David had bent close. 'Two wax dolls.' He glanced up at Natalie. 'They're witch dolls!'

She nodded. 'I think so.'

'Shit.' He shook his head. 'The real thing. Who do you think they're supposed to be?'

Natalie shrugged. 'Look at that one's head.'

'A crown?' He glanced at Joss. 'It's Edward, isn't it; King Edward.' He reached out.

'Don't touch,' Natalie cried sharply. 'Whoever made those dolls was evil. Those dolls spelled disaster: disaster for the two people concerned, disaster for their child and their descendants and disaster for this house!'

The rain was growing heavier. Standing round the table the four looked down at the pathetic little figures of melded wax as a pool of rainwater formed around them on the grey oak soaking the wood until it turned black.

'Their child?' Joss echoed. She looked up from the dolls. The rain was plastering her hair round her face. 'You think they had a child?'

Natalie nodded.

'He was called Edward,' David put in. 'I found it in the

495

records. The house was inherited by Edward de Vere after the death of Katherine's father in 1496. She had no brothers, and no other more distant relations who would fit. Her husband as far as we can tell was called Richard and his inheritance went to his brother so my guess is that Edward de Vere was the son of Edward IV – the pregnancy that the marriage to Richard was designed to legitimise.'

Natalie was watching Joss's face. 'That boy was your ancestor, Joss. The last man to inherit Belheddon.'

'And he died at eighteen, as soon as he had a daughter.' David's voice was awe-struck.

They were all staring down at the table. Joss's face had drained of colour.

'I think we're looking at the beginning of the curse.' Natalie studied the dolls sadly.

'So, what do we do with them?' Joss's voice was husky.

Natalie shook her head.

'Do we separate them?'

'I don't know. I don't *know*.' Natalie turned away in anguish and looked up at the sky, feeling the rain on her face. 'We have to help them; we have to release them. Both Edward and the girl.'

The girl.

Katherine.

They were all watching her. Natalie could feel their eyes first on her shoulder blades, then on the poor misshapen dolls and then back to her again. She had set herself up as some sort of expert and they were relying on her to save them; to save Joss's two children and to save Luke.

The rain was running down her face, dripping off her short hair into her collar. It was cold and clean and fresh.

She couldn't do it. Not on her own. She couldn't fight Margaret's spell by herself.

Slowly she turned. They were still watching her, the

two men uncertain, David understanding the implications of what they were dealing with and a little afraid, Luke self mocking, practical, still not letting himself believe that the small two-headed lump of wax on the table could threaten the lives of his two sons, even his own.

And why did it threaten them? It was a love charm, one of the commonest objects a witch was asked to produce, a piece of child-like sympathetic magic, meant to bring a man and a woman together. So why did it give off such evil vibes? And why did it threaten Joss, or the women of the house; the women who were wooed by a king?

No one said anything; they were all watching her, waiting for her to tell them what to do.

And suddenly she knew.

'Joss –' Her hands had gone clammy. 'How strong are you?'

Joss looked away, first into the distance towards the lake and then down to the figures on the table. Her face was white and very strained but her eyes when she raised them at last to Natalie's face were steady. 'Strong enough.'

Natalie nodded. 'Luke, I want you and David to go away. Right away from the house. Go to the little boys and stay with them. We'll tell you when you can come back.'

'I'm not leaving Joss.' Luke caught his wife's hand.

'Please Luke, I'm not asking lightly.' Natalie glanced at David, sensing an ally.

He picked up the cue. 'Come on old chap. I have a feeling this is women's work.'

Natalie's face relaxed into a smile. 'That's exactly what it is.'

'I'll be all right, Luke.' Joss stepped closer to him and reaching up kissed him on the cheek. 'Please, go with David.' He wrapped his arms around her and for a moment they clung together then reluctantly she pushed him away. 'Go on.'

'You're sure?'

'I'm sure.'

She and Natalie stood where they were in the rain and watched as the two men walked slowly back to the gate. As David pushed it open Luke looked back. Joss raised a hand and blew him a kiss then she turned away. When seconds later she glanced back the two men had gone.

Natalie was watching absent-mindedly. The illusion of reality was slipping away, withdrawing to the periphery of her vision as she reached down towards her intuition. 'Are you ready?' She frowned. 'This is going to be hard.' She hesitated. 'Joss, you do know you're pregnant.'

Joss stared at her. 'Don't be silly; I can't be.'

Natalie nodded. 'It's because you are carrying a little girl that we can do this, and it's because it's a girl that we have to do it soon.' She took Joss's hands in her own wet cold ones. 'In a minute we're going into the church with these,' she nodded towards the dolls, 'and we're going to separate them.'

'What about that stuff we saw in there?' Joss's mind was spinning, beating against the blackness, grappling with Natalie's certainty. 'I'm not pregnant you know. I can't be.' Luke and I – well we took precautions. It's too soon after Ned. We didn't want any more children –'

Natalie frowned. 'Just for now believe me, please. We have to be together in this, Joss. David was right, this is women's work and there are some things that women know.' She hesitated, wondering how she could explain. 'The spell was cast by someone who knew what they were doing. It worked. These two people,' she gestured at the wax dolls, 'were tied together by magic –' she smiled uncertainly, used to people's raised eyebrows when she used the word ' – magic that was powerful – a force of nature, harnessed and directed so well that it lasted beyond death for the people who were bound together.'

'Edward and Katherine,' Joss murmured.

'Edward and Katherine.'

'But what went wrong? Why are they so angry? Why are they hurting people? Was that part of Margaret's intention?'

Natalie shrugged. 'They're trapped here. Perhaps that is all the reason they need. Perhaps there is more. Perhaps the king is still searching for her. Perhaps he's lost her somehow; perhaps he wants something else.' She glanced at Joss. 'A human lover.'

Joss shook her head vehemently, her mind trapped, cannoning against the black wall inside her head, refusing to focus, but Natalie nodded. 'Face it. You have to face the truth.'

'There isn't any truth to face. All he's done to us –' she paused. The cellar. The eyes. The arms, drawing her against him. Black velvet and then nakedness. 'No,' she shook her head again. 'No, all he has done, perhaps, is bring me roses.' She shuddered. The black wall was back in place. There was a long pause. She could feel Natalie's eyes on her face and resolutely she refused to meet them.

Eventually Natalie spoke. 'Well,' she cleared her throat. 'Come on. We'd better get on with it.' She fished a blue scarf out of her pocket – silk, Joss noticed – and carefully she picked up the dolls and wrapped them in it, then she walked towards the gate.

The lights were still on in the church. Standing just inside the door they paused. Resolutely Joss shut it behind them. The sound of the heavy latch dropping echoed round them and then it died away. She held her breath and stood watching as slowly Natalie began to walk up the aisle towards the altar. After a few steps she stopped. 'Joss? Come with me.'

Joss forced herself to move. Her legs were trembling violently and it was all she could do to follow.

'Pull back the rug.' Natalie was standing to one side of it, between the choir stalls.

Reluctantly Joss did as she was bid. Before them on the floor the brass glinted in the lights which were tucked out of sight behind the roof beams. An eerie cold seemed to radiate up from the ornate figure depicted before them. 'See.' Natalie pointed with her toe. She was speaking very softly. 'The symbols of her art are there. The cross is upside down. You don't notice it until you realise which way up she is. And are those cabalistic signs? We'd have to look them up.'

'She really was a magician – a real witch, then, not just a poor old woman playing at magic,' Joss murmured.

'Oh yes. She was a real witch all right. And I guess she was a very clever one. She may have been under suspicion, but she was never caught at it. How else would she have been buried here?'

'The king trusted her –'

'I don't think so.' Natalie was unwrapping the blue silk scarf. Her hands, Joss noticed, were trembling violently. 'He was wearing armour, remember?'

Not always. Sometimes he wore velvet.

The cold was growing more intense.

'Do you know what to do?' Joss said softly. Her eyes were riveted to the wax figures as the silk fell to the floor.

'I'm going to bless them, then I'm going to separate them, then I'm going to melt them –'

'No!' Joss clutched at Natalie's arm. 'No, you mustn't do that.'

'Why?' Natalie's grey eyes were fixed on hers.

'Help them. You've got to help them, not destroy them. They've suffered enough already.'

'He has killed, Joss.'

'I know. I know he has. But only because he's trapped

here. Please – the evil is Margaret's, you said. Don't destroy them. We have to find a way of helping them.'

They were both looking down at the dolls in Natalie's hands. 'Supposing he kills again?'

'We can stop him. There must be a way. He wasn't evil.'

Eyes. Blue. Desperate eyes, staring into hers. Arms around her. Ice cold lips on hers –

'Joss! Joss are you all right?'

Katherine

The wall in her head was crumbling.

He thought she was Katherine! He hadn't even seen *her*. It was Katherine he had held, Katherine he had kissed; to Katherine he brought the roses. Her mother, her grandmother – how many other women in the house had he pursued, believing they were his Katherine? She was shivering violently too now. 'Don't separate them.' She held out her hand. 'Leave them together.'

Natalie put the figures in her palm.

Silently Joss bent and picked up the scarf. Carefully she wrapped the two dolls up once again.

'They don't belong in here,' she said quietly.

'No.'

'Can we remove the hold she has over them?' Joss nodded down at the floor.

'We can try.' Natalie stood for a moment deep in thought. 'The rituals of the church can't reach her. We need to speak to her in a language she understands. Play her at her own game.'

'Witchcraft?' Joss shook her head.

'I prefer to call it sympathetic magic. We have to cut the ties that bind her to them and to this place. We need something to tie and something to cut.'

'In the vestry.' Joss hesitated, looking down at the blue silk package in her hands then she put it down on a pew. 'I'll have to look.'

501

The door was unlocked. Switching on the light she stared round. The flower arranging materials were stacked more or less to one side near a small sink, the church paraphernalia to the other near the locked cupboards where James Wood kept books and vessels and the unconsecrated wine and bread. Her hands still stiff with cold she fumbled across the flower shelves, moving vases and blocks of oasis, jugs and flower wire. Picking up a coil of the fine wire she considered it, then she looked round for the snips. They were there, amongst the scrabble of old dusters and dried fir cones part of a long gone Christmas display.

'Here.' She handed the wire to Natalie. 'Will this do?'

Natalie groped for the end of the wire. 'My hands are so cold –'

'I know. It's only here, near the grave. The rest of the church is bearable.'

Natalie glanced at her. 'There's an energy drain. She's using the heat in some way. Here,' she nipped off a couple of yards of wire, 'wind this end round the dolls. I'm going to try and hook this end into the brass somehow.' She knelt down, the end of the fine wire between her fingers. 'It's worn so flat. For five hundred years people have been walking over her.'

'It doesn't seem to have done her any harm!' Joss commented tartly. The wire was fiddly, hard to twist. 'There, I think that will hold.'

'Good. Put them down here, on the step, while I try to fix this.'

'Natalie!' Turning from putting the dolls down Joss had glanced at the back of the church. 'Look!'

The strange mist was there again, level with the back pews; it was thinner this time, less distinct, but the shape was clear.

'She's going to manifest!' Natalie breathed. 'Oh Jesus Christ!'

'What do we do?' Joss groped at her throat for the little crucifix and realised with a lurch of terror that it was still where she herself had put it, around Luke's neck.

'Stand firm. Visualise a solid wall of light between us and her. Remember she can't hurt you,' Natalie went on urgently under her breath. She dropped to her knees again, frantically jabbing at the brass with the fine end of the wire, trying to hook it into the figure.

She could hear Joss's breath rasping harshly in the back of her throat. 'Shall I pick them up?'

'Yes. Carefully. Don't pull the wire.' Natalie's voice was hoarse.

Joss picked the figures up and stood, her back to the altar, her hand out in front of her. The image was stronger now. They could make out the shape of the woman clearly, her long dress standing out stiffly from the hips, some kind of a head-dress over her hair.

'Stop!' Natalie's voice was surprisingly strong suddenly. 'You are in the house of God! Stop now, while you have time.'

The figure didn't hesitate. It was coming closer, seeming to drift towards them without quite touching the ground.

'Margaret de Vere, in the name of Jesus Christ, I command you to stop!' Natalie raised her hand.

'She can't hear you,' Joss whispered. The woman's face was slowly becoming visible. It registered no expression at all. 'What do we do?' Her voice slid up into a cry of fear.

'She must be able to hear us – or at least she can sense us. Why else is she here?' Natalie jabbed at the brass frantically. 'Stick, damn it. Stick in, will you!'

The figure was drifting closer, with every moment becoming clearer to the eye. They could see the heavy embroidery on her gown now – the jewelled girdle, the detail of her head-dress with its floating veil, and above all her face. It was a strong face with heavy features, the mouth a hard narrow line, the skin almost colourless, the eyes open, the colour of the winter sea, unseeing and expressionless.

'We've summoned her presence by interfering,' Natalie murmured. 'Somehow we have to stop her!' She pushed the wire frantically, bending it almost double with the force of her gesture and with a slight click the hook caught under a rough edge of the ornate head-dress of the figure on the ground.

'Done it!' She scrambled to her feet, the snips in her hand.

'Margaret de Vere, you have been guilty of sorcery in this holy place. You have made images of your king and of your daughter and because of your evil spells they cannot rest in peace. This wire which holds you all together I am now going to cut. Your influence will be over. Your time on this earth is finished. Go from this place and find peace and light away from Belheddon. Go!'

She put the snips to the wire and pressed the handles together as hard as she could.

No! *No! Nooo!*

The scream which filled the church came from neither woman, nor from the shadowy figure standing before them. It came from the air, from the echoes, from the ground beneath their feet.

Natalie hesitated, the wire slipping out of the blades.

'Go on! Cut it!' Joss called. 'Quickly. Now!'

Using both hands Natalie managed to jam the wire back between the stumpy steel blades and chopped as hard as she could. This time the ends parted. The longer piece sprang free and coiled itself down onto the brass, whilst the shorter end snapped back round Joss's hand and the wax figures in it. Her eyes hadn't left the figure before them. It was barely ten feet from them now, still moving. 'It hasn't worked,' she gasped. 'Natalie, it hasn't worked.'

She was getting closer. Joss could feel the cold so intense now, that the air seemed scarcely breathable.

'Natalie,' her voice had risen to a scream. Pressing herself back against the pew out of the way she felt and saw the woman pass within three feet of her, drift on over the top of the brass, up the chancel steps, through the altar itself and out through the east wall of the church.

'Dear God,' Joss looked down at the figures in her hands. She had clutched them so tightly they had grown soft in her fingers. 'Has she gone?'

'She's gone.' Natalie sat down in a pew. She was white with shock.

'Did you do it?' Joss was staring at the wax puppets.

'I don't know.' Natalie bent over and put her head on her hands as if she were praying. 'I don't know.'

For a moment they both sat there too shocked to move, then Joss straightened. 'Let's go back to the house.'

Natalie looked up. 'What do you want to do with the dolls?'

'I think we should bury them. Together. Come on, let's go.' Joss kicked the rug back across the brass. 'I'll turn out the lights. I don't want to stay here.'

Both still very afraid they left the church, closing the door behind them. The dolls once more wrapped in the silk scarf were clutched in Joss's hand. 'Let's get back in the house. I'm too cold to think. We'll need to find a spade.'

Hurrying to avoid the heavy rain, they threaded their way down the path and into the back door of the house. Joss put the scarf down on the kitchen table. They could both smell the heavy honey of the wax. 'What about the boys? Georgie and Sammy. Have they gone?'

Natalie threw herself down in a chair. She was exhausted. 'I don't know.'

'Suddenly you don't know much.'

'I'm sorry, Joss.'

Joss was rubbing her hands hard on the front of her coat. 'No, it's me who should be sorry. You're helping me and I'm not being grateful.' She looked at the bundle of blue silk. 'Poor things. I hope they're free.' Biting her lip she was silent for a moment. 'There's only one way to find out. I'll go upstairs.'

'I'll come with you.'

'No.' Joss hesitated. 'No. This is something I have to do on my own, Natalie. Just be here, if I shout, OK?' She shook her head. 'I've never called him – summoned him, I mean. But I think if he were still there he might come.' The blue eyes had been gentle; full of love.

'And so would Georgie and Sam, Joss. They always come when they're called.'

The two women looked at each other grimly. Joss put the dolls gently into the dresser drawer. 'Just for a while. Until we can bury them.' She took a deep breath, visibly steadying herself, then she smiled at Natalie. 'Wish me luck.'

43

At the bottom of the stairs she stopped, her hand on the newel post and she looked up. The landing was always in deep shadow. On even the sunniest day the light never penetrated there. Listening carefully she put her foot on the bottom step.

'Edward!' she called in a low voice. It came out croakily, barely audible. Edward, sire, your grace . . . your majesty? How did one address a king who had been dead for five hundred years?

Her fists clenched, she began slowly to climb the stairs, one step at a time, her eyes and ears straining into the emptiness.

'Are you there? Georgie? Sammy?'

She reached the top and looked round. The landing was deserted; the door into her and Luke's bedroom ajar. She moved towards it carefully, consciously avoiding the creaky board near the coffer chest with its pewter candlestick.

'Is there anyone there? Georgie? Sammy?' She could deal with them, her own brothers; little boys.

Her hand outstretched she pushed open the bedroom door and looked in. The curtains were half drawn and the room was almost dark. Outside, the rain streamed down the window panes, slamming every now and again against the glass with extra force.

She loved this room; it was beautiful, gracious, redolent with history, and yet cosy. She could see Tom's discarded teddy in the corner; an old jumper of Luke's still inside out on the floor where he had dropped it. She smiled affectionately.

Moving towards the bed, she rested a hand on one of the bedposts. The black oak turned and carved, was warm beneath her fingers and she stroked it gently. 'Was it here? Did you lie together here?' She spoke out loud without looking round. 'She's gone, my lord. No one else can take her place, not here. You and she belong together in another world.'

Her hand dropped from the bedpost and slowly she moved up the side of the bed, trailing her fingers on the crewel work cover. 'I'm going to bury the effigies Margaret made of you both in the rose garden down beyond the lake.' She smiled ruefully. 'I'll find a white rose, a rose of York to put there so you can rest in peace.'

She jumped at a sudden clatter in the corner of the room near the back window. The draught had stirred the curtain which had knocked a small wooden car onto the floor. Walking over to it, she stooped and picked it up. 'Georgie? Sammy? Is this yours?'

There was no answer.

Slowly she turned round. The palms of her hands were wet; the small hairs on the back of her neck were tingling. Something in the room had changed.

He was standing near the front window.

Joss held her breath. Her stomach turned over with fear. He was tall; very tall and as she moved closer she could see the greying hair, the anguished narrow eyes, the strong chin, the broad shoulders, shrouded by a dark cloak and beneath it again the plate armour of a man who feared assassination in this house, the house of his mistress.

He was coming closer. Suddenly she was terrified; she

had called him, but now she knew she could not control him. 'Please,' she murmured. 'Please . . . no.!' Again she could smell the roses.

He was coming closer still.

'I'm not Katherine,' she whispered desperately. 'Please, listen to me. I'm not Katherine. Katherine has gone. She's not here any more. Please, please, don't hurt me. Don't hurt my children or Luke – please –'

She took a step backwards and felt the bed immovable behind her.

'Please. We've cut the link. Your love was cursed. It was evil. Margaret made it happen. She tied you together and to this house with her magic, but we've released you; you can go. Please –' she held her hand in front of her face. 'Please. Go.'

He had stopped moving; for several seconds he seemed to be watching her then slowly he lifted his arm towards her. She shrank back with a whimper, but the bed stopped her as his fingers brushed her cheek. It was like the touch of cold wet leaves.

Katherine

His lips hadn't moved but she heard the name inside her head.

'I'm not Katherine,' she sobbed. She retreated further, bending backwards away from him across the bed. 'Please, I'm not Katherine!'

Katherine

She had ordered them to send for him.

Lying in the high bed as the contractions tore her apart she asked, then she begged, then she screamed for him.

It was her mother who told them to wait; who forbade them to go.

As her seventeen-year-old daughter's belly had swollen with the king's child Margaret had smiled and nodded and watched. The girl's revulsion and panic were nothing out of the ordinary.

509

After her milk sop husband had been removed – so easy a task, she blew him out like a candle – it was a matter of time only before she would grow used to her kingly lover, a man whose early stunning good looks had turned to corpulence in middle age; the man who, once so attractive he could have had any woman in England, was now enslaved by her – so enslaved that he would grant his little mistress's mother anything she asked.

As she stood looking down at the bed where two frightened midwives were sponging her daughter's sweat-stained face she smiled again and firmly shook her head.

Though he was only a few miles away he could not be summoned yet. He mustn't see Katherine looking like this. She was ugly, she stank, she screamed and tore at the bed clothes shouting obscenities which might have suited a London tavern but which sounded bestial from the lips of a gently born girl of seventeen.

Let the child be born – the daughter, the precious pretty treasure who would captivate and hold her father's affections, then he could come. Then he could shower Katherine, cleansed and rested and smelling of sweet flower waters and perfumes, with gold and jewels and fine silks, and bring his child ivory rattles and coral beads.

Katherine!

'No!' Joss flung herself away from him across the bed, bunched her knees and threw herself onto the floor. With the bed between them she faced him, panting. 'I am not Katherine! Can't you see that! Katherine's dead! You're dead!' She was sobbing desperately. 'Please. The link is cut. Margaret's spell is broken; it's all over, you are free of her at last. Don't you see? It's finished!'

He hadn't moved any closer to the bed. He stood for a long time looking at, or perhaps through, her, then slowly he put his hand to his waist and she realised for the first time that beneath the long shadowy cloak he was wearing a sword. He drew it without a sound.

'No,' she gasped. 'For Christ's sake, no! Haven't you heard me? Please –' she retreated backwards away from the bed towards the windows which overlooked the garden, moving carefully step by step, her stomach knotted with terror. 'Please –'

'So, does the great king, the sun of York, terrorise women with a sword?' Natalie's voice from the door was harsh with fear. 'Are you going to kill her? Are you going to put your sword to the throat of a woman who is carrying a child. Your child!'

She ignored Joss's gasp. 'Put away your sword. You have no enemies here any more. You have no place here. This is not your time!'

Joss staggered backwards against the wall, her arms crossed across her breasts and suddenly her legs wouldn't support her any more. With a sob she found herself sliding to her knees.

Natalie stepped into the room. 'Put up your sword. You cannot hurt her. She is nothing to you, don't you see? Nothing. She is from a different world. Let her go. Let her and her family live in peace. You have to leave Belheddon. The time has come. It's time to go.'

The swordpoint wavered, then slowly it began to fall. Joss watched mesmerised. It looked very real. She could see the glimmer of the steel as his hand dropped to his side.

Katherine

'Katherine is waiting for you,' Natalie's voice was gentle suddenly. 'Let your child live. I'll take care of her.'

They were watching the man's face. The pain and anger etched into every line of it were clearly visible as was the velvet trimmed neck of his shirt beneath the breast plate and the cords which held the cloak in place.

'Let him go, Joss,' Natalie murmured. 'Release him.'

511

'What do you mean?' Joss was watching him, mesmerised.

He was holding out his hands to her, the heavy ruby ring on his forefinger catching the light dully.

'Give him your blessing and your love –'

'My love!' Joss recoiled.

'It will help him to leave. Send him away in love and peace.'

'What about the people he killed?' In spite of herself she raised her eyes to his. The anger in his gaze had gone but the pain was still there.

'They will be released as well. Love is the healer, Joss. Love and forgiveness. You are the spokeswoman, the one who has to do it for all the women – your mother, and your grandmother, and her mother and all the women through the generations who have lived in this house.'

'And what about the men? What about the children who have died?'

He was shaking his head slowly back and forth.

Katherine

'You cannot speak for them. They must speak for themselves. If we fill the house with love we can help them do it.'

Katherine

Joss shook her head. She could feel it like an intense pressure inside her ear drums: the name of the woman he had loved: Katherine.

'What is it?' Suddenly she was talking to him again. 'What are you telling me?'

The room was growing darker; the rattle of rain on the window was louder and for a moment she felt her attention shift. There was an almost imperceptible movement of tension in the room and he had gone.

For a moment she stood gazing at the place where he had been standing then she spun round. Natalie was only a few feet from her now and for a moment they stared at each other.

'What happened?' Joss sat down on the bed. She was shaking violently.

Natalie shook her head. 'Something happened out there in the world he inhabits. The energy discharged itself in some way.' She hauled herself up onto the bed beside Joss and sat with her head in her hands. 'We so nearly did it. We had reached him – or at least, you had. He was listening.'

'He was trying to tell us something –' Joss broke off. From upstairs came the sound of children laughing.

'No. Oh no, I can't bear it.'

Natalie took her hand. 'At least they're happy, Joss.'

Joss shook her head. Sliding off the bed she ran to the door. 'Georgie? Sammy? Where are you?' With the last vestiges of strength she possessed she ran up the stairs and threw open the door of the first empty attic. 'Where are you?' There were tears pouring down her cheeks.

The room was very cold. In the silence she could hear the rain on the windows. 'Georgie? Sammy?'

Behind her Natalie stopped in the doorway.

A gust of wind buffeted the end gable of the roof and in the distance they both heard suddenly the sound of a child singing far away in the distance.

tum tum te tum te tum tum tum

Joss rubbed her nose on her sleeve, staring round helplessly – the sound was so distant, lost in the wind.

tum tum te tum te tum tum tum

She took a step into the room. It was empty – bare, dusty boards, the old shabby wall paper, a damp place on the ceiling where the water had begun to seep in.

tum tum te tum te Kath-er-ine

She could hear it more clearly now, from beyond the door. With hands stiff with cold she fought the latch to pull it open. The sounds were louder now. More clear.

513

It was my Lad-y Kath-er-ine

The chant echoed across the next attic above the howling of the wind.

It was my Lad-y Kath-er-ine
It was my Lady Katherine

Joss moved slowly towards the sound. It was coming from the end attic.

The melancholy little refrain echoed in her ears as she fumbled for the key and pushed open the door. As it creaked back the words were cut off abruptly.

She stared round.

'Where are you?' she cried. She could hardly see for her tears.

'Joss.' Natalie had come up behind her softly. 'Let's go back downstairs.'

'No.' She shook her head violently. 'No, I have to see them! Where are they?'

'They're not here, Joss –'

'They are. They're singing about Katherine. Can't you hear them?'

'Yes, I can hear them.' Natalie put her arm round Joss's shoulders. 'Come on down. If they want to tell us something they will.'

Joss let out a sob. She had not stopped trembling. 'I can't cope with this.'

'Yes, you can. You're doing fine. Come on down, out of the cold and we'll talk about it.' Firmly she turned Joss round and half led, half pushed her down the passage towards the stairs.

It was my Lady Katherine

The little song, masked by the wind and rain, echoed in the distance as they reached the stairs.

Natalie squeezed Joss's arm. 'Don't take any notice. They'll come if they want to.' Leading her back into the bedroom she went over to the bedside table and turned on the lamp. In the sudden light she could see Joss's face puffy with grief and tears.

Joss wrapped her arms around herself. 'You said I was carrying his child,' she whispered. 'You said it was his daughter –'

'I was speaking metaphorically, Joss.' Natalie kept her voice calm.

'It's Luke's. I remembered. We made love in the bathroom. That's when it must have happened –'

'Of course it did.'

'It can't be his,' she gestured at the empty air near the bed where Edward had stood. 'That's not possible. It's not. That's obscene!'

'Joss, I said metaphorically –'

'You are saying he made love to me in the cellar –' Joss rushed on not heeding her interruption. 'He put his arms round me and he kissed me and he held me. I think I must have fainted – I don't remember what happened next.'

His eyes. She could remember his eyes, close to hers, full of love and compassion, the black velvet, then the touch of his hands, warm, commanding . . .

'He could have done anything –'

'Joss, calm down. He couldn't have done anything. He has no body; no real body.'

'Supposing he did the same to my mother. Supposing he raped my mother!' She was rushing on now, her thoughts out of control. 'Supposing –'

Forgive me, Jocelyn, but I can no longer fight your father's wishes. I have no strength left. I am leaving Belheddon, with all its blessings and its curses, but he will only let me escape if I give in. He wants Belheddon to be yours and I have to obey. If you read this letter then he will have got his way.

515

'Supposing he's my father!' She stared at Natalie, numb with shock.

'No, Joss. Don't even think it –'

'The women of this house. Laura, Lydia, Mary Sarah – all of them! He made love to all of them!' She sat down abruptly, her arms wrapped tightly around herself. 'My mother knew. That's why she tried to send me away. She tried to break the spell! To save me! But she couldn't. He wouldn't let her!'

'The spell was very powerful, Joss. A real spell.' Natalie knelt in front of her and took her cold hands in her own warm ones. Her voice was very gentle. 'But we're going to break it. It's half done already. Then Belheddon will be a safe, happy, place again.' She smiled. 'I promise. We can do it. You can do it.'

'The others couldn't.' It was a whisper. Her lips were cracked and dry.

'The others didn't know how to. We do. The time is right and you aren't alone as your poor mother was. You can do it, Joss.' Natalie's large grey eyes were fixed unblinkingly on Joss's. 'You can.'

'How?'

'We have to call him back.' Natalie was trying to will some of her own strength into the woman sitting in front of her. 'We have to call him back and release him so he never wants to come back.'

Joss bit her lip. 'He's buried at Windsor. In St George's Chapel. I looked it up,' she said slowly.

'His body may be,' Natalie said firmly. 'And when this is over you can go and see his tomb if you want to, but his spirit is at Belheddon Hall.' She stood up and walked across to the window. Rain was slanting across the garden, pitting the lake, soaking the grass. It was almost dark. As she watched she saw a faint flicker on the horizon. 'There's a storm coming.' She turned. 'Joss, we have to summon Katherine.'

516

'Call him! In the name of Christ and the Virgin, bring him here!'

Her mouth was too dry; the words she was screaming were barely audible.

'Let him see what he has done to me!'

'Hush sweeting, save your strength!'

The old woman who had been her own nurse wiped her face again with the piece of linen wrung out in rose water, soothing the sweat-soaked hair off her face with a gentle hand. She looked up at Margaret. 'You should send for him, my lady. Now.'

The message conveyed in the direct gaze was clear. Send now or it will be too late. Your daughter is dying.

Margaret half closed her eyes and looked away. The spell was a powerful one. It had worked well. It would not fail her now. The king was in thrall; the daughter who would hold him long after the child's mother had lost her attraction, nearly born.

She smiled and walked across to the side board. Pouring a cup of wine she sipped a little herself, then turned back to the bed. 'Here, child. Drink this. It will give you strength.' Raising Katherine's head a little she held the cup to her lips, then dabbed them gently with a fine linen napkin. 'There. Rest now.' She bent low, putting her lips to her daughter's ear. 'Remember your mother's art. You have my strength and my power, and through me, the power that lies sleeping in the ground beneath this place. With it you can do anything.'

The last word was a hiss of triumph as her daughter caught her hand and, convulsed with new waves of pain, began to scream again.

'How do we call her?' Joss was staring at the floor. She shook her head slightly, trying to rid it of the noises – the voices, echoing in her ears just beyond her hearing.

'We could try her name.'

'In here?'

'Why not. I suspect this has always been the main bedroom. They could have made love here. Perhaps even in this very bed.'

They both stared at it in silence.

'I don't think I can go through with this.' Joss rubbed her eyes wearily.

'Yes, you can. I promise.' Natalie came and knelt in front of her again. 'Think of your two little boys. You can do it for them.'

Joss took a deep breath. She looked up as the lightning flickered at the window again. 'Yes, I can do it for them.'

There was a veil of red across her eyes. Beneath her hips the red soaked into sheets and mattresses and dripped into the thick-strewn herbs. Behind the red there was darkness.

Power.

Summon the power.

Remember the words she had heard her mother cry in the black candleless undercroft of the hall, the cry that would summon the powers of darkness from the very bowels of the earth.

Shrinking back from the woman in the bed who only seconds before had been her child, the old nurse stared into the shadows of the room. The whole household was there, watching in terror.

'You,' she caught the sleeve of the steward as he was slipping with the other men from the room, 'call the priest and then ride for the king. Don't stop for anything or he will be too late.'

'But the Lady Margaret said –' the man's face was pasty with horror at what he had heard and seen.

'This is not the time to obey the Lady Margaret. Lady Katherine's wishes rule this house now.'

He nodded and with a final glance at the bed he slipped from the room.

For a while she drifted in and out of consciousness, then, slowly, her body began to tense, preparing for its last convulsive effort to rid itself of the burden that was killing it.

518

Her eyes flew open and she grabbed at the hands of the woman who still dared to come near her.

Behind them the priest, his hand outstretched to form the holy cross, had begun to murmur the words designed to bring her peace.

'Per istam sanctam unctionem indulgeat tibi Dominus quidquid deliquisti —'

'Stop!' she screamed. 'If God cannot help me, the devil will. The devil conjured by my mother to oversee my daughter's birth.'

She half sat up, galvanised by one last burst of energy.

'Go! Go priest! I don't need you. If I die I will be buried in the devil's earth! Go!' Her voice had risen to a shriek.

'Lie back, my lady, lie back. The little one is nearly here.'

The midwives had long gone, it was her own old nurse who pushed her back on the pillows, who reached amid the bloodied sheets and who at last held up the limp, half dead baby.

'It is a boy, my lady,' she whispered. 'A little boy.'

'No!' Margaret pushed her aside. 'It can't be a boy!'

'It is, my lady, a sweeting boy.'

The nurse busied herself with towels from the rail by the fire, rubbing the small cold body back to life. Behind her Katherine lay inert, her own life pouring from her.

'See, my love, see your baby.' The nurse wrapped the child tightly in a blanket and tried to push it into Katherine's arms.

She opened her eyes. 'No,' she whispered. 'No! No —'

The last word was a scream.

'I curse the man who got that child on me! I curse all men. I curse my son. He took my life from me. I curse that baby — the devil's child — and I curse my mother for her sorcery.'

The hot tears trickled down her cheeks.

'I wanted to live!

'I wanted to live. Forever!'

It was my Lad-y Kath-er-ine!

The childish treble sounded in the room suddenly.

It was my Lad-y Kath-er-ine!

'Georgie!' Joss stood up. She took a deep breath. 'Georgie, I want to see you!'

He was a dark haired boy, sturdy, with a scattering of small freckles over his nose. Standing near the door he seemed very small, an uncertain shadow amongst deeper shadows. He grinned at Joss and she found herself grinning back.

'Do you and Sammy want to go to heaven, Georgie? To be with our mother?' She found she could speak quite steadily now.

He didn't seem to hear her. He was staring past her at the window. 'It was my Lady Katherine!' he sang again, his voice more husky this time.

'Shall we call her, Georgie? Shall we call the Lady Katherine here?' she asked, but he had gone.

A flicker of lightning showed at the window followed by a low rumble of thunder as the lights dimmed.

'I'm afraid.'

'So am I. So was Georgie. That song. He was trying to warn us.'

'Of what? That we had got it wrong? Is it Katherine who is the killer?' Joss was still standing by the bed. She stared down at the crewel work cover as though she could find the answer stitched into the faded wools.

'I don't think she's buried in the church, Joss. I don't think she can be buried in consecrated ground.'

'Not here! You don't mean she's somewhere here?'

They stared at each other in silence. It was Joss who spoke at last. 'She's under the cellar, isn't she. Oh God, what are we going to do?'

'We're going to summon her.'

'Down there? In the cellar?' Joss took a deep breath. 'Yes, that's the best place. I don't want her here. Oh God, Nattie, what are we going to do?'

'Come on.' Natalie took her hand. 'Let's get it over.'

'Will Edward come down there? We need him. Katherine is the one who has killed. He never hurt anyone. He never hurt Tom or Ned, or not intentionally. He carried them. He hid them. He hid them from her.' Joss's face was white with strain.

'You don't know that, Joss. We must be careful. That's all. Careful of everyone and everything.'

Her jaw set, Natalie led the way to the staircase. Lying on the top step was a white rose.

Joss stopped and picked it up. She stared round the shadowy landing.

'Help us,' she whispered. 'Help us help her.'

It was my Lady Katherine!

It was my Lady Katherine!

The high voice was barely audible now, echoing down from somewhere in the attics.

She took a deep breath and, still holding the rose, she began to walk down the stairs.

44

e can't wait here, David. We've got to go back.'
Luke was staring out of the window in Janet's
kitchen. Janet and Lyn were making sand-
wiches, spreading strawberry jam on thick slices of home-
made bread. 'What the hell do we know about that
woman? For all we know she's a complete fraud. Or
worse.'

David didn't bother to ask what he meant by worse.
He was feeling very uncomfortable. Out there in the rain
on the terrace at the Hall he had been carried away by
Natalie's calm. He had believed that this was something
almost mystically female, something from which men
were excluded, something mysterious and movable and
watery, like moonlight on the lake, something born of
thousands of years of female secrets, but now he wondered. If Margaret de Vere was a practised sorceress – not
just a witch with her herbs and her healings and her wax
dolls to help with her spells and curses – what if she were
more powerful than that?

Janet put down her knife. 'If Lyn is willing to look
after the children, I'll come with you.'

They all looked at Lyn who shrugged. 'I don't mind.
I'd rather stay here anyway.' She glanced at David and
sighed. She had admired him so much when she first

met him; he was such an attractive man, but now. At least Luke had had more sense than to believe all this. David had proved himself in the long run as neurotic as Joss!

She watched from the window as they all climbed into Janet's car then she turned back to Tom who was cheerfully eating jam sandwiches sitting in the old oak carver at the end of the table, his legs stuck straight out in front of him.

He looked up at her and gave her a jammy grin. 'The tin man is cross,' he said conversationally.

'Oh Tom, I wish we could forget about the tin man,' she said as she pulled her cup of tea, long cold, towards her. 'Your mummy thinks he's real, whereas we both know you made him up, don't we. The tin man on the yellow brick road, looking for his heart.'

Behind them Ned let out a gurgle of delight. He abandoned the brightly coloured bunch of plastic keys he had been playing with on the hearthrug and reached for the white flower which had appeared on the floor in front of him. One by one he began to pull at the petals. Tom was watching. 'Ned's made a mess,' he said to Lyn.

She glanced round and let out a cry of dismay. Falling on her knees she took the flower away from him and stared down at it. It was cold and wet, every petal perfect and unblemished. For a moment she stared down at it in her hands, then gathering up the scattered petals she threw it in the bin with a shudder. Behind her Ned began to cry.

The house was in darkness. Pushing open the back door they peered into the kitchen. Luke groped for the light switch, clicking it up and down. Nothing happened.

'There must have been another power cut.' He groped his way towards the dresser. 'There's a torch here somewhere.' He couldn't find it and as he scrabbled for matches and candles Janet went back outside for the Maglite she kept in the glove compartment of the Audi. On the doorstep she took a deep breath of the cold evening air. The atmosphere in the house had been poisonous.

None of them spoke as she handed the torch to David. Pushing open the kitchen door he peered out into the passage. He looked back at Luke and gave a faint grin. 'Householder first?'

Luke nodded. He was beginning to feel very uncomfortable. 'Fair enough. Give me the torch.' He pushed past him and led the way into the great hall. They stood still as Luke shone the beam round the room, up into the empty gallery, towards the fireplace, across the table and on towards the door in the far wall.

'Where are they?' Janet's voice was tremulous.

'They must be upstairs.' Luke headed in that direction, closely followed by the others. 'Why are all the lights out?' Janet whispered. 'I don't like it.'

'Neither do I.' David sounded very grim. He stopped, as Luke headed up the stairs, staring at the cellar door. The key was in the lock. He frowned. 'Luke,' he called softly. His voice contained enough urgency for Luke to stop. He shone the torch back down the stairs.

'The cellar.' David pointed.

'They're down there?' Luke could feel his stomach churning uncomfortably. 'We'd better look.' He stepped forward and put his hand on the key. It was unlocked. Pushing the door slowly open he peered down into the darkness. There was no sound at all.

Jimbo was parked near the main gate in his old Cortina when he saw Luke and David drive back into the house. He had been sitting there, smoking, for some time, his fingers drumming on the wheel, torn between fear and curiosity as he thought of his sister alone in the house with Joss. Tossing the stub of the cigarette out of the car window he leaned forward and watched the tail lights of the Audi disappear between the laurels. There had been three people in the car. It was Mrs Goodyear driving, he was fairly sure. So Lyn was alone with the kids over at the farm. He sat for a minute deep in thought, feeling the chill of the evening air on his face from the open car window. At last he came to a decision. Winding up the window he reached for the ignition key and gunned the engine into life. There was no harm in checking that Lyn was all right – her and the boys. If she was there on her own, maybe she could do with some company. She wasn't that bad, Lyn, when he came to think about it. In fact, he grinned sheepishly to himself as he changed gear and pulled out into the lane, he could quite fancy her, if he thought about it.

On the road behind him his cigarette butt flared for a minute on the wet tarmac and then went out with a hiss.

Joss and Natalie were standing near the hole in the wall where they had found the wax figures when the lights went out.

Clinging together they stared round in the darkness their eyes and ears straining against a thick impenetrable blackness which seemed to wrap itself around them.

'The torch,' Natalie whispered. 'Where's the torch?'

'I don't know.'

'Matches?'

'No.'

'Shit!' She put an experimental hand out in front of her, half expecting to meet something or someone, but the darkness was empty.

'Has she done it on purpose?' Joss moved closer to her companion.

'I don't know. What we need to do is get out of here,

mend the fuse, or get a torch and candles or a floodlight or something and then come back.' She took a cautious step backwards, one hand linked to Joss's, one held out in front as she slowly turned back to where she thought the arch through to the first cellar was.

Joss followed her. 'It's this way. It must be. We left the door open at the top of the stairs. There'll be some sort of light.'

The movement of air behind them was so slight Joss thought she had imagined it. She stopped, her fingers digging into Natalie's arm, the hairs on the back of her neck prickling.

Natalie stopped too. Neither of them said anything; they were both listening hard.

Slowly Joss turned round. In the far corner of the cellar she could see something moving against the blackness. Her throat tightened; she could hardly breathe.

'Be strong,' Natalie murmured. 'We have to win.'

Joss was very conscious of the huge old house above them empty, listening as they were to the silence. Panic swept over her, drenching her in cold sweat. For a moment she was sure that her legs were going to collapse under her, then she felt the steady pressure of Natalie's hand on her arm. 'Deep breaths. Arm yourself with the light – visualise it all round you, fill the cellar with it,' she whispered. 'Don't let her see you're afraid.'

Her?

She could see it too now: the faintest outline of a woman's shape glowing like dim phosphorescence against the wall . . .

It was my Lady Kath-er-ine

The words echoed faintly in the back of her skull, a child's song, the song of a little boy, lost in the shadows of time.

'Katherine?' She found her voice suddenly. 'Katherine, you have to leave this house. You have done enough here. Enough people have paid for your pain. Don't let it go on.'

She waited, half hoping for an answer in the silence.

'You need to move on into the light, into happiness,' she went on. Her voice had begun to shake.

'We can help you, Katherine,' Natalie put in. Her words were clear and strong. 'We're not here to banish you to hell. We can help give you strength to move on. Please, let us help you.' Her eyes were closed; inside her head she could see her clearly, not a mad witch but a girl, scarcely more than a child, crazed with pain and grief, cheated of life by the greed and ambition of the mother she hated, killed by the child she never wanted.

'Don't hurt any more children, Katherine. They are not to blame,' she went on softly. 'Their fear and agony can't help you – it adds to your own. Please let us give you our blessings. Let our love and strength help you.'

She took a cautious step nearer the corner of the cellar, her eyes still closed. It was Joss who was watching. The glowing outline of the figure had grown stronger. It had a shape now, clearly a slim, not very tall girl.

'Are you buried down here, Katherine? Is this where you lie?' Natalie had dropped Joss's hand and held her own out towards the spot where she sensed the girl was standing. 'Shall we move you? Would you like to be buried outside in the garden somewhere? Or in the churchyard?'

They both felt the frisson, the cold shiver in the air.

'In the garden here, then. Under the sun and in the moonlight,' Natalie went on. 'We can do that for you, Katherine. Just show us where they buried you.'

There was a long breathless silence. It is not going to work, thought Joss. She is not going to tell us. The atmosphere was stifling. There seemed to be no air in the cellar. It had been growing steadily colder but now she felt a wave of heat roll over her. She put her hand to the collar of her sweater and ran her finger round under it, feeling her perspiration like ice.

'Where is it, Katherine?' Natalie went on. 'You must give us a sign. You must show us what you want.'

It was my Lady Kath-er-ine

Georgie's voice reached Joss's ears very faintly.

It was my Lady Kath-er-ine

Something dropped in the silence. It rattled on the ground like a pebble. The noise came again, then nothing more.

In the corner of the cellar the light slowly faded; in seconds it was gone.

Neither of them moved. Joss put her hand out to Natalie. 'Has she gone?' she whispered at last.

'She's gone.'

Natalie spun round; behind them they could suddenly hear the sound of voices. The squeak of the cellar door opening was followed by a flash of torch light.

'Joss? Natalie?' It was Luke's voice.

With the help of a torch they found Katherine's sign, unmistakable on the cellar floor. A scattering of small bricks and stones lay in the shape of an equal-armed cross on one of the old flagstones in the corner. They stood in a ring looking down at it.

'What do we do?' Luke was holding the big torch, focusing the beam steadily on it. His scepticism had dissolved.

'We have to keep our promise. We have to dig her up and rebury her in the garden.' Joss was very firm.

'What about coroners and things?'

'What about them?' She put her hands on his shoulders. 'Luke, this is Belheddon's business. No one else's. Katherine belongs here. She doesn't want to be buried in the church or in the churchyard. She wants to be buried in the garden. Quietly. With our blessing and love.'

'This is the woman who murdered your brothers, Joss.'

'I know.' Joss took a deep breath, trying to steady her voice. 'She's so unhappy, Luke. She's lost. I don't believe she was really evil. She was in too much pain to know what she was doing. I think we can help her – and make Belheddon safe for children. Our children.'

He shrugged. 'OK. Let's go for it. I'll get a pick.'

They mended the fuses first and it was in a cellar full of light that they met again, half an hour later with pick-axe and shovel.

'You realise this whole thing could be a waste of time.' Luke gazed round them. He was feeling stronger now that the cellar was lit. 'We are digging on a flash of intuition and the word of a ghost, who might or might not be imaginary.'

Joss smiled tolerantly. 'We're never really going to convince you, are we. Just dig.'

'OK.' He shrugged. Lifting the pick he inserted the point under the edge of the flag and began to try to lever it up. Taking turns in the cramped space David and Luke managed to lift four flags, then stood back exhausted. Janet had at some point left the cellar where Joss and Natalie stood, eyes riveted to the floor, and reappeared with a jug of Lyn's home-made lemonade and some glasses.

'Come on, rest for a moment,' she said, setting the tray on the ground. They stood in a circle, looking down as they drank, staring at the sandy earth, aware of the acute silence around them.

It was Luke who put down his glass first. He had barely touched his drink. 'Come on. Let's get it over.' He picked up the spade and drove it into the soil.

'Gently, Luke. We don't know if there's a coffin.' Joss

put her hand on his shoulder. He straightened and looked at her for a moment, then he nodded.

'Right. Gently does it.'

An hour later they had found nothing. A hole about three feet deep and as much across opened at their feet.

'There's nothing here.' Luke put down the spade and reached for his glass.

'There is. I'm sorry, Luke, but you have to go on.'

'It could be six feet down, I suppose.' David looked exhausted. There was a smear of earth across his face.

'Perhaps you could ask her, Natalie?' Janet was sitting on an old wine crate. 'See if we're on the right track.'

Natalie stepped forward. 'Katherine?' she called. 'Katherine, you see. We're trying to help you, but we must know, is this the right place?'

They all waited in silence. Joss was staring at the cavity in the wall where they had found the wax figures. Natalie's eyes were fixed on the hole where the spade stood alone, shoved into the soil as Luke stood back to pick up his drink.

'She's got tired and gone off to bed. And I think that's what I'm going to do as well.'

'No. No, wait. Let's try for just a while longer, please.' Joss dropped to her haunches and picked up the trowel. She dug it into the earth and heard the small chink of metal. The sound electrified the others. They turned. Luke moved closer and knelt beside her. 'What is it?'

'Here.' Joss lifted the trowel full of soil and ran it through her fingers. Left lying in her palm was a small gold ring.

Joss took a deep breath. 'It's her message.'

Luke nodded. He caught her eye and gave a rueful, private smile. He dug more carefully this time, inserting the spade almost gently, transferring the lifted earth to the steadily growing pile on the floor behind them.

They found the body at about a metre depth. There

was no coffin; there were no clothes; no flesh now, just the bones, lying on a floor of earth much harder than the soft friable soil which had lain on top of them. Using the trowel Luke lifted away as much of the earth as he could without touching the bones and they stood looking down at the skeleton before them. There were two other rings on the finger bones and a gold chain around the neck, an earth-encrusted enamelled pendant lying amongst the narrow, fragile ribs.

It was my Lady Katherine

Joss knelt down. Her eyes had filled with tears. 'Poor girl. She was so small.'

'How are we going to move her?' David put his hand on Joss's shoulder.

She shrugged. The face she raised to him and Luke was white and strained. 'First we must dig the new grave.'

'Tonight?'

Joss nodded. 'Tonight. While it's dark. Then the sun can warm her in the morning.'

Natalie offered to stay with the bones; it seemed somehow indecent to leave them alone now they were exposed. The others went out into the garden with torches. Joss had already chosen the spot in her mind. It was perfect: out beyond the lake, where the wild roses tangled over the old pergola and the sun dial registered the passing of the hours.

They dug the hole in the old rose bed, the earth soft and cold under the clogging November mist which had closed over the garden as the wind dropped and the rain petered away.

Joss emptied the carved cedar box from the study which contained piles of old sheet music. She lined it with her own fringed scarf of rough wild silk and then on her knees lifted the skull from the earth as the others watched. The rest of the bones she picked from the soil and put them reverently into the box and with them the

531

rings and chain and pendant, then last of all the wax dolls, still wrapped in their blue scarf from the dresser drawer, then she closed the lid at last.

Luke picked up the box and carried it slowly up the stairs.

The garden was dank and cold as they walked after him across the wet grass and under the pergola to the little grave. Puffing he set the box down beside it. 'Are you going to say something?'

Joss stood staring down. 'I don't know what to say. I don't think she wants our prayers.'

'She wants peace, Joss. Peace and forgiveness,' Natalie murmured quietly. 'Then all the other spirits here can rest too; the lost boys from all the centuries and their fathers, the poor men she cursed and hounded to their deaths in her pain and hatred.'

'And the king.' Joss met her eye. 'What about the king?'

'I think you'll find he's already gone, Joss. You were very special to him, remember.' She smiled. She would never, Joss knew, reveal what they had talked about with Edward of England, the sun of York, who, had he been a man, would have fathered Joss's unborn child and who might have been her father, and her mother's father, and her grandmother's father before that, and who was, with Katherine de Vere, her ancestor by blood and true descent.

'I wish the moon was out.' Joss looked down into the blackness of the hole.

'It will be, look.' Janet had been the only one looking up at the sky. Behind the mist the full moon was a wraith high up above the wrack. As they watched it found a gap in the drifting cloud and for a moment shone down into the garden.

David and Luke between them lowered the box into the ground and Joss and then Natalie each threw down a handful of soil. For a minute they waited as the moonlight ran light fingers over the carved wood then as the mist returned like a veil across the garden David lifted the spade. As the first shovel full of earth poured down into the grave they all saw the spray of white roses as the darkness returned.

It was my Lady Katherine

Muffled in the mist the voice seemed to drift across the lake.

It was my Lady Katherine
It was my Lady Katherine

Each time the voice was further away.

They looked at each other.

'I shall miss them.' Joss smiled.

Natalie shook her head. 'Rascals,' she said. 'Let them join their mum. The only children at Belheddon should be real children.'

'It's done, Joss.' David had patted down the last of the earth with the back of the spade. 'Are you going to put something here to mark it?'

Joss shook her head slowly. 'I don't know. Perhaps.' She gave a deep sigh. 'I just can't believe that it's really over. That there's no more danger.'

'There's no more danger,' Natalie said firmly. She took Joss's cold hand. 'Come on. It's time to go in. Leave Katherine to her moonlight.'

Slowly they made their way back across the grass. On the terrace Joss stopped and looked back. The garden was silent.

The echoes were gone.

Daily Telegraph

17th July 1995

To Luke and Jocelyn Grant a daughter (Alice Laura Katherine) a sister for Tom and Ned.

Sunday Times

September 1995

Son of the Sword by Jocelyn Grant (Hibberds)

An accomplished first novel written with wit and pace. Set largely in the author's own house during the years of the Wars of the Roses, Richard Mortimer and Ann de Vere tread a heady tightrope of romance, adventure and near disaster which culminates in an extraordinarily satisfactory ending, leaving the reader clinging to the edge of his chair. Highly recommended. I shall look forward to seeing more from this author.

AUTHOR'S NOTE

Belheddon does not exist. Nor did this branch of the de Vere family. King Edward IV had many mistresses during his life time. The names of the last two are unknown; the story of Katherine de Vere, woven through this tale, is entirely fictional. Accusations of witchcraft and sorcery were made at Edward's court both against his queen and other high born women around him, but whether these were merely political propaganda or substantiated in truth is for the reader to decide for him or herself.

As always so many people have provided me with help and information in the research of this book. I should particularly like to thank James Maitland of Lay & Wheeler in Colchester for his suggestions on the contents of the Belheddon cellar, (any spelling mistakes in the wine names are my fault entirely) Janet Hanlon for her assistance and Carole Blake for her attempts at keeping my characters' drinking habits within bounds! Also Rachel Hore for her editorial advice during what must have been the hottest days in East Anglia since the reign of Edward IV! I should also like to thank my son Adrian for his help with research and Peter Shepherd, Dr Robert Brownell and my son Jonathan for their help in sorting out my computer crash, computer crises and computer panic! I think I prefer to use a quill pen!